ALSO BY CATHERINE COOKSON

CATHERINE COOKSON

THE
Golden Straw

A NOVEL

LARGE PRINT BOOK CLUB EDITION

SIMON & SCHUSTER
NEW YORK LONDON TORONTO SYDNEY TOKYO SINGAPORE

SIMON & SCHUSTER
Rockefeller Center
1230 Avenue of the Americas
New York, NY 10020

Originally published in Great Britain by Bantam Press, a division of Transworld Publishers Ltd.

Manufactured in the United States of America

ISBN 0-684-81177-4

**This Large Print Book carries the
Seal of Approval of N.A.V.H.**

BOOK ONE

PART ONE

1879

1

Emily Pearson cast her eyes around the bare room from which the last piece of furniture had just been taken out to the horse-driven removal van, and she asked herself how they had ever been able to move about in that room or, for that matter, in the bedroom, or in the kitchen, for the contents of the small house had filled the van. From where she was standing she could see through the uncurtained window into the road, where the driver of the van was urging his horse into motion with the flick of his whip.

Thinking, That's that, she now took a key from her bag and walked toward the door; but there she stopped and turned, and again she gazed around the room. Was she sorry to leave this house? No. No. Yet she had been born here, and she had lived happily here until she was sixteen, when her mother had died. She could say, too, that she had lived somewhat contentedly during the following two years. Then she had married Jimmy Pearson and had spent the first night of her married life in that bedroom over there.

Marriage had startled her, frightened her. It wasn't as she expected it would be, full of tender loving, and evenings sitting by the fire, he describing his day at Parker's warehouse, and she responding by telling him about some of the customers at Madam Arkwright's, milliners. But it didn't turn out like that. He was dry, he would say, after a day in the warehouse, too dry for talking without something with which to oil his throat. True, he had invited her to go to the pub with him. But what did that mean? Sitting in the snug with women to whom she couldn't talk. It was as if they spoke a foreign language. After the second visit she had put her foot down, saying she had something better to do than sit with a lot of blowzy women, while he golloped beer next door in the men-only bar.

The following morning she had arrived at The Bandbox for the first time with a discolored cheek. It was on that morning, too, that Mrs. Arkwright had stopped being madam and had behaved more like a mother, for she had upbraided her for her silliness in being taken in by such a common individual as that warehouse man. Hadn't she warned her she was out of his class? Her mother had brought her up respectable and she herself had aimed to instil some style into her; but now here she was being treated like any waterfront slut.

She could recall the scene now: Mrs. Arkwright, who never seemed to lose her composure, gripping her by the shoulders and saying, "The next time he raises his hand to you pick up something, anything, and hit him with it, or throw it at him. At first they try it on, but it quickly develops into a habit. If you don't do as I say, by the end of the year you won't be able to see out of either eye. I know the type."

And she had been right. In the middle of the following week, when she had refused to give him five shillings out of her savings for him to back another sure winner, he had lifted his hand to her. But she had been prepared, and she had whipped up a brass candlestick from the low mantelpiece and as his fist was about to come in contact with her face he felt the weight of the brass across his knuckles. So fiercely had she aimed the blow that he cried out, then stood away from her, his pain not unmixed with amazement. The quiet, docile young lass who, as he had bragged to his mates, would do what he said, or else, was now confronting him and telling him what she would do if he dared to raise his hand again to her; and, what was more, that he wasn't getting any of her pay, but that she wanted some of his to keep the house . . .

Emily now leaned back against the door, closed her eyes, and bit on her lip as she savored her recall of the scene. It had been the most satisfactory moment of their marriage, and in a way it had brought her out of her girlhood into womanhood, much more so than the marriage bed had done.

But then, following this incident, life had become almost unbearable. There came the period when he did not return home at night. But she had been glad of this: it was the respite from which no brass candlestick could have protected her. Then came the day when he said to her, "You're on your own from now on. I'm not coming back." And when an expected reply was not forthcoming from her he had blustered, "Who d'you think you are, anyway? Your old man was nothing but a stoker on an old tramp steamer." But to this she did reply, yelling at him, "My father was second mate on a cargo boat and he was a gentleman."

She had always thought of her father as a gentleman. He had been drowned when she was five years old. Apparently she had seen him only twice, on each occasion after his return from a long voyage, and she had cried both times when the strange man held her.

It had been her mother who had imbued her with this feeling about her father: "In all ways your dad was a gentleman," she would continually say to her, creating the picture in her mind of him as a gentle sailorman, and more so as she later realized that it had been her father's half-pay notes which, added to her mother's earnings, had helped to buy this house.

It was on that night of parting from her husband that he brought up the ownership of the house by saying, "And you try to sell this place, mind, and I'm having my share, if not the lot. What's the wife's is the husband's. In fact I could sell it over your head. And I will if you try me too far and interfere with me life."

As yet she knew nothing about the law as regards women's rights, so she had remained quiet. This was something to ask Mrs. Arkwright about.

When she had told Mrs. Arkwright that he had left her, that lady had said immediately, "That's that! Good riddance! But don't go in for any legal separation, go for a divorce."

Divorce! That was only for the upper class. Yet, with the guidance of her mentor that's what she had achieved. Although the whole procedure had taken nearly three years, the fact that he had three children by the woman with whom he was living had helped matters, also it dispelled his idea that he could still claim on the property that was hers.

That the money she had received from selling the house had gone mostly on solicitors' fees for fighting her case didn't matter any more, for she was now going to make her permanent home with Mrs. Arkwright. What was more, she was going to be taken as partner into the business. And what a partnership! And what a house! In fact, what houses!

Now, she moved from the door, opened it, and stepped into the street, put the key in the lock and turned it, then muttered, "Goodbye. Goodbye, old house, you've served your purpose."

After five minutes' walk she boarded a horse-bus, and there being few passengers at this time of day she sat on one of the wooden-slatted seats at the front and gazed out of the window. She always did this, very often without seeing where the bus was going, so accustomed had she become to this journey over the years.

When she had first taken this route with her mother it had only been a five-minute ride to Bertram Close, where Mrs. Arkwright had set up her first Bandbox. Then later it had seemed a long jump, yes indeed, it had seemed a long jump to that tall, narrow house in Maddock Street. But they hadn't stayed long there, only two years. The stairs had been too much for everyone: two rooms on each floor and three floors; and, what was more, it wasn't suitable for their kind of business. But the new premises, Frontlea House in Willington Place, were, even though it was certainly not a business area as such. It was a small residential district, the occupants of the houses being definitely real middle-class. And it could be said that Mrs. Mabel Arkwright had just squeezed into it, for number thirty-five was the last house and only partly in Willington Place. Being situated on the corner its other half extended into Barclay Street and had a small business window, which set it in line with a number of shops in this particular street. Yet the businesses were all of some standing, with such as a high-class florist, a stamp and coin collector and, at the far end of the street from Mrs. Arkwright's, a gentlemen's hatter, which caused that lady some amusement.

But now, after occupying Frontlea House, number thirty-five, for four years, the business lady, Mrs. Arkwright, astounded the residents of Willington Place by taking not only a lease of ninety-nine years on these premises, but also a similar lease on the one next door, in which Rear Admiral Proggett had lived for years.

Now who would think there was so much money to be made out of hats? But of course there was this other business that was rather mysterious. There was talk of the garments in her ladies' outfitting department being not quite, well . . . new. Yet no one in Willington Place would have dreamt about investigating this for themselves; it was just what they had come to learn from a friend of a friend.

After three minutes' walk from the horse-bus Emily entered number thirty-five by the shining dark-green-painted door, which color was picked out in the window sills on each side and on the iron rails that fronted a small patch of garden. She stepped into a small lobby, then opened the frosted-glass door, and so entered what always surprised a new visitor: an extraordinarily large hall. It was an odd shape, which had been achieved by removing a sitting room wall and thus leaving the entire space in the shape of a stunted L. A number of doors led off the hall and a broad staircase gently rose from the far end of it.

The walls of the hall were covered with red-flock paper and the two long windows, one each side of the door, were draped in a gray silk material, the color repeated in the three small couches and two chairs, which were upholstered in a heavy brocade. There was a round table in the middle of the room and, set in strategic positions, three tall hat-stands holding large ribbon-and-flower-be-decked models.

Emily paused and looked about her. There was the sound of muted voices coming from a room opposite her, and from one to the far right, which meant there were clients being attended to, special ones—those who paid up within a reasonable time.

She had turned to move toward the corridor to her left when one of the doors to the right of the hall opened, and a laughing voice said, "He'll kill me. The first thing he'll say will be, 'You can't wear three at once.' Well, all I'll do is put the blame on you, Miss Esther: I'll tell him to come and try to get past you with one hat . . . Oh, there you are, Mrs. Pearson." The big, over-dressed, florid lady sailed toward Emily, continuing to explain her apparent extravagance: "I came in for a toque and go out with three pokes. That's another of Wilson Fairbairn's sayings. Anyway, what odds? What are we here for if not to wear hats? You're looking very well. I haven't seen you for some time, nor Madam Arkwright. No"—she now leaned her big smiling face close to Emily's—"I only glimpse Madam these days when I'm settling up."

"Oh, Mrs. Fairbairn, Madam would be pleased to see you at any time, you know that. You are her oldest and most favored customer."

"Not so much of the oldest, dear, not so much of the oldest." She was wagging a hand in front of Emily's face, and Emily laughed, saying, "That's but a saying. Some people are ageless, and you, Mrs. Fairbairn, I'm positive, are one of them, because you were one of the ladies I met when I first came to work for Madam, and you haven't altered one jot."

"You know, Mrs. Pearson, you talk just like Wilson Fairbairn. I don't believe a word of it. But," and now her voice changed to an exaggerated whisper, "I like it, you know. I like to hear it, nevertheless. Goodbye for now, my dear. Goodbye. You'll see I get those tomorrow?"

"Yes. Yes, of course." Emily swung round and opened the door; then passed into the lobby and opened the outer door. And the big lady, looking up the street, cried, "Ah, there's Benson. He's been trotting the carriage round the block." Then, turning her laughing face to Emily, she added, "He hates that. Upsets the horses, he says. So I stay all the longer."

Emily watched the florid figure trip as lightly as a young girl down the three steps, along the short path, through the iron gate and onto the pavement to where her carriage was drawing up; and she did not close the door until the carriage was being driven away.

Esther McCann was waiting for Emily and remarked, "By! she's a card. But you know, I could love her. I heard the other day that his firm's in a bad way. I wonder if she knows?"

"Likely she does but has decided to take no notice," said Emily, nodding her head now. "Sufficient unto the day is the evil thereof . . . How's things been?"

"Not bad at all, quite good; in fact. Lady Steele was in."

"Oh, that was nice . . . just for hats?"

"Yes, for the present. Funny about titles, isn't it? There's her without tuppence, so to speak, and having to keep up the style, but she's got no edge, and there's the other one, Lady Wearmore, I can't stand her. I really can't."

"We're both of the same mind, Esther . . . Where's Madam?"

"Now where would you expect? She's never out of next door. But it's going to be fine, isn't it?"

"Yes, grand." Then lowering her voice, Emily said, "Before you and Lena go off tonight Madam would like a word with you. It's really to finalize things, you know, about Lena's taking over the alterations and your giving her a hand, because you know almost as much as she does about it. But the point is, there'll have to be another two trained for the shop here and Madam wants your opinion as to who we should bring into the workshop."

Esther McCann nodded, saying, "Yes. Yes, we were talking about that ourselves earlier on. And I can speak for Lena and for meself an' all when I say we would rather be doing the alterations upstairs than carrying on down here. Although"— her voice changed—"not that we don't like it, but you know what I mean."

"Yes, I know what you mean. I'd rather do that

myself, too. Still, hats are my business so I'd better stick to what I know best. What do you say?"

They both laughed as they said almost together, "We say, right!"

She was still smiling to herself as she made her way along the short corridor and through the new door that led into the recently acquired house and into a half-paneled room that was bare of furniture, from which she entered the main hall. This, too, was paneled, but from floor to ceiling, and was furnished with an ornamental hall table, a tall hat-stand, and three slat-backed chairs.

She opened the door leading into the drawing room. This, too, was furnished, but so sparsely as to suggest a feeling of space, which was further emphasized by the pale-blue-flock-patterned wallpaper.

Not finding Mrs. Arkwright there, she entered the dining room. Here was more panelling, but only to chair-back height. The room had an already-lived-in appearance, right to the silver entrée dishes on the rosewood sideboard. This room had, as Mrs. Arkwright termed it, an eatable look.

Emily did not bother going down the passage and to the door that led into the basement, where Mary Pollock, the cook, having been reluctantly transferred from next door, would likely at this moment be showing her spleen and still be going for poor little Alice Milton, who was not only termed her assistant but also the housemaid; rather, she turned about and went upstairs.

The stairs as yet were uncarpeted, as was the landing, and she was walking across this to where the attic stairs led off when a muffled voice hailed her, saying, "You'll not find me up there, Emily."

She was smiling as she pushed open Mrs. Ark-wright's bedroom door. "How did you know it was me?" she said. "It could have been any one of us."

"Oh, I know your footsteps by now. And anyway, only you would expect to find me rummaging again in the attics. But my! the things they've thrown away over the years, you wouldn't believe. D'you know there's a couple of Sheraton chairs there? The mice have been at the seats, but what does that matter? A bit of tapestry and they'll be as good as new . . . Now what are you staring at? My old tin trunk opened at last? You've been curious about it for years, haven't you? And your mother before you. And why I've always kept it in my room covered with a chenille cloth? Oh, I know, I know." The elderly woman flapped her hands toward Emily now, then went on, "Well, to put it in a nutshell, I've kept it all these years to remind me not to get big-headed. One day, after I'd had a slice of luck, I was for clearing it out and dumping it. In fact, I did clear it out, and banged down the lid, and there it sat staring at me. And you know what it said to me?"

Smiling softly, Emily shook her head but made no reply.

"Well, it said, put a devil on horseback and it'll ride to hell. And I'd seen this happen so often with people who'd come into a bit of money. What did they do but cast off their past and their own folk with it. Anyway, enough about me. How did it go?"

"Very smoothly. They just managed to get the odds and ends into the van."

"I bet they did. You were mad for letting that lot go for five pounds. Twenty-five would have been more like it. You had one or two nice pieces, you know. I gave your mother that horse-hair sofa."

Emily made no comment on this, for the horse-hair sofa had caused both laughter and pain; laughter because her mother couldn't refuse it, nor could she give it away in case Mrs. Arkwright paid them a visit. And no matter what material they used, the horse-hair would find its way through the material. Her mother used to say that they were dray horses in that sofa, those with the big hairy feet, and they were fighting to get out.

"Anyway," Mrs. Arkwright said as she now rose from her squatting position and sat on a low chair to the side of the tin trunk, "that's that episode of yours closed, and good and proper. You should have done it years ago. In fact, as I told you, you should never have started it. I took his measure from the first sight of him. But you wouldn't listen, would you?"

"No, I wouldn't listen," Emily agreed, "and I learned my lesson, as you've often told me."

"Yes. Yes, I did. But it was only for your own good. Are you still going to use his name?"

"No. I'm going to go back to Ratcliffe."

"Well, that's sensible. But don't call yourself miss, keep to missis and your ring on your finger. It'll be a safeguard."

At this Emily gave a short laugh, saying, "Against what?"

"Don't be stupid! woman. Don't tell me you don't look in the glass, and the long mirror. With a figure like yours . . ."

"I haven't any figure, which you've told me for years. You used to say I could even do with carbuncles up here"—she pointed to her breasts—"to make mine stand out."

"Yes. Yes, I did, and I talk through the fat of my neck sometimes. But you mark my words, there'll be a day, and not long ahead, when all the big backsides and the battleship breasts will be cut off amidships. I can hear the Rear Admiral turning in his grave. Remember"—she almost choked on her next words—"when he was in his cups we could hear him through the wall, yelling his nautical terms? He was always yelling at somebody called Harry, wasn't he?"

Emily too was laughing now, so much so that she had to wipe her eyes as she muttered, "And he used to swear like a trooper; but when you met him in the street he was such a gentleman, so courteous, and he had a lovely voice."

"Yes"—Mrs. Arkwright nodded now—"he was a gentleman. He once kissed my hand, you know. Yes; yes, he did." She was nodding. "It was when I first set up next door and I invited him in to prove that his neighbor was respectable, and as he was leaving he kissed my hand. Yes. Yes, he was a gentleman.''

Mrs. Arkwright now paused a moment before saying soberly, ''And here's another gentleman . . . or was.'' She bent and picked up a photograph that was lying among others at the side of the tin trunk and, handing it to Emily, she said, ''You haven't seen him before, have you?''

Emily looked at the photograph. It was of a tall, quite handsome-looking man with a slight moustache and a mass of fair hair. And when she looked enquiringly at Mrs. Arkwright, that lady said, ''He was a gentleman, indeed, and in more ways than one: he was a gentleman's gentleman. But apart from that, he was a gentle man. That was my Oscar, my husband.''

''He . . . he is very handsome, very smart.'' Emily's voice was soft.

''I'm going to tell you something now. Sit down there.'' Mrs. Arkwright pointed to the chair. ''I've always meant to tell you, because you know very little about my early life, do you?''

''Nothing at all really,'' Emily said, the while shaking her head slowly.

''Well, my dear, I was a lady's maid. Yes, a lady's maid. I dropped into that just by chance. I was put into service when I was twelve. They were upper middle class, no lineage whatever, simply got there through business.'' She pulled a face now. ''Dreadful, isn't it, to get into the middle class through business? Tut, tut! Tut, tut!'' And Emily smiled as she added her confirmation of the statement: "Disgraceful, really. There should be a law against it."

"Many a true word spoken in jest. And there nearly was, my dear. Anyway, as I was saying, I started when I was twelve, in the kitchen, but by the time I was seventeen I was second house-maid. The mistress died—the master had been dead for some years—and now there was only the one daughter, Miss May, left. She was then thirty and rather prim. And one day it should happen she left the house to go to tea with some friends, but on the way she ran into a storm and she bid her coachman return home. But there was a bigger storm when she got in, because there she found her lady's maid and the footman disporting themselves. And where do you think they were at it?" Mrs. Arkwright's face stretched, her blue eyes became round, her mouth was drawn into a thin line, and she held this pose for some seconds before enlightening Emily: "On Miss May's own bed. Oh! what a day! What a day! What a day! Screams and faints all round. But Miss Elsie Wilson went out and into that storm quicker than the lightning was flashing, and someone had to go and comfort Miss May. Now, as I said, I was second housemaid. But the first housemaid was Jane Battle, although it should have been Jane Sniffles, for her nose was in a perpetual state of running, and Miss May couldn't stand the sight of her; and so, who had to go and see to milady but your humble servant. And that's how it started. She took to me and I took to her and her funny little ways; and so it went on for three years. And then one day she happened to go to a garden party at a friend's house, and who should be passing through but a Major who had been discharged from the Indian Army because of a foot injury. He was a man in his forties and she was thirty-three. It was known that she had never had a man-friend in her life before, but she fell for this one, hook, line and sinker, and he for her; and two years later they were married."

She smiled at Emily while continuing to finger the picture of her husband. And then she said, "As it says in the Bible—And so it came to pass— they were married and went to the South of France for their honeymoon. And it should happen also that the Major was accompanied by his man, and his new wife by her lady's maid," and she now dug her breast with her middle finger, before going on, "Oscar had been the Major's batman in the Army and had been discharged with him, through rope-pulling, as he was wont to say. You know, Emily—" She now laid down the photograph among the others, but she didn't take her eyes off it as she went on, "There are times in your life when you say, that was the happiest period I've ever known. And that month in that lovely hotel outside Nice, Oscar and I fell in love. He was twelve years older than me. It was almost a repeat of the Major's situation, although I was only twenty-three."

She paused here as if gathering the past back into her mind before she went on, "While the happy couple were out driving or sailing, we, after duties were done, would stroll along the beach and we would talk and laugh together. We could always laugh together. And it was such a heavenly place. The hotel had only fifteen bedrooms; but I remember the proprietors were so nice, so welcoming, nothing was too much trouble, and that went for the staff, too. Oh yes, it was a wonderful time, and a week after we returned to England, Oscar asked me to marry him. As I recall, he had to put it to the Major first, and the Major was for it. But not so Miss May. Funny, I never could think of her as anything else but Miss May, because to me marriage didn't seem to alter her much: she remained prim, if you know what I mean. At first she said, oh no, I couldn't keep the position if I married because I might have children, but at the same time she didn't want to lose me. Anyway, the Major must have talked her round because she then gave her consent. I can always remember what she said." Mrs. Arkwright's head now began to bob. " 'Mabel,' she said, 'I hope you will find no necessity to have a family.' Funny way of putting it, wasn't it? But anyway, we didn't have a family, although it wasn't for lack of trying."

She now looked at Emily as she said, "But she had one, poor dear, when she was thirty-eight, and she died during the process. The baby lived twelve days. It was a beautiful boy, and the poor Major, he was so cut up and all the zest went out of his life, because he had really loved her. Although we found out later she was his second wife; he had lost the first through death, too. But that was through one of the diseases they catch in India. Anyway, it was from then on our life seemed to center around him, so much so that he couldn't seem to bear either of us out of his sight for very long. And he talked to me by the hour of his dear wife, although he never called her by name and he seemed to think I knew so much about her; that, in fact, I'd grown up with her. It was unfortunate that she hadn't had any close relatives. And neither had he, except a nephew somewhere in Switzerland and a cousin, a very old lady down in Dorset.

"Anyway, I was thirty-two when he died and Oscar about forty-four, and at the time we were living in Northumberland in the Major's old home. The Little Manor, it was called. It wasn't a big estate, some forty acres or so. It was a lonely place, well outside of the village. But on the day he was buried all the inhabitants of that village followed the hearse, for he was highly respected. As for Oscar and me, well, we didn't know where to put ourselves, we felt so lost. And then came the reading of the will."

She sat back in her chair now and nodded at Emily as she said, "Life's funny, you know, girl. When you think you're facing a blank wall and you can't see ahead, a door suddenly opens and sometimes you're blinded with the light. And that's what happened to us. You see, we were worried because we knew we would have to find other service. We hadn't much saved up because our wages weren't great. We had our uniform and our keep and we had to take that into consideration. We felt that the master would leave us a little bit, but then we thought he hadn't much to leave. Well, we knew he hadn't because it took him all his time to keep the house and staff and the little estate going, because from what Oscar gleaned he refused to dip into his wife's money whilst she was alive, and then I think he felt reluctant to do so after she died. He was certainly a very high-principled gentleman, was the Major. Anyway, there we were all sitting in the hall and the solicitor started to read the will. He read that each servant was to have a hundred pounds. Well, that seemed to please everybody; and he read out the names, but ours weren't included. There was a thousand pounds to his nephew and a thousand pounds to his cousin. Then, in a special piece of reading, the solicitor announced: 'To my faithful servant and friend Oscar Arkwright, I leave five hundred pounds and what jewelry I possess; to his wife, Mabel Arkwright, who has cared for me so tenderly since my dear wife died, I leave two hundred pounds.' Seven hundred pounds between us. And the Major's timepiece and chain and cufflinks and odds and ends, all except his medals. These were to go back with the remainder of his money and property to his regiment. The money was to be mainly used, as I understood it, for the wounded men in the regimental hospital. And you know what Oscar and I did when we heard what he had left us? We both cried, Oscar unashamedly. He cried without making a sound and the tears ran down his face. And so we were set."

She now drew in a long breath before adding, "I've always meant to tell you that story, and I have a reason for telling it now, but that will come later."

"Oh, Mrs. Arkwright." Emily rose swiftly from her chair and, going to the elderly woman, took her hand in both of hers and pressed it, saying, "Thank you. Thank you for telling me. I . . . I might as well admit that I've often wondered about your life and how you started. It's like a fairytale."

"Oh no, my dear, it was no fairytale, it was work all along the line, I mean from the time we started the business. Oscar had said to me, 'What do you want to do, girl?' and I said, 'You know what I'd like to do, Oscar? I'd like to start a hat shop.' And he said immediately, 'Why not, my dear, because you've got such a touch with hats. Look at those you made for the mistress. It must have saved her pounds.' And so we bought our first premises and the real hard work began. Your mother was one of my first trimmers: and then you came along. Well, you know the rest. But at last I've got what I always wanted: a house detached from my business. And we'll make it lovely and homely, you and I." She now put up her other hand and touched Emily's cheek, and there was a note of pleading in her voice when she said, "You will stay with me, won't you, dear?"

"Stay with you? Of course, of course. It's all settled. Where else would I go? Who have I got but you?"

"Huh! Huh!" Mrs. Arkwright pushed her away almost roughly, saying, "I'm not going to say you're footloose and fancy free, but you're free, and you're bonny, more than bonny, my dear. And now, when it gets around there's no impediment, you'll have them here like jackals after you."

"Oh, nonsense, nonsense. Anyway, don't forget what you once said about me." Now it was her turn to wag her finger at her mistress: " 'You only look attractive when you're smiling,' you said. 'You want to take that stiff, haughty look off your face.' "

"Well, yes, I did say it," admitted Mrs. Arkwright, "because I was thinking of the effect you would have on the customers. And I've always told you, you should never look superior to a client nor outdo a client in dress."

"I know all that, but it's years ago you dished out that advice. And I've learned a lot since then."

"Yes. Yes, you have, my dear . . . Now, after all this rigmarole that would fill a book, what about a cup of tea? Oh, there's one thing I must show you. I threw it in the cupboard there." She pointed across the room to an old Dutch wardrobe, saying, "It was in a box lying on top of twenty others. I'll have to get them out and see what I can do with them. And by the way, there's some good material up there, too; some of it time-worn in parts, but we'll sort it out."

Emily opened the wardrobe door and immediately paused at sight of a hat lying by itself on the shelf opposite. It was a very large hat. Presently, she drew it from the shelf, saying, "You found this up in the attic?"

"Yes; what am I telling you?"

"Good gracious! I've always thought straws look bare without trimming, but this one! This one looks naked. I don't think it's ever had a trimming on, either." She examined it. "And what a strange color! How on earth would they get that color?"

"Oh, a mixture of white, yellow, and light brown, I would say."

"It's a straw, but it's stiff."

"Well, it would have been dipped and must have been well dipped, I should imagine, to be as stiff as it still is. What do you think of it?"

Emily put a hand in the crown and turned the hat slowly around before she said, "Well, it's very unusual. It really is a beautiful straw; and the color, I've . . . I've never seen anything like it. Not quite corn color, much lighter."

"Pale gold, I would say."

"Yes. Yes." Emily nodded. "Pale gold. This side's a bit bent. But if it's been in a box for years, it's a wonder it isn't crushed up."

"Yes, that's what I thought, too," said Mrs. Arkwright. "But it was laid flat on top of the others. As to the tilt of the brim, I think it sets it off. Anyway, it could be straightened under the steam kettle. What do you think we should trim it with?"

"You mean to trim it? Somehow it looks just right naked." She started to giggle, and felt compelled to add an explanation: "Well, it does look naked, doesn't it?"

"Yes," Mrs. Arkwright joined in her chuckling. "As you say, it looks naked as it is. What do you think we should trim it with?"

"I don't know. Funny, but somehow I can't see it trimmed."

"Oh well, it won't be sold naked. You can take my word for that."

Impulsively now, Emily went across to the dressing-table mirror and, sitting down, she put the hat on at a slight angle, and then sat staring at herself in the mirror, before slowly turning about on the stool and facing Mrs. Arkwright. It was a matter of seconds before that lady exclaimed, "Good gracious! It could be made for you, that hat. It picks up the color of your skin."

"You always said I hadn't any color in my skin to speak of."

"Well, that's what I mean. They both match now. Anyway, we'll sell that, my dear. We'll stick that on a main stand right opposite the front door. It will have to have a little trimming of some kind on it, though."

"Oh no, no." Emily got to her feet now, protesting, "Don't put anything on it."

"Oh, don't be silly." Mrs. Arkwright pulled herself to the edge of the chair. "Can you see me or anybody else in this country selling a hat without it being swamped in ribbons or flowers or feathers or some such?"

"Yes. Yes. Start a new vogue."

"That'll be the day. No, it'll have to have some kind of trimming."

Emily now took the hat off and again she put her hand in the crown and turned it around; then quietly she said, "A flat bow of wide green watered silk ribbon lying on the back, just there." She pointed. "Not too big, mustn't come over the edge of the brim in any way, nor creep up the crown; just let it lie flat."

The older woman and the younger one stood now, the hat between them, watching it slowly revolving on Emily's hand. And Mrs. Arkwright said quietly, "Yes. Yes, I think you're right. It'll have to be a soft green, the apple variety. And it'll have to have a name; the hat, I mean."

"The Golden Straw, how about that?"

"Yes. Yes." Mrs. Arkwright nodded. "Yes, The Golden Straw. That's clever. And would you like to take a bet on how long it's going to be there on that stand before being put in a bandbox?"

"It will have to be a large bandbox," Emily said, then added, "What about half-a-crown it goes within the next month?"

"I bet you five shillings it doesn't go within the next three months."

"Oh . . . Well, I'll take that on. Yes. Yes, I'll take that on. But no trimmings, just the bow, mind."

"As you say, miss, no trimmings, just the bow.

But wait, what about if a client takes a fancy to it and wants it trimmed up?"

"Well, we'll have to dissuade her otherwise with that silence, you know, that speaks louder than words when clients ask what we think."

"You have very little left to learn, have you, Mrs. Ratcliffe?"

"Very little where hats are concerned, Madam Arkwright. And you should take credit for that, shouldn't you?"

"Go on with you. Go on." Mrs. Arkwright pushed Emily toward the door and followed her, saying, "I could die in this house and nobody would bring me a cup of tea. Let's get downstairs. But don't take that thing with you." She snatched the hat from Emily's hand and flung it onto the bed, saying, "I've got a funny feeling about that thing; I'll likely lose my five bob. I might be sorry I ever found it. Go on, get yourself out. It'll be there when we come back."

"What is it, doctor?"

"A heart attack."

"Oh!" Emily shook her head slowly. "That's serious."

"Well, it can be in many cases, but she'll survive; only she'll have to be careful. Is there a room down below that could be made into a bedroom? because the stairs aren't going to help her in the future."

Emily thought for a moment, then said, "Oh yes, yes; there's the study. It leads into the other house, but it could be made into a nice bedroom."

"Well, I would see to it."

"She'll be all right?" Emily asked tentatively now. "I mean . . . ?"

"Yes, I know what you mean. And yes, she'll be all right, as long as she takes care. But this is a warning. All such attacks are warnings. The next time it happens she mightn't get off so easily, and as she is subject to bronchitis she should be extra careful . . . Has she been worrying about anything recently?"

"Not that I know of."

They were standing in the hall and he was looking about him. "Never could understand why she wanted to take on this place," he commented. "Wasn't next door big enough for her? There were plenty of living-rooms upstairs. Is she going in for buying property now?"

Emily looked straight into the doctor's face. She had never cared much for him. Not only was his manner brusque, but also he was nosy. And so she answered without satisfying his questioning: "Why she took this place, doctor, was simply because she wanted a home to live in, not a business house with people coming and going all the time and surrounded by the evidence of her work."

"Huh! Well, to my mind, she shouldn't have been concerned, because her work, as you call it, has put her somewhere, hasn't it? Hats. Who would think there was money in hats? Stupid falderals, in my opinion: women going around looking as if they were growing gardens on their heads, or had been bird shooting. I actually saw someone the other day with a complete bird perched on top of her bonnet. My God! the money some women must spend." He now buttoned up the collar of his coat, picked up his hard hat from the hall table, then added his final comment, "Some people profit from others' vanity, don't they? Well, keep her quiet. I'll be in tomorrow."

Emily opened the door. She did not say, "Good day," or "Thank you, doctor"; and when he gave her one last look she returned it and just as coldly. But then to her utter surprise he thrust his face toward her and, sounding even jovial, he said, "You don't like me, do you? But don't worry, you're not alone." And on this he turned from her and walked down the stone steps, through the gate and into the hansom cab; and the driver, perched high on his box, flicked his whip and away they went.

When at last she closed the door, she had to resist the desire to bang it, and she asked herself why she had stood there for so long. He was right; she didn't like him. Doctor Smeaton would never have acted like that, but this partner of his was a detestable individual, and had much to learn, in her mind, before he could be considered a real doctor. She imagined he couldn't be thirty years old. Well, whatever his age, he still had a lot to learn, at least in how to deal with people. She recalled his first visit when he had stood in the hall next door and gazed at The Golden Straw perched between but above two elaborately decorated hats. And he had grinned as he said, "What's happened to that one? Somebody forgotten to put the clothes on it?"

She had lost her bet over the straw hat. Many had remarked on it, but only one person had asked to try it on, and then had actually shuddered at the result, and her comment was, "I can't see it suiting anyone, even if it was trimmed. It's such an unusual shape, so large, and has no height to the crown, to speak of."

She couldn't quite understand the feeling she had come to have for this particular hat. And when the three months were up and Mrs. Arkwright had won her bet, she had magnanimously said to her, "You may keep your five bob; and besides that, I am making you a present of the hat. Anyway, right from the beginning I felt it must have been made many years ago exactly for you or somebody like you. Although it will always puzzle me why it had never been trimmed and was laid so carefully on top of that box."

The hat now reposed in a large bandbox in her bedroom, and every now and again she would take it out, put it on her head and sit before the mirror adjusting it this way and that. And the more she did this the more she became so enamored of the straw as to ask herself why hats had to be larded with so much flippancy, feathers, flowers and ribbons of every description and very often piled one on top of the other. The only shapes that didn't get imprisoned in such a way were the winter felts. Ribbons, yes, and a feather here and there. But then she recalled that some clients demanded a very large quantity of feathers on their velours, with ribbons trailing from the back, the fashion at the moment. And with regard to current fashion, there was the new corset. In her opinion, whoever had designed it must be a descendant of a member of the Spanish Inquisition.

When she voiced this to Mrs. Arkwright, that lady had laughed heartily and said, "Oh, I know where you got that idea. You've been reading those books that were left on the shelves down-stairs. You're an odd girl, and funny." Then she had added: "You throw aside *The Ladies' Journal* and yet sit reading that kind of stuff."

On that particular day she had looked in the mirror and had nodded to her reflection as she thought, "Yes, I suppose I must appear odd," but as for being funny, she could recognize nothing funny about her thinking: that was made up of shadowy thoughts and questions and almost a craving for something that stemmed from a feeling of deep loneliness, which she couldn't understand, for her daily life was a contradiction, it being filled with people. But what she did understand was she was tied to this business, to this house, and to Mrs. Arkwright. But then, wasn't that a good thing? She recalled she had never given herself an answer but had got hastily up and gone about the business of the day.

And now again she was dealing with the business of the day. First of all, she went back upstairs and into Mrs. Arkwright's bedroom, saying, "I don't like that fellow, you know. And you know what he said?"

"No; what did he say?"

"Well"—she bent over the bed—"he pushed his face almost into mine, like this, and he said, 'You don't like me, do you?'"

"He never did!" Mrs. Arkwright laughed softly.

"He did; and then he walked away, without giving me the chance to say either yes or no."

"Huh! Anyway, what else did he say? I mean, about me. Am I for the box?"

"Yes, in about ten or fifteen or twenty years' time, I would say. But I wouldn't choose the wood yet."

"He thinks I'm spoofing about the pain?"

Emily's attitude and voice both changed now as she said quietly, "No, he doesn't think you're spoofing about any pain. You've had a heart attack, and if you don't want another, and soon, you've got to take it very quietly"—she held up her hand—"at least for a time, until you've properly pulled round. And what's more, he's ordered that you sleep downstairs. No more trotting up and down." And again her hand went up as she said, "I emphasize, it's just for a time. Anyway, I'm going to see Alice, and I'll get Molly Stock to help her. We'll turn the study into a bedroom for the time being."

"You're going to do no such thing."

"But we are, Mrs. Arkwright, and you can do nothing about it, only hold your tongue and rest."

Mabel Arkwright lowered her head, and when she made no tart reply to this, Emily went to her again and sat on the side of the bed and, taking her hand, spoke to her gently: "It is just a temporary thing, and it will help all round. It's the nearest room to next door, and I'll be able to pop in and out all the time as if you were actually there. And then when you're on your feet again it'll only be a step for you to put on your bossing boots."

"Well!"—the head came up—"it needs somebody to do some bossing. You're not stiff enough.''

"No, I'm not when you're there, but you leave me on my own and you'll see the difference. Anyway, there's no need for pushing with any of them; they're all such good workers. We're very, very lucky, you know. And they'll do anything for you. They're all upset; they can't imagine you being ill. It's as if God has gone down with the measles.''

Emily now sprang from the side of the bed beseeching the elderly woman, "Now don't laugh like that, please! Oh, don't.'' But she was laughing herself while she still implored, "I shouldn't say such daft things.''

Mabel Arkwright was holding her hand tightly across her ribs, and her voice came out between gasps as she said, "It's better medicine than he could give me. But you do say the daftest things, girl. Nobody looking at you and your lady-like pose would ever couple you up with some of the things you come out with.''

"It all comes from my common breeding.''

"Oh, don't you believe that. Your mother wasn't common. By the account she gave me of your father, he was very like my Oscar . . . Emily?''

"Yes, my dear?''

"Why is it things like this happen to one? I've just got the house as I wanted it, always wanted it. It's nothing like Miss May's place, but it's got an air about it, an air of . . . well, I don't know what.''

"Refinement?"

"Yes. Yes." Mrs. Arkwright nodded once in compliance, then repeated, "Refinement, that's the word. But without the falderals. You said to me once you couldn't stand bobbed mantel borders, buffaloes' horns on walls, or occasional tables on which you couldn't lay a pin down flat."

"I said that?"

"Oh yes, years ago. Your mother took an order to one of those big houses in The Strand. The family were away. It must have been just for the day, but the housemaid proudly showed your mother round. And you must have seen the horns decorating the hall and she must have taken you into a drawing room, because when you came back that's what you said."

"I can't even remember that occasion."

"Well, even before you started work with me at fourteen she used to bring you along now and then. But anyway, I thought of what you said, so I've knocked the bobbles off the mantel border, left enough space on the table for a few pins, and, as much as I would have loved to decorate the hall and the whole house with bulls' antlers, I've resisted."

They were laughing together again now but gently. Then Mrs. Arkwright's hand went out toward Emily, and when she took it and leaned slightly forward, the other hand came onto her head and brought her face down and she kissed her. Then, in a thick voice and striving to strike a humorous note, she said, "That's never been done before, has it? And I don't know whether it will ever be done again. But you should never leave things too long, nor hold back what you want to say, because one never knows the hour, or the day, when it will be impossible to come out with anything. So I'll say it now. Lass, since you changed your life some months ago and came to live with me, I've known more comfort and peace than at any time since I lost my Oscar, and you've really become the daughter I never had. And you'll never know what it means to me, the fact that whether my days are going to be cut short or left to be long, you'll be with me."

Emily found it impossible to speak, so she pressed her lips against the thin sallow cheek, then hurried from the bed. But as she reached the door Mrs. Arkwright's voice, returning to its old tartness as if it had never touched on softness or emotion, said, "But I'm only sixty-two, mind, and you could have your hands full for the next ten or fifteen years. And don't forget there's an old girl and an old gent at the top of the street who are pushed in basket-chairs around the park every day, rain or snow. They tell me they're in their eighties. So you've got a job ahead of you."

Emily turned about and in the same vein she said, "Oh no, I won't have any such job ahead of me, for I'll engage at least two day and two night nurses to see to you while I go gallivanting like any young divorced lady looking for a husband. Now, lie there, Mrs. Mabel Arkwright, and dwell on that."

They stared at each other across the room and their chuckling joined. But after Emily had closed the door and had crossed the landing to her own room, she stood for a moment thinking: ten . . . fifteen years. It could be; these things did happen. And she looked ahead and saw her life spent between hats and Mrs. Arkwright meandering into senility.

Doctor Montane called the following day and pronounced that his patient's heart was settling into place, and yes, she would be able to walk quietly downstairs and into her new room. But there she must rest in bed for at least a week.

As he was walking away from the bed Mrs. Arkwright said, "Would you care for a cup, doctor?"

"Coffee?" He turned and looked at her; then his face breaking into what might have been a semblance of a smile, he said, "Yes. Yes, I would indeed. Thank you very much; it's chilly out."

"Would you like it laced, then?"

"Laced?" His eyebrows had moved slowly up and his full lips had gone into a pout, and he made the slightest movement with his head as he said, "Laced? Oh, thank you very much, but not at this time of the morning. If you would care to invite me any time after seven o'clock at night, I'd be delighted to accept a laced coffee, perhaps two. Who knows where to stop once you lace coffee?"

He was actually smiling now, and when he turned to Emily, who was holding the bedroom door ajar for him and enquired of her, "Do you like laced coffee?" she answered, "Yes, now and again."

"Well, well! who would have thought it? The things that go on," he said and turned his still laughing face toward the bed and Mrs. Arkwright; then with a flap of his hand as though to emphasize, yes, who would believe it? he went out and downstairs, accompanied by Emily. And there she said, "If you will come into the drawing room I'll see that one of the girls supplies you with an unlaced coffee."

"By! you're a starchy piece, aren't you?"

"What?"

"You heard what I said: you're a starchy piece. Yet you have your coffee laced. One lives and learns in this business."

"Well, I hope you live a long time, doctor, because you've got a lot to learn. One thing I would advise you start on right away, and that's tact."

"Oh my. Oh my." He walked away from her, up the room, looking about him and remarking to no one in particular, "Bit different from when the old admiral had it. Woman's taste definitely, and yet very few furbelows. Could be a male touch, what do you say?"

He turned and was slightly surprised when he found he was addressing an empty room.

Down in the basement kitchen, Emily said to the cook, "Mary, will you make a cup of coffee, strong, black, and ask Alice to take it up to the drawing room for Doctor Montane?"

"Oh! Doctor Montane. Is he come, miss?"

"Yes, Doctor Montane has come, and everybody knows it."

"You don't like him, miss?"

"No, I don't like him, Mary."

"Funny that, miss, 'cos he's got a good name. Well, so I'm told. Four bob to those who pay, two to those who find it a bit difficult, and nowt to some folk."

"Oh, he should have a medal pinned on him for that. But you should believe only half of what you hear, Mary, so I'd cut the last two out."

Mary gave a deep-throated chuckle as she said, "I'll make it black, miss, just as you say. But I'll have to stick a jug of cream on the side, you know. Anyway, how's the missis?"

"Oh, she's doing fine, Mary. We'll have her downstairs today."

"Oh, that'll be a blessin', for what with the basement steps an' goin' up the main staircase, Alice's legs were dropping off her last night. Not that the exercise isn't good for her, but enough's as good as a feast. And I wanted to have a word with you, miss. You know, we should have another help; I mean, I'm no softie on Alice, as everybody knows, but now that she's still got to see to next door she's skittering around like a scalded cat from six in the mornin' 'til nine at night."

"Yes, I know, Mary. I've thought about that for some time, and I'll have a talk with Mrs. Arkwright."

"Thanks, miss, you do that, and we'll be grate-

ful, 'cos madam's never been one for over-staffing, has she?''

They looked at each other. It was a knowing
look and required no answer. So Emily went out
of the kitchen and up the ten half-circle stone
steps and into the hall, thinking as she walked
that Mary was right, Mrs. Arkwright had never
been one for over-staffing. Very odd, that. She
was so generous in other ways, that is with regard
to wages, for she was always a halfpenny an hour
up on other hat establishments. But, of course,
she expected expert work done for it. Her mother,
as a girl, had started on a penny an hour. But a
twelve-hour day could bring in six shillings a
week, and in those days that was not to be sniffed
at. Then she went up to three-halfpence and then
tuppence. She was on tuppence an hour when
she died. She herself got nothing for the first year,
because she was what was called apprenticed.
But of course she got her bowl of soup in the half-
hour dinner break, and it was always good strong
stuff. She was on tuppence an hour when she
married; it had risen to threepence an hour by the
time she was divorced; now she was no longer on
a weekly wage but on what Mrs. Arkwright termed
a salary: fifty pounds a year and, you could say,
board and lodging thrown in; and what was more,
free hats and outdoor apparel. She was fortunate
. . . oh, yes, she was fortunate . . . In a way
she was very fortunate.

She was about to mount the stairs when she

thought, I'd better go and tell him his coffee will be brought to him in a moment or so.

When she opened the drawing room door she found him peering into a china cabinet. He did not turn fully around to her, but over his shoulder he called, "Some of these pieces are Dresden, aren't they? And that's a complete tea-set of Spode, isn't it?"

"Yes, so I'm told."

He had turned from the cabinet now, saying, "So you are told? You know nothing about china, then, just what you're told?"

"No one knows anything about anything except what they are told. Right from the beginning one is told." She stressed the "told." "A child is told what to say, what to do. Isn't that so?"

"Yes: yes, you're right there; but some children are more clever than others; they not only maintain what they are told, they take it up and work at it. For instance, if I'd just been told that was a full set of Spode, I would have wanted to know where it was made, and who made it. *We're not just told things,* we've got to extend on what we are *told.*"

"Yes. Yes, you're right. And, of course, you'd be one of those people who would definitely extend on what they were told."

"You've got a bee in your bonnet, haven't you?"

"What?"

"Oh, you say *'what'*, and not *'pardon'*. Young ladies say 'pardon', ordinary people say 'what', and I can't imagine you being ordinary . . . Mind out of the way!" He thrust an arm out in her direction. "You're going to be pushed in the back with that tray."

She had not heard Alice's approach and she stepped quickly to the side, while keeping her gaze on the obnoxious individual.

Alice passed her now, smiling widely, and walked up the room and put the tray on the edge of the table, pushed a few knick-knacks to one side; then, looking at the doctor, she said, "Cook put a couple of scones on there, doctor. They're fresh out of the oven. She said you might like 'em."

"Oh, you thank the cook very kindly for me. She's a very thoughtful woman. Tell her I haven't had any breakfast yet because I've just come from bringing another fortunate human being into the world. The mother, being a sensible woman, had decided she wasn't going to let it be born at all if she had her way. You tell the cook that."

"I will, doctor, I will."

As Alice went out laughing, the young man laughed with her; but Emily's cream-tinted skin was showing an almost rosy glow: she knew that this distasteful individual was out to shock her. By mentioning a baby's birth he imagined that he was infringing on the sensitive feelings of a maiden lady. In her opinion this man should never have been a doctor: at least, he should not yet have been practicing, for he had no idea how to handle people. He was uncouth, and being so, his nature was, as it were, up in arms against what he imagined to be a prudish streak in her. There was something else about the man that made her angry.

She knew her face was flushed and this annoyed her further; and so, trying to keep her annoyance from her voice, she said as quietly as she could, "Well, if your patient was so long in labor that you apparently had to spend some part of the night with her, would it not have been advisable to send her to a hospital where she could have had specialist treatment and perhaps a breech-birth?"

For a moment she felt a spurt of elation filling her: his eyebrows had gone up again, his mouth had gone into a slight gape; but then he said, "Well! well! human after all. And you read the papers, don't you? the parts not fit for young ladies' eyes. You have just given a brief description of N. Bates, and the case of the family bringing a case against the doctor for not doing his job. Well! well! we live and learn. I knew young ladies did read such things on the quiet, but to express them, never!"

"I'm not one of your young ladies, doctor, I am a working woman. And whatever you have against middle-class young ladies, you've come to the wrong shop to vent your spleen, and I emphasize that, the wrong shop. I, sir, was married when I was seventeen. I've been divorced for some time now. I began working when I was fourteen . . . unpaid for a year, apart from a bowl of soup. Years before that, of course, I would have been carried by my mother into a freezing attic, where she and many others sewed until blood ran out of their finger ends, with their babies lying in wash-baskets beside them. When children became old enough they were put to work untangling wool or the knots out of string. I have worked every day of my life, and among very ordinary people. I have also, through the business, met and talked with the middle class, and I have yet to meet anyone whom I would take for the person you imagine me to be."

There was silence between them and the whole room seemed to be still. Then, in a very calm voice now, she said, "I would drink your coffee, doctor, before it gets cold."

He took a step away from the cabinet as he said, "And you hope it chokes me, don't you?"

"Yes, something like that." And having said this, she turned away and left the room.

The door closed behind her and she stood for a moment, head to one side, her chin up, as she listened to his unusually deep and bellowing laugh. It was like something that could have been emitted by a very large man. But he wasn't large, he wasn't even tall, he was slim and of medium height. And a more aggravating person she hoped never to meet.

3

It was Easter of 1879 and the transfer to the downstairs bedroom was suiting Mrs. Arkwright very well: she could walk through the door into the hall; she could see to the work-rooms on the ground floor where Amity Lockhart, Margie Monkton and Jean Felton were working away, piling feathers and flowers and ribbons onto all shapes and sizes of blocked crowns, some tall, some round and some even square, at least on the outside, the inner shape being rounded to fit the head. And there were bonnets by the score, capped with frills and trailing ribbons. A few were entirely in black, to satisfy mourning orders; but in the main, the room presented a gay scene of ribbons, flowers, fruit and feathers.

There were two new apprentices, Molly Stock and Sarah Hubbard, but these divided their time between the hat-room and the alteration-room upstairs, over which Esther McCann and Lena Broadbent now presided . . . And as Mrs. Arkwright had been forbidden to climb the stairs in number thirty-four, so she was forbidden in number thirty-five. Therefore she'd had to make a concession of having a room in "her house" where the girls could bring the models to her for examination and advice as to further improvement, or, in many cases, the deleting of this apron front or that bushel-like back. Also to this room, at frequent intervals, would come the ladies' maids with whom Mrs. Arkwright dealt and had done for many years. At one time she had been in touch with only four, but now she had nine such visiting her, mostly at some evening hour when their mistresses would be dining out or doing a theater. And she paid them well for the gowns, costumes and lingerie they brought. There were times when she might not see certain of them for a full year, but most of her stock was made up after the season of balls and presentations at Court, and the like.

It might be a strange talent, but Mabel Arkwright could detect if an article of top apparel, such as an evening gown, or a dress, or a suit, had been worn more than a few times. She had been known to pick up a dress and with a lift of her nostrils would say, "Not more than three times." And an evening dress would cause her nostrils to sniff before she pronounced, "Once."

She was of the opinion that no matter how often a woman bathed or scented her body, she had an odor that penetrated her clothing, and the more she wore a garment the more of that odor it absorbed. Occasionally, she would briefly handle a dress, then say, "Tear that up; don't use any part of it; and in future we'll cut that supply out."

Now, with the new arrangements, it was Emily

who saw to the ladies who would ostensibly come to look at hats, but who would discreetly wonder if Mrs. Arkwright had anything that might interest them in the dress line. And Emily would say, "Oh yes, madam, I think she has," and then would lead the client to a room that was allotted for such visits.

However, such business would never have thrived had she ushered more than one into that room at any time. In consequence, there were no cubicles, only a chair, two wardrobes and a large swinging cheval-mirror.

Outside the workroom, there were few opportunities for laughter; or other occurrences which might sow the seeds for laughter and which would be allowed to bubble over and be enjoyed later. One such had occurred yesterday. A new customer had come to view hats. She was accompanied by a gentleman. And Molly Stock's description of her was very accurate: empty-headed; eighteen at the most; very pretty and very common. As for the gentleman, he was very middle-aged and apparently very rich. The girl had a wedding ring on her finger, but if they were married, said Molly Stock, then she herself had just swum from Borneo and her hair was still wet.

After the couple had left with the coachman, who had been brought in to carry out five bandboxes, apparently Molly and Sarah had laughed until they cried.

What did Mrs. Arkwright think about it? Well, what Mabel said to Emily was, "They bought five hats, and as long as she stays with him they'll come back again. Being a man of the world, he brought her here likely because it's a bit off the beaten track; he couldn't very well take her into Finlays or anywhere along Bond Street, for he would likely run into the wife of one of his best friends, or even his own." And she had added musingly, "Five hats in one go. Where's she going to wear them?"

When, with a little smile on her lips, Emily said, "Perhaps in bed," they, too, laughed until they cried; and when Emily added, "They won't be much use afterwards," their laughter increased.

Life was pleasant. Life was good.

And then the following day they were given another laugh; at least, the incident started with a laugh; but it caused Emily, reluctantly, to change her opinion, be it so slightly, of a certain person.

Doctor Montane had got into the habit of dropping in once a week to keep an eye on Mrs. Arkwright, and on this occasion he brought with him not only his doctor's black bag, but also a round box covered with brown paper.

After examining Mrs. Arkwright, he looked at her hard for a moment before asking, "Have you been doing what you shouldn't do?"

"I don't know what I shouldn't do, except go up and down stairs."

"Well, that's what you've been doing, isn't it?"

"No, it isn't. There's no need."

"Been outside walking?"

"No, I haven't been outside walking, either. I

haven't been out since last Sunday, when I went for a drive. We hired a carriage and Emily and I did things in style: through the park we went and down The Mall.''

"*Oh! Oh!* Looking for husbands?''

"Don't be cheeky, young man. Let me tell you, Emily has no need to go looking for a husband, they're on the doorstep.''

He didn't speak for a moment; but then he said, "Yes, I can see that.''

"You married?''

"No, I am not married.''

"Going to be married?''

"Well.'' He now looked up toward the ceiling as if thinking, then said quickly, "Not that I'm aware of, but I hope. Yes, I do hope, some day.''

"Anyway, why do you ask about the stairs?''

"Well, it's evident, isn't it? You've been over-doing it again in some way, and if it isn't that, it's your diet. Do you eat a lot of fat?''

"I like fat. What is meat without fat? Tasteless.''

"May I ask what you drink in the way of wine?''

"No, you may not, young sir. But nevertheless I will tell you. I like my drop of port and I also like my nip of whiskey, and I'm too old to change now. So let this do its worst.'' She now flapped her hand against her chest; and he answered with an air of indifference, "Well, yes, it's yours to do what you like with. Who am I to stop you? The only thing is, I don't want to lose a patient. I'm speaking purely from personal reasons: I need the money.''

Mrs. Arkwright now bit on her lip while her eyes twinkled and she said, "You'll go too far, young man. But in the meantime let us go into the drawing room, where the coffee will be waiting, minus nips."

"Oh, what a pity!" he said as he stooped to pick up his medical bag and the other brown-papered box that was tied with string.

As they entered the drawing room Emily was about to leave; but he stopped her by saying, "Ah, Mrs. Ratcliffe, the very person. I would like your advice on something. Have you a minute to spare?"

Emily cast a glance at Mrs. Arkwright before saying, "Only one or two. But I'm rather curious as to why you should want advice from me."

"Oh, on your own subject, Mrs. Ratcliffe; hats, of course. I could have asked Mrs. Arkwright here, but two heads are always better than one, I'm told."

"Hats? You want advice on hats, ladies' hats?"

"What else but ladies' hats? When *I* want a hat I go to my hatter."

Emily inclined her head as she said, "Yes. Yes, of course." Then the three of them walked up the room, and he, having placed the bag on a table, proceeded to take off the wrapping from the papered box. Having done so, he lifted the lid and extracted from the box a bonnet, a very, very worn bonnet, an old-fashioned bonnet, and holding it in his hand, he looked from one to another, saying, "I brought it for size, but I want something much more modern and, I'm told, apparently on good authority, although I don't know what you ladies think about it, that hats are getting smaller and not so heavily trimmed."

"You are wrong there, sir," Mrs. Arkwright put in sharply. "There are hats for every occasion: the races, the regattas and such like require large hats, especially if they are expecting sunshine. But not only that, there is a vying, a competition for the largest and the best-trimmed hats on such an occasion. Then there is the country-hat occasion, generally not so large. For city wear, I admit, and with those people or ladies who have to attend to business of one sort or another, the hat remains small. And, of course, the bonnet is small by nature."

"Oh, yes. Yes, I see." He nodded at her. "I have been misinformed, I can see that. But my aunt . . . and family live in the country, you know."

It was Emily who now said in a tone that implied simple enquiry: "You need a bonnet for your aunt?"

He turned on her sharply, saying, "Yes! Mrs. Ratcliffe, for my aunt. As I have yet no wife and no fiancée, and definitely as yet I cannot afford a mistress, I can assure you this bonnet is for my aunt."

Mrs. Arkwright's shoulders shook slightly, and when Emily's head went up and her chin was characteristically thrust out, Mrs. Arkwright could only remind her: "Well, you asked for that, Emily. Oh yes, you did."

"I asked for no such thing, Mrs. Arkwright. But I think it unnecessary that I should need an explanation from the doctor that he has neither wife, fiancée, nor"—she now stretched—"mistress." She had spoken as if he were not present; but he, taking two steps in order to stand in front of her, said quietly, "Believe me, I had no intention of embarrassing you."

"You did not embarrass me. Do you think the mention of the word 'mistress' embarrasses me?"

"No. No." His voice now rose slightly. "I couldn't imagine anything embarrassing you, to tell you the truth. But I just want to make it plain to you that I sincerely need help in choosing a suitable bonnet for an aunt, who is fifty-nine years old and is termed eccentric. To my mind she is not even peculiar. The eccentricity seems to have its origins in the fact that she has worn that"—he pointed now to the bonnet that was resting on the lid of the box—"for the last twelve years, both inside and outside the house. Every now and then the surmise arises as to whether or not she goes to bed in it."

There was a titter now from Mrs. Arkwright, and even Emily was unable to suppress a smile. "You see, if you will let me explain," he went on, "she is my father's half-sister and she has always lived in this house in which she was born, as I said, fifty-nine years ago. I was brought up with her. When I was three years old, she seemed old to me, but she has never seemed to change: she remains a dear sweet person. There are nine in the family; I happen to be the youngest." He now turned and addressed himself to Mrs. Arkwright, adding, "The failure of the family, because who but an idiot would go in for doctoring unless he meant to get into Harley Street or to become a great cutter-upper of other human beings? So I am what you would call the black sheep. However, in the eyes of the others I do possess a favorable quality: I can manage Phoebe, at least in most ways, except with regard to her dress. Whether she changes her underwear, I don't know, but I do know it takes almost the combined effort of my three sisters, my mother and two maids to get her top dress off and then to burn it. She often goes to bed in it."

"You're joking, doctor."

He shook his head as he looked at Mrs. Arkwright, and quite solemnly said, "I'm not, Mrs. Arkwright, not a word am I saying in joke. That is Aunt Phoebe. As for the bonnet, I have seen her in bed with that on, too. And as you will notice"—he tentatively picked up the black ribbon attached to it—"that could stand up itself with grease, now couldn't it? because she wipes her fingers on it. It hangs down the back. But don't let me give you the impression that she is mad, or anything in that line; she is not. She will discuss any topic of the day: she has studied history more deeply than is usually done in schools, and she can also play the piano, by ear." Now he was chuckling, as was Mrs. Arkwright, and even Emily was laughing.

"But unfortunately she is the reason for many disputes in the house, especially with Father. When he is away from court he likes a little peace at the weekends. But does he get it? Not when Phoebe wishes to argue a case he's been on. Yes, that's true."

"Your father is Sir Arthur Montane! the big judge?"

"He is Sir Arthur Montane, the judge, Mrs. Arkwright. He is not the big judge, he is really a very small man. But then, of course, it can be said he has a very big head with a lot of brains inside and a greater amount of common sense."

"Well! well! And he *is* a 'Sir', you say?"

"Yes. Yes, he is a 'Sir'."

"Well! well! So you are the son of Sir Arthur Montane."

"Unfortunately, yes. I say unfortunately, not because I am my father's son but because, he being a judge and a 'Sir', people expect so much more from me. I think I'm a great disappointment."

"Don't be silly." And Mrs. Arkwright flapped a hand at him. "Are you fishing for compliments? Well, you're not getting them from me. Although I will say this: you're a very good doctor, and I'm not the only one who says so; I hear of it from my women in there"—she pointed in the direction of the next house—"and who would vote for you to get into Parliament tomorrow, that is if women had the vote, of course. They know about you, that you attend to those further down the river, while old Smeaton sees to the moneyed lot. It's a wonder you got the chance to come here."

For a moment he did not answer, and when he did he said quietly, "You're well informed, Mrs. Arkwright. But let me tell you, and in saying what I'm going to say I'm not besmirching the middle class, in which, of course, my people reside, or those lower down the social scale who have money enough to pay, my sympathies are with those who can't pay at all. And, you"—he pointed toward Emily—"don't come back and say that I'm making myself out to be the defender of the poor."

"I wasn't going to say any such thing."

"No, but you were thinking it. I know you. Oh, by now I know you, Mrs. Ratcliffe. But I'll say this to you while I'm on, that I am not alone, there are a number like me who do give of their time and would gladly give up more if they possibly could, to go out and help what is usually termed the scum of the earth. Have you ever been down Pink Lane, that leads to Baker's Wharf, or to Catherine Street? Oh no, you'd never have been along there. Well, even out of curiosity, I'd advise you not to attempt it even in the daylight, unless you have a good escort. Oh, perhaps you wouldn't be knocked about, but any money or valuables you might have on you when entering that quarter, or the countless courts and alleys thereabouts, would be missing when you came out, which would ensure that somebody that night would eat better than they'd done for some days."

"You should be in Parliament."

"Yes, I know I should. And as our good friend here, Mrs. Arkwright, suggested, if it were left to the women, I would be; and I wish it were left to the women. Oh yes, I do."

"You'll never be rich."

He turned back to Mrs. Arkwright, saying, "You never know. You just never know. I won't be rich at this game, no, but I have my plans. I'm going to marry a rich woman; well, a woman with enough money to keep me in good cigars, good port—like you, I like a glass of port—a holiday on the continent when I'm feeling tired; and with the rest of her money I'll take hordes of youngsters into the country or to the seaside, and filling empty bellies; and in the meantime, seeing that pregnant women have decent attention, and, too, that my father jails other women who take the lives of young girls by back-street abortions."

They were standing now as if in a triangle, and their eyes moved from one to the other, portraying their different thoughts but not voicing them, until he suddenly said, "Well, what about this bonnet? I promised the family I'd bring a new bonnet back for her because there she is, they tell me, sitting up in her room. Apparently, Josephine wrenched it from her and she brought it in this morning, and I have to catch a train back tonight so that the family will be able to sleep in their beds."

"I can't believe this. It's one of the funniest things I've heard in years. But look, sit yourself down there for a moment. I'll ring for the coffee, and in the meantime we'll go and choose a bonnet for Miss Phoebe. Come on, Emily."

Emily did not move straightaway, but remained staring at the young man, this surprising young man, this exasperating, annoying . . . but very human young man.

But of a sudden, as if coming to herself, she swung round and followed Mrs. Arkwright from the room. And when they were about to pass through the bedroom and into the workshop that they now called number thirty-five, Mrs. Arkwright stopped Emily by taking her by the arm, and, looking into her face, she said, "He's one in a million, and he more than likes you. You want to think about it."

"What!" Emily pulled herself away from the hand on her arm. "You're joking. *Him?* I . . . I really can't stand him. Oh, and all that talk . . ."

"That wasn't just talk, those were facts, and he meant every word of what he said. I know men. You'll be a fool if you don't jump at the chance."

"Don't be silly, Mabel. He's looking for a rich woman, you heard what he said, a rich woman to carry out his ideas. He doesn't want a wife, he really wants a bank account."

"Don't you be silly, girl. The last was just a cover-up. But anyway, who's to say you won't be rich one day?" They stared at each other for a moment before Emily cried, "Oh, please, please! don't hold that out as any carrot. I want nothing more from you than what you've already given

me. You've given me everything. Oh, please, leave what you have to whom you like; I've got a pair of hands on me, I could start up a business anywhere. I . . . well, if we are speaking plainly, I'd likely be glad to carry on like I do next door, but in a smaller place. Oh no, I beg you, don't hold any carrots out to me. Anyway, I wouldn't accept them. As for him, never! He's the last man in the world I'd marry, and believe me on that."

"I believe you, the way you feel now, but time will tell. Come on now, let's choose a bonnet for Phoebe. I'll be dying to hear the next episode on Phoebe. I've never heard anything so funny for years . . . And to think his father is Sir Arthur Montane, the judge! But it's odd, isn't it? because he himself seems so ordinary, even though he's a doctor. What I mean is, he doesn't appear as if he's come from that class. He said himself he's the black sheep, but what he meant, I think, was a rebel. That type of family always seems to have one. There was a family living near Miss May when I was there. They had a son like him: he joined the Army as a private and his people got him hauled out and sent him to a big Military School, but he did a bunk from there and went to sea. He became quite a hero to the villagers."

They had crossed the hall and were about to enter the workshop when Mrs. Arkwright stopped and, appealingly now, she said, "Try to think differently about him, lass. You know something? It would ease my mind if I thought you were going to be settled for life with a man like that."

"And who, may I ask, would look after you and this business?"

"Oh, he'd come and live here."

Emily closed her eyes, and drew in a deep breath before saying, "I'd like that and I'd be quids in pocket every week from his non-paying patients. Just think of that now, just think of that."

And Mrs. Arkwright's mind immediately adjusted to this line of thinking, and she leaned closer to Emily and softly said, "And think of marrying into a titled family. Think of having a judge for a father-in-law. Think of that now," to which Emily answered in an equally quiet voice, "And you know what I think, Mrs. Arkwright? I think you're going up the pole, and the sooner you reach the top and are put into a strait-jacket the better I'll be pleased. Now we'll go and choose the bonnet, shall we?"

As they entered the showroom it was to see Mrs. Glenda Brompton trying on a blue leghorn hat heavily trimmed with pale blue ribbon, and she greeted them loudly, saying, "Ah, Mrs. Arkwright, how nice to see you. Are you feeling better? You don't appear much these days; but then things run smoothly and always will under Mrs. Ratcliffe's orderly hand. Do you like this? Do you think it suits me? They tell me that large hats are going out. I saw it in the *West End Gazette* and they are nearly always right, you know. Also they say curves are slightly vulgar now, that the figure is to be flatter. But as I said to Lady Knowle"— she nodded from one to the other—"what will our dear Queen do, eh?" The "eh" seemed to come from well back in her throat; and she said again, "Eh? Poor dear, she's stuck with her front. Yet if she says busts are immodest, then they are immodest. But how to get rid of them and to become flat, shapeless? You, Mrs. Ratcliffe, you'll have no trouble. Your figure is very much . . . well, in the coming fashion, so says the *West End Gazette.*"

"I think the *West End Gazette* was only referring to city day dress, Mrs. Brompton. Yet the slim fashion has been in vogue in Paris and Brussels for some time now and they prophesy that the three-tier skirt will be returning next year. It went out in the seventies, you know. The fashion there for hats, too, is tending toward the small and high, at least for ladies who drive in open carriages."

She pointed now to a hat-stand where a concoction of tiny flowers and feathers was perched on a small straw hat, partly shaped as a bonnet with ribbons hanging from each side. "The ribbons are for tying under the chin, you understand." She now looked at Mrs. Arkwright, saying, "We saw one such, didn't we, Mrs. Arkwright, when we drove in The Mall last Sunday?"

"Really?" The big lady was slightly nonplussed. She was not tactless enough to say, "You drive in The Mall?" but her expression spoke for her, and Emily answered it by saying, "We're so busy during the week, it's the only time we can use the carriage."

"Would you please excuse us, Mrs. Brompton?

We must go to the workroom. We've been asked to design a bonnet for Sir Arthur Montane's sister Phoebe. She's a friend of ours, you know . . . I do hope Miss Stock will find something suitable for you. That model, if I may suggest, is a little too flamboyant; try something a little less ornate. See that Mrs. Brompton is satisfied, will you, Miss Stock?"

"Yes, Mrs. Ratcliffe. Yes."

As they passed through the door into the workroom the hands of the three girls became still and their mouths were slightly agape as they listened to their mistress saying to Mrs. Ratcliffe, "You're a bitch."

"Yes. Yes, I know I am. And it was a delightful experience."

"We'll lose her."

"Well, for my part I couldn't be more pleased. I cannot stand the woman."

"That's the second one today you cannot stand. It isn't the way to do business, or keep it."

"I've no intention of ever doing business with your first illusion, Mrs. Arkwright. As for the second one back there, it irks me that any one of us has to do business with her type."

"Business means dealing with all types, girl."

"You're a hypocrite, Mrs. Arkwright. You've been wanting to have a go at that woman for years."

"Yes, I might have, but I knew I had to earn a crust."

"Poor soul, poor soul. I'm sorry for you. Well,

now you're past the crust-earning, you're on the bread and jam, and that being so I should have thought you could afford to stick to your principles."

"You know something, Emily Ratcliffe? I take back my first suggestion; he's much too good for you and I wouldn't wish him onto you." Then swinging round, she looked at the three gaping girls and said, "And you close your mouths and your ears, too. You've heard nothing. But bring out what bonnets you have; I want one for a woman of fifty-nine named Phoebe."

Amity, Margie and Jean were all looking slightly bewildered; but then they began to scatter around the room, pulling out deep drawers at the bottom of cupboards, and putting finished and half-finished bonnets in a row on the long polished table. But they even stopped doing this when they heard the strange sound, and simultaneously they looked toward Mrs. Ratcliffe, who had dropped into a chair and, with her arms folded, was hugging herself tightly and laughing in such a way as to sound almost hysterical; only to be further surprised when Mrs. Arkwright, too, hugged herself tightly and also dropped into a chair and started to laugh. And such was the infectious sound, the girls joined in, with giggles at first, then hiccuping into loud gusts of laughter which must have penetrated to the select apartments above, for the far door burst open and Lena Broadbent and Esther McCann rushed in, only to stop immediately and to stand aghast for a moment, before they too began to chuckle, calling, "What's . . . what's it all about? What's the joke?"

It was Jean Felton, pointing a trembling hand first to Mrs. Arkwright and then to Emily, who spluttered, "They seem to have had a row over . . . over a bonnet for somebody named Phoebe."

"A row over a bonnet for somebody named Phoebe?"

This statement seemed to increase both Mrs. Arkwright's laughter and that of Emily, until suddenly Mrs. Arkwright stopped laughing and, her head going back and her mouth opening wide, she muttered, "Emily! Emily!"

Emily's quick reaction in jumping up and crying, "Oh, my God!" immediately silenced the others. Then addressing no one in particular, she cried, "Doctor Montane is in the drawing room. Fetch him! Quick! . . ."

He came in at a run, felt her pulse, put his hand on her heart, but did not speak to her. Then looking up at Emily, he said, "Anything in the way of a stretcher, flat board, anything like that?"

"No . . . hos . . . hospital," whispered Mrs. Arkwright.

He looked down at the pallid face and said, "All right: no hospital; but don't move."

Emily looked in bewilderment from one to the other of the five women, and they, one after the other, shook their heads. Then Esther said, "The ironing boards . . . but they're only about three to four feet long."

He was again holding Mrs. Arkwright's wrist and once more he addressed Emily: "A light basket chair, then?"

"Yes. Yes." She nodded at him; then turning toward the girls, she said, "In my bedroom, there's two. Bring the one with the high back."

Amity and Molly Stock had now come in from the showroom and it was they who turned and ran to do Emily's bidding.

The doctor now bent over Mrs. Arkwright, as she attempted to say something: "Don't talk," he said.

"Die . . . laughing . . . good . . . good w . . . ."

"You're not going to die. Don't talk."

The girls returned at the run, carrying a basket chair between them, and when they placed it to his side, he looked at it dubiously, then back to the patient, as he exclaimed, "I could carry her, although I don't think I would last the distance; but that chair's going to be as heavy as she is. Look," he bent toward Emily, "if I were to pick her up, could you and one of the others support her legs?"

"Yes. Oh yes, of course."

"I'm going to lift you up, Mrs. Arkwright. Now just try to let go, relax. You'll soon be in bed. Now, here I come. I'm putting my arms around you. Just lie back on them."

So saying, he lifted her bodily from the chair and Emily and Esther McCann placed their arms under her legs, and thus, crab-wise, they went as quickly as they could from the workroom, past the gaping Mrs. Brompton, across the hall and into the paneled bedroom.

Having laid her on the bed, they stood panting for a moment, until Emily said, "Shall we undress her?" And to this he replied, "No. Not for a while anyway. Let her rest." Then addressing Esther, he muttered, "Would you mind bringing my medical bag from the drawing room, please?"

They were standing side by side near the bed head, when he asked in a low voice, "What brought this on, d'you know?"

"Yes." Emily's voice too was hardly above a whisper. "Laughter mostly, but preceded by an argument; or rather a heated discussion."

"Between you and her?"

"Yes."

"I can't imagine that, not a serious argument."

"I had been rude to a customer, purposely rude. She's an objectionable woman. We passed her in the hall. Her opinion, I mean Mrs. Arkwright's, was the same as mine, but she had more sense and had kept it to herself."

"And that's what caused you to argue?"

"Not entirely. There was another reason."

"To do with your opinion of me?"

"*What?*" The question was sharp yet still in the continued whisper.

"Well, you didn't believe a word I said . . . ."

He got no further, for the door opened and Esther came in with his bag, and he immediately went to meet her, then took it from her, saying,

"Thanks," and quickly opened it. From a small bottle he took out two pills, then he poured out a glass of water from a carafe at the bedside table. Bending over Mrs. Arkwright, he spoke to her as if she were awake, which she seemingly was, for when he said, "I want you to swallow these two pills, they'll make you feel better," she repeated what she had said before: "No . . . hos . . . pital."

"No, no; you're not going to hospital. Anyway, no matter what I might want to do with you, your defender here would balk me. Now, that's it; that's a good girl. Now you'll feel better."

Then swiftly turning to Emily, he said, "We'll get her clothes off."

"Oh; Esther will help me."

"Just as you wish. Just as you wish." He stepped back, went to his bag again and, taking out a piece of paper, wrote on it and together with a bottle of white tablets he placed it on the bedside table; then left the room and made his way to the drawing room, picked up the old bonnet from the table, put it back in the box and re-wrapped it in the brown paper, which he tied in place with the string; so that by the time he returned to the bedroom carrying the box, Emily and Esther had finished the task of undressing Mrs. Arkwright and getting her into a clean gown. He lifted up her hand and felt her pulse; then turning toward Emily, he said, "It's steadier. She'll sleep for a while. May I have a word with you?"

At this, Esther, looking at Emily, said, "I'll get back, then. Just call me if you need me."

"I will, Esther. Thanks"; and as she went out of one door, so he walked to the opposite door and into the hall; and Emily, after glancing toward the bed, followed him.

"Will she be all right?"

"Yes and no," he answered. "It all depends on herself. Earlier on I thought she had been over-exercising, but then she tells me that she indulges herself with fat, and she seems to enjoy her port and whiskey. So, if she were to cut out these, the answer to part of your question could be, yes, she'll be all right, at least for a while. But if she doesn't, I wouldn't be accountable for how long it'll be before the next attack, which could be the last one."

Emily let out a long slow breath before she said, "Then the attack couldn't just be the result of the argument or the hysterical laughter?"

"No; you can wipe both suspects off your conscience. But apart from me coming into the argument, what, may I enquire, caused the hysterical laughter?"

Emily looked away for a moment, then said, "It doesn't seem to be much of a laughing matter now; but at the time it sounded hilarious. It was about your aunt's bonnet and the name Phoebe coupled with it, I think, and . . . and I suppose its coming so quickly on our hot words. And the girls didn't know what we were laughing at, but laughter is infectious."

"Well," and a faint smile crossed his face, "as she endeavored to say herself, it would have been a good way to go, to die laughing. And it has happened, you know."

"Really?"

"Oh yes. I wouldn't mind going that way myself. Yet I can't imagine it happening, for I see very little to laugh at these days."

When he did not go on but continued to stare at her, she said, "I . . . I must see about the bonnet."

"No need. I'm taking the old one back. Anyway, as I told them at home, I doubt if she would accept a new one."

"Well, you could take a new one back with you, too. They might be able to interest her in it."

"We'll see about that later, but not today. I . . . I have a number of patients to see before I can leave for home, but before that I must come back again. By that time she'll likely be awake. I have left some pills and directions on the table, and I think someone should sit with her tonight, just in case. I shall be back from the country round about eleven o'clock."

He did not add, "I intended to stay overnight as it is my free day tomorrow," but went on, "You can send for me any time after eleven. But if you should feel you need help before that, get in touch with Doctor Smeaton. And . . . and don't worry." He checked his hand moving toward her, and as he turned from her to go back into the bedroom, he said quietly, "I'd get as much rest as you can, for her recovery might be slow. It all depends on herself from now on." Then pausing, he asked, "Has she easy access to the spirits?"

"Yes. Yes, of course; and I can't see me . . . well, forbidding her or hiding them from her."

"No. No, of course not. So, as I said, it will be entirely up to her. Being the dominant character she is, she will likely refuse to deprive herself of what she has always considered a very moderate intake. But that moderate intake has taken its toll. Anyway, it's up to her." Again he turned to her, saying now very quietly, "And you must try not to worry. She's an elderly woman."

She bit on her lower lip before she said, "Yes, she is, but she's all I've got, all I want."

He stared hard at her before replying softly, "Then all I can say is, she's a very lucky woman, and at the end of her life, too. It isn't a situation I come across very often." And on this he went into the bedroom.

But she remained where she was. And when a moment later he returned, carrying the bag and the parcel, she preceded him toward the front door and opened it, and he passed her and went down the steps without a word.

Her closing of the door seemed to sweep away any softened feelings she might have had about him, and she actually muttered aloud, "Marry him? Never!" Jimmy had been one source of trouble, but that one would outdo him in a thousand

and one more irritating ways. Oh no! And she actually marched across the hall as she said to herself, "I'll do anything to please her, anything but
that!"

4

"Come and sit down, girl. For days you've been flying around there like a bluebottle."

"Well, if that's the case, I'm seeing you as the flypaper, and I'm not going to be caught by one of your discourses on my future life. My future life, Mrs. Arkwright, is in my own hands."

"And God's . . ."

"Oh, I don't know about that. If I look back I don't believe He's been aware of my existence, and, for that matter, me of His. So look, woman, it's nearly two o'clock and you haven't had your rest; and I've got business to see to."

"Yes. Yes, I know you have, dear; and that's what I want to talk to you about."

The changed tone brought Emily to a stop, and her own voice, too, had a different sound as she said, "The business is all right. Are you worrying about what they say in the newspapers, that this is the worst year we've had since, oh, I don't know when? That things are becoming as bad as they are in Ireland? et cetera, et cetera. Anyway, we are still selling hats."

"Yes, my dear, but not as many and certainly less trimmed. The plainer the cheaper, they seem to think." And more to herself, she added, "It's amazing the changes that can come about in a year."

"You're not the only one who thinks that way. You prefer to believe the newspapers. The whole country is bewildered by the changes that can come about in a year or two, or three. Mr. Disraeli comes and goes. They dislike him one minute and bring in the Liberals, and out they go and back he comes, and both are blamed for the bad harvests. But oh, these, the bad harvests, they'll blame anybody but God, Ireland and Palmerston . . . Oh, Palmerston! . . ."

"I'm amazed that you give yourself time to read the papers."

"Well, I can only do that when you're resting, really resting, asleep."

"I'll be asleep for a long time shortly, girl."

These words and the way they were said silenced Emily. She stood gripping the bottom rail of the brass bed and looking to where this dear woman was propped up on her pillows. The next moment she was round to her side, holding her hands and saying, "Don't upset me by talking like that. If you would only do what he says and go on that diet, you'd be your old self in no time."

"Don't talk silly, girl. You know as well as he does that it's just a matter of time. Look; pull up a chair and sit down; there's something I want to say to you. I know I haven't said it to you before, it's something new."

"Well, that'll be a change."

Emily drew the chair to the bedside; and now Mrs. Arkwright said, "And I don't want to be interrupted or any tut-tuts, or such. Now I'll begin. It's like this. I know that when I'm gone you'll miss me"—the pressure on Emily's hand tightened for a moment—"and your whole way of life will change. Oh, you'll still run the business, but there'll be a gap in it, the gap left by me. Now, as you seem determined that you're not going to think along the lines I've suggested with regard to a certain person, you'll be very much on your own and wide open to sharp-suitors. The world being what it is, they'll consider your looks and your position as just a bit of interest on the main deal. Well, it's like this. I've been asking myself for the last three days why I should dream every night about Nice: I can always see us arriving there, then driving in the carriage for some miles along that beach road until we reached the hotel. It was just a large country house. I recall they didn't like the name of the hotel. Apparently it had belonged to the one family for years right up to the revolution, when, as the story goes, it was stripped. But later, one of the younger sons returned and restored it. And it has passed through the hands of his family ever since. But there I am again in this dream, and I'm recalling the feeling that I had on my first sight of the place: the broad white steps leading up to the long verandah; the white-painted shutters, some partly covered with a tangle of green from branches of a huge creeper; then the gardens sloping away down to a beach with white-frilled waves running up it. Everything seemed to be white or green and the sea *was* green.

"Well"—she turned to look at Emily—"it was as real as on that first day when I glimpsed it. But what is strange is that although they were the happiest four weeks of my life, and I've thought about it again and again over the years, I have never before dreamt about it. The first night I dreamt about it and I woke up excited, but wondered why I hadn't seen Oscar there, or Miss May, or the Major. No, it was just the house and the garden and the sea. But then in the second dream I saw people moving about, always in twos. Then, last night, the dream was very vivid. At first the sun was blazing down and I couldn't see anything; I knew only that the house was there, and the garden, and the sea. Then the sun went in and I saw the place. It looked the same, yet it was different: the shutters were no longer white, they were painted green, as was the verandah; only the steps leading up to it were white. And for the first time I went inside and I felt a chill on me. And then"—she smiled now—"I saw Oscar. He was just as he had been all those years ago, and he came hurrying toward me and took me in his arms, and then immediately looked about him and said, 'Where's Emily?' " Her head was moving slowly now. "Yes, that's what he said to me, 'Where's Emily?' And you know what I said? I said, 'She's coming on the next boat. She should be here tomorrow.' Then I woke up."

They sat staring at each other for quite some time until Mrs. Arkwright said, "Now, what d'you make of that?"

"I don't know what to say, only that it's strange that after all this long time you should dream of that place."

"Yes, that's what I thought, too. And it's as if it were telling me something. After I woke up this morning I lay thinking for a long time, and now I'm going to ask you something, and it's something you can do for me, and which is not going to hurt you or stir you up. Now, when the time comes, when you're alone, would you think about taking a little holiday there? I've got this feeling strong on me that I want you to see it. Ah. Ah." She held up a warning finger. "Don't say that you couldn't travel alone. Women are doing it all the time now: they're visiting Africa, India, even Timbuktu."

"I wasn't going to say any such thing. Don't I travel alone now, all over London?"

"Oh, that's different, dear; you see, once you cross the Channel it's a different prospect. And anyway, as you know, a real young lady must always have a chaperon, whether male or female."

"Well, I'm not a real young lady, am I?"

"You know what I mean, and don't you start twisting my words. But will you do as I ask?"

"Yes, my dear. Some time in the future, I'll do as you ask, because, you know, quite candidly I've been intrigued by that place since you first told me about it."

"Yes, but you'll travel as a missis, won't you?"

"Oh! Oh! You want me to do that as well?" Emily pulled a face at her. "You think, then, I wouldn't get as many hawks after me as if I went as a pure young thing?"

"Very likely. But in that case they'd be looking not only for money and looks, but also for virginity."

When Emily rose quickly from her chair, saying, "Oh, you are a terrible woman, you know," Mrs. Arkwright said, "Oh, don't act so shocked."

"I'm not acting, I *am* shocked."

"Yes, of course you are, about as shocked as Steve Montane would be if I came out with something like that."

"How do you know his Christian name?"

"He told me it, and I think it suits him. And I'll tell you something else, madam: lately, I've wished I was young again because he's the only man I'd put in Oscar's place. Now there, put that in your pipe and take long draws on it. It'll give you something to think about."

"Yes, indeed, indeed."

"And by the way, if I'm not going to have a drop of what I know will do me good, then do you think I could have a cup of tea? because I'm not going to sleep or doze."

On her way out of the room now, Emily said curtly, "I'll see about it; that's if I have time."

Esther was coming down the hall stairs and, seeing Emily crossing the hall, she took the last four at a run. "D'you think you can spare a minute, miss?" she quietly called to her; "we've got a new customer up above. She's the one Mrs. Darcy recommended, you know. And Mrs. Darcy mustn't have explained the rules to her. The price is stated, and that's that. She wouldn't get that costume for that amount anywhere else. She's complaining that there's only one overskirt and the fashion now is at least two, if not three."

"I'll be up in a minute. I'm just going to see about a cup of tea for madam," Emily said, and her tone prompted Esther to put her hand on her arm, saying, "You all right? You look so tired. You'll crack up next and then where will we be? You've never had a break for weeks. Why don't you get a nurse in? And it's not helping you, is it, lying on that couch next to her at nights?"

"I'm all right, Esther."

"Well, my eyes must be deceiving me, because you don't look all right. What you want is a holiday, and a good one at that. I've got to say it: when this is all over you must get yourself away. You know me, I can see to things, except ones like that." She jerked her head backwards. "I could have managed her, but she demanded to see somebody in charge . . . the young woman, as she said, not 'the young lady.' That's the type she is."

"I'll be with you in a minute," Emily said and made for the kitchen but then turned again as Esther was about to mount the stairs and said, "Look, Esther, just you go up there and tell her that the young woman is unable to see her, and that she has authorized you to tell her that this particular costume has been withdrawn from sale. Then finish up by saying, 'Good day, madam.' See how that works."

"I'll do that. I'll do that, those very words."

Emily now made her way to the door leading down to the basement kitchen. It was at the end of a short passage and sheltered by the overhead staircase; however, she didn't open the door, but put her forearm against the stanchion of the door and leaned her head on it.

A holiday. Yes, a holiday. But she'd be thankful now for just some quiet place, with not a soul in sight, where she could sleep unbroken sleep for eight, ten, twelve hours. She could not remember ever having felt so tired and exhausted as she did now, and if another person were to tell her that she looked pale and tired and that she needed a holiday, she would cry on their shoulder . . .

She did not exactly cry on his shoulder when, on the following day, Steve Montane stood in the hall with her and said, "I'm going to say this, and to you it might sound callous and in character with me, but the sooner she goes, the better it will be for you. This is the fourth attack she's had in six months. I'm surprised she's still here. But the next one will surely take her, and then we'll have to see to you, if we haven't already. You should have put your foot down about having a nurse in, even two. She's got the money, so there's no excuse, only selfishness. Oh yes, like all the old, she's got her share of that, and she's sucked you dry. Oh yes, she has. Yes, she has, so don't you

argue with me about that!" And she had to ad-
monish herself: Don't cry. For God's sake, don't
cry. That would be the last straw, in front of him.
And don't go for him, because he's right. In this
he's right.

His next words, however, almost sent her into a
paroxysm of laughter that would surely have
ended up in hysteria had she given way to it.
"What you want to do now," he was saying, "is to
go into your room, throw yourself on the bed and
have a damn good cry, wallow in it."

When her hand went to her mouth he smiled
and said, "Well, you're laughing, and that's something. Keep it up as long as you can, but don't let
it run into hysteria." And with this he turned and
went out, leaving her gaping after him.

He would have been surprised if he had witnessed what she did next, for she went to her
room, not to throw herself onto her bed, but to sit
near its head and lay her face on the pillow. And
she asked herself how it was that he managed to
see through her. Was that why she disliked him so
much? But then, the feeling wasn't really out of
dislike, because he had proved himself to be a
kind and thoughtful man, where his profession
was concerned. But it was that tongue of his that
seemed to be bent on putting her in the wrong.
He never seemed to make an effort to get on the
right side of her, always the reverse. Oh, what did
it matter? But again she must admit he was right
about the nursing: she should have stood out at
the beginning. But then, would she have wanted

anyone to look after her friend? No, no, because she owed her so much, and she was needed; and it wasn't to be dismissed lightly, to be needed.

She brought herself up from the pillow and sat looking across the room, her thoughts ranging from one thing to another, then culminating in a statement that seemed to encompass her life. She had always wanted to be needed. It seemed to be the most important thing in life, greater even than wanting to be loved. When you were needed you were giving of yourself, whereas wanting to be loved, you were taking. Could there be a combination of the two? Her mind told her that would be too much to ask; such partnerships rarely came about. There couldn't be many Mrs. Disraelis, or Queen Victorias . . . and yet . . . and yet . . .

Oh dear! Oh dear! She must get up, and out, and see to the business, or else she would really do what he had prophesied. She almost sprang away from the bed now and made for the door, muttering, *"That man!"*

5

Mabel Arkwright lingered on until the end of November, 1879. She died at six o'clock on a Sunday morning during a severe attack of pain that morphia could not abate.

Emily was alone with her: she held her in her arms until the body went limp, when she laid her back on the pillows and, taking the lifeless hand in hers, brought it to her cheek as she whispered, "Oh, my dear, dear friend, rest easy, no more pain, and wherever you are, wherever you're going, you know you take with you my love and deep thanks for all you have done for me."

She crossed the hands on the breast, but did not cover the face: and saw no reason for this, for it looked more peaceful and relaxed than she had ever before seen it.

As she turned to leave the room, she wondered why she wasn't crying. But she felt no need to cry at this moment. There was no feeling of emotion in her that warranted tears. She did not know why, she knew only that she just did not want to cry.

She went through the doorway leading into the business house, and so came into the hall. From there she went up the stairs to the attics and the staff quarters and, tapping on a door, called, "Esther! Esther!"

"Yes? Yes, I'm up. Come in."

Esther was just putting on her dressing gown, and Emily said quietly, "I'd get into your clothes, Esther, and take a cab and fetch Doctor Montane."

"She's worse?"

"She's gone."

"Ah. Ah, no . . . But what am I saying? We've been expecting it for days. And now, poor soul, she'll be out of her misery . . . You all right?"

"Yes, Esther, I'm all right."

"I won't be a couple of shakes getting dressed . . . Was it easy? I mean, her going."

"No, I wouldn't say it was easy."

"Poor soul. Now . . . now, don't you do anything more." And Esther carried on talking as she pulled on a pair of fleecy-lined bloomers that fell well below her knees. "Cook and me will see to what has to be done," she was saying. "I know all about it. I helped me mam lay out me dad. Then shortly after I laid her out meself. So just leave that end of it to me, will you?"

"Yes. Yes, Esther, and gladly."

On the landing again, she turned up the gas-mantle that was covered by a frilled-bottom pink-glass globe; and when she reached the hall she repeated the operation on the two bracket gas-lamps that were affixed to the wall on each side of the main door. Then she went downstairs to arouse cook, whose room was in the basement and whose duties did not begin until half-past six on a Sunday. But she found her up already and the kettle boiling, and when informed of what had happened to her mistress she said frankly, "Well, I'm glad for your sake, miss, for you'd be the next one that would need the doctor. It would kill a horse what's been expected of you these past months."

When she returned to the hall, there to see Esther turning down the gas-lamps, she said, "Why are you doing that, Esther? I've just turned them up."

"Oh. Oh, miss, it isn't respectful to have them full blazing with a death in the house."

"Esther, turn them up again. That's how she would have liked them. And once she leaves here the blinds will be pulled right up. It was her wish."

"Well . . . well, I'll say this: she was good in many ways, but she had her oddities about her. And mind, it'll cause some talk in the street, because some folk keep the blinds at half mast for a month."

"As she herself would say, Esther, we are not some people, but indeed a bunch of oddities, as you say."

With a slight shrug of her shoulders, Esther said, "As I'll have to walk to the main road to pick up a cab, I might as well walk the whole distance to his house. Anyway, I'll be back as soon as I can."

"Thanks, Esther."

She had her "oddities" about her. Yes, indeed,

Esther was right: Mrs. Mabel Arkwright had had a lot of oddities about her, but they were always kind oddities. You could even say advanced oddities, because only last week she had said to her, "Mind, when I go, don't you put the house in mourning. I know I'm on about them all wasting gas, but it's got to be done in some quarters, else they would ruin you. As for myself, as you know, I always like brightness both in hats and houses, and so do me the favor of letting me lie in light. And I don't want any black drapes on the doors or windows, nor plumes on the horses. And as soon as I'm out of the front door, pull up the blinds."

She had replied to her, "Oh, be quiet! woman. You're getting morbid." And to this Mabel had answered, "Morbid? I would say I was just the opposite. And there'll come a time when many will say the same. There's changes coming, you mark my words. But they won't be given their sway until the old girl at the top takes the same road as I'm going on shortly." The words, in this instance, were not lightly said, but with enough apparent lightness to cause Emily to chuckle and cap with, "A few years back, you know, you would have ended up in the Tower; and the Queen's no age yet."

"No, but some of her ideas are. Of course I understand her: she's never got over Albert, for the simple reason she hasn't had to work for her living. I got over Oscar because I had to."

Emily now went into the drawing room, and there she put a match to the three gas-mantles in the chandelier hanging from the ceiling. Then she took the bellows and blew on the dying embers of the fire. Following this, she sat down in an easy chair to the side of the fireplace and looked across to the one opposite, where, of an evening, her friend and benefactress would sit, relating some story of a client, and here and there dropping a private secret about a covered-up scandal in a well-known family, at times shuffling to the edge of her seat when she herself was insisting on pressing home some point about which she felt strongly.

It would seem that sitting on the edge of her seat helped her to bring more force to an argument, more often than not one centered around something in the day's newspaper concerning "that lot up there." Whether they were Tories or Liberals, it was the stupidity so evident in both political parties that annoyed her. But such stupidity did not make her welcome with favor the third force raising its head. It was named the Labour Representation Committee, and its object was the return of working-class MPs to Parliament. She could hear her now saying, "Working-class MPs! You need education to rule." Oh yes, she was all for the working man having a decent wage, but as for ruling the country: "Well!" she had ended that particular discussion, "we needn't worry about that because it will never happen."

Strange, when Emily came to think of it, there was a woman who had worked herself up from a kitchen-maid to someone owning a thriving business as well as two fine properties. Yet, if anyone had said to her, "You are of the working class, therefore, according to your reasoning, you haven't got the brains to run a business, or the foresight to buy property," she would have been up in arms. Or should they have dared to utter, "Your Oscar could never have got into Parliament, because he wouldn't know how to address people or how to deliver a speech," her wrath would have shrivelled them.

As Esther had said, she had a lot of oddities. But she was going to miss those oddities. Oh, how she was going to miss them.

There was a tap on the door and Alice Milton came in carrying a cup of tea, saying, "I took it next door, miss, and I got the shock of me life. Cook hadn't told me. Well, I was late getting up and she went for me. But oh my! I nearly dropped it, your tea. I spilt some in the saucer, I'm sorry. I forgot to put it on a tray. She'll go for me when I get back. I can't help it, I'm dozy in the mornin's."

"Don't worry, Alice. Put it on the table there. By the way, how old are you now?"

"I'm seventeen, miss."

"Is that all you are, seventeen?"

"Yes, miss. But I started half-time when I was ten, you know."

"Yes. Yes, I remember. You were taken on full-time shortly after."

"Not until I was twelve."

Emily reached out to the cup and took a sip of

the tea before she said, "Have you any ambitions? I mean, what do you really want to be?"

"Oh, miss." It appeared that Alice thought this a very strange question, and, moreover, a very odd time to ask it; and what was stranger still, Miss Emily showed no signs of having cried. She looked about her, then down to her house slippers, the tops partly covered by a blue print dress and white waist-apron, before saying on a half giggle, "Cook says I'm like all the daft lasses. Well, I mean, that's what she said to me when I told her what I thought I'd like to be. There was as much chance," she said, "of me bein' what I wanted as she bein' cook to Queen Victoria."

"And what was it you told her you wanted to be?"

Again Alice looked to one side and then the other and finally down to her slippers; then the answer came so quietly that Emily said, "I can't hear you. Speak up. Is it something terrible?"

"Well, it's a daft idea, miss, 'cos I've never done anything like it, and am never likely to. But I first got the idea when I learned to read more through the *Family Friend.* There was a young girl like me in it and . . . and she rose in the world."

"Yes? And what did she become, a princess?"

"Oh no, miss, nothing as silly as that. No. She became a . . . a lady's maid."

"A lady's maid? Is that what you want to be?"

"Yes." There was another giggle. "I know it'll never happen. Eeh! and I must be off. And fancy troubling you with such talk. Cook'll knock my block off, she will, if I was to tell her, but I wouldn't dare. Your tea must be half cold. Will I fill it again, miss?"

"No, Alice, no. Thank you very much."

"Thank you, miss. . . ."

Yes, fancy talking about such things at a time like this. What was the matter with her? Since she had left the figure on the bed and had walked out of that room she had felt strangely different. She couldn't put the word "lighter" to the feeling, but there had followed that discourse with Esther, and then she had sat here talking amiably to Alice. She had never before taken much notice of Alice. But then Alice and the cook and the general staff had been Mrs. Arkwright's province. She had always spoken nicely to the girl and had given her a Christmas present, and occasionally odd articles of clothing and shoes. Like herself, Alice was thin and tall for her age, and so she looked much older than seventeen. She could pass for nineteen or twenty. That's what hard work did for you, she supposed. But why had she bothered herself on this particular morning when Mrs. Arkwright was lying dead upstairs?

She should now have been dressed and ready for the doctor. Here she was sitting in her dressing gown and slippers and feeling that she didn't want to get out of this chair. The fire was blazing brightly, the room was quiet and it was Sunday. Sunday was always a quiet day. Sundays were strange days. She could lie back and sleep here all day. How long was it since she had had a full night's sleep? Six months? Eight months? Well, it was at Easter, and now it was nearly December. Eight months at least, and although the couch wasn't made of horse-hair it certainly wasn't like a spring mattress. And it hadn't been quite long enough for her feet; at the end of it she'd had to put a chair end with a pillow on it. Eight months? Yes, eight months she had slept on that couch, but never more than two or three hours at a time. Not that the patient had made any demands on her during the night, but being aware that Mrs. Arkwright was awake she would rise and give her a drink, or have a word with her, re-arrange her pillows, do the usual things one did in a sickroom. And then there had been the day to get through: the workroom to see to, the clients to appease, hurried visits to the factory, a new range of ribbons, feathers, or flowers to view, and then onto where the basics were made: the straws, the leg-horns, the felts; choosing the dipping, a light navy, a dark blue, shades of brown, all with fancy names: Autumn Leaf, Summer Green, Pea Green; and, of course, there were the blacks, just blacks. The sun could bring out and enhance colors but it would have nothing to do with black. Black was of the night, black depicted death, and death was just a long, long sleep. She was feeling so comfortable, so relaxed. Mrs. Arkwright was on her way. Esther and cook were dressing her for the journey. There was nothing to worry about. She could sleep.

She had the desire to stretch out but there was

something in the way of her shoulders and her head, and her feet weren't on the chair. They were warm, though. Through the narrowed slits of her eyes, she looked down to her feet resting on a footstool. She must have put them there before dropping off for a minute or two. She supposed she'd have to get up, get dressed. Dear! dear! she hadn't got dressed; but she felt so comfortable, except that her neck was a little stiff. She moved her head. Her eyes had closed again, but just before the lids had met she imagined she had seen someone. Likely it was Alice; she had come back for the cup. Oh dear me. She tried to stretch. Her body seemed cramped. She was tired of this couch, she must get up. She screwed up her eyes tightly, wetted her lips with her tongue, then pushed out her arms, her hands palm-upward and her fingers stretched to their fullest. And this last effort opened her eyes.

"Now, don't jump up. Lie where you are until you come round," said Doctor Montane.

"I'm . . . I'm sorry. I must have dropped off. I . . . I meant to get dressed."

"Don't bother talking or making excuses. Just lie and relax again."

She pulled herself up straight in the chair before saying, "You have been in?"

"Oh yes, yes. Everything's done. Now, what you want to do is to go upstairs and have a bath and get into some clean clothes, then have a good breakfast."

She stared at him. He looked different. He

sounded different. But he was telling her to have a bath, change her clothes and have a good breakfast. She'd had a bath last night before lying down, and she always changed her clothes, at least her underclothes, practically every day. As for eating a good breakfast, she hadn't eaten a good breakfast for months, not what she imagined he would call a good breakfast.

When she made to rise from the chair, the doctor was by her side, his hand on her elbow, and he was saying, "You're bound to be stiff lying in that position for so long."

When she turned her head swiftly to look at him a crick in her neck made her grimace, and she said, "So long? What do you mean, so long? I've just sat . . ."

Having turned her head, she was now facing the mantelpiece where stood the French clock under its glass dome, and she could hardly believe her eyes. The face read fifteen minutes to eleven, and so great was the shock of realizing that she must have been asleep for four hours she leaned forward and thrust her hand toward the mantelpiece, in doing so almost overturning a luster vase standing on a small table to the side of her, causing its glass pendants to jangle against each other. The doctor put out a hand to right it, at the same time saying, "Yes, you've been asleep since before seven o'clock; and that was a much needed rest, if you want my opinion."

"But under the circumstances . . ."

"Under the circumstances, it was reaction."

"How long have you been here?"

"Since you sent for me."

She opened her mouth to say something, then closed it and lowered her head as she muttered, "I'm sorry."

"What are you sorry about? This is a very nice room to relax in. And it happens to be my free day, so you need not apologize for keeping me. You know—" He pressed his lips together now before adding, "I nearly dropped off myself sitting there." He pointed to the other armchair. "Well now, I'll leave you for the time being. Do as I say, and I'll look in again later in the day, because there are certain arrangements to be made, and I can give you advice in that quarter."

"Thank you."

"And may I say something further to you?"

In a little of her old spirit, she said, "Is there any possible way of stopping you?"

"No, I don't think there is. So I will say that once this business is over, you must get away for a holiday. Not just for a weekend or a week, but for a good month at least; and some place where no one can get at you. I don't think you need worry about the business. It seems to run itself in any case."

She must get away for a holiday, and the business runs itself. The first part she could agree with because she knew she must have a break of some kind. But as for the second, the business ran itself . . . Oh! she was too tired to come back at him. She could only endorse in her mind that he was the most tactless man she had ever come across or ever would . . .

The funeral took place four days later, and Emily was surprised at the number of people who joined the cortège. There were at least three carriages from this very street, and this, when she came to think about it, spoke volumes for the respect in which Mrs. Arkwright had been held in this semi-select quarter of this city. There were other carriages, too, and hired cabs, besides the one that held the doctor and herself.

He had tried to persuade her not to attend the funeral: not that he was against women taking part in such affairs, he had said, but he felt she was in no fit state to stand in the bitterly cold cemetery on a day when there was even snow in the air.

Afterwards, the pallbearers were regaled with hot soup, cold roast sirloin, and new bread, cheese and a glass of either port or ale, as to their taste. Up in the dining room were those followers who had returned to the house, among whom, Emily noticed, were two residents of the terrace, the others, apart from the doctor and the solicitor, being business associates. They had gathered first in the drawing room, where they were offered the choice of whiskey, port, or gin, or mulled beer; and then they were asked to help themselves, if they so wished, from the table in the dining room. Spread on this was a variety of pies, cold meats, cheeses, and pastries, and it was evident from the beginning that a number of those present were rather baffled by the stand-up display, as cook had prophesied they would be. "It's a sit-down meal they have, miss, always a sit-down meal: a soup, a roast and veg, a pudding, and cheeses." And later she voiced her opinion to Alice: "What on earth is miss up to? It is the end of a funeral she was laying a spread for, not one of these fancy do's they talk about now that the gentry have at balls and such. It's a Frenchified name. I read about it only last week in the *Ladies' Friend*. My! My! Times are changing. And you mark my words, there's going to be a change in this house, too."

And cook wasn't the only one who thought there was going to be a change in the house, for the staff as a whole had been disturbed that something was happening to the miss and that if she wasn't careful she'd soon be following the mistress: she had turned so quiet, no come-back chit-chat. Of course, they could understand it at this time, but certainly not the way she walked about and how she kept sitting in the chair in the drawing room. It wasn't as if she was short of sleep now because, for two mornings running she hadn't woken up until nine o'clock. And Esther had taken things over and did the ordering for the day and such. And when she ordered the table to be set as it was for the mourners, everyone in the house became convinced there was, other than just sorrow, something radically wrong with her.

And then, when the mourners were leaving, she wasn't at the door to see them off and to accept their commiserations with her loss, as was usual. It was the doctor and the solicitor who took over this duty.

All the staff had been asked to assemble in the drawing room. And there they were now with the doctor sitting next to Mrs. Ratcliffe and all facing the solicitor, who sat behind a sofa table on which papers were spread out.

Emily was looking at the solicitor, whom she thought was a kindly man, but she wasn't seeing him, for she was thinking that this was how Mabel must have felt after the old Major died, when he had left them the small fortune and they had both cried. She wondered if *she* would cry. She hoped she would, for she wanted to cry. There was a great, hard block of crying inside her that seemed would remain there for ever because no emotion she felt could touch it. But then, she didn't feel very much of anything at the moment, except she was thinking she hoped Mabel would have remembered all the staff and remembered them well, because they had all given her good service, some of them for long years.

But the solicitor was talking about the staff now, and her attention was caught by his voice saying, "Two hundred pounds to Esther McCann; to Lena Broadbent, one hundred pounds; to Mary Pollock, one hundred pounds; to Amity Lockhart, fifty pounds; to Margie Monkton, fifty pounds; to Jean Felton, fifty pounds; to Alice Milton, fifty pounds."

An audible gasp came from somewhere behind

her, and she thought of Alice and her lady's maid dream.

"To Molly Stock, twenty-five pounds; to Sarah Hubbard, twenty-five pounds; and to anyone who has joined my staff within the past month, I leave ten pounds. To Doctor Steve Montane, one thousand pounds, together with my deepest thanks for his care of me."

There was a smothered gasp now from the man at her side, and she knew he had turned his face fully toward her; but she still stared ahead and listened to the solicitor, saying, "To my dearest friend, who has been like a daughter to me for many years, and whom I have loved dearly, I leave 34, Frontlea House, hoping that she will continue to make it her home, and number 35, Frontlea House, where my business has been carried out; and this I hope she will continue to carry on, and together with these the remainder of my money and investments, which, when last accounted for at January of the year 1879, were estimated to be in the region of thirty thousand pounds."

There wasn't a murmur in the room.

The block inside Emily seemed not to be touched at all: she had no desire to cry, yet at the same time she was overwhelmed by a feeling of amazement and of some bewilderment. The two houses and thirty thousand pounds and the business. It didn't seem possible. She knew she was to be left something, she knew that. She had the idea that Mabel would give her what the Major had given Mabel, as a sort of link-up. But no, she had left her the result of a lifetime's work and that of her husband, too. Thirty thousand pounds and these two beautiful houses. She had known nothing about her business affairs. Was there so much money in making and selling hats? She couldn't think so. But then the solicitor had mentioned investments. Yes. She had been a shrewd woman where money was concerned. Generous in one way, very tight in another. And she must have invested as she went along over the years. Thirty thousand pounds. She never needed to work again. She never needed to move her hand again. And she could sleep all she wanted. Oh yes, that's what she wanted to do still, sleep.

There was a buzz of excitement all around her now. Steve was standing in front of her. He was saying, "To leave me a thousand pounds! That's amazing. And you're set for life, no more worries. Come on, my dear." He took her hand and drew her up and through the members of staff, bunched together now and exclaiming in different ways at their good fortune. But it was Alice Milton who drew her to a stop, her hand held out.

Emily now found herself actually shaking the hand and smiling at the girl and saying, "First step to a lady's maid," which brought some smothered titters, and she thought, Yes, they would be amused at poor Alice dreaming of becoming a lady's maid, because of all of them she looked the most unlikely for such a position.

They were in the little study at the end of the hall

now, and Steve was saying to Esther, "Bring a glass of sherry and some biscuits."

When the door closed, he bent over Emily where he had pressed her down into the chair, and, a hand on each arm, he brought his face close to hers, saying, "You're not feeling very much at the moment, are you? Kind of numb?"

As would a child, she nodded at him.

"No real emotion; not even becoming a rich woman has touched you, has it?"

Again, like a child she moved her head, but from side to side this time.

"Well then, I'm going to tell you something. You're not ill, not in the ordinary way, but you need a rest, a long rest. You understand me? No more business . . . nothing for some weeks ahead. But, and I mean this, if you don't follow my advice you really will be ill, really ill. You understand?"

Yes, she understood, in a sort of dim way. She looked into his face. He seemed to be concerned for her; but then he was a doctor, wasn't he, and Mabel had left him a thousand pounds. That was nice of her. And what had she left her? So much, so much; she wouldn't be able to cope with it. She should be grateful, so very, very grateful. But there seemed to be nothing within her to evoke the feeling of gratitude. It was silly, but at the moment all she wanted was to lie down, just to lie down.

She was aware that he had left her side and was talking to someone, and she heard herself saying,

"Excuse me," but she wasn't quite sure to whom she was addressing the remark: there was a wave of something sweeping over her. She couldn't put a name to it, she knew only that she was afraid.

She was in her room and Esther was there, and she was helping her off with her clothes, which, part of her mind told her, was ridiculous. Yet she knew she could never have got them off by herself. What was the matter with her?

"Am I going to die, Esther?"

"What did you say, miss?"

"Die. Am I dying?"

"Huh! Well, I've never heard of anybody dying of pleasure, miss, at their good fortune . . . There you are now. Lie down. Alice is bringing a water bottle for your feet. And here's the doctor."

His face was hovering over her again. "You're going to be all right. Just rest. Go to sleep. Go to sleep."

And she went to sleep.

6

Later, Emily was never able to describe how she had felt during the weeks that followed. All she was really aware of was the desire to sleep, and at times she would wonder why they had woken her up. She could hardly grasp that it was she who was being fed by a spoon. That would never have happened to her. Never.

That time passed and there followed a long period during which she just lay and watched them coming and going. She was never alone, and when Esther would say, "How are you this morning, dear?" her mind would say, I'm all right, Esther; but there was no way to voice her thoughts. The doctor never said, "How are you?" He rarely seemed to speak to her these days. But he would put his hand on her brow and stroke her hair back, which she thought odd. But she didn't resist him because she couldn't be bothered. She was also aware of two uniformed nurses, one during the day, the other at night. She didn't mind the night nurse because she seemed to like sleeping, too, but the day one was very fussy. And in some strange way she always felt relief when the woman left the room and young Alice would slip in and take a seat by the side of the bed, and would say, "She's gone for her coffee," or "She's gone for her dinner," or "She's gone for her tea," and while saying these things Alice would always hold her hand and stroke it. Sometimes she would say something very strange, such as, "Come on, miss, come on." Where did she want her to go?

Then there came the morning when she felt very irritated. The nurse *would* persist in washing her face and hands. Surely she could wash her own face and hands. And when the woman said, "There now, dearie, there's only your tootsies to see to," she felt she could stand no more and so she slapped out at her and, in order to avoid the slap, the nurse stepped quickly sideways and only just saved the basin of water from falling off the side table, at the same time exclaiming, "My! My! Well! well! That's something!"

She didn't like that woman. She treated her as if she were a child. Nonsense. Where was Esther? What was the matter with them all? Oh yes, she knew she hadn't been well, but it was just tiredness. And there was the nurse going out now and Alice coming in. She liked Alice.

As usual, Alice took her hand and alternately stroked it and patted it, and when she again said, "Oh, come on, miss, come on," in such a coaxing way, she heard a voice saying, "Where to, Alice? Where to?"

Dear, dear. Her thoughts were giving voice again. But she had startled Alice, for the girl was on her feet. In fact, she was halfway to the door when she turned back again and, gripping her hand once more, she said, "Oh, you're all right, miss. You'll be all right now."

"Ye . . . s. Yes, Alice. What . . . what is . . . the . . . time?"

"Oh, miss. Well—" Alice turned round and looked at the small clock on the mantelpiece, saying, "Twenty to eleven, miss. Twenty to eleven. Eeh! I'm so glad, I want to rush downstairs and tell them. Oh, it'll be a happy Christmas after all. By! it will that. And cook was just sayin' this mornin', 'There'll be no decorations going up with her like that.' She was meaning you, miss. Eeh! the doctor's due, too. By! he'll be pleased. Cook says if she could get a doctor like him she would go to bed and stay there. Eeh! what am I sayin' . . . ? You're smilin', miss. You feel all right now?"

Emily studied this question, then said, "Yes. Yes, I feel better. Still a bit tired."

"Well, you shouldn't be, miss, you've had plenty of sleep."

"Yes . . . yes, I have. But I feel . . . I feel sort of . . . refreshed."

When the door opened and Esther came in, Alice cried to her in a voice that was almost a shout, "She spoke! Esther. She spoke! Talked."

"You sure?"

"Of course I am sure."

Esther stopped a moment and looked at the girl

and said, "Watch your tone." Then she was bending toward Emily. "How are you, dear?"

"I'm all right, Esther."

Esther straightened up, looked at Alice and said, "Well, well. Thank God. I thought it would never happen. Go down and tell the nurse. No, don't; stay where you are, the doctor will be here in a minute and he'll never get a word in for that one giving her reports, as she calls them. As cook says, there's been more running about after her than the patient. Oh, listen! There's the doctor coming. Go on, get yourself downstairs and on with your job. I'll see to him."

Alice and Steve passed each other in the doorway. And when he said, " 'Morning, Alice," she answered in that awed tone she always used when he addressed her, " 'Morning, doctor."

"Alice says she's spoken."

"Yes? When?"

"Just now. She said she talked."

"Well, if she has spoken, Esther," he said as he laid his bag on the table, "we mustn't talk over her or at her, but to her."

"Yes, doctor. Yes. Yes, doctor." She moved back from the bed and he, standing by the side of it now and looking down on Emily, said, "Then we are better, are we?"

"Yes. Yes, we are better."

He turned his head away for a moment and seemed to sigh deeply; then, looking at her again, he said, "That's good, that's good. Now we're off on another road."

First, Alice would keep saying, "Come on, come on," now he was saying, "We're off on another road." Where to?

"Would you like your coffee here, doctor?" Esther said.

"Yes. Yes, I would. Thank you."

When they were alone he pulled up a chair toward the head of the bed. He did not, however, speak for some time, but put out a hand and when he stroked her hair from her brow she told herself she hadn't dreamt that; he had been doing that a lot. He was saying, "Don't hurry anything. Just lie quiet and rest."

"I've been ill?"

"Yes . . . yes, you've been ill."

"What with?"

"Sheer exhaustion. I would say it was complete exhaustion. The result not only of the past nine months or so looking after an invalid, but also of the stress of the years before. Nothing is lost, you know, not of anything that goes into the mind. And it all has to be paid for. Now what you've got to do is to be patient and lie there for another week or so, and be fed and . . ."

"Not washed?"

He smiled now. "Her ministrations are very thorough, I must admit," he said. "I've seen her at it . . . oh, it's good to know you're back."

"Back?"

"Yes. From your long sleep."

"How long?"

"Oh, let me see. Nearly three weeks."

"What!" With a jerk, she brought herself up from the pillow, then fell back again, her face crumpled as if with pain, and she put her hand to her head as she repeated, "Three weeks? I've . . . I've been like this . . . three weeks?"

"Yes. And it'll be another three weeks, my dear, before you're fully on your feet. I might as well tell you, you've escaped a very serious illness."

"What kind of an illness?"

"Well, you like straight talk and I think you'll be able to stand it, seeing that you're partly yourself again. But you were in for a complete breakdown."

"Nervous breakdown?"

"Yes, a nervous breakdown. Your body and mind were exhausted. Every now and again the best machine in the world has to be oiled and overhauled, which process takes the form of rest. Your machine got neither oil nor rest. If you had given your machine a decent holiday it would never have got into this state. Anyway, I'm going to do no more talking, and you're going to lie there and do what you're told . . . all right, apart from being washed."

He smiled gently down on her, and she looked up into his face. It seemed different. Yet it had looked different for some time now. She could recall faintly seeing it in different lights: sometimes the sun would have been shining on it, sometimes it would have been the gaslight; and as faintly too, she could recall snatches of things he had said: "There's air in the mantle. Turn it low.'' Plop, plop, plopping. Then she could hear his voice, saying, ''Emily . . .'' and something else. At the moment she was too tired to try to recall it. But she wasn't going to die. No, she wasn't going to die. She knew that when she went to sleep now she would wake up.

During the following days the periods of sleeping grew fewer, and the day came when she put her feet out of the bed for the first time in weeks, and almost fell over.

Of course, she said to herself, he would have to be here to prove his words right: ''Make haste slowly,'' he was always saying, or, ''Stop galloping. Even a horse has to slow up sometimes.'' That was another thing that irritated her about him: he always qualified what he was saying with some quotation or quip. And from this she gathered, although somewhat grudgingly, that he was probably well read . . .

It wasn't until the day before Christmas Eve that she was able to venture downstairs. And there she was met with what could be called a reception committee and the sight of all the staff, her staff now, and their ''Merry Christmas, miss,'' ''So glad you're better, miss,'' or ''It's good to see you, miss,'' brought the tears to her eyes. So touched was she by their greetings that again she lost her voice, at least until she was in the drawing room and ensconced in the armchair with a rug around her knees, which was to her a symbol of illness or age, and which brought forth from her a quick return of her speech and a protest against the pampering.

Alone now with Esther, she lay back in the chair and looked about her before saying, "Oh, the room is lovely. When did you do all this?"

"I didn't even have a hand in it; at least, only as far as saying we'll have a Christmas tree in here for you. But what does that Alice do? She goes out and spends her money on two boxes of glass baubles." She pointed now toward where the blue, green and gold swans and half moons and bells were dangling from the branches of the snow-spangled and tinsel-decked tree. "And she and Molly Stock made the holly wreaths. There's one hanging on the front door, would you believe it!"

"She seems a very thoughtful girl," said Emily. "I recall her, a number of times, sitting by my bed and she always seemed to be saying the same thing, "Come on, miss. Come on.""

"Oh yes; any excuse to get into your room. I had practically to haul her out at times because cook was getting testy, she wasn't seeing to her other work, and, as she said, ever since madam had left her that money she had become a different girl."

"In what way?"

"Oh, she goes around like a busy bee. I couldn't tell you in what way, but cook says there was a time when she would never dream of opening her mouth until she was spoken to. But there she is now, talking ten to the dozen. In fact, she informed cook that she intended to make this room for you the same as the Queen's in Buckingham Palace. Apparently she had seen a picture of it in some paper . . . What are you smiling at?"

"Oh, just the thought of young Alice daring to stand up to cook."

"It's good to see you smile. It's good to see you downstairs. Neither house has been the same: there was madam gone and you, as we all thought at one time, about to die. You know, I never realized before what a close-knit unit we are, or were. Madam was like the mother-head and you the young daughter, and it was felt, if we lost you, the whole family would be split up. It wasn't just the feeling of losing jobs, it was something deeper than that. Anyway—" Esther's tone changed and she said briskly, "it's all arranged for Christmas Day. Dad and Mam are going to our Peggy's for their dinner and so I'm coming here. As for Lena, she's on her own most of the time anyway, and since losing her mother she has usually been invited to her sister's for Christmas dinner; although she doesn't like her brother-in-law, nor her five nieces and nephews, who apparently are still at the rampaging stage, being under ten years old and undisciplined, so she's jumped at the chance of joining us. And of course there's cook; and too, I thought you might like young Alice to be invited as I don't think her home life is very pleasant. You know something?" She now leaned forwards toward Emily and, her voice dropping, she said, "She's a surprise, that girl. Behind her docile manner, there's a lot goes on in that one's head. Do you know what she asked me?"

"No. No, I don't, unless you tell me."

"Well, she asked if madam's will would be published in all the papers—she meant the individual amounts—and I said, I didn't think so. Perhaps it would if she had died in a small town, but this being London, it would likely be only titled people's wills that would be so published. I said I thought that anyone could go to a particular office in London and find out what people left. But why was she asking? And so the answer I got, and very briefly, was that her money wouldn't reign long if her family got to know about it. I pointed out to her that they weren't her real family. She was one of a number of foster-children, wasn't she? And she said, yes, but that wouldn't make any difference; they'd want her to stump up for her lodgings over all these years. Oh, she's got things worked out, has our docile Alice."

"Good for her, I say, Esther. Good for her. And thank you, my dear, for offering me your Christmas Day. But I'll be all right on my own for a day, and there's always cook; and I'm sure the little lady in question, Alice, would stay with me."

"It's all arranged, so be quiet. But I'll tell you something: I'm going to give myself two Christmas boxes on that day."

"And what are they?"

"First, I'm going to smoke one of those cigarettes in a holder; and secondly, I'm going to get drunk."

"Oh, well, since doing those two things would make you sick, I think I would get drunk first, because getting drunk by itself will make you sick and so you would be killing two birds with one stone."

Her chin made an impatient movement as was her wont: she was getting as bad as him, trotting out old maxims; and anyway, that particular one didn't fit such a situation as Esther's Christmas boxes presented.

"Well, if I am sick it will be worth it." Then, looking at the clock, Esther said, "Oh my! It's turned eleven; the doctor will be bouncing in any minute. Shall I wait till he comes to bring the coffee in?"

"Yes. Yes, please, Esther."

The room to herself, she wondered what his greeting would be this time. Would he upbraid her for daring to come downstairs without his permission? Or would he accept it and make a joke of it and say, "Not before time; I'm sick of climbing those stairs," or something to that effect?

When the clock on the mantelpiece chimed the half hour, she thought, He's late this morning, but she sat back and waited. And minutes later, Esther actually voiced these thoughts when she said, "He's late this morning, isn't he? He's generally here on the dot of eleven."

"Likely he's had a lot of patients to see."

"Yes, I suppose so. But I don't see why you should wait for your coffee any longer."

"No, neither do I. . . ."

On this Esther had left the room. But she must

have returned countless times during the day to say, "It's funny, isn't it? Perhaps he's gone down sick himself. In that case the old one should have come."

"Oh, I don't see any reason for any doctor's attention any more. Not really."

"Don't be silly. You're not out of the wood yet, and you know it. . . ."

It had been an odd day, she had told herself, when she was once more upstairs and in bed. But then it would have felt odd anyway, for she had been downstairs, hadn't she? and at first it seemed so strange, and years since she had made that journey. Of course it had been an odd day.

Christmas Eve laughter echoed through the house, especially when a bouquet of flowers was delivered from Mr. Arthur Pendleton, of number 16, together with a note expressing his pleasure at her recovery. Then a Mr. John Beeton called. This gentleman, when informed that Mrs. Ratcliffe was unable as yet to have visitors, left his card. He was from number 27. He was a bachelor of middle years, whereas Mr. Pendleton was a widower and had been for some time, it was understood, and he was past his middle years.

"Well now," said Esther, "what d'you make of that? It's started."

"Don't be silly," said Emily.

"I'm not being silly. But what we need now is for

the women to call, and then we'll know you've made it.''

"Well, on that point," said Emily, "you'll have a long wait for, don't forget, I'm in business, and as you well know, business isn't respectable; at least, not for a . . . lone woman.''

"Don't be silly.''

"Stop telling me not to be silly, Esther.''

"I will, 'cos there's numbers of women running businesses on their own now. There's The Flower Garden, that's run by a woman. There's The Haberdashery in Percy Street, that's run by Madam Powers.''

"Yes. Yes. And there's the house of ill-repute run by another madam. It was in the papers yesterday. Her house was closed down, but likely the judge or her prosecutors will soon find her another place. And what about here? I've got a house full of women; I could start a sideline: Madam Ratcliffe's Racy Rascals or some such title.'' She laughed, and Esther joined her, spluttering, "That would close Willington Place altogether.''

"I wonder. There's some lonely men in it, by all accounts.''

"Speaking of lonely men or not lonely men, it's on eleven again. There's one thing though; you're not waiting for your coffee this morning: I'm going to bring it on the dot. But if he doesn't show his face today, I think we'd better send for another doctor, hadn't we, to go round there to see what's up with him?'' Then, her manner and voice sobering, she said, "You know, he's been very good to you; there must be a reason why he hasn't dropped in . . . I wonder if anything's happened to him? I hope not, for by! he'd be a miss, you know; and not only here, I can tell you. Anyway, I'll go and make the coffee."

Doctor Montane did not come at eleven, nor did he visit during the afternoon. All day there had been a great deal of coming and going of carriages in the street; and for a time she had stood by the window and watched them. And, too, whenever she had had the room to herself she had got to her feet and walked about, so as to strengthen her legs. She had also been thinking a lot today about Mabel and the things she had said, foremost in her mind being her description of the hotel in France where she had spent such a happy time. She knew that she herself must take a holiday, a break away from here, from the work and the bustle that was impossible to shut out even in this private house, for the atmosphere of the workshop next door penetrated it. She felt she owed it to Mabel to carry out at least one of her wishes, and she could do that by traveling to France and to that hotel. But it was a long journey, and she had never been abroad. She couldn't possibly go alone, and so whom would she take to accompany her? She could travel through London alone, yes, but not abroad. And the way she was feeling now she certainly wouldn't be able to attend to luggage or the business attached to travel.

At half-past three, Alice came in and lit the gas. The girl's face was bright, and her look of happiness hurt Emily in some ways. Here was a girl who had so little to be happy about, yet happiness seemed to be shining from her, especially when she said, "It's a lovely Christmas, miss, isn't it? It just wants to snow buckets an' that would cap it."

She was drawing the curtains covering the front windows when she exclaimed loudly, "Oh! Here comes the doctor, miss. I'll let him in."

Emily lay back in the chair, and took her feet off the footstool, which she pushed aside with her shoe. Then there he was, striding up the room and blowing on one doubled fist like a young boy.

"It's enough to freeze you out there. How are you?" he greeted her, and as she answered, "Fine," she watched him put his bag on the table as usual but then realized that he had not expressed any loud surprise at finding her downstairs.

After checking her pulse he remained quiet for a moment; but then he said, "Have you missed me?"

"Not particularly."

"Oh, I'm glad to hear that. It puts you back in your old form: you are getting better."

"I am better."

"Yes. Yes." He stressed the two words. "You are better, although I would add, better than you were, miss, or missis, or madam, whichever title will fit you today."

He was in one of those moods, was he?

He was sitting opposite her now when he said, "I didn't get in yesterday. I was for asking Doctor Smeaton to look in; but then I thought, oh, you could manage for a day without me."

"Well, yes, just." It struck her at this point that he wasn't talking like a doctor. He never talked like a doctor, he talked like . . . Her mind closed down on the next thought.

He had risen from his chair and had gone to his bag again; and from it he took out a small parcel and, handing it to her, said, "Happy Christmas."

"Oh! Oh, thank you. And the same to you."

He was seated again when he said, "Open it. It doesn't have a fancy wrapping."

She did as he commanded and revealed a thin volume. It was bound in red Morocco leather and the title was *Friend of Mine* by S. Petersen. And as she opened it, he said, "Do you like poetry?"

"Some."

"Oh well; these mightn't be to your taste. They're very simple, no Byron's *Childe Harold,* or Swinburne, or John Donne, or Swift, but just ordinary thoughts put down as they come."

"You like poetry so much?"

"Yes. Yes, I like poetry so much . . . You are surprised?"

Yes; yes, indeed she was surprised. The last thing she imagined he would read was poetry, but then he was an odd individual altogether, not easy to understand. She again looked down at the book, and then asked, "Who is S. Petersen?"

"Oh; I understand he's a man who just . . . well, writes poetry or whatever you would call it. I think, perhaps, he has a different slant on things, since he comes from Norwegian stock. Petersen is derived from a Norwegian name."

She turned the page, and slowly she read the first poem entitled "Need":

I do not need love and passion deep,
Or sonnets sung to lull me to sleep,
Or poems written on which my cheek will
 rest at night;
I do not need kisses on my lips,
Or odes voiced to my eyes;
I do not need children about my knee
Who might grow to despise me;
I do not need prestige or power
Which with age will grow sour;
I do not need to possess another,
Claiming a debt,
As do mother, father or brother,
Or rest of kin;
I do not need to seek admiration
 to sustain life;
I do not need one of these, for I will
 never need a wife.

She glanced at him, then turned the page and went on reading:

I only need a hand to hold in friendship,
To exchange words without spleen or hate,

To link thoughts on topics great and small,
A friend to be a metaphorical bulwark or
  a wall
Against which I can lean and draw new breath
To continue the fight for life and . . .
  against death,
That ultimate, that final blow,
Against which all knowledge cannot defend.
To that end . . . I need a friend.

She now raised her head and looked at him, "It was written by a man?" she said.

"Yes, it was written by a man."

"But . . . But how would he know how a woman felt?"

"Oh well, I suppose, through observation. And there are all kinds of women, you know. There are some who don't want to marry, and others who can't wait to jump . . . I mean, who can't wait to get into that state."

She smiled and said, "Why didn't you finish what you were going to say . . . jump into bed? You don't usually choose your words when talking to me."

He allowed his head to fall back onto the chair and started to chuckle; and presently, still with his head back, he said, "You think you know me, don't you? You think I'm rather an uncouth individual . . . No; I won't put that name to myself, not uncouth . . . a brusque, and irritating person, yes; no sensitivity."

"How do you know what I think? What I do think

is, you're very dogmatic in your thinking, pretty much like the author of this book; at least, where he thinks he knows what a woman wants or doesn't want."

He was looking at her again as he said, "I've told you that there are many types of women . . . and men and, inside the types, a variety of shades. You know, we are, each one of us, a very, very odd mixture, capable of reaching the heights and of doing the most self-sacrificing things, or falling into the depths and committing the most hideous crimes. We are all, as I said, a mixture. It all depends upon circumstance. It's circumstance that breeds events either good or bad, self-sacrificing or selfish, it's all down to circumstance. And we can never choose the circumstance, not really. There is talk of free will. There's no such thing. We are drawn to this or other circumstance by an unknown force and there we act what that circumstance dictates. You're in the position you are through circumstance; I'm in the position I am through circumstance."

In the ensuing silence she could find nothing to say. He disturbed her. In all ways he disturbed her. His attitude disturbed her. His thinking disturbed her. Oh yes, yes, his thinking. And his liking for poetry actually amazed her.

She put her hand flat on the book, and her fingers stroked the cover as she said softly, "It's beautifully bound."

"Yes. He . . . he apparently likes good binding. It's one of a limited edition."

"Oh! Well, thank you very much. It's very kind of you. I'm afraid I have nothing to offer in return."

"No? Well, I think there's something you can give me . . . my name, for instance."

"Your name?"

"Yes. My name is Steve. I think we've known each other long enough for you to use my Christian name."

"But you are my doctor." There was a half-bewildered smile on her face.

"Yes, I'm your doctor, but I am also a human being with a Christian name: *Steve.*"

She lowered her head and bit on her lip; then, laughing gently, she said, "I couldn't call you Steve; I think of you as Doctor."

"Oh, being you, I know it will be hard, but you could give it a try . . . Emily."

Again she was biting on her lip. "You're impossible. You know that?"

"Yes. Yes. I'm well aware of that. I've been told that by my family since I was a small boy. Half of them don't own me now, except, of course, Aunt Phoebe. You remember the bonnet? Of course you do. That was rather tactless, for at the time it almost put paid to our benefactress."

She was smiling widely now as she said, "It was funny, though. What happened? You never said."

"Oh, my father climbed the ladder and pushed the bonnet through the window, because she wouldn't open the door, and afterwards things went back to normal."

"And she's still wearing it?"

"She'll wear it till the moment she dies. We're a very queer family, with funny traits running through us. I've a brother who tinkles with explosives and has twice almost blown up the house, and all of us with it. Of course, he's now into it in a big way at the War Office. But there, I think, they let him deal only with the paperwork. And I've a sister who does good works, which means interfering with other people's lives. One such good work resulted in her having a black eye from an irate husband who didn't want his wife to be emancipated. And, oh yes, I have a brother who's a Catholic priest. Nobody speaks to him, only me of course; but then I'll speak to anybody as long as they'll listen."

She wasn't smiling as she said, "You're not joking for once? Are they really members of your family?"

"Yes. Yes, really. And no; I'm not joking. But it gets odder as we go into nieces and nephews."

"You're to be envied."

It was perhaps a full minute before he answered, "Yes—" And then seriously, "Yes, you're right, Emily, I am to be envied. They're a marvelous crew, all independent spirits going their own way. It's an honor to be one of them. That's where I was yesterday. They have a roaring time at Christmas; I'm only sorry I couldn't join them. Nevertheless, we had a party last night; at least"—he smiled now—"to be correct, it was in the early hours of this morning. We didn't get to bed until about two o'clock. There were nine of us rogues, besides Mother and Father, and cousins and neighbors and the staff, which, incidentally, isn't very large but very loyal. Most of them are at the doddery stage, where they seem to have been since I can remember. Yes, I'm very lucky to be of such a family, more so when, in my work, I come across all the lonely people in the world."

"That's why you favor this kind of poetry?"

"Oh . . . oh yes, you could say it is. He and I think alike in many ways. Of course I criticize his work: it's over-simplified, but then I think it's in his mind to write simply so that those of us who have to run through life can take in some of his ideas."

He now pulled himself to the edge of the chair and looked back toward the drawing room door, saying, "Am I ever going to get a cup of tea or coffee in this house again?"

She was smiling and her head was shaking as she put her hand out and pulled a long cord that was hanging by the side of the mantelpiece. And when almost immediately the door was opened and Esther came in carrying a tray, he got up from his chair, saying, "Now that's what I call service. It couldn't have been answered sooner if it had dropped from the skies." And he quickly took his bag from the table to make room for the tray, so causing Esther to remark, "You *were* in need of a cup."

"I wasn't only in need of a cup, Esther, I was gasping for it."

"Well, there it is." She now turned toward Emily and said, "Will I pour out?" But before Emily could answer, Steve was saying, "No; I'll do it. I'm used to pouring tea. Anyway, you're wasting time; get back to your work, woman."

"Eeh! Did you ever hear such! and from a doctor?" Esther asked of Emily, but Emily made no reply: she was watching him take the lid from the teapot and stir the contents with a spoon he had taken from a saucer.

What she had learned about him today was that there were a number of sides to him, and she didn't know if she liked him better for the discovery, for he was obviously more clever than he made himself out to be, and there was a depth in him she was finding disturbing.

"Here." He was handing her the cup of tea while saying, "She never even brought a piece of cake in, and it's Christmas."

"Would you like a piece of cake?"

"No. No." His voice had changed; it was quieter. "I haven't time anyway to stay much longer; the surgery was filling up even as I left. There's a kind of feverish running cold going about. I hope it stays like that and doesn't develop into anything further. And I'm on duty all tomorrow; but, then, it won't be just colds I'll be attending to, but drunks and broken heads, or beaten-up wives."

"No! Really?"

"Yes. Yes, really. But that'll be nothing to New Year's Day. The first year I qualified I worked through, non-stop, for twenty-four hours over the New Year, and this set the pattern."

"How many patients, those who really pay, have you?"

He turned from her, saying, "Oh, I don't know"; then added quickly, "Four. I'm not a private-patient man. I haven't got the bedside manner; I leave that to the old fellow," to which her reply was somewhat pert: "Oh I quite agree with you on that point with regard to your bedside manner," she said, for which he turned on her quickly, almost startling her with, "Do you know what a bedside manner really is? It's keeping patients in bed or sitting tucked up under shawls much longer than is necessary; it is encouraging them to think they're the only patients he, the doctor, cares about; in the case of a woman who doesn't want to bear any more children, it is the chaise-longue treatment and the pampering of nerves. If I had anything to do with half of those women I would, metaphorically speaking, kick them in the . . . backside. Yes. Yes, I'd kick them in the backside and back into real life again. The bedside manner pays mostly where there is money. And this you don't find being doled out by male patients; they're not so damned gullible." He now threw off the remainder of his cup of tea; and then almost glaring at her, he said, "This is the point where I should say how sorry I am for using such expressions, but I'm not going to, because after you've given this one-sided conversation some thought you will know I am right. Anyway, I won't be in for a day or two; raw humanity needs me more than you do now. From now on it's a matter of using your common sense." And a touch of his wry humor returning, he added, "I think you've got enough of it to keep you from the chaise-longue. Anyway, for the next few days the only advice I'll give you is to start planning where you're going for a holiday."

He was picking up his bag as she said, "I already know where I'm going for a holiday."

"Oh, you do? Where?"

"Oh, I can't explain now, but if you deign to call again when I shall be up and about my business, I will tell you where, and why."

"Good. Good. I'll look forward to that."

With his bag in his hand, he said quietly, "One day you'll get to know me, Emily."

And she couldn't resist answering, with a touch of sarcasm, "Oh, that'll be something to look forward to . . . Doctor."

He remained staring at her for a few more seconds before he turned and went from the room; and he did not close the door quietly after him . . .

Of all the strange men in this world he was one, and the most exasperating. However could anyone be expected to live with such a man! How on earth did Mabel imagine that she could ever think of that man in a loving way! In spite of his claim to some form of good looks and his well-set-up physical appearance, and taking into account that he was very good at his profession, he was the most unlovable kind of man.

7

The unlovable man did not put in an appearance during the following week, nor did he visit on New Year's Eve as she had thought he might, indeed expected him to. Usually, even slight acquaintances would drop in to wish one a Happy New Year. Instead, apart from the company of Alice, she saw in the New Year of 1880 alone.

Those of her staff who lived out were naturally spending the New Year with their families.

In the past, Esther and Lena and cook had seen in the New Year with Mabel and herself. But this year, circumstances had altered the pattern. Lena had been gone these past four days. She had taken the long journey to Devon to attend the funeral of her one and only aunt, probably, Esther had pointed out, in the hope that the aunt had remembered her in her will, which Lena really thought unlikely, after the long years of neglect . . . on both sides. Still, Lena had gone hoping. As for Esther, she had slipped out at ten o'clock to wish her people a Happy New Year. However, the New Year came in and Esther hadn't returned, which could only mean she had been held up by her family or by the crowds parading the streets.

So, here she was standing at the window of the drawing room with Alice by her side. All the church bells in London were vying with each other. Boat horns were hooting from the river, church bells were ringing; there were the distant sounds of people singing; and here she was, standing alone but for this young girl, as a New Year came into being. And she wondered what it would hold for her. She knew how she was going to begin it. Oh yes. During the past week she had made her plans: she was going on a holiday, to that French hotel near Nice. There was one snag: she knew she couldn't travel alone. She had been over this before in her mind: whom would she ask to go with her? Not Esther; Esther was needed here to run the business. She had been doing this on her own for weeks now. And not Lena. No, Lena was an excellent dressmaker but would be a poor companion. Amity Lockhart? Oh dear, no. No. Margie? Jean? Molly Stock? Sarah Hubbard? No. No. No, again. So that left Alice, the girl whose one ambition in life was to be a lady's maid. Well, she could never imagine herself needing a lady's maid; but having her as a companion? Well, no again. Yet the girl was bright. Speaking candidly to herself she acknowledged that Alice was brighter and, for her age, more intelligent than any other member of her staff. But having said that, she couldn't really take her with her as a companion, it would have to be as her . . . lady's maid, and only in her own mind would the term hold a large question mark. Yet, after all, she,

Emily, was a person of wealth and that alone, in many cases, earned the title of lady; the young, eager housemaid-cum-maid-of-all-work was already a lady's maid in her own mind, even if only in a dream.

So it was settled, although she hadn't voiced her plans to anyone, not even to Esther from whom she could already hear the high exclamation of, *"What! Her!* as your lady's maid? Dear God! What are things coming to?"

It was odd, she thought, this business of prestige among workers. It was the same pattern that held sway in the big houses, where the hierarchy of the staff was often more stressed downstairs than it was above stairs.

As the sound of the bells died away Emily turned from the window, and Alice, pulling the curtains, said, "Will I pour you a glass of something, miss?"

"Yes, please, Alice, a sherry . . . Do you like sherry?"

Alice pulled a slight face, saying, "I've never really tasted sherry, miss. I've had a sip of port now and then, but I wasn't much taken with it, nor with beer. I don't like beer."

"Well, see if you like sherry."

"Oh. Oh, thank you, miss."

So Alice poured out the two glasses of sherry, placed one on a small tray with a plate to the side, then said, "Will you have a piece of cake with it, miss, or a sandwich?" She pointed to the side table on which, on a lace cloth, were placed a number of plates holding a variety of meats, and a fruit cake.

"No, thank you, Alice; just the sherry. But you help yourself."

"No, thank you, miss. I had a good supper; and I made it, an' took it in to cook. She's very much under the weather . . . Well, she was in bed."

"Here's to 1880."

"Yes, miss." Alice now raised her glass, repeating, "To 1880." And after she had sipped at the wine, she smacked her lips, saying, " 'Tis nice. I could take to it."

"You had better not."

The girl laughed, saying, "No, I had better not, for 'tis another form of mother's ruin."

Emily went and sat in the big chair near the fire and, motioning with her hand to a chair near her, she said, "Come and sit down."

"What, miss?"

"I said, and you heard me, come and sit down."

"Oh. Oh, all right, miss."

"Drink your sherry."

"Yes, miss." Alice drank the remainder of her sherry in one gulp . . . and choked and coughed; then, her hand over her mouth, she said, "What . . . what were you sayin', miss? I'm sorry, it went down the wrong way, catched the back of me throat. What were you sayin'?"

"I was saying, Alice, that you must be eighteen now."

"Yes, I am, and I don't know whether it's today or Christmas Day."

"You don't?"

"Well, there's a doubt about it. Sometimes Granny Milton says I was born on Christmas Day and other times she says it was New Year's Day, an' there's nothin' to show when I was. I've asked her many a time to tell me what she knows about me, but as she only talks when she's half-canned, I can't believe what she says."

Emily felt that she wanted to laugh, yet she didn't; what she said next resulted in the stem of one of the wine glasses being broken as it bounced off the arm of the chair; it was, "Would you like to be my lady's maid for a month, Alice?"

"Oh! miss. Oh! miss. Look what I've done! Oh, I am sorry, I am. Esther'll go for me. She'll raise the flat."

"Leave it where it is for the moment. It's only in two pieces, it doesn't matter. Sit down. I asked you a question."

"Yes. Yes, I know, miss, and . . . and that's what startled me. I mean . . . well, did you mean it?"

"I'm not in the habit, Alice, of having my best wine glasses broken for the fun of the thing. I asked if you would like to be my lady's maid for a month. I intend to take a holiday abroad and as I'm not yet fit, so I'm told, to travel alone, and moreover we're given to understand that it's something that ladies don't do, I was looking for someone to accompany me."

Emily stared at the girl, who was sitting almost rigid. Then she herself was actually startled as

Alice flung herself on her knees and, grabbing her hands, kissed them as she cried, ''Oh! miss, miss, I can't believe it. Oh! miss, thank you, thank you. I'll work for you till the day I die. I will. Honest to God! I promise Him I'll work for you . . .''

''Alice, get up, please, and stop it. I'm not asking you to work for me till the day you die, I'm just offering you a post for the next month. What will follow after that I don't know, I can't promise, I only know it will be an experience for both of us. Now stop it! please. Stop crying. This is New Year's Day. You know what they say, whatever you do on New Year's Day you do all the year round.''

''Well''—there was another gulp—''well, if that's the case, miss, I'll . . . I'll be a lady's maid for a year. Oh! miss, miss. Never in me born days have I thought that that would come true. But—'' She now sat back on the chair and, all the excitement seeming to have gone from her voice, she said, ''But I don't know the duties. I won't know how to carry on.''

''Well, we've got another week, or perhaps a fortnight before we start out. It'll give us time for some practice, won't it?''

Much to her surprise Emily found that she was enjoying the prospect of going on the holiday with a lady's maid, and such a one as this young girl. Yes, she would have to be trained but she was sure she would be a very quick learner. And she, too, would have to assume a part. And so she said further: "But listen: say nothing about this until I tell Esther of my plans. You understand?"

"Oh yes, miss. Oh yes. But at the same time"— she smiled broadly now—"I . . . I want to do a bit of a jig and shout it. You know what I mean?"

"Yes, Alice, I know what you mean. But you must suppress your desire to jig for a little while longer."

"Yes. Yes, I'll do that, miss. Oh, there's the front door going, miss. That'll be Esther coming back."

"Yes. Yes, it will be. Well now, your first lesson is to take that look of delight off your face; you are merely Alice the housemaid."

"Yes, miss, I am merely Alice the housemaid." And on this she stooped and picked up the broken glass and waited, as Emily did, for the opening of the door and the storm that would assuredly beat down on her when Esther should see what she was holding in her hand.

8

It was a month before Emily was able to start preparing for the holiday. There had been much to
arrange and she found she was glad of the extra
week or so, because she was made to realize that
as yet, her strength did not sustain her for long
intervals. And the weather was so inclement that
she could not take any outdoor exercise. What
was more, although she had known that her
choice of companion would cause a little stir, she
had never imagined her announcement that the
least amongst them would be accompanying her
to France for a month would result in such resent-
ment.

Not least from Esther, who had been piqued
enough to ask what else she might have expected
and then to go on and say that she might as well
also tell Emily that she, herself, would have been
glad of the opportunity. And to this Emily had
said, "There would have been no opportunity for
you, Esther, because you are the only one I could
leave in charge if I were to be satisfied that things
would continue to run as usual."

Esther, however, was not at all mollified by this,
and the rest of the staff, too, right down to Sarah

Hubbard, with one exception, made it plain to her that they thought the boss's choice had been unfair. The apprentices would have accepted the choice had it been any one of those in the workroom: Amity Lockhart or Margie Monkton or Jean Felton, but to have picked Alice Milton, who was really nothing more than the cleaner was, after all, a bit too thick.

Then, what was more puzzling still, was the exception to this general thinking among them: human nature being what it is, made up of a tangled cord of thoughts that created emotions which were sometimes formulated into opinions, brought forth, first, the favorable reaction from cook, quickly followed by a storm against her from the others of the staff: "Well! Would you believe it!"

"She's treated her worse than a dog for years."

"She's never had a good word for her."

"And she's got the last ounce out of her."

"And now she's saying she's glad for her," against which unexpected onslaught cook could excuse herself only by saying: no matter what she had said before or how she had acted, she had done it for the girl's own good. Everybody had to be trained. What she didn't say was that Alice had been the only one who had thought she should be in bed with her cold, and had brought her hot-water bottles and a hot drink and had seen to her meals; and even more than that, she had kept her tongue quiet about her particular weakness for the bottle, whereas the others, even Esther, had let her stand on her feet for days while her head was splitting. No, she was glad the lass had got her chance, and she knew she would make the best of it, although she knew it would then be hard on herself having to knock somebody else into shape.

Then the day had come. It was the 2nd of February. Since early morning the house had been full of bustle, and now the last of the packing was almost completed. Esther was once again going for Alice. She was saying this time, "She's not taking that with her."

"Madam said it had to be packed."

"Madam," said Esther, stressing the word, "would say no such thing."

Alice now straightened up and, holding the large straw hat in her hand and her voice as stiff as Emily's herself could have been, said, "I had my orders to pack this hat. Madam wants it—" She paused on the next word, searching in her mind for it, then she said, "She wants it . . . *accessible.*" She pointed now to the large bandbox at the foot of the bed.

"Don't you speak to me in that tone of voice. Who are you anyway? Nothing but a young skit stepped out of your place. A month is only a month, mind, miss, and you'll be back where you were. I'll see to that, or else . . ."

Then the door opened and Emily was standing there looking at Esther, saying, "Oh, Esther, give over, else I won't move a step out of the house."

Red-faced and so angry, Esther couldn't speak

for a moment. When she could it was to say, "Am I to understand you're taking that with you?" She pointed to the hat.

"Yes, Esther." And Emily's voice held a stiffer tone as she went on, "Mrs. Arkwright liked that hat, Esther. We often talked about it. She thought it was my type of hat and that I should wear it when the opportunity arose. Well, Esther, I think the opportunity has arisen, or will do when I get to France. You see, I trimmed it yesterday with a green silk bow on the back."

"Trimmed? You call that trimmed? They'll laugh at you if you go out in that. I thought you would know better; it isn't a felt."

At this point Emily felt like saying to this dear woman what she herself had just said to Alice, and which had been audible as far as the end of the landing: "Who do you think you're talking to?" But what she did was more effective: she stood straight, silently staring at Esther until the woman, her head drooping, said, "I'm . . . I'm sorry, but I'm all worked up, and you know why. And I can't help it."

"Alice, take that bandbox downstairs, together with my handbag."

"Yes, madam."

When they were alone, Emily's tone changed and she said, "Oh, Esther, why can't you give her a chance? Look back: you got *your* chance, I got mine."

"Yes, but not such a one as she's getting. And

the airs she's putting on. And this 'madam' business."

"She had to be trained, as far as I know how to train her. I am still called 'miss'; she couldn't go on calling me 'miss'."

"A month'll soon pass, and when you come back, what then?"

"We'll see."

"What I can see is that her head'll be so big she'll go off and advertise herself as a lady's maid."

"Well, won't that be a good thing? You'll be rid of her."

"Oh dear! I've never felt so worked up in my life."

Emily went to her and, putting an arm around her shoulders, she said, "I thought I understood you inside out, but I can't about this silly little business. You know, if it wasn't I had you solely running the place, I wouldn't be going." And then she lied diplomatically by saying, "Or if there had been anyone else that I could have left in charge, you would have been the one to have accompanied me, and you know that."

The words had the desired result, and Esther said, "Yes, I know; and I'm sorry about this last fracas. I wanted you to go off knowing everything would be all right, nothing on your mind."

"I am going off just like that, knowing everything will be all right under your care. But as for nothing on my mind, I'll still have a lot on my mind. I hate to see you like this, Esther. It isn't you."

"No. Well, I've never felt like this before. The fact is, I thought she was stepping into my place, and you know I would do anything in the world for you."

"Oh, I know that, Esther, and you've proved it. Nobody will step into your place, take my word for it. Now, have I got everything?" She looked here and there about the room, then went toward the bedside table and from there picked up the slender volume of poems. And as she did so, Esther said, "I should say you've got everything! You have enough luggage to give you changes for a year. But anyway, enjoy yourself. Although how you're going to get on among all those foreigners remains to be seen, doesn't it? And you'll write to me, won't you?"

"Of course, of course."

"Can you speak any French now?"

"Just about enough to get me to the hotel and there remark on the weather and ask the way to the ladies' room."

At this, Esther pushed her in the shoulder, then said, "My goodness! it had gone out of my head. Well, it would with that one, wouldn't it? The doctor's downstairs."

"He is?"

"Yes; that's what I came up to tell you, but . . . well—" She now leaned forward and kissed Emily on the cheek. Then, as if she regretted the impulse, she turned quickly and went out. And Emily stood for a moment, the book in her hand; then she looked around the room, wondering how she would feel when she returned: as good as she was feeling now?

Such was her contentment that when she reached the drawing room and saw Steve standing there, she actually apologized to him, saying, "I'm so sorry I've kept you waiting, I didn't know you had come. It is nice of you."

He said nothing until she was well into the room, when he looked her up and down before remarking, "You look very elegant."

"Oh, thank you."

"But then, you've always known how to dress."

It crossed her mind that not only was she feeling different, but so was he. There was a quietness about him, no bustle, no fuss.

He noticed the book in her hand and said, "You're taking that with you?"

"Yes. I . . . I like it very much; at least some of the poems; others rather puzzle me."

He smiled, saying, "They puzzle me at times."

After a moment of staring at her again, he said, "I'm going to miss you, you know."

Dear, dear. This was another side to him: he was quite human . . . well, ordinary.

"You'll not be the same when you return. You know that?"

"Of course I shall."

"No. No, Emily, you won't. A month in France experiencing a different way of life, meeting all types of people, from weird to wonderful, no, you'll never be the same again."

"Well, Doctor, can you tell me how I shall be affected?"

"Yes, you will be a more understanding person. Your views will be wider. You'll be looking below the surface, not judging the animal by its fur."

Oh, she had thought it wouldn't . . . it couldn't last long. Here he was, off again, criticizing her.

"Well, in that case, I hope you are right," she said, "for then I'll be able to tolerate all types . . . that cross my path."

He laughed, "I'll take back some of what I said, for now I see the old Emily is too deep to erase. But," and now his tone softened again, "I want you, speaking as your doctor, to have a good rest and to enjoy it; in fact, have a wonderful time. And"—he took a step nearer to her—"may I ask one special favor of you?"

"Yes, you may."

"Don't forget me entirely. And when you read this"—he now put his hand into his inner pocket and drew out a letter which he handed to her— "remember it's from the same person you left in England, no matter what you might have imagined otherwise."

She placed the letter on top of the book and now was holding them in both her hands and gazing directly into his eyes, unable to believe what they were telling her. When his hand came out she lifted one of hers from the book and met it, and his grip was firm.

"Goodbye, Emily."

"Goodbye . . . Steve." His name was slow in

coming, but he smiled at the sound of it and said, "Thank you"; then added, "I'll leave you now, for my presence is needed in a two-roomed flat where the sixth baby is waiting to be born. We are very lucky, Emily. As Petersen says somewhere in that book"—he pointed—"privacy, space, and a garden, and a friend to drop in would eliminate much sin. Startling in its truth, isn't it? Goodbye again, my dear."

She thought for a moment he was going to lean forward and kiss her. Then he went abruptly from her.

She did not turn to watch him leave the room, for she was disturbed in a very odd way, and for a brief moment she wished that she wasn't going away, leaving the house, leaving England.

When her thinking became almost audible with the words "and him," she thrust them away from her, saying to herself, "No. No. It's ridiculous. As he himself would say, leopards really don't change their spots. They have resting periods when they don't eat you alive; in other words, dominate you, be sarcastic, and, on the whole, be objectionable."

She now swung about and went from the drawing room into the hall where the staff were waiting, and so into a new phase of her life.

PART TWO
1880

1

From the balcony of his room Paul Anderson Steerman admired the view over the gardens toward the sea. There was no movement on the water today, not even a ripple; in fact, it looked as if a sheet of sky had fallen onto a wide plain, for there was no distinction between the colors.

He lowered his gaze to where the figure of Miss Kate Forester was emerging from the cypress walk, as usual pushing her mother in a wheelchair. Often over the past years his visit had coincided with theirs, and he had repeatedly thought of the waste of a life. Kate must be in her late thirties, and she must have spent at least the last ten years pushing the old girl around. At first she had put a bright face on it but then a dullness seemed to have settled on her countenance. Yet what could one expect: from what Walton had heard she had twice been engaged to be married, but each time the old dragon had put a stop to it.

He half turned now and spoke to someone behind him in the room, saying, "Who's expected today, Walton?"

"A Mr. and Mrs. Crouch, sir. They are new. And Sir Arthur Cartermere and his lady."

"Oh, they are early this year, aren't they?"

"Yes, sir, a little early. And there is another new guest, a Mrs. Ratcliffe."

"Alone?"

"As far as I can gather, sir, apart from her maid, naturally. Are you going to rest now, sir?"

"No, not yet, Walton . . . I'm tired of resting. Is it my fancy or has everyone suddenly become very old in this place?"

"I think it might be your fancy, sir. I suppose it's just that you meet up with the same people on your yearly visits."

"How long have we been coming here?"

"Oh, sir, on your own, sir, or with your parents before that?"

"Don't forget my grandparents, too. No, I meant since I married."

"Well, actually each year since your honeymoon, sir."

"Well, I think we'll make this the last visit, Walton."

"But you must rest, sir. That's the reason why you are here. And it's a very good place to rest."

"Yes, and be bored to death."

"Would you like, sir, that I arrange for a visit to Cannes, perhaps to the Casino?"

"Feeling as I do now, Walton, if I went to the Casino and lost even a guinea, I would sit howling my eyes out."

When he heard his man chuckle, he turned and walked back into the room, saying, "We're booked for a month and this is only the fourth day."

"Well, your irritability, if I may say so, sir, proves that you are much better; and you know your headaches have eased since you came."

The sound of a vehicle on the gravel drive made him nod to his valet, almost naturally indicating he should go onto the balcony; and Walton called back, "It's the waggonette arrived, sir."

"Oh, well, let's see what it spills out."

As his man came back into the room Paul Steerman himself returned to the balcony and, glancing down toward his left, he saw the Cartermeres descending from the waggonette, and he smiled as he saw Lady Flo adjusting her garments; first, her hat; then her waist at the front, and then the back; lastly, tugging at her gloves as if to bring them more firmly on her fingers even though a few minutes later she would be discarding them.

It was as if it were but yesterday that he had first watched this routine, for she was forever adjusting her clothes to her body. Then there were the new people. Well, he thought, thank goodness for that; by the look of them they haven't seen thirty yet.

Now he was staring at the young woman standing near the luggage brake and talking, presumably to her maid. When she turned and walked toward the main door, he could not see her face for she was wearing an outsize hat. Well! Well! he'd understood from the chatter that went on between Irene and his mother that large hats were out, worn on state occasions only.

How odd!—he had almost uttered the words aloud—the hat was quite untrimmed, except for a little something hanging at the back. How strange. Its owner had stopped now and had turned and was looking over the gardens toward the sea. Then she turned again and slowly began to survey the façade of the house until her eyes rested on himself.

Her face was pale, her skin appearing to be almost the color of the hat, which seemed to be a pale yellow. No, no; he dismissed that; her skin wasn't yellow. Of course, that was likely from the shade of the hat. Golden, he would say, or deep cream. She was wearing some sort of linen costume. Fashionable, in a way: tight in the waist but not so full in the skirt. He supposed she was slim, rather shapeless, and overall a bit too tall for fashion.

"I wonder if she wore it on the crossing?"

"What was that, sir?"

"The hat our latest companion is wearing. Look; she's going up the steps now."

"It is a very large hat, sir, and rather plain."

"Extremely so, I would say, except for that bit of ribbon on the back. Someone must have forgotten to trim it for her. You'll have to find out why she is wearing it, won't you, Walton?"

They exchanged a knowing glance and the valet said, "I'll do my best, sir."

"Discreetly, of course."

"Always discreetly, sir."

Again there was the exchange of glances.

"It's warmer than usual today; I think I shall lie down, Walton."

"Do that, sir. And you won't be going down to tea?"

"Oh no, no. I've done my duty; I've put in one appearance. Dinner will be trial enough the way I'm feeling now."

"Will I arrange to have it brought up, sir?"

"No, no, I don't want to be treated as an invalid, Walton. There's enough of them kicking around here as it is. I'm telling you, this is our last visit here; it's becoming like a home for old fogies."

"Yes, sir, yes. I agree with you."

"And I'll soon be one of them."

"Nonsense, sir. Nonsense, if I may say so. Is there anything more you want at the moment, sir?"

"No. No, thank you, Walton. Go and do your ferreting."

"Yes, as you say, sir, I will be about my ferreting," and when his master laughed, he too smiled broadly, then went out.

"It's a beautiful place, isn't it . . . madam?"

"Yes, Alice; it's a beautiful place. But from what I've glimpsed in the hall and the lounge, it's full of elderly people."

"Oh, I saw a young lady and a young man when I was being shown to my quarters."

"What is your room like?"

"It's very small, just a single bed, a wardrobe, a chair and a little dressing-table, which is just like a box with a standing mirror on it. But I'm glad I'm on me own. I thought I might have to share with somebody. But when I was told that the ladies' maids and the valets eat together I . . . I felt really nervous; well, a bit jittery."

"Now you mustn't be nervous. You will be probed. But you know what to say: your mistress is a widow; her husband was lost at sea. You don't know much about him, as he died before you came into my service, which was five years ago. Right?"

"Right . . . madam." Alice smiled broadly now.

"And where do we live?"

"Thirty-four, Willington Place. It's a very good address."

"I wouldn't add that, Alice. All those servants you'll come in contact with will likely have the map of London at their fingertips. Let them find out where the Place is and judge for themselves. But you could say that your mistress's house was occupied by an Admiral before she took it. You could be forgiven for forgetting to prefix 'Admiral' with 'Rear'."

"Rear being less than a real Admiral, miss? There I go again!" Alice beat her forehead with her knuckles. "When we are talking like this I always think of you as 'miss'."

"Well, you must forget that I am a miss. In any case, it's a long time since I was a miss. But far better use 'miss' than 'missis'. Better still, stick to the 'madam', eh?''

"Yes. Yes, madam."

"You're doing very well so far; in fact, splendidly."

"Oh, thank you. Sometimes I'm so excited inside that I want to let go. You know?"

"Yes, I know, do that jig. Well, jigs are out, Alice, quite out, especially here."

"Yes, especially here, madam. Yes."

"Now down to business. I'll wear the blue satin with the voile overskirt for dinner, and the white shoes with the half heels."

"Are you going to lie down now?"

"No, I'm not going to lie down, Alice, I'm going to sit by the window here."

" 'Tis a pity there's no balcony to this room. There was some balconies at the front."

Emily made no remark on this. Yes, she knew there were balconies at the front, and that she had been observed from one of them. He had looked down on her with a kind of astonishment, as if he were surprised at seeing her. Perhaps it was the hat. Yes—she chuckled to herself—likely it was the hat. It had already caused some comments when she had donned it just before she had left the boat. But why had she decided to wear it then? She had experienced a very odd sensation when she had first put it on in her cabin: it had been as if Mabel were standing by her side, saying, "That's it! It's you, and this is the place to wear it." But now she wasn't so sure. Likely, the size of it wouldn't have caused any comment had it been trimmed; it was the bareness of it, its nakedness, as she had first described it, that must draw the eyes. Still, here she was, hat, baggage, lady's maid and all. It seemed fantastic. Yet, stranger still, she did not feel out of place. She certainly wasn't dreading going down to dinner, whereas, in the ordinary way of things, she should be, because the tables would likely be dotted with titled people. What was it he had written at the end of his letter? "Never be afraid of a title. It is just a name; it cannot alter the man below the skin, who is merely a human being, except that if he was rotten before, he will be more rotten still."

It was odd, but since she had first read his letter, the one that had disturbed her so much, she was seeing him in a different light. And a short while ago, when she was being greeted in the foyer by Monsieur Albert Fonyère as if she were a long-lost relative, for a moment she had wished he were there just to hear his comments on the greeting; and also to have watched those passing through the foyer, all seemingly languid, their steps slow and stately. She felt that he would have likened it to a play.

After Alice had gone into the dressing room and closed the door, she rose from her seat by the window, reached for her bag and, taking out the letter, she again sat down and re-read it:

The substance of this letter was written weeks ago, long before Mrs. Arkwright died,

but in a slightly different vein; yet the sentiments expressed now are the same.

"Your feelings for me haven't changed
much over the intervening time: in your eyes I
am a most unlikeable person.

Here she stopped reading and shook her head,
for that was indeed how she once thought of him.
It is strange that he had put it into words. The
letter went on:

"And I haven't done much to erase this image from your mind. Yet strangely, that has
been my one desire, to make you see the
man beyond the acid tongue. But right from
the beginning you were a challenge. I knew
how you viewed me and so I played up to it.
Yet dear Mrs. Arkwright saw beneath my dis-
guise and I knew she took my part, and that
she tried to make you see me as she did. But
no, you couldn't stand the sight of me. And,
you know, Emily, that hurt. Yet such is the
complexity of human nature, as I've pointed
out to you before, we take delight in slowly
killing ourselves, whether physically or mentally. This is the self-conceit in one, especially
enlarged in the male. But now that I'm going
to be deprived of your presence for a short
while, I'm writing what I should not find difficult to say, but which I know you wouldn't sit
or stand still long enough to hear and that is: I
have a deep affection for you. And as things

stand now I have no hope of it being returned. However, I ask you in all humility,
could we not be friends? Leave the battle-
ground, as it were, and walk on the plain for a
little way, in the hope that some time in the
future you might climb the mountain?

As I said to you before you left, you will
come back a different person. Personalities
impinge on personalities. Manners rub off.
Ideas are absorbed. In short, you'll see people who live a different way of life. Such a
place as that hotel will likely be thick with
titled people. All of this will press on you like
a pattern, and you'll be unable to do anything
about it. Naturally, you will be a little awed at
first in your new surroundings, but by the end
of a month you'll be asking yourself why.

Emily, my dear friend, don't change too
much. Hang on a little to the spark-flying
business lady. It was she who first touched
my heart.

Steve.

Then, as a PS, followed the reference to titles.

She folded the letter slowly, returned it to its
envelope and then placed it back in her handbag,
feeling a deep sadness within her as she did so.
He loved her. Yes, he must love her. Strange,
really strange. But could she ever love him? She
shook her head. No. No. Be his friend? She considered a moment. Yes. Yes. She could be friendly
with him and perhaps enjoy the sparring that

would evolve from such a friendship. Well, that was all he was asking at the moment. Should she write back and tell him so? No. No, not yet. She *could* send him a few brief lines on a postcard indicating that a friendship was possible. Yet, no, she mustn't do that, either. She mustn't give him the impression it could lead over that plain to the mountains, as he had put it.

There was another note in the letter that touched her. It was as if he was lonely, really lonely inside. Yet he seemed to have a loving family, and practically every hour of the day he would be in contact with people. However, from her own experience, she realized that such contact did not take away that empty feeling, and it was because of this feeling he liked that man's poems.

She had spent quite some time on the train reading them. They were strange poems, sad even. There was one on aloneness, and he himself had once mentioned aloneness, saying it was different from loneliness.

She picked up the volume from the table and, flicking through the pages, she came to the one poem headed ''Aloneness'', and she read:

I had all the world could give,
A wife, a family, and a fine house in which
   to live;
Yet deep in me a want cried out
And asked what life was all about.
I put this question to my wife and my son,
And they advised a holiday, a little fun.

How could I have said, "I have a need
Which can't be quenched with what I eat or
    see or read?"
Then one day at my club I sat with a
    member
To whom I'd never taken
Thinking he was dour, and unlikeable,
And about character I was never mistaken,
But this day he cornered me
And began to talk haltingly;
At the end of which
He said, "I'm rich,
I have everything on which a good life
    should depend,
Yet I've never been able to make a real
    friend:
Inside, I'm alone.
Now, on all heads there is snow;
But the port is good.
And the cigars draw well
And the fire is aglow."

Strange, even pathetic. "Oh." She let out an audible sigh. Why was she bothering about him, or the poems, or anything else? She was here on a holiday, a recuperative holiday, and she was not going to spend it just resting: she was going to see the sights; visit places she had never even dreamed of; talk to people she might like or dislike; but do it all before she went back to the old life.

Change her. That's what he said, it would

change her. Well, well! if it did, what matter? Perhaps she needed changing. Perhaps she needed softening, to get rid of the bristle he found so attractive in her. Yes. Yes, she would welcome a change all round. She'd had enough of numbers thirty-four and thirty-five, Willington Place; they had eaten half her life already. This was a break, an escape, a month of exploration before she returned home . . .

To Steve and friendship?

Yes, perhaps, to Steve and friendship; but nothing more. No, nothing more.

Paul Steerman had a single table at the far end of the dining room. It was placed near the window with a distant view of the sea. Monsieur Fonyère always saw to it that he had the same table, for he had an abhorrence of tête-à-têtes; having to make polite conversation with another while eating always gave him indigestion.

Most of the other diners with whom he was acquainted were already seated when he entered the room, and as he made his way to his lone seat, he stopped here and there to speak to them.

"Ah! Good evening, Mrs. Forester. Have you had a good day?" and as usual without waiting for a reply, turned to her daughter, asking, "And Miss Forester, too?" More often than not Kate Forester did not reply.

But it was different when he came to Mrs. Winifred DeWhit's table, for her greeting always beat his.

"You're looking better already, Paul," she said, "tonight."

"Thank you, Winnie," he answered. "And where have you been today?"

"Oh, to Nice, shopping. Always shopping. But

we are going onto Monaco tonight to have a little flutter. What about joining us?''

"Thank you, Winnie, I would love to, apart from two reasons: I'm too tired and I haven't any money.''

Her high tinkling laugh filled the dining room as she replied, "The first I believe, the second is a joke.''

"Just as you say, Winnie, just as you say.''

Lord and Lady Huxton's table was too far away, but Lord Huxton raised his hand, and his wife bowed toward him. Their daughter, however, did neither; she just stared at him with large hungry eyes.

He had just seated himself at his table and was glancing toward the sea, when his head was turned again by that certain sound that only a lady's gown could make. The sound was hardly a rustle, but rather a swish; and this evening it was distinctive, and the reason for it was a single lady being led to her table by the head waiter. She was wearing a blue evening dress with voile overskirts in various delicate blues.

As she advanced toward a table quite near his, he thought again that she was too tall, yet she had style. Who was she? Her pale face was topped by a mass of brown hair swept upward, and as far as he could see it was quite unadorned, as were her ears and neck. She was devoid of any jewelry, even a necklace. Her hands, too, were bare of rings as far as he could make out, except for a significant gold one on her left hand, indicating her marriage state. It was odd, but she looked almost as bare as that hat she had arrived in. She was so bare that she stood out from every other woman in the dining room.

But was it to her advantage? Yes. Yes, he supposed it was, because she was rather unusual. How old would she be? About thirty? Well, perhaps not that. But she must be used to traveling alone, because, except for her maid, she was here without escort. Well, wasn't it becoming the fashion these days? Of course, though, you had to be of a certain age before you could have the liberty of traveling unattached. So she must have reached that certain age, yet it was well camouflaged . . .

Some two hours later, most of the diners had adjourned to the lounge for their coffee and liqueurs or whatever else they liked to drink; but she hadn't followed them, having been accosted, a word he always put to any approach Mr. Harry Cloche made to a woman. But, apparently, whatever invitation Harry had offered was refused, because he had bowed, and she inclined her head and departed. Poor Harry. If he didn't soon find another wealthy supporter he would indeed be on the rocks . . .

Later, while strolling in the garden enjoying his cigar and aiming to avoid the other guests, he noted that the new arrival was sitting at the far end of the terrace, partly hidden by the palm tree. And he wondered if she was seeking isolation:

had she noticed that there were steps leading down from the end of the terrace onto the path that led to the beach, a way often used by the more agile of the guests?

Some time later still, on entering the lobby, he saw her sitting talking to Kate Forester, which indicated that Kate must have left her mother in the hands of the nurse and escaped for a while. And he was again made to wonder, this time about Kate, why she was talking to the newcomer, because she was anything but good company these days, which, of course, was understandable.

When he reached his room, Walton asked him, "Are you retiring early, sir?"

"Yes. Yes, Walton. This hectic life has worn me out." His valet smiled as he helped his master off with his coat. Then he said, "Did you enjoy your meal, sir?"

"Yes. Yes, it was very good, as usual. And did you enjoy yours?"

"Oh yes. There's nothing to grumble about, sir. There never is here."

Paul Steerman did not push his enquiries further and ask, "Well, what have you found out about the newcomer?" because this wasn't done. He was content to play the waiting game; and Walton, being aware of the game, did not proffer any information until his master was in his dressing gown. And then he said, "The new influx, sir, the Crouches, as far as I can gather, are retired. I think they have been in business. He hasn't a man with him, but she's got a maid. I should think they're a very ordinary couple. Then there is Sir Arthur and Lady Florence. Well, you are acquainted with them, aren't you, sir? But they weren't at dinner, they were dining with friends in Cannes.'' There was a pause before he added, ''The single lady, I mean the lady who arrived alone, is a Mrs. Ratcliffe, as far as I can gather, sir. Her maid was very quiet, had little to say, and what she did say was touched with a London accent, not broad, but distinct to the ear.''

''Well, it's been a very dull day, Walton; and I suppose it will be a duller one tomorrow. You know, I'm positive I'll not be able to stand this for a month. I'd rather go up to Scotland; at least there'd be the shooting.''

''And the family would be so pleased to join you there, sir; Northumberland is only a giant step away.''

''Walton, you know, there are times when I want to yell at you, or even hit out at you, times when you stress the obvious . . . Anyway, there's always London.''

''Perhaps you have forgotten, sir, that the house is being redecorated.''

''Yes, upstairs, but there's always the kitchen quarters. And even they in their present condition are much more comfortable than those in either of the other two houses, especially the Little Manor. If any should have been redecorated it should have been the Manor, not the London house. Even the dogs don't favor the Manor kitchen; it's so damned cold. Any maid who ever worked down there developed swollen feet and bronchitis. I've put that to the pater over the years, but he doesn't seem to see it my way. Northumbrians are used to cold, damp, and freezing winds. You know something, Walton?" He started to laugh now. "My father can't understand why I developed pneumonia just through falling off a horse and splitting my head open. Yes, of course, he said, I lay out for hours in the rain; but he himself marched for days, soaked to the skin, as did his men, and none of them contracted pneumonia. Scurvy, dysentery, rotten meat; yes, these were natural, but not pneumonia. I often wonder, you know, Walton, how my mamma has stood it all these years. But then, as the pater points out, she was born in Northumberland. In fact, from what she told me, she was very nearly not born at all, at least alive, because they couldn't get a doctor or a nurse to her, the snow was practically up to the roof-tops." And the thought made him shiver as he took off his dressing gown and got into bed, and Walton, straightening the quilt, said, "Well, you're certainly in the best place, sir. And you've always found it very restful here before. Monsieur Fonyère looks after you so well."

"Yes; but all that does nothing for boredom. Anyway, good-night, Walton."

"Good-night, sir. I'm sure you'll feel much better tomorrow, and it'll turn out to be a pleasant day."

"Prophecies. Prophecies."

They exchanged a smile.

3

She had been here for three days. It seemed much, much longer, because during this time she had come to know the background of most of the guests, and this from Miss Forester. If ever there was a lonely creature in this world, it was that girl, or that woman. And if you could call an acquaintance of three days a friend, then she supposed they were friends.

It was really strange how it had come about. That first night she was sitting in the lounge wondering why she was here at all among all these elderly people, when Kate Forester passed close by, and so she had smiled at her, and the woman had stopped. She hadn't smiled back, but she had taken a seat beside her and had said straight-away, "I'm Kate Forester. I noticed you at dinner. I'm . . . I'm at the table with the wheelchair. My mother is an invalid."

"Oh, I am sorry," she had said in sympathy, and the reply elicited by that statement had startled her somewhat. It wasn't so much the words but the way they were uttered and repeated: "So am I. So am I"; to which Kate Forester had added,

"Have you come here for a rest, as most people do?"

"Yes, I was ill for a time."

Then she was more amazed when the woman said, "I'm surprised you couldn't find a livelier establishment, because this has become a rest home for the jaded, or those who want to revive memories of what it was like in their young days; oh yes, and for here and there a gentleman out looking for a rich wife."

Emily couldn't help but laugh at this and responded, "You are very frank, Miss Forester."

"Yes, that's the only liberty I have left to me, frankness. That's why I'm sitting here talking to you like this. And, I will add, you're so young and so fresh-looking, so composed. As I looked at you at dinner I thought how out of place you were. And then that hat, the hat you arrived in. It was amazing."

"You think so?"

"Yes, I think so; and so thought many others, I should imagine. Why haven't you had it fully trimmed?"

"Because I prefer it like that."

"Did you have it made?"

"No. A friend of mine found it in a trunk in the attic of a house we had just moved into in London."

"And it was like it is now?"

"Except for the bow at the back."

At this, Kate Forester had turned to look toward the door and to a part of the garden that was visible, and what she said hurt Emily in a strange way: "I've envied many women for many things in my life, but I envied *you* most of all when I saw you arrive in that hat. Not because of your looks or your dress but . . . but for something within you that gave you the courage to defy fashion and the talk and the sly looks in wearing that startling piece of straw on your head. And that quality that gave you the courage to wear the hat and defy convention and every *blasted* thing in it, and also took you into the dining room without a single bauble on you. Oh, how I envy that. I do. I do."

She had turned again to meet Emily's gaze, and there was silence between them. But in the silence a strange thought occurred to Emily, who was asking herself why it was that she had not cried over death, the death of Mabel, for instance; and why it was that she could not remember mourning her mother. Yet now, listening to this lady who had just sworn, she wanted to let the tears flow in order to ease the pain that the woman's words had created. It was this business of being aware of and affected by loneliness . . . no, aloneness, just as the poems in that book expressed, the feeling that Steve was always talking about.

"You think I'm strange?"

"Oh no, no." She found her hand going out to this woman, because she felt she understood her. And she heard herself saying to this stranger, "It is not too late to make a stand, at least in some way . . . in part," to which Kate Forester's answer was to smile and then to press Emily's hand, rise from the seat and say, "Perhaps we can talk again some time."

"Oh, yes, yes. I should like that."

And that's how it had begun.

The following day Kate Forester had come to her after breakfast and said, "My mother is resting in bed this morning, so I am going into Nice to do some shopping. Would you care to come?"

And so they had gone shopping, and they had talked, and she had learned a great deal about the "old hands" who came to the hotel year after year. She had been warned against the handsome, middle-aged, military type of man, Mr. Harry Cloche. He was seeking another wealthy widow to escort and to be paid for his services. When Kate had asked, "Are you a wealthy widow?" Emily had replied, "Well, yes, you could say that in a way," and Kate had come back with "Well, look out. You have been warned."

They found they could laugh together.

She had also learned that Mr. Paul Anderson Steerman used to visit the hotel with his parents now and then, but since his honeymoon, ten years ago, he had been a regular visitor. Kate herself had been here at that time. She said his wife was half French and very petite. They had both been so young but, as she recollected, the wife would stay only a week at a time; and he, too. But he had recently suffered a bad accident, she understood, and he was here for a month. He was very pleasant but rather aloof. He didn't mix easily. He had three children. His grandparents used to patronize the place in the old days. They were the Steermans of the fishing line. The Anderson part of the name headed their other business, big haberdashery stores. There were two in London, others in the provinces. The London stores dealt mostly in fine materials.

On the third day Kate met her after breakfast and said, "I'm afraid our drive will have to be postponed. Mother insists on getting up and going out"; but on Emily's suggesting, "Well, couldn't I walk with you? I would like to meet her," Kate came back swiftly, saying, "Oh no. No. She would want to know your ancestry back to Adam. Anyway . . ." She paused and her expression assumed a blank, even dark look, the look Emily had noticed when she first saw her, and she explained this now, saying, "She has managed to spoil, ruin, or check every nice or decent thing that could have happened to me. And now, if she thinks I have an acquaintance . . . even a . . . semblance of a friend, she will find some way to squash that."

"Oh no, surely not."

"Oh, yes, surely yes! Have you ever thought it possible to love and hate somebody at the same time?"

"No; not yet."

"Well, I hope you never will. Anyway, I'll see you later in the day and perhaps we could have that drive, say, tomorrow?"

"Yes. Yes . . . Kate."

Kate had half-turned away to make toward the stairs, but then stopped and looked at Emily again. She didn't smile, or say anything, but her eyelids blinked rapidly before she turned away.

As Emily walked along the verandah to where the large potted palm stood shading a rustic chair, she thought to herself that Steve would have found Kate's situation most interesting, and once again he would have read her a kind of parable from Kate's life: a woman wealthy enough to travel and stay for weeks on end in a hotel like this, yet deprived of liberty, and to such an extent that even a working woman would not have stood such treatment without open retaliation.

She sat down on the seat. She liked this corner, and for the last three days she had made it her own. It gave her a view of the gardens and of the people walking about, and, way beyond, the strip of coastline bordering the sea that during the day remained perfectly blue.

Today, she wasn't enjoying sitting here: the disappointment brought on a feeling of being at a loss. What should she do today? Well, she could go back to her room and write a letter to Esther and one to . . . yes, she would write to Steve. But what would she say about his offer of friendship? Well, she could accept that, couldn't she? Yes, she supposed so. Yes, she would write and tell him; and that would fill the morning. But what of the afternoon? Oh, she knew what she would do. She would hire a carriage and take Alice into Nice . . . one could be escorted by one's maid, she thought cynically. And Alice, of course, would be delighted with such a trip. Whereas she herself had made a friend, there seemed little hope of Alice doing the same from among the servants. They were a snooty lot, upstarts, most of them, was Alice's opinion, especially the valets. Although she herself didn't speak . . . proper like, she had said, she knew when other people weren't speaking proper. And half of them down there were no better than she was, if you went by their talk. The difference was they could put a twang to it. And what's more, some of the men say "ain't".

It was here Emily had felt she must interrupt and say to her, "Well, I think that is a common phrase among the gentry, Alice, so I read."

"Well, 'was you' isn't, surely, miss?" she had said. "You never say, 'was you,' nor did Mrs. Arkwright. And I know, if I know nothin' else, I know it isn't 'was you.' It's common, is 'was you'; and there's one or two down there tryin' to make out they're not common and yet givin' themselves away every time they open their mouth. Some of them say 'is you?' with a twang. My foster-mother always says 'is you?' and she's as common as muck, God knows."

Oh, she was glad she had brought Alice with her: Alice was unconsciously funny. It wasn't only what she said, it was that peculiar way in which she voiced her comments.

Well, that's what she would do, she would take

Alice sightseeing this afternoon, and buy her something . . . nice, not common!

She rose from her seat, walked along the verandah and was about to enter the inner lobby, when she was pushed to the side near the stanchion of the door, then brought upright again by two hands on her arms:

"Oh, mademoiselle, I'm so sorry. I . . . I was talking . . . Yes, yes, talking." Monsieur Fonyère was by her side now. "We were laughing, my good friend and I."

Now she was seeing the smiling face of the Englishman as he, too, remarked, "Yes, we were laughing, my good friend and I, and I wasn't looking where I was going when I turned about. Are you all right?"

"Yes. Yes, of course. It was nothing."

"Oh, I don't know. If you had been near the steps you could have gone tumbling down."

"Well, fortunately I wasn't."

He stood aside now, raised his hat and smiled, to which salute she inclined her head, then walked on.

It was later, after dinner, that they met again. There were a number of people sitting on the verandah, and they gave her smiling acknowledgments as she passed them on her way to the beach, for at this time in the evening it would be chilly and so deserted. But as she was about to descend the wooden steps, she saw that a couple had already preceded her and were about to make their way along the path to the beach. And so, deciding to wait a while, she sat down again on what she now called her seat. But she had hardly sat down when she was approached by the gentleman against whom Kate had warned her.

"Good evening," he began. "I'm afraid we haven't been introduced, even though I spoke to you briefly. My name is Cloche, Harry Cloche. This is an old haunt of mine"—he spread his hand wide as if taking in the whole hotel—"but I have been rather preoccupied in the last day or two so haven't had the pleasure of making your acquaintance. You are Mrs. . . . ?"

"Ratcliffe."

"Ah, yes, Mrs. Ratcliffe. I've heard your name mentioned. Well, Mrs. Ratcliffe, I have come on a special mission. There is a party of us going to the Casino this evening. Mrs. DeWhit was to make up a foursome but unfortunately she has developed a slight cold. So our square has become a triangle, and we were wondering if you would care to join us?"

"I do not play cards, Mr. Cloche."

"Oh, that is wonderful; I would be only too pleased to become your tutor."

"Nor have I any wish to gamble."

"Ah! Ah!" He raised his eyebrows while giving a little shrug. "Gamble, you say. Well now, we don't gamble as such. A little flutter, a very little flutter on my part, because I couldn't really afford to . . . what you call *gamble.* But part of the fun is in watching others who can, both win and afford to lose. And the company, I can assure you, Mrs. Ratcliffe, is very entertaining. You will be highly amused, and I think a little amusement is required after a day or two spent in"—again his hand waved—"this . . . atmosphere, however delectable, which unfortunately"—his voice dropped now—"gets heavier with age."

"I find this delectable atmosphere, as you name it, quite to my liking."

"Oh, come now, Mrs. Ratcliffe; you are young and beautiful and, I must say it, so elegant and . . ."

"Ah, there you are."

She started slightly as from around the palm tree came the man who had unwittingly thrust her aside some hours earlier. He was smiling at her. Then turning to Mr. Cloche, he said, "I think your company is getting impatient, Harry; at least, the steeds are pawing the ground."

"Oh. Oh." Harry Cloche looked back over his shoulder; then turning to Emily, he said, "You're sure you won't accompany us?"

"Quite sure, thank you."

"Oh well, hi-ho! But there may be another time. Good-night, Mrs. Ratcliffe." He said nothing to Paul Steerman, although he made an odd gesture of flicking his chin with his finger and thumb.

"Did he annoy you?"

"No. No, he didn't annoy me."

"Perhaps he amused you. I hope he didn't, because that would be fatal."

"No, he didn't amuse me, either. But why should it be fatal if he had done so?"

"Well"—he, too, now shrugged his shoulders—"if I don't pass this information onto you, somebody else will. Our charming Harry is an inveterate gambler. He has already lost his own fortune and bits and pieces of other people's. Do you follow me?"

"Yes. Yes, I follow you, and thank you for the information."

He stood looking down at her for a moment, then asked, "Are you enjoying your stay here?"

"Enjoying?" She cast her eyes to the side to the steps leading to the beach before saying, "The word doesn't fit my feelings. I feel rested, quite calm and, well, lightly entertained."

"Entertained?" The word was a question.

"Yes. Yes"—she nodded at him—"because quite candidly, sir, I have never met up with such a mixture of people who, at the same time, seem to have been cut from the same pattern."

"Oh, dear! dear! Oh, dear! dear! I see we're going into deep waters. And I suppose I have the honor, or the disadvantage—it's how one looks at it—of being part of the pattern?"

"I can't say that, sir, because my judgment is merely a surface one. So far, I have only been able to have any kind of conversation with Miss Forester."

"Ah, you have talked with Kate. And may I ask how you found her?"

"Yes, you may." She paused and stared at him

for a moment before finishing, "I find her a very interesting person. And further, I think it's a great pity she has to spend most of her life in hotels such as this."

Now there was another pause, longer this time, before he spoke again, when he said, "Would you care to take a walk with me along the beach?"

"Thank you. That would be pleasant."

When she immediately rose to her feet, he took her arm to assist her down the steps. Her quick response to his invitation, he found, to say the least, most unusual, but was in line with her manner, which was very direct. He was already aware that she wasn't used to the kind of society that she was seemingly studying, for she was too blatantly direct in her speech. In his class, only the aged could claim the privilege of being frank and saying what they actually thought.

At the foot of the steps he released his hold on her elbow; then they were walking side by side along the narrow, shrub-bordered path that sloped down to the beach.

Matching her frankness with his own now, he said, "Dare I enquire of the reason why you chose this hotel?"

"Yes. The reason is it was the wish of a friend of mine that I should, one day, come here, because when she was a young girl she spent a month here."

"Honeymooning?"

"No, not exactly."

She now asked herself if she should speak the

truth. What if he passed it all round the hotel? It would explode poor Alice's story, too. Yet, she didn't think he would be the kind of man to gossip. But how did she know what kind of a man he was? This was only the second time they had spoken and, although he had a nice face, he was of the class that gossiped. She'd had plenty of experience of that among the hat clients who had repeated the tales their husbands had brought in from the club, or the shoot, or the house party, or even the office. There flashed through her mind a picture of Steve. What would he do? What would he say?

She turned her head as she said, "She was lady's maid to the bride."

"Oh. Oh, really? Well, she must have had a very happy time."

"She did. She married the groom's gentleman . . . valet."

His laugh rang out; it seemed to echo over the dunes. When he stopped laughing he dabbed at his eyes, saying, "Excuse me. It . . . it wasn't that I found it funny; just unbelievable. And did they live happily ever after?"

"Yes, both couples. Very happily ever after."

"And . . . and the lady's maid, what really happened to her and her husband? Did they continue to look after the bride and groom?"

"Yes, until they were quite old; and after the lady died they continued to care for the gentleman."

He was no longer smiling but he kicked gently at a pebble, as he said, "How very fortunate for him.

Very fortunate. Then . . . then, he had no family?"

"No; nor any close relatives."

"And what happened to your friend after that?"

"Well"—she sighed now—"he rewarded them by leaving them what was, in those days, a small fortune, and she invested in a business in which she had always been interested."

When she didn't expand on that, he asked, "And what was that?"

"Millinery." Now she turned her head quickly toward him as she said, "Hats."

"Hats?"

"Yes. Yes, just hats." She was smiling broadly now and he was too, as he said, "Result, the golden one you wore the other day?"

"No. No, that wasn't the result. That came into our hands by chance, and only recently. Do . . . do you know London well, sir?"

"Pretty well. Yes, pretty well."

"Do you know Willington Place?"

"Willington Place? . . . Willington Place? Yes. Yes, of course. I went there twice when I was a boy. Willington Place? Yes. My father had a friend there. They had a large family, all girls. And you live in Willington Place?"

"Well, my business is in Willington Place."

"Your business?" It was a soft enquiry.

"Yes. The Bandbox. My friend left it to me. She died last year."

He stopped now, and she stopped, too, and they faced each other. There was a soft smile on his countenance as he said, "That's a remarkable story. But it isn't just a story, it's a piece of life, real life. And . . . and that large yellow hat endorses all that you have told me. You will never be afraid of life, will you?"

"Oh yes. Yes, I will. I am. I am now."

"No." He shook his head. "Troubled now and again, but not really afraid. No one"—he was laughing again—"who could wear that hat with such aplomb could ever be afraid of anything or anyone."

It was strange, but Kate had said those very words; and she told him: "Kate, Miss Forester, said something very similar. But it isn't true. I . . . I am afraid of what life holds for me, deep inside I am. I think only fools aren't afraid of life."

He held her glance for some long moments, then said, "You talk with Kate?"

"Yes. We have become . . . well, acquainted."

They were walking on again before he said, "Poor Kate. There is a life ruined through domination. To my mind that is the greatest evil, the greatest sin in the world: the domination of another human being in any way. With Kate, it has not only sapped her life, it has sapped her very soul. That mother of hers is a tyrant. Weak and selfish women dominate; beautiful and charming women dominate. Ruthless men dominate. Each dominates the other. They dominate their children. But I think the worst of all of them is the mother, at least with regards to the man. A mother is the first woman in a man's life; she bred him.

And the wife, no matter what love is there, is only psychologically second best. With the mother and the son, the foundation of the domination springs from love, but with the mother and the daughter, it comes entirely through selfishness. Utter, un-refined selfishness.

"Dear! dear!" He gave a shaky laugh now as he said, "I don't remember making a speech like that for, oh, I don't know how long. I'm sorry; I must have bored you."

"Not at all. But it's odd. I have a . . . friend back home, a doctor, who goes off at a tangent, just as you did, when he gets heated about any-thing. But I think most of his talk—he is very brusque—is to hide his other self, because he loves poetry."

"Well, I can't say I'm all that fond of poetry but I love reading . . . My goodness!"—he pointed—"there're the caves. We have walked some way; you must be tired."

"No, I'm not tired; I think, though, I'll turn back. But are they large caves?"

"Well . . . there are three of them, but they are quite small. There's a tale of a French farm laborer who lived in one, and died in it. There was a hurri-cane one night and higher seas than usual, and he was drowned. But they never found the body. It was only a villagers' tale, like all such, and yet people fight shy of going in that one, neverthe-less."

"I can understand that."

"You can?" He sounded surprised.

"Well, when I was young the people who lived just three doors down from us had to leave their house because of strange things that happened: ornaments were thrown about, and furniture was moved. The house remained empty for years. It was still empty when we left there."

"Poltergeists."

"What did you say? Poltergeists? What are poltergeists?"

"I think the conclusion is that they must be evil spirits. But not all of them throw or move things about; and so I suppose some of them could be good spirits. What they call 'psychic associations' are springing up now."

"Really?"

"Yes; trying to find reasons for these happenings. Not for me, though; I'm quite willing to let others delve into such things."

"Yes. Yes, indeed." They had turned about now and their conversation became spasmodic, until, nearing the steps that led to the terrace, he turned to her and said, "I've thoroughly enjoyed our walk, Mrs. Ratcliffe. May I hope it will not be the last, that we may perhaps do it again?"

She answered as he expected, quite straightforwardly: "That would be very nice."

"Well, I'll look forward to it. Anyway," he went on, "it hasn't cost you as much as it would have done if you had accompanied our friend, Mr. Cloche."

"Oh, about the same amount, because I wouldn't have gambled."

"Oh, I don't know. Once you get into the Casino you have to be very strong not to risk a franc or two."

"Well, I learned very early in my life to value a farthing, for nine hundred and sixty farthings make a pound. And you may not know it, but a farthing will buy a row of pins; in a draper's, instead of a farthing change you will be given a row of pins"; and this caused him to laugh and his steps to slow as he said, "Are you originally from Scotland?"

"No; I was born in London. Do I sound as if I'm Scottish?"

"No, not really, but it was the row of pins. We have a house in Scotland which we use mostly for the shoots—it's very isolated. There was a gillie there when I was a boy who would frequently say, 'For a row of pins I would skelp your ears for you' . . . well, yes, it might be a different part of one's anatomy. He was no respecter of children's rights, especially when they wanted to play tricks. I've also heard the saying in Northumberland at the Little Manor. But there it would be 'For two pins'; they didn't go as far as a row."

She put up her hand as if to check him speaking, then said, "You have a house in Northumberland, too?"

"Yes. But our main home is in Scotland; the Little Manor is sort of a halfway place."

"And it's really called the Little Manor?"

"Yes, and it isn't so small as it sounds, nor yet so large as to be termed an estate; it has no more than forty acres . . . What is it?" He was bending toward her now for she had her hand over her mouth; and when she muttered, "How strange," he asked, "What is strange?"

"That you should live in a house called the Little Manor in Northumberland, because I don't suppose there are two so named. You see, the Major, for whom my friend worked, lived in a house of that name, and in Northumberland. Apparently the Major had been born there."

"Do you recall his name?"

"Yes; I . . . I think, in fact I'm sure, it was Wrighton, Major Wrighton."

"Well! well! well! what a coincidence. The previous owner of the house was a Major Wrighton. It is in the deeds, and the family went back some long way, but died out, I understand, with the Major. How I know this is, after my father bought the property, he attended a sale of the effects and bought one or two nice pieces of furniture, together with the contents of the library as it stood. And years later, browsing through it, I found a sort of diary relating to the family and its origins. It is a very unusual piece of work, with entries from different members of the family. But, dear, dear me! isn't it most strange that you should be acquainted with the Major and the Little Manor?"

"Oh no; you could hardly say *acquainted,* except through my friend's employers."

"But even so, don't you think it strange?"

"Yes. Yes, I do."

They were smiling at each other now, and then

he said, "When we go up later in the year for the shooting, I shall look up that book again. There are all kinds of people mentioned in it. What was the name of your friend?"

"Mrs. Arkwright."

"Arkwright. Arkwright." He put his head back now, thought a moment, then said, "It seems to ring a bell. It isn't a common name, Arkwright." Then on a laugh he thrust out his hand, saying, "Under the circumstances, Mrs. Ratcliffe, I feel we have been formally introduced through a mutual friend, somewhat distant but nevertheless mutual."

She, smiling now, took his hand and their laughter joined.

And there it began.

Later, when Walton enquired of his master if he were fatigued, as he seemed to have had an extra long walk, his master replied, "Not at all, Walton. I met and talked with Mrs. Ratcliffe."

And to this Walton replied, "I hope her company proved to be pleasant, sir?"

"Very pleasant, Walton. She turned out to be a lady . . . and, like her hat, very unusual . . ."

On the other hand, Emily made no mention whatever to her maid that she had spent a very interesting hour walking and talking with Mr. Steerman.

4

It was the end of the second week of her holiday, and not a day had passed since she had first walked on the beach with Mr. Steerman but that they did not meet and exchange words. At first it would be only for a few minutes, when on the way in or out of the hotel; at other times, it would be after dinner, sitting on the balcony, or in the lounge. On such occasions, of course, they would both exchange words with other guests, he mostly with Mrs. DeWhit, and Emily with Kate Forester.

Twice that week, Emily had been on short trips with Kate, and the more she saw of her the more she liked her, and the more she felt sorry for her.

During the second week, conversations between them became longer and more frequent, and occasioned walks in which to indulge them. But weren't they both guests and, among such, weren't walks and talks not unusual? Perhaps, that is, until a bright and warm Friday morning when Mrs. Ratcliffe left the hotel wearing that extraordinary yellow hat and was helped into a waiting carriage by Mr. Paul Steerman, and they were driven off together.

Then again, it was surely not unusual for guests to be driven off in carriages, a carriage being the only means of transport, except if there was a party, when a brake would be used. Again, if a carriage was hired, a party of four would be formed, two gentlemen and their wives. There were exceptions, of course, such as Mrs. DeWhit and Mr. Harry Cloche, but they were old and established friends, whereas Mrs. Ratcliffe was a young widow and Mr. Steerman a married gentleman and of a well-known family . . .

In the carriage he was saying, "If I could get under that hat, I would see that you were smiling."

She turned toward him and she *was* smiling.

"I suppose," he went on, now smiling back at her, "you are well aware that it has caused some comment back at the . . . retreat? Do you wear it knowing that it will raise eyebrows?"

"No. I wear the hat because I like it. I've always liked it; it has something about it."

"Oh," he shook his head, "to my mind and to others, it has nothing about it. I think it must be the barest hat to be seen on the Riviera; but then, too, the most beautiful . . . at least, it appears so when you're wearing it."

She turned her head away again and looked toward the sea. She should have responded with some sharp rejoinder about cheap compliments; but she didn't want to, nor did she want to question, or think about, anything, only that she was enjoying this holiday as she had never imagined she would. She felt so different, she couldn't believe she was the same person who had driven along this road to the hotel on that first day, feeling slightly nervous, as if she were here on false pretenses. Well, in a way, she had been living under false pretenses, but not any more, at least to this man sitting by her side. He knew everything about her, how she had come into the business and the money, even that she was divorced. That, she knew, had surprised him, and when she had commented on it, he had said, "Well, divorces are very difficult to achieve and not very popular, and costly into the bargain."

And to that she had answered, "Yes, I am very well aware of those three points. Nevertheless, it was achieved."

He hadn't followed it up and asked on what grounds the divorce had been granted, nor had she informed him.

"Now," he was saying, "may I ask what you would like to do today on this our first excursion?"

"Learn French."

"What?"

She turned toward him again. His face was screwed up as if with merriment. "You did say learn French?"

"Yes, that's what I said."

"Oh, my dear Mrs. Ratcliffe; then French you shall learn. Everywhere we go I shall speak in the desired tongue, then you will repeat it . . . and mind, repeat it again until you get the accent right. . . ."

And so the day was spent in sight-seeing, lunch, then afternoon tea, all coated with laughter.

And then as they strolled along the promenade he summed it all up by saying, "It's been the most delightful day, and wouldn't it be more delightful still if we finished it by going to the theater?" And she agreed immediately. "Yes; that would indeed be delightful." She loved plays. Whenever the opportunity arose she had gone to see a play in London.

But they didn't go to a play as such; instead, they went to see a burlesque and laughed loudly, as did the rest of the audience. And once, when her hand touched his, he held onto it for a time. But it was all part of the gaiety of the evening, not a familiar hold.

But then, on the drive back, she knew it *was* a familiar hold when his hand sought hers, with the moonlight enhancing all about them, and he said, "What a pity this day is almost ending; it has been extraordinary, delightful, and never again will I think of you as Mrs. Ratcliffe. It would be impossible; you will always be Emily to me. And may I ask that I be Paul to you?"

She gave him no immediate answer; but instead she slowly pulled the pins out of her hat, then took it off in order that she might lean against the padded head of the carriage. She knew what was happening, what had already happened to her, and that she shouldn't have allowed it to happen.

He was a well-known gentleman; he was married and had three children; and because of this it must go no further. Her reasoning really meant nothing to him, she was sure of that: he was a man of his class, in which men enjoyed women's company freely . . . that is, women of their own class. She wasn't of his class, and he knew that. So how did he hold her? . . . Cheaply?

Very likely he was amused by her difference. Well, she was no silly girl; she must put a stop to it: this delightful day, as he had termed it, must be the beginning and the end.

Pulling herself up straight, she turned toward him, saying, "I think it should remain Mr. Steerman and Mrs. Ratcliffe."

The trotting of the horse and the grinding of the wheels on the gravel road filled the silence. Then he said, "As you wish, Mrs. Ratcliffe . . . Yes, as you wish"; and after a further short silence, he added, "But that formality will not wash away the pleasure of today, and may I hope it will be the same for you?"

"Yes. Yes, of course. Today has been most enjoyable and very instructive."

"Well, now and again I can take your lesson further?"

She paused before saying, "Yes. Yes, of course."

The moon was no longer romantic. The elation she had previously felt was now a sort of ache.

*   *   *

It was noted by guests sitting on the verandah in the cool of the evening that Mrs. Ratcliffe had stepped out of the carriage with her hat in her hand. That unusual, untrimmed, big yellow thing. Really, there must be a question mark about Mrs. Ratcliffe with regard to her station in society.

5

She had written a short letter to Steve. It began:

> This is my last week. I am feeling so much better. You said I would feel different, and you were right, especially about one thing.
> I don't know how I'm going to take to spending my days selling hats again, or put up with London weather, because here, one can't believe we're just into March; it's more like the usual English early summer. However, everything must have an end, and this time next week I shall likely be pushing my way from the station through thick fog.
> Yours sincerely, Emily.

She also wrote a shorter note to Esther in which she finished, "I'd like to live here forever," knowing that that was far from the truth, for there was only one person—no, two—who had made this holiday bearable: after the first two or three days of rest she would have become irritated by the inane pleasantries, the slowness of the days, the dressing up for morning, afternoon, and evening. Oh, yes, dressing up for the evenings and those almost ceremonial and interminable dinners. And then there were the musical recitals in the drawing room.

She turned to Alice: "Will you take these letters down to catch the post, please?" And Alice, glancing at Esther's name, repeated what she herself had said a few minutes earlier, "We'll be back there this time next week, won't we, madam?"

"Yes, Alice, we shall. Will you be sorry?"

Alice pursed her lips for a moment, then gave a little shrug and said, "Yes and no," only to add quickly, "Well, if I was speaking the truth, I won't be sorry to be back. They're a very starchy lot down there. I've learnt a new word since I came here: pre-ce-dence."

"Precedence?"

"Yes, madam. Oh, my, I'm gonna get mixed up with that when I'm back an' all," and she smiled widely. "Still, it's been an experience, don't you think so . . . madam?"

Emily turned about before answering, "Yes. Yes, it's been an experience." She knew that Alice was no fool and that, when discussing the guests, she herself, after the first few days, had not referred to Mr. Steerman, which would not have gone unnoticed. She now added lightly, "I am taking a walk with Miss Forester this morning, Alice. But I'll be back in good time for lunch. By the way, will you press the mauve chiffon? I'll be wearing that this evening."

"Yes, madam."

When the door closed she repeated to herself: Will you press the mauve chiffon? I'll be wearing that this evening. Then she turned to the window and stood looking out across the water. He was right. He said she'd never be the same again. How could she be after these three weeks? especially after the last two. What was she going to do? What could she do? Nothing. It was an impossible situation. Every day it was becoming more like a play, a tragic play, and she wished the curtain would come down quickly. But the knowledge that when it was down it would never rise again filled her with such pain as to be almost unbearable. Yet, at the same time, she asked herself how this could have come about, and how, having happened, it could have struck her with such intensity? She was not a silly girl, she was a woman and she was of a perceptive turn of mind. She could, to put it plainly, see through people, take their measure. So what was his, and what did she see in him? She had to admit she didn't know. It wasn't just his charming manner; it wasn't his wry sense of humor; it wasn't his understanding and sympathy with what could be called the common people, which had been revealed during their conversation; it wasn't any of these things, and yet it was all of them put together: his gray eyes so clear and bright, and the way he smiled and laughed; the way he walked; the way he stood; and then it was his tolerance, yes, his tolerance, for he made excuses for the lives led by those in his class, those in this hotel.

He had described little vignettes about different residents, and all showed, in a way, a sympathetic understanding of why each one acted as he or she did—with one exception, and that was Kate's mother.

She must get downstairs; Kate would be waiting . . .

A number of people were in the hall: Mrs. DeWhit was leaving, and quite noisily, as was her wont.

"Goodbye, darling. See you later. No, no, not in the autumn; I'll be fluffing up the pheasants then for DeWhit," which brought laughter all around. And then she was speaking to Paul Steerman. "Goodbye, my dear Paul. I'll take your love to Irene. Now, try to be a good boy." She was patting him on the cheek and he, taking her hand, kissed it, saying, "I've never been a good boy, not since they took me out of short trousers, you know that. Now you be a good girl . . . a good girl, do you hear that?"

There was more laughter.

As Kate and Emily circled the group to reach the main door, Mrs. DeWhit turned to Kate saying, "Goodbye, Kate." But when the gurgling voice added, "Give my fondest love to your mother . . . dear soul," Kate made no reply. Then the voice, the tone slightly changed now, with perhaps a slight haughtiness in it, murmured, "Goodbye, Mrs. Ratcliffe," to which Emily replied in an almost similar tone, "Goodbye, Mrs. DeWhit."

She and Kate had walked across the verandah

onto the drive, then into the garden before either of them spoke, when it was Kate who said, "There goes a woman who was baptized with snake-venom." And when Emily gave a short laugh, Kate turned her head toward her saying sharply, "You shouldn't laugh, because she can't get back to London quickly enough to tell Paul Steerman's wife that he has been enjoying your company."

"Oh, Kate!"

"Oh, don't try to shut me up. I know this crowd and you don't. And you're not a fool, so you must know that you've caused comment, having been seen with him so often."

"What about other people walking together and talking?"

"Yes; but they've changed over now and again. These last two weeks, except for the short jaunts we've had, you and he have spent your time together. He's a married man, Emily, with three children. He's a well-known figure. You came out of the blue. Nobody knew anything about you. They still don't and that's what makes them curious. And you're not like the rest of us . . . I mean, everybody back in that hotel knows everybody else. They winter together, they summer together, they're at the same balls. Most of them were presented at Court together. God knows how long ago."

Trying to veer from the serious subject, Emily said, "Were you ever presented at Court?"

"Yes. Yes, I was; and what good did it do me?

My mother gathered up her pains shortly afterwards and took to her bed, only becoming agile again when she thought nobody wanted me. Then when somebody did, back would come the pains. And I suppose, in a way, you could say God gets his own back on some people, because now she really is crippled and"—her voice dropping, she ended, "so am I."

"Oh, Kate, don't talk like that."

"All right, we won't talk like that; we'll get back onto this other subject, because I know where I stand, but you don't. You're either going to have your heart broken or you're going to do something damn silly that's going to wreck your life. It won't be in the same way as mine has been, but you'll go through as much, if not more."

They walked on in silence until they came to the end of the gardens that opened onto the beach. And they continued to walk, past the bathing huts that had been pushed to the rim of the water, past the long basket chairs dotted here and there, and onto where the path came down from the steps at the end of the verandah. And as they walked on Kate said, "There hasn't been an evening for weeks now when you and he haven't walked along here. Our side window looks onto this stretch."

Emily made no reply to this statement, for she felt annoyed. She had the desire to turn on Kate and say, "Will you please mind your own business!" yet she knew that would be stupid, for here was someone who was honest and straightforward, the only one, so far, that she had met in this new society who was; for when she came to think of it, Paul wasn't straightforward: he never mentioned his wife or children, and rarely touched on any part of his life. It seemed that his main object, when they were together, was to get her talking and make him laugh.

Kate was speaking again. "I've never had a real friend in my life, no one I could talk to openly, until I met you. And now you'll go out of it at the end of the week and that'll be that."

Now Emily stopped and, putting her hand out on Kate's shoulder, she pulled her round, saying, "That's something that needn't happen. You live most of your life in London and that's where I live, too. There's no reason why you can't come and see me whenever you like. It might be more difficult for me to come and see you, considering how your mother views me. Oh, I know, I know."

"Yes. Yes, so do I know." Kate nodded at her as she smiled now and said, "I'd like that, Emily. Yes. Yes, I would." Then impulsively she put her arm through Emily's and, like this, they walked on in silence now for some way until Kate, pointing across the water, said, "Look at that haze. I bet there'll be a storm later on today. There always is when it's like that, a sort of bluey-gray."

Emily looked to where Kate was pointing but she didn't seem to see any change in the sky or the sea, for at the moment she was more concerned with the storm that was brewing inside her. And had Steve been reading her thoughts he would have said, "It's up to you whether you weather it or not. . . ."

In the afternoon the sky was overcast. Kate's forecast storm seemed in the offing. But she kept walking along the beach toward the caves. She had turned now and again to look out to sea while glancing back along the beach to see if he was sauntering toward her. Whenever they met, his manner would always be circumspect: his step was never hurried, suggesting that he had just come upon her while taking a stroll. But today there was no sign of him.

She could no longer see the beach huts in the distance, and even the outline of the hotel was blotted out. There was certainly going to be a storm. She should turn back.

When, suddenly, a streak of lightning almost seared the sand a few feet away from her, she actually jumped and cried out in alarm. And when the following crash of thunder almost deafened her and the rain pinged on her face like small stones she stood gasping before discarding the idea that she could reach the hotel without being soaked. And so she now took hold of her skirts and, pulling them well above her ankles, she ran toward the first of the caves, and as she neared its opening another bolt of lightning and its almost instantaneous attendant clap of thunder seemed to lift her through it where, gasping, she fell onto her knees and clutched at the sandy floor.

She had been in this cave once before. She didn't know if it was the haunted one or not, but she remembered that it had been icy cold. But the cold she was feeling now was mostly from fear. Yet her body was sweating. She had never liked thunderstorms, but up until now they had held no great terror for her, probably because she had never had the experience of being caught in one in the open.

For a while it seemed she was being attacked by sheer noise, with the sound of the rain aiming to outdo that of the sea, and occasional bursts of thunder that seemed bent on splitting the rock above her head. One such burst brought her crawling as for protection to the wall of the cave that she had glimpsed in another flash of lightning. And there she hitched herself along to the furthest point . . .

It was after the rolls of thunder had receded and the rain had eased off that she raised her head from where it had been lying in the crook of her arm and looked toward the entrance. It was light outside, for the sun was shining again. She couldn't believe it. Even so, the relieved feeling in her was not enough to make her rise to her feet and dust herself down; instead, she again hid her face in the crook of her arm and slowly and painfully began to cry.

Like a child she sat, her feet half tucked under her, her arms resting on her knees, supporting her head, and she sobbed as any child might. And she longed as she had never done before to be back home, her life divided between the bustle and chatter of one house and the peace and serenity of the other, and where she had only the self she knew to deal with, not this new being, full of all the emotions which, in her case, could create only pain.

She let out a cry bordering on a scream when a hand came on her shoulder, and when she lay back against the wall of the rock, gasping, she was gazing at Paul's face peering down into hers and saying, "Oh, my dear! My dear! What is it? I didn't know you were out in the storm. Kate just told me she saw you going along the beach some time ago. And when your maid said you were not in . . . oh, my dear, my dear, why are you crying so?"

He was kneeling by her side now, his arms about her. "Are you so afraid of storms? It was dreadful while it lasted, but they're always very short. Oh, don't, don't, my darling, don't. Please don't cry, I can't bear it. Anyway, it's all over now. Come. Come. Get up."

He put his hands under her arms and drew her to her feet; only for her to find that she was unable to walk, and she had to lean against the wall of the cave.

"You're so cold. You're freezing."

She made no reply, for she was finding it quite impossible to speak, her mind registering only one thing at the moment: he had called her "darling".

He was now holding her chin in one hand while he wiped her face with a handkerchief, and he was saying softly, "I . . . I can't bear to see you cry. I don't associate tears with you at all. You're such a lovely person, an independent spirit. I've . . . I've never met anyone like you, Emily. Never. Nor have I felt for anyone like I do for you. You know that, don't you? You know that." His face was moving nearer to hers now. "I . . . I can't bear the thought that I may not see you again. No, I won't bear that thought; I must see you again. Do you understand what I'm saying, my dear, dear Emily? I care for you. I really, really do. You . . . you sprang upon me as quick as the lightning that has just gone . . . from the moment I saw you in that ridiculous hat. Oh, Emily."

She had been kissed before. Oh yes, Jim had kissed her, almost eating her alive at times, but with as much gentleness as a dog worrying a bone. But she had never imagined being kissed like this, gently at first, lovingly, until her arms went about him, then passionately, but still wonderfully.

How does one measure wonder? She was lost in it. It went on and on until it wiped out her past life, and there was no one in the world but him and her.

And his wife and children?

Gasping now as if she was still weighed down with the fear of the storm, she pressed herself from him with the flat of her hands, and her voice was loud as she cried, *"No! No!* What are you doing? What am I doing? I . . . I am having none of it. *No! No!"* Her head was shaking violently from side to side, and almost hysterically she cried again, *"No! I tell you. No!"*

As she made to stagger toward the opening of the cave, he gripped her by the shoulders and shook her, saying, "Listen to me, Emily. Please. Please listen. It will be all right. Everything will be all right. We can be discreet. Anything; but I can't let you go out of my life. Do you hear me?"

"Yes. Yes, I hear you, and . . . and I can't let you into my life. You have a wife and three children. Do you forget that?"

"No, Emily, I don't forget it. But . . . but I must say this: you seem to have forgotten it these past days; you have known all along that they were there, but you couldn't help yourself any more than I could."

She pulled herself away from him and went to the opening of the cave. The day was glorious in its own way again. The sky was blue and mirrored in the sea. The air was like wine. The bathing huts were back in view, as was the hotel. Everything was as it had been before the storm, except for within herself.

She looked down at her gown with the damp sand clinging to it and she dusted it away. Then she stroked her hair back from her face and under the small hat which, secured by two pins, had remained on her head all the while.

She said now, "Would you like to leave me, please? I would prefer to walk back to the hotel on my own."

"No, Emily, I would not like to leave you. Nor am

I going to leave you. We'll go back together, and after you have changed your dress, we'll have tea in the small drawing room. Nothing is going to change outwardly. I won't let it. We have only five more days together. Whatever happens after that will have to be arranged."

"No! No!"—Steve would have recognized the tone of her voice now—"It won't have to be arranged. It can't be arranged. What are you proposing? That I become your mistress?"

"Oh, Emily, one of your attractions, your charms is your openness. But you are putting the rough edge to it now. I hadn't thought to ask you to become my mistress."

"No? Then, even knowing how you say I feel about you, this was to be just a holiday romance? A pleasant episode before you move onto the next amusement of hunting or yachting?"

"Such talk isn't worthy of you, Emily. You have sprung into my life and created a feeling that, hitherto, I never imagined possible. And truthfully, Emily, this last week, I have felt that I have been touched by the gods. And so my dear"—he moved a step toward her—"I can't bear the thought of not seeing you again after this holiday is over."

She literally had to force herself not to be melted by his words, and to this end she said quietly, "Then what, may I ask, are your intentions? A divorce?"

He stepped back from her and his body seemed to stiffen as he said, "No, Emily. Oh no. There could never be a divorce. As you know, I have three children and . . . and they are dear to me. And their careers are in my care. And having said so much, I can say further that my wife and I now lead our separate lives. We occupy the same houses, but we go our own ways, and have done for some time now. My wife, I have to say, is a very charming woman, but we don't see eye to eye on a number of issues. So, therefore, we tolerate each other.''

''Oh, I see.''

''Oh, no, you don't see, Emily.''

''Oh, yes I do.'' Her voice was harsh now. ''Being a man of your class, you have the license to have a mistress. It is the done thing. And what is more, if your choice had been among one of your own set, this discussion would not have had the raw flavor to it that it is having at this moment, would it?''

He turned his back on her now as his head drooped, an action that admitted she was right in pointing out how one of his own class would have dealt with the situation.

When she added, ''Now, would you please let me return alone?'' he swung round on her and, as harshly as she had been speaking, he answered, ''No, I shall not let you return alone. If you want tongues to wag, that's the way to do it. Even from this distance we can be seen from the upper rooms of the hotel, and I'm sure your new friend, Miss Kate Forester, has had us under observation for some time. Now do me the courtesy, please, to walk back with me to the hotel. And during our walk I will not mention love to you again, but I would ask that for the next few days you will meet me as a friend? Please, Emily. Promise me this one favor.''

She was staring into his face now and her whole being was telling her that she would promise him anything in the world if only he were free. But, as he implied, even said as much, he would never be free, and she knew now that neither would she: she would never be free from the want of him. How near she had been back in that cave to succumbing to him wholly. Well, there was one thing sure in her mind: once she left this hotel she would never see him again, because he was one man she could never be friends with. A friend to Steve, yes; in the long run, a friend to Steve. But not with this man, for it would be all or nothing. And it must be nothing.

6

Emily occupied Tuesday by going into Nice to buy specific presents for Esther, Lena and cook. For the others, she bought boxes of candy and sweetmeats. She had lunch in the town and filled the rest of the afternoon visiting the places that she had already visited with him. Then she hired a cab to take her back to the hotel.

When she entered her bedroom Alice looked at her closely, and having relieved her of her packages and helped her off with her dust-coat, she remarked, "You look peaked, practically the same as when you came. You've been overdoing it. You should rest before you go down to dinner; there's an hour yet. What would you like to wear tonight?"

She wanted to say, "It doesn't matter;" and so when it was some time before she answered, "The gray," Alice came and sat down beside her at the foot of the bed, a liberty which a real lady's maid never would have taken, and she said, "What is it, miss? You look so sad all of a sudden."

Emily turned to her and it was only with an effort she resisted putting her arms about her and laying her head on Alice's shoulder and blurting out just *how* she felt. It would have been the action of some young girl disillusioned over her first love. But when Alice put her hand on hers and asked quietly, "Are you worried over Mr. Steerman?" she actually jerked her body further along the bed as she exclaimed, *"Alice!"* The name was a reprimand, and it caused Alice to hang her head and her body to rock slightly as she said, "I'm . . . I'm sorry, miss . . . madam, but . . . but they chatter down there. It isn't so much what they say, 'cos they only say it in halves, it's how they look. And they quiz me. His man doesn't; Mr. Walton. He's a quiet fella, like a gentleman himself. He spoke to me the first night I was at the table."

"What do they say?"

"Oh"—Alice now lifted her head—"they . . . they talk mostly about him, Mr. Steerman, and his family. They're . . . they're all old patrons of the hotel. Then, one or two have quizzed me about how long you've been a widow, and how long you were married. And what did you do? They meant, where did you spend your time during the year? They all seem to be drifting from one place to the other."

"And what did you say to that?"

"Oh, I told them that you own houses, property like. Well, you do, don't you? and that one of them was run as a big business."

"In hats?"

"Well, yes, miss. I had to sort of . . . to put it

something like that, that you owned a big establishment for hats and such.''

''And what did they say to that?''

Alice looked down again for a second, then bit on her lip before turning to Emily and, with a suppressed smile on her face, saying, ''Well, sort of . . . that it was a pity you didn't get that big one trimmed.''

Emily smiled and, rising from the bed, she said, ''Yes, perhaps it is.''

''Oh, no, miss.'' And Alice immediately attempted to correct herself by making an impatient sound in her throat and saying, ''It's funny, you know. It's . . . it's very funny, it's odd, but sometimes it's quite easy to call you madam, while at others, like just now . . . talking, I think of you as miss.''

''Well, Alice, we'll soon be back to the 'miss' stage, and . . . and, between you and me, I won't be sorry.''

''Ah, Miss Emily, don't say that. You've looked so bonny lately, beautiful; and you wear the clothes wonderfully. You look better than anybody in this place. And you've enjoyed it up till now. Don't . . . don't mind what anybody says. Go on enjoying it. It's only a holiday, and everybody is entitled to a bit of fun now and again.''

''Oh, Alice. Alice.'' She had to turn away because otherwise she knew she would burst out crying again, and she could only mumble, ''I will lie down for a while. You . . . you had better press the gray, it is apt to crease at the back.''

"Yes, I'll do that." Without either the miss or the madam, Alice turned away and went into the dressing room. And Emily, lying down on the couch below the window, closed her eyes and put her hand tightly over her mouth, telling herself she must pull herself together: if a change of front was so noticeable to Alice, then it would be to others, and it would give them more to gossip over. And now speaking plainly to herself, she said, "You deserve all you've got. You knew what you were getting into." But when memory brought his voice back to her, soft as it was in the cave, and she whimpered, "But he feels the same. He loves me," the answer she was given seemed to come from Mrs. Arkwright, saying "That's what they must all tell their mistresses." And that was what he was offering her: to be his mistress. Well, she would never be his mistress, or any man's. Never! Never!

On the Wednesday they met in the afternoon and sat for a time on the verandah. He asked her what she thought of the present situation in London: Parnell was on his hind legs again. In his opinion that man aggravated the troubles in Ireland. He did not pause to give her a chance to answer, but went onto discuss the Queen, and expressed his opinion that mourning could be carried too far, and that it was a wonder she hadn't copied the fashion here in France of staining the furniture black.

And when she did speak, saying, "You are not a

Royalist, then?'' he came back strongly with, ''Oh yes, I am. I am. I love them all; I admire Albert Edward, Prince of Wales. There's a man who has not been used to his full capacity. He's a fine ambassador.''

As he went on talking about the Prince and his journeys, she told herself that, of course, he *would* admire him: the Prince was noted for the number of his lady friends, especially the one who was openly his mistress, and in defiance of his beautiful wife, Princess Alexandra. What must she feel? Why was it that men could claim this liberty as a right? whereas, if a woman were to leave her husband for another man, she would be, if not actually barred from, at least ostracized in society, even though she might have had to put up with her husband's mistresses for years. It was a very unfair situation, a cruel situation.

She recalled Mrs. Arkwright's advice to her before she married Jim Pearson: ''Don't give in to him,'' she had said, ''because once you do, you're finished. And if he knows you're pregnant he'll likely go off. Most of them do. And then what happens? The lasses are thrown out of their jobs, with no references, and the bairns carry a stigma for life. So remember that, when he starts messing about with you.''

And she had remembered it, although mostly through fear of the terrible prospect of having a baby before she had a ring on her finger.

Yet here Paul was sitting, praising the Prince of Wales, a notorious womanizer . . .

"Would you like a stroll in the gardens, Mrs. Ratcliffe?"

"Thank you, yes."

They passed two couples reclining in basket chairs: the Arnold-Fawcetts smiled at them, but Lady Huxton and her daughter just stared; and Lady Huxton even raised her lorgnette in an endeavor to follow their progress into the garden until they were cut off from her vision by a high hedge.

"How are you feeling?" he asked, after they had walked some distance.

"Quite all right, thank you."

"Oh, Emily, please don't wear that stiff coat. What's done is done; it can't be undone for either of us. I should say I am deeply sorry it has happened but, in truth, I am not. And if we never see each other again after we leave here, I shall never forget you, because I shan't be able to. So why not let us act as friendly friends for the next few days?"

"I'm going to find that difficult." Her voice was low. "I am not used to having affairs, and so I am not as yet practiced in putting a face on such things."

"No, my dear, I'm well aware of that, which makes this affair, as you name it, so very, very different."

She was quick to pick this up and, turning her head sharply toward him, she said, "From others you've experienced?"

He did not come back at her but smiled tolerantly as he said, "No, Emily, not from others I myself have experienced; but I am a man, and not having been brought up in a monastery, I've lived in my world."

"And followed its pattern?"

"Yes. Yes, you're right in some ways, I have followed its pattern. But I can't repeat too often, you are not in that pattern. You are something outside, something quite different and I fear I'll never be able to convince you of that, but nevertheless it's true."

"Good morning," a voice said.

They were passing an old gentleman who was bending over a bush, but his head was turned toward them and he said, "Lovely smell. I've tried to grow this in my garden but it just dies on me. Bad storm we had yesterday, wasn't it?"

"Yes, Colonel; yes, it was." Then, having passed on, Paul remarked quietly to Emily, "I wish I was his age and my desires and appetites were concentrated on a scented bush."

"He makes me feel sad," she said; "he seems so old and alone, yet living among all these people, and of his own class. But he puts me in mind of a poem I read in a book a friend gave me. It ends with two old men finding each other and sitting before the fire, smoking their cigars and drinking their port: they've each found a friend."

"Good gracious! Petersen's. S. Petersen."

They were looking fully at each other now and she said, "Yes, that's the author of the book."

"I have it. They're very odd poems. This is his second book."

"You know him?"

"No, not personally, but a friend of mine says that he's a psychiatrist in some hospital. I think he must be to write as he does. Very odd poems, some with no claim to poetry at all, but the sense is there. I like him. I understand he's Norwegian."

"Really?"

"Yes. That's why he writes rather oddly, I should imagine, and doesn't think quite English. You know what I mean?"

She didn't answer; but when he stopped and with his hand gently on her arm drew her to a standstill, and his voice low, he said, quietly, "There you are, you see, we do have something else in common. Who knows, we might end up like those two old gentlemen: me with my port and cigar and you with your tapestry."

She forced a smile as she said, "A very comforting picture, but unfortunately I have never done any tapestry, and I'm not at all inclined that way. The gentle pursuits of ladies don't attract me."

"Oh, Emily, we *can* be friends. I know we can. I love just being in your company. It makes me happy just to be walking with you like this and waiting for your . . . pithy comments. It is you, you know, who insist on putting people into classes. Oh, yes, yes, I know." He now closed his eyes and wagged his hand at her. "There definitely are two classes; no, three really, and always will be. But if you were a member of the one you criticize most, do you know you would be highly respected and feared . . . ? Oh yes, because no one would be able to stop you saying what you think, and that is a privilege allowed only to dowagers of great age."

"In other words, I have an acid tongue."

"No, no, no. There you go again. That's an unfortunate habit you have, too, of turning one's meaning. There's no acid in a pithy remark because it comes within the category of wit. . . ."

And so the conversation went on during their walk; and she got through Wednesday and most of Thursday.

He had come upon her casually as she watched a game of croquet and when it was finished they strolled together from the green and into the hotel foyer. They were crossing the threshold and she was slightly ahead of him, when she heard him gasp and mutter something like, "Oh no!" before exclaiming aloud, "Why, Irene! What a surprise!" And he brushed past Emily and approached the lady who had turned from the man she had been talking to, and his hands were held out to her. "How lovely to see you! But I didn't know you were coming. I thought you were going onto Rome."

"Yes, we are, darling, on Saturday. The luggage has gone on but I thought I would drop in to cheer you up. I saw Winnie DeWhit in London. She said you looked lonely."

They were staring at each other; then the

woman turned her head and stared at Emily. And he turned too, saying, "Oh, by the way, this is Mrs. Ratcliffe. Mrs. Ratcliffe, my wife."

"How do you do?" They both spoke and inclined their heads at the same time. Then the woman turned away. "I've just reassured Monsieur Fonyère, who tells me that the hotel is fully booked, not to worry; I have shared a room with you before." Her laughter was light and high to match her person; not that her appearance was in any way heavy, for her body was slight, but her hair was jet black, as were her eyelashes, which were accentuated by the paleness of her skin; her upper lids were heavy and shaded her eyes which seemed to take up the color of her hair, for they were bright and very dark.

Before following his wife, Paul Steerman glanced quickly back at Emily, but she had no way of interpreting his expression, although she felt that, apart from his greeting of his wife, he wasn't over-pleased to see her. And so, as she now made her way toward the stairs, she thought, well, that's that. So much for them living apart. In a way it was just as well that Mrs. DeWhit's tongue had wagged.

She made the effort to fill up Friday by again taking Alice into Nice so that she could buy some small gifts for her friends back in the house. Then, after lunch, she showed her the same places as she herself had first been introduced to, managing to arrange the outing so that on returning to the hotel she had no time other than to change before going down for her last meal. And with a show of defiance she put on the blue chiffon that she had worn on the first night here. It was a dress he had remarked upon, telling her that he would always remember her as he saw her that first night.

As she entered the dining room and wended her way to her solitary table in the far corner, there was some slight turning of heads, a here-and-there issuing of tight smiles: How would she react now that his wife had arrived? And so unexpectedly. Winnie DeWhit had surely been working on her mission in life, which could be termed a courier of scandal. Against the principles of her own class, of course; but then their society would be very dull without the Winnies of this world.

Emily could almost discern the thoughts as she, too, here and there, returned a smile. And all during the meal she aimed to keep her expression pleasant, having a word with Henry, the waiter who had most often attended her during her stay.

Madame was leaving tomorrow then? He was sorry to see her go.

She, too, was sorry to leave. But then, life could not be one long holiday.

"No, madame, life cannot be one long holiday." And when he added, "Not if one is wise," they exchanged a single motion with their heads as if they were in complete accord with his statement.

And so the interminable meal ended and as usual she walked into the lounge to take coffee, and there was joined by Kate, whose mother had been obliged to dine in her room. They were scarcely seated before Kate remarked, "What a turn of events!"

"Please, Kate."

"Just making a statement. But to my mind it's just as well; you can now see how the land lies. Anyway, when you're back in town, may I come and see you?"

"Oh, of course; I've told you, I'd like that very much."

"Thank you. You won't believe me when I say that I envy you, for no matter what you are feeling at this moment, you're free. You are your own mistress. You work for your living and get paid for it. I work for my living. Dear God! How I work for my living. And what do I get for it? My food, my clothes and traveling expenses. But I don't see a penny of that. Do you know, Emily, that I haven't one farthing of my own?"

Emily found it was quite impossible to say anything at this moment, for here was someone pouring out her heart to her as no one had ever done before. Steve talked of friendship. Paul talked of friendship, but neither of them really needed friendship. But here, this middle-aged woman, this lady, because Kate was a lady born and bred—her plainness, her stodgy body could not hide her breeding—here she was saying she envied her, telling her that she hadn't a farthing of her own.

"My father left everything to my mother, even

though she had disappointed him by not providing him with a son, and he didn't care for the substitute. No, no"—she shook her head—"he never cared for the substitute." And she turned her head away now, seemingly to look around at the guests here and there as they sipped at their coffee and liqueurs. But when she again looked at Emily she said simply, "He never spoke a civil word to me in my life, and all this chatter of mine may appear that I'm begging sympathy. I'm not. But what I'm pointing out is that in my . . . this class that you've found yourself in, the pain of rejection and such is harder to bear than in any other division in society, because we must put a face on things. It is very bad form to yelp, and for the very first time in my life I am doing just that, for I feel I can with you. You're different, quite different from anyone I've ever met, and . . . and I don't want to stop seeing you. I know you think I've latched onto you, and I have. Meeting you was like coming across an oasis in a desert. My desert is upstairs." And she pointed her index finger discreetly toward the ceiling; and then she sat back in her chair, sipped at her coffee, and remained silent, until Emily, who had never taken her eyes off her, said briskly, "How old is your mother?"

"Seventy-four."

"Is she really ill?"

"She's crippled with rheumatism and she claims her heart's in a poor state, but I've only got her word for that."

"Well, she can't live forever. Just hang onto that thought. And you've got another life before you."

"I'm forty-one, Emily."

There was a sad finality about the words. Perhaps it was this that brought into Emily's mind the picture of her husband coming in drunk and singing his usual comic music hall ditty. He had done so toward the end of their marriage and for a time she had feared him because the ditty, such as it was, pointed out that should anything happen to her, he'd be the better off through the sale of the house.

The ditty had a swing to it, and so, what she did now was to lean forward and, putting her face close to Kate's, sing in a voice just above a whisper, and in staccato tones, emphasizing the last word of each line:

> "The missis of the house
> Had a mouse up her blouse,
> And she couldn't get it down again;
> And she coughed till she died,
> And I laughed till I cried
> 'Cos of all I stood to gain."

There was a splutter, a cough, and when Kate Forester's laugh rang out high and loud it seemed to petrify all the other occupants of the lounge for a moment: raised cups became stationary, heads jerked to the side and remained still. Among those so affected were Mr. and Mrs. Paul Anderson Steerman. When Kate's laughter ebbed, heads were turned back to each other again, each one holding enquiring looks; then expressions as if of amazement were directed again toward the woman they all knew so well, she who was drying her eyes while her shoulders were still shaking with her mirth. Her companion, Mrs. Ratcliffe, who had apparently supplied the cause of Kate's outburst, was evidently trying to suppress her own laughter, for her fingers were across her lips and her eyes were cast down.

But when Emily raised her head she found that she had met the eyes of Paul Steerman, and he wasn't smiling; nor was his wife. But the expression on his face gave her the feeling that he was slightly hurt. Perhaps, she thought, he was disappointed that she wasn't in the depths of despair over his wife's unexpected appearance having, as it were, severed the last link between them. And she experienced a moment of satisfaction that was like salve on the constant ache within her; and she noted that after he turned abruptly away, his wife continued to stare at her.

Her attention was brought to Kate again, for she was saying on a gasping breath, "Oh, Emily, I've . . . I've never laughed like that in my whole life. Where on earth did you find that piece?"

"It was in my husband's repertoire when he was drunk."

Now it was Kate who put her hand tightly across her mouth, muttering, "Please, Emily, don't . . . don't set me off again. But . . . but you really mean that he sang that to you?"

"Oh, yes. Yes; but perhaps not to me, but rather *at* me. He was a patron of the music halls; that is, when he wasn't spending his evenings in bars."

Kate now wiped her face and the laughter off it as she said, "That must have been an awful time for you."

"It was."

"You must have been very brave to go through with a divorce."

"I didn't see anything brave about it, but it did seem to take forever."

"Yes, it would. Divorces are very difficult things to achieve, especially from the woman's side. And they can kill careers and blast the family apart. I've seen it happen . . ."

People were now leaving their tables to mingle with others or to make their way outside. And when Mr. and Mrs. Steerman passed them there was no acknowledgment from either side.

"You'll get over him."

"Kate, please."

"Oh, you've got to face up to it. Others have, and you're really no different."

"What do you mean, others have?"

"Well, he's a charmer. I had to get over him at one time."

"You?"

"Yes, me. Oh yes, me. He's so pleasant; he's so kindly; he has the power to make you feel that you're the only woman in the world with any sense. At least, that's how he made me feel. He was sorry for me; he's that kind of man. But that's not to say he was sorry for you. Oh, no! That was a different attraction altogether. In my case I was older than him by three or four years. That didn't make any difference. Of course, he never knew how I felt, but there it is. That's my second confession tonight. Anyway, I'll have to go up now; I'd hate that nurse to come in search of me, bidden like a schoolgirl back into the classroom. Anyway, I can call on you? I know your address. We shall likely be back in London within the next fortnight, unless, that is, she decides we're going to try the waters somewhere.'' She stood up now, but, leaning down toward Emily, she said, "This has really been the best holiday for me for a long time, and I thank you for it.''

"Oh Kate, I, too, thank you for the holiday, because you set me on the right road in many ways during our first talk.''

"I'm going up the back way, because if I go by the front stairs I'll be politely stopped and asked what you said to make me act in such an undignified manner,'' and her face breaking into an unusually broad smile, she said, "Do you think if I put a *mouse* down *her* blouse, it would do the trick?''

"Try it, Kate. Try it.'' They were both laughing now.

"Goodbye, Emily.''

"Goodbye, Kate.''

Kate was moving away from the table when she turned and said more quietly, "There will be formal goodbyes in the morning, of course.

Mother will insist on coming down to see you off, because you've been a bad influence on me . . . And thank God for it. Goodbye again, dear."

Emily sat for a while longer at her table, and she was thinking: If she had met only Kate during this holiday, she would be returning home blithely, because she knew she had found a real friend in that lonely woman . . . And she too had been in love with Paul. Well! Well! She had suggested, too, that she was but one of many. And now she herself was of that number. She had been a fool. But the damage was done and the wound was wide open.

She was standing in the hall drawing on her gloves, her handbag dangling from the crook of her arm, and facing her were Mr. and Mrs. Steerman. Mrs. Steerman was smiling at her: her dark eyes were shining and they tended to illuminate the whole of her face. And her voice seemed to match them, for it was unusually deep and surprising coming from such a petite figure.

"I do hope you have a pleasant journey back," she was saying. "You are likely to find London quite empty and dull at this time of the year. I hope that you have fully recovered your health, and also that my husband has been his usual charming self and helped you to enjoy your stay."

"Yes. Oh yes, he has. He has lightened a number of days that otherwise would have been very dull." She forced a wide smile to her face as she added, "I found him very entertaining . . . and amusing. But I'm sure there's no need for me to extol his talents to you. Yet I must thank you for giving me the opportunity to benefit from the lighter side of life he portrays so well."

She now looked fully at Paul, his face pale and his expression utterly blank; but her smile was still wide as she said, "I must get out of the habit I have acquired during my stay, that of talking about people as if they weren't there . . . Goodbye, Mr. Steerman."

She did not hear his reply as she turned to his wife, saying, "Goodbye, Mrs. Steerman."

"Goodbye, Mrs. Ratcliffe."

Mrs. Steerman's smile was no longer bright, nor was her tone so airy, and her eyes appeared even darker. It was as if she was slightly surprised at losing a battle, the success of which had been assured before she went into it.

At the door Monsieur Fonyère was awaiting her, and after kissing her gloved hand, he earnestly hoped, in stilted English, that she would return soon, and then dropped back naturally into voluble French to express how they would all miss her.

Although she had heard him go through the same performance with other guests, she smiled at him, too, and thanked him for all the courtesy and kindness she had received.

As she now made her way toward the brake, which awaited her at the far side of the drive, she was stopped here and there by a guest wishing her a good journey. But while she was answering them politely she was aware that Alice was not awaiting her by the brake but was standing at the far corner of the house talking to a man whom she recognized as Paul's valet.

When she saw them actually shaking hands she thought, Good gracious! Not Mrs. Arkwright and her Oscar all over again?

They happened to be the only passengers going into the town that morning, so Alice was being allowed to accompany her in the brake, and when they were seated she looked intently at Alice, and she, returning the look, said, "I know what you're thinkin', madam, but I'll tell you in a minute when we get out of this." "This" was the open drive, and not until they were out of it and bowling along the road did Alice open her hand to reveal a crushed small envelope. Pushing it toward Emily, she said, "When he shook my hand, that was in it. That . . . that was the only reason he shook hands. And what he said was, 'Will you kindly pass that on to your mistress?' Then he hoped that I would have a good journey and said that he had been pleased to meet me. And that was that. It was the closest I've come to a conversation with him, or with any of them, for that matter. And I'm telling you, miss, here's somebody who'll be glad to get back home."

Meanwhile, as Alice talked, Emily had smoothed out the small envelope, but she did not attempt to open it. What she did was put it into her handbag as, somewhat belatedly, she answered Alice's remark: "You're not the only one, Alice. But one thing I must ask of you: whatever you think you know, I beg of you to keep it to yourself."

"Now, you know, miss; you've got no need to say that to me. Give that lot back there a smell, I mean a hint . . . well, you know what I mean."

"Yes, I know what you mean, Alice. But what is more, we must both act as if we are sorry to be back, and that it has been the most wonderful holiday."

"Well, that's true, miss, in a way. It has been a most wonderful holiday for me, 'cos I've learnt a lot about people and their ways. And one thing has stuck out: that servants of that type put on more airs an' graces than their masters or mistresses. You know what one cheeky cat said? She said I should take elocution lessons. That's the word she used. It stuck in me mind, el . . . o . . . cu . . . tion. An' you know what I said to her, and this only yesterday? I said I had more sense in me head and brought it out on me tongue than she'd ever learn in her whole life. 'Cos she's the one that said, 'is you', but in a high-falutin' way. Anyway, I pointed it out to her, and strongly, and her face nearly took fire. Oh yes, miss, on the whole, I'll be glad to be back where people are normal. But don't you worry, miss. They'll get sick of listening to the marvelous time I've had. And if I look at it in the right way, I have had a marvelous time, because never in me born days could I have ever got to a place like that, without you pickin' me up. So, don't you worry, miss. We'll act it out together. What d'you say?"

Emily looked at this young girl who was, as she herself had suggested, wise. And once more she felt like putting her head on her shoulder and feeling the comfort of her arms about her. Back home, there would be nobody else's shoulder she could cry on. Certainly not Esther's; no. No. Esther must never get an inkling of this business . . . no one must get an inkling of this business. It was finished. She had put the final touches on it back there in the foyer. That blank, dead look on his face had told her that it was over, that he saw her acting as one of his own class, vitriol dripping from her tongue, and she wasn't the one he had thought he was in love with . . . But what had he said in this note?

She wasn't to find out until they were in the refreshment room, waiting for the train that wasn't due for half an hour. And there, in the ladies' room, she read his note. It was brief.

Emily,
Please, please don't judge the situation as it appears. This is merely a façade. I must see you again and explain. I may not be able to be in London for another fortnight. But I shall call upon you at my earliest opportunity. Believe me again, things are not as they appear.

It is impossible for me to change my feelings for you, but I sign myself as you would wish . . .

Your friend.

7

She had been back home for almost five days, and every now and then she had asked herself if she had ever been away. Only the pain that was deep within her gave her the answer. Both she and Alice had acted their parts, particularly on the Monday morning with the arrival of all the staff.

And now, at this particular moment, Alice was being cornered by Esther, who was pulling her into the lower study, saying, "I want a word with you, miss," to which Alice answered, "Well, you can have your word without putting your hands on me."

"I'll put my hands on you and around your face one of these days."

"Oh, oh! but you won't. Let me tell you: you try that with me now, Esther McCann, and you'll get double what you give out."

Esther stepped back from the young girl, as she still continued to see Alice; and when Alice went on, "I had enough ear-cuffing and knocking about from cook and bossing from the rest of you to last me a lifetime. But no more. I'm where I am today, and I'm going to stay there. As I see it, I've earned it. And I fit in; and madam wants me . . . and

repeat, *madam* wants me and she needs somebody.''

Esther's mouth gaped, and she thought, yes,
she needs somebody, but that somebody should
be me. But what could she do against this young
skelp who had turned, seemingly overnight, from
a skittering maid into a . . . ? She was lost for a
description of the new Alice. But when the saying,
''If you suck up to the corporal, you'll soon be a
sergeant'', came into her mind, she immediately
discarded it as being too low a tactic. But in its
place her thoughts jumped to ''There's more
ways of killing a cat than drowning it'', and so she
brought her voice down and turned her gaze off
her opponent, as she said, ''Well, since you've
grown up so much lately, you should understand
how I feel. I've been Emily's friend for years, long
before you came on the scene at all.''

Slightly mollified now, Alice said, ''Well . . .
well, I know that, and . . . and I've always given
you your place. And it wasn't me that started
this.''

There was silence between them for a moment;
then Esther said, ''I . . . I think there's something worrying her. She doesn't look any better
now than when she went away. And I don't take in
all this talk about the wonderful time she's had.
Can I ask you''—she paused now—''did anything
happen to upset her when she was away? Did
she make any friends?''

''Oh yes,'' Alice replied quickly. ''She got very

friendly with a Miss Kate Forester. They went about a lot together."

"Was she some . . . well, fancy piece?"

"Oh, no." Alice's head wagged now. "Plain as a pikestaff; no figure, and . . . and she was oldish. Well, middle-aged. But she was a lady. Oh, yes, yes, she was a lady." Her head was nodding now. "One thing I learnt while out there was never to go by looks. 'Cos as soon as she opened her mouth, and the manner she had, oh, she was a lady. But she took to miss, and they went about together."

"Were there any men there?"

"In the hotel?"

"Yes. Yes, in the hotel." There was an impatient note in Esther's enquiry now.

"Of course. Of course there were men there. They were nearly all couples."

"Did she get friendly with any of them?"

Now playing her part well, Alice looked down at the floor as if she were trying to recall something. And then she said, "Not more one than another. There was a single man there but he was a gambler. And miss soon showed him where to get off. He invited her, I think, to go to the Casino, but she wouldn't go. And there was the Colonel, but he was a very old man. There was Lord and Lady Huxton. His valet, the lordship's, I mean, was snootier than the lord. Oh my! Some of the ladies' maids and the gentlemen's gentlemen, the airs they put on. Eeh! Esther, you wouldn't believe. And the way they used to talk about their bosses! I mean, their masters and mistresses. Gossip,

gossip, all the time. 'Twas a different world." She paused now before looking straight at Esther and saying, "It was a different world, Esther. Not one I would like to live in. Nor do I think would the miss have liked to stay there much longer."

Esther sighed; but then, after pulling her lower lip tight between her teeth for a moment, she said, "Well, if nothing happened there, I wonder what's the matter with her?" and as if light had dawned on her she actually poked her face toward Alice's, and whispering now, she said, "Do you think it's because the doctor hasn't called?"

"Oh. Oh, Doctor Montane? Oh no, Esther. Well, she was always arguing with him, wasn't she?"

"Oh, you can't go by that; and she's always been slow to show her feelings. Well, whatever it is, I feel there's something worrying her. Twice I've come across her and she was in the dumps. She didn't know I was in the drawing room and she went to the mantelpiece and laid her head on her arm, and nearly jumped out of her skin when I coughed. She said she had a headache. She's always bragged that she never had headaches. So, it could be the doctor." She straightened up; then went toward the door, saying, "Well, she could do a lot worse. By! she could that. I like him."

"Yes, so do I, Esther."

Alice allowed her superior some seconds to advance into the corridor, which gave her time to draw in some deep breaths before following, while her lips emitted a "Whew!"

It was about three o'clock in the afternoon when Alice scampered through the study and into the hallway of number thirty-five, bringing forth from Amity Lockhart the acid comment, "My! My! Where are we off to now in a rush? Going to pack again for another holiday? Some people are lucky."

But Alice gave herself time to answer: "Yes, Amity," she said. "And I'm dead sorry it'll never come your way." Then she fled up the stairs, across the landing and into the dressing room, where Lena, in the act of lifting an evening gown out of a glass-fronted case, checked Alice's move toward the further door, saying, "Where d'you think you're going?"

"I want to have a word with miss."

"She's busy seeing to a client. And what d'you want up here, anyway? This is not your quarter."

Again, one of the older women was amazed to be turned on by this skit of a girl, saying, "Wherever miss is, that's my quarter. I've got a message for her."

"Well, you can give it to me."

Alice drew in a long breath before she said, "Well, you can tell her the doctor's come. He's waiting in the sitting room."

"Well, now get yourself back to where you belong," said Lena; "and you can tell the doctor she'll be down when she's ready."

"You'd better tell her he's here, 'cos he mightn't be able to wait."

"Go on! Get yourself away."

Alice got away, but slowly; and when she opened the sitting room door Steve turned from the window as she said, "She'll be here directly, doctor; she's with a client," adding, just in case miss didn't come directly, "Some of them are very fussy. They won't have the others tendin' them."

"Well, I can understand that, Alice. Anyway, tell me, did you enjoy your vacation?"

"Well," and her head wagged, "yes and no. I wasn't sorry to be back."

"No?"

"No. Stuffy they were, some of them. Too big for their boots, the ladies' maids and the valets. Even some of the coachmen were stiff-necked."

He laughed, saying, "Some of the coachmen are stiff-necked here. It all depends on whom they are working for."

They both looked toward the door as Emily appeared, and before she was halfway up the room Alice hurriedly made her exit, and Steve, walking to meet her, exclaimed, "Well! Well! So here we are again. But—" He peered at her; then turning his head in an exaggerated fashion as if to see her from both sides, he added, "You don't look a bit different. I thought you would come back not only with roses in your cheeks but with different parts of your anatomy showing the results of the good and high living."

She stared hard at him before replying, "Well,

that means neither of us has changed, for your tongue has lost none of its acidness."

"Good gracious! There was nothing acid in that remark. Old habits seemingly die hard; you picked up my words in the wrong way. I was only meaning to point out that you looked rather pale, almost the same as when you left . . . How are you feeling, really?"

"Oh, much better. Do sit down."

"Yes, I will for a moment. But I can't stay long, I have a lot of work to catch up on. I've been away for a few days: I was called home; my father was ill."

"Oh! Oh, I'm sorry." Her tone altered. "Has he recovered?"

"Yes. Yes, he has; but it seems like one of those small and rare miracles. We thought he had cholera and, what was more, a number of people in the village were suffering from the same attacks. But then it was discovered it was food poisoning, caused by tainted meat. How it had got into our house and past the cook, I don't know. But so far no one has died. So we are fortunate." He smiled now, saying, "Did you wonder why I hadn't called in before?"

Her usual answer would have been, "Why should I?" Instead, she said quietly, "Yes. Yes, I did."

"Oh. Well, that augurs good for our future relationship."

"Please!"

"All right, all right. You read my letter and I read

yours, so we can go on from there. What do you say?"

"I . . . I don't know."

"Why don't you know?"

When she did not answer, he stared hard at her before saying, "My prophecy was right, then: I said a month in France, and in such a place, would change you."

"Yes. Yes, in a way you were right."

"Oh." He passed one lip over the other, then said, "You met some interesting people, I suppose?"

"One or two."

"Anyone in particular?"

"Oh, yes, one in particular." She paused. "Oh yes, there was one in particular: a Miss Kate Forester. Looking back, I don't think I would have been able to put up with the company so long as I did if it hadn't been for her taking me under her wing, so to speak."

"Was she old?"

"Not really, about forty; the victim of her demanding mother, who was in a wheelchair, mostly." She smiled now. "She put me in mind of you in a way: her turn of phrase, her cold summing-up of the members of her class."

"I don't sum up the members of my class, more than I do of any other class, high or low."

"Yes, you're right. Well, she was like that, too. Anyway, we became friends and she's going to call on me when her mother decides that they come back to London."

"Well, that'll be nice for you. What else did you learn during your holiday among the upper crust?"

Without hesitation she said, "That the majority of them seem to be leading false and empty lives. Flitting from one resort to another, even sponging on each other."

He was grinning as he said, "So, from all this, am I to take it that you are glad to be home?"

"Yes, you could take it like that."

"Are you sorry you went and had this experience?"

"In some ways, yes; in others, no. It will be something I shall always remember."

When he stood up she said, "Won't you stay for a cup of tea?"

"No, thank you; another time. They were packing the surgery before I left and Doctor Smeaton was on the verge of apoplexy. But . . . but I just wanted to welcome you back . . . Emily."

"Thank you . . . Steve."

They were looking directly at each other when he said, "My mother asked me to extend an invitation to you to lunch, on any Sunday that you feel like a change. It's a family day, quite mad at times, but very relaxing. Would you care to come?"

"Yes. Yes, thank you."

What else could she have said? It would have been ungracious to refuse to meet his people. Yet what impression would it give them? At least they would imagine she was agreeable to his intentions. Well, he knew how far his intentions could go: she couldn't have made it plainer: they were friends; and there it would stop.

What he said now was in a tone so unlike his usual bantering manner. "I'm so glad you're back, Emily; I missed my visits." And some part of her was touched by this side of him. But then he had to revert to character as he added, "Even knowing I should have to face gunfire, shot and shell, every time I saw you. Goodbye, my dear." He turned briskly from her and went from the room. He hadn't brought his bag with him today.

She sat down again, asking herself, why did he stir her up so? There was a different side to him, she knew that, so why had he set out to annoy her by making her out to be a bristling person: gunfire, shot and shell! She could think of no one in her life, not even Jimmy, who had got under her skin as he did. And it was beyond her how he could express such tender feelings for her as he had done in that letter, when he seemed set to pick holes in her.

Oh!—she was on her feet again—she must get back to work. Her feelings with regard to him were very secondary compared with those that were, at the moment, tearing her apart with the knowledge of their futility.

8

It was on the third Sunday after her return that she went to lunch with Steve's people. And she knew that if she hadn't been eaten up with longing for the sight of a man she could never have, she would have considered that particular Sunday one of the happiest of her life.

After an hour's train journey, they were met at the station by a horse and trap and her first introduction was to Newton who, after getting over the surprise of the tall lady in the large, strange, yellow hat, said, "Very pleased to meet you, miss."

Following on this, she was given a summary of Newton's history, which brought from the elderly man only grunts and grins, until he was about to turn the pony into a twisting drive, when he said, "Never be any better, you. I've always said that. A hard case from the day you were born. Wouldn't have you doctoring me; no, I wouldn't. Now, I'll tell you . . ."

They hadn't gone very far up the drive before Steve said, "These pot holes want doctoring. I thought you were going to see to them?"

"Haven't got ten pairs of hands. Anyway, grit ain't come."

The trap bowled along from the drive into an open space, flanked on one side by a long, rambling house, seeming at first glance to be made up of at least four odd houses, and on the other by a stable yard. Beyond was a large lawn, which seemed to be crowded with both adults and children, and all yelling at each other.

After being helped down from the trap, she stood for a moment taking in the scene, Steve by her side and he said, "It's rounders they're playing." Then, turning her about, he added, "Come and meet the sensible folk."

The sensible folk were two elderly people standing on the stone terrace that lay flush with the graveled drive.

The white-haired lady came forward swiftly, followed by a grizzled gentleman.

"Hello, my dear," was Steve's mother's greeting as she kissed him, and when he said, "This is Mrs. Ratcliffe, Mamma," she said, "How do you do, my dear? I hope you have had a nice journey."

"It was very nice indeed; the scenery was lovely."

"Hello, sir. This is Mrs. Ratcliffe. Emily, my father."

"You're very welcome, Mrs. Ratcliffe. You're very welcome. But I hope this renegade son of mine has told you what you're in for. Just look over there!" He pointed to the running figures on the lawn. "Is that any way to spend a Christian Sunday?"

Emily noticed straightaway that in his eye he had the same look as would show in his son's when saying one thing and meaning another. She turned and looked at the shouting mêlée on the lawn and replied, "There could be worse pursuits, I should think."

"Oh, I don't know. People should spend Sunday after church reading the Good Book."

"Oh." His wife now pushed him none too gently, saying, "Don't give Mrs. Ratcliffe the wrong impression. Anyway, don't be such a hypocrite; you are not on the bench now." Then looking up and raising her voice she called, "Mickey! Mickey!" and a boy standing on the edge of the lawn, and poised ready to catch a ball, raised a hand above his head, but didn't turn around, causing her to cry, "Do you hear me, Mickey? Tell them ten minutes." Then, turning to Emily, she said, "Come along, my dear. I'm sure you would like to wash your hands after that train journey; they make one so sooty."

As they turned toward the door, there appeared to Emily what looked like someone dressed up for a stage comic act. She was a slightly built woman, her face heavily lined, with her hair drawn tight back from her forehead into a knot that was hidden by the bonnet.

The bonnet. This was Aunt Phoebe, and that was *the bonnet* that had been the instigation of Mrs. Arkwright's first seizure.

As Lady Montane began, "This is my sister-in-law, Miss . . ." she was checked by the odd person exclaiming loudly, and with more than a touch of impatience, "Oh, she knows who I am," and nodding her head toward Emily, she added, "You're the one who makes bonnets, aren't you? And you were going to make one for me. Well, if you had I wouldn't have been here now. No, I wouldn't. And you make hats an' all." She looked up at the big stark yellow hat, then said, "Well, 'tis about time you learnt to trim them."

"Aunt Phoebe!"

"Oh you! Steve Montane, you're not going to shut me up. Anyway, you only come when it suits you; you should be here all the time." And on this the dowdy, gray-clad body swung around and marched into the hall, leaving Lady Montane to excuse her, saying quietly, "I am sorry. She is not usually so rude. She's been upset this morning. I hope . . ."

"Oh, please!" Emily was smiling now. "Don't apologize. She's . . . well, she's rather refreshing."

"Oh, that's a new one for her," said Sir Arthur Montane now. "One day there'll be a startling court case, and I'll be in the wrong seat—in fact, in the dock because I've drowned her in the mere."

"Do that, Pa," Steve was nodding at his father, "and I'll see you get off because of extenuating circumstances."

They were in the hall and Emily stood for a moment looking about her. The hall in number thirty-five was large, but it wouldn't have taken up one third of the space of this one. And then there was the atmosphere, created by the low and beamed ceiling, the broad, shallow oak stairway leading from it that was uncarpeted, as was, she realized, the hall floor. She was standing on a rug and there were others lying around on stone flags.

"Come this way, my dear."

Emily followed her hostess up the stairs and along a narrow gallery from which led a number of doors.

"Be careful, dear, there's a step down. This house is all steps up or steps down. Even after years of usage one forgets about them and then has a tumble. Now, I hope you find what is necessary." She pointed to a wash-hand stand and then to a dressing-table. "Will you excuse me while I leave you for a few minutes? I must demand that the horde come in, else lunch could be put back to whatever time they felt hungry. Then cook would carry out the threat she's been holding over my head for years."

She laughed, a gay, youthful laugh, denying her white hair, as did her lovely pale skin.

Left alone, Emily looked around the room: it held a four-poster bed from which hung rose-colored drapes, and they were so fresh and new-looking that they shouted at the old heavy wardrobe and large matching wash-hand stand and dressing-table. There was a couch at the foot of the bed and an easy chair near the window, both with tapestry seats and these much worn. The whole room gave her a sensation of years of use and wear . . . and comfort. Moreover, at the end of the room, there was a half-open door that showed a water-closet.

She took off her hat and dust-coat and laid them on the bed; then she washed her hands and combed her hair. Afterwards she sat for a moment in the chair near the window and gazed out toward a large orchard. It was well set out with paths between the trees, and as she gazed there came into her mind a strange thought: if she had come to some place like this to recuperate, how different her life might have been. One thing was certain: it would have held no emptiness, and her heart would not be aching as it was now.

She re-arranged the overskirt on the front of her dove-gray colored dress, then went out of the room and into a commotion; for pushing and laughing up the stairs came a number of children, only to come to a stop at the stair-head and stare at her, while a middle-aged woman appeared and cried at them, "Behave yourselves! Where's your manners?" and a man disengaged himself from those now appearing in the hall and bounded up the stairs, saying, "Oh, I'd better explain the horde and who they belong to. By the way, I'm Matthew. I have the honor of being the eldest. How d'you do?"

They shook hands, and then he turned and, pointing to a rather lanky boy and a chubby girl, he said, "For my sins those are the twins, Mickey and Meg. Twelve in years and twenty-four in devilment. And that is James." A smaller boy grinned

at her. "And this is Flora, the least of the tribe."
He ruffled the fair-haired little girl's curls. "And
those three are Susie's. That's William, the
cherub, ten years old; and here's some more
twins. They run in the family. Betty and Nell, imps
as ever were." Then, turning to the woman, he
said, "Nanny, get them all out of my sight. I've
had enough of them for one day."

"We're coming down to tea!" This was a chorus
from his twins, and he shouted back at them,
"We'll see about that." Then, his voice lower, he
turned to Emily, saying, "You must think we are a
weird outfit"; then lowering his voice even further,
he said, "I understand you've met Aunt Phoebe."

Her voice was as low as his as she answered,
"Yes; but I knew about her long before I made her
acquaintance."

He laughed. "Come down and meet the rest of
us," he said.

In the hall he introduced her to Cissie, a stout,
middle-aged woman. She had keen eyes and a
bright smile and she said, "I'm very pleased to
meet you. I've heard about you and your hats.
Phoebe tells me you've come in an extra large
one. You must show it to me. I love hats, but I've
got a very mean husband."

"Huh!" grunted her very mean husband, but
then called across the hall, "Vera, stop arguing
and come and meet Mrs. Ratcliffe."

Vera came, accompanied by her husband John,
and also Steve; and after saying, "Hello, there.
How are you?" to which Emily replied, "Very well,

thank you," she asked, "How on earth do you put up with him?" and thumbed toward Steve. "He's ignorant, rude, and unattractive. And I should know because I was stuck with him from when he was a baby."

"I'm John," said a quiet voice. "I don't know how I got into this family. The only thing I can tell you and warn you against is Sundays. Always, if you can, have an excuse not to come on a Sunday."

"Well, why do you?" This came from a bushy-haired, quite good-looking woman in her thirties. "It's only because it's the only decent meal you have in a week. By the way, I'm Susie. For my sins I'm the mother of William and the twins, Betty and Nell."

"Well, now, you've all had your say, but she won't remember one from the other."

Emily looked at Steve, saying, "Who says I won't? I already know there are two sets of twins, seven children altogether, and that I have met Matthew, Vera, John . . ."

"Mistress says meal's on the table," a voice came from a corridor down which a middle-aged maid was now disappearing, followed by a younger one, who was grinning widely.

The dining room, like the hall, was beamed. It was a long room. It had to be to take the dining table. There were eleven of them seated, but it could take as many again. And for the next hour Emily forgot the weight on her heart, for she laughed and she listened and she learnt quite a lot, not least about Doctor Steve Montane.

First of all she learnt that there were members of the family absent: the two younger sons, Raymond and Charles, were both in America, and there were younger daughters still, Kate and Maggie. Kate was married to a solicitor in Devon. Maggie was married to a laird in Scotland. But it seemed they would all be together for Christmas, even the two from America.

At one point Cissie, leaning across the table and above the buzz of conversation, said to Emily, "Have you always been in the hat trade?"

"Yes, and my mother, too. I used to go with her when I was a child and sort out the ribbons and things."

"Steve says you've got a fine establishment, not a shop, but a sort of house, or houses."

"Well, one is used for business and the other as my home."

"I think all women should have careers. I'm all for it, but we're just used as breeders."

"That's what you were made for," came from the far end of the table; and Cissie answered, "Well, elephant ears, let me inform you there's a change coming and it's already in the air."

"Well, that's the best place for it. If God had intended women to have careers He would have given them brains."

"Oh!" Cissie's hand went toward the glass water-jug, and it seemed only that her mother's voice crying now "Cissie! Cissie! Stop it. You know what happens? you'll only get the worse of it," deterred its flight.

And Steve, who was sitting opposite Emily, said, "What did I tell you? I warned you they were savages. They've never been away from this neck of the woods. They're hardly civilized."

Now Vera put in loudly, "That's what old Parson Horner said this morning. 'Why collect money for the natives when this country is so uncivilized?' and promptly forgot his theme and resorted to mythology: I'm sure he's only kept on through the patronage of The Hall and because Lord Bias believes in feeding the souls of the workers on his farms."

"Well, he'd get a better reward in heaven, which is what he's after, if he paid his workmen a living wage, enough to feed their bodies, and build them decent habitations, not the stinking sties some of them live in. They talk about the condition of the pit folk. Their houses are palaces compared to that lot on the high bank."

"Now, now," said Sir Arthur from the top of the table, "no politics, Steve. We've been through all this."

"And we'll be through it again, Pa, and more as time goes on. You'll see, you'll see." The laughter had gone from the table. "You expect to come across hovels and ten sleeping in a room in the cities, but in parishes like this . . ."

"Well, if you're so concerned, Stevie, you could see to their bodies in your own way, because old Raymore is retiring, and when he goes, the nearest medical help will be in the town, ten miles away."

There was a lighter note now all round as voices came at Steve, saying, "Now there, you could put some of your theories into practice." This was from Matthew; and Cissie's husband, Harry Spencer, added, "That's an idea; and we could all have our medical treatment free. What do you say, father-in-law?"

They all looked toward Sir Arthur and he, looking down the table toward his son, said, "I have found that it would be easier to turn the wind from North to South than turn Steve's mind from the direction he had set it." And with all eyes now turned on him, Steve laughed shortly before saying, "You seem to know me well, Daddy. Yet I wouldn't go as far as to agree with you whole-heartedly. Things happen that turn lives upside down. But as far as I can see ahead my course is set, and the wind is in the right direction."

It became noticeable to Emily that during the whole course of the meal Aunt Phoebe hadn't opened her mouth, except to eat. But now her voice came into it, holding a soft, plaintive note as she said, "But it would be lovely if Stevie doctored us all, and round about, too. They need a good doctor round about, especially in the village."

"Now, Phoebe"—it was Lady Montane speaking—"you know that Steve can't come back; he's needed in the town. There are a lot of sickly people there."

"Well, there are a lot of sickly people here." The voice had changed. "And I'm one of them. There's different places to feel sick in besides your stomach; and he understands that."

It seemed that Cissie was out to save the day by saying, "Who's having tea or coffee in the garden? We might as well enjoy it before the horde comes down again."

"That's a good idea, Cissie," her mother said. "We'll have it in the garden. It's the first really warm day we've had so far this year. . . ."

As Emily, with Steve by her side, walked across the hall toward the front door, she was shown another side of the family feeling toward him when Cissie, slipping her arm through her brother's, said softly, "Aunt Phoebe was right, you know: it would be lovely if you came back. And we do all need you."

He patted her hand where it lay on his arm as he said, "I wish I were two people, Cissie. When I'm here I don't want to leave, because life is easy, yet quite disorganized, as always." He laughed as he turned and looked at Emily, adding, "No routine or pattern to it. I've never visited any house where such chaos was the order of the day." Then turning again to his sister, he said, "But you know yourself the need here is nothing to what it is there. You have no idea, Cissie."

"Oh, I would argue that," she said. "The need is the same here, although perhaps there is more of it in the city."

"Well, yes, perhaps. Anyway, here we are for the

afternoon and I want a game of croquet. Have you ever played croquet, Emily?"

She looked at him and smiled and her voice was low as she said, "That's a stupid question."

"I don't see why. Anyway, that means you haven't played croquet. Well, you're going to learn. . . ."

For the next hour or so Emily learned how to handle a croquet mallet, to get the balls through the narrow hoops, and how to score. And when some time later, sitting in the shade with Lady Montane and watching the three men and the women playing the game, there came a call from the house and Lady Montane, looking to where her husband stood beckoning her, said, "Excuse me a moment, dear. I wonder what it is now; likely something to do with the imps."

As she hurried away, almost immediately and appearing as if out of the air, Phoebe took her seat, causing Emily to gasp.

"Why did you wear that big hat when you were traveling?" And the question with no lead-up again caused Emily to gasp. "Well," she said; then smiled as she went on, "I . . . I was persuaded to wear it. I was going to wear a smaller one, but Steve said, wear that big straw."

"Do you always do what he says?"

"No; very rarely."

"It won't get you anywhere, you know."

Emily paused before she asked, "What won't get me anywhere?"

"That hat."

"Oh! Well, what makes you think that?"

"Because it's like my bonnet, it's fated."

"Fated? Why should it be fated?" Emily was no longer smiling.

"Because it's odd. It's got nothing on it except that bow. It's too big and too bright and it upsets people . . . like my bonnet. Years ago my bonnet upset people. It was pretty then, beautiful. It still upsets people. That hat will, too, because some hats bring trouble. They take on what's inside you. That's why they pick you in the first place. You don't pick them, they pick you."

Emily now turned fully toward the odd little woman and as she stared at her she felt a shiver pass through her body. She was uncanny, she was weird. But she was right. In a very strange way she was right.

As Phoebe saw her sister-in-law advancing toward them again, she rose hastily from the seat and, looking directly at Emily, she said quietly and quickly, "He's the best of the bunch. And I don't know much about you yet, but I don't think you're worthy of him." And on this she turned away.

"Has she upset you?" Lady Montane was looking down on her.

"No, Oh, no; only, she's very observant, isn't she?"

"Yes . . . yes, she's very observant. And, you will have gathered, she's not like an ordinary person. She isn't an ordinary person. She could be called an eccentric. She has never taken on any of the niceties of manner or speech that would have classed her as normal. But nevertheless, to my mind, in fact to all our minds, she is very normal."

"Has she experienced some tragedy?"

"No! No!" Lady Montane's voice was bright. "Never crossed in love, although we have to use that at times to explain her oddity. But no; she's been like that since she was small. She was born when my husband was four, that's sixty years ago, and she seems to have been under his care ever since. The only real oddness about her is that during any period he has to be away for any length of time she keeps mostly to her room. She had a private tutor until she was sixteen, and she's very well read, although you wouldn't imagine it from her manner and her talk." She now changed the conversation suddenly by saying, "Have you known Steve long?"

"No; not very long. Just from the time he began to attend my employer." What question Lady Montane would have asked next was checked by her rising and saying, with a touch of impatience, "Oh, excuse me again; here are some friends of ours."

As she went toward the terrace, the game of croquet ended, and Vera and Cissie, coming toward her, flopped down into chairs. And Vera, nodding toward the visitors who were now coming on to the lawn, said, "They must have got wind that Steve is here." Then, looking toward Emily, she added, "Neighbors of ours."

Emily was introduced to the Misses Braize. Miss

Nan looked to be somewhere in her middle twenties, a plain and severe-looking young woman; but as for Miss Biddy, Emily couldn't place her, for she had a giggle like a frivolous young girl's and a manner tending toward affectation. And Emily soon discovered they were very curious to know all about her: Who was she, what did she do? Had she been presented at Court? How did she come to know dear Stevie? The questions came coated and cleverly mixed with odd topics of conversation.

Afternoon tea followed on the lawn and it wasn't lost on Emily how the elder Miss Braize felt about Steve, for if she wasn't near him she couldn't take her eyes off him. She also noticed that his manner was kind and caring toward her, for he didn't treat her to any quips and challenging remarks.

Emily felt it was only because it was considered bad form to outstay one's welcome to afternoon tea that the sisters left when they did, amid waves of goodbye and unmistakable lingering looks on Steve from Miss Nan Braize.

When presently it was time for them, too, to leave, Emily could not help but be surprised at the friendliness of all of them in wishing her to come again. But it was Lady Montane's last words to her, as they stood alone together in the hall, that filled her with guilt, for she was saying, "I feel sure we'll be seeing a great deal of each other in the future, my dear." What could she say to that? All she could do was manage to smile and thank her for a wonderful day.

It wasn't until they were sitting in the train opposite each other and with the compartment to themselves that he said, "Well, tell me truthfully, what did you think of that lot?"

And so she told him truthfully. "I think they were wonderful as a family, so close, yet so free, and the homeliness and lack of . . ." When she paused, he said, "Order?"

"No, no . . . pretense. That's the word I was looking for. Your father and mother are what is termed quality, but they acted . . . the whole family acted like . . ."

Again he cut in: "Ordinary human beings?"

She laughed now as she said, "Yes. Yes, you could say that, ordinary human beings. Even Aunt Phoebe."

"She was funny about your hat, wasn't she?"

The smile slowly faded from her face as she answered, "She was very perceptive about the hat. We had a talk about it later."

"No!"

"Yes. Oh, yes. She likened it, in a way, to her bonnet."

"She couldn't."

"Oh, yes, she did, and she was right. She said she didn't choose her bonnet, her bonnet chose her; and it was the same, she said, with me and this hat. And, you know, in a way, she was utterly right."

He said, "At one time, you know, we thought she had second sight, but then she turned out to be so wrong in most of her predictions that we didn't take any further notice of them. But now and again she hits the nail right on the head. She's a very special person, is Aunt Phoebe. Not likeable, not lovable, but special."

They sat looking at each other until he said, "You'll come again, then?"

"Yes. Yes, I'd like to very much, but I feel that my visits might be misunderstood."

"Perhaps. They might think we are . . . courting. And we're not, are we?"

"No, Steve. No, we're not."

"Well, more's the pity, on my part, anyway. But still, I'm a patient bloke."

"Please, don't let us spoil a wonderful day, and it has been wonderful. I can't remember a time when I've enjoyed anything so much."

"As you say, don't let's spoil a wonderful day. But would it be spoiling it if, as a friend, I sat beside you?"

"Oh, Steve." She closed her eyes, shook her head and laughed. And at that time he left his seat and sat beside her; and when he took her hand she left it in his. And so they remained for the rest of the journey, hardly exchanging a word, even though their thoughts were racing in different directions.

When she reached number thirty-five she gave an impatient gesture as she said, "Oh, I came out without my key and I don't expect Alice will be back yet. She was going to visit her people. Anyway"—she smiled—"it'll stir the cook from dozing; the bell rings down in the basement." And she pressed a bell to the side of the door.

When it was opened there was the flustered cook saying, "Oh, miss! Look at me. I didn't expect to have to open the door. I thought you'd have your key. Good evening, doctor."

"Good evening, cook."

"Dear me." She fussed at her blouse, saying now, "I haven't even got me apron on. But it's a good job I had it on when I answered the door before. I didn't expect any visitor. Did you, miss?"

"No; not at all, not today."

"Well, there's a gentleman called. I told him you were away, and he left his card. There it is." She pointed to the table. "He said he would come back tomorrow; I was to tell you."

"Thank you. Thank you, cook."

"Do you want a drink, miss?"

"No. No, thank you."

"Will . . . will you let the doctor out when he's goin' "—she nodded toward Steve—"or will I come up?"

"No. No, of course not. I'll see him to the door, and then lock up."

"Ta, miss; an' Alice'll come the back way. Good-night, doctor."

"Good-night, cook." His voice sounded flat and remained so when he turned to Emily, saying, "One of your friends from the holiday?"

"Yes. Yes, as you say, one of my friends from the holiday."

"You've lost all your color."

She gulped, but could say nothing; and he said, "I'll be going now, then. Good-night."

He went toward the door and opened it, and as he did so she said, "Good-night, Steve; and . . . and thank you."

He made no answer, nor did he turn around, but pulled the door closed behind him. And she stood there, her teeth pressing into her lip, the card crushed in her hand, the while muttering, "Why had he to come today? Today of all days. I won't see him. I mustn't see him. I'll tell Esther. No. No." She swung round. "Not Esther . . . Alice. Alice must see him."

In the sitting room she pulled the pins out of her hat and flung it onto the sofa, and as she did so she remembered Aunt Phoebe's words. And she turned now and looked at it. It was lying there, one part of the brim supported by a cushion. It looked a live thing, just as if it were about to spring down from the couch. If she hadn't worn it in the first place he might not have noticed her. It was the hat that had caught his eye. She had a strong urge to pick it up and rip its brim apart. Instead, she went out of the room and up the stairs. She'd have to think, and try to be calm. She must prime Alice in the morning. She herself would keep upstairs next door all day. It was the only way.

9

She did not, after all, prime Alice. Her thinking in the night told her that she must face up to him and make him realize that their association was completely ended. It had ended back in the hotel. And his wife had put the stamp on it.

When Alice brought her breakfast into the dining room, she said, "By! you slept late, miss. Your tea was dead cold."

"I was some time in getting to sleep, Alice."

"Was it the excitement of yesterday? Was it a good day?"

"Oh yes." She could say this honestly, and she repeated, "Oh, yes, it was a lovely day."

"Are . . . are his people nice?"

"Wonderful. He has a wonderful family."

"Is it a big house?"

"Oh, yes, very big and right in the country."

"With grounds and things?"

"With grounds and things."

"Have they got a lot of servants?"

She paused here before she said, "Well, there were two waiting on at dinner, and there's a cook. But I suppose there were kitchen staff, too."

"And have they got horses?"

"Yes; and a very nice trap. And I think there's a carriage."

"My! My! And the doctor mucking it about among the scum of Westerley Place."

Emily looked at Alice inquiringly now, as she repeated, "Westerley Place?"

"Yes, he gets down there, I'm told. Behind Piccadilly Circus, in the alleys and warrens. Me foster-dad knows that quarter. Well"—she wrinkled her nose—"he used to live there. Brought up there, I think, among rats an' sewers . . . an' stink. 'Tis terrible, can't believe it's just behind posh streets. There's mile of it! Well now, get your breakfast before it gets cold. And is there anything special you want me to do this morning?"

Talking of rats and sewers, and then told to eat! Emily tutted to herself, then said quietly, "I'm . . . I'm expecting a visitor today, Alice; I don't know what time. I should imagine it will be in the afternoon. And I should like you to be at hand somewhere around the hall to open the door to him and show him into the study."

Alice looked at her mistress; but her mistress's eyes were looking firmly down onto the breakfast plate, which held a slice of bacon and an egg, the latter reposing on a piece of fried bread. And it was some seconds before she said, "Yes, miss."

When the door closed on Alice, Emily pushed the plate away, poured herself a cup of tea, drank it, and then another one, before rising from the table and thrusting the dining-chair back into place. Then she stood gripping the top of it, her head bent over it, as she muttered words that could have been a prayer: "Dear God! Let me get through today."

Paul Steerman called at three o'clock.

When Alice opened the door he smiled at her, saying, "Good afternoon. I have called to see Mrs. Ratcliffe."

"Come in, sir."

He passed her and stood in the hall looking about him as she closed the door, then said, "Will you come this way? I'll . . . I'll have to tell miss that you're here."

She left him in the study, and again he stood looking about him. And as the maid hadn't taken his hat or gloves or walking stick, he laid the hat and gloves on a chair, and leaned the walking stick against it. Then walking to the window, he looked out onto a courtyard, one side of which was framed by a coach-house and various out-buildings, a row of potted ferns and such flanking one wall. There were double gates at the end of the yard.

Turning about, he now inspected the bookcases that lined two walls. Many of the books were old, dealing, it seemed, mostly with the sea and ships. But one section, he noted, held a number of modern writers. Among these books was S. Petersen's book of poems. He took it out and was fingering the pages when the door opened, and there she stood.

Hastily he put the book down on a small table

that stood to his side, and went toward her, his hand outstretched. But when she did not take it, he stood silently before her for a moment; then he said, "I had to come, Emily. I had to see you. Please! Will you listen to me?"

She moved from the door; then, taking a seat, she pointed to another some distance away; but still she uttered no word, because she found she couldn't. Just the sight of him, the sound of his voice, seemed to have taken all the strength out of her, the strength of resolve to end this business finally.

He was sitting now bent forward, his hands joined on the edge of his knees, as he said, "Believe me, Emily, I've tried, just as much as you have, to put the holiday episode out of my mind, but I find it impossible. I . . . I don't know why I find it so hard. Oh yes, I do." He now hung his head for a moment before looking at her again and saying, "I've never met anyone like you. You seemed to belong to a different species from all the people I've ever associated with."

She found her tongue now. Her back was straight and her head up as she said, "Yes, in other words, I was out of your class, and you recognized it."

"Nonsense!" He went to rise from the chair, but she lifted her hand as if to press him back. And he said, "It has nothing whatever to do with class, but everything to do with personality, viewpoints, honesty, that refreshing honesty that hitherto has been unknown to me. All I'm asking, Emily, is that

I may come and see you, talk to you . . ." Her voice cut in sharply here, "And be your mistress?"

"Oh, that you would be, Emily. Oh, yes, that you would be; though not in the sense you mean. But . . . but I cannot hope for that, yet at the same time I can hope that you care for me a little . . . and I know you do. Oh, yes, I know you do; but not to the extent that I care for you. All I want you to say is we can meet and talk and . . . and be friends."

Friends. There was that word again. Steve using friendship to cover love. Association with Steve would be honorable; it would mean marriage. But this man could offer her nothing but disgrace if she gave way to the weakness inside her.

Her voice had lost its sting now as she said, "That would be impossible and you know it. You have a wife and children. And you . . . you have likely had a mistress or two."

Her mind flatly denied the latter suggestion. And when she saw him bow his head again, she said, "I'm . . . I'm sorry. But that is the way of men today; I mean, gentlemen of your class."

After a moment he looked at her again, saying, "Yes. Yes, that is the way, for the needs of the body are very powerful. But that is a different thing from loving, needing companionship, needing understanding. Emily, I must tell you that what you saw before you left the hotel was a charade. For more than two years now my wife and I have lived together, yes, but have gone our separate ways. We've had no need of each other since my young son Robert was born. My eldest daughter Annette is now five years old and Marian's three. There will be no more family. But my wife is very socially minded and demands that we put a face on things. And although she does not want me she is still very possessive. 'Tis a strange contradiction in her nature; and she hates to think that I might have an interest in anyone else. Our mutual friend, Mrs. DeWhit, I surmise, couldn't get back to London quickly enough to inform her that her husband was taking walks with a very attractive young woman. The result was she broke her journey to Rome, where she was to visit her married sister, and made sure she stayed long enough to put on a show for the onlookers, particularly you."

"Well, can't you see it happening again? Perhaps she's had you followed here."

"She's in Switzerland at the moment, and she knows I'm in town on business, with boardroom meetings and such. And I am staying with my father, as our own house in town is closed, and my father being in a poor state of health and rather demanding of my attention, she would see no reason to have me followed . . . Oh, please, Emily, don't look like that. That isn't how I see you in my mind all the time. And you are in my mind all the time. But . . . but, my dear, I'm willing to comply with any of your wishes if you will only agree to my visiting you now and again."

"I can't do that. It should be evident to you that I can't, because your visits would create the wrong impression. Don't you realize"—there was now a plea in her own voice—"I am surrounded by my staff in both houses. What would they think? And there are those among them who would not be above probing to find out who you were, and then I would lose their esteem. You may not be able to understand their point of view, because in your eyes they are just servants, but I have friends among them, close friends. So you see, I cannot agree with your suggestion."

"Need they know?"

"Need they know?" Her voice was rising. "They answer the door, they let you into the house, and you say need they know?"

"Is there no other way into this house?"

She drew her head back into her shoulders, but didn't answer him. He was suggesting coming in the back way, furtively!

As if he was reading her mind, he said, "There must be a back way. And I don't mind acting furtively as long as I'm able to see you, be with you just for a little while . . . . You really have no idea of my feelings for you, Emily. You are like a window in my life that has been smeared for years, but has now become clean, bright, shining."

"Oh"—she tossed her head impatiently—"that is nothing but romantic nonsense."

He laughed gently. "That's another part of you I find so refreshing," he said; "you say what you think. You have no façade at all, have you, Emily?"

She rose quickly from her chair; and he rose

from his, saying, "All right, my dear; if I cannot sneak in the back way, I shall continue to call on you through your front door."

"Oh, please!" She was now appealing to him. "If you really think of me in the way you say you do, please don't set out to spoil my life. I, for my part, will get over any feeling that I might have for you. So, please, I beg of you . . ."

"Emily!" He was gripping her hands now. "I don't want to spoil your life. I have no intention of spoiling your life, I want to bring happiness into it. Behind all the smartness of the business lady there is a very lonely young woman needing to be loved, to be cared for, and I want to be the one to do it. And we would be hurting no one, believe me, we would be hurting no one. Unfortunately, it would be only at odd times that I would be able to call on you, because I, too, have a business to run, one which forces me to take journeys abroad, besides the family ties." Immediately he could feel her hands attempting to jerk from his, and hastily he explained, "I am meaning my children. I am fond of my children, and they of me. It is a sort of compensation; at least, it has been up till now, until I met you."

He was drawing her slowly to him, saying as he did so, "I saw a gate at the end of your courtyard. Your other house is the last one in Willington Place, I noticed, and part of it is in the other thoroughfare. As I looked for the number I saw an alleyway there. I suppose it must lead into the lane. No one would see me come in that way, and it would just be for an hour or so, now and again. Perhaps less, just enough time to say hello . . . and to look at you."

She tugged herself away from him and, turning about, laid her hands against the bookcase as if for support, and muttered half to herself, "I . . . I'll have to think."

"Very well, my dear. And may I say when I next call, I will make it late in the evening, and if the back gate is open, may I assume I . . . I shall have my answer?"

He moved toward her now, and when he put his hand on the back of her hair and stroked it toward her cheek, she shivered.

She did not turn around, but she knew he was taking up his hat and gloves from the chair, and retrieving his walking stick as it fell to the floor; and not until she heard the door open and close did her whole body slump against the bookcase.

Her mind was in a turmoil, crying loudly that she must not give in to him; it would be the end; yet through it all there was rising the knowledge that he would find the back gate open, and that sooner or later she *would* become his mistress.

10

During the following ten days she had three visitors. The day after her emotional encounter with her would-be suitor, Kate Forester called, and they greeted each other with affection. Kate was all in black, but this conveyed nothing to Emily because her new friend had very little taste in the way of clothes. But they hadn't been sitting together for more than a few minutes when Kate said, "You're looking pale. More in need of a holiday than when I first saw you," to which Emily countered: "Well, you're not looking very bright yourself. You look tired."

"Yes, I am a bit tired and I may not look bright outwardly, but I am very bright inside. I buried Mother last week."

Emily actually started. "Oh, no! Oh, no! I *am* sorry."

"Now, now, Emily. Don't let's be hypocrites. The little you saw of her you disliked, and she disliked you more. As for me, I hated her. And inside I'm very bright. I'm not going to be a hypocrite; and what is more, I am very rich. She hadn't a chance this time to alter her will in order to try to frighten me. She had done so several times. Last year when she thought I was really leaving her she made a will leaving everything to me, but I knew that in a very short while she would change it, as she has done over the years. Cat-and-mouse business. Anyway, I'm free to do what I like with the rest of my life that's left to me, and I'm going to India."

"India? Why India?"

"Oh, simply because we never got that far and I've always wanted to go to India. But there's one obstacle. I don't want to travel alone."

"Then you'll have to take a companion."

"Yes, and that's why I'm here. What about you coming with me, just for three months or so?"

"Oh, Kate, thank you so much. It's so good of you to want me to go along with you. But, you know, I have a business to run."

"I think you told me you had two very good women, one of them practically running this business when you were a girl."

"Yes. Yes, I know. I've still got her, but we've expanded and there's a lot of work, and people to be seen to."

"What you're saying is, you don't want to come."

"Oh, Kate. Under other circumstances I would have been only too glad to accept, and it would have been wonderful to see India. But it's impossible . . . well, there are other reasons."

Kate sat staring at her hard before she asked, "Have you had a visit from Paul Steerman?"

Their eyes held before Emily replied, "Yes. Yes, I've had a visit from him."

"And where does it go from there?"

"Oh, Kate." She hitched herself along the couch, saying, "Really! What are you suggesting?"

"I'm not suggesting anything. I'm just asking you, where do you go from there? No good will come of it, you know. It's impossible, and he's got three children . . ."

"Yes, and a wife. I know all about that, Kate. I know everything I need to know."

"You don't know everything you need to know. He's a charming fellow, is Paul, and if I didn't like him myself I'd call him a charming rat. But Emily"—her voice dropped low now and she put her hand out—"I also like you. I've never had a real friend and I felt we could be friends. In a lot of ways we think alike. So that is why . . . well, I'm afraid of you being hurt."

"Thank you, Kate, I understand. But . . . but I am not a fool . . ."

"We're all fools, Emily, in different ways. I was a fool years ago to give in to fear. Fear of the woman who bore me and who demanded payment by turning me into her slave. She owned my very soul. It is said that one should always forgive the dead, and even if you don't, you feel guilt. Well, I feel no guilt; nor can I ever forgive her."

When she now sat staring straight ahead Emily said quietly, "Will you have another cup of tea?"

"No, thanks. I have an appointment with a

dressmaker. This"—she pulled at her black coat—"is the last time I'll wear black; from now on I'm going in for all the colors of the rainbow."

Emily smiled before saying, "Well, start by going to a hairdresser and getting your hair styled. It's beautiful hair, but no one would think so the way you screw it back."

"Oh, yes; I intend to do that, as well as having my fingernails manicured. And I'll have my toe-nails done, too."

They were laughing together now.

As Emily walked with her to the door, Kate said, "If you read in the papers about an Englishwoman being abducted, I hope you will be filled with re-morse about letting me travel on my own."

"You can take a maid."

"I can't stand maids. I suppose it's because I myself never had their attention. Mother, of course had a lady's maid, but she managed to gollop up her every minute. Anyway, dear—" She turned and looked into Emily's face and very qui-etly she said, "Make use of that good head of yours in this particular case, my dear Emily, for fairy stories are never based on fact, only on wild imaginings." And with this she was gone, leaving Emily's mind once more in a whirl and asking what she meant to infer by those cryptic words? Was she implying there was more, much more for her to know about Paul; but, not being a Mrs. DeWhit, she had kept it to herself?

*   *   *

The following night a male visitor nearly scared the wits out of Alice as she came up from the basement and almost ran into a man closing the back door behind him. She was about to scream when she recognized his voice saying, "It is all right, Alice. Your . . . your mistress is expecting me."

She peered at him in the turned-down gaslight on the passage wall, then gasped and muttered, "Oh! Mr. Steerman."

"Where is your mistress?" His voice was just above a whisper, and she whispered back, "When . . . when I last saw her she was in the drawing room."

"Thank you. I'm sorry I frightened you."

She stayed where she was and watched him make his way along the passage and into the hall and pause before the drawing room door. And out loud she said, "Oh my God!" And in this moment she wanted to run back down the basement stairs and straight to cook, because she felt she needed some support with this burden. But then, not cook, and not Lena. Lena would be shocked. There was Esther. No, no, not Esther, either. She couldn't tell anybody . . . And how would the miss face her tomorrow morning? There was the doctor. Oh, why couldn't she take the doctor? He was a fine man, was the doctor. But she wasn't so sure of this one. No, she wasn't, not at all. He had a wife and family. Eeh! dear! If anything should come of it . . . Well, she'd better get to bed. She couldn't show her face to the miss tonight, 'cos she wouldn't know how to handle it.

"Are you awake, miss? I've brought your tea."

"Yes, Alice; yes, I'm awake. Thank you."

Emily opened her eyes to see Alice walking toward the door, and her words stopped her, saying, "Come here a minute, Alice."

Alice walked slowly back up to the head of the bed and stood dutifully still while she listened to what the miss was saying. "You saw Mr. Steerman coming in the back way last night, and . . . and you're thinking the worst. It's not like that, Alice. We . . . we are friends, just friends. But if he were to come in the front way people would get the wrong impression. You see what I mean?"

"Yes, miss."

"His wife and family are away on the Continent. He is all alone. And you know, Alice, you can be alone when you are very rich as much as you can be alone when you are . . . well, destitute."

"I wouldn't know, miss, about that."

"You are very shocked, aren't you, Alice?"

"Oh, no, miss. No, I'm not shocked. Well . . . well, I know these things go on. In all quarters they go on. You just have to look at the Prince. But . . . but I'm worried for you, miss."

"Oh, Alice, you needn't worry about me, dear, because there is nothing really to worry about. He is a friend, that's all, the same as Miss Kate Forester. They are two people I met on holiday and would like to remain friends with. But society being such as it is, he cannot visit me as openly as Miss Forester can. You understand, Alice?"

"Yes, miss, I understand."

"And—" Emily now reached out and picked up the cup of tea from the side table before she ended, "you won't mention this to anyone else?"

"Oh, no, miss. Oh, good gracious, no."

"Thank you." She looked toward the window. "It's going to be a lovely day; the sun is shining. By the way, tell cook I'll just have a lightly boiled egg and toast this morning."

"Yes, miss. Yes, I'll do that."

When the door was pulled to softly, Emily lay back and closed her eyes tightly. She had climbed that hill better than she imagined she would, and she had an ally in Alice, which was fortunate. But now there was a mountain looming up, and that one would be more difficult to climb . . .

It was almost a week since Steve had looked in on her, but when he next came she must tell him plainly how things stood. But could she say she was in love with a married man with three children, someone from the upper class, with a wife who was a socialite? This being so and the fact that Paul's father, Mr. William Anderson Steerman, was a big name in the City, which meant dealing with money . . . No. No, she couldn't. It was strange but she didn't want to hurt him, especially now that she had met his family, and through them had understood him more.

But how was she going to put it? Could she say

he is merely a friend, like you, Steve, but he has to visit me at nights simply because of the rules laid down by a narrow minded society, the patron of which was the Queen? And now her mind, like Alice's, jumped to the Prince. The Queen had no control over him in that way, had she?

She got up suddenly, telling herself now that she would climb that particular mountain when she reached it . . .

When Steve hadn't put in an appearance for ten days she thought to herself, He knows. Some way he's found out; or perhaps he put two and two together when she had picked up the visiting card on that particular Sunday and the sight of Paul's name had drained the color from her face.

She asked herself why one could not have a number of friends, only, as it were, to come back at herself with a slap in the face by saying, Don't act stupid, woman! Yet, that's all Paul was, a friend. During the three visits he had paid her over the past week they had talked and he had held her hand, and he had kissed it before leaving her. That had been all. And at the end of that third visit he had told her he would not be able to see her for the next two or three weeks: the family were going up to Scotland, and his father and mother were going with them. So, although the last two days had been filled with work, designing new shapes to meet the growing demands of large hats for the races, and so busy was the dress-renovating department upstairs that she'd had to refuse to take new customers, part of her remained empty inside.

She had tried to keep her manner as light as possible toward Esther and Lena, but, nevertheless, she felt that they were viewing her with some kind of suspicion. The camaraderie that had existed between them before her holiday was no more. And this, too, troubled her at times when she lay in bed, thinking it was as if she now had the weight of the world on her shoulders. It seemed impossible that making the acquaintance of a man on holiday could turn one's life topsy-turvy, could arouse emotions you couldn't imagine yourself capable of feeling. During his visits she had felt an almost uncontrollable desire to put her arms about him and feel herself being pressed into him, lost in him. Nothing seemed to matter when she was in his presence but that he should remain there.

She was now in the workroom watching Sarah Hubbard trimming a hat that was perched on a high-standing block, and she put out her hands and said, "No, Sarah; you don't want deep red roses there. Try the pink, and lay them on the mauve ribbon, like that," she demonstrated.

"Yes, yes," Sarah nodded, then added, "You don't think the red ones will go anywhere on it?"

"No; they clash with the mauve. Now bring the soft green leaves and place them behind that rose. Then repeat that around the brim. Keep the roses small, just the ones that are about to open. You can add a bud here and there later."

As she moved away to another table, Jean Fulton came up to her, saying, "There's five bandboxes ready, miss. Which of us have got to take the cab?"

"Well, who went last time?"

"Margie did, miss."

"What about Amity?"

"She hates cabs. They make her sick."

Emily now smiled and said, "Well, that only leaves you, doesn't it, Jean?"

"Well, you could say so, miss." The girl grinned and hurried away, and as she made to open a door at the end of the room, it was pushed open and Alice entered. And Jean, jumping to one side, said, "Oh, make way for the lady's maid."

"One of these days I'll slap your mouth for you."

"And that'll be Tuesday; or you could try Monday or Whistlecock Sunday."

A titter followed Alice as she hurried toward Emily, to whom she said, "The doctor's called, miss."

"Oh, all right, Alice. I'll be there in a moment."

She did not leave the workroom immediately; but going to another table she sorted among some buckram shapes, and having picked out a medium-size one, she took it over to Amity, saying, "Sew a head band into this, Amity. I'll be back shortly and we'll start trimming. I think that shape will suit Mrs. Wilson Fairbairn." Then she walked slowly from the room, across the hall and through the connecting door, and so into the study of number thirty-four. And there she stood for a moment drawing in deep breaths while asking herself, What am I going to say? But she was given no answer.

As she opened the sitting room door Steve turned from where he had been standing looking down into the grate, which was all set with paper, sticks and coal awaiting a match. But it wasn't until she was standing before him and then after some further seconds that he said, "How are you?"

"Oh, I'm quite well, thank you;" and her tone held a touch of jocularity as she added, "And how are you?"

"Oh, I am as you always see me. Well, that isn't quite right. Perhaps you will notice that I'm decently dressed for once. I've had to make an effort as I am about to escort two young ladies to the theater, and dinner later."

Her eyebrows were raised as she said, "May I guess at the Misses Braize?"

"Yes, you guess right. They are two very interesting young ladies when you get to know them."

"I'm sure they are, especially the younger one . . . the one with the giggle." Why was she talking like this? It was as if she resented the fact that he was taking these two spinstery-looking young women out. It was ridiculous.

"Her giggle, as you call it, is just the sign of nervousness. She is not used to company: they've both led a very, not exactly a sheltered life, but a restricted one."

"Oh, I see. I'm sorry. I was judging on first appearances, and . . . and one should never do that.''

"No; you are right there.''

He now pulled at the bottom of his coat as if tugging it into place. Then pointing toward the table, he said, "I am lost without my bag. I usually leave it there; but then I think, in the future, it will be quite unnecessary for me to bring it, you are looking so well. Have you entertained your new friend during the last few days? He promised to call, if I remember cook's message for you.''

She drew in a sharp breath before she said, "Yes. Yes, I've entertained both my new friends during the last few days.''

"Both of them?''

"That's what I said. Miss Kate Forester and Mr. . . .'' She paused then said, "Steerman.''

"Oh, Mr. Steerman?'' He tilted his head to one side. Looking upward and his eyelids blinking, he said, "It's an unusual name, Steerman. It wouldn't be one of the Anderson Steermans, would it?''

She remained silent, her face tight: his voice and manner were getting her on the raw again.

"My! My! If you're being visited by one of the Anderson Steermans, you're getting into high society. I know a little of that family, not that I've met any of them; it's through hearsay. My father and the elderly Steerman spent some little time together at an academy. But that was many years ago. I understand they have a very large estate in Scotland, and besides their town house, they have another in Northumberland.'' He paused;

then, his tone changing and his face taking on a look of concern, he said quietly, "If it's the same Steerman, then there's only one son, and as far as my knowledge goes, I think he is married." There was another pause before he said, "Is he married, Emily?"

She took one step back from him before turning and dropping down into the corner of the couch.

He remained where he was for some minutes but he didn't take his eyes off her. Then moving slowly toward her he looked down onto her bent head and, quietly now, he asked her, "Have you . . . have you an affection for him?"

When she did not answer, the bawl he gave startled her so much that she flung her head back to the demand, "Answer me!"

And now she was staring up at him, her face scarlet, saying, "Don't you dare shout at me. You have no right, none whatever, not even to question me. How dare you!"

His voice only slightly lower now, he answered her: "You know why I dare. I've made it plain to you why I dare. And you sit there and you tell me that you've got an affection for someone you've met by chance in an hotel, and he a married man. Tell me something more. Do you intend to become his mistress? Because that's all such associations lead to. Don't you know that? Of course you know that. You are no girl; you have been through life: you have been married and divorced. And still you remain somebody that one could admire . . . and love. But that, I see, was a mistake, a big mistake on my part."

He turned from her now, saying, "My God! I can't believe it, not of you, a mistress. One of the whore tribe." Then swinging round again, he demanded further, "Have you asked yourself where you will come on his list? His type change them as they do their shirts. It's the done thing."

She had dragged herself to her feet now, and finding her voice, she cried angrily at him, "I am *not* his mistress!"

His head drooped and he drew in a number of deep breaths before he said, and more quietly now, "But you allow him to visit you, and on your own admission you've got an affection for him: it was written all over your face. I know now why you came back from that holiday so disturbed and, as the weeks went on, you became more miserable about something. But now it is evident what was making you miserable: he hadn't called. There was a different look on your face today as you entered this room. Well, now you know my feelings for you, so I think I'm entitled to ask you not to see him again, to promise me . . ."

"I will promise you nothing," she snapped. "What is more, you have no right to take it upon yourself to speak to me in this fashion. I will do what I like with my life and take the consequences. Yes; do you hear? I will take the consequences."

The color had drained from his face, and so tight were his jaws that his cheekbones were pressing against the skin. And when he spoke it seemed he had to sift his words through his teeth as he said, "I will transfer your name to Doctor Smeaton's calling list." And with this he turned about and walked slowly from the room.

Emily put both hands to her head, her palms over her ears, but she could not shut out the closing of the front door.

Instead of flopping down on the couch she began to pace the room, still holding her head. And when the tears began to run down her face she made no effort to wipe them away. There was a moaning sound inside of her and contradictory voices fighting each other. She hated him. How dare he speak to her like that! "One of the whore tribe." She had a vivid picture of sitting in a cab with Mrs. Arkwright while driving from a factory, the manager of which had become a friend and had kept them chatting long after the workers had left, and the cabbie, either through perverseness, or extending his fare, had driven them through the back thoroughfares and Mrs. Arkwright had pointed out of the window toward where street after lamplit street was dotted with women of all ages, mostly sparsely dressed and blatantly offering their bodies, and she had said, "God help them. If I had my way I'd lynch all their keepers. Look at that one! She can't be fourteen; and there's her master in that doorway, if I'm not mistaken."

The memory of that night stayed with her and

she was ever conscious of what went on behind the respectable façade of the city.

But why was she now feeling she had lost something, something good, durable? Something that would never come her way again, for he was a bully? And what business was it of his anyway what she did? He had no hold over her, accusing her of being Paul's mistress!

But she would be, wouldn't she?

No! No! It mustn't happen. She would be disgraced. She would lose all respect. And it would be dreadful if . . . if . . .

If what? *If what?*

It would mean now that she would never be married again. Never have a family . . . like his family . . . that wonderful Sunday. But there would be no more Sundays: he had gone; his door had closed, and finally . . .

"What is it, miss? What is it? Has he upset you? Come and sit down. Oh, you are in a state. Will I get Esther?"

"No. Please, no, not Esther."

"It's a clean handkerchief, miss; dry your face. There now. There now. Will I get you a cup of tea?"

When Emily nodded, Alice hurried from the room; but outside the door she paused a moment and, looking toward the front door, she said to herself, "Poor doctor. If only she would have sense. But who could with a man like Mr. Steerman?"

11

"Politics is like a seesaw, Emily, and the main seesaw has been between Disraeli and Gladstone. First the Liberals are up and then the Tories. There have been atrocities in Bulgaria. Of course, when there's trouble between the Turks and the Christians we must do something about it; oh, yes, even between the Turks and the Russians; the spark of one fire lights another. It goes on endlessly. So why am I wanting to join the Government? Can you tell me that, Emily?"

She smiled, but remained silent as she always did when he was talking about politics. But she had learned a lot. Yet she knew she could have acquired the same information from the daily papers; but she never had time to peruse them. So much was going on in the world, and the more she learned of it through him, the more ignorant she felt. She knew that her busy hive was set in a backwater, where the conversation ranged between ribbons, brims and crowns. Two of her staff could neither read nor write. But they were intelligent and had memorized the names of most streets and byways in the city, and could also recite the names of shops in many of the thoroughfares and what merchandise each dealt with. And a girl she had taken on recently, Brigid Mc-Mahon, had informed her proudly that she went to night classes where they read out pieces from Mr. Dickens.

Something that he was saying now linked up with her thoughts: "It covers mainly a poor constituency and it's going to be a very hard fight. It's quite new territory to me. Quite candidly, Emily, I'm not very enthusiastic about it all, but my father is very anxious that I should put up for it. You know, the poor in the country are different altogether from the poor in the towns, and I'm not including staffs like our own, they are very well off: housed, fed and clothed and with a wage. Of course, they obviously appreciate it, for some of them have been with us since they were children. My father had the same valet since he was a young man. They're both growing old together. However, those I am referring to, Emily, are farm workers and such. But there again, they, too, are housed and fed and get a wage . . ."

"Yes, but from what I hear, it hardly keeps them alive." She was surprised at herself, for it was the first time she had questioned anything he had said. It was as if she were talking to Steve.

"Oh, my dear," he was laughing at her now, "what do you know about farm workers? You're a city girl . . . young woman . . . lady . . . a beautiful lady. And here I am stupid enough to waste our time together talking about politics and the conditions of the poor. Oh, my dear"—he reached out from his seat at the end of the couch and gripped her hand—"you must excuse me, but I can never talk like this to anyone else. I don't want to talk like this to anyone else. And, in a way, you are quite right to question my opinion; and I hope you will not only continue to do so but also do it more often, because I know you have a deeper insight into the working class than I have, or ever will have."

She was smiling now as she said, "Yet you're going to represent them: as you've already told me, in your constituency are many mills and factories, and a coal mine thrown in for good measure."

He laughed aloud now, then put his hand over his mouth and looked toward the door as he said, "Has Alice retired?"

"Yes. Yes, quite a while ago."

"Oh, Emily"—he moved closer to her—"I hate this hole-in-the-corner business as much as you do; if only I could come in the front door and say, 'Good evening, Alice. Where's your mistress?' or"—his voice dropped—"better still, 'Good morning, Alice. No, I won't have any breakfast, just a cup of coffee.'"

She closed her eyes now, murmuring. "Don't. Please, Paul, don't."

"I love you, Emily. I wish I didn't. I've tried to put you out of my mind, but I find it impossible. I kept away for a whole week, remember, determined to put a stop to this madness. But it was no use. As long as I could see you, talk to you, feel you near me, I told myself that would be enough; but I know it isn't, and never will be. What are we going to do, Emily?"

"I . . . I have my staff to think about." Even to herself her voice sounded prim. "I . . . I couldn't bear the disgrace if . . . if . . ."

"My dear, my dear, what disgrace? No one need know. No one has the slightest inkling that I'm here, have they?"

Her voice sounded a little stiff as she replied, "Alice is no fool."

"No; but she's your maid, and she seems a discreet kind of girl."

"She is not a maid in that way, the way you infer; she is really a housemaid."

"Well, whatever she is, personal maid or housemaid, from what I've seen of her, she seems very fond of you."

"As fond and discreet as many are, there's always a slip of the tongue and I wouldn't be able to bear it if . . ."

"If what, my dear? Tell me, if what?"

She dared not look at him straight in the eye as she said, "If I were to have a child."

"Oh, Emily, Emily, that would never happen. I . . . I can assure you that will never happen. It mustn't; it couldn't . . . no!"

His arms were about her, he was holding her close; and then for the second time in their acquaintance their lips met and held as they had done in the cave. And when at last it was over she lay back against the sofa and, muttering, she said, "Please, Paul, go now."

"Yes. All right, my dear, I will go. But I shall be back tomorrow night." He was holding her face between his hands; then kissing her on the lips, but softly now, he repeated, "Yes, until tomorrow night, my love."

She watched him put on his coat; then as he picked up his hat and gloves and walking stick from a chair, she pulled herself up from the sofa and walked to the door and quietly opened it; and although cook's quarters were still next door, and Alice would be asleep in her room in the attic, they both walked somewhat stealthily down the passage. Then with her hand on the key of the door she turned to him and again he kissed her gently.

It was after she opened the door and looked out into the night that they both gasped, because the thick fog floated into the house like smoke.

"Good gracious!" His voice was a whisper now. "It was just a night mist earlier. I've never known such a fog this late in the year. I can't see the gate."

She, too, whispered as she said, "Perhaps when you get into the street the lamps will help. Perhaps you'll see a cab. They generally lead the horse and swing a lantern. Give me your hand. I can find my way to the gate."

Outside the gate she peered along the alleyway to where, at the end, a lamp from the street always gave a glimmer of light. But there was nothing, only this thick yellow-gray mass that was choking her and making her want to cough.

Silently now she tugged him back into the yard and groped for the bolt and eased it into the stanchion. Then, still holding his hand, she led the way back to where she imagined the door to be. But so thick was the fog that she came up against the wall to the side of it. It was with a choking gasp of relief when, stretching out her arm, she found the door and thrust it open. And then they were both inside and standing with their backs to it, he, too, trying to smother his coughing now.

In the sitting room he divested himself of his coat before walking over to Emily, who was bending over the fire, hands held out to the blaze; and he drew her shivering body into his arms and held her close for a moment before saying gently, "It seems, my darling, that the weather has taken a hand in our destiny, wouldn't you agree?"

12

She was happy. She had never felt like this in her life before, simply because she had never been loved like this before. She imagined that no woman could ever have been loved as he loved her. Her days were now spent waiting for the nights. How many times had they been together during the past month? Oh, she didn't want to count, she only knew that when a night passed without his coming she spent it fitfully. She would not allow herself to ask where it was going to lead, or how it would end. She did not even worry when her monthly occurrence did not take place, for her body acted erratically in that way, it always had. The only regret she had was that almost always he had to get up and leave her after perhaps only an hour's stay. Once or twice he had fallen asleep by her side and she had been tempted to let him go on sleeping all night. Only the thought that she, too, would fall asleep and Alice would come in and find them in the morning had made her arouse him gently.

Did Alice suspect anything? But how could she? They had been very, very quiet, and Alice herself had admitted she was a heavy sleeper; moreover she was always in bed before ten o'clock. But what about Esther? Well, Esther's eyes had held a trace of suspicion for some weeks now. Before anyone else, she had detected a change in her.

It had been difficult lately to hide her feelings and adopt her ordinary businesslike manner when in the sale room or the workshop, and particularly upstairs when re-designing the dresses, for she had had to resist the temptation to pick out one or two for her own use. This would have been questioned by both Esther and Lena, for they were hard at it to keep up the supply for the customers.

She happened to be up in the dressing room when she heard Lena say, "Look, Esther, there's that boy standing on the corner again, looking across here. You remember, he was there the other day."

"Perhaps he's a messenger."

"He couldn't be a messenger, else he would be about his business."

"Oh, yes. Yes, of course." Esther put the scissors down on the table, then walked to the window. And after a moment she turned to Emily, who was fitting a bodice on a dummy stand, and said, "Look here a minute, Emily. Have you any idea who he is?"

Taking two pins from her mouth and sticking them in a small pin cushion attached to a ribbon strapped around her wrist, Emily walked to the window and stood between them looking down on the figure standing on the opposite pavement. And her comment was, "He's beyond a boy, I think. He looks sixteen or seventeen, and he's too well dressed for a messenger. He's been there before?''

''Yes. I saw him one day last week. Why I took notice of him was that he was outside here, outside our door; and I spoke to him. ''Are you looking for a number, son?'' I said; and he stared at me for a moment before saying, ''No.'' Then he walked off. Funny for him to be standing there again. D'you know there was a robbery in Marlborough Terrace the other night?''

''Well''—Esther laughed and turned from the window—''what d'you think he'll be after here, a hat?''

''There's money in the till,'' said Lena.

''Aye, you're right: there's money in the till. But imagine if he tried to get it, we'd all claw him to death.''

They both laughed then glanced toward Emily. She was still staring down at the young man. But his gaze was directed, seemingly, to the lower part of the house, likely the doorway. Presently he turned and walked away. He walked well, strode out, not unlike a soldier; and even after he had disappeared from her view, she remained looking down. Why was he watching the house? By what the girls had said, this must have been his third visit. She had an uneasy feeling. In the ordinary way, if someone were watching your house you would inform the authorities. That's if you had nothing to hide, of course.

She did not go back to the model but took the

pin-strap from her wrist and without making any comment went out of the room. This caused the two women to exchange glances, and Lena to comment, "I would like to know what's the matter with her these days. She's as moody as a hen on a clutching of chalk eggs."

" 'Tis the doctor. He's never been here for weeks. I got that out of Madam Alice. I know he could be here and gone, and in this end we wouldn't know anything about it; but I would sometimes knock into him when I went through to her. But not having seen him I asked that 'un if the doctor had been lately, and when she came back at me and said she didn't know, I went for her: 'You know or you don't know' I said. 'If you didn't open the door for him, he could have got in down the chimney and went out the same way, couldn't he?' Well, this reply must have tickled her fancy because she laughed and then she said, no, he hadn't been. And I asked if they'd had a row; and her answer to that was, no more than usual, because they always argued. But, you know, Lena, there's arguing and arguing. And there was good arguing that went on between them, because I've heard them. And he was for her. Oh, yes, that stood out like the nose on his face. Not that his was over-big, but you know what I mean. All his argufying was just to hide his feelings . . . She's a fool."

"I agree with you there, Esther, yes, she's a fool. There's not many about like him who'd work as he does down by the river. And that's just one part of him;'' and when she ended, "I wish he would notice me. I'm ready and ripe and only forty,'' Esther pushed her so hard that she fell against the model and just managed to steady it, crying, "Look out! you idiot; she's spent hours on that bodice. And look, some pins have dropped out.''

While together they endeavored to put the pins back into the folds of the bodice, Lena remarked, "I wonder what that lad's really after? By! I'd like to know. He's not standing there for nothing, that's for sure.''

He was dressed, ready to leave, and sitting on the side of the bed, her hands were tight within his and his voice was thick with emotion as he said, "You're beautiful in the daytime, Emily, but you are exquisite at night. How am I going to bear the days ahead without the thought of seeing you?''

"How long will you be away?''

"I couldn't say, darling . . . not this time. It's a birthday celebration, the highlight of the year for my father. And, oh dear!'' he sighed, "they can become so tedious: the celebrations go on for ever, with the same faces, the same talk, the same senseless chatter; although''—he pulled a face at her—"it'll be slightly different this year. It will be politics every night in the smoking-room and I shall have to listen to advice from the old ones on how to tackle the political life ahead of me. But . . .''

"Will it be a week, a fortnight or . . . ?''

"Oh, probably a fortnight, my dear; but a barren

fortnight without you." He lifted her thick loose hair from her shoulders and spread it over the pillow. "Your hair's like wings and so strong."

"Will . . . will all the family be there?"

He raised his eyebrows as he answered, "Oh . . . oh, yes. Yes, of course, my dear."

"The children, I mean."

"Oh, the children? Oh, yes, yes, of course; but I'll see very little of them; they'll be up in the nursery."

"You never talk of them."

"Well, quite honestly, although I would like to, I rarely see them. I remember I caught my first glimpse of my own mother when I was seven. She was Mamma, a lady who patted my head and said, "Be a good boy." And I was twelve before I had any kind of conversation with my father. But I must say it seems that we've never stopped talking since. Children, you see, dear, in certain—" he checked himself from saying "classes" and substituted, "households, are kept in the nursery until they are sent to boarding school, the boys at seven and the girls at nine. The strange thing is we are brought up by servants. In an ordinary household, of course, one would get to know one's parents. The system, as I said, in our type of household is, well . . . no different. So, I don't suppose I shall see much of my children. Of course, there are exceptions. Should my son take to a pony at four or five, then I shall ride with him."

It was in her mind she could recall him saying he

enjoyed spending time with his children, but the thought was pushed aside when he went on: "Anyway, my dear one, you know by now that nothing, nor anyone, can fill the time that we're apart. I only wish . . . oh"—he shook his head—"how I wish that I could take you away and have you all to myself, and that I wouldn't have to sneak in the back door, but march through the front door and straight into your arms. Have you ever thought of giving up this business and taking a house somewhere quiet, a place where we wouldn't have to hide so much?"

Slowly she pulled herself a little further up the pillows until her head was on a level with his, and then asked quietly, "If I did, would you be with me every day and every night for always?"

"Oh, my darling!"—both his look and his manner expressed his hurt—"you know how things stand. You know that I am tied. I have explained it all to you and all with regret. And one thing is sure: she will never divorce me, no matter what I might do. And she never behaves in such a manner that would give me the right to divorce her. She is clever that way, tenacious and clever. And then there is my father. He is a very dominant man, the family is everything to him, and my future career comes under that heading, which means politics. I'm very fond of him, but I'm also not blind to the fact that his love for me and his concern for my future are because, in a way, he wants to live again through me. He was never successful in the political field. In business, yes, but then it was a ready-made business, with the wealth having been garnered by his ancestors. All industrialists. So, you see, my dear, I . . . I am tied in all ways. You are my only liberty. Anyway, we'll talk about this later. One thing I do know: I could never give you up."

When she held his face between her hands and said, "Nor I you. There's only you," he replied, "And for me there is only you. . . ."

The door closed on him and she lay back and put her hand across her eyes and as the tears ran through her fingers she asked why fate should have brought her such a love, and having done so, why it had arranged it to be enjoyed only by stealth. And then with no hope in the future of it being otherwise. She turned now and took the pillow on which his head had lain and held it to her.

The first morning she felt a wave of sickness overtaking her she put her hands behind her head and gripped the brass rails of the bed. And she knew that if she were to release her bottom lip from her teeth she would scream, for the scream was loud in her head and yelling, "No! No!" He had said . . . he had promised her there was nothing to fear. Nothing. No, he had said; that would be the very last thing he would want. Then, why? Why? It was seven weeks now since he had first lain in this bed.

Suddenly she sat bolt upright. That night, he had not been prepared. It was that night of the thick fog. But . . . but could it have happened then? Yes. Yes, it could and it had. Her monthly time had long passed. Oh, dear God! What was she to do? The disgrace. An illegitimate child. She must think. She must think. And her staff . . . she would lose their respect.

She could go away for the birth. What? Stay away for eight months or more? People weren't fools. And why didn't he come? He had been away over a fortnight now. Why couldn't he have written to her? There came a tap on the door and Alice entered with her morning tea. "Oh, you're awake," she said. "It's a lovely day. What's . . . what's the matter, miss? Aren't you feeling well?"

Alice just managed to put the tea on the side table when she was pushed aside as Emily rushed toward the wash-hand stand and vomited into the basin.

When it was over Alice put a wet flannel to her face, then went to dry it, but Emily, taking the towel from her, muttered, "I'm . . . I'm all right. Something that I ate."

It was some seconds before Alice said, "Likely the fish last night, miss. I don't like hake meself; a bit of cod's my fancy. Lie down again and have that cup of tea. There's nothing spoiling."

Emily allowed herself to be led to the bed and tucked up again. She found that whereas the sight of the tea had caused her to vomit, now she was glad to drink it. When the cup was empty she handed it to Alice, saying quietly, "Don't . . .

don't tell Esther about this. She . . . she'll only fidget me."

"No. No, miss."

When the door closed on Alice, Emily muttered, "It's likely the fish." Dear God! If only it was. What am I going to do . . . ?

On the second, third and then the fourth morning, she managed to reach the closet along the corridor in time, and on that morning when she almost staggered back to her bedroom and found Alice there, she dropped onto the side of the bed, hung her head and murmured, "Oh, Alice."

"It's . . . it's all right, miss." There was a break in Alice's voice. "It happens. Nobody wants it but you can't do anything about it. It happened to the girl I was brought up with, and she was only fifteen."

Emily raised her head. "Fifteen?" she said. "What happened to her?"

"Well, she had to go into the workhouse. My foster mother put her out an' she's no better than she ought to be. But don't you worry, miss."

She had an almost hysterical desire to laugh; it was as if Alice was saying: well, we won't let that happen to you . . . She felt ill, and not only with the sickness but with the awful feeling that now prevailed all day. If only she could take something to allay it. If Steve had still been coming . . .

Her mind seemed to spring away from the name, but after a moment was brought back with the thought: what would he think? She had a mental picture of them all sitting round the dinner table on that wonderful Sunday. She could still think of it as a wonderful Sunday. What had it then led to? . . . *This.*

But what was she going to do?

Why didn't he come back? It was nearly three weeks now. What if he didn't come back at all? These things happened: gentlemen got tired of their fancies. Oh, what was she thinking? This was different . . . they loved each other and under different circumstances would have been married . . . What was Alice saying?

"I . . . I think you should tell Esther, miss. She'll . . . she'll be pleased . . . I mean, she'll want to help you. And when it begins to show . . ."

"*Be quiet! Alice. Oh, be quiet!*" and with those final words she sprang from the bed and, pushing Alice aside, began to pace the room . . . Tell Esther because soon she'd be beginning to show! She stopped suddenly as she realized that it was the thought of how her staff would react to her condition that was troubling her most. If she had been living alone she would have accepted the situation, because she had always wanted a child. Yes. Yes, that had been her girlish dream when she first married, to have a child; and not just the one, but two or three, a family.

And, oh dear! It wasn't only the reaction of her staff; there were the neighbors. She had been accepted by most of them. Although they might not call on her, they would bid her the time of day. Even the Misses Pearson, from the top end, who drove out in their hired carriage, had smiled at her. And she had been alone at the time, and few ladies from this area went out unaccompanied; in fact, none of them, for it would have relegated them to the servant class.

Damn the neighbors! Damn the staff! She was having a baby and it was his, and it would be a wonderful child. So, come what may, she wouldn't be ashamed of it. She turned to Alice, saying, "Has Esther been quizzing you?"

Alice wagged her head, then pursed her lips before saying, "She's always quizzing me, miss. But she's concerned like, so I think you should . . . well, put her in the picture, like."

Emily sat on the chair now, and some seconds passed before she again looked at Alice. "I can't see myself doing it, Alice," she said, "because I know it will come as a shock to her, in fact, to them all. I know I'll lose any respect they have for me . . ."

"Oh no, you won't! miss. Oh no, you won't! She's a crab at times, is Esther, an' Lena an' all, and as for the others, every one of them would stick by you, miss, if they were called upon to do it. But after the first sort of . . . well, shock, and it's no use sayin' one thing and thinkin' another, it will be a shock, they'll . . ."

"Was it a shock to you, Alice?"

"Yes and no, miss. You see, I knew he was visiting."

"How? How did you know that?"

"Oh well, miss . . . sounds, you know. Me bed

is just above the passage. Usually it's as quiet as a graveyard at night . . . and the slightest difference, well . . . an' that door creaks a bit."

There was a tender smile on the girl's face and such was its effect that once more Emily wanted to lay her head on the girl's shoulder and feel her comforting arms about her. Instead, she put out her hand, saying, "You're a friend indeed, Alice; so can I ask you to . . . well, when the time comes, talk to Esther? I'm . . . I'm a coward and can't face her with it. She'll be so shocked. They all will."

"No. No, miss; these things happen. They're happenin' all the time. Don't you worry about that. But I'll tell you what I think you should have . . . well, will you be seeing the doctor? But . . . but as you won't, I suppose you should have something to try to ease the sickness. A bottle from the chemist. My foster mother used to get one and it helped her. Quietened her stomach, like. You know, I think in the ordinary way you shouldn't be feelin' so sick in the mornings. And when you get over it you'll likely feel fine . . . different, but fine. Lots of people do when they are carryin'. So should I slip out and get you a bottle later on?"

"Yes; that would be very kind of you, Alice. Yes, please do that. And if you are going out, you can do something else for me. You can drop a note into the warehouse. I should have been there this morning. I had an appointment with Mr. Burton for eleven o'clock. It's a bit out of the way, but you could take a cab."

"I don't need to take a cab, miss, I like walkin'. And I know enough short cuts to get me there in half the time it would take a cab. And—" she gave a little laugh now as she added, "it's cheaper on your feet. . . ."

About an hour later, she was in the middle of dressing when there was a tap on the door and Esther's voice said, "May I come in?"

"Yes. Yes, Esther."

She was pulling another waist petticoat on top of a lawn one, and as she fastened the strings at the back Esther stood looking at her, saying, "How are you feeling today?"

"Oh, quite a bit better."

"You don't look it. You should see the doctor, you know that?"

"I'm all right, Esther."

"Where's she off to?"

"Who?"

"Your maid, of course." The words were heavily laden with sarcasm.

"Oh, I sent her with a note to the warehouse."

"You sent her? Isn't Jean fit enough to run messages? She generally does."

Emily's voice was sharp now. "She was going out with a message for me and it was like killing two birds with the one stone. Now, can you find any fault in that?"

"Yes, I can, since you ask. Messages are treats which, and again since you ask, are usually taken in a cab. And another thing, that one's getting much too big for her boots, and there's going to be a showdown shortly. Now, I'm telling you, Emily," and with this she turned and marched from the room, leaving Emily to flop onto the end of the bed. A showdown. She was nearer to a showdown than she knew. It was odd: she seemed to be surrounded by caring people, yet she felt so alone. It was as if she was on an island . . . No! No!—her mind rejected the isolation the word indicated. More as if she were in a prison, barred in.

Why didn't he come? It was weeks now and not a note or anything from him. But he had explained that to her, hadn't he? It would be difficult to write letters when he was with the family.

When she had finished dressing she stared at her reflection in the mirror. Her cream-tinted skin seemed to have lost its warmth; her face looked pasty-white; her dark eyes were deep in their sockets, which seemed to have enlarged. He had said she was beautiful, but she could see no beauty there now. It was a frightened face. But hadn't she told herself she wasn't going to be afraid, that she was going to have this child because she wanted it? She wanted something completely her own. Something permanent, because . . . she shut down the thought that her association with its father might not be permanent. Yet the thought attacked her again; why not? Most men in his position had mistresses, many of whom were accepted. But she didn't want to be accepted as such, she just wanted him. Oh, yes, she wanted him; in fact, she ached for him.

She turned from the mirror and sat down in an easy chair, telling herself that she just couldn't go next door and face the others. They must be talking among themselves already, because she certainly hadn't acted like her old self these past few weeks. She no longer joked with them or laughed at the repartee.

She lay her head back, closed her eyes and tried to shut out the future, but all that happened was that she found she was longing for the past.

It was as if she had been waiting for Alice's return, for when Alice closed the front door behind her, there was Esther, demanding, "And where d'you think you've been?"

"Out, else I wouldn't be coming in."

"I want none of your cheek. I've had enough of you. What's all this about?" Then, as Esther grabbed at her arm, Alice turned and said quietly, "Take your hand off me."

"I will when I get something out of you. There's something goin on up there and I want to know . . . Ooh!" The side of Alice's hand had struck Esther's wrist, bringing the warning from her: "You young devil, you. You dare to strike me."

"That's nothing to what you'll get if you do that again. And yes; there's something goin' on, and I could tell you about it; and I would have done before now if I had been given me place. But you forget I'm no longer in the kitchen. You can't get over that, can you?"

Alice now stepped back before adding, "All

right, then, I have got some news and I'll give it to you and Lena there. So, I'll see you in about fifteen minutes' time next door." And adopting a manner that could have been Emily's and speaking in a similar tone, she said, "And I would advise you both to take a seat before I start talkin'," then swung about and went up the stairs, leaving an open-mouthed Esther watching her progress.

Without divesting herself of her hat and coat Alice entered Emily's bedroom to find her still sitting in the chair by the window. She handed her a bottle she had taken from a paper bag. Emily took it, saying, "Oh, thank you, Alice," and read the label, "Guaranteed to cure sickness, bile, dizziness and fever." Then she started as Alice, her voice low, said, "He'll be here tonight, miss."

"What? What did you say?"

"Well, I mean, Mr. Steerman. I saw him. He was in a cab. There was a hold up near the circus, and there he was in a cab. There's not another like him; it was him all right, and I had a second look before it moved on."

Emily closed her eyes and said, "Oh, Alice, of all people for you to see in London."

"Yes, miss, 'twas funny. I thought so meself. But now I'll away and get your cup of coffee. Then I'm goin' next door." The smile now left her face as she said, "You suggested I should put them in the picture, miss, an' so I think I should do it now . . . . Esther knows there's something amiss with you an' she'll only ferret it out for herself an' likely upset you."

Emily looked up at the girl for a moment or two before she said, "In a way, I'm beginning to think we must be guided in our choices, at least some of them, because, at this moment, I don't know what I would do without you, Alice."

The smile was back on Alice's face and her head wagged as she said, "Oh, somebody would have stepped in, miss. There's lots of the likes of me kickin' around London, just waitin' for a chance to be useful. I was lucky. Well, I'll go and get that coffee."

"Thank you, Alice. Thank you for everything."

"Oh, there's nothing to thank me for, miss." The head wagged again before she turned about, red with embarrassment, and hurried from the room, leaving Emily musing to herself, " 'I was lucky,' she said. She thinks she's lucky. It all depends on what you expect from life."

And she *had* seen him. Alice wouldn't have made a mistake about that: as she had said, there isn't another like him. And if he were back, he would surely come here, and as soon as possible—tonight!

She rose from the chair and went to the mirror again. There was a little color in her cheeks now and her eyes were no longer lost in their sockets.

"Stay where you are for a minute, Alice; Lady Steele's next door. She's just going. Esther'll see her downstairs," said Lena.

They both stood listening now to Esther's voice:

"I'm so glad you're pleased with it, m'lady. I'll have it sent onto the house this afternoon."

"Thank you so much, Miss McCann. And will you please tell Miss Ratcliffe I'm sorry I didn't see her and I hope that her cold will soon be better?"

"I will, m'lady. And . . . and would you like to go out the side door? There's nearly always a cab passing on the side street."

There was a pause before the refined voice said, "Yes. Yes, I'll do that. Thank you. I'm to meet my sister-in-law shortly at Claridges."

As the voice died away Lena turned to Alice, saying, "Claridges, and there's not a penny between them. How they keep going, God only knows. And they used to be rolling in it at one time. That's what happens when you put your faith in gold mines. Still, she's a real lady in all respects. Well, come on in. I understand you have something to say."

Alice followed the rotund, middle-aged Lena into the fitting-room and watched her seat herself down on the couch the while saying, "We had our orders to sit;" but she made no direct reply to this other than, "Well, you'll see what I meant in a minute or so."

"I can't wait."

Alice hadn't been invited to sit, so she stood holding onto the back of a chair while Lena talked at her. "You've got yourself ensconced nicely next door, haven't you? Mind, I'm not blaming you altogether, because you had a rough time under cook. Esther says the change has gone to your head too suddenly and you forget yourself at times. But anyway, there's one thing I can tell you: cook wishes you were back downstairs; in fact, she's had to get extra help in. I never heard much about your holiday. I suppose that gave you high ideas. But, of course, out in a foreign hotel they'd be no better nor no higher than the ones we get in here. Not likely such good class, either . . . Oh, there you are." She was now addressing Esther, who had come into the room. "I've taken me seat. You'd better plant yourself down beside me as you've been ordered." Lena was laughing now.

Esther did exactly that: she sat down beside Lena. Then looking at Alice, she said, "Well now, get on with it. What can you tell us about the mistress of this house and next door that we don't already know? I'm very anxious to find out."

Such was her manner that Alice was once again aroused to say, "I have a good mind to walk out and leave you guessing."

"You start that, madam, and for two pins . . ."

"Oh, you and your two pins!" Alice flung her hand wide. "I'll bring you a whole paper load of pins the next time I go out."

The two seated women turned and looked at each other in blank amazement at the effrontery of this girl who, up to a few months ago, was classed as a skivvy.

"You can't stop gettin' at me, can you?" She now bent her head and when the tears came into her eyes, Lena said, "All right, lass. Go on.

There's faults on both sides here, I suppose, but let's have your news."

Alice blinked, then looking from one to the other, she said, "She's going to have a baby. She's pregnant."

If someone had sprung into the room and levelled a gun at them they could not have been more surprised or shocked, and instinctively the hands of the two women went out toward each other and gripped. And it was Lena's voice, very quiet, who asked now, "It's right? No mistake?"

"No. No mistake, Lena. She's been sick four mornings in a row."

"Oh, God in heaven!" Esther now lay back against the couch, and putting one hand tightly over her mouth, she said, "I could be sick meself at this minute. I could! I could!" Then, shaking her head, she said, "No! Not her!" When she turned to Lena and said, "What are we going to do?" Lena, in a helpless tone, said, "Don't ask me. It's what *she's* going to do."

They both looked at Alice now and almost spoke the words together, "So what . . . what is she going to do? Have . . . have it taken away?"

"No. No, she wants it. As far as I know, she wants it."

"Whose is it?"

Alice looked at Lena but said nothing. Then Esther answered for her, saying flatly, "The doctor's, of course."

"No. No, it isn't."

Again they were startled as they gazed at the girl in front of them, who was leaning over the back of the chair now, saying, "The doctor would never have taken her down. He's a gentleman, is the doctor."

"Well! Well, who's the gentleman who took her down, then?"

Again Alice bowed her head as she muttered, "Somebody she met while we were on holiday."

Lena was on her feet now as she said, "The man cook let in that Sunday? And he came back the next day. But it couldn't have happened then. Did . . . did it happen on the holiday?"

Alice sighed as if she were weary, saying, "No. No, it didn't happen on the holiday. And . . . and she did her best to push him off. But they became friendly, like, and then . . . well, these things happen."

"Is he of the gentry?"

"Yes, Lena, he's of the gentry."

"Well, will he marry her?"

Both Esther and Alice now looked at Lena in silence.

"Well, he could have been of the gentry and not married her just because she's a working businesswoman. They don't have open doors in the upper class. So"—she turned to Alice now—"he's married, then?"

"Yes. Yes, he's married."

"God in heaven! Her above everybody on this earth. So sensible, so proud . . . and she was beautiful, so smart and beautiful she could have had anybody."

"She couldn't have had anybody," said Esther, "not to suit her. She could have had the doctor; he was ready and willing. Oh aye, and he was of a good-class family. But still, they weren't out of the real top drawer . . . Is this one the top drawer?" Esther was looking at Alice again and she, nodding, said, "Yes. Yes, you could say that. Aye, he's out of the top drawer."

"But how do they meet? Does he come every day? Anyway, what's his name?"

"I . . . I can't tell you that."

"Why? You've told us enough."

"You'll have to ask her yourself." Alice was now addressing Esther.

"I don't know how I'm goin' to face her."

"Well, when you do, try to be kind. She needs kindness. She's . . . she's sort of lost an' she's feelin' bad all the time, inside and out, because she doesn't know how you'll all take it. So be kind to her."

The two women stared at the young girl before Lena said, "All right, Alice; don't worry. We'll make it as easy as we can. And I'll see to the others, too. Anyway, I know they'll all rally round her. Go on back to her now and sort of . . . well, reassure her. You know what to do."

Alice turned slowly away and went out of the room, while the two women, after looking at each other, resumed their seats on the couch. And it was Esther who said, "I can't believe it. I just

can't believe it.'' Then turning to Lena, she added,
''And wait until it gets out up the street. They had
accepted her and the whole business, but now
they'll shun her: all the frocks in the world
won't hide what she's carrying; and then, when
it's born, it'll be illegitimate, a bastard. Oh dear
God!''

''Perhaps she'll go away to have it and then
farm it out. And being her she would do it decently; it would go into a good home.''

''Don't bank on that, Lena. You heard what Alice
said: she wants it. And if she wants it, she'll keep
it. She's as stubborn as a mule in some things, I
know that. Well, that's knocked the stuffing out of
me. I'll not get over this in a hurry, I can tell you
that. And how I'm going to face her I just don't
know. And that 'un said to be kind.''

''Yes. Yes, she did. And, you know, I think
there's more in that lass than meets the eye . . .
Well, are we going up to see her? We'd far better
do it right away, and we've nobody coming for
another hour.''

They stared at each other for a moment; then
Lena pressed her hair down from the middle parting to each side of her head while Esther pulled
the velvet belt on her frock in another notch. And
they both left the room . . . to get it over.

The door opened quietly. He came in, stood for a
moment looking at her, then quickly divesting
himself of his coat he hurried toward her and without a word took her in his arms and kissed her. It

was a long, tender kiss. Then they gazed at each other, and presently he said softly, "I've kept conjuring up your face, but I could never visualize you as beautiful as you really are. Oh, Emily, how I've missed you." Again he embraced her before he asked, "Did you miss me?"

"Is there any need for you to ask?" She touched his cheek gently with her fingertips, then said, "If only you could have written me a note."

"Oh, my dear, it was most difficult. The house has been like a railway station for weeks, with all the comings and goings. And . . . and then there was the accident. You see, my wife was thrown off her horse and hurt her back. And then I had to accompany Father back to town, twice."

"You've been back here twice?" Her head came up from the pillow.

"Yes, my dear. But on this parliamentary business I had to visit my proposed consituency. I told you about it: a Member died and I'm hoping to take it over if I am selected and then successful at the by-election. But father was with me all the time; and the evenings we had to spend at his club. Talk, talk, talk. Meeting this one and that one who could be of help in my future career." He pulled a face at her now. "Anyway, if it happens I shall be in town more often than not: I'm told one must show oneself to the people one represents, and be ready to put their demands, which I understand will be more than a few, before Parliament. However, dear, I am here for the next three days.

Father has gone back to Scotland and I am off the leash. Oh, how I've missed you. You will never know." Again she was in his arms. But before his lips sought hers once more she pressed him gently from her, saying, "I have something to tell you."

"Yes? I . . . I hope it is something pleasant, something nice."

"I hope that you may think so. I . . . I am going to have a baby."

When, with a look of amazement, he actually recoiled from her, she felt as if a great weight was dragging her heart down through her body. And when he murmured, "No, no, it can't be," she forced herself to say, "It can. It is."

"But . . . but I always came prepared."

"There was . . . there was that first night. Were you prepared then?"

He stared at her; then he closed his eyes and, his head drooping forward, he said, "I'm . . . I'm sorry, my dear, dreadfully sorry. But don't worry." He was looking at her again, and as he hitched himself back into his former position on the side of the bed, he added, "I will see to everything. It can be done quite discreetly. There are places . . ."

"No!" It was she who moved back from him now, pressing her head into the pillow. "I don't want it taken away. I want to keep it."

"But my dear, that would create an impossible situation. It would bear a stigma and . . . and I don't wish it to happen . . . Emily"—he was gripping her hands now—"believe me, I have reasons for saying this."

"Yes; yes, of course you already have three children. Well, you needn't worry. I shall lay no claim on you."

"My dear! My dear! Don't talk such nonsense. It is only you I am thinking about. You could be disgraced. It . . . it might affect your business: people are often narrow minded about this kind of thing. And, too, I can't bear the thought of you being burdened with a child. I know the difficulties of child-rearing. Oh, yes, yes, I do indeed. And I want you utterly for myself. Believe me, my dear, and I can't bear . . . well, the thought of losing you to a child. Emily!" His voice now was full of pleading. "Do this for me. I beg of you. Let me make arrangements. You could, presumably, take a short holiday in the country and after the business is over, recuperate for a time. I'm . . . I'm only thinking of you."

"I want this child, Paul. It might be the only child I shall have in my life."

Slowly he drew away from her, saying, "My dear, already it is putting a wedge between us, even the tone of your voice is that of the Mrs. Ratcliffe I first met, and I never thought to hear it again. Never!" He now rose from the bed and, looking down at her, he went on, "I shall leave you now, Emily, and give you a day or so to think over my suggestion. I beg of you to comply with it, for one way or another your decision will decide our future life."

"What life, Paul? If I were to do as you ask, what future have I in your life? A stealthy night now and again? It's almost a month since I last saw you, and you tell me you have stayed twice in town during that time. Surely there weren't the comings and goings and calls upon you that could describe the life of a busy railway station?"

"Oh, Emily, please don't talk in that tone of voice; sarcasm doesn't suit you. There were reasons why I couldn't write, and I had no time to do so when I was in town. But I won't go into them, for in your present state of mind you would not believe me. Good-night, my dear. I am very sad for both of us at this moment."

She could hardly believe it. It was impossible. Surely this wasn't happening to her. She could hear Esther's voice resounding through her head, asking, "Will he stand by you, him being married?" And she had answered so firmly, "Oh yes. Yes." And Lena had said kindly, "Well, you won't be the first woman to be mistress to a gentleman; you'll be in company with one or two of our best customers, too; and they're accepted in society, seen at the races an' all, and one of them could be you wearing that yellow hat."

The yellow hat. Every now and again that hat seemed to pop up into her life. And now within her there was a child and the chances were that it might never have been there but for that hat. As she had thought before, it was the hat that had caught his eye.

She now turned onto her face and, gripping a

handful of pillow, it would seem that she was attempting to ram it down her throat, whereas she
was only using it as a gag to dull the wail that the
gush of tears had wrenched from her.

13

"You're a silly girl, Brigid. But don't cry, it'll be all right. The doctor'll be here soon. What on earth made you plunge that steaming kettle into cold water?"

"It had boiled itself dry, miss, an' . . . an' I did it in a rush so cook wouldn't see."

"Well, cook noticed." This came from cook herself; and addressing Emily, she added, "She's an idiot."

Emily made a warning motion to cook, then said to the girl, "Dry your eyes. You don't want to be howling when the doctor comes, do you?"

"Will . . . will I lose my job, miss, an' have to go back to . . . ?"

"No. No, of course not. Don't worry about that. Jenny there will help you until your hand is better. It won't take long."

Emily doubted her own words as she examined the badly scalded hand; then turning to cook, she said quietly, "Make her a cup of tea."

As Mrs. Mary Pollock turned somewhat reluctantly away to do her mistress's bidding, she muttered, "It's having two kitchens; I can't be in both at once. And only idiots to see to things when I'm away. I've told you before, miss, it should be one or t'other . . ." Her voice trailed off with the sound of steps coming down the basement stairs and a man's voice speaking.

"That'll be Doctor Smeaton," Emily said, but when the figure entered the kitchen she saw that it was his partner and her hand went automatically to her abdomen as if to conceal the bulge. And then there he was standing before her. She knew that he was taking in her condition, and for a moment she felt the urge to turn away, so that he should not see it.

Abruptly, he moved to the seated girl who was holding her scalded hand; then without a word he put his bag on the table, opened it, took out a jar of ointment and some dressing and spoke for the first time. "How did you manage to do this?" he asked.

When she told him, he nodded, saying, "Natural reaction. Yes, natural reaction. But you'll not do it again, will you?"

"No, doctor, no."

As he finished dressing the scald, he said, "Now, don't touch that. No matter what it feels like, don't take it off. Doctor Smeaton will be back tomorrow to see to it." Then, looking toward the grim-faced figure of the cook, he said, "I'd let her rest for the remainder of the day."

There was a reluctant mutter of "As you say, doctor," from cook.

He now lifted his bag from the table, nodded to

the girl and walked briskly up the room; and after a moment's hesitation Emily followed him.

In the hall she stood watching him getting into his overcoat and said quietly, "The weather is very raw today."

The look he gave her was definitely disdainful, and for a moment she wilted under it; then, drawing herself erect, she said, "You can think what you like, but it's my life."

"Yes. Yes, of course it is. If you wish to degrade yourself who am I, or anybody else, to try to stop you. Of course it's your life."

Again she was wilting and again her head drooped, but it drew no sympathetic, understanding reply from him, just, "I often have inquiries about you from my family; I'm sure they'll be interested to know of your condition. And by the way, I'm sure it'll interest you, too, to hear that I am to be married."

She was looking fully at him now, saying, "Yes, that is interesting news. To the Misses Braize, I suppose?"

"Well, hardly both of them. Miss Biddy will be doing me the honor."

"Miss Biddy's the younger one?"

"Yes, the younger one."

She could clearly visualize the doll-faced young woman, who still thought herself a young girl, and hear her giggling.

"She's a very sweet, kind and understanding person."

"Oh yes, I'm sure. Well, I hope you'll be very happy."

"That goes without saying. But thank you for your good wishes. Goodbye."

"Goodbye."

She stood with her back to the door thinking: he's taking that stupid little piece. Why? Why? And the answer was clear: Because she's the opposite to you, Emily, in every way.

Hearing the work room door being opened she moved from the door and Esther inquired, "Is that the doctor just gone?"

"Yes."

"Well, she wouldn't get much sympathy out of old Smeaton."

"It was Doctor Montane. Doctor Smeaton is away for the day."

"Oh! Oh!" And their glances held for a moment before Esther said, "If I were you I'd tell the authorities about that lad. He only comes now at dinner times. He must be working somewhere and it's in his break. But yesterday he had a woman with him, a big piece. And there she was again this mornin'."

The presence of that boy, as he stood gazing at the house, had puzzled her, too, for some weeks now. It wasn't that he came every day, and he didn't always stand on the opposite side of the road: only yesterday she had met up with him on the pavement outside here. And she had said to him, "What are you after? Why are you watching my house?" but he hadn't answered her; he had simply looked her up and down before turning and hurrying away.

She had known some time ago that she should have informed the authorities. Then, why hadn't she? She couldn't rightly say, except that one didn't voluntarily get involved with the police.

She turned now to Esther, saying, "I've just had a thought: he might be a distant relation of the Admiral's, you know, the man who lived here for years, and perhaps he was brought here to visit as a child."

"Oh no; that's farfetched, to my mind. Although he's decently put on, he's working somewhere, I'm sure of that, because it's the time he comes. And then there's the woman who's been with him. If she had been any relation to the Admiral, she would have made herself known."

"Perhaps she was a poor relation."

"She didn't look all that poor to me. She was pretty well put on, even if she looked flashy."

"Well, all right," Emily said, coming to a decision, "I'll go tomorrow to the station and explain things to the sergeant."

"PC Cooper is on the beat. Why don't you have a word with him?"

"No, he would likely just chase him and then we would never find out why he persists in standing there."

"Perhaps you're right. Anyway, I'm glad you're going to do something, because I find myself going to the window to see if he's arrived"—she started to laugh now—"and if he doesn't put in an appearance, I start to worry. Something might have happened to him . . . been knocked down by a horse, anything."

"Go on with you." Emily pushed her in the shoulder, then went into the sitting room. And this room in number 35 still remained the sitting room, although the rest of the house had been turned over to the business. For it was in this room that she received the special clients who . . . had just called in and wondered if Mrs. Ratcliffe had anything suitable for them in the way of a tea gown, or an evening dress, or perhaps a cloak, or yet again, something suitable for travelling.

For more than a month now she had been no longer able to camouflage her shape, and so she had left this part of the business entirely in the hands of Esther and Lena.

But her thoughts now were not dwelling on anything to do with business, but on the face that had shown such contempt of her. Her hands were gripped tightly on her knees and she found that she was rocking her body slightly. His presence had always affected her, for he was the most disturbing person, although never more than within the last few minutes. And he was going to marry that silly, stupid giggling girl. In a way, she could have understood him taking the elder one but not that simpering . . . Her mind would not supply her with any more adjectives, but what it said to her now was, why are you letting him disturb you like this? It doesn't matter whom he marries. And she answered it with, No; no, it doesn't; but he looked at me as if I were the lowest creature he had ever come across.

Calm yourself, don't get angry, it'll do you harm.

That was what Paul had said to her last night in the sitting room next door: "You are angry and, you know, anger in your condition can only do you harm." He no longer added, "If only you would do what I ask," for it was too late for that now anyway.

Yes, she had been angry with him, for he hadn't been near her for more than two weeks, and when he did visit he seemed to expect her to be in bed. But now that Alice knew all about the situation, she had told him he could call earlier and they could meet in the sitting room.

Strangely, it was his companionship that she needed now: she wanted him close, their hands joined as they talked, or rather, as he talked and she listened. He was very taken up with the coming election. He would talk incessantly about it, often becoming vehement about Parnell and Ireland. But then there were times when he would suddenly stop talking and hold her face between his hands and tell her how she had changed his life and his outlook, and how this house was like an oasis in a desert.

She had admitted to herself it was strange that, if Steve had been making the same statements, she would have questioned them, and vehemently in her turn, especially about conditions under which the factory workers were employed. But with Paul she just sat and listened, because his voice was different from all others, and he had a way of putting meaning into the simplest compliment. She loved the readily changing expressions of his face, the movements of his hands. She loved all of him. That was the trouble. At times, she would tell herself that she was besotted and that her feelings weren't natural, that one day she would wake up from this dream; yet, at the same time, she hoped she never would. Last night she almost had when she discovered that he had been in town for more than a week and had not looked in on her, even though he knew he could call at any time after six o'clock in the evening when, other than herself, the only people in the house were Alice and the cook; and often cook would go to her room quite early.

When it had inadvertently slipped out that twice during the week he had been to the theater, she had dared to say, "Some men, I understand, have been known to take their mistresses to the theater;" but on recognizing a momentary look of alarm on his face, she had come back swiftly, saying, "Oh, don't worry; I don't want to be known as that," which he had countered by saying, "I never think of you as my mistress."

"Then can you tell me what my position is?" she persisted, for it was her intention that he should clarify the situation. "The wife whom, unfortunately, I cannot acknowledge," he said.

"And never will be able to, I suppose," she had retorted. Then she had dared further by saying, "If your wife were to die, Paul, would you marry me?"

A momentary silence followed before he said, "Oh, Emily, how can I answer that? It is like wishing my wife dead. She is a very healthy woman . . ."

"I thought she had injured her back?"

"Oh yes . . . yes, that; but apart from that, Emily, don't you realize how much I love you? Yes; yes, if my wife were to die I would marry you. Of course. But why ask such questions now? Oh, I know; it is your condition. As you may remember, I told you in the beginning things would change, didn't I? The very carrying of a child changes the personality; at least, for a time. You had the option, my dear, but you were stubborn."

"Should I have a son or a daughter, will you recognize him or her?"

She had watched him shake his head as if in bewilderment before he said, "Recognize him . . . or her? There will be difficulties. You understand that?"

When she said, "I'm beginning to think, Paul, that I understand very little," it was then he had said, "You are angry," and had left her without another word.

The sound of the door-bell ringing broke into her thoughts, which meant another customer. She hoped it would be someone Alice or Esther didn't need to bring in here. But she was already looking toward the door when Alice came hurrying into the room, whispering, "It's a woman. She wants to see you. She doesn't want a hat. I think she's a foreigner, from her voice.''

Emily noted that Alice had classed the visitor as a woman, not a lady. ''What is her name?'' she asked.

''Well, I got the first part, Mrs. Maria, then it sounded like Dimarca. She's foreign, I'm sure.''

''I don't want to see anyone today, Alice. You'd better go and tell Esther to deal with her.''

''Oh, I did. I said I'd get the manageress to see her, but immediately she said, 'No. Your mistress, that's who I want.' That's what she said, and like that, sharpish.''

A feeling not unmixed with fear nagged at her, so much so that she hesitated while looking at Alice; and then, drawing in a deep breath, she said, ''Show her in.''

As the woman stepped into the room, Emily straightaway took her to be about forty. She was handsome in a florid way, for her face was full, her hair abundant, and hanging from under her hat in loops over her ears. It was black hair and seemed to match the woman's eyes; and not only that, her expression, too, appeared dark. She was big made with a high, full bosom and wide hips, and when she walked slowly toward Emily her skirt swung as if her body were rocking slightly.

She was within two arms' lengths of Emily when she stopped and, poking her head forward, gazed on Emily's waistline, and her words came startlingly deep and frightening, ''You are not full of consumption, are you? No! Your belly is full of his child. Isn't it?'' Her arm was thrust forward now, a be-ringed finger pointing at Emily's abdomen.

At this Emily demanded, ''Who are you? And how dare you come in here and accost me in this fashion!''

''Who am I? I will tell you who I am, Miss Sneaky Woman. I am his mistress, his legal mistress, recognized by his family. He is my husband in all but name and the father of my son and daughter. That is who I am. My son has been watching for weeks, looking for the poor, sick woman. His father supposedly visits a distant relation. That's what you are, a distant relation, disowned by the family, huh! huh! because you keep a hat shop. I believe, yes. I am a fool . . . I believe, but not my son.''

Emily felt she was going to faint or that something was going to happen to her: her eyes were blurred, she could hardly see the woman. She listened to her voice now, high, almost screeching. ''You think to take him? You never will. He is mine for eighteen years. He bring me from Italy. I could not speak a word of English then. I give him Benito. He love me, but he marry. His wife know I am his mistress. We have nice house; my son and daughter in position, in big office. He stray. Yes, he stray, like all men, but he always come back. I am everything he needs, always . . . until''—her hands began to flap the air—''until he come back from Nice. He is change. I think nothing, just that it is a man's humor. But my son, he think much, very much and he see him come in your door one day; and from then is the tale of the poor, ill member of the family. Dear Mother of God!'' She now threw her head back and pressed her hand on the top of her hat as if to keep it from flying off.

''Get out! Get out of my house!''

''Out of your house, you say, miss? No. I not go until you give me promise that you leave him alone. Do you hear?'' She took a quick step toward Emily. ''Do you hear me? Leave him alone!''

Emily's vision was quite clear as she thrust both her hands against the woman and almost overbalanced her. What followed was so quick that she could not attempt to save herself from the blows. She only knew that she screamed and tried to fight off the hands that were beating her face and body. And when she fell and the weight came on top of her she let out a piercing scream, and wasn't aware that there were others, too, screaming all about her.

She knew she was lying to the side now and that Alice was holding her head; but that there was a mêlée going on somewhere in the room. When her mouth filled with blood and she swallowed it she made an effort to pull herself upward. But she remembered nothing more after falling back into Alice's arms . . .

She came to gasping for breath. Someone was wiping her face with a cold cloth, and through her blood-bleared vision she saw the woman being dragged to her feet by two uniformed men. And one of them was saying, ''It's all right, girls. Leave go of her. It's all right. She'll behave." And then the other one, turning to look at Esther, who was making an attempt to put her hair up again, said, "We'll be back, ma'am. We'll be back for a statement."

"How are you, love?"

Emily blinked up into Lena's face. She wanted to say, "I'm dead, Lena, I'm dead."

"Oh, miss. Oh, miss." They were crowding round her now.

"Get yourselves out of the way. Let her have air. Let's get her to bed."

"Well, get her on the couch first. She'll never make the stairs."

She didn't know how many pairs of hands went beneath her, but she seemed to float to the couch, then sink into it.

"Will I get her a glass of sherry?"

"No." Esther's reply to Alice was unusually soft. "It's the worst thing you could give her. A cup of tea, lass, a cup of tea, because she's in shock."

Yes, she was in shock. They were whispering all around her. She was in shock. Her brain seemed to be swinging like a pendulum, repeating her thoughts: tick-tock, tick-tock.

"She had the strength of a bull."

"Just look at the sight of this end of the room."

"Eeh! Poor miss. Her face is in a mess. And her clothes torn off her."

"And that woman kept yelling, 'He's mine! I'm his mistress. I'm recognized.' "

"What a thing to say."

"Be quiet, the lot of you! Get yourselves away and tidied up. Never mind the room. That can be done later."

Emily closed her eyes. Someone said, "How are you feeling, lass?" She didn't answer. Another voice said, "Has she gone off again?" And the answer to this was, "I think so."

Then the whisper. "He must be a swine. Married, and that big fat hulk on the side, and then taking her. God! He wants lynching."

The pendulum was still swinging in her head. It was saying, If you will it strongly enough, you can die . . . If you will it strongly enough, you can die.

A far-away voice said now, "Did you send for the doctor?" And the answer was, "Yes. Yes, of course."

"Well, I wish he was here."

The clock was ticking again, crying loudly now, Dear God, bring Doctor Smeaton. Bring Doctor Smeaton. Bring Doctor Smeaton; she could stand no more from the other one. If she saw that look on his face again she would die. Surely she would die.

14

For four successive days Steve had come, and she hadn't spoken a word to him. But then she had hardly spoken a word to anyone, because she could scarcely move her lips.

First he had flashed a light into her eyes; then he had put cooling pads over them. He had put ointment on her bruised cheeks and over her mouth. He had forced her to swallow something that had put her to sleep for almost two days. He had wrapped a bandage round her bruised neck and put a splint along the broken first finger of her left hand. He had put a plaster over the torn skin on her shin bone where the skin had been ripped off on the side of the brass fender when she fell. And he had sounded her chest. He had not touched, or mentioned, her abdomen.

On the fourth day, as he was leaving the bedroom, he said to Esther, "I may not be able to get in until late tomorrow. Doctor Smeaton has to go into hospital; I want to see him settled, and so I'll be busy otherwise."

"Thank you, doctor," said Esther. "She'll be all right now, I think . . . won't she?"

"Well, the face is going to be rather painful for

some time, as is her leg and finger. But give her the drops every four hours; at least, for tomorrow, but we'll have to reduce them after that."

"Yes, doctor. Thank you, doctor. I hope you have time to stay for a cup of coffee. Alice will have it ready downstairs."

"Thank you. Goodbye."

"Goodbye, doctor."

Alice was waiting at the sitting room door. "Will you have time to take your cup of coffee?" she said.

"Yes. Yes, Alice. I'll make time this morning because I want a word with you."

"Oh, yes, doctor? Yes?"

She followed him into the room, closed the door, then went to the table and poured out the coffee and after she had handed it to him, where he was sitting on a chair to the side of the couch, he said, "Sit down a moment, Alice."

"Yes, doctor." Alice sat.

"Now"—he bent toward her, saying quietly, "you are the one, I think, who is closest to your mistress. I want you to tell me all you know about this affair."

"Oh, well, doctor." Alice bit on her lip before saying, "You mean from the very start or just what that woman said?"

Steve seemed to hesitate for a moment; then he said, "Yes. Yes, Alice, from the very start."

And so she told him all that had happened at the hotel; at least, as far as she knew. And she ended that part by saying, "He must have told her that he had nothing to do with his wife any more, because when the wife landed there the day before we left and they were arm in arm and as chummy as could be, she must have felt she had been hoodwinked, because she was vexed, real vexed. I knew that. So much so that I thought, that's the end of that. She must have realized that he had told her a tale. Anyway, she was very down when we came back and she had to put a face on things and pretend she'd had a marvelous time. Well, I think she had an' all, until she found him out. And then''—she paused now and shook her head—''she was getting over it, really right over it. I knew that on the day she went with you into the country to see your people. But it should happen it was on that very day he called, and he came back the next afternoon an' all. And I know for a fact that he plagued her after that. It was all done underhand.''

"What do you mean, underhand?"

"Well, doctor, it had to be, hadn't it? She didn't want all of them here to know what was going on, so he used to come in the back way. I wasn't supposed to know, either, but me bed's just above the back door and so I twigged. And then, well, you know as well as I do what happens. I say that''—she laughed now—''I'm not supposed to know anything about it, I'm too young. But, you see, I was brought up by a foster-mother who was as loose as a packet of Epsom Salts. Oh, I mean . . . well—'' She again bit on her lip, bowed her head, and Steve said, "I get your meaning, Alice," and smiled at her.

"Well, doctor"—Alice's voice was full of concern—"she was in a very bad way when she found out. Oh my! She was so sick, so ill morning after morning, and she had nobody to talk to. In fact, she couldn't say it, she couldn't admit it. It was me that had to say to her, it was all right, I knew, and about him. And it seemed to relieve her a little bit. But she was so bad. And then he didn't come for weeks. He was at his shooting place in Scotland, and when he did come I knew about it. Oh, it was a very short visit, I can tell you. He wasn't for her having it. She didn't tell me, but . . . well"—she sniffed and hunched her shoulders—"I've got a good pair of lugs on me, doctor. He went on alarmingly. She did an' all. And she said it was all she had in life to look forward to and no matter what he said she was going to go through with it. And I seem to think that things haven't been the same since. Then, all this time— I didn't know about it at first—there's a young fella been standing watching the house."

"Watching the house?"

"Yes. Yes, doctor, watching the house. He would stand the other side of the road on the pavement, mostly at dinner times, Esther said. So that meant he was in some business or other and came there at dinner time. Then Lena and her saw a woman join him. That was the day before this happened, and it was me who let her in. She was a foreigner, like in the way she spoke. She spoke English of course, but in a funny way."

"What was her name?"

"Well, it sounded like Maria Dimarca. But that mightn't have been her last name. And then, when she was in, all hell was let loose. I heard her start straightaway and I stayed outside the door. From what I could gather she said she was his mistress and had been for years. He brought her over from Italy. She had a grown-up son—that was the lad who used to stand outside—and a daughter an' all. She kept saying that she was recognized as his mistress by his family, and from what I could gather he must have told her that miss was a relation not recognized by his family because she kept a hat shop, and that she was consumptive and ill. Then I heard miss order her out of the house. And after that, well, all hell broke loose. And I knew they were fighting and I screamed and I ran for the lasses in the workshop. We all went in and pulled her off miss. She was a great big woman and as strong as a bull. And when the constables came she kept telling them she was his mistress and recognized by his family. Well, she's in the clink now and that's where she'll stay until the case comes up. She could have killed miss; she meant to. Mind, I had me suspicions about him once or twice. When he spoke to you he was so polished, so nice, you couldn't believe he would do anything bad. But they are the worst ones, aren't they, the polished ones?"

Steve stared at her for a moment. He did not answer her question, but what he said was, "I'm glad she's got a good friend in you, Alice."

"Oh, it runs both sides, doctor. She's been a good friend to me. She gave me a position I never thought I would get. You see, I was just in the kitchen for years. I started with Mrs. Arkwright. She was a tough one, too, an' what with her and the cook I was run off me feet. But me life changed completely when the miss took me in hand. She's got me for life or as long as she wants me."

He rose to his feet saying, "Oh, you'll meet someone soon, Alice. You're a pretty girl, you know."

"Oh, not me, doctor. I've seen too much of it, both sides of it. An' you know, doctor, it makes you older than you look. And I'm a lot older than I look."

They both laughed gently together now. Then she pointed to the coffee, saying, "Oh, look at that, doctor, it's clay cold."

"Don't worry about that. Hot or cold, it makes no difference to me. I'll drink it."

And when he had drained the cup he placed it on the table again, then stood looking down into it as he said, "She's going to need some gentle handling from now on, Alice. She'll be very low in spirits. You'll have to do everything to cheer her up. But besides that you'll have to be patient with her, because I think for the time being she's lost the string of life."

Alice pondered on this for a moment before she said, "Yes, you could be right, doctor." Then she grinned at him as she added, "A good argument with you again would likely do her a lot of good."

He didn't smile at her remark and his voice was flat as he answered, "Those days are past, Alice . . . unfortunately."

She preceded him to the door, opened it, then in a voice as flat as his had been, she said, "Good-night, doctor."

"Good-night, Alice."

Emily had been in bed for a week, when at eleven o'clock on this particular day Alice entered the room. Esther was standing by the bed with a comb in her hand and she was saying to Emily, "I'll see to your hair. Just you sit still. Just you sit still;" then she turned to Alice and inquired, "What is it?"

Alice looked from her to Emily and hesitated before she said, "There's a lady downstairs asking if she can see you."

It was Esther who said, "Who is it?"

Again they exchanged glances before Alice answered, "She's Mrs. Anderson Steerman."

When Emily dropped back on her pillows and closed her eyes but said nothing, Esther, turning to Alice, whispered, "Go down and tell her that your mistress is unwell and isn't seeing anybody. Make it plain."

Alice meekly nodded and hurried out of the room, and Esther, turning to Emily again, spoke softly, saying, "Now, don't distress yourself. But I must say, she's got a nerve . . . Now, forget about it, her and everything else. It's all over."

The pendulum had stopped swinging in her head, but nevertheless, her mind repeated, it's all over. It's all over . . . But it wasn't all over. For her, it had hardly begun: she had some two months to go; and what then? Did she still want the child? Yes, and no. Candidly, she admitted to herself, she didn't know what she wanted, for she couldn't, as yet, believe that she had been so easily deceived. That anyone could lie so convincingly when you would have sworn your life away on their integrity. The question was, how many others had he beguiled before her while still supporting his mistress? That big, fierce, terrible woman, whose face haunted her sleep and caused her to cry out as she felt her nails tearing at her face.

She turned toward Esther, saying, "May I have a pill, Esther, please?"

"Oh now, love; doctor's cut down on them. He told you just one in the morning and one at night."

"Please, Esther; I . . . I feel awful."

"Oh well, I suppose you were on three to start with." She now went to the side table and, taking a white pill from a cardboard box, she poured out a glass of water and returned to the bed, saying, "That's all you needed this morning, another upset. When the doctor comes I'll tell him and he'll deal with her."

"Oh, no, no; please don't mention it."

"All right, all right, don't get yourself agitated. There now, lie back and you'll go to sleep again soon." . . . Esther didn't tell Steve about the visitor. But later in the day he had hardly entered the house before Alice informed him. However, his only response was: "Mrs. Anderson Steerman. Well! Well! We *are* going up in the world, Alice."

Two days later Mrs. Steerman called again, only once more to be refused a meeting with Mrs. Ratcliffe. And the following day, on his visit and on hearing of it, Steve brought up the subject.

Emily was seated in a full-length basket-chair near the fire, and after examining her finger and her leg he commented, "They're doing nicely," but then by-passed making any reference to the discoloration of her face in order to say, "When Mrs. Anderson Steerman calls again, I should see her, if I were you."

"What! No."

"I think it would be wise."

"I . . . I can't. Don't ask me to, please."

"Would it help if I were present at the meeting?"

She turned her head slowly toward him and looked at him for some seconds as if thinking. Then she said, "Why do you think she wants to see me?"

He turned from her now and walked toward the table behind her chair and, picking up the box of pills, he gave it a little shake, then replaced it before he said, "She likely wants you to save his public face by dropping the charge against that woman. From what I gather, he's into politics; at least, he's aiming for it, and although his father's shoulders might carry him some way toward his ambition, it's the people's votes that count in the end. That's how I see it. I may be wrong, but as I said, I think you should see her and in the presence of a witness."

Some moments passed before she said quietly, "You may not be here when she calls."

"That could be arranged. I could write to their town house and give her a time that would suit me."

She wanted to ask, why are you doing this? Why are you taking all this trouble on my behalf? It wasn't, she felt, that he had any affectionate feelings left toward her; he was going to be married, and a man like him wouldn't just marry out of pique; he would have to feel there was some foundation for future happiness. So why was he going to all this trouble? She could only imagine it was professionalism. He would likely do the same for any one of his patients similarly placed.

She raised her head. She hadn't been aware that he was standing looking at her.

"Esther tells me you're not eating," he said, "apart from bits and pieces. That's no good. You must eat proper meals. Well, I'll be off now. I may not be in tomorrow; I have to visit the hospital again to see how Doctor Smeaton is surviving, and I must also tackle his patients. I've put in for a locum and the sooner one appears on the scene the better I'll like it. Well, take care. Don't stay up too long. Goodbye."

"Goodbye."

The fire was blazing merrily, the room was full of late autumn sunshine; everything in it looked warm and colorful. It was only herself who was cold and drab. Never before in her life had she needed to apply that word to herself, but now she knew she *was* drab, her thoughts, her body, her face . . . oh yes, her face. The swelling was reduced from around her eyes but the discoloration was still there and her lower lip was still almost twice its normal size. Then there were those deep scratches on her right cheek. She hadn't asked him if the scars would leave a mark; it didn't seem to matter what she looked like. There was only one thing she was certain of: never in her life again would she trust anyone. Never! No matter who it was. Never! The gullible girl was dead. The divorce should have killed her off years ago, but it hadn't. Her mind had to be attacked by exposure to the truth and her body by nails and fists and feet before the woman emerged.

And she was drab and would remain so.

15

It was her first trip downstairs. She was seated in the big armchair, dressed in a dove-colored loose gown. Her hair was swept up from both sides of her face into a pile on the back of her head and its soft waves were a stark contrast to her face, one side of which showed three long red weals, the other from her brow down to her lower jaw, which held a faint, patchy purple hue. The hand with the bandaged finger was lying on the arm of the chair, while the other, doubled into a fist, was resting on the mound of her abdomen.

When Alice, opening the door, announced Mrs. Anderson Steerman, the woman walked slowly up the room toward Steve, and he, bowing slightly to her, said, "Good afternoon. Please be seated." And he pointed to a chair almost three yards away from where Emily was seated. And the woman, after looking from him to Emily, said, "Thank you," then sat down.

Steve took up a position to the side of the fireplace and eyed the visitor. He could not help but be surprised at her appearance. He had expected a very tall, stately, fashionable woman. This one was definitely dressed fashionably, but she was small, petite. She had dark hair, and dark eyes. She was beautiful, in a way, and he could imagine that she was vivacious. She was returning his look now and saying, "I would like, sir, to speak to Mrs. Ratcliffe privately, if you don't mind."

"I'm sorry I can't grant your wish, madam. I am Mrs. Ratcliffe's doctor and also her confidant. She has been through a very harrowing time and it is only because you have persisted in calling on her that she's seeing you now, for she is far from well, which I hardly need to point out to you, madam, do I?"

"I . . . I'm very sorry. I'm very sorry to be intruding on you at this time, Mrs. Ratcliffe." Mrs. Steerman was now looking straight at Emily. "But it is imperative that I speak to you. First of all, though, let me express my sincere regrets that . . . through my husband's duplicity you have experienced such a dreadful ordeal."

She stopped speaking and now seemed to be waiting for Emily to make some response. But when Emily simply stared at her, Steve said, "May I ask why you feel it so imperative that you talk with my patient if it is just to express your sympathy?"

"Oh, I wish it were just that, sir. Oh yes, I wish it were. But no; I am here to beg her clemency, not only for my husband's sake, but for that of my father-in-law and my children and the stigma that will touch them and our house should that woman appear in court. And so"—she was again looking fully at Emily—"I appeal to you, Mrs. Ratcliffe, to

. . . to drop the case against her. She has so far kept her tongue quiet, but once she is in she will talk, or her lawyer will talk for her, and . . . and my father-in-law wouldn't be able to stand the disgrace. He is not a well man."

When again Emily did not speak, Steve, moving toward the chair, sat down and said quietly, "As I understand it, your husband is standing for Parliament, and you are anxious to conceal the fact that he has kept a mistress for the past eighteen or twenty years and has a son and daughter by her; that your family has approved of this, but that unfortunately they have not been able to control her, so that when she finds him out in yet another deception she attacks my patient, who finds herself in the unenviable position of carrying his child, after having been deceived into thinking that his marriage to you had long been over in all but name."

Of a sudden he felt sorry for the woman who was now sitting with her head bowed, her hands joined tightly on her lap. However, he could not relent, and so he waited; and presently, she lifted her head and, looking at Steve, said in a very low voice, "Everything you say, sir, is true. My husband is a charming man. He is also a very weak man, an inveterate liar and a wastrel. He has never been able to achieve anything in his life, except, perhaps, to enchant women. His father has carried him, as it were, on his shoulders. He has got him out of scrapes. He has paid his debts. He has provided for his mistress and her brood. I, myself, knew he had a mistress before I married him, but at the time he convinced me that was all over. I was actually persuaded to go on believing him up to the birth of my third child. It was then I discovered that she had two children by him. I could, I suppose, have divorced him; but two things prevented me. First, I did not want to bring any more trouble into his father's life—I am very fond of his father. Secondly, I could not throw off the love that I had for him. Naturally it is not what it was and has become threaded with pity, because, seemingly, he can't help himself where women are concerned. And then we were all strangely happy when, a year ago, he seemed to become interested in politics. He also had a bad fall from his horse and was ill for a time, and it appeared he was having a change of heart, so much so that I felt no trepidation of what was to come when he spoke of recuperating in the quiet little hotel in France. It was a place we had often visited and was usually frequented only by elderly people or semi-invalids. But then, Mrs. Ratcliffe, you happened to be there and you were neither elderly nor infirm. A close friend of the family, Mrs. DeWhit, knew all about him and his weaknesses. She saw what was happening and she suggested that there might be more trouble in the offing. So, once again, I put on a show of family unity in order to scare off the young and unsuspecting victim. But, in your case, it didn't work; and it was unfortunate that Maria Dimarca's son should see him visiting your house. He is, I understand, a very highly strung boy and has been known to follow my husband around when he is in town. He always wants to claim his attention, yet is sensible enough, I suppose, through his mother, not to go too far and claim relationship. She knows, or at least she fears, their allowance would be cut off, together with the post my father-in-law obtained for the boy, because he's really not equipped for it."

Her head drooped again and she heaved a sigh as if she were tired. And when she spoke now she did not look up, and her refined voice became almost a mutter as she said, "I beg of you, Mrs. Ratcliffe, not to press charges against this woman. I know he is not worth begging for, and I feel humiliated in having to do so, but he is of an old-established family and the newspapers will have a field day. He will be ostracized from society. Of course, there will always be a section that will accept him, but those that matter will close their doors to him . . . One mistress, yes, but not two . . . or more. And further, when that woman opens her mouth, and in court she would, she will even brag on how she has attacked you. Your name, too, would be blazoned . . ." She gestured with both hands to imply the resulting effect on Emily and the business; and this did bring a reply from Emily:

"Having taken a case up against her, I would expect to appear in court, and for my name and perhaps character to be blazoned abroad," she said. And this brought a small sigh and acknowledgment from the small figure in the chair.

"Yes. Yes, of course," she said; "I am not thinking straight. My mind has been in a turmoil for some time. I will go now, I can do no more."

When she went to pull herself up from the chair Steve went quickly forward and put his hand on her elbow. As he did so, he said, "We will leave the matter open until tomorrow. I shall let you know Mrs. Ratcliffe's decision then."

Irene Steerman looked at him and said quietly, "Thank you very much, sir. I . . . I shall be at home all day." She now turned toward Emily and their eyes met. Her voice still low, she said, "Believe me, I am so sorry you have had to suffer in so many ways on his account: he is not worthy of your affection, or of my love."

She added no word of goodbye but turned and walked slowly up the room with Steve by her side.

In the hall he helped her into her fur cloak and handed her her gloves and handbag that had been lying on the chair; then, bending toward her, he said very quietly, "I will see what I can do, madam."

"Thank you. Thank you, doctor. Good-day."

"Good-day, madam."

He opened the door and she went out and into the carriage that was waiting for her.

After he had closed the door he walked slowly back into the sitting room, and there, his manner quite offhand, he said, "She's right, you know. If you do go through with it, this house will be stormed. And it won't finish there. When your child is born they'll resurrect the case. Anyway, what do you intend to do? It's up to you."

"What should I do?" Her voice was very small.

He did not answer immediately, but went and stood in front of the fire, looking down into it the while the fingers of one hand beat a tattoo on the ridge of the wooden mantelpiece, then said: "I'd let the matter drop, not only for your own sake but for that poor creature who has just gone out. And I can call her a poor creature: she is rich, she is well known in society and from an honored house, and she is so unhappy it was painful to look at her; in her case she's got to hide it all behind a façade. Do you know," he looked up now, "there are families living on the waterfront. They cannot sleep for the rats at night, and what they eat is the rotten food thrown out from hotels or butchers' shops. Many of them die young, especially the children, and the women are old at thirty. Yet, given the opportunity and the facts, I doubt if one of them would change places with Mrs. Anderson Steerman, this day. Anyway," his voice had risen a couple of tones, "I'll leave it to you. Sleep on it."

"No. I asked your advice and you've given it to me, as usual, in the form of a parable."

He smiled, saying, "I don't speak in parables. I never use parables. That bit about the waterfront is true, every word of it. Anyway, does it mean that I can tell her that you are going to drop the case?"

"Yes, I suppose so. But . . . but how do I go about dropping it?"

"Oh, just get in touch with your solicitor and he'll get in touch with hers and that'll be that. If you don't want to press charges, they can't do anything about it. But now I must be away; I've got so much to do. And tomorrow I'm slipping home. It's nearly a fortnight since I had a breath of fresh air."

"When . . . when are you going to be married?"

He half-turned from her before saying, "Oh, it'll be Easter. Yes. Yes, Easter. But first they'll be getting the house ready for Christmas. They all go mad at Christmas; they land on it like locusts. Yes, I've told you this, haven't I? I try to get a couple of days there, either at Christmas or the New Year. But I don't know what it will be like this year with Smeaton still convalescing. Anyway, he's retiring shortly."

"What will happen then? Will you take over the practice?"

"I don't know. It's a toss-up whether I stay there or go back into the country. At home they're all pulling strings to get me back. Perhaps under coming circumstances it might be the thing to do. But that's in the future; I must be off now. Take care. You should sleep tonight, knowing that you haven't got that business to face up to. Don't stay down here too long; I'd get up to bed as soon as possible. And tell Alice that I'm going now. Good-bye."

"Goodbye."

He was turning away when she said, "And thank you," and he looked back at her for a moment, but made no response. Then she was left alone. Her head drooped onto her chest and slowly she began to cry.

She had written a letter to her solicitor stating that she wished withdraw the charge against Mrs. Maria Dimarca and had sent it by hand to his office in the City. Then, although it was early, she had gone upstairs.

It was while Alice was helping her undress that she suddenly put a hand to her side and gritted her teeth, and this brought from Alice, "Have you got a pain, miss?"

"Just . . . just a spasm."

"Is . . . is it the first time you've had it?"

Emily did not answer for a moment; then she said, "No, not the first time. It's a sort of cramp I get."

Some time later, when in bed, she again experienced the cramp, and Alice made her way quickly through the communicating door, upstairs and into Esther's department. There, taking her aside, she said, "She's got a funny pain and she must have been having it for some time. She looks awful. I think you should come and have a word with her. . . ."

Standing by the bed and making a great play of straightening the eiderdown, Esther said, "I hear you've got a bit of pain, love;" and she was more than disturbed when Emily, looking at her, said, "I . . . I feel ill, Esther. I think something's happened inside."

"Oh, no, no. Since when? I mean, when did the pain start?"

"It's been niggling for a day or two."

"A day or two? My God! Why couldn't you say, girl? Do you feel any movement?"

"No, just a pain."

Esther now turned and said to Alice, "Why couldn't this have happened a while back when he was here? You'd better get your things on and go and fetch him. Wrap up, it's freezing, and take a cab."

The fact that there was no protest from the bed further disturbed them. And after exchanging a knowing glance Alice hurried from the room; and Esther, turning to the bed again, took hold of Emily's hand, saying, "It's going to be all right. He'll see to you when he comes. It's going to be all right," while her mind was saying, best possible thing that could happen if she gets rid of it now . . .

It was more than an hour later when Steve arrived, saying to Lena, "I couldn't get here any earlier; I had a surgery-ful. I've left half of them. What's the trouble?"

"I'm not rightly sure, but Esther thinks she's losing it."

"Losing the baby?"

"Yes, doctor; that's what she thinks."

When he stood by the bed he took Emily's hand

to feel her pulse. Then he said, "Not feeling too good?"

"No. I'm not feeling too good."

"Why didn't you say when I was here earlier?"

There was a pause before she answered, "There was enough being said then, don't you think? without me adding to it."

"I'll have to examine you."

When she made no reply he turned to Esther, saying, "I'd like some hot water and towels."

He got the hot water and towels, and when a little later he pulled the bedclothes over her again he looked down on her, saying, "You're going to lose the baby, but I think you know that," and turning to Esther he said very quietly, "I'm going to need help with this."

"You mean you want a nurse, doctor? Well, there's one in Carlton Road, she's a mid . . ."

"No. I think I'm going to need the help of another doctor. The baby is dead and, as far as I can determine, it is misplaced."

"Oh!"

"I'll be gone for perhaps half an hour or more. It all depends if my doctor friend is still in his surgery. However, I'll be back as soon as possible. And if I can't get help I'm afraid she'll have to go to hospital."

It was almost eight o'clock when he returned with his associate, who appeared to be a middle-aged man with a kindly manner. And he talked to Emily as if she were a little girl whom he was about to entice with a sweet before giving her the medicine.

Less than an hour later they had taken the dead child from her womb, and fortunately she had known nothing about it.

16

They had all rallied around her. Although she was back on her feet and was even doing a little work next door, there remained about her an air of lassitude that was causing them all some concern. As the girls in the workroom expressed it, they could never see her really getting back to her old self. At the same time, they would reason, well, you couldn't expect her to, could you? After all she had gone through: being used by that no-good, so-called gentleman, then being battered almost to death by his mistress; and on top of that, losing the child. And she had wanted it, too, hadn't she? So after all, her quiet demeanor was to be understood.

Although they had had Christmas Day and Boxing Day off, they all, without exception, had looked in on her on Christmas Day and brought her a little gift. Even the doctor had made time to pop in. But Esther hadn't seen him, and so had inquired of Alice, "Did he bring miss a present?" And Alice had to admit, not to her knowledge.

"No flowers or anything?"

"No. No flowers. . . ."

The staff worked till late on New Year's Eve in

order to have New Year's Day off. In the ordinary way of things she would have been left with only Alice and the cook; so she couldn't help but be pleased when, around half-past eleven, both Esther and Lena appeared at the front door. The fact that they hadn't left the shop till well after seven, but had still arranged between themselves to come back in order to bring in the New Year with her, touched Emily deeply.

She held out her hands to them both as they came laughing into the sitting room, and all she could say in greeting was, "What's brought you two back? You must be frozen."

"Of course we are frozen," said Lena; "and it's starting to snow. But it won't hit the pavements because you can hardly get through the streets for people, and the square's already thick with them. As usual, some of them'll stay there dancing till two in the morning. Mad as hatters."

Alice, now smiling widely, went up to Esther, saying, "May I divest you of your coat, madam?"

"Not before I divest you of one of your ears, miss."

They were all laughing now as Emily said, "You'll have to fetch more glasses, Alice."

"And a kettle of boiling water," chipped in Lena. "I want my whiskey hot."

"But if your breath's anything to go by, madam, you've already had it hot."

"None of your business, miss. Get goin'."

When Alice scampered from the room and the three of them were seated on the couch before the fire, Emily in the middle, Esther looked at her and said, "You've changed your dress. I've always liked you in that plum velvet. It does something for you, shows up your skin."

Automatically, Emily's hand went to her cheek and at this Lena said, "Oh, there's hardly a vestige left. You wouldn't notice them if you didn't point them out. Another few weeks and they'll be gone. He said so, the doctor. Has he been in?"

Emily turned and looked at Lena, saying, "Doctor? No. No. Anyway, I don't need the doctor now; I've had all the doctor's attention I want for the rest of my life."

"Oh, well, all I can say, Emily, is that you were very lucky to have him at the time you needed him most."

"You said last week he was going to be married in the spring. What's she like?" asked Esther.

"Young, girlish, very pretty."

At this Esther said, "I couldn't imagine him marrying a type like that . . . well, as you describe her."

And Emily thought, nor could I. She had been a fool. Oh, such a fool. The more she dissected herself now, the more she despised her stupidity, her ignorance of human character. She, who was supposed to have a head on her shoulders . . . yes, for hats, and that was about all. She'd had to tell them about his forthcoming marriage a few days before, when Esther had remarked on the fact that not many doctors would be as attentive as he had been to a patient, but that then perhaps he saw her as a special patient. Yes, he had, but that seemed a long, long time ago now. It seemed like something that had taken place in another lifetime. Yet it was only a matter of months. But in that time she had been born to love, and died of love, for she was dead inside. And the knowledge of her escapade, for that's what it had been, had killed the love of a man who had broken down her defenses to the point where she recognized that pride alone was stifling the affection that was growing in her for him . . .

"Here she comes!" Lena was crying now, "spilling the kettle. Hold it straight, can't you?"

"I haven't got four pairs of hands, an' if you were any use you would have come and helped me."

Lena now clicked her tongue as she said to Emily, "I'm not puttin' up with her cheek, and anyway, why can't you engage a proper butler. Girls are so slap-dash."

"D'you want this hot whiskey in your lap or down your gullet?" Alice was now pouring the hot water into the glasses that were well laced with whiskey. "And who wants sugar in it? Do you want sugar, miss?"

"No. No, Alice. And look, I don't want all that whiskey, either. And shouldn't we keep it until twelve o'clock strikes?"

"There's ten minutes to go," put in Esther now, "and I might be dead by then. My stomach's going into collywobbles; give me the glass here."

A few minutes later they were all holding their steaming glasses up to each other.

"A Happy New Year."

"A Happy New Year."

"A Happy New Year, when it comes."

"Sit down, Alice!"

"Are you going to cut the cake, miss?"

"Oh, leave that till later."

Lena, looking toward the table, said, "There's enough there to feed a regiment. By the way, where's cook? Isn't she coming up?"

Alice shook her head, saying, "She had a crying bout; she's gone to bed."

"Oh." Esther pulled a face now as she said, "Another one of them? Well, that means she's got a little load on. The funny thing about it is, she's not supposed to drink. She denies it. But she throws it back on the quiet . . . has done for years. Some people are funny, the things they think they can hide."

"Do you think she'll go to sleep?"

Alice, grinning now, said, "Well, miss, I don't think she'll hear the bells or the hooters. And neither will we if we sit muffled in here. Come on, let's go to the door, but we'd better wrap up 'cos the air would take the nose off your face. But thank God it isn't fog. Oh, how I hate that fog."

Esther shuddered, as did Emily.

Muffled up in their coats, and with scarves round their heads, they opened the front door and heard the first siren sounding from a boat on the river. Almost immediately, it was joined by hooters and a ringing of bells, until the cold air seemed to become dense and weighed down by the volume of the sound. A cab passed up the street and someone shouted from it, "A Happy New Year," and they all called back, "A Happy New Year." Then as the sounds gradually died away, other sounds took their place as door-knockers were banged and first-footers entered the houses amid distant cries of "Happy New Year! Happy New Year!"

They stepped back into the hall now and Alice closed the door, and rather soberly they made their way to the sitting room again, where Alice handed round the sandwiches and the sausage rolls, and lastly the cake. And not until they had all had a glass of port did the conversation again become threaded with laughter. And the threads turned to uproarious laughter when Esther, exhibiting a hitherto unknown talent, began mimicking the walk, manner, and accent of some of their well-known customers, especially those of Mrs. Glenda Brompton and Lady Wearmore, two of the regulars, but the two least liked among their clients.

It could have been at the height of the laughter that there came the sound of the front door-knocker being banged twice, and they all looked at each other as Alice said brightly, "It'll be your first-foot, miss."

"Yes. Well, let's make sure, Alice, that he's a welcome one. I'll go to the door with you," said Esther.

When Alice opened the door, both she and Esther exclaimed together, "Oh! Hello, doctor. A Happy New Year."

"A Happy New Year to you, too. Are you having a party? I've knocked three times. I had to bang the knocker at last."

"Oh, well, doctor"—Alice was laughing now—"Esther here was doing a turn. And she was very funny. But there's only miss and Lena here."

He had taken off his hat and overcoat and was now loosening his tie, as he said, "Just four of you, and all that racket?"

"You are our first-foot, doctor, and a dark man, so you're bound to bring luck."

He was entering the room as he said to Esther, "Well, that's why I came, especially to bring you luck."

He was walking up the room toward Emily, who was now standing, and it was Lena who called to him, "A Happy New Year to you, too, doctor," and he replied, "A Happy New Year to you, Lena." But not until he had reached Emily did she say quietly, "A Happy New Year. How nice to see you."

She did not know why she had added that. It had just been a thought in her mind that had slipped out.

He now handed her a narrow bag with a corked head protruding from it, and he said, "I brought gin. I understand women prefer gin."

"Oh yes; I like gin, doctor." And Lena was nodding toward him when Esther put in, "Like it or

not, you're not having any more tonight. The mixture of whiskey and port is enough. And anyway,
we've got to get home, and you're shaky on your
legs already.''

"I'm not. Fancy saying that, Esther. I'm not
shaky on me legs.''

"Well, you will be if you have any gin . . . Look
at the time! Almost one.''

"Oh now, don't let me break up the party, else
I'll be sorry I came. It's New Year's Day.''

"She's right, doctor. We were just about to be
on our way, in any case. But she's not right about
the gin. Anyway, I'll have my drop tomorrow, Emily. Will you keep it for me?''

"Yes. Yes, I'll keep it for you, Lena.''

She did not press them to stay; and after they
had said goodbye to the doctor and again wished
him "A Happy New Year," she followed them
from the room.

In the hall she thanked them quietly, saying, "It
was so good of you to come. I . . . I don't know
what I would have done tonight if I had been left
on my own.''

Their mumbling replies were to the effect that
there was no need to thank them, as they had
intended to come round in any case. And then
with an unusual show of outward affection they
both kissed her.

After closing the door on them she stood looking toward the sitting room. Then as she walked
slowly toward it Alice came out bearing a tray on

which were the used glasses, and she said, "I'll
. . . I'll make a cup of coffee, shall I?"

"Yes, that would be nice, Alice."

"And . . . and when I'm down there I'll slip
through and see how cook's faring. If she's still
asleep I'll leave her, but if she isn't, I'll sit with her
a bit because she always gets the hump at holiday times, especially Christmas and New Year."

"All right, Alice, all right. You do that."

As she entered the room to see him standing
alone, she thought to herself, it's a pity they didn't
realize that their maneuvers could come to nothing.

"Would you like a drink?" He was now pointing
to the bottle of gin that she had placed on a side
table.

"No, thank you. That would be mixing them, as
Esther said. But you have one, by all means, or
would you like a whiskey?"

"Yes, I would like a whiskey, but I'm not going to
have one. Thanks all the same. I've had my share
for tonight. Doctor Smeaton had some friends in
and they were helping him to empty a number of
bottles. So I thought one of us had better keep
our sea-legs intact, just in case we were needed.
And New Year's morning is often a busy time with
split heads, you know."

"It was good of you to look in."

"Oh." His manner was offhand now. "Oh, I go
round visiting friends. Anyway, I was glad to hear
you were having a merry time. You've got a really
good staff, you know. They're very thoughtful for

you. And it's rather unusual, I mean, a staff's regard for the boss. It's generally us and them up top."

"Yes, I'm very fortunate." She could have added, in some ways.

She was sitting on the couch now and he in a chair to the side of it, and he turned his head and looked about him for a moment, then presently remarked, "This is such a colorful, comfortable room. I haven't been in it often at nights when the lamps are lit. They add to its charm. The only other room comparable with it is our drawing room at home."

She said now, "Did you manage to spend any time at Christmas with your people?"

"Yes, most of Boxing Day. But, as usual, it was like bedlam; the party was still going on, so to speak. They were all there, Matthew, Vera, the twins, and James and Flora, and Cissie's three, and of course Harry and Kate managed to get down for the holidays. Oh, they were all there. And of course others from round about dropping in. I wish I had been there on Christmas Eve when Aunt Phoebe told one of the neighbors, a rather stuffy individual, exactly what she thought of him, and in no small voice. Oh dear me!" He laughed as he so easily envisaged the situation. "The man is a farmer of the kind who owns farms but doesn't work on them himself. He has a manager, as he calls him, and in this case the manager, on the orders of his master, had dismissed one of the hands, an oldish man, because he had been found helping himself to vegetables or some such. And, of course, being dismissed meant he was put out of his cottage. My father and mother had apparently discussed this between themselves, saying how bad it was, without having the nerve to tell the man what they thought. That was left to Aunt Phoebe. And Vera, that's my eldest sister, you met her, she said it was as good as any play she had ever seen, especially when Aunt Phoebe said that she was only expressing the thoughts of all the village and the neighborhood, and if he didn't give old Roland his cottage back, there would be a curse put on him.'' Now he was laughing loudly as he ended, ''Imagine being confronted by Aunt Phoebe uttering a curse. Vera said the man literally blanched and that my father had to ply him with a very tall whiskey. But that wasn't the end of it. At breakfast the next morning, that was before I arrived, Aunt Phoebe had upbraided the lot of them for not abetting her. You know what it's like on a Boxing Day morning, with children still excited and running up and down stairs, and the elders with splitting heads. And I made matters worse when I arrived solid and sober and with a clear head and laughed until I cried as it was related to me by Vera, for she can mime Aunt Phoebe to a tee.''

She was sitting looking at him: his face was still animated from the telling, his whole manner relaxed. And during the telling she had been back again in that house on that long Sunday, and so had pictured the scene clearly, and there swept over her a feeling of such poignant nostalgia that no amount of willpower could stop the tears welling up in her eyes.

He was looking toward the fire now as he said, "They'll be bringing the New Year in with a vengeance at this moment. The village won't sleep tonight or this morning. They'll be in and out of each other's houses, and when in ours they'll join in the dance. The place will be packed. As far back as I can remember they have always danced on New Year's morning. I think it's the Scottish strain in my father, because he certainly lets himself go on New Year's Day. The word circumspect is forgotten. And in between times, when my mother is almost run off her feet ordering, arranging, and welcoming this one in, and goodbyeing to that one going out, he'll whirl her round the room. Oh, it used to be a grand do, all New Year's Day."

He turned to her now and exclaimed in amazement, "Oh, my dear, what is it? Oh, I'm sorry—it's my chattering. Don't cry! Please! What have I said?"

She was rubbing her eyes briskly as she muttered, "Nothing, nothing; it was all so vivid and I . . . . I recalled that particular Sunday, and yours was such a family that I had never seen before, never knew existed. I'm very sorry. I'm all right, I really am."

The door was pushed open and Alice came into the room carrying a tray of coffee, saying, "Cook's out for the count. I doubt, miss, if you'll get any breakfast. By the look of the empty bottle on the bedside table, she'll sleep till dinner time."

Alice looked at Emily and was about to say, "You got a cold coming, miss?" when something in the doctor's face checked her words, and so she said, "There's plenty to eat on the table, doctor. Can I get you something?"

"Thank you, Alice, but I'll help myself." He smiled at her. "I'll get more that way."

"Oh, doctor." Alice wagged her head; then went quickly from the room.

As Emily made to rise from the couch to pour out the coffee, he stayed her with a hand gently on her forearm, saying, "Sit where you are, I'll see to it."

When he handed her the cup of coffee, she thanked him; then he resumed his seat and for the next few minutes they sat sipping at their cups, and in complete silence now.

It wasn't until he had taken her empty cup and placed it next to his on a table to his hand that, sitting back in his chair and looking toward the fire, he said, "It was a good Sunday that, wasn't it?"

"Yes." There was a break in her voice. "Yes, it was a very memorable Sunday."

She was going to cry again and she mustn't . . . She must not. What was the matter with her? It was this bodily weakness, it was still on her. She didn't seem to be able to shake it off. She gave a slight start when his hand caught hers and he said, "Now, you mustn't . . . you mustn't cry again. You know what they say about the things you do on New Year's Day: whatever you do today, you'll do all the year round. And you've done all the crying that you're going to do, because you've got your whole life before you. You are free again. It's a painful freedom and will be for some while. But that pain will pass; I promise you it will. You can do anything you want with your life from now on. Look at all your assets: you have a thriving business; you have a number of good friends, and you know, good friends are not to be thought of lightly; you will soon be strong again in yourself. In fact, you have surprised me with the recovery you have made, and your face is back to normal.'' He went to put his hand out toward her cheek, but withdrew it, saying briskly now, ''Well, I must away and get a little sleep, because I know I'll have a heavy day before me tomorrow . . . I mean, today. As for you, I'd advise a long rest in bed; and this you can do as there won't be any business to attend to. Come along now.'' He took her hand again and drew her up from the couch.

They were standing facing each other, and then he said very quietly, ''As we can be nothing more, Emily, I would like you to look upon me as the friend I once offered you.''

''Thank you.'' Her reply was small, for the words had to mount the lump in her throat.

''Well, that's settled.'' He stepped back from her and his tone became brisk: ''If I'm not caught up by some mad hatters on my way back, I'll be asleep within the next half hour."

He was pulling the collar of his overcoat up around his ears when his hands became still as she asked a question: "Does your family know all . . . about me?"

There was a pause before he said, "Only my mother."

"Oh."

"Does that disturb you?"

"No."

"My mother is a very understanding woman, as are most of my family. Perhaps not my father. Like most men he expects his life to run as set down by rules and, of course, the hour."

"How is it that you are different, then?"

"Oh, I am no different in many ways from the majority, except that I'm a doctor and I come up against life on all planes. You could say that men in our profession have a little further education, or expressing it in a more colloquial term, we get eye-openers and we see the bed of roses and the happy-ever-afters in their true light. And you know"—he poked his head toward her—"one could write volumes about what takes place when front doors are closed, be they attached to mansions or to hovels. Life in the main is a game of pretending, for most of us. There now"—he pulled his hat further onto his head, adding, "get yourself to bed and try to work that out. It'll send you to sleep. Good-night, or good-morning, and again, a Happy New Year."

She repeated neither of his farewells but said, "Goodbye, and thank you."

She was still in the sitting room when Alice came in, and the girl, looking at her where she was lying back on the sofa, her eyes closed and her face wet, exclaimed softly, "Ah, miss, don't cry." Quickly she sat down beside her and taking up the limp hand she patted it while saying, "You've drowned the New Year, miss, but everything's going to be all right in it. It's had a good start. We had a good laugh an' it was lovely him dropping in; now, wasn't it?" There was a break in her own voice. "He's very caring, is the doctor. He's a very caring man."

When Emily turned and laid her head on Alice's shoulder, the girl put her arms about her and, her own tears flowing now, she muttered, "It'll all come right, miss. You'll see. It'll all come right. Everybody makes mistakes, an' you're not the first one that's been hoodwinked out of your mind. My! When I think of it, I could murder him meself. I hope he dies lonely; that's what I wish for him, that he dies lonely."

17

The bleak weeks of January dragged into the even bleaker ones of February. Then, on the Wednesday of the third week, the sun showed its face in earnest, which brought the perennial words of hope: Spring will soon be here.

It had been a busy morning in the shop. Emily was upstairs talking with a client when Alice, beckoning from the inner room to Esther, whispered, "Lady Montane's downstairs."

"Montane? Who's Lady Montane?"

"Doctor's mother. Doctor's mother."

"*The doctor's mother?* Lady Montane? Good gracious!"

"You'd better tell Emily."

"Yes, yes. You go on back. Tell her she'll be there in a minute or so."

It was five minutes before Esther could tactfully extricate Emily from the somewhat demanding client. Then she whispered urgently, "Get downstairs; the doctor's mother is there."

"Who?"

"Lady Montane."

"Lady . . . Montane."

Definitely surprised, Emily hurried downstairs,

through the communicating door and into the sitting room, where her visitor rose from a chair, saying, "I'm so sorry."

"Oh, Lady Montane"—Emily cut off the apology—"I'm terribly, terribly sorry I kept you waiting. I . . . I had a customer, a very finicky one, and the girls, they couldn't advise me of your visit."

"I've called at a busy time, and unannounced. I shouldn't have done so."

"Please! Please! Oh, do sit down. Will you have a cup of tea, or a cup of coffee?"

"I should love a cup of tea, dear."

Emily pulled the hardly used cord to the side of the fireplace and almost instantly Alice appeared.

"Would you bring a tray of tea, Alice, please?"

"Yes, miss. Yes, miss."

"You must have a very busy life," Lady Montane said. "I was shown into your business house first and your kindly little maid brought me through into what she called your house. And if I may remark, it's . . . it's a very pleasant house. This is a lovely room. But then I know about it, because Steve has described it to me."

"Really?"

"Yes; and you must be wondering why I've called. It is really rather cheeky of me, but I am, as it were, marking time between visits. You see, my husband has been in town attending a case all this week, and it should happen that my daughter Cissie, you remember her . . . and William; well, William has something wrong with his blood, and this afternoon he is having tests at a hospital. The arrangements have been hastily made and we hadn't informed Steve, but I went there thinking he would still be tending his surgery. Unfortunately, he had just left; and when I asked where I could find him, his housekeeper, a very, very, grumpy woman, I must say, said, 'He'll be down there.' When I asked where 'there' was, she said, 'Well, among that lot. He always does an hour in the morning among that lot.' "

"She couldn't have realized who you were."

"No. And I didn't bother to tell her, because I couldn't bear the thought of waiting under her beady eye for his return, which, she muttered, would be at about one o'clock. Well at one o'clock I am to meet up with my husband and Cissie and the boy, and we're taking them to lunch. But in the meantime, I thought, well, I'll do some shopping, which I intended to do in any case. And then I thought of you. I knew that your place was not all that far away from the surgery. So I took a cab and asked for The Bandbox in Willington Place, and here I am."

"And I'm so pleased to see you, too, because I hold very vivid memories of our first meeting."

"And I, too. And I, too, my dear. It's a pity we haven't seen each other since. But then your life is very busy."

Emily now looked down at her hands, where they rested on her lap and said softly, "Not so busy that I haven't made drastic mistakes. I . . .

I understand that Steve told you what happened?"

"Yes, my dear, he did; and I was terribly sorry . . . terribly sorry. Such things always seem to happen to the nicest people. Steve was very disturbed about it. He is, as you may have guessed, very fond of you, and is very unhappy about your situation."

After a lapse of some seconds Emily said, "He . . . he has been a good friend. I am glad he has found happiness. I am sure you will be getting very excited about the wedding."

"The wedding?"

"Steve's wedding to Miss Braize."

They both turned toward the door as Alice entered with the tea tray. When she had placed it on the table, she said, "Will I pour, miss?"

"Yes, please, Alice." Then, turning to her visitor, Emily said, in a polite conversational tone, "It's lovely to see the sun. The weather has been atrocious. February is the worst month of the year, I think."

"Yes. Yes, it is. But then comes March and the spring. I love the spring, don't you?"

"Yes. Yes, indeed; for then the parks all about the city are a delight from April onwards. Thank you, Alice."

They were both holding a cup of tea as Alice made her exit and Emily reverted to the conversation, saying, "And the spring is a lovely time for a wedding."

"Yes. Yes, indeed it is. Did . . . did Steve tell you all about it?"

"Well, merely the fact that he was going to marry Miss Braize, and that they had known each other for years."

"Oh yes, yes, that is right, they've known each other all their lives. At least, Steve was about twelve when Nan was born and older when Biddy came on the scene."

"Will it be a very big affair?"

"What? Oh, Steve's marriage."

Emily watched as her visitor turned her head to the side and seemed to think a moment before she said, "Well, as far as I can gather from this distance I should imagine it will be a quiet affair."

Then, much to Emily's surprise, even amazement, her visitor began to chuckle and when she said, "You know, Emily, I have the strangest family, each one of them so unpredictable. But, to use my husband's term for Steve, he's an obstinate cuss. Excuse my language. He's always gone his own way, oblivious to persuasion. I must tell you that we are all trying to persuade him to take on the opening that needs to be filled when Doctor Raymore leaves. It would be ideal and—" she paused again now, and once more there as the slight chuckle as she said, "Under the circumstances it would be very fitting. But there, Steve will go his own way in the end, and at the last minute surprise us all. My husband calls it deviousness, Steve calls it strategy. But I must not keep you any longer. I'll drive back and leave a

message for him. But should he manage to call in
. . . does he call in often?''

"Well, he tends to the needs of my staff and he
looks in on me sometimes.''

"Well, should you, by any chance, see him before he gets back to the surgery, would you tell
him I've called?'' And now she gave a little hunch
to her shoulders as on a laugh she added, "He'll
be very surprised, I can tell you. And he'll want to
know everything we've talked about. He's always
curious to know what people talk about. It's the
doctor in him, I think: he wants to probe . . .
Goodbye, my dear, and let me say that I would
like you to come and visit us again any time you
feel so inclined.''

"Thank you. Thank you very much indeed.
Goodbye.''

Back in the sitting room Emily stood looking out
of the window. She could see the cab disappearing into the distance. So he had told his mother all
about her and yet she had still come to see her.
She was a very nice woman. Not only a nice
woman but a great lady, full of charm and kindness. In a way, he took after her. Oh, no, not with
her charm; but he had likely inherited her kindness. With regard to his marriage, she had
seemed to take it as a matter of course; and yet
on that Sunday she was sure she had looked
upon Emily herself as a prospective daughter-in-
law. But perhaps she had been mistaken in that:
they had all been so kind, so welcoming.

She turned from the window. She had that deep

feeling of aloneness on her again and it was only with a great effort that she made herself go back into the next house and up the stairs into the dressing room.

For the rest of the day she felt extremely weary. She had had no more visitors. Somehow she had expected Steve to call in and speak of his mother's visit. So nine o'clock found her upstairs and ready for bed.

She had taken to reading in bed—it helped her eventually to get to sleep. Also, she had found that she couldn't sleep in a darkened room, because when she had the recurring nightmare of the struggle with that woman the fear was intensified if she woke up in the dark.

She now reached out and picked up the book of poems from the bedside table. She had never asked herself why she should read these poems, because there was nothing soft or gentle about them; rather, they stirred the mind like the one she was reading now. It consisted of a few lines only and was set out in the middle of the page, the words seeming to convey they had just been dropped there. There was no rhyme in them, and they read:

Where are you, God? I can't find you,
But you know where I am,
Forty-six B, top floor, under the skylight.
Will you see that I'm warm when I'm dead?

She closed the book with almost a snap. He was such a gloomy writer, was S. Petersen. She didn't know why she continued to read him. Even those words had made her feel cold. And yet, behind them, she knew what the man was getting at, because not all the very poor were feckless. And as she had done before, she asked herself what she could do to help such people, and as always her answer was, nothing. Yet Steve did something.

Oh! Steve. Why must he always come into it?

She stretched out her arm and, reaching back to the wall and the gas-bracket, she dimmed the light . . .

She didn't want to think about him, and his mother had brought his forthcoming marriage so close. Once again she told herself that if he had been marrying someone other than that silly little creature she could have understood it. But why was she saying that? She was the last person who should criticize another for their choice of a mate. Look what she had done! Oh!—she turned on her side—she didn't need to be reminded of what she had done, for she hated the stupid gullible creature that she had been.

Her mind jumping from one thing to another made her weary, and she quickly fell asleep . . .

When the nightmare seemingly became real, she thrashed from side to side to avoid the hands that were on her face until suddenly she was brought stiffly and freezingly still by a voice, saying, "Oh, my dearest Emily, it's me, it's me." Her cry was stifled by a hand over her mouth.

Staring up into Paul Steerman's eyes, his wine-thick breath wafting over her, she arched her body in an attempt to rise, but he had one knee on her and was muttering, "There now; there now, my dearest Emily. Listen, listen, I must talk to you. Listen!"

She lay taut, her eyes wide as he went on, "I . . . I had to come. I . . . I had to see you. I'm like a prisoner, my life is finished. I can explain. I haven't anyone now. No one! No one at all! I might . . . I might as well be in prison, darling. I've had to give up everything and I've done it for you. No more politics. They stopped that, they stopped that. Do you know? I wanted to come. Oh, yes, I wanted to come to you but they threatened me. But my love is so great, Emily. Emily!"

"Get away from me! I hate you. Do you hear? I loathe and hate you." Emily's voice was shrill.

"No! No!" His voice was loud now. "You could never hate me. You love me too much."

"I never loved you. Never! I couldn't have loved you."

"But you did, Emily. You had my baby. But don't worry, I'll give you another, and another, and . . . Don't struggle. Oh, Emily, don't. I love you. I do."

When he tore back the bedclothes and his body rolled onto hers, she let out a high scream, crying, *"Alice! Alice!"*

It was only minutes before Alice dashed into the room, but by then it had been done and she was lying inert: only her voice was active, and it was whimpering, "Alice! Alice!"

"You beast, you! You dirty rotten beast, you!"

Alice was dragging the man from the bed where he had rolled onto his side, and when he dropped onto his knees she took her fist and punched him in the mouth.

"She . . . she understands. I . . . I had to come back."

"You're drunk, you dirty rotten sod! Get out!"

And now, gripping the foot of the bed, he pulled himself up and turned from her as he adjusted his clothes. Then, stumbling to the door, he looked back at her, saying, "Shouldn't leave kitchen doors open. Just by chance found it. Your cook has drunk more than me. Dead asleep. I . . . I still love her, you know, Alice . . . I do. I do . . ."

Alice's reaction was to pick up a stool and aim it at him, but he had already hurried through the door; and then she heard him call in a high voice, "I know my way out. I know my way out, don't I, Alice?" And he could have been laughing.

Alice was now chafing Emily's limp hands, saying, "Oh, miss! Oh, miss! I'm so sorry! I . . . I came down as soon as I heard you. But I never thought . . . no! I never thought it was that. Let me cover you. Oh, miss! Oh, miss! He should be locked up. He should. He should be locked up. Miss"—she was patting Emily's face—"speak to me, miss. Say something. Come on. Come on, miss, say something. Look, I'll get you a cup of tea. Shall I? Shall I get you a cup of tea? I'll be back in a minute." She didn't move away immediately but continued to pat the eiderdown; then she turned and flew from the room. She didn't, however, go down into the house kitchen, but next door and into cook's quarters and, there, she actually slapped cook's face as she cried, "You, you drunken old bitch. Why couldn't you lock the back door?"

"Wh . . . at? Wh . . . at? What's the matter with you? Did . . . did you hit me, girl?"

"I'll more than hit you. You don't know what you've caused this night. You left the back door open and he's been in."

"Who? Who you talkin' about, girl?"

"You know who I'm talking about. The one that used to come before. Look! You get the kettle on quick and get a cup of tea ready and bring it up. I don't care if you fall on the stairs and break your neck. If I had anything to do with you, you'd get the sack, drunken old hag that you are. She's too soft with you." She now turned and ran from the room and rushed back upstairs the way she had come. But the bedroom was empty, the bed was empty. She looked about her in bewilderment, then ran to the closet room, only to find the door was locked; and she cried, "Miss! Miss! It's me, Alice, open the door. Come on, miss, open the door!"

There was no answer to her plea, and so she started to hammer on the door, crying, "Miss! D'you hear? Open the door!" When after some minutes there was still no answer, she turned and leaned her back against the wall, her hand tight over her mouth. Then she dived up the attic stairs, pulled on a skirt and coat over her night-dress, rammed a shawl onto her head, and ran down the stairs again. And when once more she banged on the closet door and there was still no answer she ran out of the house, stopping only to lock the door on the outside. Then she took to her heels and ran up the street.

When she heard the sound of a horse-drawn cab, she hailed the cabbie; and he, being without passengers, pulled up, saying, "Where d'you want to go, miss?"

When she gave him the doctor's address, he said, "Oh, I know that place."

"Hurry up! Please! hurry up. Someone's dangerously ill. . . ."

She was now hammering on the doctor's door while shouting, "Doctor Montane! Doctor Montane!"

A window opened above her head and a female voice called down, "What's the row? What do you want? The doctor's in bed."

"Well, get him up! Tell him it's Mrs. Ratcliffe. She's very ill."

Before the window closed the door opened and a strange man stood there, saying, "Yes, what is it?"

"I . . . I want Doctor Montane."

"He's in bed. I'm Doctor Nelson. What's the trouble?"

A voice now came from somewhere behind the man, saying "What is it?" And then Steve was looking down on Alice, saying simply, "Alice?"

"It's . . . it's the miss; she's . . . she's been attacked again."

"What!"

"Yes. Yes." Her head was bobbing. "But she's locked herself in the closet and . . . and I can't get in. I'm . . . I'm afraid."

"I'll be with you in a minute. You've got a cab there?"

"Yes. Yes, doctor. . . ."

He was lacing his boots in the narrow hall, and he had hardly straightened up when the young man almost pushed him into an overcoat, and then he himself was pushing Alice into the cab . . .

In the house, Steve took the stairs two at a time and on the landing he found cook standing outside the closet door and she greeted them with, "Not a sound out of her, doctor. I've been batterin' on it. I brought the tea up and then I heard something fall in there."

"Emily! Emily!" His voice was stern. "Emily! Open the door! Do you hear? Emily!"

He now waved his hand toward Alice, saying, "Keep back, and you, too," and he pushed the drink-sodden woman to one side. Then, from the opposite wall of the corridor, he made a run at the door prior to thrusting his foot against the lock. But it took four such efforts before the wood split and he was able to push the door open.

She was lying on her side, her face buried in her arms, with an empty pill-box on a small table near the sink.

He lifted her into a sitting position; then, after pulling an eyelid down, he hauled her up to her feet, shouting to the cook, "Support her. Take her arm on that side."

"But she c . . . can't hardly walk, doctor."

"She's got to walk, woman. And you, Alice, quick as you can, bring up a jug of hot water with two tablespoons of salt in it."

"Salt?"

"*Yes, you heard me. Go on.* And now, you, cook, you hold her up as well as yourself. And by the way, I'm telling you, if you don't give up the bottle, you won't be here much longer to drink from it. Keep her up! Now walk. Walk!"

They had walked the corridor four times, holding up the trailing body between them, when Alice appeared with the jug. And now Steve said, "Let's get her into the bedroom and sit her down. Did you stir up the salt in that, Alice?"

"Yes, doctor. Yes, I did."

"Well, pour a glass of it out."

"It's . . . it's hottish, doctor."

"It'll cool when it goes into the glass."

When he held the glass of salted water to Emily's lips her mouth remained closed until, roughly, he nipped her nose hard, and then she gasped, which allowed him to pour the liquid down her throat. What she didn't swallow ran over her neck and under her nightdress.

When, after two glasses of the salted water, the body made no response, he smartly slapped her on both cheeks, and so hard was it that the sound made Alice wince.

When she heaved, then heaved again, he said, "The chamber pot. Quick!"

When she vomited and Alice muttered, "Thank God!" he muttered back at her, "Don't thank God yet." Then he again held her nose and attempted to pour a glass of the salted water down her throat. And when her body jerked, he said to the cook, "Take her arm again." And, once more, they were trailing her up and down, with cook muttering her thoughts aloud: "'Tis rough treatment," she said. "I think I'd prefer to go."

"And you will, as I've told you, without the rough treatment, if you don't watch out."

"You're a hard man, doctor."

"When I bury you, I'll tell myself I wasn't hard enough."

"Eeh! the things you say. Doctor Smeaton used . . ."

"Shut up! woman, and keep walking."

Not until she had retched for the third time did he now say to Alice, "Get her a clean nightdress. But before you do that, change those sheets."

Emily was now lying on the couch at the foot of the bed. As it wouldn't take her length, her feet were resting on a chair and he was sitting on another at her head. When the bed was ready he said, "Get the nightie off her, then we'll get her to bed."

While they were undressing her, he went to the wash-hand stand and there he not only washed his hands but sluiced his face of sweat.

When they had got her into bed he turned to cook and said, "Now you can get yourself away to your bed, but don't, I advise you, take anything more to make you sleep. I'll have a talk with you tomorrow, and as a pre-warning I'll tell you now: I will advise your mistress that she cannot afford to keep someone in her service who is incapable of locking doors at night. Do you understand me?"

The woman slowly shook her head, then glared at him before she mumbled, "Yes, only too well, doctor, I understand you." And on that she turned and went out.

Now Steve said quietly to Alice, "Have you told her what actually happened?"

"Yes, doctor. I . . . I think I did; but I was in such a state, I don't really know."

"Well, that's understandable. Anyway, I'll see to her tomorrow. Now . . . now, don't you cry. You've been very brave and very helpful."

"It . . . it was awful, doctor. He was like a maniac. And . . . and she fought him; she did."

"All right. All right. I understand. Now what I want you to do is to go upstairs to bed."

"But somebody . . ."

"Yes, somebody should sit with her, so I'll make myself comfortable on these two chairs. And don't worry about her any more. She's going to be all right."

"Oh, doctor, there's only so much anybody can

stand, and she's had more than enough, don't you think?"

"Yes, I do, Alice. Yes, I do. But I can promise you that there is going to be a change."

"You can?"

"Yes, I can. Now, go to bed, because you will have a busy day tomorrow running up and down stairs. I myself will likely go fast asleep, for I've had more than a busy day. So there's nothing for you to worry about. Good-night. It's close on twelve. Oh, listen, there's Big Ben telling us about it."

"Good-night, doctor."

"Good-night, Alice."

He moved the bedside table, then arranged the chairs so that he could watch her, pulling a rug over himself and settling back. But as he lay there, he wasn't so much thinking about her but of what he meant to do the following morning.

When she awoke, she found herself staring at him. She was feeling ill, but her mind was clear. She remembered everything that had happened up until she had taken the pills. She even remembered Alice's voice begging her to open the door. She could only guess what had happened after that. But there he was. Why did he do it? Such kindness could hurt. Oh, she wished she had died.

She saw the door being opened quietly, and there was Alice with a tray holding two cups of tea. She watched her put it down, then come to the bed.

"How you feeling, miss?" It was a whisper. "You could do with a cup of tea, eh?"

She made a small motion with her head toward Alice. Dear Alice. In a way she was like him, so kind, so thoughtful for others. Why did they do it? Oh, if they had only left her alone . . . She couldn't face today. Nor the future . . .

A long slow grunt came from the chair, then a sound of a slight splutter, and there he was sitting up. "My! My! There you are again, Alice. What time is it?"

"It's on seven, doctor."

"Seven o'clock? My! I must have slept."

"Well"—she smiled at him—"you said you were tired. Would you like this cup of tea?"

"I would indeed." He swung his legs from the chair, but, still sitting, he drank the cup of tea. Then, standing up and looking at Emily as if he had just noticed her, he said, "Hello, there!"

She could make no answer, but just stared back at him.

"Feeling rotten?"

When he still received no reply, he said, "It would be a surprise if you didn't. Well now, I think I'll go along the corridor and have a wash. I'll be back in a minute."

After he had gone from the room Alice busied herself pushing the chairs back into place, before moving to Emily and, stroking the straggling hair back from her brow, saying, "You're bound to feel awful, but it's going to be all right. He says so. My! he was in a state. But it's going to be all right, miss. Lie quiet now."

It was as if Emily had made some protest, but her body felt so weak, it was as much as she could do to hold the cup and saucer in her hand. And after she had managed to drink the tea and Alice said, "I'll wash your face and hands in a minute, miss; it'll make you feel fresher," she did not protest, for at the moment there was no fight left in her, either to live or to die.

When Steve came back into the room, Alice picked up the tray and went out, and he, sitting by the bedhead, looked at her as he repeated Alice's words, "It's going to be all right. Don't worry."

She now turned her head on the pillow and, looking into his eyes, she asked quietly, "Why didn't you let me go? It would have been a further kindness."

"Oh, no, I couldn't have done that, let you go . . . because . . . well, you see"—he lifted one shoulder—"I happen to love you."

This statement brought her head up from the pillow, only to drop back again; when she stared at him, her eyes wide, he said, "Don't look like that; it shouldn't really be any surprise to you. From the minute I first saw you I've always loved you, and I always shall. You're a stubborn cuss. You're an irritating cuss. In all, you're an aggravating woman. But there it is, I love you."

"You . . . you are going to be . . ."

"Married? Huh! Oh that!" He was smiling gently

at her now. "I'm a man; my ego was attacked; you were pushing me aside for someone else; I wasn't going to let you think you were the only pebble on the beach. Not me. I'm not made like that. No, I was out to show you . . . using the platitude that there were other fish in the sea just waiting to be netted. So I picked on the one that would irritate you most."

Somewhere deep down inside her there was the beginning of a smile, and although she couldn't bring it to her face she could only wonder at what she was hearing. He was so human, this man, possessed of all the frailties, yet so determined, so thoughtful, so kind.

"I'm a jealous individual. You'll find that out. And I do things that are quite opposed to ordinary standards. My family know that. Yesterday, my mother couldn't get over the fact that I was going to be married and to Biddy, of all people, someone almost as odd as Aunt Phoebe, and Mother said that if ever our crew, that's the family, got wind of this I would never hear the last of it until the day I die. Well, what have you got to say?"

"Oh! Steve—" She gulped before she said, "How . . . how can you love me after all that's gone before?"

"Well, that's the same question I've asked myself a number of times. But, as I said, I can't do anything about it: I love you; I want you; and there is a hope in me that some day you will love me as much as I do you. Oh now, now. Look, don't start to cry; but tell me, do you think you'll ever really love me? Really love me?''

"I . . . I think, Steve, I've . . . I've always loved you, and not really known it. Well, yes, I have, but I've fought against it. But now, please, please don't say anything more for the moment. I . . . I really don't want to think about it, or talk about it, for something happened last night that could make all the differ . . .''

"I know what happened last night. It's been graphically described to me. And inside I am raging because of it. But not against you, never against you. But last night apart, I meant to come clean within the next day or so. In fact, this very day, after learning what transpired between you and Mother. What a pity I didn't call in last night. Yes. Yes''—his head drooped—"it's a pity. But now I say to you, you must put it out of your mind. Will you marry me?''

"Oh! Steve.''

"Never mind 'oh Steve'. I'm asking you, will you marry me?'' He moved closer to her as he spoke.

"Thank you. Yes. Oh, thank you; I'll marry you, Steve. But . . . but wait.'' She now pressed his face away from hers and, closing her eyes, her head drooped to the side and she said, "If . . . oh dear me! I've got to say this, it's dreadful. This is what made me . . . well, take the pills; I couldn't bear the thought of the consequences again. You know . . . what I . . . I mean?''

"Yes, my dear, I know exactly what you mean; that if you'd had to bear the consequences again, you would have been on your own. But that is not going to happen to you."

"Oh"—she drew back from him—"you're not just doing this to save me . . . embarrassment or . . . ?"

"Oh, don't be silly, woman. I'm doing this, as you say, *this,* because I love you . . . as *I* have said, and always will. And I want you, woman. Don't you understand? I want you as my wife . . . with your stiff neck, and your argumentative mind, and your business head, and your beauty." His voice had become lower, and now he stroked her cheeks; then slowly he put his mouth to hers, and when her arms came about his neck he held her close. Then he released her, saying, "None of this should have taken place this morning, you know, not when you're feeling like nothing on earth. This is an event that should have been celebrated by gambolling around the sitting room, or Trafalgar Square, or the workshop . . . Please! Please, dear, stop crying. Oh, here comes your guardian angel." He laid her back on the pillows and turned to look at Alice, who had stopped within the doorway; and she, her face bright, looked from one to the other and he called to her, "Yes! Alice. I told you everything was going to be all right. I must be out of my mind, but I've just asked if she'll marry me."

"Oh, doctor. You're the most lovely man on God's earth. Oh, miss." She was now holding their hands. " 'Tis the happiest day of me life. But where're you going to live?"

"Oh." He looked from her to Emily. "We haven't got that far yet. We might go and live in the country: there's a nice opening for a doctor there."

"Oh." Alice sounded disappointed for a moment; but then she said, "Well, would you take me with you?"

"We'll always take you with us, Alice, always. Won't we?" He looked at Emily. And Emily's answer was in the look that she gave Alice.

"Well now, I've got some business to do this morning, so I must be off. But you'll take care of her, won't you, Alice, until I get back?"

"Of course, doctor, yes, doctor."

He did not bend to kiss Emily again but brought her hand to his face, and then went from the room. But on the landing he called, "Alice!" And when Alice joined him, his manner changed and he said, "Do one thing further for me. When her friends come to see her, tell them that . . . well, there was an intruder last night. You can tell them who it was, but not what actually happened. You understand? You can put it over that he tried to kiss her, or something similar. You know what to do. But before they do arrive you had better explain to her what you intend to say, so that she won't inadvertently tell them the truth. You understand what I'm getting at? And also, and more important at the moment, get at that cook and tell her what she's got to stick to—or else it'll be the door for her. Make it plain, until I can see her myself."

"I'll make it plain all right, and to the others as well."

Their glances held; then he put his hand on her shoulder: "She should thank God she's got you, Alice," he said. "Now, I may not be back this morning; I have some rather serious business to attend to. I may not be back today, in fact. We'll see how it goes. But you stay with her and buoy her up, because even the surprising news I pelted at her this morning cannot have erased how she's really feeling, and that is quite ill."

"I'll see to her, doctor. Never fear. And I think it was the right time to pelt your news at her."

She smiled at him, and he smiled back at her and said, "I think so, too, Alice. Yes, I think so, too." Then he hurried away.

He rang the bell of the highly polished door of the house in the select square. And when it was opened by a man in livery who said, "Yes, sir?" Steve answered, "I wish to speak to Mr. Steerman."

"Which Mr. Steerman would that be, sir?"

After a second Steve said simply, "The son."

The man hesitated now before asking, "Your name, sir?"

"Doctor Montane."

The word "doctor" seemed to impress the man, for he drew the door further open as he said, "Will . . . will you wait a moment, sir?"

Steve stood in the hallway. He did not look about him in surprise; he had visited a number of such houses. There was the elaborate wrought-iron staircase going off to his left, and a number of doors to his right, and opposite, a corridor. He saw the man hesitate for a moment, glance toward the stairs, then decide on the corridor, and it was along there he walked.

It was as Steve heard him knock on a door that there appeared on the stairs the figure of a man in a velvet dressing gown. As he descended further, Steve could make out that the man's face was puffed and his eyes bleary. He had never met Paul Steerman, but instinctively he knew this was his man.

When the figure reached the bottom step Steve was waiting for him. They stared at each other. Then Steve said, "Mr. Paul Steerman?"

"Yes. What do you want?" The voice came thick and guttural.

"Just this."

Steve's fist, landing between the unprepared Paul Steerman's eyes, knocked him back on the stairs and had him clutching at the banister. But after a moment, during which he shook his head, he pulled himself up and almost threw himself on this stranger, and in the scuffle Steerman's head caught Steve on the side of the mouth and the salt taste of the blood infuriated Steve still further, causing him to lash out wildly. But then being aware that someone was tugging at his shoulders calmed him sufficiently to aim a blow that again caught Steerman between the eyes and sent him reeling against the paneled wall.

A commanding voice now filled the hall. "What . . . what is this! Who are you?"

Two men, the liveried butler and Paul Steerman's valet, were holding onto Steve, who cried at the tall white-haired man standing before him, "I am Doctor Steve Montane and—" he gulped for breath now and licked the blood from his lips before going on, "I am here, sir, because last night your son broke into Mrs. Ratcliffe's house and raped her . . . yes, raped her. He took no heed to her protests and screams, although eventually they brought her servants flying to her aid. But it was too late, and the distress became so much she attempted suicide."

The old man's lips moved, and the sound could have been "My God!" Then, authority returning to his voice, he commanded the two servants, "Let him go!"

Released from the men's hold, Steve staggered back a step or two. Then, taking a handkerchief from his pocket, he wiped the blood from his chin; and the tall, thin, stately figure that had not moved since first coming to the hall looked at his son and, again addressing his servants, said curtly, "See to him." But when the men went to assist the drooping figure along the corridor they were checked by the loud command of, "To his room!"

When Paul Steerman attempted to throw off the servants' hands, his father cried at him, "Up to your room, sir!" It was as if he were addressing a recalcitrant youth. Then, turning to Steve, he said, "The woman in question, is she . . . ?" And to this Steve answered, *"The lady* in question, sir. Yes, she is still alive, but in great shock." And then, because Paul Steerman was still in earshot as he was being assisted up the stairs, he cried, "But should she not survive the attack brought upon her by your son, then the courts will see that he pays for it, and dearly."

The men on the stairs were momentarily brought to a halt by these words, and this caused the elderly man to look upward, before turning again to Steve and remarking stiffly, "As to the person in question, you seem to take an interest above that of a doctor, sir; an undue interest, if I may say so."

"As the lady is to be my wife, I would say my interest is not undue, sir."

The white head was slightly bent now and the voice muted. "This knowledge can only add to my regret with regard to this affair. And . . . and I promise you, sir, that it . . ."

"Huh! Please don't add that it will never happen again, for I'm here to tell you that after this exposure you son won't dare show his face in decent society."

"Please!" The tall figure took two steps toward him. "I . . . I beg of you not to make this matter public. I promise you he will suffer for this."

"Just as he suffered through the previous attack on her? Your daughter-in-law had to humble herself to save his skin then, and now you are asking that it be saved again."

The old man was now standing very straight,

and his voice was low, as he said, "Yes, I am asking you, sir. As my daughter-in-law did, so I am demeaning myself to ask for your clemency."

Being the man he was, Steve felt a surge of pity for this man, the head of an old family who had bred a wastrel son. Such cases were not unknown, and he'd heard of them, but he had rarely experienced the trauma at first hand. He'd had no intention of making the matter public. It was the last thing in his mind, or that she could have tolerated. Yet he could not resist pursuing the suggestion that such an exposure could take place, because he wanted not only physically to hurt that cad of a man, but also to ruin him socially for good and all. But still, such were his feelings, he could not help but refrain from giving any promise. And so, after a long pause, he said, "I will do what I can, but it all depends on the lady's recovery."

"Thank you."

A servant now appeared from the far corner of the hall and, picking up Steve's hat from where it had fallen onto the floor, he handed it to him, then quickly opened the front door, and without further words Steve left the house. His lip was still bleeding, his knuckles were sore. He also had a strange feeling in his legs. He wanted to sit down.

He hailed a passing cab and gave the address of his surgery, and there John Nelson, the new assistant who had just finished with the last of the string of patients, the result of overnight revelling, looked at Steve and said, "Good Lord! sir. You been at it, too?"

"Yes, it looks like it, doesn't it? I think I'll need a stitch or two in this lip."

"Well, I never! What happened? Was it about last night's business?"

"Yes, you could say so, but stop dithering and get the needle."

The young man turned away, saying, "Do you want your knuckles looked at, too? You certainly don't do things by halves, do you?"

As Steve dropped into the chair before his desk, he thought, how times are changing. When he had first come here, he wouldn't have dared to have any repartee with old Smeaton; the old fellow would have wiped the floor with him. Yet he preferred it this way, and this young whippersnapper had good material in him. He was caring, and that was something to start on.

"Ouch!" Then again, "Ouch!" as the needle went in for the second time, but he managed to wait until the third stitch was finished before, putting his hand to his mouth, he said, "That's one thing you need a lot of practice on."

"Oh, I thought I was pretty good with the needle and thread."

"Yes, about as good as a bricklayer would be. There's a right way to put a needle in and a wrong way. Another time, I'll show you how it's done on some loose skin of yours."

The young man laughed now and said, "I think what you need, sir, is a drink."

"Yes; but bring the bottle in without Mother Shipton seeing you, else she'll have Doctor Smeaton here in no time, and the less said about this business the better." He looked up at Doctor Nelson, saying, "You understand?"

"Yes. Yes, I understand. Did . . . did you have any sleep?"

"Yes, I had some sleep."

"How is she?"

"She'll survive."

"Good! Good!"

Steve closed his eyes and repeated to himself, "Good! Yes; but then, only so far. What if . . . ?" But then he pushed himself to say, "Wait and see. Anyway, just in case, see that you're married before another month is out." But the distant voice persisted: "Why are you doing this? What if she does have a child? She had one before . . ."

"Well, we'll meet that obstacle when we come to it."

However, he still hadn't answered the question of why he was doing this, because the fact that he was in love with her was all too simple. Being in love was like a passing fancy . . . loving was something different. Perhaps that was it.

18

He did not visit Emily again that day, but on the following morning when Alice opened the door to him she greeted him with, "Oh, I am pleased to see you, doctor."

"What's the matter? Anything happened?"

"Well, nothing serious, but she's up and . . . and she's in a bit of a tear inside herself . . . she destroyed the hat."

"Destroyed the what?"

"The hat . . . you know, that big yellow hat. It was a lovely one."

"Oh. Oh, that. What has she done with it?"

"Well, she had already torn the crown from the brim and I don't know what she would have done next: thrown it on the fire, I think; but I took it from her and put it upstairs in my place. I didn't show it to Esther or Lena, because then they would start asking questions; well, more than they've done already. They're like ferrets, those two . . . But you've had an accident, doctor?" She pointed to his lip and the discoloration on his cheek.

"A slight accident, Alice. I bumped into a lamp post, and the piece at the top that sticks out . . . well, it bent down and retaliated."

She didn't smile but said, "You went for him, doctor?"

"You could say that, Alice."

"Well, all I can say is I hope you laid him out."

"I did my best, but then one's best isn't always enough. But you know what I need now, Alice, is a very strong cup of coffee."

"You'll have it, doctor. In a jiffy you'll have it."

He ran up the stairs, paused before the bedroom door and knocked gently; and when there was no reply, he opened it slowly and poked his head round it. She was just coming out of the dressing room and was fully clothed, so he went in, saying, "Who told you you could get up?"

She didn't answer, but her eyes showed alarm as she saw the damage to his face and the bandage on the knuckles of one hand. She started to ask him what had happened, but he put his hands on her shoulders and, leaning forward, he gently kissed her on the lips, sore though his own were. Then, afterwards, when their arms went around each other, he said, "I'll tell you all about it some other time."

After a moment, she said, "Oh, Steve, I . . . I feel so awful."

"Well, that's understandable, if you *will* go and do silly things."

She looked into his eyes again, saying, "I must talk to you."

"Well, let's sit down and you can talk away. But before you start, I have something important to say to *you.* Come on." He drew her to the couch at the foot of the bed, and when they were seated, he said, "We are to be married a week today. I already have the license."

She now pressed herself from him and, her head wagging, she said, "No. No. Please, not yet. Wait until . . ." Her whole body seemed to heave with an effort to bring out the next words which he checked by saying, "We are going to be married a week today. I am not waiting any longer." He now put his hand out and turned her face toward him. "If I put it off till next month the result would be the same, I'm sure. We are going to be married sooner or later and I consider I've waited long enough. Anyway, I've informed my mother and she will tell the others, and those who can, I'm sure, will be here. And then there is your staff. So there will be quite a number and I don't think"— he smiled now—"that cook is up to preparing a little reception. So we will have to choose an hotel. As for the ceremony itself, it can be either in a church of your choice, and that should be easy because we have both been within the parish, haven't we? for more than three weeks; or it can be in the office of the registrar, whichever you prefer. And it's no good pulling away, my dear."

She leaned against the back of the couch, her head turned toward him, and she asked herself why she should be so lucky as to have this man: for she could only look back on a life of egotistic stupidity and stubbornness: first with Jim, and then . . . with that creature, for that is how she thought of him now; and yet throughout that time there had been this man loving her—this extraordinary man who did good by stealth, and whose exceptional qualities she had refused to recognize. She really was a stupid woman, because she had been aware of her own attraction to him from the first, yet she had been foolish enough to do everything in her power to stifle it with cheap and terse repartee.

"I . . . I don't know why you want to do this." Her voice was low.

But when he came back at her with, "Now don't be silly or coy," her head came up and a shadow of her old self appeared as she said, "I am not being coy. I'm never coy. I . . . I leave that to the ladies."

"Yes, you are coy. I know all about you." He now pulled her toward him repeating, "Do you hear what I said, I know all about *you*. But . . . but, my dear, you don't know all about *me*. I carry a dark secret and I think I'd better let you into it before next week, because from then on when I come to live in this house . . . yes, for the time being I'm coming to live in this house, you will see what I do in my spare time. You have never guessed, I know, for you don't care much for the work of S. Petersen. It puzzles you and annoys you at times, doesn't it?"

He watched her mouth fall into a slight gape and her eyes widen, then she whispered, "You're not . . . ?"

And he whispered in return, "Yes, I am. But only

one other person knows, and that is my mother. Dreadful, isn't it?''

Her face broke into a smile, and now her hand gently covered his cheek as she said, ''Oh, Steve, I've never really known you, but I want to so much. Oh, how I want to.'' And now her arms went about him and she stroked the back of his head, while he, his voice thick with emotion, replied, ''You will, my love. You will.''

At the end of the first week in November, readers of *The Times* might have noticed in the ''Births'' column an announcement that on November 3rd, 1881, twins—a boy and a girl—had been born to Dr. and Mrs. Steve Montane of Willington Place, London.

BOOK TWO

Passions

PART ONE

1902

1

It was the second week in October, 1902. The sky was high, its color a clear blue, but the reflection in the Isis was steely gray. The two men on the bank watched the sculler pulling away into the distance, the cleaving of the boat making an arrow of thin froth and creating a momentary perfect formation of flying duck.

"He's good."

"Who is he?"

"I think his name is Montane, or some such. He was certainly up last year, because I saw him on the river."

"You haven't spoken to him?"

"No. Although I think he was on the next staircase to mine. He must be reading history, now I come to think of it, because I've seen him going into old Stokes, likely for his tutorial."

"Could you get to know him?"

"Yes. Yes, I suppose so. No reason why not. He would fit in well at three or four, wouldn't he?"

"Would he be heavy enough?"

"Yes. Yes, he's quite a big chap."

"Well, look; ask him to come to tea in my rooms, for the quicker we get fixed up the better. Torpids will be on us before we know where we are; and then the build-up for Eights."

The young men turned about and walked toward the boathouse, where they had tea and biscuits while waiting for the sculler to come back up the river.

*   *   *

Dear Mother and Father,

So sorry I'm a bit late with my news, but things have been happening here. At least on the water; on the land, things are much the same. A few days ago I was approached by one Hector Mills-Cotton, a rather uppish individual, as Alice would have put it, the kind that gets up her nose. Anyway, he was extremely civil and asked if I would like to have tea with his friend, a Mr. Robert Anderson. And at tea I was given the reason for the invitation: would I be willing formally to join the boat club and train regularly and hard in preparation for Torpids next term? In case your poor senile minds have forgotten, Torpids are the bumping races which take place in February.

Yes, thank you very much, I said. Why hadn't I joined the rowing club during my first year, I was then asked. Because I was into rugby, said I. Oh. Well, would I give up rugger?

I may as well tell you that I paused for some time before agreeing to do so. But I gave in only through fear: there were five pairs of eyes on me, and you know what a coward I am. Anyway, they seemed a very nice lot. When I got back and told David and Michael, they weren't at all pleased. Traitor, they said, because the team is thin on the ground at the moment. They also said that Cotton's crowd is a boozy one, which I cannot see and said so, for the College has a very good eights record and to keep fit enough for racing you cannot or shouldn't indulge overmuch.

I rather liked Robert Anderson. He's in his third year, reading maths. Altogether it was a very interesting evening. When they got off the year's prospects they got onto politics, and oh my! there nearly was skull and hair flying. One, Bruce McVain, got very heated over the Irish question, and from there he jumped to the Chinese troubles. He put me in mind of you, Father, going round the whole block before you come to the front door . . . Now, now; keep your hands down, I don't want to hit an elderly man.

It's odd, my dears, but I haven't been up three weeks and here I am longing for the Christmas vac. When I get these feelings I ask myself why I was ever persuaded to come up here. Oh, I know, I can hear you, Father, it's the greatest place in the world and it's an honor to be here et cetera, et cetera. And truthfully, I do enjoy it because the city, the university, I suppose I should say, and some of the architecture is out of this world. Yet frankly I'd exchange it at this minute for those three houses in Willington Place, where I could stride from the hats, through our house and into the surgery, and yell upstairs to Uncle Nelson and his tribe. Do you know, dear parents, that you own one quarter of Willington Place? Have you ever thought about that, Doctor Montane? You with your socialistic ideas are really a plutty aristocrat . . . Well, no; perhaps not quite that. Seeing that your lady wife runs a business, you are likely both termed middle-class manufacturers.

Well, enough of this nonsense; I really haven't got time to chatter to you. I have a paper to get out for my tutor, dear old Mr. Stokes. Why everybody calls him old, I really don't know. Old Stokes they call him, and he can't be fifty. But then, that is rather aged. How old are you now, Father? Fifty-seven? Fifty-eight?

Oh, good night to you both, dear people. By the way, how is Janet surviving? She promised to write, but she's likely up to her eyes in bedpans. Why you ever let her go in for that lot, Mother, I'll never know. Hard labor isn't in it; it turned me sick the last time I went to that hospital.

Love to you both always,
Jason.

PS Tell Alice I'm dying to nip her behind.

2

"Well, Montane. You've been sitting there with your ears spread, not saying a word, and you're the historian. How do you think England, with the Queen dead and her son, who at long last has taken his seat on the throne and hasn't had all that much practice, will manage? Will it be in the same, conquering, steady British way?"

Jason looked at Hector Mills-Cotton. He wasn't fond of him. In fact, he didn't need to probe very hard to discover he disliked him. And so his reply was rather curt. "For a start, I think you can drop the 'conquering': the events over the last decade of the past century have given warning that change is inevitable. The nineteenth century has been a hotbed of tension between the Mongol world and Europe, and China was the mother of it all. Then what happened? We and others pressed her too hard through both war and commerce and we bled her and left her wounds open for the Japanese to do the rest."

"You're making China out to be a poor, misjudged, misguided and bullied nation," Mills-Cotton snapped back, adding, "What about the Boxer Rising? What about the massacre?"

"Yes, what about it? To my mind that was the result of a nation's despair, an ancient civilization's despair, brought about by the Japanese, the Huns, and the British, and their overall greed for trade. The old Dowager Empress ordered the massacre, but no one takes into account the scores of Mandarins who endangered their own lives in warning the British of what was coming. And you hear of the terrible destruction the Chinese wreaked, not only upon the aliens, but on themselves; but you don't hear so much about what the soldiers from the West did as they rampaged and smashed to bits wonderful carvings and ancient records, things which were absolutely irreplaceable, artifacts that would never again be found in this world. Copies of them, yes, especially made by the Japanese, who are the greatest imitators in the world. And this is not something that happened in the last century. It has happened practically on the doorstep of our time. It is very unfortunate, though, that the conquerors cannot imitate the philosophy of that great nation, whereas it is fortunate today that many survivors of the Rising were already ingrained with the philosophy of Confucius, so that generally they believed, and still believe, in peace."

"My! My! You *are* hot under the collar, aren't you?" Bruce McVain shook his head. "Are you one of the new socialists?"

Slightly taken aback and embarrassed, Jason said, "No, not one of the *new* socialists; but neither am I an old Tory, nor am I a middle-of-the-road Liberal."

"Ah, there sits the next Prime Minister who, like the present one, doesn't know which side he's on."

"Oh, I know which side I'm on," and Jason continued to nod at the young man now, but restrained himself from adding, "and it isn't yours." Since joining the club, he had come to dislike McVain even more than he did Mills-Cotton. He liked Robert Anderson, perhaps more than any of the others; and Jim Fordyce was a decent chap, too. But it was Robert Anderson who was now saying, "Look, let's leave politics for the time being and get down to the business in hand, shall we?"

"I will if you'll offer me another glass of that wine. You're very stingy with the wine, Robert, you know."

"And yes, Hector, I must be," said Robert, nodding, "because you've nearly finished that bottle on your own. Now listen, you fellows. This is my last year and I mean to make more bumps in Torpids and then in Eights than we've made for years, even if I have to walk upon the waters and bump the beggars myself."

"Oh, we'll do well in Torpids, never fear," said Hector Mills-Cotton, "but I'm not so sure about Eights. I know we've got till May, but so have Balliol and Magdalen, and we've got to get them before having a go at Oriel and the headship."

Jim Fordyce pulled himself up from the deep

leather chair in which he had been lounging, placed his hands on Robert's shoulders and said, "My dear, dear Robert, we'll all see you through, even if we have to overbump to do it. And we'll carry you shoulder high through Oriel, and afterwards, if we're still alive, we'll have High Mass said for you at the . . ."

"Stop it! you fool, and get yourselves off. I've got a paper to do for tomorrow, and so have you if I know anything."

"Sums, sums, sums: two and one are triplets; triplets and one are quads; quads and one are . . ."

"Take him away, will you?"

Amid much laughter, they were going from Robert's room when Bruce McVain, nearing the door, turned to Jason and said, "Did you cheer on Mafeking night, Montane?"

The small party remained still and quiet, for all were aware that the intent of the question was to test Jason's loyal patriotism, and so when the answer came, "No, McVain, I did not cheer on Mafeking night: my cousin had died out there during that week. His name was Major James Montane, and he left a young wife and three small children," and as he turned to hurry down the staircase, no one followed him immediately, and he did not hear Robert Anderson say, "That was in very bad taste, Bruce."

"Perhaps," said McVain; "but I don't like the fellow and I don't mind saying so. I don't know why you needed him in the boat; Cassidy was doing well enough."

"That's my business."

"Yes, well, I suppose it is. Good-night."

No one answered him, and now he too went on his way and there now remained Jim Fordyce, Hector Mills-Cotton, and Robert. And it was Jim Fordyce who said in a low voice, "No; he wouldn't like him, would he? for Montane doesn't need to force his Britishness. He's fair, gray-eyed, tall and with an enviable body on him, even for other oarsmen; very much like yours, Robert, whereas our dear Bruce has a lightly telltale muddy depth of eye, and although there's nothing wrong with his shape his mind's as narrow as his face. And he always gives himself away by his over-zealous defense of royalty."

Mills-Cotton now pushed Jim Fordyce onto the landing, saying, "You're tight, and I notice you always start dissecting character when the wine has flowed. You should have been a doctor."

"His father's a doctor . . . Jason's is."

"Yes, I know he is," Robert Anderson put in. "Somebody's got to look after the ills of the world, those brought on by old age, and yes, especially on young fellows who drink wine between meals. Get yourself downstairs."

After closing the door on his friends, Robert Anderson remained standing with his back to it for a moment, taking in the table strewn with bottles and glasses. There were magazines and papers on the floor, the ashes from the fire had spread onto the hearth; the room looked a mess. But that was his scout's business; he was going to bed. It hadn't been a pleasant evening. They were all his friends . . . or were they? He had considered Hector his friend up till now, but Hector was a rank snob; and yet he was pleasant with it. But the new fellow, Jason . . . he liked him. Yes. Yes, he did. There was something about him, an open honesty, a frankness that was almost fearless. He wished he too was fearless. Oh, let him get to bed; he couldn't tackle that paper tonight; he would get up early in the morning. But he must get down to work; he mustn't disappoint his grandfather. It was a little over a month before the Christmas vac. Lord! how he was dreading it.

3

It was Robert who proposed that they journey down together, at least as far as London, because from there he would have to take a train into Sussex.

It was a Saturday and the end of the first week in December. The term had finished the day before and last night there had been a rather uproarious party, with much toing and froing and horseplay among the occupants of the staircases and which ended in many of them congregating in McVain's rooms, where more wine was drunk, and stories told that evoked rocketing laughter. And Jason faintly remembered standing up and singing a pantomime song, with the others joining in the chorus. He was quite good at mimicking, and he had obliged with a called-for encore, taking off a well-known music hall singer. He didn't remember doing this, but Robert had laughed about it this morning.

Apparently, Robert could hold his wine; he was used to it. He had also remarked to Jason, as he had done once or twice before, "Take no notice of Bruce; he doesn't mean half he says. He's fighting an inner battle, you know. His father's a very ordinary chap, pots of money, but very ordinary. But he will keep harping on about his maternal grandmother. She is one of the DeWhits. That's what he kept on telling you last evening, that his grandmother knew all about you. Do you know the DeWhits?''

Jason had replied that he knew no one of that name.

They had found an empty carriage and after the porter had deposited their luggage on the racks and had touched his cap in deference to the tips, because each gentleman had been generous, they settled down in opposite seats.

''It's an early train so we may be lucky and have the carriage to ourselves; at least, before it starts picking up at the stations along the way.''

''Yes, it's surprising the number who stay up over the weekend, isn't it? Something I can't understand,'' said Jason; ''I myself can't wait to get home. But I had a job to get up this morning. Lord! I had a thick head; and I've still got it. No more nights of wine and merriment for me. It isn't worth it.''

''You should have taken a Seidlitz powder.''

''I did; two.''

When Jason lay back and closed his eyes, Robert sat staring at him. He had never before felt like making a firm friend of anyone as he did of this fellow. Over the past two weeks he had gone out of his way to seek his company, using the subterfuge of conversation about boats and their crews, practice times; anything that would involve Jason.

And so he was surprised now when Jason suddenly opened his eyes, stared at him and said, "What do you do with yourself over the holidays?"

"Oh; well, I seem to have to spend it in a"—he paused—"sort of triangle. I visit my mother and father in Sussex. Then, it all depends where my grandfather is staying: if he's in Scotland I skip up there; if he's in town then I stay in town. But he doesn't keep the town house open all that much. There's a caretaker and his wife and they see to things. But when he comes down on business he uses the house mostly for sleeping, and eats out most of the time. I, too, when I'm with him. And my mother uses it when she comes up for a day. But Grandfather's living is divided between London and Scotland."

"I suppose you're in great demand for do's and parties. Do you hold them in Sussex or in Scotland?"

Robert sat forward on his seat, so as to get his hand into the inner pocket of his greatcoat. From it he took out a pipe and a pouch of tobacco and set about filling the pipe. Then he gave a slight laugh as he said, "What makes you think *I'd* be in great demand for parties?"

"Well, because I imagine that would be the pattern of your life. Three houses, so to speak . . . having such, you would likely do the rounds."

The pipe was lit and Robert was drawing on it before he replied, "It may surprise you to know I've only been to one so-called party in my life.

That was at my elder sister's wedding. Of course, there are the shoots, but I wouldn't call such a gathering a party. Our Scots neighbors and friends are nearly all as old as my grandfather, and they are staid." He smiled.

"But you have another sister, you said. Doesn't she go to parties?"

"Oh, Marian. She doesn't care for parties; as long as she has a horse she's happy. She lives in the stables most of her time, and when not there she's racing across the hills. I've never asked you, but do you ride much?"

"No, not at all."

"Really?"

"Well, we live in the center of London."

"But there's always Rotten Row."

"That's never attracted me."

"Well, what do you do with your time, I mean . . . ?"

"Oh, numerous things. I do enjoy our family evenings out: we'll do a play or perhaps the music hall. Some days I spend digging up historical information; more often I go visiting with my father."

"Visiting patients?"

Jason smiled now and said, "Yes, visiting patients. But not those who come to Father's surgery at home. Those, or most of them, would never have heard of Pimlico; perhaps the East End, yes, but they've never been there."

"And your father has a surgery there?"

"Well, he runs a kind of clinic. He started it years and years ago, before I was born, I understand."

"But surely they would have their own doctors in that quarter?"

"Yes, perhaps, but if you're not in their penny clubs or you haven't a shilling to pay for one, what do you do? Just fade away and die in some back alley, or let the sores run until they become gangrenous and then have your legs chopped off."

Robert gave a short laugh now, saying, "I'm sorry, and don't get hot under the collar. I haven't had your experience and so should be forgiven for my ignorance. Anyway, if you felt so strongly about it, why didn't you become a doctor like your father?"

Jason's tone was different now as he said, "Oh, well, I suppose I'm selfish. I saw how my father's life was eaten up by other people, and I knew I wouldn't have the stomach or patience to put up with those who spend their money in gin-shops, or those whose lives are drained in sweatshops, or the plight of homeless children. You've read Dickens, I suppose?"

"Yes, I've read Dickens. But, I might as well tell you, he annoys me at times, the ramming home of the fact that only the poor suffer. Physically they might, but give them enough to eat and drink and in the main they are content and happy; while the others, the middle classes and such, have more than enough to eat and drink, but they, too, suffer. And their suffering, to my mind, Jason, is more difficult to bear than that of your waifs and strays.

Those your father deals with, his clientele, if you like, can shout their feelings to the world; in fact, expose their sores, whereas the upper class, as it is called, have to erect a shield to hide their pain. If I had to choose between mental and physical suffering I know which I'd plump for."

Jason stared at this man who had become his friend. He had, at times, gleaned something in him on which he could not quite lay his finger. Earlier he had thought it was loneliness; but then he dismissed the idea as ridiculous, because he was really very popular. He himself, in a way, had felt honored that he could be classed as one of his friends because, strangely, he had felt drawn to him from the very first. He could recall thinking, Father would like him; and this aroused the thought that they could amicably continue this discussion of the advantages and disadvantages of class, whereas if this question had come up at home, the whole family would have been drawn into it, with Uncle Peter and Aunt Mary and their three, and it would finally degenerate into Speakers' Corner in Hyde Park on a Sunday. He smiled at the memory. He was longing to get back into the home mêlée again. But then, as he continued to look at the man who was now staring out of the window, the sad thought struck him that home life couldn't be the same for Robert. He seemed to be dreading going down next year and more than once had voiced the opinion that he might stay up for another year. It all seemed to depend on his grandfather. It was strange too that he never mentioned his father.

He said now, "You're going straight onto Sussex?"

Robert turned his head and answered briefly, "Yes."

"Will you be staying long in London at any time?"

"Perhaps; it all depends . . ."

"On your grandfather?"

"Yes, on my grandfather." There was a terseness in the tone of his reply.

"Well, I was only thinking that, if you were staying, you might like to drop in on us?"

"Thank you. Yes, I would like that. Indeed I would, because I've heard you yapping on so much about your father and mother and your sister that I've created my own picture of them."

"Oh, I doubt that you'll find them as you've painted them. And there's not only them, there's the conglomeration between the three houses. I told you about my mother's hat business, our home, and then father's partner next door and *his* family, James and Harry and Rosie. If you happen to drop in on a working day, you'll think you've landed in bedlam. But anyway you'll be very welcome."

"Thank you."

"Look, I'll write down the address. Our houses are at the end of Willington Place, thirty-three, thirty-four and thirty-five. Knock on the middle door, thirty-four, and if it's opened by Alice, she'll likely say, "The surgery's next door." And if she's in a very testy mood, because she gets very tired of opening that door, she might address you with, "It's doctors to your left and hats to your right." It all depends, as she'll tell you, whether she spots she's answering the door to a lady or gentlemen, or *them.* And 'them' covers a multitude, from beggars to delivery boys, evangelists selling religion, rag men asking for any old clothes, pamphleteers, to name but a few."

Robert was smiling widely now as he said, "It sounds like a menagerie."

"That's the word for it, that's the exact description. Anyway, you are very welcome to come and view the oddities. . . ."

They said their goodbyes outside Paddington station: each took a cab, Jason to Willington Place and Robert to Victoria Station.

4

"How are you, Mamma?"

"Just as you see, Robert. Time stands still here; or, at least, sometimes it does. At others it seems to race back into the past. But don't talk about me—there's plenty of time for that and your tea's getting cold—I want to hear about Oxford. Does time stand still there?"

"No. No, Mamma, it flies much too quickly, and I want to slow it down."

"Did you ask your grandfather about staying up another year?"

"Yes; but he's not for it. He wants me on the board; or, at least, on one of them. He says they've got need of a mathematician."

"Huh! What nonsense, with all those accountants about. All he wants is for you to be near him. That's one thing I regret: giving in to him and letting you stay with him so much when you were younger. But then, of course, we were up in Northumberland at the time. Yet, I must be fair, this is no place for you, either."

Between them there fell a silence broken only by the replenishing of the tea cups. Then he asked a question he had wanted to ask since his arrival two hours ago. "How is he?" he said. And as always she emphasised her answer by saying, *"Your father* is much about the same."

"Any incidents lately?"

She sipped from the thin china cup before she replied, "Only one of any note. Walton left him fishing quietly by the lake. He was so much himself that Walton felt he could leave him for a time. But when he returned he was gone. So Walton, as usual, made straight for the village inn; but surprisingly he hadn't been there and no one in the village had seen him. And when the afternoon wore on and it was raining heavily and becoming dark, I . . . we didn't know what had happened. Marian had been out riding all afternoon searching the countryside. And it wasn't until about nine o'clock that night that Jamie Grayson came to say he had been doing a last round of the farm with the dog, when it became excited and . . . well, there was your father lying in a ditch. He must have been making his way across the muddy field and slipped into it."

"And he was loaded, I suppose?"

"Yes." Her voice was slightly tart now. "As you say, he was loaded. He was also soaked to the skin, and this resulted in a temperature, which kept him in bed for a fortnight."

"Does . . . does he still get his daily supply?"

"Yes; but apparently it isn't enough. The doctor says the trouble with your father isn't just taking one or two drinks, but a craving that overwhelms him at times and becomes unbearable."

"Oh, nonsense, Mamma." Robert rose abruptly to his feet and walked over to the fireplace and there, putting out his foot, he thrust a half-burnt log into the middle of the open grate, and when the sparks flew out from the shelter of the surrounding walls she cried, "Be careful what you're doing, Robert! And why do you get so angry?"

He turned about and put his foot on a spark that was still gleaming on the hearthrug, not answering her for a moment. When he did, his tone was low but grim as he said, "For the simple reason, Mamma, that you go on defending him when he's ruined your life. He's a drunk of the worst kind, and he's a liar with it. How many times have I seen him stand in this very room with his wine-laden breath wafting over you and carrying on in that hurt tone of his, "I have never touched a drop. How dare you accuse me!" And at such times, Mamma, he could barely stay on his feet. How do you put up with it? And why have you put up with it? He should have been left in the clinic years ago. But what happened then? He succumbed to his other vice, didn't he? And a young girl . . ."

"Please! Please, Robert"—she too had risen to her feet—"don't upset me, I beg of you, any more than you can help. I long to see you, but every time we meet this happens."

Swiftly now, Robert moved toward his mother and, arms about her, he said, "It's no use me saying, yet again, that I'm sorry, but I cannot bear to see you wither away, nursing him, protecting him and being so unhappy."

"It's all right, Robert. It's all right, my dear; and . . . and I am not all that unhappy, and . . . and everything isn't black. There are days that even stretch into weeks when life . . . well, runs quite smoothly. And there is always Marian to keep me company—" A little smile spread across her face now as she added, "when she can manage to get off her horse."

He touched her cheek gently before walking back to the fireplace again and from there he said, "Do you hear much of Annette?"

"Oh, she writes now and again."

"But she doesn't visit?"

"Well, Devon is some distance away, isn't it? And from what I gather, she is expecting a baby," she said, and straightaway stopped pursuing the matter by asking, "Does your grandfather mention your father at all?"

"No. Never."

"He doesn't ask what you find when you come down here?"

"No. He never enquires. He only tells me . . . well, not exactly tells me, but puts it that he would like me to spend a certain time at High Gully during the vac, or suggests that we might stay in town for a few days before we travel up to Scotland."

His mother now sighed as she said, "It might have eased things considerably if he had allowed *us* to go up there for a time each year."

"Oh, I don't think it would, Mamma, oh no. In fact, as I see it, and I'm sure Grandfather does too, Father would get his supply secretly from either McBrien or Jock Taggart; or from Phil or one or other of them. None of them, you know, looks upon drinking as a curse. And Johnny McBrien is himself so soaked in whiskey one can never tell whether he is drunk or sober . . . No, you are better off here, Mamma, under the circumstances."

"Will you go up and see him now?"

"Couldn't I wait until dinner?"

"I would rather you had a little talk with him before dinner."

As he made for the door she called to him softly, "Be kind, Robert."

He paused as if about to answer her, then just sighed and left the room.

In the hall he saw Oswald Walton descending the stairs. The valet seemed always to have been part of his life, at first like a nanny, and then as a counsellor, and he greeted him now with, "Your fire's nicely away, Mr. Robert. No matter how often that chimney's cleaned, it always smokes. But it's all right tonight as the wind's in the right direction. I've laid out your change. I anticipated you might be wearing the deep navy; you are partial to that suit."

"Thank you, Walton." They were standing at the foot of the stairs now facing each other, and Robert made the expected enquiry, "How is he, really, Walton?"

"Oh, not too bad at all, Mr. Robert. Don't worry. And the attack hasn't done all that much harm; it only affected one side slightly, making his arm and leg a little stiff in their movements."

"Attack? Attack? Mother never mentioned an attack."

Walton looked away for a moment before he said, "No, Master Robert, she doesn't care to recognize it and what it might portend. But we all look at things differently. As I see it, it's a deterrent to his . . . well, his wanderings. You were going to call in on him?"

"Yes, I was."

"Oh, he'll be pleased about that, for he may not come down to dinner."

Robert nodded, then went up the stairs, across the gallery and down the corridor.

He tapped on his father's bedroom door before opening it and, putting his head round and with forced brightness, said, "May I come in?"

"Oh, Robert, my dear boy. Of course! Of course! How nice to see you."

Robert walked up the length of the room to where a couch was placed at an angle before the fire, and he looked down on the man resting there, his once fair hair now a pure silver and framing the face that was hardly lined, yet revealing an appearance of age well past his fifty-eight years.

"Sit down. Sit down. You get taller every time I see you."

When Robert had taken a seat to the side of the couch and away from the blazing fire, his father stared at him for a moment before saying, "You look just as I did at your age. I was just thinking the other day of what I used to do when I was up at Oxford. Oh, the larks we got up to. Do you get up larks?"

"Not very often, Father. There's no time. I . . . I have a lot of reading to get through."

"Oh, yes, yes. But, strangely, I never took to mathematics. That's the only difference between us, isn't it? Now the head was wagging. "You're so like me in many ways. I keep telling your mother you are so like me in many ways."

It was only by a force of will that Robert kept his seat and didn't stand up and cry at this pathetic creature, "I am like you in *no* way, sir! you who have ruined my mother's life and, by what I gather, those of a number of other women, too. And simply because I don't want to be like you I have become afraid of women and seek the company of men, because they are safer." But he remained seated and listened to his father making parental conversation:

"I was saying to your mother that we might go up to town for a few days and do the shows. We used to have such wonderful times at Christmas. Oh, and the parties we had in the North, and here, too. Do you remember the parties we had when you were small, and I used to dress up? Do you remember that? I used to dress up."

Robert could stand no more of this, and so made himself rise slowly from his chair, then say, "Father, would you excuse me? I must go and change; I still feel dusty from the journey; the trains never get any cleaner."

"By all means, dear boy. By all means. I'll tell Walton to run a bath for you."

"No; don't bother, Father. I'll see to it. Be seeing you later."

"Yes. Yes, of course."

As he made for the door his father called, "Are you staying for Christmas?"

"I . . . I don't know yet, Father."

"What about the New Year?"

"Yes. Yes, perhaps."

"That will be nice. We'll bring in the New Year together. That will be so nice."

Dear Lord! He stood on the landing for a moment. How did his mother stand it? That blocking out of all reality; that charming voice that could never speak the truth; and those eyes of his. Yes, those eyes. There was always a strange plea in his eyes, like that of a child. He likened it to one that had been promised a whipping and couldn't understand why.

He had only been in his room a few minutes when a knock came on the door and a voice called, "May I come in?"

As he said, "Yes, of course," and pulled open the door to see his sister Marian, she laughed and said, "Hello, there. Nice to see you."

"And you. How are you? But need I ask? My! you look fit." He was admiring her plump red cheeks.

"Well, so would you be if you worked as hard as I do."

"Sitting on a horse, working hard?"

"I've been breaking one in. Boy! is he tough? How long are you staying?"

"Oh, just a few days."

"You going up to Scotland?"

"No, not right away. I think Grandfather's spending a short time in London. But I have to hear from him yet."

"I would like to go up to High Gully again. I've only a dim memory of it. Do you think he'd let me?"

"Yes, of course he would. But believe me, you'll be glad to get back to civilization. It's pretty rough up there, especially at this time of the year."

"Mamma said that they used to have marvelous times there; great big house parties that went on for days."

"Yes, so I understand, but I've never experienced them. It's dull and grim and cold," a statement which seemed quickly to moderate any enthusiasm for such a visit, and so she turned toward the door again, saying, "Have you seen Father?"

"Yes."

"What do you think?"

"Well, you know what I always think."

"He can't help it. That's how he's made. You might find that out some day yourself."

He turned on her fiercely, saying, "Don't you suggest, Marian, that I might become like him."

"No, I'm not suggesting that, but you know, you're not dead yet, and it's mostly circumstances that make people do what they do."

"It wasn't circumstances that made him do what he did. And whatever it was it must have been pretty bad for Grandfather to disown him."

"He hasn't disowned him."

"Well, you tell me what to call it when he won't see him and forbids him to visit either London or Scotland. What amazes me is how Mother puts up with it and has done all these years."

She was holding the handle of the door as she paused and, looking over her shoulder, she said, "Oh, we all have our compensations . . . Horses are mine, I'm thankful to say." And on that enigmatic remark she left him to his ablutions.

But the enigmatic remark was clarified some time later . . .

He'd had a bath; he had changed; and he was now sitting by the fire, thinking of the claustrophobic atmosphere of this house, where visitors weren't encouraged, apart from his mother's close friends, Winifred DeWhit and the Musgraves in St. Leonard's; and there was no hospitality shown to immediate neighbors. He knew there must be a reason, but he hadn't determined what it was. Only one thing he did know: his father hadn't always been a drunkard, and he could recall times when the house seemed to be bursting with people.

His thoughts turned to the train journey down ealier in the day and to Jason talking about his family and longing to be among them. If his grandfather should decide to stay in London any time next week, he would take Jason up on his invitation and call at the Middle House. It would be a break from the monotony. And perhaps if he stayed in town for a few days, Jason and he could do a show. He would like that. He thought again that he had never been drawn to anyone as he had to Jason. Maybe it was because he was so uncomplicated, so frank, with nothing to hide; whereas his own life was so complicated that at times he felt he was hiding from things about which he knew nothing. Why had his grandfather insisted that he use only his first name of Anderson? He had been told this when he was first sent away to school, where he was known as Robert Anderson, and it had stayed with him ever since. Yet his father was known as Anderson Steerman. He had once asked his mother about this and she had been very evasive, dismissing it simply as: "Well, if Grandfather wants it that way, so be it." And at the time it was easy to accept when he surmised that, anyway, there was nothing to be proud of in the name of Steerman, especially around here.

He leaned forward, his elbows on his knees, and sat staring into the fire as though asking: had his father done something criminal in his early years? But then that would have meant he had likely spent time in prison, and his memory told him that he had always been there when he returned from boarding school for the vacs, and also that he had never seen him in any other place but this house—whereas of the house in Northumberland he had only a vague recollection. So was it only the drinking that had made him a kind of recluse . . . and his mother, too? He would like to know more. He would like to get to the bottom of something. But what?

He got up, went to the mirror, straightened the bow tie on his shirt, pulled his cuffs down below his jacket sleeves, then glanced at the clock. It was a good twenty minutes before the dinner bell would ring. Nevertheless, he would go downstairs, perhaps go into the kitchen and have a talk with cook and the maids. They liked him to go into the kitchen, always making a fuss of him. It was nice to be made a fuss of; at least, in some place or other. His mother didn't usually come down for dinner until the bell rang. It was a sort of pattern, a way of life.

When he reached the foot of the stairs, instead of crossing the hall, he turned and made his way to the dining room, which had access to the breakfast-room and onto the kitchen.

The dining room door was ajar. He pushed it open and, walking up by the side of the long table, with a dozen chairs at each side, he saw through the arch and reflected in the mirror above the fireplace his mother and Walton. They were standing close together. He could see only the upper part of them. But Walton was holding his mother's hands in his and, his head bent toward her, he was evidently speaking to her in very soft tones, because no sound of his voice came to him. But what he could see in their profiles caused him to freeze for a moment, and as their heads moved closer together he closed his eyes, turned about and went slowly and quietly from the room.

His mother and his father's valet! No! No! But yes; his eyes hadn't deceived him.

We all have our compensations.

In the drawing room he stood gripping the back of a chair. What was he going to do about it? What *could* he do about it? His mother, his lady mother and a servant! But wasn't Walton more than a servant? He had been in the family for years. He had been with his father long before he was married, so he must be a man in his sixties, although his hair was merely pepper and salt in parts and quite dark at the back. And there was his mother; she was in her middle fifties. What on earth could they mean to each other?

Oh, don't be so damned naïve! He almost thrust the chair from him, then went and dropped onto the couch. But the man was *a servant,* old family retainer or not, he was a *servant.* Yet perhaps it was because of him that she was able to stand this life. Such memories might now be vague, but he could remember her being quite different from what she was now: memories of her as being bright, gay, and so pretty. She was still pretty.

Did his father know of this, even sense it?

Oh, what did that matter. He didn't deserve anything better than to have a wife who would consort with a servant.

Oh dear God! What was the matter with him? Hadn't he been out in the world? Hadn't he learned anything?

The answer was attacked by a crying inside himself, Yes, he *had* learned something . . . to be afraid of showing emotion. But now that his father's valet and his mother were showing emotion, he was shocked.

When the door opened he stiffened, then relaxed a little when he saw it was Marian; and she must have noticed his changed expression because she asked, "What's the matter?"

He swallowed deeply before he said, "You mentioned a little earlier that everybody needed compensations. What did you mean by that?"

"What do you think I meant? Just that. We must all have something to keep us going, especially in this set-up."

"Were you referring to Mamma?"

She turned a sharp glance on him as she said, "What do you mean?"

"Just what I say; were you referring to Mamma?"

She lowered her eyes now and said, "All I can say to you in answer to that, Robert, is, *we* have to live here. And since Grandfather cut Daddy off without a penny and only gives Mamma a bare subsistence, life has been anything but easy."

"But Mamma has money of her own."

"She had, but it had dwindled, what with supporting this place and allowing me my pastime. She knows, and I know, there's very little hope of some gallant knight galloping here on a sixteen-hands white charger, and whipping me up into his arms. As I was once told in school, I'm as plain as workhouse fare."

"Don't be silly; you're not plain at all!"

"Don't try to be kind to me, Robert. We know each other too well." Now she smiled as she said, "We've fought too many battles, and yet"—her voice softened—"since you went up to Oxford you have changed. We were always battling each other before that, weren't we? Now you don't seem to want a fight." Her smile broadened, taking away her actual plainness. Then, her voice softening further, she added, "Leave Mamma alone, Robert. Try to understand. Quite candidly, you don't belong to this household at all. You've never really been in it for any length of time. Grandfather's seen to that. You are his substitute son. You know that, don't you?"

"Marian, tell me, because you know much more about it than I do, what has Father really done?"

"Oh!" Her voice was loud now. "Don't let's go into that. In fact, *I'm* not going into that. I'll just answer you in the quip of the music hall: wine, women, but, in this case, no song. Now, there's the dinner bell. Please!" Her voice had softened again; then linking her arm through his, she said, "Shall we go in to dinner, brother?" And more quietly still, she whispered, "And for the Lord's sake! take that pulpit look off your face."

As he allowed her to lead him out of the room and into the dining room, he was not the Oxford student in his third year, down for the vac, he was not the popular captain of boats, he was not the young man who held debates in his rooms: they peopled another life; here, he was like a callow youth who had yet to go out into life and learn about love, loneliness, desire and pain.

5

"Oh, there you are, dear." Emily rose from the table in the breakfast-room to greet her daughter, who had just entered the room. "You've had a good sleep. And oh, you needed it. But you needn't have got up; you could have had your breakfast in bed. Alice looked in half an hour ago and said you were still sound asleep."

"It's force of habit. It's a wonder I didn't wake up at six, because it takes me half an hour every morning to pull myself together in order to get on duty by seven."

"What will you have? Bacon and egg, kidneys? They're still hot."

Emily had lifted the cover of the heated dish on the long sideboard.

"Oh no! Mother," and Janice grimaced at her stomach's reaction. "I couldn't face that this morning, especially when there's a Christmas dinner looming ahead at one o'clock. You know, Mother, when I asked Sister if I could delay my leave until the middle of the week and as usual she asked the reason, I had to say it was so that I could have Christmas Day dinner with my family on the day before Christmas Eve; and she peered at me with that steely look of hers as if I were some weird creature who had evolved out of thin air, not that Nurse Montane who had irritated her for the past year and who could never do anything right, and she repeated, 'Christmas dinner the day before Christmas Eve!' And then do you know what she said, Mother? 'Your attitude, nurse, always prompts the thought that you come from a strange family,' and she sniffed in her usual way and said again, 'Christmas dinner the day before Christmas Eve. Get about your work, nurse!' " Janice laughed as she added, "And I wanted to say, 'Yes, you're quite right, Sister. We are all oddities!' "

"You should have told her exactly why we have Christmas dinner when we do."

"I don't suppose she would have believed that my doctor father and his wife and their son spend Christmas Day down at Westerley Place, cooking and serving meals to the waifs and strays, and that's not counting the preparation on Christmas Eve and the work that goes into raking in the volunteers."

Janice took a piece of toast from the rack, and as she buttered it, she said, "How long have you been doing that, Mother?"

"Oh, since you and Jason were about seven, I think. The first year I took you both with us, but you were sick, not once, but a number of times, and so I dared not repeat it. Some of the poor souls had been giving you bits from their plates: fat pork and such. I remember that year because I had to bring you both home in the afternoon and so missed the best part of the day: the sing-song at night, when they are all warm and relaxed, and some of them even look happy. I suppose that for a while they have blotted out the coming day . . . Your father has done marvelous work down there, you know.''

''Yes; but he's had to work twice as hard next door to be able to accomplish what he has. And you, too. Neither of you ever seem to stop and lead an ordinary life.''

''Oh, we lead an ordinary life all right, and a very fulfilling one. And we're not the only ones in this particular field, you know. There are many caring people in the world. The only thing I wish is that more of them would get into Parliament.''

''Where's Jason?''

''Next door, of course, arguing with James and Harry. They finished school last week, you know.''

''How are things going with Rosie and him?''

''Oh, my dear, I just don't know. I think he still sees her as someone he was brought up with and pushed around when she was a baby. But it isn't the same with her, and she's such an intelligent girl, if a bit too possessive at times; and she's so good at her secretarial post. That seems to be the latest craze. Even the debs, I understand, who haven't managed to find a suitable husband in the marriage market are attending the secretarial colleges. Times are changing, and rapidly. It all seems to have happened since the Queen died and they've got over the mourning period.'' Emily smiled now as she said, "Your father is all for the King. He's putting the change down to him, because he's a traveled man and, in a way, also a deprived one, denied his rights to the throne for so long. But, moreover, as your father says, he really is a human being."

"Yes, of course, Mother, he's a very human being with a mistress on the side for so long, with the princess, as she was, having to put a face on it."

Emily rose from the table, saying, "I . . . I must go into the kitchen and see how things are moving there. Your father has a special appointment at three o'clock, so we must have our Christmas dinner on time. And we thought we might all go to a show tonight. So get your heads together and see which one would be the jolliest."

In the hall she was stopped by a young girl in uniform, blue print dress, bibbed white apron and starched cap, who said to her, "Can I clear now, ma'am?"

And Emily, looking back toward the breakfast-room door, said, "Oh, give Miss Janice another ten minutes. And Annie?"—she now turned toward the maid—"she's had only one cup of tea so far and, as you know, she nearly always empties the pot."

"Very well, ma'am." They smiled at each other before going their different ways.

There was the sound of voices and laughter coming from the drawing room, when Alice, on her way toward it, paused as there came a knock on the front door. Looking back, she called to Annie Smears as she was making her way hurriedly toward the kitchen, "See who that is, Annie."

Annie ran to open the door, and there was an exchange of voices; and it was just as Alice was about to enter the drawing room that the young maid beckoned to her, saying "It's . . . it's a gentleman. He wants to speak to Mr. Jason."

When Alice reached the front door, it was to see a well-built young man standing on the front step. She had to look up to him and she stared, and her mouth fell into a slight gape; then she half-glanced back to the drawing room before saying, "Yes, sir?"

"I . . . I'm inquiring if Mr. Jason Montane is at home."

"Oh, yes. Yes, he is, sir. What is your name?"

"Robert Anderson."

"Oh, Robert Anderson." The name died away on her lips. Then on a higher tone, she said, "Come in, sir. Come in a moment."

Robert stepped into the hall. He was holding his hat now and he watched one maid hurry toward the right-hand side of the long hall, while the other servant, in uniform, approached and entered a room opposite, from which the noise and chatter then ceased, before the door was pulled open and there was Jason.

"Well! Well! Oh, I am pleased to see you. Come on in. Take off your coat. When did you arrive? I mean, how long have you been in town?"

"Since yesterday. But wait, you have company. I'll call again another time."

"You'll do no such thing. Look; take off your coat. Let me have it." He almost pulled the overcoat from Robert, saying, "You couldn't have come at a better time. The mob's all here. We are just going to have our Christmas dinner."

"Oh, no, no." Robert now grabbed at his coat and said, "I can't intrude. No! please; another time."

The door was again opened and another man appeared. He was of medium height and had gray hair and very bright eyes. He didn't approach them, but stood some distance away staring at them, hearing Jason calling to him excitedly, "This is my friend, Father, the one I've told you about: Robert. Robert, this is my father, Doctor Montane."

"I'm very pleased to meet you, sir."

Steve shook the hand held out to him as he stared into the visitor's eyes. Surely he had seen this young man before. But where, he didn't know. Still, he had so many patients next door, and down on the waterfront, too. Yes, it could be one of them. He was fair-haired, not unlike Jason, although Jason was of a darker shade.

"Come and meet the family. But I must apologize for them beforehand; in fact, I should make excuses for all those present." He was walking back toward the drawing room door, Jason behind, his hand on Robert's arm.

"Quiet a minute, you lot of hooligans! This"—he

put his hand back toward Robert—"is Jason's friend from Oxford, and as he has only just arrived I have yet to find out how this menagerie will affect him. This, by the way, sir, is my wife."

Emily took the hand extended toward her, and as she did so she was puzzled by the shiver that ran through her body. But she smiled as she said, "You're very welcome. And this is my daughter, Janice, Jason's twin."

"I'm often asked," Steve put in quickly now, "why Janice and Jason? Well, Janice was the name of my wife's mother, and Jason was my grandfather's name."

"And I'm the elder," Jason said.

Robert was still holding Janice's hand as she said, "How do you do? Yes, he's the elder by four minutes, but mentally he's deficient by four years. He has a lot of catching up to do."

Amid the laughter, Robert gazed at the girl whose hand he was holding and, joining her mood, he acknowledged, "I detected the deficiency in the brain some time ago. But that doesn't detract from his brawn, which is quite useful in the boat."

"Oh, well capped! Well capped."

Steve now turned and said, "This is my partner Doctor John Nelson, and his wife Mary. And, for their sins, their daughter Rosie, and their sons James and Harry." Steve had pointed to each in turn, and when the introductions were finally over Steve, glancing at the clock on the mantelpiece, said, "Well, it's close on one; let's away to the dining room."

"I . . . I feel that this is an intrusion; I would rather . . ."

"Say no more, young man, if you don't want to spoil our Christmas dinner. You see, we have it a couple of days beforehand because we're so busy on Christmas Day and there's no time for it. But perhaps Jason has already told you all about the odd arrangement by which we live . . . Alice!" He now called down the room to where the maid was standing at the open door. "A piece more cutlery on the table, please. That'll make a straight ten. I like even numbers."

Five minutes later they were all seated around the long dining table, Steve at the head and Emily at the foot, with Janice sitting to her father's right and Robert to his left. Jason sat to his mother's right, with John Nelson and his family filling the vacant seats.

The chatter was hushed when Steve stood up and said a very strange grace: "May the gods never provide less for others than we have on this Christmas dinner table."

The concerted "Amen" was followed by Jason rising and pouring out the wine; and when he was seated again, their glasses were raised as Steve toasted: "Let's drink to all our loved ones who are gone and those who are still with us, particularly our wives and children . . . not forgetting our very welcome guest," and with this all the raised glasses were swung in Robert's direction; and his pale face was tinged slightly pink as he, in turn, raised his glass and replied, "Thank you, and to you all."

Now, turning his head toward the door, Steve cried, "Alice! Bring it in," and almost immediately Alice entered, carrying a very weighty dish on which rested a large turkey. She was followed by two maids carrying trays of side dishes.

When the turkey had been carved and the vegetables served, and the cranberry sauce passed amid noise, laughter and chatter, they ate their way through the heaped course. Following this, more wine was poured, the pudding was brought in and set alight amid "Oohs!"and "Ahs!" and brandy sauce passed around. And it was during the eating of the pudding and amid comments that it was the best that cook had ever achieved, which was said every year, that Steve, his voice raised to make himself heard, said to Robert, "You must feel you are in very strange company."

Robert answered brightly, "It couldn't be better, sir. It's a long time since I've enjoyed such a meal. You're given small helpings in hotels. There are always several courses, but very often you don't care for half of them."

"Have you been long in town?"

This came across the table from Janice and he shook his head as he replied, "No, just since yesterday."

"Are you staying over the holidays?"

"I . . . I hope so. It all depends upon my grandfather."

"Your family is here?"

"No. My mother and father are in Sussex. My grandfather lives in Scotland."

"I didn't catch your name." This was from Steve.

"Anderson, sir."

"Oh, Anderson. Are you the only one in the family?"

"No, I have sisters, one married and one still at home."

There was a great deal of laughter now from the end of the table and Janice, her voice raised, leaned toward him, saying. "Your sister's in town?"

"No." He shook his head. "She's with my parents. It takes a lot to get her away; she is horse mad."

"She rides a lot?" It was Steve speaking to him now. And as the laughter had subsided somewhat from the other end of the table, Robert had to lower his voice as he said, "Indeed, sir, she rides a lot. She would sleep in the stables if she had her way. That's all she thinks about, horses." Then he gave a slight shake of his head. "No," he said, "not quite. I'm always surprised at her other hobby which is reading, mainly . . . well, poetry. It has always surprised me."

He was also surprised at himself, for he was feeling very much at his ease, even talkative. He put it down to the enjoyable meal, and the wine, which was so good.

"Why does it surprise you that she likes horses and poetry?"

He looked across at Janice now and answered, "Well, the two don't seem to go together. Not the type of poetry she reads, anyway. It's mostly modern stuff, quite a lot by a fellow . . . well, I don't know if it's a man or a woman. I myself cannot understand what she sees in the work, but every year, when I ask her what she would like, her answer is always, "Oh, just get me a Petersen book, if there's a new one out." I think he's published about eight . . ."

There was a coughing and spluttering from the far end of the table, and Steve chastised his son, saying, "Really! Jason. You were always an untidy eater, even as a child. Why can't you see to him, Mother?" He was looking down the table toward Emily. But Emily had her elbow on the table, her head resting on her hand, her eyes cast down. But now all eyes were turned on Janice who was addressing Robert. "You don't care for Petersen's poems?"

"Well, they are not in my line. I would say they appeal more to women . . . ladies. And yet . . . no, I'm sometimes puzzled to know whether Petersen is a man or a woman."

"Then you read him?"

He laughed now, "Only when I buy them for my sister. I have a volume in the pocket of my coat." He thumbed over the back of his chair now. "It's the man's latest . . . or *her* latest. Don't know which. Yet, I'm always amazed that Marian . . . my sister, enjoys them, because there's a bitter streak running through some and . . . er . . . and a religious touch to others. And some I can't make head or tail of."

When the sound of combined coughing came from the end of the table, Mary Nelson's voice checked it quietly. Then it was Emily who spoke. Looking down toward her husband, she said, "Steve, please ex . . ."

"No, my dear, stay. Your daughter likes Petersen, so let her deal with this argument. And by the way"—he was looking at Robert now—"I've never known this family to eat a meal, whether Christmas or otherwise, unless heated discussion of some kind or another takes place. So today we are keeping to pattern." Then, nodding, he said to his daughter, "Go on. Say what you were going to say, dear."

Janice laughed and, looking at Robert, said, "I was just going to ask you if you had read any of those in the new book?"

"Well, I just skipped through them in the shop and there was a short one that caught my eye. It was called, 'Waterloo Station.' " He laughed.

"And did you read it?"

"Yes. Do you know it?"

"Yes, I know it, and I love Petersen's work. I love Petersen altogether, and I particularly like 'Waterloo Station.' " And now she sat back in her chair as she began to quote:

It was in a station,
Waterloo;
I saw two lovers leave a train.
Separate, they walked toward me,
Went past, and on again,
Both tall and straight and beautiful
Their eyes shining in love's first youth;
Then shyly their fingers touched and clung.
Who were they?
Whence did they come?
Whither did they go?
To what future I do not know,
I only know on that day
My heart sang
And I was touched as if by a spring
From the fountain of their love,
And the pages of my life rolled away
And I was old no more,
But young and gay,
Walking straight through Waterloo
After meeting the train
And you.

There was silence at the table. Robert's face was very red now. He stared at Janice for some time, then glanced along the table and found all eyes directed toward him. He turned to his host, who was staring down at his plate while his hand was stretched out and gripping that of his daughter. And Robert, his voice stiff now, said, "I . . . I feel that I have made a great *faux pas* somewhere. Yet I don't know where." He turned his head sharply and looked toward Emily, asking now, "Is it your pseudonym, Mrs. Montane?"

"No. No, Robert, it isn't my pseudonym. It is my husband's. And I feel that my family have behaved very badly."

"No. No, we haven't." Steve's head was up, his voice loud. "No, we haven't. This was a discussion, and I'm not going to apologize to our friend here because I write poetry that sometimes appears womanish. He is a young man who should know by now that in all of us there is but a very, very fine line between the male and the female. The latter in the male may be deep, but those of us who can touch or detect it are enabled to understand more than we would have done had we been strongly male, probably arrogant male. So I make no excuses, sir, for my tendency to confuse, not only you, but many others. Yet at the same time"—his head wagged from side to side—"I'm always amazed that anybody wants to read them. You see, in the first place, they were written on scraps of paper during the time I was walking the wards and learning my trade, which led me to the waterfront and the misery I witnessed there; and they were put down in simple language. It's only when I try to be clever and profound, two difficult things for me, that nobody seems to know what I'm getting at."

The tint was fading from Robert's cheeks and now he looked down the table toward Jason, saying, "No wonder you spluttered into your pudding;'' and amid the ensuing laughter he went on, ''Why couldn't you tell me, or give me a hint?''

''Why should I let myself down by telling you my father wrote stuff that has neither rhyme nor reason? It's nothing to be proud of.''

From all quarters shouts were rained on him like blows, and one of the Nelson boys actually threw an orange, which bounced off his head and onto Mary Nelson's plate, causing Emily to command, but in no way as a reprimand, ''Oh, please don't start on the crockery,'' and for Steve to suggest: ''Well, shall we have coffee in the sitting room? It'll give them a chance to get clear of this clutter and get on with their own dinner,'' which was immediately taken up by both Mary Nelson and her daughter Rosie saying almost simultaneously, ''We will see to things,'' and Steve adding, ''Yes; why not?'' to be followed by more laughter when Jason, patting Mrs. Nelson on the shoulder, said, ''No; you sit down, old lady, and rest your poor old bones, together with my mother: Rosie and I will see to things.'' And as he was given a push by Mary Nelson, he took hold of Rosie's hand and almost at a run took her out of the room.

As the rest of the party made their way toward the sitting room, Robert found himself walking by Janice's side. And he noted that she was extra tall for a young lady; she must be the same height as her twin; and she was very like him in looks, although not exactly: you couldn't say Jason was beautiful, but this girl was. Where Jason was fair, she had brown hair and deep brown eyes and alabaster-tinted skin. She moved her head toward him and, under cover of the chatter that went on ahead, said, "You didn't really mind me ribbing you, did you?"

He forced himself to smile and say, "Not at all, not at all," yet at the time aware that he had felt most embarrassed and slightly angry even, for he had never been able to stand being the butt of jokes. Oxford was a place for practical jokers, and while there one had to grin and bear it. But it always annoyed him inside, because the only person who seemed really to enjoy a practical joke was the perpetrator. But he was already telling himself he wouldn't mind being ribbed again in such a way by this girl. And that was a strange thought for him; and strange, too, was the immediate feeling of being at ease with her. It was odd, but she had the same effect upon him as had Jason. Well, of course; why should he wonder about that? They were brother and sister. Moreover, they were twins and so alike in all ways except in coloring.

She was now asking, "Are you having a big do at Christmas?"

"A big do?" He gave a derisive "Huh! If you knew my grandfather you would realize that his days of big do's are over. Although yes, he sometimes recalls them when he is well warmed in the evening with his port and cigars and a big fire."

They were seated side by side now on a couch some way from the fire when she asked him, "Do

you spend most of your holidays with your grandfather, then?"

"Yes—" He kept back the word "unfortunately."

"Couldn't he join your family in Sussex?"

When there came a blank look on his face and
he didn't answer, she said, "Oh, I am sorry. There
I go. I'm as bad as the rest of our tribe. I'm always
asking questions. I'm so . . ."

"Please, don't be sorry. You have such a close
and uncomplicated family that it must seem natural to you to spend all your holidays in the same
place. But, you see, my father is rather unwell and
he doesn't leave the house very much, and my
mother attends him. And, as I've already said,
Marian gives her life to the horses and"—he
pulled a face at her now—"Mr. Petersen-cum-
Montane's poetry, while my grandfather lives
most of his life up in Scotland, which I may tell
you is a very dreary and isolated place; at least,
the part we live in."

"Is he very old?"

"In his middle eighties. Yet he's surprisingly agile for that age; mentally, I mean. His wits are still
very keen, as is his business acumen. He still
keeps overall control, which is really what brings
him to London now and again."

"Do you do the shows?"

"Very, very rarely, because he likes my company in the evening."

"Oh, what a pity! It would have been so nice if
you could have joined us tonight. We make it a

point every year to do a music hall or a pantomime. Something you can laugh at, you know.''

When he made no reply but just continued to
look at her, she said, ''Well, I know it's not the
opera or the proper theater . . . not very 'Oxford' . . .''

She did not say, Really! but looking into his
eyes, she thought she detected sadness; in fact,
if it didn't seem so outrageous, she would have
said he looked lost, and it was as if, in the few
hours he had spent in this house, he was emerging as a butterfly might from a chrysalis. Yet she
recalled that Jason had mentioned him constantly
in his letters; of how well he was liked, what a
good sportsman he was on the river, how he
ralied the crew; of the discussions in his rooms;
and of how he felt about him in general. And she
guessed that her brother felt quite honored by the
fact that this third-year man had taken him, as it
were, under his wing.

Yet, despite all this, she sensed his unhappiness
and so, impulsively, she said, ''Do come with us
tonight. We may be going to the Royal Strand.
Louie Freear in *A Chinese Honeymoon.* She's so
good as the maid Fi Fi. She sings 'I want to be a
Lidy'; or perhaps to the Gaiety. Gertie Millar's on
there. There'll be a family meeting presently to
decide where we'll land up, because somebody
will have to dash round to book. We always get in
somewhere; perhaps we'll end up at *Quality
Street* at the Vaudeville. So do come. You'll enjoy
it. And leave your grandfather to his wine, his ci-

gars and the fire for one evening. It isn't as if it was Christmas Eve or Christmas Night; you couldn't leave him then, but tonight is different. Will you come?''

There was no hesitation in his voice as he said quietly, ''Yes. Yes, I should love to.'' And then a feeling of excitement grew in him when she jumped up and went straight over to her mother, who was at a side table pouring out the coffee, and his mind went back to when his own mother was still entertaining and he considered what would have happened if one of the mammas had heard her daughter asking him to go to a vaude-ville show, where they could all join in the singing. There would have been either a polite and hasty exit, or an assumed faint to attract the erring daughter's attention.

Times had changed, but not to the extent of the freedom that was prevalent in this family. It was like breathing pure clean air after being suffocated by fog.

As he watched the tall, elegant girl coming toward him carrying two cups of coffee, he knew that never again would he be afraid of women's company, for this girl had broken through the barrier.

6

The man knocked at the door and when it was opened by the footman he thrust his foot in the gap, saying, "This is the fifth time I've called here lately and I know he's at home. So don't give me that. Just tell him it's Benito Dimarca, and that I've got news for him."

The butler did not fully open the door but turned and spoke to someone crossing the hall. Then the door was pulled out of his hand and Jock Gibbons stood there, saying, "It's no use, the master won't see you. In any case, he's not at all well."

"Well, he'll feel much worse if he doesn't hear me out, 'cos I'll open me mouth and set his closed world on fire again. He won't be able to hush it up like last time."

Gibbons stared down into the dark, swarthy face; then pulling the door open, he said, "Step inside, but no further," and after closing the door and intimating to the footman to leave, he again said to the young man, "I repeat! the master won't see you. But tell me what this is all about and I will see what I can do."

"You've said that before and nothing came of it. And it's bloody-well odd to me that from the time he stopped the money when my mother died, I should then get the push. That's eighteen months gone, and I've been living from hand to mouth since, scrabbling bits here and there. And it shouldn't be, for I'm related. By law he's my grandfather. Give my bloody father his due, he always stumped up."

Gibbons put his face close to the man's and said, "Your bloody father, as you call him, never stumped up; it all had to come from *his* father."

"Well, whoever it came from, we got a little bit of our rights."

"Never mind your rights. What is it you have found that you say is of such importance that you can use blackmail?"

"I'm not using blackmail. And anyway, if you had me up for that I would likely get justice when it all came out. But what I've got is . . ." The man shook his head. "No, I want to see him himself. I'll tell him myself."

"I can assure you now that you will not see him. You will either tell me, or you will go."

The man drew in his lower lip tight between his teeth before he said, "Well, it's like this, if you want to know, and it's something I've known for a long time, although I've kept me mouth shut: I'm not the only other grandson, bastard or otherwise, of the old fella's. You mind when the doctor came and bashed my father up after he had been at that one who sells the hats? Well, why does he go and marry her the next week or so? And why were twins born after just nine months? And why, when you see the boy and the old man's grandson standing side by side, are they almost as twin-looking as the fella and his sister? But that's only half of it, because the lass, who's a nurse, the twin, is thick with my dear half-brother. And when I say thick, I mean thick, because he was at a party there at Christmas and I've seen them since together. They were at the Tate. I was sitting there, not looking at pictures, but to get out of the cold. But there they were. And now the latest I hear is, he's taking her to a dance at Oxford."

Gibbons remained silent for at least a minute before he said, "How have you come to know all this? You have no connection with that house."

"Well, having nothing to do, mister, I keep me eyes open. And every now and then you can pick up a delivery job for a few days, when it's possible you find yourself, as the Bible says, talking to the least of these, the scullery maid. They're all great chatterers, are scullery maids. They're even proud of the goings-on upstairs. And as I can't pick and choose my jobs now, I go for where my interest lies. D'you get me?"

"Yes. I get you. And I would like to get you by the neck and fling you out of that door."

"It would take someone younger and bigger, mister, to do that. Now, what are you going to do about it, eh?"

Again Gibbons stared at the man, then said, "Stay where you are. Move toward one of the rooms and I'll have you out of that door. Information or no information."

He now hurried along the corridor and into the smoke-room where, stretched out in a long cane chair, sat his master. He had a portable desk across his knees, on which were a number of papers, with more scattered on the floor.

"May I have a word with you for a moment, sir?"

"Yes. Yes, what is it, Gibbons?" The white head remained bent over the papers.

"It's that man Dimarca, sir."

The head came up with a jerk and the voice was stiff: "I've told you, Gibbons, in no way am I . . . ."

"Excuse me, sir, but he has come up with something . . . well, I think, rather important; that is, I mean, if he should make it public."

The master and man stared at each other. There was nothing they did not know about each other. And when the old man remained silent, Gibbons went on, "Following the episode of Mr. Paul, the doctor married Mrs. Ratcliffe. I'm not sure whether it was a week or a fortnight later. But what transpired was that she was delivered of twins, a boy and a girl, born within the recognized time for Mr. Paul to have been the father. And Dimarca has been aware of that, but remained quiet as long as the allowance was being paid. But, from what he says, I imagine that since then he has made it his business to probe once more. And . . . and . . . ."

"Yes? Yes? Go on, man. And what?" The tone was icy.

"It has come to his knowledge that Master Robert is . . . er . . . well, friendly with . . . er, in fact associating with the daughter of the house."

"Robert and the daughter?"

"Yes, sir, the daughter. Probably brought about after the young man had become a friend of Mr. Robert's when up in Oxford. You may remember that he went to a friend's house at Christmas, and if I may remind you, sir, you were annoyed that he didn't give you pre-warning that he was staying out that evening. So, therefore, he may not have mentioned the name of the people he was with, which happened to be the doctor's family. The name is Montane, you recall, sir."

"Dear Lord! Dear Lord! Indeed I do. I do recall the name of Montane. Yet what can that scoundrel do? Eh? What can he do with this new piece of surreptitious information?"

Gibbons would have liked to answer: he can inform the world at large that you have two other grandchildren; instead, he said, "He could make it uncomfortable for the young people, sir. And there is always the chance that their association might continue to develop."

The old man did not immediately react: he thoroughly gathered up the papers before him, squared them off top and bottom and placed them in a folder before, clapping his hand hard down on it, he said, "I am not going to be subjected to blackmail by that crawling, sneaking individual. And you tell him that, Gibbons: he does not get another penny out of me." He paused, then said, "What about his sister?"

"I . . . I think she went back to Italy some long time ago, sir. She was of a different caliber from the rest. If you remember, her mother brought her here once, actually by force, and the girl was sensible enough to say openly that she wanted nothing from you. She did not seem to like either her parents or her brother. May I suggest, sir, it might be wise to give him a little something."

"No, it would not be wise, Gibbons. Not only would I have him around my neck, but when I am gone he would be around Robert's, too. No, let him do his worst."

Gibbons was turning slowly away when the old man said, "Wait!" and Gibbons waited; then, as he knew it would be, the more thoughtful decision was made: "The answer to that man is still the same. But tomorrow morning I shall get you to take a letter to Doctor Montane, asking him to visit me. He is, I think, a man of honor, one who will deal with the situation that has arisen. Yes, that's what we'll do, Gibbons." And with a nod of his head he dismissed him.

In the hall, Gibbons gave the answer to the man, whose immediate reaction was shown on his reddening face as he muttered, "Well, you can tell him that I warned him. If I have nothing to gain, I'll see he has something to lose and that is his pampered grandson." And he turned toward the door, only to swing round again and with a break in his voice say, "It's bloody unfair. D'you hear that? it's bloody unfair. All my life I've been looked upon as

an outcast, not given my place. But from now on
. . . well, we'll see. . . ."

Benito Dimarca walked briskly until he came to
Willington Place, and there he knocked on num-
ber thirty-five. And when the door was opened by
Alice, who stared at him open-mouthed, he said,
"I want to see Doctor Montane."

"This isn't the surgery"—she jerked her head—
"that's next door. And anyway, what's your business?"

"What's my business is *my* business." He
turned from her to go next door, and she craned
forward to watch him stare at the brass plate on
the wall, before he rapped on the door.

When this door was opened she heard him say,
"I want to see the doctor." And although she
could not hear the answer, she knew it would
have been: "Do you have an appointment? Because the surgery hours are over." She did hear
him say, "No. But I want to see him privately,"
and also the reply, "Then you should either come
back in the morning or go down to his other surgery."

"Where's that?"

Having anticipated the answer, "Westerley
Place," Alice closed the door, but remained there
until she heard the footsteps pass: then she
nipped on her lip. She knew who he was. It was
around Christmas time when she had last seen
him outside the house. What had drawn her attention to him then was that he should be stand-

ing where the young lad used to wait, all those years ago.

She looked toward the door leading to the workroom and she said to herself, don't tell me something else is going to start! And it wasn't today's visit of this young man; the feeling inside her had been growing for some time now; ever since Christmas, when she had begun to put two and two together, but then had tried to stop, thinking it was mad. But now, please God, the idea *is* mad, for Miss Janice is in love with that fella, if ever she had seen it. What should she do? She had better have a word with Esther.

She hurried across to the workroom, now holding twice the number of assistants it had once housed; then through the new machine room and up the stairs to where the top floor had spread into the attic. And when she saw that Esther was alone she hurried to her, and in a low voice asked, "Where's the mistress?"

"Upstairs with Lena. What is it?"

"That man's been at the door. You know the one"—she pointed to the far window—"that used to stand outside."

"Him? What did *he* want?"

"He wanted to see the doctor. I sent him next door and I heard cook directing him to the surgery lower down."

"He spells trouble, that man. He did as a lad. But what in the name of God! could he be after?"

"Money, likely. Perhaps the old man is not stumping up enough."

"Well, he won't get any out of the doctor."

They looked at each other; then Alice said, "You know, Esther, I haven't said much, but I've had a funny feeling since Christmas. Well, you know." She nodded her head. "All these years past, things have gone very smoothly, too smoothly, too happily. And then, well at Christmas, when that young fella visited, I don't know what it was but . . . but he put me in mind of somebody."

"Who?"

Alice did not speak her mind now and say of whom he put her in mind, but said, "I don't know. Haven't been able to put me finger on it. Anyway, the sight of that fella's made me uneasy. Do you think we should tell her?"

"No! No! Don't do that. My goodness! After all this long time you don't want to start that again. She went through enough, and there's not two happier people in the city than them two. And look at this business, it's doubled. And look at the doctor's business, too."

"Yes." Alice nodded now. "But most of what he makes in his business goes down to that mucky lot on the river front. And then there's the rescue places. I would say more than what he makes goes down there, and a bit of the missis's too, because he's got her as daft as himself. I'll tell you something:"—she leaned toward Esther—"I didn't tell her, but I found two lice on the bottom of her skirt fringe last week."

"Uh!" Esther wrinkled her nose, then said, "Well, I'm not surprised. Sh! she's coming; you'd better get yourself away. Say nothing for the time being. Say nothing.''

"Come and sit down.'' Emily beckoned from the couch to her son, adding, "I've hardly seen you since you came home and you're off again tomorrow.''

"Well, I lead a busy life, Mother.'' He pulled a long face at her. "Didn't I have to go and see about the last fitting of my dress suit this afternoon? I always thought one stopped growing at eighteen.''

"You're not growing upward, you're growing outward, you're putting on too much weight. I wish Janice would put on a little more; she's run to skin and bone. I finished her dress today. It looks beautiful. She'll look wonderful in it, that's if she gets the chance and that beastly sister doesn't find something else for her to do at the last minute.''

"She'd better not, else I'll go round there and drag her out myself. If I didn't, Robert would.''

"Why did he have to go back to Oxford yesterday?''

"Oh, it's something to do with his tutor. He wanted to see him because his grandfather is against him doing another year. He must be a mean old scrub. Apparently he wants him to get to know the business, or businesses, or whatever he runs, to be able to take over. You know, I feel sorry for Robert at times; and more so the other day when I was introduced into his ménage.''

"Yes, I was going to ask you about that. You didn't say what happened, only that you had met his mother and father."

"Well." Jason lay back on the couch and put his hands behind his head and looked up toward the ceiling before he said, "It was odd, really, how it came about. Hector Mills-Cotton, you see, has got this new automobile. He bought it in Oxford but he wanted to get it home—he lives in Sussex, not far from Robert's mother and father, but they are right out in the heart of the country. Well, you know Robert and I always travel up and down together, at least from London, but Mills-Cotton apparently didn't relish this first long journey on his own. He's only had the vehicle for a couple of weeks and he wanted Robert to accompany him. But Robert said he always went by train with me. And then Mills-Cotton said, well, the three of us could squeeze in, and after he dropped Robert he said he would take me to Horsham station, from where I would get the train to London. So there we were, rolling madly along country lanes, scattering chickens, being held up by cows and sheep, making horses rear in the shafts. He was going at over twenty miles an hour and he was bragging it would do fifty or more. Anyway, the idea was just to drop Robert off, turn about and take me to the station. Well, we went up this drive, got into this big yard and there pandemonium broke out. There was a young girl with three horses, and what did that fool Cotton do but blow his horn? And the girl, I tell you, was marvelous.

She yelled to a man to take one horse, while she hung onto the other two. Eventually they managed to get the three stabled, even though they were still kicking like mad. She then came straight over to us and, taking not the slightest notice of either her brother or me, she glared at Mills-Cotton, who was still seated behind the wheel almost as petrified with fear as the horses had been. His face was a picture." And now Jason started to laugh. " 'What the hell do you think you're up to?' she yelled at him. 'Get that damned contraption and yourself out of here before I bring one of those animals out and make it kick in the front of this monstrosity.' And Robert had to try to calm her down. 'Oh, do shut up, Marian,' he said. 'It wasn't intended. These are my friends, Hector Mills-Cotton and Jason Montane.' It was then she looked at me, and after seemingly weighing me up, she let out a puff of breath and said, 'You're all stark staring mad. Get that thing out of sight, away from the horse boxes—it must look like a dragon to them—and then come inside. I expect there's some tea going.' "

Jason sat up straight now and looked at his mother, and laughing again, he said, "That part of it was funny, when I look back on it. There she was, not the size of sixpenn'orth of copper, different altogether from Robert in looks and everything else, not like a girl at all. She wasn't in a riding habit, but wore breeches and leather boots; and she marched into the house ahead of us, not even wiping her feet." He chuckled now, saying,

"You would have sorted her out, Mother, if she had done that here. But there she went, leading us across the hall and straight into a drawing room, where we all came to an abrupt stop, because her mother was sitting on a couch and the butler was pouring tea. There were two cups on the table, and it was the butler who turned and said, 'Good afternoon, Mr. Robert. We didn't expect you so soon'—and the girl said, 'Didn't you hear the commotion in the yard, Walton?' and he said, 'Yes, Miss Marian. But there's often a commotion in the yard, isn't there?' He struck me as a very friendly kind of man, not at all like a butler. Robert introduced Mills-Cotton to his mother, and then me. And when he said, 'This is Jason'—an odd thing happened, for she slowly stood up and stared at me before holding out her hand and saying, 'Jason who?' And I said, 'Montane, ma'am. Jason Montane.' And you know, Mother, she pulled her hand away as if she had been stung. She did. And then she sat down again and the butler handed her the cup of tea, then turned to us and said he would get some more cups and a fresh pot. After that the conversation became more general." And the memory of it brought a smile to his face, and he continued the scene: "The little horsewoman sat next to me. And, you know, Mother, she smelt strongly of the stables, she did. But she was so entertaining in a very strange way and so curious and inquisitive. She wanted to know all about me. And when I told her you had a very stylish hat shop, she laughed and asked if you made bowlers, and I said, I didn't think so, only bonnets. Then the butler came in and served the tea.

"It was some little time after, when I was about to make my excuses—I thought we had over-stayed our welcome, and Robert's mother, who looked a delicate sort of woman, was very pale and had little to say—that the door was opened, and a man came into the room. He was slightly stooped to one side, and on his appearance Robert and his mother sprang up from the couch and, as they went toward him, the man said, 'Oh, I didn't know you had a gathering, my dear. I just felt like a stroll. I was actually looking for Walton.' Then he looked from Mills-Cotton to me and said, 'How do you do?' It was then that Robert said, 'This is my father,' then added hastily, pointing toward Mills-Cotton and me, 'These are my college friends.'

" 'Oh, how do you do?' The man greeted us again. He had the most charming voice. He looked pretty old; at least, he had white hair; but his face was oddly smooth, quite unlined. Yet, at the same time, he had a vacant look. But altogether there was a certain pathetic charm about him. And when I answered his greeting, saying 'How do you do, sir?' he looked at me hard, I thought, before he said, 'I am very well young man. How are you?' I recall I felt embarrassed, but said, 'I am very well, too, sir.'

"It was then that Robert's mother took him by the arm, saying, 'Come along, dear. You must rest.' And they went out of the room. Then I noticed something. All the while this had been going on, Robert's sister Marian had never moved from her chair. But after the door had closed on her mother and father, she looked at Robert and said, 'Well! well! Of all the times . . .' But he cut her off sharply, saying, 'You'll want to catch your train, Jason, won't you?' And I said, 'Yes. Yes, of course.' And so we all went outside. And when Mills-Cotton and I were seated in the car and Robert said, 'I'll meet you and the girls at the station on Friday morning,' his sister piped in, 'I'm not coming, because they won't let horses in.' Then she bent forward and leaned on the door, so unlike the young girl, or young lady that she is, because she's over twenty, and said, 'Will you come again?' And I said, 'Oh, yes, yes, if I'm invited.' And she laughed and said, 'You're invited.' "

He now shook his head, saying, "It was most unusual, Mother. She was quite an unusual girl. In fact, she wasn't like . . . well, a female at all; and yet she wasn't masculine."

Emily looked at him for some moments before she said, "What are you going to do about Rosie?"

"Rosie? What do you mean, Mother?"

"You should know what I mean. When are you going to . . . well, speak to her, make your feelings plain?"

He inched away from her and said, his voice

rising, "What are you getting at? You mean . . . ?"

"Of course I mean . . . you care for Rosie, don't you?"

"Yes, of course I care for Rosie. But we've been brought up together."

"Oh, don't be silly, Jason. Anyone half-blind could see how she feels for you. And you must have noticed it."

He turned and looked toward the fire, then said, "But she's hardly eighteen."

"I've known people who have two children by then."

"You . . . you think she expects me to speak . . . really?"

"Well, my dear, just look back. Whom do you take out when you're home? Whom do you go to see first before you're hardly in the door? You dash next door. It isn't the boys you go to see."

"Yes, it is." He shook his head. "I'm . . . I'm very fond of her, but I hadn't thought of speaking . . . well not like that; in fact, I don't know how she herself really feels. I mean, other than as a sister."

"Oh, don't be silly!"

"I don't. I didn't! Anyway, she's so pretty, she's so bonny, she could get anyone."

"She's neither pretty nor bonny, Jason, she's beautiful; and she'll become more beautiful still as she moves into womanhood. And then you'll find you're not the only pebble on the beach. Some girls, you know, get very perverse at her age and think, oh well—to use another cliché—there's more fish in the sea than has ever been caught. And so she might not dangle her line again."

"Oh, be quiet, Mother; you're talking like a penny novelette."

"Well, let me tell you, big man, that life is often *like* a penny novelette, more often than otherwise. The only thing that's wrong with a penny novelette is that there's no real happy-ever-after." She now got to her feet and he rose, too, and he said in surprise, "You're annoyed with me?"

"Yes, I am, because Rosie's unhappy, and I'll tell you why: you stupidly told James and Harry last night about the fascinating girl-cum-boy, or boy-cum-girl, who turns out to be Robert's sister."

"Oh dear Lord!" He closed his eyes and then shook his head slowly. "I was explaining about her rig-out and her swearing at us, and I suppose I said she was so unlike any female I had ever met."

"Well, that in itself was the most stupid thing to say. If you have any sense and if you want to have a happy dance tomorrow night in Oxford, I think you should go in tonight and tactfully make amends of some sort."

As Emily made for the door he called after her, "I have another year before taking Finals, after which I have to get a job, which will all depend on my degree. Am I expected to saddle myself with a wife before that?"

"No, indeed you're not. But girls and women

live on hope for years; that is, as long as they've got something to hope for."

As he heard the door close none too gently behind her, his expression showed amazement. Really! he had never heard his mother go on like that, and all about Rosie.

He walked back to the fireplace and, standing there, stared down into the flames and asked himself how he would feel if he were to come home and hear that some other fellow was interested in her. Say, Robert. Oh, he wouldn't like it at all. No. But, then, Robert had fallen for Janice. Yes, he had indeed; and he hoped they would bring it off, for then his friend would be his brother-in-law. He liked that idea . . . But Rosie?

Did he love Rosie? He must do; it was just that she had always been there and so near that he hadn't really seen her. But he must now go next door and look at her in a different light.

The thought was not unpleasing.

7

When, all those years ago, Steve had first seen Westerley Place, it seemed to be a conglomeration of warrens and alleys, with tall tenement houses leaning over single-story ones; there were derelict buildings, but they were empty only during the day, for at night they would be filled with both old and young.

Now, almost thirty years later, most of the derelict buildings had gone and sweat factories had been built in their place. Some people had moved to what were called decent streets, which spread from the outskirts into the main East End of the town. But in that quarter where Steve had first set up his hut clinic, the inhabitants seemed not to have changed at all: some worked when they could get it, others lived by their wits; there were as many clever pickpockets among the children as was described in Dickens's *Oliver Twist*. There were frequent district gang wars, in which one or another person would disappear. If a body was found in the river, it was accounted for; if it was not found, it was said the person or victim had gone to America.

Steve's clinic was no longer in a hut but in a

house. At one end of the street and on the same side was a cheap lodging house, at the other end a corner grocery shop; in between these were two gin shops and a pawn shop.

It had been noticeable over the years that Steve's surgery windows had never been smashed, nor were his three-roomed premises ever broken into. Perhaps it was because of the now faded but still legible words painted above the one window at the front of the house and which read: ANDS ORF. He had found it there one morning very shortly after he had taken the premises. Neither the corner shop nor the pawn shop had any such inscription, but they too were never broken into. Yet the gin shops and the lodging house frequently had their windows smashed, as did the offices of the junk yard opposite and the warehouse and the Mission Hall to either side of it.

It was six o'clock in the evening and drizzling with rain when Steve's assistant, known by the name of Crabbe—whether it was his surname or Christian name Steve had never inquired—came from the waiting room and said, "There's a bloke out 'ere, doc; 'e's been standin' 'ere this last hour. Could 'ave taken 'is turn but said, no, 'e wanted to talk to you private, like."

Steve was writing at a small desk set in the corner of the room, which also held a high single bed with a curtain hanging round it, and a long, narrow table attached to one wall, and on which were a number of medical implements. Without looking up, he said, "What's his name?"

"Didn't say, doc. Forrin-lookin' bloke. Might come off one of the boats, but speaks English all right."

Steve now wrote something on a pad; then looking up at the tall, burly man, whose brown overall reached only his knees, showing the bottom of a pair of moleskin trousers resting on a pair of heavy working boots, he said to him, "Two or three new faces tonight. D'you know them?"

"No; not clapped eyes on 'em before. But one put a tanner in the kitty. Must be well-in somewhere."

"Which one was that?"

"'Im who said 'e'd an abscess on 'is arm. Looked to me as if a bullet 'ad said 'ow do? to it, sometime or other. What d'you think, doc?"

"Much along the same lines, Crabbe, much along the same lines. If he's not careful he's going to be one arm short."

"Well, you'll likely see 'im again."

"Very likely," said Steve; then added, "Well, tell the man, whoever he is, to come in, and then clear up inside." He motioned toward a far door. "And rinse those bottles well, Crabbe. I picked up one today with sediment in it."

"Did you now, doc, did you now? Must 'ave been 'ard and took no notice of me shakin' it, 'cos me bones rattle at times the way I go at them bottles."

Steve smiled as he watched the big man now go

to the door of the surgery and beckon, then stand aside to let in a man whom he had described as a foreigner.

Before addressing the man, Steve nodded toward Crabbe, who then slowly walked to the far door, but he did not exactly close it behind him.

"What can I do for you?" said Steve now, and the man answered, "It's more like what I can do for you, doctor."

"Oh, yes?" And Steve's eyebrows moved. "Well, tell me your business."

"Perhaps my name will enlighten you a bit. I'm Benito Dimarca. Remember the name?"

Steve felt a shiver pass through him, but he made no response. And the man now said, "I thought you would. So I don't have to remind you that what you call your family and mine are sort of related."

"What do you mean, my family?"

"Well, you call them your family, don't you, doctor? But you know, and I know who fathered them," and when Steve sprang to his feet and moved menacingly toward the man, the latter immediately assumed a fighting stance, shouting, "Don't you come that with me! You might have knocked *him* about when you found out; but you'll find I'm a different kettle of fish. Anyway, like it or not, your two are my half-brother and half-sister."

"Get out!"

"I'll get out when I've had my say, and it's just this. We were looked after by the old fella, who had a right to, anyway, because he is my grandfather. And that went on until my mother died. But from then, not a penny. I'm out of work and I've been along there to him. But anyway, I've told his man what I'm going to do if I don't get enough to live on. 'Cos I'm tellin' you, I'm not going around begging. Why should I? So it's up to the pair of you, one or t'other, because that's the only thing that's going to stop my mouth this time. And the papers will pay a bit for a scandal like that, the old boy being one of the kingpins of the City. And that's not all. There's something going on under your very nose, doc . . . tor, that'll make your hair rise. And I'll tell you . . ."

He got no further, for Steve's doubled fist shot out; but the man was quick to move and the blow just grazed his ear and Steve's knuckles came in contact with the brick wall.

At this moment the door of the other room was pulled open and, without a word, Crabbe gripped the man by the shoulders and almost lifted him from his feet, then dragged him through the waiting room and threw him out of the front door with such force that he fell on his knees and scattered three boys who were playing chucks in the gutter. And Crabbe remained standing there until he saw the fellow rise to his feet, turn and glare at him, then stumble off. At this, he called one of the boys to him and, whispering urgently, he said, "Follow 'im, but don't let 'im see you. Find out where 'e lives. I'll be in the Three Bells," and he pushed the boy, saying, "Quick, now!"

When he returned to the surgery Steve was

again sitting at his desk, but not writing. He had his hand on the table and was rubbing salve into the bleeding knuckles.

"Nasty piece of work that, doc."

Steve made no reply.

" 'E's up to no good."

Now Steve got to his feet. He felt shaken and his voice betrayed it when he said, "Forget what you've heard, Crabbe. Do you hear?"

" 'Eard, doc? I 'eard nowt, only your knuckles 'itting that bloody wall. But you get yourself away 'ome, doc, an' forget about 'im. Scum like that are no good. Blackmailers, the lot of 'em."

On another occasion Steve would have smiled at the idea of Crabbe condemning blackmailers but now, as the big man was helping him into his coat, saying, "Now, don't you worry your 'ead any more about . . ." Steve turned quickly around and, lifting his painful hand, he wagged it at the tall figure, saying, "Now, Crabbe, don't you dare do anything. I'm telling you. I'm warning you."

"Me, doc? I 'adn't the thought in me 'ead. Me? What could I do? I don't know the bloke. 'E's gone."

"Oh, I know you, Crabbe, and you know I know you; you've got your ways and means. Now, if you organize anything I'll know. I tell you, I'll know."

"Doc! man, you're gettin' in a state about nothin'. D'you think I want to swing?"

"If the truth was known about you, Crabbe, you should have swung years ago."

At this the big fellow let out a roar of laughter, saying, "Aye, an' I might 'ave if it 'adn't been for you, doc. There I was, not eight years old an' I pinched ya watch an' your wallet from that very desk there. An' you 'auled me up by the collar of me rags; then ya took me outside an' you dipped me 'ead in a bucket. Yes, you did, doc, you dipped me 'ead in a bucket, and I thought I was gonna drown. There was the river, an' I'd never been in it, but I swallowed a lot of that water. Ya nearly choked me, you know. Ya could 'ave done me in."

"Crabbe, I'm not in the mood for reminiscences. I know you, and you know I know you, as I have to keep reminding you, and I'll say now I'm grateful for your loyalty over the years. But please! Please! Don't interfere in this business."

"As you say, doc, as you say. An' when you're grateful for me loyalty, let me tell you I'm grateful to you for me way of life. A few years back I'd 'ave ended up in Australia. But even in these h'advanced times, I know I would 'ave ended in the clink more than once if it 'adn't been for you. I'm your man, doc, as long as you need me. But go on 'ome now with an easy mind an' forget about that stinkin', blackmailin' bugger."

Steve went home, but not with an easy mind, and at the sight of him Emily was immediately perturbed. But before she could say anything he said, "I'm all right. I just fell against the wall and hurt my knuckles."

She shook her head as she said, "Were you attacked?"

"Me, attacked? Don't be silly. As you know, I can walk into that place any time of the night or day and have my wallet in one hand and my watch hanging openly from my Albert chain and it would still be there when I got out of the place. More likely to be pinched by some fancy well-spoken fellow when I come up this street. Get me a drink, dear, and let me sit down and put my feet up."

She brought him a drink, then sat down on the couch beside him, and when he glanced at the clock and said, "The ball is just about to start," she nodded and said quietly, "Didn't the girls look lovely? I mean, last night when they dressed up in their evening dresses and their velvet cloaks. I thought Janice looked magnificent; she made me want to cry. And Jason always looks so handsome in his dress suit. I was so proud of them, weren't you?"

"Oh, yes, yes, I was, dear."

"What is it? There's something wrong."

"There's nothing wrong; I'm only tired."

"Steve Montane, you can't tell me there's nothing wrong. I know your every thought, your every mood."

"No, you don't. No, you don't. I think of some things that would scare you stiff. I do." He pursed his lips before enlightening further: "Such as murder. Yes, murder."

Then when she drew away from him so as to look him fully in the face, he bowed his head and said, "Yes, there is something afoot. I can tell you, but I'm not going to tell you tonight, and perhaps not tomorrow. I may have to tell you later on."

Her voice was a mere whisper as she said, "About . . . about the children?"

There was a long pause before he answered, "Yes, darling, about the children."

"Oh, dear God!" She now got to her feet, but he did not rise with her, and she had not walked the length of the hearthrug from him when, her back to him, she said, "I should have done it years ago. I wanted to, you know, just in case . . ."

"Well, dear, I didn't want it. We were married, they were mine. To all intents and purposes they were mine."

She turned now and looked at him, saying pitifully, "But you knew they weren't yours."

"Never mind what I knew; I took them as mine. I've loved them as mine, and they love me, both of them. I am their father, and no matter what happens I shall remain their father. But now, darling, come and sit down and do this one thing for me: leave it for the next day or so. There is a way out but it goes against my nature, yet I may have to resort to it."

He was reckoning up in his mind what he would offer the man for his silence. It would have to be on a weekly basis. But then again, how long would that go on? And once he submitted to that line he would be in the man's power. Yet, if it was going to save her anxiety, he would do it.

The door opened, "Supper's ready, ma'am."

"Thank you, Alice. We'll be there in a moment."

Steve rose from the couch, saying, "I'll go and have a wash first. Stay quiet until I come back." He bent and kissed her on the brow, then went out, and she repeated to herself, "Stay quiet," when her whole being was churned up. What would her children think of her if that story ever came out? The second mistress of a married man, and to lose her first child by him, then to be raped by him and be delivered of twins. What on earth would they think? Janice was always saying things were changing, and changing fast, but she herself knew that morals would not be counted in that change. She suddenly thought of the hat. That hat. It was an evil thing. Two years ago Janice had found it up in the attic, its brim severed from its crown. She had brought it down full of excitement and had stuck the brim on her hair, saying, "Isn't it a lovely shape! Why on earth is it up there? And why was it torn?" And Alice had come forward and said, "Well, I used to have it in my room. I had thought I could do something with it, then couldn't, so I threw it upstairs."

"Well, something could be done with it," Janice had said. "It just wants sewing up again—it's a clean tear—and a velvet band put around it. May I take it to the girls to be done, Mother?"

What else could she have said but "yes?" But

every time she had been off duty during the summer months, Janice had worn that hat; even this morning she had gone off in it. And now here was her beloved Steve telling her the past was to be brought into the open again, the past that had begun with that hat, for, as she had always thought, it was the hat he had noticed. There was something bad about it; it was evil.

8

The ball was at its height. Janice and Rosie were sitting fanning themselves as they sipped at the long, cool, minted drink. And they smiled at each other as they listened to Robert and Jason discussing the reason why they had been bumped by Balliol in the February Torpids and bumped by Magdalen in the Eights during the past week. The blame seemed to lie not with the rowers, but with something they referred to as the Gut, where the Cherwell flowed into the Isis, a place where they themselves should have made their bump; but the weather being what it was, *they* were bumped instead.

The girls were saved from more river discussion when the band struck up once more and a waltz was announced. And at that moment a tall young man came to the table and, standing to Janice's side, said, "Our dance, I think, Miss Montane."

"Oh. Oh, yes. Excuse me." Janice got up, and as she was waltzed away by her partner, Robert muttered, "He's got a nerve. That's the second one he's had already."

"Well, you should have filled up her card straightaway; you were slow off the mark."

Robert looked at Jason now and said quietly, "But it isn't done, you know."

"Oh, sir, I stand corrected."

"Well, I'm glad you do."

It said something for the friendship between them that they could laugh at this. Then, taking Rosie's hand, Jason said, "One thing I do know. I have the next three with this lady."

"Well, I'm sure she gave them to you only out of politeness."

"You're right, Robert," Rosie said, as she rose to her feet. "He reacts like a child if he doesn't get what he wants."

Jason looked at this girl he had known all his life. Her ease in company surprised him, especially this kind of company; he had expected her to be somewhat gauche.

On the floor, he said to her, "Enjoying yourself?"

"Yes, it's lovely." Then she added, "Wouldn't it be lovely, too, if Robert were to become serious about Janice?"

"Oh, I think he is serious enough, and she, too. They've already met a number of times out of term, you know."

"Really?"

"Yes." Then putting his lips near her ear, he whispered, "And wouldn't it be lovely, too, if a brother and sister married a brother and sister? Marian looks lovely on a horse. Well, the horse looks . . ."

When his soft leather toe cap was trodden on

hard he gave a smothered groan. It said a lot for what had transpired between them last night.

What he said next, and not in her ear, was, "You're a little vixen at heart," and smiling sweetly into his face, she responded, "Yes, I know." Then, their brows touching, they laughed together.

On the way back to the table, he stopped at the buffet and collected the drinks; but when they reached their seats it was to see Robert and Janice disappearing through a far door . . .

"Shall I go back and get your cloak? It's chilly."

"No; I like the cool air. It was so hot in there."

"Are you enjoying it?"

"Oh, yes, yes. It seems so far removed from the wards, the routine of the 'Nurse, nurse, nurse' and 'Yes, sister.' "

"Is she such a dragon?"

"Yes, she is a dragon-plus. I promised myself that should I ever become a sister, which is a very faint hope, but that being so, if I ever wanted to tell anyone off, I would count ten, close my eyes and say 'Sister Brown' three times."

He laughed as he said, "I can't imagine you ever being a starchy sister, or even a starchy nurse."

"Oh, the only things starchy about nurses are their caps, aprons and cuffs; for the rest, we are pliable peasants."

They crossed the quad and he guided her to a seat close to the high stone wall and invited her to sit; and then he sat beside her. And there was silence between them for a moment, until they each turned and looked at the other and he said, "Janice."

"Yes, Robert?"

"I love you."

She did not droop her head as she said, "And I love you, Robert."

"When did you know?"

"I don't exactly recall. I think it was when I sat across the table from you at our Christmas dinner. It couldn't have been before Christmas, because I hadn't met you. But from then I . . . I haven't been able to get you out of my mind."

"Oh, my love." He had hold of her hand now and was pressing it close to his shirt front. "It's been the same with me, every minute. Quite candidly, every minute of the day, because I couldn't get you out of *my* mind. There was something about you, I couldn't tell what. It wasn't only your beauty or your manner, it was something wonderful. You are wonderful. I . . . I must tell you something. Such has been my home life, especially in relation to my father, that I became . . . sort of afraid of girls, or women. But from the moment I saw you, that feeling went. I knew you were the one."

Their faces drew slowly together, and when their lips met her eyes were closed and his arms were holding her gently. Their kiss was long and sweet, though not passionate. And when their faces drew apart their cheeks were moist and their eyes deep and shiny.

"If I had the gift of words like your father," he whispered, "I would speak to you now in a poem. But what I can say is, we have just put the seal of our love on our lives, our life together. We will be married soon."

She did not coyly say, "But you haven't asked me, and I haven't said yes;" her answer was, "Yes, soon, darling."

"Oh, you're wonderful, wonderful." He was pressing her close to him now, muttering, "No coyness; no pretense; no, 'You must see, Papa'; none of the advice of the *Young Ladies' Journal.*"

She pulled herself from him laughing now, saying, "Well, if you would like it that way, I could throw in a swoon; I'm very good at swoons. I mean, I've had a lot of practice watching others."

His head went back and his laugh rang out. Then, again looking at her and his fingers tracing her features, he said, "I'll be unable to get back quickly enough tomorrow to tell my grandfather; and then to run into your house, crying, 'She's going to marry me! You're going to lose her. She's going to marry me.' "

Her voice was sober now as she said, "Well, promise me one thing: you won't come to the house first; you'll give me the chance to tell them."

"As you wish, my dear. As you wish. Yes, of course, that's only right. But . . . but what about tonight? Shall we tell . . . ?" He nodded his head back; and she thought for a moment before she said, "No; but only because I think it would be stealing their limelight; because, as Mother said, Jason has just opened his eyes and seen Rosie. I think they, too, came to a sort of understanding last night, but it hasn't been made public yet. Let them have the first shot."

"Just as you say, darling. Just as you say. But at the same time I want to shout it from the hills. I . . . I think I'll dash up to High Gully tomorrow—that's our place in Scotland—there's some pretty stiff mountains behind and I'll yell it from there. You know, I never cared much for High Gully; it was too isolated, too lonely. But now, and for days ahead, all I'll be able to think of is getting you up there to myself. Just you and I alone on the hills. In a way it's like a desert island, for it's a good half hour's trot to the next house. The stores are brought up once a month. Yes, that's what I'll do as we are married, I'll whisk you off."

"Is it big?"

"Yes. Yes, it's quite a large place."

"Oh well, then, we'll turn it into an isolation hospital. I've always wanted to manage an isolation hospital."

They were laughing again, clasped tight. Then looking toward the illuminated building, she said, "That's the second time the band's stopped. Good gracious! What's on my card?" She opened her Dorothy bag that had been lying on the seat beside her and when she looked at her card, she said, "The first one was yours, but that doesn't matter, does it? And the last one was Jason's. Well, that matters less. But we must go in."

"Let me hold you once more and kiss you once more." They were standing now, their lips tight, their bodies entwined. Then when, breathless, they drew apart, he gripped her hand and, like children, they ran across the quad toward the brilliantly lit hall, the light from it matching the glow from within them both, and which, in spite of circumstances, was never to die.

Steve had seen his last patient of the morning, and was about to go next door for his usual cup of coffee with Emily, when a letter was delivered to him.

"A man came to the door, sir. He asked if it could be given to you at once."

When he opened the envelope, his eyes went first to the address, and this caused his gaze to drop to the signature; and on the sight of it the anxiety that had been in him since he had been visited by that man was intensified.

The letter was brief.

Dear Sir,
Would you be kind enough to call on me at your earliest convenience? The matter is of great importance.

And was simply signed,

William Anderson Steerman.

He stood staring at it and repeating "Anderson Steerman." And there was a pause between the two names and as he folded the letter up he said to himself again, "Anderson . . . Steerman."

In the hall he said to the maid, "Will you slip next door and tell Mrs. Montane that I have been called away? I'll be back as soon as possible." Then, after donning his hat and coat, he hurried out.

He did not need to take a cab or be reminded of the location; he remembered the last time he had gone there twenty years ago. But, as on that day he went in anger, now the feeling was more one of trepidation.

Ten minutes later, when he entered the hall, it was as if he had left it on the previous day: everything looked the same, except for the man coming toward him. This man walked with a slight stoop and his hair was white.

"Good morning, doctor," he said politely. "I am Mr. Steerman's valet. Will you please step this way?"

Steve followed the man toward a door before which he did not hesitate but straightaway opened it and announced, "Doctor Montane, sir."

Although so many years had passed since they had last met, Steve recognized the figure sitting in the long chair. The hair was whiter, the face more gaunt, but the head was still erect and the shoulders straight.

"Good morning. Will you kindly be seated?"

Steve took the chair that was being pointed out

by the long, blue-veined hand. But he was hardly seated before the old man began, saying, "It is some years since we met, doctor. On that occasion the matter had to do with an escapade of my son. On this occasion it is, I would say, much more serious, for it is to do with the result of that escapade. May I ask, sir, have you met a man called Dimarca?"

"Yes. Yes, I have."

"Then I have no need to tell you why you are here, for the news that that man suggests is indeed of a most serious nature. You are aware, I am sure, that you are not the father of the child . . . or children born to your wife. The recorded dates of your marriage and their birth leave no doubt in the matter. May I ask, at this point, if they know anything of the circumstances?"

The answer came brief and harsh, "No."

"Then, from what I have to say, that is a pity, for that man informs me that my grandson and the young lady who is recognized as your daughter have become associated."

Steve closed his eyes: Anderson Steerman. Anderson Steerman. His voice was a mutter now as he said, "The young man's name is merely Anderson."

"He is known as Anderson."

"My son met him at university."

"Yes, yes, I am sure you had no inkling of his real identity, otherwise there would have been no need for this meeting. It was I who suggested that he, or rather the children as they were then, should be known simply as Anderson. At that time I did not know what steps your wife intended taking against my son: whether he might be brought to justice for a rape, which would have sullied our name, and that wasn't to be borne. I was thinking of the children's future and what my grandson would have to put up with when at school, and later perhaps at university, if he were to be known as the son of a man who had three children, but was keeping two mistresses and had raped the second because she had repulsed him. I was looking ahead for them. As for myself, I was strong enough to weather the disgrace for what time I had left, so I imagined at that period, for I was suffering an illness which righted itself. But I never expected to live and have to deal with this present situation. You understand what I mean, sir?"

It was a bark that came from Steve now. "Of course I understand, sir, and the ruin of the lives of two young people, who unfortunately have grown to care for each other. *Understand what you mean!*" He was now on his feet glaring down at the man. "As I see it, it is damnable that these two young people will have to suffer, perhaps all their lives, for the licentious swine of a man whom you bred, and fostered by paying for his kept woman and her brood, while he was breeding another in your household, besides looking further afield to satisfy his lust. The blame, I see, sir, lies as much with you as with your dirty offspring. And now my son has to be told that he is of your line, which stinks in more ways than one; for what have you done, sir, but spend your life making money: owning companies that run factories where a living wage would hardly feed a dog? I spend part of my life, sir, attending people who can't afford to pay for a doctor, people who spend *their* lives in *your* factories and sweatshops owned by *your* companies. I have followed your career, sir, the career, I now understand, you hope to push your grandson into. And I say push, for the young man whom I know as Robert Anderson has told me how he hates the idea of going into business. What he desperately wants is another year at university. But *this grandfather* of his doesn't see it like that. He wants to swallow him up. You may be an old man, sir, and perhaps I shouldn't be talking to you like this, but your age is only in your features, for your mind is still on money. The newspapers speak of your agility in that way. Well, may it do you some good, sir. May it do you some good, for I'll tell you this now: you'll never hold the young man I know as Robert Anderson. He'll never become my son-in-law as I had hoped he would, but from what I've judged of his character, he'll never be another you or, please God, his father. And . . ."

The door was opened at this moment and a voice said quietly, "Did you ring, sir?"

"No, Gibbons, I didn't ring"—there was a slight tremor in the voice—"but I think the doctor is ready to go."

Steve did not immediately move: in a lower

voice he said, "One last word, sir. It has just dawned on me that my son has already met his father and he described him as a poor, pathetic-looking, weird creature, partly paralyzed. Well, all I can hope, sir, is that your son lives for many, many years, aware of his condition before he roasts in hell." And on this he swung about, almost knocking Gibbons off his feet as he pushed past him, and then, grabbing up his hat and coat from a hall chair, he pulled open the door, not even pausing to close it behind him.

He was seething with such fury as he had never imagined himself being capable of: he had the desire to smash something, but nothing seemed big enough to alleviate the agony he was feeling for his family: his happy family was to be rent open within the next few hours and the results would be unbearable to watch. He saw Emily's guilt being dragged into the light of day, the guilt he knew she had never been able to throw off; he felt his son's disdain when he recalled the picture of his real father; but, above all, there was his darling Janice and that fine young fellow. Yes, a fine young fellow, for whatever he had sprung from he was as yet untainted. He was sure of that. But now . . . Oh God! He came to a dead stop in the street, put his hand out and gripped the lamp post that was to his side. The feeling of its cold iron was such that he wanted to put his brow against it—he felt he was in a fever.

Slowly now he began to walk back toward his home; and his step actually faltered as he reached the door: for the first time in his life he was reluctant to enter his home. Always, wherever he had been, he had been eager to return; and should she not be in the house to greet him, but in the shop, he would become irritated until she did put in an appearance, when he might greet her with, "You spend your whole life in that damn head factory," and she would reply to the effect, "Well, if you would stop having two practices just to prove you're right, I might be at home more often."

This time, however, he hoped she *was* next door, for he had to settle himself and think of a way to break this news. But of course it had to be to the contrary, for there she was coming down the stairs toward him.

He turned his back on her as he took off his hat and coat; and when he hadn't found any chirpy words with which to greet her, she approached him and, gazing into his eyes, said, "What *is* the matter, dear?"

He could not answer her for a moment, because he was swallowing deeply, and so she asked him, "Are you feeling ill?"

"Yes. Yes, my dear, I *am* feeling ill, but . . . but not physically. Come into the sitting room."

In the room, he said, "Get me a drink, will you? Not tea or coffee, but something hard."

She paused and stared at him, then hurried out and into the dining room. When she returned with the decanter and a glass on a tray, he lifted the decanter before she had hardly put the tray on the table, and pouring himself out a good measure of whiskey he threw it off as if it were water, which in itself caused her to exclaim, "The children! Has anything happened to the children? What is it?"

"In a way. Yes, in a way."

"An accident?"

"No, no. Sit down . . . give me your hand."

When she put her hands in his, he found that they were both trembling and she almost whimpered now, "What is it, Steve? Please tell me."

He turned his head away from her now and lay back on the couch, then said slowly, "I received a summons this morning to go to see Mr. Anderson . . . Steerman." When her hand jerked in his he held it more tightly, then went on, "It appears that from the time I first went to his house he must have followed the proceedings, and so he informed me that I wasn't the father of those I have come to think of as my son and daughter. But, worse still, we could have weathered that, I think, had not the fact emerged that Robert Anderson is really Robert Anderson Steerman. He had arranged that the children should drop the name Steerman in order to avoid being stigmatized through their father." He now turned and looked at her. Her face was ashen as she muttered, "Janice. Janice."

"Yes, Janice and him."

"*Oh dear God! Oh dear God!*" She now drew her hand from his and brought herself to the edge of the couch.

After what seemed a long silence she muttered,

"Why? Why has it all come out now?" And he answered, "Apparently, after that . . . that woman Dimarca died, the old man refused to support the son. I don't know what happened to the girl, but the son must have lost his job. He . . . he came to me yesterday to offer a form of blackmail for his silence. He had already been to old man Steerman, but it hadn't worked there. So I was his last resort. But I didn't know then anything about Robert and his real identity. He would likely have told me, but I went for him before he could say more. However, he had told Steerman, and that is why I was summoned."

She rose to her feet, her hands now wringing each other as she said, "What must we do? They'll be back shortly."

"We must tell them, dear, that's all; we must tell them and leave it to them."

"But . . . but Janice, she's . . . she's in love with him, with Robert, and he with her."

Steve bent forward and, with his elbows on his knees, he cupped his head in his hands and muttered, "I know, I know. The revelation would have been bad enough without that situation. Well, there's no way out, there's no cure for it."

"All through me."

He almost bounced up now and, taking her by the shoulders, he said, "Now, stop that! You've carried that on your shoulders for years. At times it has loomed like a shadow between us."

"No, no. Oh, no, Steve. There's been no shadow, not on my part. I've loved you from the beginning and I never imagined love could grow greater; but it has, with the years. I love you so much it is painful at times, because you're so good, so kind, forgiving.''

"I'm neither good, kind, nor forgiving. Anything I did for you was from a selfish motive. I loved you. I wanted you. I meant to have you. And when those children were born they were mine, to all intents and purposes they were mine, and I've loved them as mine, and I'll go on loving them as mine.'' He now put his arms around her shaking body. "It'll be against the grain, but I'll pay that man to keep his tongue quiet. And we'll have to put up with what reactions we receive from Jason and Janice. But it's this other business that's going to be the tragedy, because nothing can alter that. But come, try to keep calm. Don't, as yet, mention anything of this to Alice. As for Esther and Lena, those other two old fogeys up in their loft, not a word, else you'll have them wailing like banshees over us.''

"Alice will probe.''

"Let her probe for the time being; she'll know all about it later.''

"I . . . I can't go next door.''

"All right, dear—you've got a very bad head. I'll give you a couple of tablets and I'll get Alice to bring you in a strong cup of tea . . . What time are they expected back?''

"I should imagine it will be between two and three. Janice is on duty tonight, you know. It's the start of her night shift for the next three months.

That's why she's had the two days off. What if he comes back and he comes in with them?''

''Well, in that case, dear, I'll send him straight back to his grandfather. Following that, we'll soon know his reactions. If it is anything like what I expect Janice's to be, I won't want to witness it.''

They came in like two careless children who were bursting with some glorious news. Their eyes were bright, their faces wide with smiles. They practically tore off their outer clothes and after glancing at each other Jason shouted, ''Where are you, you pair of old dodderheads?''

When Steve and Emily appeared at the drawing room door, they fell upon them, almost forcing them back into the room.

Steve made himself say somewhat brightly, ''No need to ask if you two have enjoyed yourselves.''

''Oh, it was wonderful, Father, it was wonderful. The place, the ball, everything, every . . . thing.'' Janice split the word up into two syllables.

''We have something to tell you, both of us.''

Before Jason got any further, Steve held up his hand saying, ''All right, all right. But . . . but first of all we have something to tell *you.* By the way, where are the others?''

''Oh, Rosie dashed indoors''—Jason pointed to the wall—''and Robert dropped off to see his grandfather. They both had news to impart.''

''Please. Wait.''

The words ''please,'' then ''wait,'' sobered them both, and they glanced at each other before simultaneously asking of Steve, "Something wrong? Something wrong?"

"Yes. Yes, my dears. Something has happened, a very important something. Come and sit down." With this, Steve turned and, taking Emily's arm, led her back to the couch. There they sat side by side. And now pointing to two chairs, Steve said, "Bring them up, Jason, and sit straight opposite us."

Janice looked at her brother. The smile had gone from her face, as it had from his; and when Jason had brought up the chairs and placed them exactly opposite the couch, he motioned to his sister to sit down, then slowly he, too, sat down, and quietly now he asked, "Is . . . is it bad news?"

"Well, the first part depends upon how you will look at it; the second part, yes, very bad news; at least, for one of you."

Again Jason and Janice glanced at each other, and this time their looks held, until Steve began. "I've got a story to tell you." He cast his eyes sideways to where Emily was sitting with her head bowed. "I will go into each detail as I know it happened. You already know how your mother came into the possession of the business through the kindness of Mrs. Arkwright. But what you don't know is that she looked after her for so long that she herself became ill and had to take a rest. She decided to go to an hotel in France. It was a place that Mrs. Arkwright had always talked about, because it was there, as a lady's maid, that she met her husband, who was a valet to a gentleman. And so, naturally, she retained romantic ideas about the place, and she would often say to your mother that she should go there. And eventually this is what she did. I may say at that time your mother was a very beautiful young woman. She is still beautiful, of course!" He again glanced toward the bent head. "And at that time too she was very high-spirited, and being in the hat and dress trade she was always beautifully attired. She wore, I may tell you, Janice, the very hat that you have just left in the hall, the day she went on this holiday. It enhanced her as it does you, my dear." He now wetted his lips and swallowed deeply before going on, "Well, at the hotel she met a gentleman who paid her attention, and naturally she thought he was unattached. When, toward the end of the holiday, she discovered otherwise, she fled the place, terribly upset. But this man pursued her. At that time, I, too, was in love with your mother, but each time we met, with my perverse nature and her high spirits, we would argue and set sparks off each other. And so it was a very sad young woman who went on a sort of convalescent holiday. Although she had been married and had divorced her husband a few years earlier, she was still of a romantic age. And when this man forced himself back into her life, presumably just as a friend, she accepted him. Then, inevitably, something happened and she had to face the disgrace of bearing a child. But she wanted children and so she was prepared to accept this. Unfortunately, five months into her pregnancy, one day there came upon the scene a certain woman."

He now put out his arm and placed it around Emily's shoulders, drawing her closer to him, then went on talking to the strained and wide-eyed faces before him, telling them what transpired from then on: how she was attacked by this woman; how the man's wife had come entreating her not to make a case against the woman, whom she had, for the sake of the family, accepted as her husband's recognized mistress, with whom he had sired two children. He then dealt quickly with the period leading up to the loss of the baby and Emily's recovery, during which they came to know each other. At which point he paused for a long while, before clearing his throat and saying: "She was so much better, and much of her brightness had returned, when the man broke into the house. He was under the influence of drink and he—the only word that can be used is 'rape'—he *raped* your mother. The result was she attempted suicide." The two faces opposite were now directed toward the lowered head, the while Steve continued: "It was only Alice's prompt action in coming for me late at night that allowed me to save her. After that, I had great difficulty in persuading your mother to marry me."

His head now drooped as he said, "There was a result of the attack and you were born prematurely," but then he raised his head to look at the two faces staring at him and quietly informed them, "You see, I am not your father. But from the first moment you were delivered I claimed you as mine, and I have loved you as mine and I shall always go on loving you as mine. To me, you are my son and daughter. As for your mother, she has carried this burden with her for years, and we both might have taken it to the grave, if it hadn't been that the son of this man's mistress has begun to blackmail both Robert's grandfather and myself . . ."

"Robert!" It was a cry. The chair overturned as Janice sprang to her feet crying again, *"Robert!"*

They were all standing now. Steve was holding Janice by the shoulders, saying, "Yes, my dear one, Robert is your half-brother, half-brother to both of you." He glanced toward Jason.

"No! No!" Janice pulled herself away from Steve's grip. *"No!"* And now her voice rose to a yell: *"No!* It can't be! We're . . . engaged. We are . . ."

Suddenly her hand went to her head. She, who had always disdained swooning women and fainting men, now gasped and gripped at the air with her flailing hands as a blackness overcame her.

She would have fallen to the floor had not both Jason and Steve caught her and laid her on the couch, and Emily knelt beside her, muttering, "Oh, my dear, my dear."

Jason turned to Steve and muttered, "That man, that pathetic old man, Robert's father, he is . . . ?" He could not go on: he had covered his eyes with his hand, for he was seeing the picture of the pathetic creature being led from the room. Only then did words of recrimination escape him: "Why didn't you warn us?" he said.

"I . . . I didn't know; he was just Robert Anderson, not Robert Anderson Steerman. His grandfather had dropped the last name in order to save the young children from suffering disgrace. If we had decided to sue, it would have come to light that their father had had a mistress with two children and also had children by another woman he had raped."

Jason stood thinking for a moment, then said, "Oh, God, what a mess! I suppose *I* can weather it—after all, Robert's a good fellow and we took to each other straight away—but what about Janice? She and Robert are in love—so much in love. It'll be the end of all that."

He turned as Janice, recovering from her collapse, sipped at a glass of water Emily was holding to her lips, and then said to Steve, "One thing I must say: you've always been my father and you always will be. This revelation makes no difference—well, not to me, anyway. I've always loved you, admired and honored you, and I know I will all the more now."

There were tears in Steve's eyes, and when they clasped each other it seemed to cement their relationship even more firmly.

A tearful Janice was now saying to her mother: "How . . . how could you, how could you let us go on?"

"I . . . I didn't know, my dear. I didn't know."

Yet even as Emily uttered these words, she recalled the feeling she had experienced when she
first set eyes on the charming young man at that
Christmas dinner. She remembered, too, the
shiver that had passed through her.

Pressing her mother aside, Janice swung her
legs from the couch and sat up, and looking into
Steve's troubled face, she put her hand out and
she, too, murmured, "You are my father. You'll
always be my father." Then slowly she turned and
looked at Emily as if seeing her for the first time.
Her mind now seemed very clear. She remembered every word she had heard: this woman who
was her mother and who had appeared so gentle
and, in a way, so private and untouched, had
been not only married and divorced, but also a
mistress to a married man who already had a mistress and who later had attacked her. And worse,
she had been raped and had tried to commit suicide. Then she had married this good man, and
he *had* been a good man to take on a woman with
a past like her mother's. And he had fathered the
result of her escapade. She couldn't believe that
this delicate-faced woman was one and the same
person whose history had just been unfolded.

She turned her gaze from her mother and
looked up at Steve, saying now, "How many people know of this?"

"Very few," he answered. "Only Alice knows the
ins and outs, and she is as one of the family. Even
Robert's grandfather was not fully aware of the
circumstances until recently, when he summoned

me to tell me that this man who was blackmailing him had revealed your association with his grandson and that there could be a suspicion that you had a close relationship."

"Could . . . could there not have been some mistake, since you married"—she swallowed—"Mother so soon afterwards?"

"Unfortunately, no, my dear. I married your mother, but—"he paused for some seconds now before he said, "it was at her behest that we did not come together until she was sure of the results of the attack. And I may add here that the knowledge caused her agony of mind. It wasn't until after you were both born and she saw how I accepted and loved you, that her anxiety and pain eased. Yet all these years there has been a shadow over her life. Well, now it has been lifted, but painfully, especially for you, my dear. I'm sorry to the bottom of my heart because I, too, have become very fond of Robert."

Janice pulled herself to her feet now; then after straightening her dress she ran her hand over her hair before she said, "When Robert comes I'd like to see him alone, please." And with that she walked from the room; and Jason followed her.

Emily was seated on the edge of the couch now and looking toward the closed door. Her daughter hadn't spoken one kind word to her. Neither of them had, and there rose in her now a sadness of such depth that all her past experience never reached. They disliked her. They blamed her.

When Steve's arms went about her she laid her

head on his shoulder. Her eyes were burning and dry, and when her voice came clear to him, saying, "As ye sow, so shall ye reap," he experienced a deeper pain still and he had no words to deny the statement.

At six o'clock, Robert had still not appeared, and so Janice went upstairs and donned her nurse's uniform. When she came down again it was to find Steve dressed to go outdoors, and when he said, "You're off early, dear," she answered, "Well, I start my month on nights and . . . and I've got things to prepare."

"I'm going that way to the surgery; we can walk together." Then he added quietly, "Go and say goodbye to your mother—she's in the breakfast-room, and in a bad state."

It seemed almost reluctantly that Janice turned from him to go down the passage, and when she opened the breakfast-room door it was to see her mother sitting almost crouched over the fire, and the day was still warm.

"I'm off now, Mother," she said. "You know I start on my night duty from now on."

Emily rose to her feet but she didn't move toward her daughter, nor did she speak, and it was the despair Janice could see portrayed on her face that made her go hurriedly forward and put her arms about her mother and murmur, "It's all right. It's all right. It was just the shock. I'll . . . I'll get over it. It wouldn't have mattered, all the rest wouldn't have mattered, it's just . . . Robert."

"I know, my dear. I know, my dear. It's Robert I'm thinking of, too. But please, please don't stop loving me."

"I . . . I couldn't if I tried. I . . . I love you both so much. You're both one in my mind. I couldn't stop loving one and not the other. There now, there now. Please! Please don't cry so. It'll be all right. It will have to be all right. These . . . these things have got to be faced. I . . . I'm glad I'm a nurse; one sees so many tragedies. They help you to face your own. I . . . I'll be home tomorrow sometime during the afternoon. Don't worry any more now. Please! We'll talk again tomorrow."

She went quietly from the room and in the hall she said to Steve, "It's all right."

"Oh . . . good. Thank you, dear."

They went out together and he saw her to the hospital gates, before making what could only be his circuitous way to the surgery.

There was, as usual, a crowded room waiting for him, and as usual he was met by Crabbe.

"You're a bit late, doc. Some of 'em thought you weren't comin' and 'ave gone orf. Still, there's enough out there to keep us goin' for the next couple of hours . . . You feelin' sick, doc?"

"No, no. Why do you think I should be feeling sick?"

" 'Cos you look kind of peaky round the gills. But I've one bit of good news for you. You know that fella what come in 'ere blowin' 'is mouth orf? Found in the river, he was, this mornin'.''

Steve had been about to sit down at his desk; but he swung round so quickly that Crabbe jumped back, protesting, "Now look, doc. Me . . . I 'ad nowt to do with it. Believe me, I never saw the bloke again.''

"You might not have had anything to do with it, Crabbe, but who but you knew anything about him and what went on here?''

"More than you think, gov . . . I mean, doc, more than you think. Apparently, he's the fella that's been shouting his mouth orf down in the Wild Boar. An' that ain't on our patch, you know. 'E said 'e either 'ad money or 'e was comin' into money and 'inted 'e was kind of out of the top drawer. You know what I mean, doc? So no, doc, no, 'twasn't one of our lot.''

"Then how do you know it was him?''

"Young Sparky was down on the beach when they pulled 'im out. The bobbies were there, an' there 'e was with all his clothes on, everything except 'is 'at. Now, if it had been one of our lot he wouldn't 'ave still 'ad 'is boots on. Now would 'e, doc?''

"Not unless they had been warned not to take them off.''

He stared into the big man's face and the big man stared back at him, his eyes unblinking. And as Steve knew only too well a straight stare from one of this lot was not a criterion of honesty, because most of them could lie their way off the gallows.

"Anyhow, doc, you should be thankful, I would say 'e'll not be botherin' you again. Whoever did it should 'ave a medal."

"Still, how did you know it was him?"

"Well, the bobbies got a letter from 'is pocket an' there was 'is name and address on it. An' what was more, there was still a few bob in 'is pocket. The only thing 'e 'adn't got on 'im was 'is watch. 'E used to be always swinging 'is watch, Sparky said, showin' it orf! It was a big time-keeper."

"You seem to know a lot about him, Crabbe, and yet you weren't there."

Crabbe's face went into a grin as he said, "You know me, doc, I believe in makin' friends. Anyhow, that's settled. But you've got all this lot to settle, an' there's at least two with legs that are beginnin' to smell. Old McIntyre should go to the 'orspital. You've told 'im, but he gets the skitters every time you mention it 'cos 'e knows they'll take it orf."

Steve sat down at his desk again. He didn't believe a word Crabbe had said. He was a man with power in this neighborhood: people were afraid of him because of his strength. And why he still stayed in this job when the wage he received could have been eclipsed, in a matter of minutes, by picking someone's pocket, he would never know. But Dimarca was dead . . . His hand that had been lying flat on the blotting pad went into a doubled fist as he thought, if only they had done it a little earlier. Everything that had happened during the last two days would never have come about. His beloved Janice could have married her Robert, and who would have been the wiser? There must be hundreds in the country wedded together, the blood running in them having been derived from the same source: the Paul Anderson Steermans of this world spread their seed liberally. And yet not only them. It wasn't always a rumor or topic for gossip that the outcomes of many such associations were housed in asylums or in the attic of some lonely house, for some were even kept and cared for openly in the family; incest was rife in some quarters, the proof of which he could verify from his own experience in this area.

If what had come to light had been known to him alone, would he have countenanced the coming together of his Janice and her half-brother? Professionally he would have had to forbid it; but the man of two worlds that he had become over the years would have closed his eyes to it.

As Janice left the ward to make her way to the nurses' home, the shield was gone and the pain was writhing at her again.

She had never been in love before: other than Robert, she had met no man who had attracted her; not even as a young girl had her heart fluttered with the stirrings of adolescent love. But she knew now that when she first set eyes on Robert there was born in her the knowledge that this was the one, this man was to mean her whole life. The thought of him had lightened her days, and he was ever there: he became alive in her mind in sleep. But now it wasn't the thought of a young woman crossed in love who was telling herself that she would never love again, that for the rest of her life she would be crying out at fate; there was the certain knowledge in her that she would never love again, that she could *never* love again.

Since returning here from home yesterday, so full of the wonder of love, only to have it wrested from her, she had waited for him to come, for she knew they would have to meet. They must meet. But when, by last evening, he had not put in an appearance, there was added to her pain despair and rejection, which had led to a feeling of being unclean.

When she came out into the open air she stood for a moment and drew in some deep breaths, before crossing the square to the grim-looking building of the nurses' home at the other side. Halfway across it she stopped dead, for there he was, striding toward her from the main gate. He was lost to her vision for a moment as he rounded a stationary ambulance. Then almost at a run he came and stood before her.

They stared at each other silently and then, his voice sounding strange to her, he said, "Could you . . . can you come for a walk?"

She was unable to answer, but she turned, and

he with her, and they walked toward the hospital gates and so out into the street.

There was a thin mist still hanging over from the night, but the sun was aiming to dispel it. He said, "Shall we go into the park?"

Still she was unable to answer. Twice before, they had met in the park; it had been a secret between them. They had walked together, and they had talked as they had sat, but they had never even touched hands.

Five minutes later they were walking through the park. It was practically deserted, except here and there where a man, or a youth, was curled up on a bench, his belongings acting as a pillow and his cover consisting mainly of newspapers.

For once, Janice was not touched by this familiar sight.

They had reached a corner that was backed with shrubs and in front of which there was a slatted seat, the sun, breaking through, showing up its damp surface. Taking out a handkerchief, he rubbed the seat, but to little effect. He next whipped off the white scarf from under his coat and, doubling it up, he roughly dried some distance along the slats, before indicating that she should sit down.

For the first time she realized he was still wearing the coat and scarf he had worn when they returned from Oxford yesterday. And now she became full of concern for, looking into his face, she saw it was gray with fatigue. She guessed that when he had arrived home he had been immediately told of the state of affairs and such was the effect the bombshell had had on him, he had not changed his clothes. But where had he been since? He looked different, older, and terribly agitated.

For the first time she spoke, saying merely, "Oh, Robert."

Now he had her hands clutched in his and the words were spluttering from his lips: "I . . . I can't believe it. I won't believe it. I've . . . I've been demented. I've even thought of killing him: I even got as far as the station, but then rationalized that if I did kill him I would never see you again . . . would never be able to talk about the matter . . . find a solution. Oh Janice! Janice."

"I know, dear. I know, my love; I . . . I feel the same. I can't believe . . . I don't want to believe it. I, too, want a solution, but there isn't one, is there?"

Their deep sighs came close together, their hands were clasped tight, their breaths were each fanning the other's face. "I . . . I love you, Janice. I adore you. And I know deep inside myself it's no using saying it'll pass. Because I've never felt like this before. I've never wanted a girl or a woman before. From the moment I first saw you I've . . . I've been consumed with this feeling for you. I . . . I went mad yesterday morning. I can only dimly recall what I did. I only know I upset a table and smashed a priceless vase when my grandfather told me and said my feeling was due only to the blood connection. The very thought of that almost drove me insane. I recall Gibbons and Mason dragging me out of the room. And then for a time I just walked. I've been walking ever since."

"Oh, my dear, my love." She pulled a hand from his and cupped his cheek, whimpering now, "I know. I know. I know exactly how you feel. I've had to work all night or I, too, would have been walking. I love you so much, Robert. I'll always love you. Always."

When his arms went about her and his lips brushed hers, she suddenly pressed him away from her, and her head bowing and swinging from side to side, she muttered, "No, no! Please! I couldn't bear it. We must not; you know we can't."

He turned from her now and bent his body to rest his elbows on his knees, and stared toward the gravel path; and after a moment he asked, "What are we going to do?"

It was a moment or two before she answered, "We can't do anything. You know in your heart we can't."

He swung round and looked at her now. "We . . . we could be friends, just friends. I can't bear the thought of never seeing you again, never talking to you."

"We . . . we wouldn't be able to endure that, you know we wouldn't, dear."

"Well, what the hell does it matter? After all, what does it matter? There must be many in the same boat as we are, and some must know it; some won't know it, but some must.''

"Yes," she nodded, "some must. But how are they living? In fear of the truth being told? Or, if it is known, they're ostracized. And . . . and you with your future, you cannot afford that. Your grandfather's a very old man. Shortly you will come into the business, and from what I understand it is a very big business.''

"Damn the business! I don't want the business. Never did. I only want to live my own life, and live it with you.''

It was as if he hadn't spoken, for she went on, "Then there is my side. There is the man I love as my father. I look upon him as such, I've always loved him and respected him, but I look upon him now as a great man, for he took on the responsibility of two children that weren't his own, while knowing and hating the father. And forgiving my mother for her stupidity in the first place, and for not being able to recognize good from evil. Because I see your father . . . and mine, not as a charming weakling . . . that was mainly a cover for his licentiousness. For you know, or perhaps you don't, that not only you and I are related but also two others whom he gave to his mistress. And how many more are we related to that we know nothing of? The Bible maintains that the evil that men do is passed on for generations. I had never even given those words a thought until the middle of last night. But they are so true.''

He lay back against the wooden rails of the seat now, and he looked up into the sky. There was a lowering mass of cloud, dark and threatening, but in the middle, as he had often noticed, was a deep round patch of blue. And for the first time, as he stared at it, he saw in it some significance: "You will one day marry someone else. You were made for marriage," he said.

"I never shall. Believe me, Robert, I never shall."

He turned his head slowly toward her.

"Nor me."

As she looked at him she felt compelled to quote the old adage, "Time heals. You will marry." Although there was a certainty in her own mind that she would never give herself to another man, there was also the knowledge that his needs might drive him to take on someone without any deep feeling of love. But when he said again, "I tell you, Janice, I shall never marry. No, never!" she made no assertive reply that circumstances might arise and change his mind.

She stood up now and said quietly, "I've . . . I've got to get back, Robert; I have to be in my room by nine."

Standing in front of her now, he said, "I feel utterly desolate, Janice, utterly, utterly."

"I know. I know, my darling."

"Won't you let me see you again?"

"It would be fatal for both of us, and we know it. Why don't you insist that you go back to Oxford for another year? Jason is so fond of you. He, too, was dreadfully upset about this, but there's no barrier between you. You can be a good friend, but . . . but you mustn't waste your life, Robert, for, as I see it, looking into the near future, many people will depend upon you. Your companies control a great deal of work force. You could be such a power . . ." Her voice trailed away and her head drooped as she repeated, "A power for good."

His voice was quiet, even calm now, as he asked, "And what will you do with your life?"

Her head was still bowed as she said, "Go on nursing. Perhaps become a sister. Who knows? But . . . but I must go now." As she looked at him again, he said, quietly, "Let me kiss you just once more. Please, Janice, just once more. It'll be the last time."

Slowly she moved into his arms and when their lips met, softly at first, then hungrily, their bodies pressed against each other for a moment; then she was wrenching herself away, and, turning, she lifted up the front of her long print dress and ran, the while he stood watching her until she disappeared from his view.

She ran until she reached the hospital, and there drew to a stop, wiped her face hastily of the tears that had been raining down her cheeks, then made herself walk into the nurses' home.

She went past the dining-hall, knowing that she would later have to give an account of her absence to the home matron, and into her room. There she took off her cloak and hat, then dropped down onto the end of the single iron bed and, gripping the rail with one hand, she pounded it with the other. And when her tears started to flow again she groaned, "I can't bear it. I can't bear it."

It was a full half hour later before she got into bed. Then, sitting up against the unyielding back of it, she put out her hand and brought her father's book from the side table, and she knew immediately what she was going to read. It was the first poem in his book, and it was as if he had written it for her. It was entitled "Need."

I do not need love and passion deep,
Or sonnets sung to lull me to sleep,
Or poems written on which my cheek will
 rest at night;
I do not need kisses on my lips,
Or odes voiced to my eyes;
I do not need children about my knee
Who might grow to despise me;
I do not need prestige or power
Which with age grow and sour;
I do not need to possess another,
Claiming a debt,
As do mother, father, or brother,
Or rest of kin;
I do not need to seek admiration
 to sustain life;
I do not need any of these things, for I will
 never need a wife.

She paused here and laid her head back against the iron rails of the bed. Then, after a moment, she went on reading:

I only need a hand to hold in friendship,
To exchange words without spleen or hate;
To link thoughts on topics great and small,
A friend to be metaphorical bulwark
   or a wall
Against which I can lean and draw new
   breath
To continue the fight for life and . . .
   against death,
That ultimate, that final blow,
Against which all knowledge cannot defend.
To that end . . . I need a friend."

The tears were raining again as her heart cried, "And I can't even be that to him, for neither of us would be strong enough to resist the other's need. Oh, if I could only slip away now into that ultimate that Father talks of and against which all knowledge can't defend. But Robert and I have got to live with the knowledge that we are dead to each other already."

PART TWO

1918

1

"Now, look you here! Master Steven. Stop that racket!" Alice gripped hold of the eight-year-old boy's collar. "You're not goin' in there to disturb your grandmother, she's having a nap. She's had enough of you all day . . . And don't you sneak off there, Miss Jessie." She now released her hold on the boy and grabbed the six-year-old girl's arm. "I'm surprised at you. Haven't I told you your grandmother's asleep?"

"You always say that, Alice; and she wants to see us. Anyway, we want to tell her about the parade, the soldiers and everything. Everybody's going mad out there."

"Well, let them; but you're not goin' to go mad inside. And so get yourselves next door. Anyway, where's Gracie and Freddie?"

"They've gone in home."

"Well, you go in, too."

"If it was Gracie you would have let her go in."

"Well, Gracie is still a baby and she doesn't make a row like you."

"She's no baby. She plays up to Grandad; she's sly."

"Well, she'd have to be twice as sly to match you, miss. So go on, when I tell you."

"Alice?"

Alice looked at the boy whose face was no longer bright, and he said, "Let's stay here in the kitchen for a while, will you? because it's sad at home. Mother was crying because of Uncle Harry being killed, and Uncle James's boat should be in by now and it isn't."

Alice turned away toward the oven and said, "Well, sit yourself down; or, better still, put out some cups and saucers and we'll have a cup of tea when I take these teacakes out."

"Oh! teacakes. I love your teacakes," said Jessie.

"Mary Ellen's teacakes are always flat and she never puts enough currants in them. Daddy says she counts them."

A few minutes later the children were drinking tea and eating hot buttered teacakes, and Alice said to them, "Now, stay put. I'll be back in a minute," and she was making her way toward the door when Jessie called after her, "Where's Bella?" and Alice answered over her shoulder, "It's her day off. And it's lucky for you it is or you wouldn't be sitting there stuffing yourselves."

As she entered the hall the front door opened, and with an exclamation of surprise she hurried toward a tall woman dressed in a gray coat and fur-trimmed hat, and she exclaimed, "Oh, my dear! What a nice surprise. We didn't expect you today. How did you manage to get through the crowd?"

"I had to fight my way, Alice, yes, literally fight my way. My hat was knocked off once and some idiot waved it on the end of his walking stick. I practically had to fight him to get it back. The whole place has gone mad; you can't get across the square. And what it'll be like tonight, the Lord only knows." Then, her tone dropping, she said, "Where are they?" And to this Alice said, "They are both in the sitting room. Your father's been on the go since early morning, helping out next door. He can't keep out of that blooming surgery. He's supposed to be retired, but he's been in there more often than he was before. Anyway, it's a change from him trotting down to Westerley Place. It's a good job that was flattened, I say. Give me your coat."

Janice handed Alice her coat; then, taking off her hat, she said, "I lost both my hat-pins and I nearly lost half my hair at the same time. Really! the place has gone mad."

"Well, it's over, and thank God. But what I think about, Miss Janice, is all those that won't come back and those they've left behind."

"Yes, Alice. But it would seem that for the moment, at any rate, the whole population have forgotten about them."

She now went into the sitting room and there brought exclamations from the two people sitting on the sofa. At seventy-three and his body as trim as it had always been, Steve would deny his age, although his hair was almost white and his face well lined, but it was with almost the agility of a much younger man that he rose from the couch, exclaiming, "Oh! my dear! How wonderful to see you. We didn't expect you."

Emily, too, had risen. The change in her was more noticeable: her hair was lily-white and, although her face showed few lines for her sixty-five years, it nevertheless gave the overall appearance of age. Yet her body was still slim and she was smartly dressed in a loose, mauve velvet gown that gave her a regal touch. "Come and sit down, my dear. You must be frozen," she welcomed her daughter. "Have you changed your duty time?"

"Not really. But I've got a bit of news and I felt I wanted to discuss it with you."

"Well, sit yourself down, dear"—it was Steve now propelling her to the sofa—"I'll call Alice, and get her to bring us some tea."

He hurried to the door and, when he opened it and was about to shout across the hall, from the other side of the room Alice called, "Yes, I know, I know, she'll want a cup of tea. It'll be on its way in two minutes."

"How did you manage to get through the crowd, dear?"

Janice turned to her mother, saying on a laugh, "I've just told Alice . . . with much difficulty. My hat was torn from my head and some idiot stuck it on his walking stick and waved it in the air. What I didn't tell Alice was, he bargained with me. 'Give me a kiss,' he said, 'and you can have it.' And you know what I did?'' She now turned a laughing face toward Steve. ''When he went to put his arm around me I gave it a sharp twist behind my back. And I can tell you my hat came down very suddenly.''

Steve let out a roar of a laugh now, saying, ''Good for you! I taught you that, didn't I?''

''Yes. Yes, you did, Father. Yes, you did.''

''And also how to use your knee.''

''Yes, that, too; and I can tell you that's come in handy. When I first went on night duty all those years ago some of the wide boys got a surprise. You wouldn't believe the tricks they got up to when the lights were lowered.''

''But now they're scared stiff of you,'' said Emily.

''Yes.'' She nodded at her mother. ''It's funny that. I don't have to open my mouth: I just walk through the wards and you can hear a pin drop. Sometimes, I really want to burst out laughing. If they only knew what was going through my mind.''

She leaned back and sighed now, saying, ''There's not much fun in the job, you know. When I was sister on my own ward I could let go now and then. You got to know your nurses and you could have a joke and a laugh about different patients. But now, being night sister and having a number of wards to go through, you don't really know anyone individually. Anyway, that'll soon cease.''

"Yes?" It was a double note of inquiry from both Emily and Steve.

"Well, you know, it's amazing, but I now have two options open to me. I've been told confidentially that the sister-tutor opening is mine if I want it. Then I had a letter this morning, inviting me to go for an interview for the matron's post."

"That hospital in Brighton?" asked Steve.

"Yes. Yes, that hospital in Brighton."

"Well, my dear, what will you do?"

She turned and looked at Steve and said, "Well, Father, I'm not struck on being sister-tutor. I would like the post of matron, but it seems so far away."

"Yes. Yes, it does, dear." Emily was nodding at her; but Steve put in, "There's surely a good train that runs between Brighton and London?"

Janice laughed at this and said, "Yes. Yes, I know there is, but there wouldn't be my own room to come home to on my days off. Nor would I be able to pop in to get the smell of disinfectant and hospital out of my nose. The matron's a living-in post. It's twenty-four hours for most days. And although"—she now turned her head from one to the other—"you're a very odd couple; in fact, extremely odd; I've got used to you and I'd miss you."

Their hands came out simultaneously and caught each of hers, and it was Steve who said, "That goes both ways. But it's what you want to do, and it's your life. And it's a big step-up. And by the sound of it, it seems to be a very good hospital.''

''Yes, it is, and it's a lovely town. But then so is London, except on days like today. Anyway, I've got a little time to think about it and I'll let you think about it, too. We'll talk about it again at the weekend. By the way''—the excitement had disappeared from her voice—''how are they taking it next door?''

''Oh, both sides are very down,'' Emily answered, indicating with a wave of her hand the surgery to her left and the house above, where John and Mary still resided, then to her right to what used to be the workshop and hat department, but which, for the last ten years, had been turned into the family home of Jason and Rosie and their five children. And she added, ''If James's ship would only come in, that would ease things. It's four days overdue. But I don't think Mary will ever get over losing Harry. He was such a bright spark, and to be taken so soon. He was out there hardly a month.''

''Well, it is over,'' said Steve now, quietly; ''and it's been a war to end all wars, so they say. But what for? What for? I ask you.'' He now turned to Janice, saying, ''Do you ask yourself that question when you go round your wards?''

''Yes. Yes, practically every night, Father. I asked it before the military came in, when the beds were full of the ill-nourished, the diseased and the dying. But for these past two years it has at times been hellish to see some of the cases.

Yet they put you to shame with their cheerfulness. Even the legless tell you how glad they are to be back in Blighty. It gives one just a little idea what hell it must have been over there. What hurts me most is the sight of the very young when they are maimed. Some can't even be eighteen, I'm sure. They must have faked their age. And here and there, when you hear a muffled noise under the bedclothes, it almost breaks your heart. I sometimes want to pull the clothes down and yell at them, 'Cry it out! Don't be ashamed of crying; it's a form of release.' But they would die of shame if they thought I knew."

When the door opened and Alice entered carrying a tea-tray, and behind her young Steven and Jessie, each carrying a plate of buttered teacakes, Steve cried, "Oh, that's good! But you've taken your time, all of you. Have you been making them?"

For answer, Alice said, "Of course we've been making them; you only get things to order in this house."

After the children had laid the plates on a side table, they stormed over Janice, crying, "Oh! Auntie. I didn't know you were in. Are you on leave? Are you staying the night?"

Pulling herself toward the end of the couch, Janice put an arm around each of them, saying, "No, I'm not on leave; and no, I'm not staying the night; and yes, I am in, as you can see."

They laughed at her now and Jessie asked,

"How did you manage to get through the crowd?"

"With great difficulty," she answered, "and I don't know how I'm going to get back."

"You'd better take a cab." This was from her father.

"Some hope of that, today of all days. Anyway the poor horse would be trodden on."

"You are funny." Jessie pushed at Janice's arms. "How could a horse be trodden on?"

"Quite easily in Trafalgar Square. The only way for it to escape would be to swim in the fountain."

The two children laughed. They liked their Auntie Janice: she not only made them laugh, she also gave them pocket money on the side. She was good fun. They could both recall when their mother, too, had been good fun. But since their Uncle Harry had died she had spent a lot of her time with Grandmamma Nelson. And when their father was finished at the office he spent most of his time in his study. But Grandmamma and Grandad Montane were nice to be with. Grandad was always jolly, just like Auntie Janice.

For the next fifteen minutes or so the conversation was taken up with chit-chat and with Steve teasing the two youngsters. Then, glancing at her watch, Janice exclaimed, "Good Lord! I didn't realize the time, nor how long it's going to take me to get back. It's nearly five now. Out of the way, you two ragamuffins, and let me get up."

"May we walk with you to the corner?"

"Well, just to the corner, and that's all. But you

can't go without your hats and coats; where are they?''

"In the kitchen," said young Steven.

"Well, go along and get them. I'll be with you in a minute.''

With the room to themselves once more, she now kissed Emily and then Steve, before saying, "I'll be home on Saturday morning, by which time I'll have made up my mind. But I want to hear what you think first. Right?''

They both nodded at her, then followed her into the hall; and when Steve helped her into her coat, Emily buttoned it up as if Janice were a child again. Then as Janice put on her hat, she questioned, "Will it keep on without pins?''

"It'll have to.''

"Wait a minute while I get some.''

"No. No, Mother, I must be off. Come on, you two!'' she called to the children who were emerging from the kitchen. "And just as far as the corner light, mind.''

It was Steve who now put in, "It's too dark for them to go out. But just a second; I'll put my coat on and go along with them.''

Without commenting, Emily went to the hall wardrobe, took out his coat, a muffler and his hat, and helped him into them. Then, bending to the children, she said, "Look after him, he might get lost.'' And they all went out laughing, the while she remained standing in the cold night air listening to their laughter as they passed from her view in the darkness. And then a strange thought entered her mind: he'd walk to hell for two minutes more of her company; and then a stranger thought still: she hoped her daughter would choose to go to Brighton, and then, for weeks on end, she would have him to herself, with no sharing.

It was almost eleven o'clock that night before Janice got round to ward six. In here, as over the whole hospital, there was that nightly hush, broken only by a cough or a splutter, with sometimes the cry, "Nurse! Nurse!"

She went into the duty room where the staff nurse and another were making tea, and she smiled as she said, "I couldn't have timed it better."

As she stood drinking the cup of tea, she said, "There'll be a new disease now the war's over. It will be called tanningitis. How many cups do you get through in a day?"

"Oh, I've stopped counting, sister." Both nurses laughed softly and the staff nurse's voice was muted as she said, "Sister Talbot said it's been like bedlam in here all day. Some of them had their relations in. Oh, and there was high jinks when the officers from the annex were ready to go on their transfers. Those who could hobble went to the windows, and the things they shouted! Sister said that if they had used the same words last week they would have been court-martialed."

"The annex will be empty now. They will be

starting the extension on that straightaway, I suppose?"

"No, no, sister. Not yet, not quite: there's still two in there."

When Janice raised her eyebrows in inquiry, the staff nurse said, "Well, all the other wards are chock-a-block and if the annex hadn't been empty they would have had to send them on. One had a high temperature: the captain. Sister said they had a bit of a do with him. Perhaps it was his fever, but he damned them because they put his batman in the emergency bed at the end of the ward: he demanded to know who they were going to put in the other five beds in the annex and when the sister said it was reserved for officers, he swore at her and told her to get his man back there and into the bed or he would know the reason why. Then, so they say, he passed out. Anyway, they brought the batman up and put him in the annex. Apparently, from the little he said, he and the captain were trapped for nearly three days in a dugout, up to their necks in mud. Eight of the platoon had been there, too, but none of them survived."

"Is the captain badly wounded?"

"He's wounded in the foot. It seems clean enough and is mending, but he has a bit of a fever. His temperature was really high a little while ago. Anyway, they just landed yesterday. There're the details, sister." She pointed to the table, and Janice, sitting down, picked up the first sheet of paper and read, "Private Daniel Dickinson, age twenty-nine, et cetera." She then looked down his service record to the last line, which read, "Wounded on 31st October, 1918. Admitted to field hospital 2nd November. Shipped on the 6th. Transferred to Saint Agnes's, London, 10th November."

Janice looked up, saying, "The tenth? They should have been here yesterday."

"Yes, they should. But we were full; then base must have heard of our transfers leaving the annex empty and sent them on today."

Janice lifted the sheet and put it to one side; then she looked at the heading of the next one. "Captain Robert Anderson: Aged . . ." She got no further; a wave of heat passed over her: she was back in the sitting room and her father was saying, "I am not your father," and an inner voice was yelling, what did he mean? Well, he had meant she was the daughter of Robert's father and that her mother, sitting there, had been the man's mistress.

It had all happened a long, long time ago. But never a day had passed since that she had not thought of him. Yet she had never looked upon him since that morning in the park. She had, however, followed his progress: he had gone up to Oxford for that extra year; he and Jason had remained firm friends, firmer than ever, really. Yet Jason had spoken of him but once when he said, "I was drawn to him from the beginning. It was the blood tie, I suppose."

And the blood tie remained.

"Are you all right, sister? Finish this tea. It's likely the strain of night-work and all the excitement of today. I know how you feel. Oh, I do." The nurse was talking in an ordinary way to a hospital night sister, and one did not talk in an ordinary way to such a person. But, as she said later, night sister looked as if she was about to pass out.

"It's all right, nurse. It's . . . it's just that I once knew Captain Anderson."

"Really?"

Both nurses were beaming on her now.

"It's a small world," said the night nurse, and her superior, the staff nurse, added, " 'Tis that; there's not a truer word. And you find that in here, 'cos they're from all over the world. Are you sure you're all right now?"

"Yes. Yes, nurse. I'll do the round."

Her heart was thumping against her ribs. She had a desire to run through this long ward, down the passage and into the annex. But she forced herself to stop here and there to ask questions. Some of the men were still awake, too full of excitement to sleep. "Evenin', sister," they said. And she went up to them, saying, "How's it going?" and receiving the answer, "Fine, sister. Fine," or, "I'm grand."

It seemed an interminable time before she reached the end of the ward. There the nurse opened the door and they walked along a short corridor and through another door into the annex.

A low light was burning, and Janice could see

two figures in their beds. The one furthest from her was propped up and he was awake. But the nearer one was lying well down on the pillows, and his head was moving from side to side, his face flushed. She stood looking down on him, her whole being crying, Oh, Robert! Robert! She wanted to wipe the sweat from his face, to put her arms about him. She had said that she had followed his career, but that was only in business. Three months after he came down from Oxford, his grandfather had died, and Robert had taken charge of the business, part of which, the papers said, he had sold. But for the last ten years she had heard scarcely anything of him. As for his private life she knew nothing. For all she knew, he could be married and have a family.

She shuddered and closed her eyes for a moment. Then a voice from the other bed brought her attention back to the present. He was saying, "Is he in a bad way, sister? Well, you know what I mean, for he's been through it. Kept me goin', he did, and did his damnedest to save the rest of the platoon, but they were really gonners before he started. Will he be all right?"

It was the staff nurse who answered, "Yes. Yes, he'll be all right."

Janice was now reading the chart that hung at the foot of the bed. It showed that his temperature had dropped from one hundred and four to one hundred and three. She moved back up the bed, and now she dared put her hand on his cheek. And at this he opened his eyes and gazed up at her and said, "I hate it! I hate it! Mud. Keep your head up, Dickie. Keep your head up!"

The man said now, "That's me, miss . . . nurse, that's me. I was for lettin' go. One of the best, he is. Grumpy at times, you know, nothin' right for him. But when it comes to the pinch, well, I wouldn't mind bein' in another hole with him. But God forbid. Oh aye, God forbid."

"Lie down, Mr. Dickinson. Lie down. Go to sleep."

"Can't sleep, miss . . . nurse. I dream like, you see. And me coughin' chokes me."

"Would you like a hot drink?"

"I would, nurse. Yes, I would."

Janice said to the staff nurse, "See to it, nurse, and—" Turning directly to the nurse and lowering her voice, she added something else, and the nurse acknowledged the order: "Yes, sister, one or two?"

"Two."

Left alone, Janice again stared down into the beloved face. He hardly resembled the same man she had previously known, for he was looking so much older. In fact, she might not have recognized him if it hadn't been for his name. His hair was still thick and fair, but his face looked utterly fleshless: his cheekbones were prominent; the mouth, although open and gasping for air, was thin-lipped. Suddenly, she realized that his eyes were showing some form of recognition, for he tried to raise himself from the pillow. And his lips now moved into her name, but then he said, "Dreaming?"

She bent her face close to his and whispered, "No, Robert. No, you're not dreaming. I'm here. Go to sleep. Go to sleep again, and when you wake up I'll still be here."

"Janice?"

"Yes. Yes, my dear, it's Janice."

He gave a movement of his head that seemed to deny what he had heard, then closed his eyes again. The voice from the other bed now was a whisper: "You . . . know the captain, sister?"

"Yes. Yes, I know the captain. Here is your hot drink coming. Now, you go to sleep, too. I'll see you in the morning."

"Thank you, miss . . . sister. That's good."

"What is good?"

"That you know him. 'Cos I've never known him talk of his people, not to anybody. Good-night, sister."

"Good-night." She had almost said "Dickie," for her heart was singing and she was no longer thirty-seven, but young again.

This feeling stayed with her until she left the ward and went to her own office, and there she came down to earth. Resting her hands on her desk, she bent her head over them. What was the matter with her? Nothing had changed, the barrier was still between them. Why had she suddenly felt the world was good and that she had a life ahead of her? Her thoughts had taken a ridiculous turn and for a moment she had been in love again.

But then, she had never been out of love. Her love for him had made her turn down two good men: one had repeatedly asked her to be his wife. He had distinguished himself in the war, and only last year had married someone else. As she had said, and as her father had written, she would never be a wife. So why had she felt as she had done a short while ago, like some girl rediscovering a lost love? The fact was that she had never lost the love. It would always be with her. But it could never come to anything . . .

She made her visit to the annex the last of her night round. It was half-past six, and the wards were a-bustle: there was the rattle of tea-trolleys; there were men limping to the ablutions, others were being washed in bed; here and there, men lay perfectly still, with only their eyes moving. These were the spinal cases, most of them awaiting transfer to specialist hospitals.

When she opened the annex door the light was turned on fully. Private Dickinson was hoisted up on his pillows, his face bright; but his captain was still lying flat, his head turned to the side: his eyes were wide open and he was looking toward the door.

When she stood near him neither of them spoke for a long moment. Then he said, "I . . . I wasn't dreaming, then."

"No, Robert. You weren't dreaming. It's . . . it's wonderful . . . wonderful to see you. You're . . . you're just the same. I recognized you straightaway," she lied.

"That's very kind of you. But you know you're fibbing."

"No. No, I'm not."

"Oh." He went to raise himself up, but she pressed her hand on his shoulder, saying, "Lie still. Do you feel any better?"

"Yes. Yes. Much cooler."

"That's good."

When Dickie's voice came from the other bed, saying, "He's had a good night, sister," his captain retorted, "Shut up!"

She wanted to laugh; it sounded so ordinary. It sounded as if her father were talking to Alice. No distance between man and maid, or man and his servant.

The man now said, "He's a lot better, miss. He always bawls when he's better."

She was amused by Private Dickinson's addressing of her: it would seem he couldn't make up his mind as to whether she was miss, nurse, or sister. She could imagine such a man being of some light relief, especially in sticky corners. And by the sound of it there must have been a number of these.

Robert now asked, "Is . . . is this a clearing base?"

"Well, sort of."

Then more softly he said, "Won't you sit down?"

As she pulled the chair forward, she assumed a stiff manner as she said, "No preference must be shown to individual patients."

He took her hand now and, his voice very low, he murmured, "It's been worth it all to land up here."

He was staring up into her face when he made an impatient movement and, turning his head now to the side, he said, "Don't you have to go and wash?"

"They didn't tell me, sir, what to do."

"Well, you can still walk, can't you? So get going."

"Well, I might get it in the neck, sir."

"You'll get it in the neck in any case. Get going."

Again Janice wanted to laugh, but loudly now, loudly and long, and clearly, more so when Dickinson, passing the foot of the bed, said to her, "You're witness, sister. If me shrapnel moves, it'll be the captain to blame. You're witness."

When the door closed on him Janice said, "He seems a good fellow."

"Yes. Yes, he's a good fellow. There's not much where his brain lies, but his heart's as large as his body." And now his smile widened as he said, "He was passed onto me some years ago because of his lack of deference toward his so-called superiors; he was apparently untrainable in that way." He paused, then whispered, "Oh, Janice. Janice." He was gripping her hands now. "I still can't believe I'm looking at you. It's such a lifetime ago."

"Sixteen years and a few months."

"There hasn't been a day when you've been out

of my mind. But the last time I saw you was 1905.''

''You saw me?''

''Yes. I knew your routine in the hospital; at least, when you were on night duty. I watched you crossing the square; just a glimpse.''

''Oh, Robert, Robert.'' The tears were in her voice now and, after swallowing deeply, she said, ''I mustn't cry. Good Lord! No! They would have the surgeons, doctors, the whole crew around me. Sister Montane crying . . . she must have an operation at once.''

He smiled now, saying, ''Are you such a dragon?''

''I don't think so, but I'm known to be rather aloof. I've never made friends. I've been unable to, somehow. I have the family and . . .''

''You still have them all?''

''Well, Mother and Father are now getting on, but are quite healthy. Jason married Rosie, as I suppose you know. Mother closed the hat shop and turned that into a house for them when they already had two small children. They have five now.''

''Really?''

She nodded. ''And John, you know, Doctor Nelson and Mary; they also had two sons, you met them at that Christmas dinner. Well, Harry was killed within a month of being in France, and James, he goes to sea and they're all very worried because his ship is overdue. It was rather a sad day for them yesterday. For the rest, life has just gone on by routine, getting through one day at a time. That's all, Robert, just getting through one day at a time."

"You never married?"

"No. I told you I wouldn't . . . and you?"

He paused. In the pause her heart sank and then he said, "No. I tried. Yes, I tried. I became engaged, but then like the coward I was, I had to tell her I was in love with someone else and it wasn't right that I should go on. Her father was for shooting me. I wouldn't have blamed him at the time. But oh, Janice, you've got no idea how I feel. I've found you. I've found you again. I can touch you, look at you, talk to you, hear your voice. That must suffice . . ." They looked at each other, the same thought in both their heads, and then he added, "For the present."

She muttered, "Your people?"

"I don't seem to have any. My mother and father died. I never saw my father again after I left you, although I did return to the house for my mother's funeral. He survived her for nearly three years. One good thing happened—my sister was happy for a time. You didn't know Hector Mills-Cotton. He was the young fellow who drove me back home in his car. Jason was with us at the time. That was the day he saw Father. Well, Marian greeted that car and Hector with a mouthful. I thought she was going to hit him; he had frightened her horses. She was mad on horses, still is. Well, they married. I never imagined her marrying. She was so plain, you know, but she was full of character. We always got on well. But Hector caught it in the first year of the war. They had a nice place down in Dorset and bred horses for the Army. Oh, dear, dear. To watch the death of a man is bad enough, but to watch the last agonies of a horse is even worse. That's the only thing we disagreed on, Marian and I, breeding horses for the Army. Anyway, she still runs the business down there on her own. My other sister I rarely saw. Haven't seen her, in fact, for years. As for the house, well, I offered it to Marian after our people died, but she didn't want it. So I sold it. I still keep on the London place; and Gibbons who looked after my grandfather, is getting fast on in years, but he still sees to the house.

"Walton, who was my father's man, he died within about two months of him. It had been a long association between them. It often happens, I suppose."

His voice trailed away and he laid his head back on the pillow, and she said quietly, "Go to sleep."

His face brightened now as he turned toward her again, saying, "I never want to sleep again as long as I can look at you. There's only one other thing that I want and that is to get out of here. I can still walk—at least, I could before this hit me. Yes, I can remember walking."

"From what I understand, you had a rather long mud-bath."

His eyes blinking now, he said, "Oh God! Yes. Yes. Oh, yes, that's it. It was rather a long mud-bath." For a few words his voice was low and the words disjointed at the memory: "Once . . . I'm on my . . . feet, I'm going to take . . . you to High Gully," and his intent now urged him to go on: "I used to hate that place, you know. But now, oh, for a long time I've just longed to be there in the wildness of it, and the beauty." He nodded now. "They took all the men during the war. Johnny McBrien's still there; he's the gillie. He can hardly walk now, he's so old; and the cook and two maids. They've shut up the other part, you know." He suddenly stretched his eyes wide as he said, "What am I rambling on about, Janice? They gave me a dose of something just a while ago. I'll watch that in future."

"Go to sleep, my dear." She had almost said "my love." "I'll be back shortly."

Dickinson came back into the room now. In fact, he was pushed in by a nurse and was proclaiming loudly, "I do what the captain says and nobody else. He told me to wash an' I washed."

"And I'm telling you to get back into bed and stay there."

"I've had no breakfast."

"And you are not getting any. You're going down to the theater later."

"Good God! I'm not."

"Good God! You are."

"We'll see. The captain . . ."

"Shut up! I'm the captain here. Get back into that bed!"

Robert was smiling now, his eyes closed; then,

his breathing steadier, he muttered, "That's it, Dickie, you tell 'em."

The nurse now came round to Janice's side, saying, "He seemed to sleep well until about six o'clock, so I didn't disturb him to give him the dose. But then he became so restless I thought he'd better have it."

"Yes." Janice nodded at her. "Quite right. But his temperature is well down this morning."

Janice gave one last look at Robert's sleeping face, before following the nurse out of the ward. Her heart was singing again. He wasn't married, she wasn't married. As he had said, they could see each other, talk to each other . . . and wait for what was to come.

Why hadn't she seen it this way all those years ago? The world had changed, of course. Everything had changed. No girl fainted now at the word "sex." Women had achieved a freedom that had to be recognized by men. Divorce was no longer the prerogative of the rich, and a woman didn't have to suffer the indignities of desertion or brutality before she could apply for a license to make a new life for herself. Yes, morals had taken on a different picture. Then she almost stopped in her walk up the ward, and the light went from her face: incest was still a terrifying word, and the coming together of brother and sister was equally something to shudder at. But what about half-brother and half-sister? There must be thousands of them already married and breeding families. Why should she and Robert be different? Why?

Immediately there sprang up before her the image of the man she was proud to call father, and of her mother, and she knew *their* moral attitudes had not changed.

2

In the end, Janice took neither the sister-tutor's position nor the post of hospital matron. Steve and Emily had, as promised, told her their thoughts about taking the sister-tutor's appointment. Emily had expressed her opinion earlier to Steve that the position of matron would be the better, but had then acceded to his view. But Janice had surprised them both by telling them she was taking neither, and when they asked why, she had answered briefly that she had changed her mind; that certain circumstances had arisen that might alter her future and she would tell them about it later, as nothing had been decided yet.

They had glanced at each other, then looked at her, and Emily had asked: "You have something else in your mind, dear?"

"Yes. Yes, I have, Mother," she had replied. "But I'm saying nothing about it yet." And without pressing any point, Emily again acceded: "Very well, dear, in your own good time."

What Janice didn't tell them the following week was that she had given a month's notice; and the surprised superintendent had got no further in her inquiries than Emily and Steve had previously.

By the end of November both Janice and Robert knew what was going to happen to them. He was now walking on crutches and Dickinson had had his shrapnel removed and was to be discharged. Robert had managed to hasten his own discharge: except for two missing toes, with fortunately the big toe not being one of them, his foot had healed well, and all that was now needed was a support that would balance the foot and enable him to walk, after some practice, without limping.

At this moment Janice was sitting, of all places, in the drawing room of the house in the square, and they were being attended by both Gibbons and a bright-faced, middle-aged maid. The tea-trolley had been placed before Janice where she sat at the end of a deep chesterfield couch. The trolley held a silver tea-service and china cups and saucers, and next to it had been placed the cake-stand, its round rosewood leaves holding plates of thin bread and butter, cucumber sandwiches, and an assortment of sweetmeats.

"Can you manage, madam?"

"Yes. Yes, thank you." Janice smiled up into the face of the stooped-shouldered, white-haired man, who then turned to Robert and said, "Can I get you a footstool, sir?"

"Don't fuss, Gibbons. If anyone needs a footstool it's you. I told you before to put your feet up; there're plenty of others to do the running."

"The habit of years, sir, the habit of years."

"Well, you've got many years left, I hope, in order to drop the habit."

The old man almost beamed down on Robert now as he said softly, "It's so good to have you back, sir. It's so good to have you back."

"And I am pleased to be back, Gibbons, believe me."

Robert now looked at the maid and said, "Take him away, will you, Doris? And see that he gets a rest."

The maid, smiling now, shook her head as much as to say that command was beyond her, but together they did leave the room.

Hitching himself further up the couch toward Janice, Robert said, "Judging by the time he came to Grandfather, he must be in his late eighties now, if not nineties, and he's spent most of his life between this house and High Gully. Which reminds me to ask you if you can manage the weekend."

She nodded as she said, "Yes. My time's up on the eighteenth; and anyway I have a week's leave due to me, so I could really finish at the weekend."

"Do that, then we needn't hurry back, because it will take more than a weekend to show you—" He paused, then went on, "Well, not to show you, but to see what you think of the place. It's wild, it's lonely, and in the winter it's like Siberia, but always it's beautiful and calming."

He took her hand from the tea-tray and looking

deep into her eyes, he said softly, "We keep skirting the issue, don't we? We never bring it to the foreground, but we're trimming it up with such words as, you must come and see the London house, you must come up to Scotland and see the Gully, you must do this, and you must do that, but . . . but the question is, my dearest Janice, my dearest, dearest, Janice, I repeat the question . . . Why?"

Her hand was trembling in his and her voice was low but firm as she answered him, "Because we . . . we both know why. The 'why' was there sixteen years ago, but we were young and afraid; or at least I was. But no longer."

"Oh, my darling." As he made to put his arms about her the trolley rocked and they both put their hands out to steady it, laughing self-consciously. And when he went to push it away, she said, "The tea will be cold."

"The tea will be cold," he repeated. "Oh, my dear, at this moment, this wonderful moment, all you can say is that the tea will be cold. Come here with you! Come here." She was in his arms now and hers about him, and for the first time since their lips had last met on that misty morning in 1902, they were pressed close again. And so long did the kiss last that when he finally released her she lay back from him against the side of the couch and, between short breaths, said, "I . . . I never, never thought it would happen. Never! And, you know, my dear, for most of those long years I've regretted the choice I made, because I know now it lay with me."

"Maybe, but you were wise, because we could never have lived down the storm it would have created; you could never have gone back to your people; and as for Grandfather agreeing to it, he would have cut me off." He pulled a face now. "Oh, yes, I know he would have cut me off and left the whole bang-shoot to some charity or other. For that alone I have you to thank, because I feel that I have been able to do some good with his money. That is, up to when the war started. And you know, darling, we have the war to thank for our coming together and for making our future life possible. It has swept away a great deal of hypocrisy, although there is still much left." His voice sank now as he repeated, "Yes, I'm afraid there's still a lot left. And your people, I'm sure, will hold some of it. Though perhaps not your father."

"Oh, my dear, I think you're mistaken there. I would imagine that he, on this matter, would be more adamant about the moral code than Mother would. And yet, yet I don't know, and this is the only thing that worries me: they've got to be told."

"Shall . . . shall I go with you to the house?"

"Oh, no, no." She put out her hand and touched his cheek. "Let me deal with this first."

She turned again to the tea-trolley and poured out the tea and he took a plate from the cake-stand and handed it toward her, and for the next five minutes or so they drank their tea and nibbled at the sandwiches, while sitting close and gazing at the roaring fire in the wide hearth.

When Robert asked, "Who knows about the situation in the family, besides your mother and father and Jason?"

"Only Alice, I think, because Father asked Jason not to tell Rosie. The break between us, I understand, was put down to your grandfather having other ideas for you above that of a nurse."

"No!"

"Oh, yes; and I think it was cleverly done. Who on your side knows?"

"Only Gibbons, I'm sure of that. Even Marian wasn't told. Yet she has a very keen mind, has Marian. But even if she *had* known she would have been on our side had anything come about."

He now brought her face round to look into his as he said, "I have a confession to make. It could be described as jumping the gun . . . I took out a special license last week."

"Oh!" Again she repeated, "Oh!" and louder now. "You mean . . . you mean we should be married? I thought, in fact I was quite willing that . . ."

"That we should just live together?"

"Yes; yes, of course."

"Oh, my dear!" His two hands were holding her face now and he shook his head as he said, "No. No. For good or ill, and it's going to be for good, we're going to be married. We'll tell no one until it's done; then it can't be undone."

"But . . . but Robert, have you thought if there . . . you see, although I'm nearing forty, I could still have a child."

"And you wouldn't want a child?"

"No. No, I wouldn't, not under the circumstances."

"Well, I've thought along the same lines as you, dear, and you have no need to worry. I'm going to make sure that is impossible."

Their gaze held for some moments, and her head dropped onto his shoulder as she murmured, "All I want in this world is you."

"And me, too, and in the next. Wherever we go I want to feel you'll be with me. What I have for you is no ordinary love. All right, it could be said it springs from our tie of blood, so it isn't ordinary, but deeper than any emotion created by looks or personal attraction. It is something I recognized long ago is beyond my own comprehension, because an ordinary love would have died over these past years. But mine has never wavered. Even when I would have married another it was there, telling me that the love I had for you was not wrong, but the feeling called love that I was offering someone else was a bad thing, because it was based solely on bodily desire and lies."

He lifted her head from his shoulder as he said, "I hope you like the Gully. It will likely have to be all opened up and redecorated inside. But I can see us spending the main part of our lives there, growing old there with just occasional visits to Edinburgh . . . or London. It was odd, you know, darling, but during the war, in those filthy stinking trenches, my mind would jump back to that Christmas dinner: the time I first saw you, and then the night when we all went to the Gaiety Theater and saw the musical comedy, *The Toreador.* It was brought back vividly to mind when I heard one of the men singing and in a broad cockney voice:

Keep off the grass,
Keep off the grass,
Conduct like this I won't pardon.
Play at your ease,
But if you please,
Keep off the grass in the garden!

The words brought it all so vividly back. It was a wonderful night. And remember the next time we all went out together? That was only possible because Grandfather had seen his doctor, who had ordered him into a nursing home for a couple of days for tests. And we all went to the Royal Strand and saw *A Chinese Honeymoon.*"

"Oh, yes, yes. Oh, yes, dear, I remember that. Yes, yes. Do you remember when we came back and Jason got dressed up as the little Cockney maid, Fi Fi, and he sang her song and we all stood round the piano and joined in. We were up till about one in the morning. From then on Jason thought he was for the stage, because he sang it so often. In fact, we all sang it. It went:

I want to be a lidy,
And with the lidies rank.
I want to have a thousand golden
    sov'reigns in the bank.
I want to ride a gee-gee
And wear a coat of fawn,
So that folk will say when I cry 'Who-a!'
I'm a lidy bred and born.''

She laughed now. "Everybody was singing it and the errand boys whistled it. You know, it ran for over a thousand performances. And you know, you hear of Gertie Millar, and names like that hang on, but the girl's name who sang that song was Louie Freear, a great comedienne, if ever there was one."

As they sat now gazing at each other, she said sadly, "That was the most wonderful Christmas of my life. But, you know, I hated Christmases after that. I still don't like Christmases. Although, since Jason's family came along, one has to be merry and bright for the children, because it really is children's time."

A silence fell between them; then he broke into her thoughts by saying, "We could adopt. It was amazing the number of fellows I met out there who had been brought up in homes or adopted." She smiled and nodded at him as she said, "Yes. Yes," then paused before saying, "But not for some time. I want you all to myself."

"Oh, Janice, Janice. There aren't enough life-times left to satisfy this craving to have you to myself. We . . . we must be married soon."

"Yes, dear," she said simply now. "Yes, soon."

3

Jason took the letter Steve handed to him. It read:

> My dear Mother and Father,
>   I'll be calling in about eleven tomorrow morning. Could Jason be with you, please, as I have something to tell you all?
>   With my love, as always,
>   Janice.

"Well, what do you make of that?" asked Steve. "And tomorrow morning is now and it will soon be eleven o'clock. By the way, where did you get to? Rosie thought you had gone out shopping."

"Yes; well, I had. There were things I needed and the stores get so crowded later on, or I have the tribe with me and cannot think what I'm doing or why I'm there."

"What can she mean?" Emily asked. She was sitting very upright in a straight-backed chair. Then, looking directly at Jason, she asked, "Are you in her confidence in any way?"

"Well"—he gave a short laugh—"I suppose I am and this, I think, is what it's all about. You see, for some time now, she's been learning to drive a motor car."

"A motor car? Why?"

He looked at Steve. "Just because she wanted to learn to drive a motor car, I suppose. You know Janice, she never explains her motives."

"How long has it been going on?"

"Oh, months."

"It couldn't have been months. She wouldn't have been allowed a motor car when the war was on."

"From what I understand, one of the doctors had one. He's of about retiring age. Anyway, his wife was terrified to go in the thing, so he promised that when he retired and didn't need it so much, he would give it up. I think it was from then that Janice got the idea, and so he used to take her out in it now and again. From what I can gather since then, she's bought it from him."

"Well, where is it?"

"Well, Mother, she wasn't going to bring it and stick it outside the door, was she? I suppose it's been kept in a garage or some place near the doctor's house."

Steve turned away and walked toward the window. And as he stood looking out, he said quietly, "I think there's more to it than that. She's been different of late; brighter, happier." He turned swiftly now and, looking at Jason, he said, "You say this doctor's of retiring age and with a wife? Are you sure?"

"Well, that's what she says. I don't know him."

Steve walked back to the fireside and addressing Emily now, he said softly, "It could be that, you know, she's . . . she's found someone. Evidently not that man, but someone; and that's the surprise."

"But why all the secrecy? It's true, dear, that she has been different of late. At first I thought it was the excitement of her being offered the two posts; but then she said she wouldn't be taking either and was going to stay. Oh, dear me." Emily got to her feet and looked toward Jason, saying, "And another thing, she hasn't been near us for nearly a week. She always made time to drop in for a coffee, even if it was only for half an hour. There's something wrong. I know there is. I know there is."

"Now, now. You know nothing until she comes and tells us what it's all about." Steve had gone to her and pressed her back onto the chair, saying, "Calm yourself, dear. Calm yourself."

She looked up at him and asked, "Are you calm inside?"

Without answering, he turned away. No, he wasn't calm inside. He had a fear in him on which he wouldn't allow his mind to dwell, for it would be too awful to contemplate . . .

It was five minutes to eleven when the doorbell rang, and when Alice opened it she exclaimed, "Oh, love! come away in; it's enough to freeze you." The words died away on her lips as she saw the motor-car standing by the curb. She could see it was a long affair with a canvas hood and that there was someone sitting in the passenger seat.

"You came in that?"

"Yes, Alice, I came in that, and what is more, I drove it."

"Never on your life!"

"Where are they?"

"They're in the sittin' room. Master Jason's with them. Give me your coat an' hat."

"No. No, dear Alice." Janice now put her hands on Alice's shoulder and said softly, "I'm not staying, Alice. I'm . . . I'm going away with someone."

"Ah, miss! In the name of God!"

"You will know all about it shortly. But just let me say this: I'll miss you because I love you. You've looked after me so well all these years."

"Dear Lord! Dear Lord! What's this come upon us?"

Janice learnt forward now and kissed the already wet cheek, saying, "Don't come in for a while, please." Then she left her and went toward the sitting room door. There, she paused a moment before opening it.

The three of them were waiting for her—Emily was standing again—but no one spoke until she said, "Sit down, can't you? This is going to be awful enough without you standing like the three judges."

"Dear! dear! dear!" Steve walked toward her, saying, "Judges? What are you talking about?

Come in and sit down. Why haven't you taken off your hat and coat?"

"Simply because I am not staying, Father. Please!" She looked at her mother, then at Jason, saying, "I can't talk to you or tell you anything when you're standing there already accusing me."

"Have you done something of which you could be accused?"

"You might think so. Perhaps not you so much but, *please, won't you sit down?*"

All three sat on the couch and she on the chair her mother had vacated.

After twice wetting her lips she said, "I'll make it brief. Robert and I met up again on Armistice Day. He was brought in with the wounded and from the moment we saw each other we knew we should never have been parted in the first place." As she watched her father's hand go to his head and his chin droop to his chest, she said, "I knew what the reaction would be, that is why I never brought it up. We are going away, and . . . and now."

"Oh, no! No!" This was from her mother. "You can't do this. You mustn't do this."

"Mother"—Janice's voice was low but her tone was firm—"I must say this, no matter how it hurts. I didn't start this business. And when fate threw us together it was none of our doing; and we knew we loved each other from the moment we set eyes on each other at that fateful Christmas dinner. And immediately after our situation was made known to us the following May, we knew we must part. But never a day has gone by since then that I haven't thought of him, and he of me, and we have still some time left before us, and we mean to spend it together."

"My dear, my dear, while there is still time, think of the consequences."

"Father, please don't get up." Her hand was pushed out as if pressing him back onto the couch; and there he stayed, but he went on, "I repeat, the consequences."

"There will be no consequences, Father, in the way you mean. Robert has seen to that permanently."

When the three of them bowed their heads as if they were horrified at the bold statement so crudely presented, Janice said quietly, "The world has changed. I shouldn't have any need to tell you that, Father."

At this, Steve's head came up sharply and his voice was loud as he said, "It cannot change wrong into right. He is your half-brother. You'll be living with your half-brother. It will become known."

"It won't become known, Father, unless you broadcast it. Or you, Mother, or you, Jason. And as I was married yesterday I am now Mrs. Anderson." Then when her mother made a sound as if she were about to vomit, she turned on her almost vehemently, saying, "You, of all people, Mother, should try to understand."

Emily was now on her feet, crying back to her daughter, "You are doing this to make me suffer!

When the knowledge of your birth was made known to you, you turned against me!"

"You know that is not true, Mother. You're quite wrong. That knowledge dealt me a vicious blow, and looking back I consider I acted pretty well under the circumstances, considering my feelings for Robert at that time. I could have easily given in, and he, too. But there was . . . the family on both sides and the disgrace. Oh, yes, the disgrace. A man died so that no whisper of the truth should come out."

At this Steve sprang to his feet, but his eyes were on Jason, and Jason, looking at Janice, said, "Yes. Yes, I told her a little of what had happened. We were close, practically as one; I felt she had a right to know," and immediately he walked over to her and took her hand, saying, "I can understand, dear; and I wish you all the happiness you can get."

It was too much and even her teeth going tight into her lower lip could not stop the tears from springing to Janice's eyes.

Steve shook his head, mumbling now, "Perhaps later, perhaps later. But apart from everything else, your mother and I are . . . are losing you for good. Nothing will ever be the same again," to which Janice replied, "I know that, and for my part I'm happy it won't be, because for me the past years have been very lonely. One puts a face on during the day but there're still the nights to get through. And I had thought, Father, that you of all people would have understood. In a way you foresaw my life in the last poem in your Christmas book: 'I would never be a wife and all I needed was a friend.' But for all these years I've needed more than a friend, Father. Well, now I've got one; a husband, whom I love dearly . . . desperately.''

The silence in the room seemed to scream in all their heads and it was Jason who now broke it, his words stumbling, ''Where . . . where are you living? I mean, where are you going to live? Are you staying in London?''

''No, Jason. We . . . we are keeping on the London house, but our main home will be in Scotland, on the estate there. High Gully, it is called.''

Emily and Steve were staring at this woman, this daughter of theirs, this girl whom they both loved. In different ways, yes, but loved, if not passionately, then possessively, at least on Steve's part. And she was talking about keeping on their house in London and their estate in Scotland. This alone had removed her from their world, even from his horizon. And when she said, ''He . . . he's waiting in the car. Would . . . would you see him?'' their answers came as one, and almost a shout, ''No!'' But when Emily added, ''What . . . what an indelicate thing to ask,'' Janice rounded on her, crying, ''Oh, Mother! *you* talking about indelicate things. *Classing him as an indelicate thing.*'' She stood now, her breast heaving as if it was pressing down on anger, as it really was; but she forced herself to say, ''I knew I'd meet with opposition. Yes, that was a foregone conclusion, but not in this way. You have certainly cut the umbilical cord this time." As she quickly turned about to leave the room, Steve halted her. Gripping her arm, he said, "Don't go like that, dear, don't go. It was a shock . . . a shock to us both. But . . . but we'll get over it. Yes, we will. Yes, we will. But don't put us out of your life. Please! When . . . when you're back in town, come and see us. Better still, write to us. Please, write to us. I beg of you."

She looked into the tortured face of the very good man that she knew him to be. Suddenly her arms went out and she held him close, and he her. After a moment she released herself and looked across at her mother. Emily was standing supporting herself with one hand against the mantelshelf, her face the color of lint. Slowly Janice approached her and they stood staring at each other for a full minute before Janice said, "I'm sorry, dear. I'm sorry I'm hurting you. I didn't mean it. Only I'm . . . I'm helpless. Just think of that. I'm as helpless now as you once were, where my affections are concerned."

When their arms went about each other and they kissed, it was with none of the warmth of Steve's embrace, nor in hers. And now she was stumbling from the room, too blinded with tears to see where she was going. But Jason had his arm around her shoulder. Alice was still standing where she had left her. She said nothing but opened the door.

And now Jason led Janice out into the street,

across the pavement and to the car, and there, bending down, he saw the man he hadn't met for some long time now, and he said simply, "Hello there! Robert." And Robert answered in the same vein, "Hello! Jason."

Jason now opened the car door, and as he held it, Janice turned to him, saying, "Thank you, dear. We'll look in on you from time to time; and . . . and perhaps you'll bring Rosie up, and the children."

"That would be lovely."

"Oh, Jason." They hugged each other for a long moment; then she got into the car and Jason closed the door; and now putting his head under the hood, he looked at Robert and said, "Take care of her, Robert. Be happy, both of you. It's a long time to make up for. I'll be seeing you."

Neither of them could make any answer.

As he straightened up the car hummed into activity, and he stood in the cold street and watched it until it had gone from his sight.

When he returned to the sitting room only Steve was there, and he said to him, "Try to see it their way, Father. Please. And if you accept that, you won't lose her, she'll be back. Because I tell you this much, I don't need to cut any cord. I'm with them both all the way. I liked him then, I like him now. Just ask yourself what you think her life has been all these years, especially seeing me married and having a family. I think she has played the game very well under the circumstances." And with that he turned and walked out of the room. He did not have to ask where his mother was, for he knew she would be upstairs in her room, likely crying her eyes out.

But the door had hardly closed on him when Emily appeared at the top of the stairs, and when she again entered the sitting room Steve turned to look toward her, and with some amazement, for in her hand she held that old yellow hat.

He did not speak until she reached the fire, and there he watched her take the brim in her hands and twist it in opposite directions until the straw, weakened with age, came apart. Then she ripped the whole from the crown, and when his hand came out to stop her, she cried at him, *"Leave me alone!"* causing him to step back in amazement at the tone that she had never used to him before. And now he watched as, piece by piece, the yellow straw was flung into the heart of the fire and immediately became ignited, until the whole was aflame and giving off strange, iridescent colors, until there was nothing left but a fine mush lying on top of the red coals. And when he murmured, "Why, dear? Why? She . . . she liked that hat, and it was yours," she replied, *"Yes. Yes, it was mine.* And I've just found that for some time she must have been taking her clothes from her wardrobe and drawers, but that she had left that hat to cast its spell. It was an evil thing. Right from the beginning it has been an evil thing."

"No, no, my dear." He pulled her forcibly round from the fire. "Don't blame the hat. What we each do with our life, if it is not already planned, is there for us to mould: whatever happened to you was not because of the hat.''

''Oh, yes, it was. Yes, it was.''

''All right, dear, all right. But now it's gone, and if you think it was evil, then the evil has gone with it. Perhaps she too sensed something about it; and that's why she didn't take it. Come. Come and sit down. What is done is done. We have to face up to it, for we can do nothing.''

She allowed him to lead her to the sofa, and when she lay in the protection of his arms, her mind cried at her, I wanted her away so I could have him to myself, and now I have him . . . or have I? but at what a price.

She turned her head and looked toward the fire again. That hat *had* been an evil influence. That's why somebody had stored it away in that box in the attic, where it had lain for God knows how long, unable to spin its web.

A commotion outside the door now disturbed them. It was Alice remonstrating with the children. And Steve said, ''It is Christmas Eve tomorrow, dear, and there are the children to think about; and they need you. We all need you.''

Of a sudden, she threw herself against him, begging now, ''Hold me! Please! dear, hold me tight. Never let me go! There is only you. Only you.'' And as he held her, he murmured, ''And for me, my love, there is only you.''

Perhaps it was an echo of the past, but Robert had parked the car on the curb, near to the place where they had parted all those years ago. And, her hands going out to him, Janice cried, "Hold them tight for a moment, dear, hold them tight, and know there is only you. Ever. It was awful back there. It was awful. But nothing matters any more." And he, leaning toward her, brought her face to his and there, under the gaze of a passer-by, he kissed her hard, saying, "And for me, there is only you, as it was in the beginning, and to the end."

BOOK THREE

Consequences

PART ONE
1936

1

"If you go out of this house and leave me alone for another Christmas, I'll yell the dirty facts from the house-tops. I know I've said it before but this time I mean it. D'you hear me?"

"Yes. Yes, I hear you; and I say to you, as *I've* said before, you needn't be alone: you can come with us as you used to."

"As I used to . . . while I was kept in the dark all those years, visiting that filthy pair?"

"Now, Rose, I'm warning you, be careful."

"What have I to be careful of? It's a wonder you didn't do the same as your sister."

Jason's voice was quiet and steady as he replied, "Yes, I could have, and would likely have been a damn sight happier than I am now if, the night of the Oxford Ball, my mother hadn't practically pushed me up your stairs to propose to you. And let me tell you something that you haven't heard before: I never thought of marrying you up till that minute, when she told me how you felt about me and how it was expected of me, how nice it would be to bring the two families together, permanently . . . God help me . . . permanently. Yes, but for her doing that, I would likely have gone the same way as Janice: I would have gone to live with my half-sister, because I was interested in her from the first minute I saw her. And if I remember rightly, you didn't like it, because you kept talking about her. Oh, yes, yes, Rose. If it hadn't been for Mother you wouldn't have got your delicate, refined and poisoned claws into one Jason Montane, and remember I dodged the issue for years. Why did I not go on teaching when I had read history? I said there wasn't enough money in it, that there was more in accountancy, and that meant starting from scratch, because I knew it would take me another two or three years or more to build up a position of some standing, and my dear mother kept pointing out to you why I wouldn't accept help was, being an independent sort of bloke, I wanted to provide for you in my own way; whereas all the while I was waiting for you to become fed up and tired of it all and so give me up. Now, you didn't know that, did you?''

From where his wife was sitting on the couch, a half-empty glass of sherry in her hand and a decanter on a low table near her knee, the expression on her face told him to be wary because at any moment she could hurl her glass at him. But what she did was to put it to her lips and throw the remainder of the wine down her throat in one gulp; and then she stared at him for a moment before saying, "That being so, you were pretty anxious to get into bed, weren't you? Couldn't wait, night or day, could you?'' to which he replied, "That's a facet of human nature, unfortunately, which rarely has anything to do with love."

She now drew herself to the edge of the couch, but instead of rising to her feet, she strained her body from the waist toward him and her words came through her gritted teeth. "You've condoned your sister's situation for years and encouraged my children to look forward to the trips to Scotland and mix with him and her and the four pieces of scum they've adopted. Not only that, but dear Marian has often been in the party, hasn't she? Well, then, let me tell you, from this day on the idyllic situation is at an end." Then she slowly shook her head and said, "I'll give you one more chance. I'll keep my mouth shut and I will not inform our lot about the situation, and they may go up there on their own, but you are to stay here."

Jason stood stiffly and watched her hand go out to the decanter and refill her wine glass; then he said quietly, "You know something, Rosie? You may tell who the hell you like. Bring them in, tell them the whole beautiful story, because it's as beautiful to me as it is to Janice and Robert; and that's what you've been jealous of, isn't it? Jealous of their happiness. And let me tell you something else: during these past years my visits up there have been like stepping from hell into heaven, and since you overheard what you weren't supposed to after Janice adopted Queenie, I've been sickened by you . . . and that." He now thrust his forefinger toward the decanter. "You're a lush. I have only to look back to realize that you always have been. After we had our first tiffs, that was your solace: you had to have a glass of sherry; not one on the quiet, but two, three, four, and yet you could stand up and swear to my face in deep indignation that you had never taken a drop, hadn't even seen a glass of sherry for days."

She was on her feet now, rushing at him and screaming, "It's all I've got. It's all I've ever had. Driven to it by you and your incestuous sister. That big, dirty, filthy . . ." As her voice reached almost a screech the flat of his hand came across her face and almost simultaneously the door opened, and there stood his family, the four of them all dressed in their traveling clothes, all aghast at the remnants of what they had heard and the fact that their dad had struck their mother.

There was a stillness in the room and for some seconds, her hand still cupping her cheek, she stared at the group at the door, but the stillness in no way calmed the feeling inside her, and she yelled at them, "Did you know that your dear Aunt Janice is living with her brother?"

"He is not her brother, he is her half-brother and my half-brother." Jason's voice was almost as loud as hers, and she glared at him again as she inveighed against him, "And Marian's your half-sister and you've been along of her, too."

Once more he raised his hand as if to strike her, but his elder son's shouting, "Dad! No! Not that!"

checked him, and he turned to his children, his eyes closed, and he was gulping in his throat as he said, "Go into the study, please, all of you. I'll be with you in a minute."

The two young men and the two young women seemed reluctant to move; until Freddie, stretching his arms wide, turned them all from the door as if he were ushering children; and Jason himself went and closed it quietly; then stood with his back to it and looked toward his wife and with a deep tremble in his voice, said "It's finished, Rose. You're on your own from now. I'm leaving you with your bottle and your mother. Oh yes, with your mother, for you make a good pair. She ruined your father's life as you've done mine. Unfortunately it's too late for him to do anything about it; not for me, though. I'm fifty-five years old, and what time is left to me, if not spent in happiness, is going to be enjoyed in peace. The children are children no more. Steven is twenty-six and Gracie is coming up twenty. They're all out in the world doing what they want to do. But I know that all their lives they've looked forward to Christmas: wherever they've been they've made it their business to be home so that we could all go up there together. At least, it was so until five years ago, when you overheard or purposely listened to a conversation between my *half*-sister and me. Looking back now I can imagine you welcomed such news, for it gave you an added excuse for indulging in your friend more freely than ever, didn't it? Well, now, I'll see my solicitor after the holidays and it can be a separation until, hopefully, a divorce can be arranged."

"You do. You do," she said, in a grinding whisper. "You shame me, just you shame me, Jason Montane, and what has happened now will be a fleabite, for I'll make it headlines, the great Anderson Steerman living with his sister . . . Yes, I'll say sister, not half-sister, and that he married her. What will his world think of that, his business world? I'll tell them of their adopting these poor children and trying to turn them into ladies and gentlemen, living in a house that's like a mansion, and with a London house, too. Oh, I'll make the papers sing."

He stared hard at her before he said, "Do that. Yes, do that. I'll tell them what to expect. But when you're doing it, remember we've been through one war. This is 1936 and by all accounts we could be in for another one. The world is changing, and let me tell you that today there must be thousands of married couples who are ignorant of the circumstances of their birth and are happy together. You do what you intend to do. It might bring a lot of things out of the wood; it might dispel a lot of fear. Goodbye, Rose."

As he turned to go she screamed at him, "What about your mother, the old hag! Living next door like a duchess with her dear Alice, and her cook, and her maid, and her son, because you're all she's got, for she hasn't seen her filthy daughter for years. She won't see her, yet it was she who started all this, wasn't it? Your mother was nothing more than a prostitute, a whore."

His clenched fists pressed tightly together so as to prevent himself from lashing out at her again, then he turned quickly and hurried to the door.

Now with the door closed behind him he had to stand against it for a moment before he could move toward the study.

They were standing waiting for him and he said quietly, "Sit down. This won't take long. . . ."

It took ten minutes to give a summary of their grandmother's life: of how both he and Janice came into being; of why the wonderful man who had died ten years ago was not his and Janice's father, that their real father was also the father of Uncle Robert and Auntie Marian; of the instant impact of Robert on both Janice and himself, not brought about solely by the blood-tie, for Janice and Robert had fallen almost instantly in love, and had remained so for seventeen years after their mutual acceptance that they must part; of how then and quite by accident they had met in the hospital in which Janice was a sister and he a wounded soldier; of how, during those long years of being parted, each had refused marriage; of how, knowing the reception they would get from Mother and Father, they had married on the quiet. "Yes," he nodded at them, "they got married secretly; but they arranged that there must never be any children of the marriage; which is why there is the adopted family in High Gully. As long as you live, I am sure you'll not find a happier couple; and if you yourselves marry, you will indeed be fortunate to be as happy.''

''And mother knew nothing about this?'' asked Jessie, his elder daughter.

''No, nothing, until about five or six years ago, when she overheard a conversation between your Auntie Marian and me.''

''Is that why she took to drink, Dad?'' Gracie asked.

''Don't be silly!'' Freddie replied disdainfully to his younger sister. ''From as far back as I can remember, and that's when I was about three, she was always sipping sherry; at least, she always seemed to be.''

Jason looked from Steven to Jessie and from Jessie to Freddie and then to Gracie; then, taking them all in at a glance, he said, ''Well now, what are you going to do? Are you still going up there?''

''Good gracious! Yes.'' Steven was nodding his head briskly now. ''It's really got nothing to do with us . . . well, I mean, what is between Aunt Janice and Uncle Robert. For my part, I think they are a wonderful couple. I always have done; and so have you lot, haven't you?''

Jessie, Freddie and Gracie nodded their assent, and Jessie, a twisted smile on her face, said, ''Aunt Janice was a nurse, just as I am now, and I only hope I meet somebody like Uncle Robert, and with pots of money.''

Jason's hand went out quickly and slapped his daughter's arm as he said, ''Forget about the money. They would be the same without it," and Jessie answered, "As you say, Dad. As you say," but the words held a cynical touch, which escaped notice through Gracie's saying, sadly and just above a mutter: "That is why Mam has been on at me a lot lately, I mean, going for me, saying that I'll become a museum piece, just like my work. At first she was so glad I had got into the museum. It must be because . . . well, I look like Aunt Janice."

Jason turned to her, saying, "You couldn't take after a finer person, Gracie. But yes, you may be right in your surmise."

"But why do you think this knowledge upset Mother so much, Dad?"

Jason looked at Steven as he answered, "There's a lot more to it, son, than has been said. Your mother is a jealous woman, always has been. She is a possessive woman. She takes after her own mother, your Granny Nelson. As you have heard, there were two sons. Harry was killed in the war. Then, at the time of the Armistice, James's boat was five days overdue, and they thought he had gone, too. But after his welcome home it became noticeable that his mother could think or talk about nothing but the one she had lost. It was always, 'Oh, if only Harry had lived.' So James, after sticking this for about a year, moved out and went to sea again, and later settled in Canada. He's married and has a family there, but none of us has seen him or his family. So your grandfather was left with your grandmother and the daily moanings over her lost son. She forgot she had a husband. And this has been going on for years. Well, now"—again he cast his glance over them—"I don't intend to become like your grandfather. As you know, he should have retired years ago, but his work is all he's got. But for myself, I feel there's more to life than work—there should be a little peace and happiness for us all—so, I'm leaving your mother . . . Yes"—he nodded now from one to the other—"I've told her. I've been wanting to do it for a long, long time. I stuck it until you were all grown up and able to fend for yourselves. But now it will be a separation, if not a divorce."

"But where will you live?" Freddie asked quietly.

"Oh, most of the time, down at your Auntie Marian's. Oh, oh"—he lifted his hand—"there's nothing like that between Marian and me, although I cannot convince your mother otherwise. I love Marian as my sister, although I keep emphasizing that she is my half-sister. She was happily married and she lost her husband during the war. As you know, she's mad on horses; you've all seen that, haven't you? And she's not alone: she has a good staff and she has Maggie, her secretary-cum-factotum," he smiled now, "for a companion."

"What about us, Dad?" Jessie said. "I'm all right, really, because I live in and only come home when on leave. And Steven's traveling most of his time"—she turned to her brother—"aren't you?"

And after a moment Steven replied, "Yes," then added, "but I feel I must come home at times to see how she is."

"Yes. Yes." Jason touched his son's shoulder, saying, "Thank you, Steven; that will ease my mind. Yes, thank you."

Then Freddie said, "Well, I have another year at Cambridge. I'll be home in the holidays, of course, but anything can happen in a year. That leaves only Gracie."

The tall young girl stood up and, addressing her elder brother, said, "If you'd drop in now and again, Steven, that'll help, and I'll stick it out as long as I can." And Steven nodded to her.

It was Freddie who returned to the main issue: "What if Mam makes it public about Auntie Janice and Uncle Robert?" he asked his father.

Jason said, "Well, they'll have to meet that when it comes. One doesn't seem to hear of it; but it must happen and quite unknowingly, as it could have done here, especially if Robert had drifted further away from his family."

"How did Mam really find out?" Steven was asking now.

"As I told you, I was having a talk with your Aunt Marian. I think it was at Christmas, 1930 or '31"— Jason shook his head—"but anyway, I met her in the street, your Aunt Marian. She was up shopping, and I asked her to come home and get warmed, and to have a drink. I was just on my way to the office, as a matter of fact, but I went in and left a note, and then Marian and I came back to the house. I had told her there would be no one at home as your mother had gone to the hairdresser's. And so there we sat, in this very room; and, as you know, there's the other door"—he pointed to the far end of the study—"that leads into the dining room. Well, she didn't want that kind of a drink, she wanted a cup of tea, so we went into the kitchen and made a tray of tea and brought it in here. And as we sat down, your Aunt Marian said, 'Well, Janice has done it again. It seems she must always have a baby to nurse, and she's forty-nine now! If she had been able to have her own family she would have had a dozen by now.' And I replied, 'Well, there's four lucky people going to grow up there.' And to this she answered, 'I envy her, you know, for the courage it took for her to marry Robert in the face of her mother and dear Steve.' And then she happened to say—" He shook his head now before going on, "Well, she said, 'You know, I liked you, Jason, from the first minute I saw you. It wasn't an ordinary feeling. I suppose it must have been the blood-tie, having the same father, like Janice and Robert.'" Again he shook his head and his voice was low and hesitant as he muttered, "She then asked me, 'Would you have married me, Jason?' and I can remember replying, 'I don't know, Marian. I only know that I, too, was attracted; but then you couldn't stop talking about your horses. You were happy, though, with Hector, weren't you?' And at this your Aunt Marian laughed and said, 'Yes. Who would have thought Hector Mills-Cotton, the snob of snobs, would have fallen for me, because there was no one plainer, even in the stables, than I.' "

Jason now put his head back and smiled as he said, "I remember saying to her, 'You have the same quality as your horses: you are high-spirited and finely bred. And to me you never look plain; nor did you to Hector, for he fell for you, hook, line and sinker.' "

He paused a moment and the room was silent, and then he said, "Those two were happy. They were poles apart. He was, as she said, a snob, and she anything but. Yet after he died it was discovered, as it says somewhere in the Bible, that you should never let your left hand know what your right is doing, for he had been supporting his second cousin who was in bad straits with TB. He had been keeping him and his family for years. As Marian said, he was indeed a dark horse. She was terribly cut up after he was killed. He had been out there for three years. Well, after that I took to going down now and again, because I found it so restful there; and the company good . . . sane."

As he stood up they rose to their feet and his voice had a break in it as he said, "I'm sorry about all this. There's always two sides to every question and circumstance. But the circumstances in this case have reached a point where I can't go on. Let's come out in the open among ourselves. Your mother's an alcoholic. I've tried to get the doctor to talk her into going away for treatment. But she almost hit Doctor Pike when he suggested it. She emphasized her state by swearing at him and telling him she would sue him for slander. But they can't help it, these people who drink all the time. They're finding out now that it could be a disease. But it wrecks not only their own lives, but those of all about them. It's a selfish disease because they hang onto it when they know that they could be cured." And to emphasize that was that, in a matter-of-fact voice he said, "I wouldn't go in and say goodbye; there would only be scenes. But you're still all agreeable to going up to High Gully?"

One after the other they nodded, then said, "Yes. Oh, yes." And it was Freddie who summed it up, by saying, "I can't imagine Christmas anywhere else. We've always spent Christmas there. They used to be marvelous, they still are. And the children; I mean, the youngsters; they are not children any more, except for this latest one. What is Andrew now? eighteen?" He nodded to himself. "He'll make a painter, you know. But just as painters are supposed to be, he's temperamental. But not Alicia; she's a spark if ever there was one. John's a nice little fella; he hates being at boarding school. I don't know what Madam Queenie will turn out to be, for she's a pert little miss already, and spoilt, too."

"They were all spoilt, although in a nice way," said Gracie now. "And they all know that they are adopted and are seemingly grateful for it; as who wouldn't be, considering the home they've got?"

"The main thing is," put in Jason now, "no matter what you think about this business underneath, and you're bound to, being human beings, try to act the same as you've always done toward Auntie Janice and Uncle Robert, because you all have your lives before you and, as yet, you don't know what's going to happen to you love-wise, and I mean that, love-wise. Not just falling in love but loving. Anyway—" he now tossed his head to the side as if throwing off such sentiments and said, "don't stay here. She'll only be at you. And I'm going to see my mother before I leave, and I'll explain why you haven't come in as a horde as usual." He addressed Steven now, saying, "Here are the tickets and all that is necessary. Wait for me by the buffet. But get a taxi now."

"You won't have much time, Dad; the train leaves at ten."

"I know that, Freddie. But the main point now is, I don't want you lot to stay in the house, in either house. But then you're not in the habit of slipping into your Grannie Nelson's, are you?" And he raised his eyebrows as if in inquiry. Then addressing Steven again, he said, "If the train is in before I arrive, get your seats."

"But what if you don't make it on time?"

He looked at Gracie and assured her, "There's another train at twelve and you've done the journey often enough to take care of yourselves, I hope. Don't worry about me, I'll be there on time; if not, I'll arrive before midnight."

"More like one in the morning if you don't get the ten o'clock."

"Very likely. But go on now; you are just wasting time."

He shepherded them from the room and to the front door where their luggage was stacked. Then, on opening it, he exclaimed, "Oh! there's the taxi. It's early; but just as well."

They all looked at him, and it was Gracie who voiced their thoughts: "Oh, Dad, it's going to be awful for you."

He was quick to notice that she hadn't said, "For Mam," and as he patted her cheek, he said, "One of the lessons in life, my dear; but don't worry, things will work out." He watched them pile into the taxi; none of them waved, nor did he.

He went back inside, picked up his suitcase, then walked across the hall, down a short corridor and into a room he had used as a study from his very early days. It was as he passed out of the room through another door that he almost bumped into a maid carrying a tray, on which were the remains of a breakfast, and he said to her, "Is my mother up yet, Hannah?" And she answered, "Oh yes, sir, this half hour or so. She's ready for coming down, I think." She glanced toward the stairs, and at this he nodded to her by way of thanks. Then, placing his case at the foot of the stairs, he hurried up them and to his mother's bedroom door.

After knocking gently, it was opened by Alice, who exclaimed, "Oh, there you are, then. All ready for the road? I expected the gang all to be rushing up before now. Where are they?"

"They've gone on, Alice."

Her voice low now and her head thrust toward him, she said, "Without coming up to say goodbye to their granny?" Her tongue clicked, but before she could continue with any critical comment he leaned toward her, saying, "Yes, Alice, without dashing upstairs to say goodbye to their granny. They're grown up now, you know."

Alice pulled her head back from him as if to get him into focus through her fading eyesight. Then she pulled at the bib of the starched apron over her ample bosom, for she no longer had the trim figure she had kept up into her fifties; now, at seventy, she was more than amply covered, in fact there was now no resemblance to the Alice of yore, except perhaps for her tongue.

He passed her now and went into the bedroom; and when at first he didn't see his mother he glanced toward the dressing room door. But instead of calling out to her, he waited, for he knew that her hearing was as good as ever and that she would know that he was there in the room waiting for her. He thought she was an amazing creature. At eighty-three her mind was still active and up until three years ago her body had been, too. But now she deigned to use a walking stick, otherwise the rheumatics in her left knee would have tied her to a chair for most of the day.

She came through the dressing room door, a tall, silver-haired, erect figure, elegantly attired in a loose gown. She could have been a duchess deigning to give audience to a lesser mortal. This was a manner she had adopted after Steve, or his father, as he still thought of him, had died ten years ago. It had been noted then that she had not cried at his going, and that she had remained almost a recluse for about six months. Then, as if out of a chrysalis, the figure before him had emerged. It would appear to others as if her past had never been.

"You ready for the road, dear?" she asked.

"Yes, Mother."

"And the children?"

"They've already gone on."

"Oh!" She walked slowly toward the chair, sat down, but still held onto the walking stick. This was another regal pose. She asked quietly, "Why have they gone on without coming to say good-bye? They always do."

"There is a reason, Mother." He now cast his glance toward Alice, a glance that, to anyone else, would have said, Please leave us. But not to Alice. She was of the family; in fact, she had been a second mother to him. She and his mother were inseparable, so he said what he had to say, but quietly, "I'm not only leaving for the Christmas holidays, I'm leaving for good."

A shiver passed over his mother's long body, even moving her walking stick, and after a moment when she said, "Why has this come about?" he left another space of time before he answered, "I should think you know the reason by now."

"You can't do this, Jason."

"Why not?"

"It . . . it wouldn't be right."

With difficulty, he managed to restrain himself from yelling, "You of all people to talk about what would be right or wrong!" for, apart from her being the instigator of the dark secret behind which Janice and Robert were still living, it was she who had pushed him into the marriage with Rose. When she added, "She needs you," he actually did turn on her and, bending toward her, he hissed, "She has the comfort of the bottle that she enjoyed even before we were married; and you knew about this. And she also has the comfort of her mother, who has been living with the dead all these years. Well, as I've already told my children, I'm not going to end up like her father, working day and night to save his sanity and being blackmailed into the bargain, because suicide is the worst form of blackmail."

She was sitting tight back in her chair now. This was her son and he had never before spoken like this to her. Yet she had gauged his feelings long ago for he had guessed that his adoptive father had loved his step-daughter as much as or even more than he loved her, and that from the day she had married her half-brother he had pined inwardly for her.

She would not admit to herself that there was any resemblance to Rose in her own character, in that they both demanded all the love from one man. There was a deep and niggling guilt in her that she had never loved the two children given her by that man, he that she despised so much, never admitting to herself that she had willingly been his mistress, and that it was through him that she had first come to know love.

"You'll have her on your conscience."

"Well, Mother, I won't be the only one who's troubled with a conscience, will I?"

She turned her head to the side and looked toward the frost-rimmed window. And now he said, "I'm sorry, I'm sorry, Mother, but it's been hell next door lately, and not just lately."

Her voice was low as she said, "What if she tells the children the facts?"

"She's already done that."

She actually started, and the stick fell from her grasp, only for it to be retrieved and to be put into her shaking fingers by Alice. He noticed that she swallowed deeply before she said, "And I suppose you explained the whole situation to them?"

"Yes, I did, and in the kindliest way possible."

At this, her parchment-like skin showed lines and wrinkles that were normally invisible when her face was in repose, and there was amazement in her voice as she said, "And they are still going up there?"

"Yes. Why not?"

"Knowing the facts?"

"Yes, Mother, knowing the facts, for they've had more happiness up there than they've ever had in their own home; and they weren't shocked at the news. Interested, yes, and slightly surprised, but not shocked, for they have a deep affection for both Janice and Robert, and for their family, too, adopted or not. I'm going to say this, Mother, because I've thought about it for years. You have lost much in your life by ignoring them. Dad never did. He often went up to Scotland, and he made it his business to visit them every time they stayed at the London house. It was never mentioned, was it, between you? Because you couldn't bear the thought that he loved Janice . . .''

"Mister Jason! Look, stop that!" interrupted Alice.

He turned to look at her. Her face was quivering and she spoke as if her mistress were not present: "She's had more to put up with that you know nothing about, and never will. It wasn't right what Miss Janice did. It wasn't right then, and it isn't right now, no matter how you or the children look at it. So to my mind, I think you've said enough; in fact, too much."

In the ordinary way he might have turned on Alice, saying, "You forget yourself. You have been treated as one of the family, but don't take advantage of it." Instead, he looked at his mother and said, "I'm sorry, Mother. I shouldn't have brought all that up, not at this point when I, too, am leaving you. Yet, no"—he shook his head—"I'll pop in often, because no matter what has happened, I love you, and Janice, too, loves you. I must say that, because never do we meet but she asks after you and says she longs to see you." He paused before he said finally, "I'll go now." And bending, he kissed her on the brow; and once again his nose, as it had always done, wrinkled against the strong smell of lavender. He wasn't averse to scents—he liked the smell of so many different scents and flowers—yet from the early days when he had nestled to her, he had been somewhat repulsed by this particular perfume she always wore.

As he turned away, her voice came at him soft and pleading, "Won't you think about it? After the holiday, won't you think about it?"

She never gave up. He didn't answer her, but shook his head, then turned and looked at Alice before walking from the room.

He hadn't reached the hall before Alice's voice checked his step, and he turned and waited for her to descend the stairs.

"Where will you be staying?" she asked.

He bit on his lip for a moment before he said, "Oh, I might go down to Marian's after the holidays. I know Robert will want me to use the London house . . ."

"Don't do that! Oh, Mister Jason, that would upset her. Doing either would upset her. Get a place of your own if you must, but don't go to either of them."

As he stared at her he thought how strange it was that not only had she taken on his mother's ways, but she also imitated her voice; and she had infiltrated his mother's mind until her mistress's antipathies had become her own. At one time, he felt sure, she would have said to him: "Go to Miss Janice,"—she never referred to her as Mrs. Anderson. Then she would have added, "Don't be alone. It isn't good for anybody to be alone." But not, it seemed, any more.

Harshly, he said, "I'll do what I feel inclined to do, Alice. For the first time in more than thirty years I'm going to please myself. Do you understand me?"

Yes, Alice understood him, but she said nothing more, and out of habit she opened the front door for him. And once more he picked up his bag and left first the house, then the street and the place in which he had spent his life since he was born . . .

He caught the train with only five minutes to spare. Gracie was staring out of the door window, waiting for him, and when he entered the reserved compartment she said, "Another few minutes and you would have had to get into the guard's van, if at all."

After thrusting his case into the space on the rack they had left for him, he sat down between Steven and Gracie. No-one spoke; they seemed to be listening for the guard's whistle to blow. It came, followed by the *chunk, chunk* of the engine as it began to move and send down a pall of smoke over their window. And not until it had taken on a slow rhythm as it left the station behind, did Freddie ask his father, "Was she upset . . . Gran?"

"Yes, I could say she was upset."

"She's always had her own way. She wouldn't have liked it, for she just had to look at you and you obeyed without protesting. I always wanted to protest every time I went into her room and heard her but I never did."

They were all looking at Freddie and with different shades of astonishment on their faces, because Freddie had always appeared to be the one among them who just sailed through life and wasn't affected by what others thought or said. And their astonishment rose still further as the young man, looking out of the window, added softly, "I never liked Gran. I always felt she was playing a part, that she wasn't real. And that she wasn't nice underneath, that the outside was merely a façade." He turned quickly now and looked at his father before adding, "I can say this now, Dad, because I know you've made a stand at last, and not before time."

Jason smiled softly at this son, this happy-go-lucky son. Now if Steven had spoken those words he could have understood, because Steven was the thinker and the doer. Steven, in his work as an architect, met all kinds of people. He could pick out the fakes from the tribe. Steven and he had talked a great deal, but not so he and Freddie. Did anyone ever know what went on in another's mind?

Jessie's pushing of her brother and saying, "You're a dark horse, aren't you? You've never let onto me how you felt about Gran," brought the atmosphere in the carriage back to normal, and Freddie, a smile on his face, answered, "Would I, and to you of all people? You would have had me on an operating table and dissected me from the roots of my hair to my toenails," which caused a light titter of laughter to pass round the carriage, only for it to be quelled by Freddie saying, "What will Mam do about it; about Auntie Janice and Uncle Robert? She spilled the beans to us. Will she tell on them, I mean to the children?" and they all looked toward Jason, who sighed before he said, "Very likely, and also make the matter public."

"Oh . . . no!" The words coming from Steven were drawn out, and he repeated, "Oh no! She wouldn't."

"Well," said his father, "that remains to be seen." Then in a lighter tone he said, "Let's try and forget it for a time, eh? We're all going up North to spend Christmas in a house that we love and with people whom we love. And yet, I must say, I think it's going to be the last time we'll all be together."

At seven o'clock, they were met at Stirling station by Robert, who kissed and hugged the girls, punched the two young men on the shoulder, then gripped his half-brother's hand for a second before saying, "Don't let anyone ever say a word against the Scottish timetable. Look"—he pulled out his watch—"on the minute, the exact minute."

"Only because she was pushed half the way, Uncle," said Freddie.

"We were ten minutes late leaving Edinburgh;

but then, of course, it did make up the time, didn't it? Yes; yes, indeed, the Scottish timetable," said Gracie.

As they walked toward the exit laughing, Robert said, "I'll lay a bet with you, Freddie; you won't dare complain to Johnny about the Scottish time-table."

"Johnny's driving?"

Robert turned to Gracie and he also laughed, saying, "Don't worry, he's improving. He's only once driven on the wrong side of the road and he blamed it on me for giving him wrong directions."

"He's a menace," said Gracie.

"Well, all right, Gracie, I'll have another bet with you. You tell him that to his face."

Outside the station, standing near a long brake, stood an extremely tall man, clean-shaven, but with hair sprouting thickly from the sides of his glengarry cap, which he doffed as he addressed the party, saying, "Aw, you've got here once more, have you? But again I'll say, only the Lord himself knows why you want to come to this fro-zen and Godless acre."

"Get that luggage into the back, and shut up! And I'll tell you *yet again,* if this Godless acre doesn't suit you, you know what to do," said Robert.

"Oh, aye, I know what to do, sir, and I'll do it one of these days. You'll see."

"Well, hurry up about it; I want to put the flags out. But in the meantime, get them wrapped up in there, will you?"

They were all piling into the back of the long brake; and now Johnny McBrien, with a tenderness that was touching, was wrapping up Jessie and Gracie in heavy woollen rugs, each of which must have used the wool of more than one sheep, and Gracie, tucking hers under her chin with her gloved hands, said, "Oh, thanks, Johnny. That is lovely." Then she added, "To tell you the truth, Johnny, I only ever get warm when I come here."

"Ah, 'tis tact you have, Miss Gracie, tact. 'Tis a rare virtue, tact. 'Tis a pity t'isn't more spread about."

"You're right there," came Robert's voice now from the driving seat. "Close those doors and get yourself seated."

"Am I not to come up front?"

"No, you're not to come up front. I've already told you."

"One of these days . . ." The rest of the prophecy was drowned by Robert starting up the car and saying to Jason, who was sitting by his side, "It's the same greeting, isn't it, every time? He never changes. Thank God for it." The last words were said quietly and Jason added to them: "You couldn't get on without him."

"No, I don't think I could, Jason. I was two when my grandfather brought me up here for the first time. And that's when I first saw Johnny. He was five; and even then he was working in the yard, mucking out, and the only time he's been away from the place was during the war. And, you know, it's unbelievable, but he went through it without a scratch. He and his big head, I'm sure it must have been a target many a time above a parapet. But he never even had a graze. And he imagines he's still in the Army. Jock and Rob put up with him; they look upon him as a very old bloke. I don't know how they look upon me, being only three years younger."

"Is he still warring with Angus?"

"Oh, yes. That'll never stop. To his mind, Angus is . . . a house man, no better than a woman servant. The thought that Angus sees to me and at the same time acts as butler and man of all trades, even secretary at times, gets up his nose. I don't think they've exchanged a word for years."

"How's Janice?"

"Oh, blooming, blooming." Robert's voice had changed. "But, between you and me, I hope she doesn't come across another stray. Queenie is a handful, she's like a live wire, lovable, but as mischievous as a kitten. But we've taken on a new nurse, a Miss Fanny Laidlaw." He gave a short laugh. "So I think Miss Queenie has met her match. She's no young learner like the last one; she's twenty-five years old and has been about and has handled youngsters, which is already showing in Miss Queenie: we don't come down the stairs on our bottom any more; we don't break toys when in a tantrum; and we don't splash our spoon into the middle of the pudding. That's three improvements. And apart from that, Miss Fanny Laidlaw is a very nice young woman with a sense of humor, which one needs, as you know, when living up here, where you have to look at the same faces for weeks on end when the snow's up to your chin." There was a pause now before Robert asked, "How are things back there?"

There was a longer pause before Jason replied, "Pretty bad. We've got a lot of talking to do, Robert. The boil has burst, one could say."

When Robert turned sharply toward him, the car swerved slightly, and he said, "What does that mean exactly?"

"Leave it. Leave it." Jason's voice was now a mutter; it could hardly be heard above the noise of the car, and Robert said, "What did you say?"

"I said, leave it. Leave it. Let's get tomorrow and Christmas Day over. I don't want to think about it now, because there will be a lot to think about after."

They had now turned off the main road onto a definitely unmade surface; then, about five minutes later, the car's headlights picked out two huge stone pillars, from which hung open iron gates. Once through them, the tree-lined avenue appeared to be like an enormous black tunnel, going straight for some way before turning sharply right, then left again, and from here into an open-paved stretch on which stood an enormous stone house illuminated by floodlights, the effect of which brought gasps from the new arrivals.

It was Steven, leaning forward, who cried, "You've had it done then, Uncle? I mean, you got it through, the electricity?"

"Yes, Steven, we got it through at last. We'll likely end up in the workhouse, but what matter?"

Steven made no further comment: he had heard the saying before, always from very rich men; in fact, it was mostly millionaires who talked of ending up in the workhouse.

"It looks beautiful," cried Jessie, and Gracie added, "Fairy-like."

"More like a picture house twice-nightly, brash that it is. Paraffin lamps have been good enough up till now," said Johnny.

"But smelly and more work," shouted his master back at him.

When the car came to a standstill at the bottom of a rising row of steep stone steps, there came tumbling down them a tall young man and girl in her middle teens, followed by a younger boy; then a little girl, and behind them all the big, motherly figure of Janice, an older Janice, yet still with the same warm expression on her face, the same voice and the same manner.

Above all the hubbub, Robert's voice cried, "Get yourselves indoors. If I don't soon have something warm inside me I'll stiffen."

They needed no further bidding and surged through the wide black-oak door, there to be met by the housekeeper, Mrs. MacGinney, commonly referred to as Gin, and Robert's man Angus, with Fanny Laidlaw hovering in the background. Robert remained on the steps and, turning to Johnny McBrien, said in a voice that was different from the one he had earlier used to him, "Now get yourself inside the cottage, Johnny, and something warm into you and into bed. No going round on parade tonight. The lads will have seen to everything, you know that. So don't be daft, man, and get yourself warm." And Johnny McBrien, his voice different, replied, "Well, take your own medicine. From the look of you, you need it, too . . . Night."

"Good-night, Johnny."

Robert dashed up the steps and into the hall, where the newcomers were being divested of their outer clothes or were making for the big log fire that radiated heat from the far end of the hall.

From a velvet-padded settle set at an angle to the fireplace but well away from the fire, Jessie looked up at the beamed ceiling, crying, "What lovely colored chains! Oh! how the hospital would like those. Where did you get them?"

"Andrew made them." Janice looked toward the tall young man with the thin pale face who was now sitting beside Freddie, and she said, "Andrew. Of course." And Gracie, putting her head back and looking up at a chain hanging above her head, said, "Each link has a picture on it." Then, turning to Andrew, she said, "You painted them all? A picture on each one?"

"Yes, a picture on each one, Gracie. I have nothing else to do, so I've spent the last three months on them."

"He's fibbing," cried Alicia. "He did them all in a couple of days."

"Oh, here's something to warm the cockles,"

cried Robert, as two maids, carrying trays of steaming mugs, came across the hall. And between the handing out of the hot mugs, the maids were greeted with, "Hello, Lorna. Hello, Betty," and answered, "It's lovely to see you back, miss," or "sir." And so the welcoming exchanges continued . . .

An hour later, they had changed and had eaten an uproarious meal, followed by a cross-discussion of their work and lives, and now they were making their way to bed.

Robert had taken Jason aside and said, "I must have a word with you. Come into the study."

The so-called study was a room like all the others in this house, large and high and beautifully furnished; and, like the rest of the house, too, would have been unbearable without the roaring fires, kept going even during the summer; although then they were smaller.

The outer wall of this room, like those of the drawing room and dining room, had been left bare to show its natural stone. And, as were the others, it was dotted with paintings. But two of the walls in this room were lined with bookshelves and glass cabinets.

It said something for the situation that existed between Robert and Jason that Robert dropped into a chair first, thereby showing that Jason was no guest, but his natural brother.

When Jason was seated opposite, Robert said, "I can't wait until after the holidays; there's something amiss. I knew by your face when I first saw you." He now reached for a box of cigars from a side table and, bending forward, he proffered it to Jason. And as Jason took a cigar from the box, he said quietly, "I've left her."

"You mean . . . ?"

The box now held at arm's length in mid-air, Robert added, "Finally, you mean?"

"Yes, finally, I mean, and not before time." Automatically, he rubbed the cigar between his palms, then looked down on it as he said, "I should have done it years ago. In fact, I shouldn't have done it at all; I mean, marry her. But . . . well, you know the story. Anyway, today she blackmailed me once too often."

"What d'you mean, blackmailed you?"

"Oh, if I left her at Christmas again she would tell the children about the situation here."

"No! Rosie said that?"

"Yes, Rose said that. You don't know Rose. Nobody knows her like I do . . . and the children. Well, I said, she could do what she liked; I had had enough. And so she screamed it out. She didn't tell them, she screamed it out. It's a good job the house was on the corner and the two others were occupied by the remnants of the family, or the whole street would have known. She was drunk again. She's an alcoholic, Robert; has been for years, although she won't face up to it."

Robert was now sitting well back in his chair as he asked quietly, "How did they take it?"

"Oh, slightly surprised at first, naturally, but otherwise it made no difference. This house, and you and Janice, is all they've had to look forward to for years. Even when they got into the world on their own, it was the same. But now they're grown up, and they're all going their own way. Gracie will be the only one who will stay with her; at least for a time. Jessie's home is in the hospital, Freddie will be at university, and Steven's going to take rooms."

"How did she get to know? I mean, Rosie?"

"It was shortly after you took Queenie there. Marian and I were talking; we didn't think she was in the house. We were discussing old times, and unbeknown to us she had come back earlier, having skipped a hairdressing appointment, and was indulging in the dining room."

"So that's why she stopped coming with you?"

"Yes, that's why, Robert. And every year since it's been, "You leave me at this Christmas time, and I'll tell them." Well, as you know, I've missed the last two, making excuses. But no more. There's a limit to what one can stand. What I'm worried about now, though, is that she's threatened to expose your situation."

"Oh, has she? Well—" Robert, now taking a spill from a brass pot on the hearth, lit it from the fire and applied it to his cigar, then handed the spill to Jason, before adding, "Well, if she means to do it, she'll do it. What can we do about it? We both knew that some day this idyllic situation would be punctured . . . not ended. No!" His voice sounded vehement. "Never ended. It will make no difference to us, really. We could live the rest of our days here and never move out of the estate, and not miss one fraction of the world beyond. I could do all my business from here. I wouldn't need to touch London. Anyway, there's going to be changes all round, all round the world. What I saw in Berlin the week before last staggered me. If I were aiming to be funny I would have likened the youth movement to boy scouts, but it's no boy scout formation. These are soldiers marching in ranks, young, ardent, aggressive as always. Hitler means business and his business, like Hindenburg's before him, will be war."

"You think so?"

"Well, I can't see it ending any other way. Why do you build up a great military force? Not to play at soldiers. But there, it's retaliation for what they suffered after their defeat in the last war. One should never stand on the neck of a victim, whether it's personal or national. The way to stop making the same mistakes is to bring him to his feet. Still—" He drew on his cigar and puffed out a cloud of smoke before he said, "That's international business. We've got our own war here, apparently. Anyway, Jason, don't worry about us. We shall weather it."

"What about the children knowing?"

"Oh, I suppose we'll tell them in good time. But at present we are worried in more ways than one about Andrew."

"Has his bleeding worsened?"

"No. No, just spasmodic, as usual. He can go for months and not a sign of it, and then his nose takes over for a week or more and leaves him like lint. The local GP says he'll grow out of it, and that it's natural for people to have nosebleeds. Many people are so afflicted. But there's a doctor in Edinburgh who says it could be the sign of vascular trouble called, of all things, Telangiectasia. It's very rare and he only knows one other patient who has it, and she's a woman and, as Andrew's is, her tongue is covered with the red spots."

"Good gracious! Poor Andrew."

"Oh, he's not to be pitied, Jason. At the first sign of pampering he's up in arms. He'd throw his paint brushes at you. And that's another thing: he's not going back to the school, he says."

"No? He was doing marvelously there."

"Yes; but as he said, pun-wise, one of the teachers gets up his nose. It appears that Andrew's painting, and sense of color, annoys this man. It's too vivid, not natural enough. Of course he does splash it about, I must admit. Some of his colors really are startling."

"Well, I don't see any harm in that. I dropped in to see Gracie at the museum the other day and to take her out to lunch, and there was a new gallery open nearby she wanted to see. Well, to tell you the truth, I know nothing or little about art, but I do know when I'm looking at a face. But I can't make out why an artist wants to put an eye in the middle of somebody's belly and give him three arms and one leg."

Robert laughed. "It's the new vogue," he said. "I've noticed it abroad, too. But, of course, it's one of these things that'll come and go quickly. It's the temperament of artists: they are either up in the clouds or down in the pit. During the summer break Andrew brought a friend home. Well, we thought Andrew had his moods, but this fellow made Andrew appear absolutely normal: he'd paint till three in the morning by himself up in Andrew's studio; then watch the dawn before going to bed, and come down for breakfast about one o'clock. But he had the nicest disposition and I could see why Andrew and he got on together. And he had a sense of humor that used to make Andrew laugh, make us all laugh, in fact, he would quote Burns at you by the hour, but not in a Scottish accent, nor even an ordinary English one. He never said, but it was my guess he originally came from the East End of London before his people settled in Edinburgh."

There ensued a silence during which they both drew deeply on their cigars; then Robert said slowly: "Andrew is becoming curious as to his birth, and it's worrying Janice. This has just been happening over the past few months. He's asking Alicia what she thinks about being adopted. Now, Alicia is only fourteen, as you know, but she's got an old head on her shoulders. So, what did she do? She went to Janice and said, 'I'm not asking for myself, because I know I'm adopted, and it doesn't matter to me who brought me into this world; it matters only that you and Dad have seen to me since. And I'm lucky, and so are the others. But it's Andrew I'm talking about, Mam. He's different: he seems to want to know where he came from and why. But there's one thing sure,' she said to Janice, 'he loves you both, and my goodness! he should.' Those, Janice said, were her very thoughtful words, and she's only fourteen."

"Have you ever spoken to Andrew about his parentage?"

"No, never; for the little we know won't help him. But I suppose it's natural . . . the feeling of wanting to know, the pull of the blood-tie. If anyone should understand this, we should. It's odd, you know," went on Robert now, "that I never think of you as a half-brother, but as a brother, whereas, in Janice's case, I never think of our relationship at all. It's as if I had known nothing about her but just met her and fell in love, and that's that. It's an odd situation. Yet the three of us are joined like a triangle."

"There's Marian, too; she could make the square. And don't forget the girl in Italy."

"Yes, you're right there, Jason. But that girl wanted out of it, and she's kept out of it. Thank God for that part anyway. But our father got around, didn't he? And who knows but there's a few more of us kicking about. Ah well"—he pulled himself to the front of the chair—"would you like a drink?"

"Yes, please."

As Robert got to his feet, he said, "Well, there's one thing I'm thankful for, Jason, and that is knowing how your lot took it, because they showed not a sign of their new knowledge to either me or Janice. By the way, let us keep this from Janice until after the holidays, as you suggested in the beginning, for I want nothing to mar her Christmas. She has so much looked forward to seeing you all again.''

As Jason took the glass from his half-brother's hand, he thought, with a deep touch of envy, It's always Janice, Janice first. Would that it had been like that with him and Rose.

It was Boxing Day evening and the staff party was in full swing. Johnny McBrien was playing the pipes and his redoubtable enemy, Angus Taylor, Robert's man, was playing the flute and very well too, while Billy McKenna, the woodman, was drowning them both with two spoons, which he hammered on his knees.

Present, too, were the three yard men: Phil Kilcullen, Jock Taggart and his wife, Rob Macmillan and his wife and their married son and daughter; the indoor staff: Mrs. MacGinney, Kathy Ferguson the kitchen maid, Lorna Sweetman the first housemaid, Betty Green the second housemaid, and Hannah Macintosh, the laundry woman from down the valley, and Katie, her dominated daughter; and equally enjoying it with them were Jason and his family, Robert and Janice and their four, together with their nearest friends, the Culberts, Francis and Margaret, their sons James and Glen, and daughter Kathy.

Altogether, the house resounded to the thumping of dancing, jigging feet and great hilarity. Everyone there seemed tireless where the dancing was concerned. Yet it had followed on the big meal at nine o'clock, and now it was half past twelve and into another day and no one was apparently tired, except Queenie, who was asleep and tucked up on the drawing room couch.

Andrew, who had been dancing most of the evening and who now stood near an open door, his face running with perspiration, while he clapped his hands to the beat of the music, suddenly turned away and went into the corridor. And there, pulling a handkerchief from his pocket he put it to his nose and examined it before exclaiming, "Damn and blast it!" He had just reached the hall when Gracie came running up to him, saying, "Oh no! Andrew, not tonight."

He looked at her over the top of his handkerchief and muttered, "It's nothing, it's just a drip."

"Will I get you a cold pad?"

"No, I'll just sit down for a minute. It'll stop. You go on back."

"I'll do no such thing."

They were leaving the hall and were about to enter the drawing room, when the sound of the phone ringing brought them to a halt, and Gracie said, "Go and sit down, I'll answer it."

When she picked up the phone there was no sound for a moment, even when she asked, "Yes, who's speaking?"

Still there was no answer, and she was about to put the receiver down when the voice came to her, thick and fuddled, muttering, "Andrew. I want Andrew." For a moment she paused. It had sounded like her mother; but no, it wasn't her mother. She said, "Wait a moment, then." And now running into the drawing room, she exclaimed, "There's someone who wants to speak to you."

"Oh, it'll be Pat. He said he would ring; he's coming up for New Year."

She didn't say, "It didn't sound like a man," but watched him still holding the handkerchief to his nose as he went to the phone. "Hello, there."

"Andrew? Is that . . . Andrew?"

He drew his head back from the mouthpiece, then turned and looked at Gracie, who was standing at the drawing room door, before saying, "Yes, this is Andrew."

"Dear, dear Andrew. You know who this is? This is your dear Auntie . . . Rose."

Again he glanced toward Gracie, then said, "Hello, Auntie Rose. A Happy Christmas."

Then the voice came to him, harsh and loud: "Happy Christmas, he said. Happy Christmas! Shut up, boy! Shut up! I'm going to spoil your Happy Christmas. Do you know that? I'm going to spoil all your Happy Christmases, every bloody one of you there."

He now took the handkerchief away from his nose. The drips had stopped, and he shook his head slowly as though nonplussed. Then the voice came at him again. "You're very fond of your dear mamma . . . and papa, aren't you? Won . . . der . . . ful people! Oh, yes!" He held the receiver away from his ear as the scream came at him. "They are rotten! Do you know that?

Rotten! Bad! Evil! Incest! Incest! They are not husband and wife. Did you know that, Andrew? Do you hear me, Andrew? They are brother and sister. Now, listen. Did you hear those words? Brother and sister. Well, half, but it's all the same. Your dear papa and my dear husband are half-brothers and their half-sister is your dear mamma. Now, what about that for a Happy Christmas. Eh?''

When Andrew put one hand out and pressed it against the stone wall, Gracie ran to his side, hissing at him, ''What is it? Who is it?'' And after a moment he closed his eyes, then muttered, ''Your . . . your mother.''

''Oh dear God! No!'' She grabbed the phone from him and shouted into it, ''Mam! Go away! Stop it!''

''Oh, dear Gracie. Are you enjoying yourself?''

''Yes, Mam, I am enjoying myself. We are all enjoying ourselves. And whatever you've said, it doesn't make the slightest difference. Do you hear me? Not the slightest difference. So get back to your bottle and chew on that. Your venom has only made us love Robert and Janice more.'' And she banged down the receiver; then, bending forward, she pressed her brow tight against the wall.

Presently, Andrew's arm came around her shoulder and he said softly, ''Come away. Come on,'' and he led her into the drawing room.

As he guided her to the couch his arm still remained around her, and when she muttered, ''I'm so ashamed,'' he replied, ''Don't be silly. What have you got to be ashamed of? But . . . but why is she doing this? Is it . . . ? Do you know what she said to me?"

"Yes. Yes, I can guess it was about your father and mother." And now blinking the tears from her eyes, she turned on him almost fiercely, saying, "They *are* your father and mother. They may be half-brother and half-sister, but they are good people. When you know the whole story you will realize how good they are. S . . . s . . . seventeen years they kept apart." She was stammering now.

"Seventeen years?"

"Yes, seventeen years; just because they thought it was wrong. Then the war changed everything, people's ideas and everything, so Father said. He would tell you the whole story better than I could. But they've gone through the mill just to be together. And it makes no difference to me, nor to the others. In fact, I think it draws us closer to think that Dad and Uncle Robert are related, really related."

He asked quietly, "Why is she doing this? Why has she turned against us?"

"Because Dad's leaving her. He told her flatly before we came away. Life hasn't been happy at home for any of us; we knew what was going on. Mam's been on the bottle for years. It's sherry. Just wine, she says, just a glass of wine. But a bottle a day is nothing to her at times. One of my earliest memories is of her drinking, there at the table in the sitting room, a glass of sherry in her hand as she went for us, particularly me, for something that I had done. Freddie remembers her that way, too.''

He surprised her now by saying, "What is it like working in London?''

Her bright, round eyes widened, and she repeated, "What is it like working in London? Well''—she moved her head—"very busy and interesting. So many places to see. But it's like, I suppose, every other town or city, like your Edinburgh or Stirling. There's nice people there and nasty ones. You find that wherever you go.''

"I would like to go there and work.''

"You mean at The Slade or somewhere?''

"Oh, no; no more school.'' His words came quick now, rolling over each other: "No more school. No more sitting in herds. No, I want to be on my own. I can work better on my own . . . well, not really on my own, if you know what I mean: no more classrooms; no more vindictive teachers who imagine their ancestors must have painted the Sistine Chapel along with Michelangelo, and insist that they know all about art and you don't, you're not even a beginner. They imagine you cannot understand unless you're fifty or sixty, or in your dotage, or going mad, like Van Gogh. No; no more of that. I feel, if I . . . well, if I had a room there, or a studio, I could paint . . . well, sell, make a living at it.''

Staring at him, Gracie thought about some of his wild paintings: masses of startling color; sunsets that you never see in the sky; at least, not over London, although you might up here; dawns blazing like roaring fires. His work gave her the impression that he was angry inside about something. And his next words gave her the inkling when he said, "You're lucky in a way, you know, Gracie. You know who you are, whereas I don't. I love my mother and father and I'll always think of them as my mother and father. But let's face it, they're not, they didn't breed me. I have a nagging urge to know where I came from. I lie thinking at night: what was she like? What was *he* like? Am I like him? Am I like her? Who did I inherit this damn blood disease from? Yes, I often think of that, because it *is* a disease. It isn't just nose bleedings. My tongue's starting now; even the top of my thumb the other day. And it maddens me when they say, oh, he'll grow out of it. Whatever this is, I will grow into it more, I know I will. But in the meantime, I want to paint. I want to put something on canvas that hasn't been put there before. Can you understand that?"

"Truthfully, not really, because I'm in no way artistic. I like looking at paintings, but I could never draw or paint. Yet I understand your need, because I, too, have a need. I, too, want to get away. The thought of my future, and having to live in that same house with Mam, makes me feel sick in the pit of my stomach. But I am the only one she's got left now. There is Gran, but, she too is like Mam, in a way. Gran is still mourning the loss of a son who was killed in the last war. And Grandad has suffered from it, as Dad has suffered from Mam,

because Mam is a demanding woman: she wants
all his attention, and when she doesn't get it she
plays up. Always has. So, in a way, I understand
how you feel and the want in you.''

He leaned forward now and, his elbows on his
knees, he looked toward the fire and said quietly,
"I can't stay on here, Gracie. I must get away. It's
going to hurt them to tell them, but I must go; at
least, for a time. This is a wonderful house, a wonderful place. They are wonderful people, but it's
. . . well, it's like a kind of fairyland, frozen." He
turned toward her and smiled. "Yes, a frozen
fairyland. That's how I used to look back on it
from Edinburgh and long to feel the cold again,
the ice-ripping cold, then the glorious warmth of
the fires all round the house. But"—he straightened up—"it isn't real; it isn't life the way I know it
really is. I've got to get away."

She sat staring at him for some time without
speaking, then she said quietly, "Don't say anything to Dad about the phone call, at least not
tonight. I'll . . . I'll tell them tomorrow."

They both now stood up and looked at each
other, and then he said, "I never think of you being older than me."

"Well, I am; two years; and that's dreadful, isn't
it?"

"Yes. Yes, indeed, it's dreadful." He smiled at
her. "But, on looking back, I could always talk to
you, couldn't I? Not to Steven, or to Freddie, although I've always been very fond of Freddie, but
I could always talk to you. Never to Jessie. She

seemed old to me, Jessie; and being a nurse . . . dear! dear! she represented the matron in my boarding school. But you . . . you were different."

She stared at him but said nothing, for what she would like to have said was, "Of course I'm different, because I have loved you from the time I can first recall seeing you. I feel that I am, in a way, like my mother, a one-man woman."

Janice's reaction to her brother's news was that she wasn't surprised. She now looked from him to her husband and said, "I've been expecting something like this ever since she stopped coming." Then turning to Jason, she added, "But I'm sorry for the break-up. I really am. What will you do now? I mean, where do you intend to go . . . to live?"

"Oh, I'll get a flat in London. But, you know, I like going down to Marian's. It's quiet there; yet at the same time there's always something going on . . . if it's only somebody being kicked or bitten by a horse."

As Janice looked at her brother, she almost asked, "Is Maggie still there?" But that would have been a silly thing to say: Maggie would always be there, and for Jason, too. She had known that for a long time. As for Rose, her intention wasn't a great surprise to her, and she was still worried. And so, turning to Robert, she asked very quietly, "If she gave it to the papers, what then? There's your Holland trip next week. That's so important.''

''Well, my dear, if she gives it to the papers, it will be an intended nine-day wonder that will last twenty-four hours, because as far as I can gather, papers have much more interesting material to get their teeth into today.''

''Oh, I don't know,'' which brought the attention of both Robert and Janice back to Jason who added, ''Your name's to the fore pretty often, and with this Dutch and German project in the wind it could do the company harm.''

''Yes, it could. That's true, but the company can stand a lot of harm. The company now isn't just me, as it was Grandfather. All they would do is ask me politely to leave the board.''

''They wouldn't dare!'' Janice's voice was loud. ''You *are* the board. It's *your* money, *your* work that's put them all where they are.''

''Yes, perhaps the former, but don't forget, dear, that money is limited and controlled by markets. And look at the men we've had to stand off during the last few years. Oh, yes, yes''—he nodded his head—''things are looking up, and we've taken on a good many again, but the awful thing to say is that the only time there'll be full employment in this country is if it comes to another war.''

''God forbid that!''

Robert looked at Jason now and repeated, ''Yes, I say with you, God forbid that! But as you yourself know, for you get about, there is uneasiness now that wasn't there a few years ago. Nationalism is to the fore again, people are protesting. You've only got to look at the number of Jews leaving Germany."

"Oh, I think the Jews are clever enough to look after themselves, they always have been."

Robert smiled tolerantly at Jason now and he shrugged his shoulders. It was no use talking about this feeling, but he had traveled enough over the past few years to gauge the temper of a country as soon as he entered it. And not from those in power, but more so from street level.

"One thing I am glad about"—Janice was walking toward the tea tray—"one thing that has relieved me, and that is the way Andrew took this news. He was very sweet about it. As he said, if it hadn't happened, he would likely not have happened, at least here, and he was glad he'd ended up here. Yes, he was very sweet about it . . . He had another bleeding this morning." She looked at Robert over her shoulder as she added, "Did he tell you he wants to live in London for a time?"

"Yes. Yes, he did, and I said, fine, and he could stay at the house and work in one of the attics. The staff would look after him, and would love to have him there, I'm sure. They're always saying we don't make enough use of the house."

"But what if he has a bleeding?"

"Well, he's in the right place for attention, isn't he . . . nurse?"

She thrust out her hand toward him as if pushing him off, as she said, "Yes, that might be so, but I don't suppose they know any more about his trouble there than they do in Edinburgh. The only thing they can confirm is that it's not haemophilia. But I'm of the strong opinion, and I've pointed it out to different people that, if it's an inherited disease, there must be many more like him. And they, too, are just treated as if they are having just ordinary nose bleeds. Anyway, I'm glad he's going to London; he's ready for a change. In fact, so am I; and it will give me an excuse to go down with you next week and stay there until you come back from Holland."

Robert smiled. "And you will bring the squad?" he said.

"No; I shall not bring the squad this time. Fanny is more than capable of seeing to them all. I want a week to myself and to do a bit of shopping. Do you know, Jason," she had turned to her brother now, "I've never had a new rag for years. The only things that change up here are the sheepskin coats, and they last nearly a lifetime."

"Well, my lot expect them to. They were delighted with their presents. But then they are delighted with everything up here." He turned away now and sat down in the chair facing the great log fire. And he did not speak until Janice handed him a cup of tea. Then, looking up at her, he said quietly, "What a pity we grow old, that we grow at all, away from the young years. There's one thing, I have no wish to live until I'm ninety or even eighty; especially when I look at Mother, eighty-three years old, clinging onto life and pretending every day was yesterday and things are the same now as when Father was alive.''

As Janice took her seat beside Robert on the couch, she asked quietly, ''Does she look very old?''

''Yes, sometimes a hundred; at others, you can't believe your eyes. When Alice gets her togged up for her weekly drive, she seems to . . . well, go back, to put on a new life; she could be in her sixties. Oh, yes, definitely. The only thing that gives her away is her stick. But, no; that's not the only thing, it's her face, set like parchment. You never know what's going on behind her mask. I used to love her once. In fact, right up to the time she took a stand against you. I can't help saying it, but she of all people, with the life she led, to take a stand against anyone . . . anyone at all, is sheer presumption.''

''Has she ever mentioned my name?'' asked Janice.

It was a long moment before he answered. ''No, not in my hearing, not once. And I don't think she did to Father, either. She did know he visited the London house whenever you were there. Oh yes, she knew. I could feel it in the air. And that weekend he came here when he was supposed to be going to Sussex for his last-remaining brother's funeral and see to the selling of the house—he left that all in John's hands on the quiet, so to speak, and he made the journey—oh yes, that weekend! And I'm always so grateful, as you are, that he did. You know, he loved you above everything else, he loved you. And sometimes I think he put you before her, and that she was aware of this. But again, she would never say a word. She's a strange woman." He shook his head slowly. "When I told her I was leaving Rose, she said that I shouldn't do it, that I'd have her on my conscience. It's amazing—" He turned and looked at Robert now before repeating, "It *is* amazing, you know, Robert, how people can close their eyes to themselves, to what is in them. Her attitude to life is as if she had been the most virtuous woman on God's earth. And we are simply here today because of what she thinks of as sin."

"Well, here's one, Jason, that thanks God for her own particular sin. That's all I can say."

At this, he pulled Janice tightly toward him and kissed her openly, and repeated, "Yes, thank God for her sin."

Andrew had been installed in the London house for three days. By telephone, the Pattersons had been instructed to clear one of the attics where he could work. Robert had even gone to the trouble of ordering an easel and a quantity of paints and canvases to be delivered to the house; and so all Andrew had to take with him from High Gully were his personal effects.

It was now the end of the first week in January, and during the time he had been in residence he hadn't put a stroke of paint on a canvas, nor yet taken a pencil in his hand to rough-sketch anything that might be in his mind, for he was still consumed with the real reason for his having left home, about which he had not been open to either Robert or Janice. Yet it had been on New Year's Day that he had pointedly asked her if she knew who his people were.

She had been slightly taken aback, although she was aware that he had earlier been probing this. But on New Year's Day he had put the question to her so directly that at first she was flustered, and then she had to tell him the little she knew. He had been adopted in 1919, when he was just over one year old. The only real information she had gained about him was that he was born on the 6th June, 1918. But she remained chary of telling him the little she did know about his mother: that she walked out of the hospital three days after he was born, leaving him there; that she was a working-class girl of twenty years old who had, at first, said she had lived in Bermondsey, and her name was Birchcomb, thought by those in authority to have been assumed; but not taking the child with her had somewhat puzzled them, because she had at first wished for the baby to be adopted; and so strong had been this intention that they felt she would come back for it.

It was on the understanding that the woman might return to claim the child, and because Janice had at one time been a sister in the same hospital, that they allowed her to foster it.

It was solely by accident that she had heard of the case. After marrying Robert they had both returned to the hospital for more attention to his foot, and while there she had talked to the sister in the maternity ward. And the excitement of the moment was the story of the mother walking out of the hospital and leaving the child. Apparently she had left in her dressing gown, of which the police had been informed in case she was found wandering about and appeared to be mentally disturbed. They all seemed to be convinced she had acted on the spur of the moment. Yet the doorkeeper could recall having seen a figure in a dressing gown talking to a woman outside, which at the time he had thought strange. It was also recalled that it had been visiting day and that she'd had one woman visitor that afternoon. But at the time there was also concern that it being only three days after her confinement, she should not have been out of bed or even on her feet.

So Janice had asked herself if she could or should tell him all that. What she did say to him was, "Your . . . your mother had to leave you in hospital for reasons no one knew."

When he had asked if she knew her name, she had again hesitated before saying, "The authorities thought it was a false one."

He had waited the while staring at her, and she had said, "It was something like Birchcomb." And he had repeated, "Birchcomb?"

And at this she had said, "Yes. It is an unusual name. They felt she had made it up."

"Do you know where she was from? I mean, was she foreign?"

"Oh, no, no. They were sure of that. They thought she was from somewhere . . . well, in London." She couldn't tell him that the impression was that she was definitely a working girl of some kind. They hadn't inferred "common," although it was the impression she had received. But whoever she was she had given birth to this young man, and there was nothing common in any way about him. She shut down on the thought that his environment and associations may have covered his inherited traits. But two things had certainly resulted from such traits: his blood disease, and his artistic qualities. And so she imagined that both these had come from the father, for such a girl was not likely to possess an artistic temperament. She had always told herself that the girl had likely had a short liaison with some gentleman or other. His final question on the matter was, "Do you think she might have been from London? Really, I mean?" to which she had answered, "I don't really know, Andrew, I only know we took you when you were a baby and we have loved you ever since." And then he bowed his head and said, "I know, and . . . and I love you both. And thank you for all you have done for me. But . . . but there's an unrest in me all the time, and that's why I think a break might do me good."

She had made him promise that if he bled he would go straight to the hospital, and she told him that his father was going to get in touch with a specialist he knew at the Middlesex and he would see to him.

And so here he was at this moment, sitting in the drawing room in the exact position where his adoptive grandfather's long chair had been situated for years. And he was once again looking through a number of telephone and street directories lying on a small table to his side. There were Birches and Birchtons and Birchams, but no Birchcombs; in fact, not many names beginning with Birch. Disappointment engulfed him. The poor woman, it was assumed, had given the hospital authorities the wrong name. Could she have quickly said Bircham? What had he to lose? He would try Bircham. He noted that the number was of an address in Bermondsey.

After writing the name and address and the phone number on a small pad he had pulled from his pocket, although he had no intention of telephoning, he rose quickly from the chair, hurried out of the room and upstairs. In the dressing room, he took off his house-jacket, put on his suit, thrust his wallet into a pocket, bent down and looked into the mirror, then took a brush and tried to flatten his unruly black hair.

Downstairs, he was helped into his greatcoat by Patterson, who enquired, "Will you be in for lunch, sir?"

"No. No, I don't think so."

"Dinner?" The elderly man thrust his head forward as he smiled, and Andrew, smiling back at him, said, "At the moment I don't know, Patterson. As my father says, you can expect me when you see me."

"Yes. Yes, that's a saying of Mr. Robert's all right. Racing all over the world, never in one place two minutes. That is, of course, except at High Gully. It's difficult to get him away from there once he gets set in. Of course, the weather has a lot to do with it, hasn't it, sir?"

"Yes. Yes, it has . . . at certain times."

"Will I keep the fire going in your studio, sir?"

Andrew paused a moment: "No. No; I wouldn't

bother. I . . . I have an appointment and I don't know how long it will take."

"Very well, sir. I would tuck that scarf in tight; it's a snifter outside this morning. And are you taking an umbrella, sir?"

"No, Patterson." Then turning to the old man, his voice a confidential whisper, he said, "I can't stand umbrellas, walking sticks or gloves."

Patterson laughed now as he said, "Well, I've noticed about the umbrella and the walking stick, sir, but I thought the gloves would be very necessary."

"Only on certain occasions," adding on a laugh, "when my mother is about."

He went almost gaily from the house and Patterson stood for a few minutes and watched him stride away down the street, thinking to himself, he could be the master's son at that. He's done a good job on him, has Mr. Robert. And he's a nice young fellow. Oh yes, he is. Not like some you find around: times were changing; a crudeness was appearing in the young. The smile left his face and he closed the door none too gently . . .

Andrew knew little about London except for the main thoroughfares, the museums and theaters, so he found the district in which he was now walking very strange. There were still largish semi-detached houses, with pebble-dashed council houses closing in on them, and a near-by shopping center. At one shop a queue had formed outside, and the smell of frying fish gave the reason. The whole place was busy, yet overall there was a drabness. He stopped a woman and said, "Would you please direct me to Cranwell Terrace?"

"Cranwell Terrace? Oh yes; you're not a step from it hardly. See across yonder"—she pointed—"go straight up that street and turn left and there you're into it, Cranwell Terrace."

He thanked her and followed her directions and found that Cranwell Terrace was another short row of semi-detached houses, not of any great quality, although each was fronted by a few feet of iron-railed ground on which, here and there, stood tubs of dismal-looking shrubs.

Number twenty-six had three tubs, the evergreens in them appearing gray.

He hesitated before opening the gate; then he was knocking at the door. He heard someone laugh before it opened, and there stood a tall, thin man, with a pleasant face, who said, "Yes, well? What can I do for you, dear?"

"Are you Mr. Bircham?"

"Yes. Yes, I happen to be Mr. Bircham, dear."

Andrew looked into the pleasant face and noticed that he had very blue eyes, and now hesitantly he said, "I'm . . . I'm looking for someone . . . er . . . Mrs. Bircham."

Now the face that seemed to be hanging over him from the high step of the house became slightly contorted: the lips went into a large pout, and the eyes opened widely; the man then ran his hand through his hair before laughing and saying,

"I think you've come to the wrong house, dear. There is no Mrs. Bircham."

At this moment a face appeared at the man's shoulder. It didn't look so pleasant and the voice was gruff as it asked, "What is it?"

Now the blue-eyed man turned a laughing face to his companion and said, "This young man wants to speak with my wife."

Both faces were turned to Andrew now, and the second man asked, "What's your business? Why are you looking for a Mrs. Bircham?"

"I . . . I wanted some information about . . . a family."

This gruff and shorter man now pressed the other one aside and he was taking in Andrew, from his soft felt hat over his well-cut overcoat to his highly polished shoes, and after a pause he asked, "Sure you've got the right name and address?"

Andrew bit on his lip before he said, "Well, it was the nearest name to one I am looking for. I got it from the directory."

"Nearest name?"

"Yes, I was really looking for someone under the name of Birchcomb, but I thought that those . . . well, those who had given me the name might have got it slightly wrong, and Bircham . . . well, it was just a chance."

The blue-eyed man now said, "And it's to do with your family?"

"Yes. Yes." Andrew nodded at him. "I'm looking for someone in that family."

"Could it be Birchcomb?" Now the two men were looking at each other. They had uttered the name almost simultaneously. Then the tall man said, "Couldn't be, surely, not round there," and he laughed, leaving the shorter and gruffer man to say, "There's people called Birch*comb* along"— he jerked his head to the side—"in the council houses, but—" Now a smile came on his face as he shook his head slowly, saying, "I would think you're on the wrong track there, too, son. I don't think you'd find any connection of yours with that particular Birchcomb family." Then he moved a step back and said, "Would you like to come in and have a chat?"

Andrew looked from one to the other, hesitating. They were kindly, nice enough men, but there was just something about them that disturbed him, and he answered politely, "Thank you, but I am . . . well, stuck for time." Even as he said this he thought it was the one thing he wasn't stuck for. Then he backed a step from them, saying, "I'm very obliged to you. You've been very kind and helpful."

"You're welcome, I'm sure, dear." It was the blue-eyed man smiling at him again.

Once more he inclined his head toward them and said, "Thank you. Thank you both," then almost tumbled against the small iron gate before moving into the street. And he was aware that the men had moved from the step and were watching his departure.

It wasn't until he had reached the end of the

street and turned into what immediately appeared to be a different district yet again that he drew a long breath. Then his step slowed and he said to himself, "Birchcomb. But . . . but I don't know the number." He looked now at a long stretch of these gray pebble-dashed houses, broken only by, as far as he could see at this distance, a narrow road, on the corner of which was a shop.

He stood outside the shop, one section of which was given over to fruit and vegetables, the other to dry household goods, and could see there were two people being served, but they were at the household side, so he made for the fruit and vegetable counter and was immediately addressed by the man standing behind: "Yes, sir?" he said.

"I . . . I wonder if you can help me?"

"Be obliged to. Be obliged to, if it's in my power. Now, how can I help you?"

"I am looking for a number, or the position of a house. The name is Birchcomb."

If he had brought out a pistol and said, "This is a hold up, hand over your cash," the two women at the far side of the shop, and the woman behind the counter couldn't have turned round more quickly; and it caused the man's expression to change. Then, as the previous two men had reacted, so did this man: leaning across the counter, he took in Andrew's attire and found it matched both his manner and his voice; and he said, "You're looking for the Birchcombs?"

"Yes, the Birchcombs. I'd be obliged if you could direct me to the house, please."

"Yes. Yes, I could direct you, and I will." He now came around the counter as if to get a better view of the young fellow. Then he pointed toward the shop door, saying, "You haven't very far to go, son. Just cross the back lane there and it's the fourth door down."

Andrew now turned and looked at the women. They were staring at him, hard and inquiring stares through screwed-up eyes. And as he thanked the man and made for the door, one of them said, "After last night, it could be a detective. They're young these days." And as he stepped into the street he heard a softer voice saying, "All hell was let loose last night, and him only out a week."

He passed the back lane, counted four doors down, then stood for a long moment in front of it.

The letter-box was at the bottom of the door and there was a knocker three-quarters of the way up. His hand moved hesitantly toward it, and even after he had lifted it he still paused, before finally letting it fall.

It must have been a full two minutes before the door was opened and there, standing before him, was a girl.

During his travels into this district that morning he had seen so many different expressions on the various faces, but none like the one on the face of this girl: aggressive was a mild word for it; blazing fitted it better. Her face, if not exactly red, was of a deep pink that was emphasized by a mass of bouffant blonde hair. He guessed she couldn't be more than five feet tall, but he couldn't guess at her age, which could be anything from fifteen to twenty-five; and it was nearer the latter that was indicated by her voice when it came at him, almost barking, "Yes? An' what you after?"

"I . . . I'm sorry to trouble you, but I was looking for a Mrs. Birchcomb."

Her eyes screwed up in the same way as had those of the women in the shop, and he noticed they were blue eyes, too, like those of the kindly man back in the terrace. And they peered up at him for a full minute before she spoke again when, in a lowering of her tone, she asked, "Which department are you from?"

"Department?" He shook his head. "I represent no department; I was just looking for a Mrs. Birchcomb. I . . . I would like a word with her."

Again the voice was harsh. "What kind of a word? Look, she's got nothin' to say. She's got nothin' to do with this. It was settled last night. They couldn't touch him for what he did and they hadn't any business to come barging in here. People's houses are their private places."

Now it was his turn to screw up his face as he said, "I think you are under the wrong impression. I . . . I represent no authority whatsoever. I . . ."

"What is it?" The voice came from behind her now, and then a woman appeared, and immediately the word drab came into his mind. Her hair was brown and looked as if it hadn't had a comb through it for some time. Her face was round and had once been pretty. He noted that she wasn't very old, not even as old as his mother. In such an immediate comparison it was natural that he should think of Janice as being his mother; yet, he was looking for his mother.

The woman pressed the younger woman to the side and confronted him, looking straight into his face and, almost in a whisper, said, "What d'you want?"

"I . . ." He stopped now and looked up and down the street where people were moving, before he asked quietly, "It . . . it is a very private matter. May I come in?"

She now turned and looked at the girl, and said, "You'd better let him. He's not from them; any of them."

They stood aside to allow him to walk directly into a room and immediately to inhale the staleness of it and note its general untidiness. And this first sight of the room and the first real look at the woman now staring at him told him that he should never have come here, for he felt sure in his mind who the woman was, and her appearance and everything about him in this room repulsed him.

He now took in the figure of an old woman sitting in a wooden chair in the far corner of the room, and her voice came to him now, a Cockney voice saying, "Who's 'e? What's up? Tell 'im to get the hell out of it. We've had enough. And if 'e wakes up," and the scraggy neck jerked upward indicating the ceiling, "there'll be bloody 'ell to pay again. He's 'ad enough. We've all 'ad enough."

"Shut up! Gran. Shut yer mouth!" It was the girl speaking; and now she turned to her mother, saying, "Sit down. Sit down, else it'll start again."

As if "it" had started again, the woman now put her hand into the pocket of her short dressing gown and, taking out a soiled handkerchief, applied it to her nose.

Watching this, Andrew had the distressing feeling that he could be sick.

"Sit down." The girl had pushed a chair toward him, and after glancing at her he sat down. Now he looked at the woman and said quietly, "You have nose bleedings?" and before she could answer, her daughter said, "Yes, she has nose bleeding, and belly bleedings, and the lot. Are you from the hospital? A student doctor? They say they can't do anything, so why . . . ?"

"No, I am not from the hospital, but I, too, bleed, though so far only from the nose and the tongue."

The woman and he were staring fixedly at each other, then her hand went across her mouth as if to cover the muttered words, "Oh my God!"

His voice was stiff now as he said, "You had a child and you left it at the hospital when it was three days old. Isn't that so?"

She didn't answer. The room was quiet, so quiet that a milk van rattling by in the street sounded deafening. And then he went on, "I was adopted, luckily, some would say, because they were very kind and caring people, but there's always been a need in me to know not only where I sprang from, but why I was left.''

''Because she bloody well 'ad to.''

The woman and the girl turned toward the voice now and they both cried in an undertone, ''Shut up! will you?''

The girl moved slowly toward the couch and stood beside her mother's knee, although she didn't speak, but just fixed her eyes on this nattily dressed, as she thought, young fellow who could be her . . . her thoughts didn't add the word ''brother.'' Then they were all looking at the old woman again, who was on her feet now and yelling at the top of her voice, ''Get him away! You don't want murder done. If he bloody well finds this out, last night'll be nothin' to it.''

''Shut your mouth, Gran.''

''What! What d'you say?''

The girl now rushed across the room to the old woman and, taking her by the shoulders, she pushed her back into the chair, hissing at her, ''If anybody brings 'im down it'll be you, you deaf old cow.''

''One of these days . . .''

''Yes, I know, one of these days what you're gonna do, and one of these days I'll carry out me threat an' see you're put in a home. You cause more mischief than enough in this house.''

The woman on the couch now pleaded quietly, ''Betty! Betty! Leave her.'' Then, looking up at Andrew, she said in the same tone of voice, ''Go away, will you, lad? Come back again, at the weekend. He'll be gone then."

"Will I, be God!"

The voice startled them all, for none of them had heard the room door being opened.

As Andrew watched the man advancing slowly into the room, the woman on the couch again muttered, "Oh, God Almighty!"

The man was stockily built. He was wearing only trousers and shirt, the neck of which was open and showing a black hairy chest; also the shirt appeared tight around the shoulders, indicating extraordinary breadth there.

Before her husband had reached the couch the woman had risen to her feet and, looking at Andrew, she gabbled, "You goin' now?"

Andrew did not answer her or look at her; his gaze was on the man and he asked himself, could this man be his father? Or had he been got on the side? Perhaps that would explain why the woman was looking terrified.

"Who's this? Somebody else wants bustin' up?" He had been addressing his wife, and now he looked at Andrew and said, "You got a permit to come and rake through the house?" Then he stopped, and as the others had done he looked the young man up and down before asking him in a quieter but menacing tone, "What d'you want?"

When Andrew did not answer another short silence fell on the room. But again it was broken by the old woman who was cackling, as she cried, " 'E's somethin' for you to swallow, Big Mouth.

'E's yours! the one she was terrified to tell ya about in case you wouldn't marry 'er when you got back. You didn't want kids, did you? No kids for you, you'd 'ad enough of 'em with the thirteen bastards you were brought . . ."

As the man swung round to the old woman, the girl jumped forward and, dragging at his arm, cried, "Dad! Dad! Now, look! Listen! Just listen!"

The man did not thrust his daughter off but he turned slowly from her and, looking at his wife, he said, "Well, let's 'ave it. See if I believe this one."

The woman now seemed to gain courage for a moment because she straightened up and, facing him, she said, "It's as Mum says: 'cos you were brought up with your crowd you were against bairns of all kinds, 'an I knew when you got back off your trip, if you 'ad found 'im"—she now nodded toward Andrew—"that would've been the end of it. You wouldn't 'ave believed it was yours anyway. You were such a jealous bugger. But many's the time, I'll tell you, I wished I'd gone through with it and let you take it or leave it. Anyway, as far as I can understand"—again she nodded toward Andrew—"'e's the one I left after three days. Yes, just three days old 'e was, an' me 'ardly able to stand. But she come for me"—now she was looking fully at her mother—"because she wanted me married an' respectable, not like her other ones that 'ad gone off the rails. You wanted one you could hang onto, didn't you?" she cried at her mother; "give you a home, see to you, 'cos you were always a lazy bugger. You worked it all out, didn't you?"

The man stared at his wife, then turned his gaze once again on Andrew, and the saliva sprayed from his mouth as he said, "I don't believe a bloody word of it. All right, I can believe you 'ad 'im, but 'e's not mine. Look at 'im, 'is 'air's black, and curly at the back; 'e's pale-skinned, like a bloody 'alf-caste."

With his forearm he thrust his wife back onto the couch with such force that her head bounced against the wooden rail: and some instinct in Andrew caused him to cry out, "Don't do that!"

"*What?*" The word was quiet but stressed, as were the following ones, too. "What did you say?"

"You heard what I said, and I'll say this: I would prefer I had a black man as a father rather than you, you ignorant bully that you . . . !" His words were cut off by a blow to his mouth that sent him reeling backwards, to come up against the wall of the fireplace. And as he leaned there, his head reeling, with the taste of blood in his mouth, a taste which seemed to be different from that which at times would pour from his nose and his tongue, there rose in him an anger such as only once before he had experienced, and which had nearly meant the end of him: he was seeing the farmhand that his father had engaged only the week before on a strong reference that he was a good breaker-in of horses.

He could see himself being drawn to the bottom

field by the wild neighing of a horse, there to see the animal roped to a tree on a short lead and the man flailing it with his whip. He was twelve at the time and was on holiday from his boarding school. And he himself had become like a wild animal with the feeling of rage in him, for he had jumped onto the man's back and had tried to throttle him. But the man had thrown him off and had brought the whip across him as he had hit the ground; and that's all he remembered. But while he lay prone, as if he were dead, the fellow had scuttled off and left him within inches of the maddened and rearing animal. It was only because Johnny McBrien, too, had been attracted by the wild neighing, that he had not been trampled to death.

And now, here was the man standing before him with the whip and the woman was the tethered horse. And when he sprang, it was utter surprise rather than force that knocked the man off his feet and bore him to the ground. And after his head had come into contact with the wooden stool, he lay there, quiet, apparently stunned, with Andrew sprawled on top of him.

Hands were now dragging him off and as from a distance he heard the woman cry, "Get him away, Betty, because he'll murder him. Get him away! Look! He's coming round. D'you hear me, girl?"

The mist was clearing now and dimly he saw the girl drag a tea-towel from a rail and, rolling it up, push it against his mouth; and automatically his hand went up and held it there. Then she was pulling his soft hat onto his head. Dimly, too, he was aware of her getting into a coat and a woollen hat before she pulled open the door. Then she was grabbing his arm, saying, "Come on! Come on with you!"

They were in the street now and he heard a voice saying, "He's at it again, then, Betty?" and her answering the woman, saying, "Yes, Mrs. Mc-Neil, he's at it again. Mind he doesn't start on you next."

They were some way along the street when she said, to no one in particular, "Brass-faced, interfering cow," and his buzzing brain took it up and kept repeating, "Brass-faced, interfering cow." Then she was talking rapidly: "Why did you have to come today? Why couldn't it have been on Thursday? He'll be gone then. Oh my God!" She pulled him to a stop. "You're bleeding from the nose an' all. And you've got a split lip, you know that?"

"Yes. Yes, I know that." He couldn't recognize his own voice, for now there was no maniacal anger in it: there was now no desire to kill, and he had wanted to kill that man as he had wanted to kill the horse-breaker.

She was saying, "You'd better come to the hospital out-patients." She gently lifted the tea-towel from his mouth and said, "Oh, Good God! It is a slit; it's a good job it wasn't your eye, he'd have put it out. And it would happen after last night. Oh, come on." She grabbed his arm, and he allowed her to lead him down streets, around corners, through narrow lanes; and then they were hurrying through the hospital gates and toward the Casualty Department. She seemed to know her way about, for she took him to the far end of a large room and sat him on a wooden seat, saying, "Stay there, I'll get somebody."

It was some minutes later when a nurse said, "Come this way." Then she added, "You've started early in the day."

When he was sat in a cubicle, she examined his lip, saying, "Oh, that will need something. But your nose is still bleeding. It's a wonder he didn't bust it. Or did you hit a brick wall?"

He knew his voice had a stiff sound as he answered her, "I'm subject to nose-bleedings."

She stared at him for a moment; then looked at the girl, and her mind could have been saying, two different types here. Another story I'll never get to the bottom of. "Stay there and I'll get the doctor," she said.

When he closed his eyes and leaned his head back as if searching for some place to rest it, the girl put her hand on the back of his head, saying, "Feeling woozy?" And to this he muttered, "A bit."

"You'll be all right; they're good here." She spoke as if from knowledge. And he opened his eyes and said, "It's kind of you."

"What! Kind of me to save you from being killed? Because he would, you know, he would. All I say is, God keep that banana boat on the move."

It must be because his head was muzzy, but he couldn't take that in. It wasn't connected with what they were saying.

She said quickly now, "Oh, here's the doctor. They'll be pushin' me out, but I'll be waitin' for you. Don't worry . . ."

It was forty-five minutes later when the nurse led him out of the cubicle and guided him toward where Betty was waiting, rather impatiently, by the wooden bench, and she greeted them pertly, saying, "I thought you were giving him an operation."

The nurse looked at her rather disdainfully as she said, "He's lost quite a lot of blood. He needs to rest for a while. Can you take him home?"

She looked from the nurse to Andrew, then said offhandedly, "He'll be all right." As she went to take his arm, he turned to the nurse and said, "Thank you very much," and to this she smiled at him, saying, "It's all in a day's work. But I wouldn't try to laugh too much for the next day or so else you'll open up your lip."

She was again leading him by the arm out of Casualty when she muttered, "Funny cuts. Who d'they think they are, anyway?" then continued without pause, "Where d'you live?"

Where did he live? For answer, he said, "I'm still feeling a bit woozy. Do you think we could go to a café and I could have a coffee or something?"

"Oh, yes. Yes, there's one just round the corner. Come on."

When they were seated, a cup of coffee before

each of them, she said, "It's a workin' man's place, but the coffee's good. Drink it up."

When he had drunk the mug of coffee almost without pausing, she said, "Could you do with another?" And when he answered, "Yes; yes, I could," she took his mug and went to the counter, and as he watched her, he asked himself, where do you live? Then gave himself the answer: 17, Melbourne Court. But how long ago was it since he had *lived* there? Since he had left there this morning he had been introduced to a new world, people of so many different types. He hadn't realized people lived like that, although he was used to working-class people. There was the staff at High Gully and in London, there were the Pattersons; and he had been round the markets. But had he ever thought about how these people, especially in the markets, lived? No, they were cheery, jolly men, and the tradesmen who came to 17, Melbourne Court were also nicely spoken. Some of them were broad Cockney, but they were also nicely spoken. But had he ever thought of the rows of gray houses where they lived or how they lived in them? Fighting, brawling, bashing. But they wouldn't all be like that, surely. No, there were the two odd fellows in the terrace. Their house, he was sure, would have been clean, because they, too, looked clean. Yet there had been something about them that in some way distanced them from the world he knew; but his mind wouldn't go into the cause. And then there was this young woman now standing at the counter. She was what you would call common. Yes, very common. She looked common, she talked common . . . and she was his sister. This thought brought him up stiffly in the chair. Yes, she was his sister; and that woman whom he had disliked on sight was his mother. But surely that man couldn't have been his father? No! No! No matter what he thought about the woman, he would have to own her as his mother, and this girl as his sister; but not that man; he wasn't only common, he was the lowest of the low.

The word "common" grew in his mind until it covered everything he had experienced that morning. Yet the strange feeling about it was that it was all alive and that he didn't really object to it. He had no wish to run away from it and back up to High Gully. No, no, never. He couldn't see himself ever again living in High Gully, or yet the London house. What would his mother and father think about Betty? Oh, his mother would be kind to her. She was kind to everyone. And his father would be amused by her, but he would place her in a certain category and, being the gentleman that he was, he too would be polite and kind to her. But would he accept her as his sister? If he were to take her up there, what would happen? But he would never take her up there because he wasn't going back.

Why wasn't he going back? Was it because he had found out who he was and was ashamed? No, no; it wasn't that. He didn't quite know how to express the feeling in him at the moment. When his head became clearer, he'd know then.

When he felt the finger under his chin, his head bounced up. He hadn't known it had drooped. Her voice came at him again, saying, "You should be lyin' down. Can I phone anybody for you? Anyway, where are you from?"

She had put a mug of coffee into his hand and he drank from it before he said, "Scotland."

"Scotland?" Her voice was high with surprise. "You mean you've just come down; I mean, to London. Did you travel overnight?"

He looked over the steaming mug and made himself answer her by nodding once.

"You must be dead on your feet. And then for this to happen." She said again, "You should be lyin' down. Are you goin' into a hotel? 'Ave you any money? Well, of course, I suppose you 'ave. But you'll 'ave to be careful where you go, being in the state you are. Can you afford a good hotel?"

He was just becoming aware that she dropped her "h"'s all the time; she was a real Cockney. Did it matter? No, no, it didn't matter. How old was she? Younger than him, seventeen likely, but she talked and acted like a grown-up woman. She had something about her. What was it? A sort of command? No, that wasn't the word; capable, perhaps . . .

"*Listen!*" Her voice roused him. "You've got to lie down somewhere. If me dad had been away you could've come back to our place. But then, I don't think by the way you acted that you were much taken with it, or with me mum. But she's all right. She's 'ad a rough time; she can't help not bein' able to do things. She's what you call . . . anemic . . . you know, it makes you appear lazy. Some people don't understand. Me dad doesn't. Oh, why didn't that banana boat leave yesterday?" She leaned toward him now. "He works on a banana boat, you know. They can be away for months . . . it goes round the islands collecting bananas." She paused now and seemed to give a little laugh as she said, "When he's right sober he can talk about the islands, especially Jamaica. I used to like to listen to him." Again there was a little laugh as she said, "People don't believe he works on a banana boat. As he said, folks believe bananas grow on trees. I used to think that was funny, you know. He could be at times, you know, funny."

He knew she was nodding at him and the expression on her face looked merry. Then she leaned toward him, saying, "You're not listenin' to me, are you? You look miles away. But you've got to get settled and I'll have to go to work tomorrow. I work in Woolworths, but I had to stay orf today an' send a message to say I've got laryngitis again. But after last night's do, when they ransacked the house—" her eyes darted quickly over the row of empty tables to the left of her before she went on, "they still won't believe he isn't in Murphy's lot. He had been home three weeks and he was spending, 'cos he's well paid on the boat, you know, but there had been another break-in at a jeweler's, so they swooped down on 'im. He did two years, all because he wanted to get away and go to sea. He likes the sea, and Murphy didn't like that because me dad was good when it came to the rough stuff. So Murphy planted something on him. Well, he put it in the 'ouse or got one of his lads to do it. Dad got two years and no time off 'cos he played bloody hell all the time 'e was in there 'cos they wouldn't believe 'im. 'E 'ates the police, the 'ole lot of 'em, because some of 'em are real buggers, you know, when they get it in for you."

When she stopped talking it seemed strange. Her silence brought his attention fully on her. She was sitting with an elbow on the table, one hand cupping her face, the other stirring the spoon round her empty mug. Then of a sudden she started again. "Willie," she said, "Willie could 'elp you. 'E's a friend of mine. Oh, I'm not thick with him or anything like that, 'e's Delia's fella and Delia's my friend. But Willie knows a thing or two. He should get on, should Willie. And he's got this top floor in Arthur Lynch's lodging 'ouse, but he's made it good: he runs it like an Army barrcks; he's fixed up cubicles and all that. There used to be six of them, but Bobby and Keith, they've gone to Australia, of all places, they want to get on. But there's a free bunk there anyway. Of course it all depends, if it isn't your style. But you 'aven't got much choice the way you are. So, come on, get yourself up." She paused in her rising, saying now, "What's your name?"

"Andrew."

"Andrew what?"

"Maddison." Why had he said Maddison instead of Anderson? It had just come into his mind.

"Well, by now you know that mine's Betty. I don't like it very much, not when people say it suits me. Oh, come on, let's get this finished. I've got to get back to me mum, because if he goes out tonight an' gets another skinful there'll be skull and hair flyin' again. God bless banana boats."

She was taking him by the hand now as if he were a child, and he didn't mind it. They were going down more side streets, through alleyways; and then they came to a demolition site, and the dust enveloped them and she coughed as she said, "How they stand swallowing this I don't know. They won't last long. Mind where you're goin', there's stuff lying about. I'll have to shout."

He was startled when she did shout . . . her voice seemed bigger than her body. "Willie!" she yelled, "Willie! here a minute."

He could dimly see a group of men standing round a machine; then one of them turned and walked toward them. Now she was talking again rapidly, so that he didn't get half of what she was saying, until she said, "And this is me brother, believe it or not. I can cut a long story short. Me mum had him when she shouldn't, but 'e's me dad's all right. And you know what hè thinks of kids. He nearly throttled me when I was young for cryin'. Well, can I take 'im along?''

"Aye, yes, of course. Win will be up and in the kitchen likely, as always.''

Andrew looked at the big dust-covered man and when he said, "I'm sorry to trouble you, sir,'' the man turned and looked at Betty with a sharp look of inquiry. Then turning to Andrew again and with a note of laughter in his voice, he said, "No trouble at all . . . sir. No trouble at all.''

"Thanks, Willie. I'll be glad to get 'im off me 'ands for five minutes. He's only 'alf with us. But he wouldn't be with us at all if me dad 'ad got up in time.'' She laughed now, a gay laugh. "You won't believe it, but 'e knocked me dad down.''

"Never! Not in this world.''

"I'm tellin' you the truth, he did. I'll tell you all about it later tonight.''

The man was grinning at Andrew now and he was saying, "By! that was somethin'. You knocked Sep Birchcomb down. I'd really 'ave to see that before I'd believe it.''

"It's a fact.'' She was pulling Andrew away now and he allowed her to lead him again, that was until, his mind seeming to clear, he pulled her to a stop, saying, "I . . . I'll have to phone.''

"Your home?''

He paused, then said, "Yes. Yes.''

"You want to tell them you've arrived?''

"Yes.''

"Well, I can understand that, but don't tell 'em

how you've arrived, or where you've arrived. 'Cos, whoever they are, they'll be worried." Then, more in a mutter to herself, she said, " 'Cos they've done a good job on you. Come on. Come on, there's a phone in the 'all at Arthur Lynch's."

It seemed to him that they had walked only a few yards before they came to the block of large houses which undoubtedly at one time had housed some wealthy merchants. He did not notice the stucco peeling off the walls, but in the quite large square hall he noticed the smell that emanates from stale cooking and confined bodies.

Betty did not lead him straight to the stairs, but turned to a cupboard-like structure with a half-glass front that seemed to be stuck onto a side wall. She knocked on the pane.

It was some minutes before, through it, she saw the door at the far side of the structure open and the owner of the house appear. And when he slid the window aside she said, "Could my friend use your phone, please?"

His eyes left her and took in Andrew. He was a judge of men, class and types, and he saw that this young fellow was extremely well dressed, and his face, too, was well dressed, but in the wrong way. He said to her, "Where's he going?"

"Up to the floor. There's only four there now; there's two empty beds."

"You're well informed, aren't you, as usual, Miss Facey?" Then he added, "What have you been up to now?"

"Broke into the Bank of England. He's carryin' the cash."

"One of these days, miss, your smarty tongue will get you into trouble. Somebody will smack your mouth for you."

Her voice was low now as she answered, "Well, it won't be you, Mr. Lynch. You can reckon on that, it won't be you. Now, can he use your phone?"

After staring hard at her he brought the standing phone onto a ledge outside the glass window, and then, looking at Andrew, he said, "What number d'you want?"

"I can get it, thank you." Andrew picked up the phone and looked at the man across the counter and said, "Would you mind?"

"Mind what?"

"I want to have a private conversation."

"O . . . h!" The head bobbed. "I'm sorry, your lordship. I will take my leave so you can have your private . . . conversation." The word "conversation" dropped to a growl.

As the man went out of the cubby hole, Andrew turned and looked at Betty and she, shrugging her shoulders, turned about and walked to the other side of the hall, but not as far as the wall, and what she heard her new brother say on the phone startled her and made her think immediately: he was lying, he doesn't come from Scotland.

What she heard Andrew say, was, "I won't be home tonight, Patterson. I'm . . . I'm staying with a friend." There was a pause and then, "Yes, if you phone, just tell him I'm staying with a friend." There was another pause, during which he seemed to be listening; and then he said, "Yes, it could be a day or two. Thank you, Patterson."

He put the phone down, then turned toward Betty. He didn't know what to make of her expression, but at the moment it didn't trouble him; all he wanted to do was to lie down, even in this smelly house. But as he followed Betty toward the stairs, the man Lynch appeared in a doorway and his face was screwed up in inquiry as he looked at the young fellow. He, too, had good hearing.

All Andrew remembered of that first night in Foley House was that when he reached the top of the third flight of stairs he suddenly felt very tired, and then he was in a large room, a most odd room, for one side was taken up with make-shift cubicles. In the middle of the room was a large table with oddments of chairs around it, and over-all, mingled with the other smells in the house, there was that from an oil-burning stove. He vaguely remembered a man who limped coming out of a doorway and Betty saying to him, "This is a friend of mine, Win. Willie knows all about it. He's been hurt, he needs to rest." And then she turned to Andrew and said, "This is Mr. James Winterbottom."

For some reason or other Andrew recalled that he wanted to laugh. They called the man Win, but his name was James Winterbottom, and he had a short leg. When the man said, "Would you like some hot soup? It's fresh, I've just made it," Betty said, "Not now, Win. Later, perhaps. But he's all in."

"Who did that to him?"

"Me dad . . . well, half of it."

Then she was helping him off with his coat and jacket; and when she went to lift his feet onto the low plank bed, she said, "I'd better get rid of your shoes."

As he drifted off to sleep his last thought was, "She's my sister. I have a real sister."

He woke once to a familiar voice saying, "This is Henry Hall," and on this, he thought it must be five o'clock. Then he turned slowly and painfully on his side and went to sleep again.

But now he was awake, wide awake, and aware that his head was splitting and his jaw was aching and the packing was still in his nostril and that he had an urgent desire to go to the toilet. He pulled himself up onto the edge of the low bed and looked about him. He was in a cubicle of sorts. The side walls were of plasterboard and about six feet high, with a rod stretched between them and from which a curtain was hanging, leaving a gap of about a foot above the floor. The head of the bed was pressed against a papered wall, which was faded, although the rose pattern was just visible on it. His top coat and jacket and hat were hanging from three pegs on a piece of wood nailed to the wall. His shoes were on the floor underneath.

When he went to stand up he had a fit of coughing which brought the blood clots from behind his
nose; and as he was hurriedly spitting them into a
handkerchief the curtain was pulled back and the
aperture taken up by a very large man. He
seemed to remember the face yet couldn't place
it.

"Hello, there. Feeling a bit better?"

"Oh, yes. Yes, thank you."

"You still bleeding?"

"No, not any more."

The coughing had loosened the packing in his
nostrils and his attempts to pull it down brought
the exclamation from the man: "Good God! You
should have gone to the hospital for that,
shouldn't you?"

"No; I am quite used to taking it down."

"How d'you feel?"

He looked up at the man. "I think the appropri-
ate word is 'lousy,' " he said.

The man laughed, then said, "Well, get on your
feet and come and have something to eat. A cup
of tea first, perhaps, eh?"

"Is . . . is there a wash place near?"

"Oh. Oh, that! Come on." But when he saw Andrew stagger as he pulled himself up from the low
seat, he put out a hand and, very much as Betty
would have done, drew him into the room. And
pointing to a table at which three men were
seated, he said, "Don't take any notice of them.
We'll do the introductions after you've gone about
your business." And at this he drew him toward a

door at the far end of the room and into what, apparently, was a kitchen, a room not as large as the other, but still of a good size, then through it and into a make-shift toilet room that had evidently been created out of a short passage. At the end was a lavatory pan and along one side a narrow bench on which was a large tin dish and an equally large enamel jug, together with a soap dish, while underneath the bench stood a bucket.

He did not make any comparison between the beautiful bathroom not two miles away and the huge, elaborate one in which you could freeze, even with the oil heaters on, at High Gully. He was making no comparisons whatever in this strange new world.

After he had used the toilet, he washed his face gently with the cold water, then dabbed it dry with a none-too-clean piece of roller-towelling hanging from a single wooden rod attached to a long wall. Then he smoothed back his hair. His comb was in his jacket pocket.

When he entered the living-room the big man hailed him, saying, "Well, come and sit down, and let's get the introductions over. But look, Win has made you this pot of tea. D'you take sugar?"

"Yes, please."

"One, two, or three?"

"Just one, please."

The tea was strong and very sweet—the sugar spoon being more suitable for dessert. The tea was also scarce of milk; yet he drank it quickly, and the men sat watching him in silence. When he had finished the big fellow said to him, "Well, here goes. I don't know how long you're goin' to stay, but if it's a night or two, or a week, or a month, or a year, like some of us, we need to know your name and as much about you as you want to tell us. Well, as I said here goes. My name's Willie Grabelly. You saw me earlier in the day and what I was doin'. I'm a breaker-upper, you could say. I'm a ganger on the job." And laughing, he added, "And I'm foot-loose but not yet fancy-free. And this"—he pointed to a man who was probably in his late forties—"is Dill, Dill Morgan. He's a painter. Not one that goes round the houses, you know, he's a real painter and he's got a place up there." He jerked his head toward the ceiling. But Andrew kept his eyes on the man with the stiff expression who had acknowledged the introduction only by glancing at him before biting into a slice of toast. But Andrew's interest had been immediately aroused and he said, "I'm . . . I'm glad to make your acquaintance. I . . . I, too, paint."

If he had expected any response to this not only was he disappointed, but he felt repulsed when the man said, "Everybody paints; it's the only natural gift God and the devil have dished out to us."

Before Willie Grabelly could pass onto the third man, whose name was Mickey Fenwick, this young man, who seemed to be of the same age as Andrew himself, laughed as he said, "That's Dill's manner when he's in a good temper and, as you've noticed, he's very polite. But just imagine what he could be like when he's got his rag out."

The painter took no notice of this jibe but went on eating his toast while the big fellow's introduction went as follows: "This is Mickey Fenwick. He is, what shall I say, Mickey . . . a violinist?"

"Yes. Yes, you could say I'm a violinist, because that's what I am. I'm only a busker because I'm not appreciated. But come the day, you'll see, come the day."

"Yes, come the day," repeated the big fellow. Then looking almost tenderly on the small man who could have been taken for any age, thirty, forty, or even fifty, he said, "This is Mr. James Winterbottom, affectionately known as Win. James has an art, too, he can cook." He pushed his big hand out against the man's head, then went on, "He supplies us with tit-bits we'd otherwise never see."

Andrew was taking note that this big man, this Willie Grabelly, spoke differently from the rest; not middle-class, but differently. And, what was more evident still, he seemed to be a kindly man, an intelligent man. He was saying, "We couldn't do without Win. Keeps our house clean and he cooks, and all in his spare time. Well, that's us. What about you?"

Andrew realized he had even the painter's attention now, for the four pairs of eyes were on him and as he looked back at them he said to himself, "Tell them the truth, the first part at least." So he began quite abruptly, saying, "My name is Andrew Anderson-Maddison."

"Oh. Oh, well, make up your mind. Is it Anderson or Maddison?"

He looked at the violinist and said, "Maddison. I understand I was adopted when I was three days old and by very, very kind people. But from when I was fourteen I began to wonder, as all such as me do, where I came from, who were my real people. So I set about searching, and . . . well, today I found them."

"And they were the Birchcombs?" The big man's voice was quiet and had a note of sympathy in it; and Andrew answered, "Yes, the Birchcombs."

"God in heaven! You would have got a shock."

Andrew looked at the young man named Mickey and he said, "Yes, it was, particularly when I met the man who was supposed to be my father. But I don't accept that. My mother . . . her? Yes, I do. I've got to, because I've inherited her . . . well, her disease." He pointed to his nose. "It is a bleeding; very rare I understand, and passed on through families. And there she was suffering from bleedings, as I do. So I accept her. But not him. And he insulted me, so I hit him."

There was a moment's stillness in the room; then simultaneously there was a great burst of laughter; even the painter was laughing. As for Mickey Fenwick, his head was on his folded arms on the table. Only James Winterbottom was looking at him, and his eyes were wide with surprise while the tears ran from them.

When, gradually, the laughter died down and they were looking at him again, Willie said, "You know, son, I've seen three burly cops trying to get that fella into the Black Maria and before succeeding they all lost their jackets. And you say you hit him?"

Andrew said nothing, but for a moment he recalled the fierce wild anger that had risen in him, and the awful thought now struck him that perhaps, after all, that man *was* his father and that his bashing brutality had merely been channelled differently within himself.

"And what happened after you hit him?"

It appeared that he had caught the painter's interest, and he replied, quietly, "Well, first he hit me"—he pointed to his chin—"and at that I got a bit mad and I jumped on him, and . . . and we hit the floor. He must have been knocked out for a time, and so Betty . . . well, she insisted I leave."

Each man at the table seemed to be in pain, and Win spluttered, "He's noted, you know. There are some big bruisers at the Beef Joint . . . that's where I work every night from ten till six, washing up, you know. Well, the man you jumped on could take the lot of them and knock their heads together. They would scarper at the sight of him. You . . . you had better keep out of his way, and not let on you're here."

"Oh, as I understand it, he'll be gone tomorrow, or the next day, on a banana boat."

There was another splutter, and then a repeating of his words: "A banana boat . . . a banana boat. A . . . a *banana boat,* you said?"

"Yes; he works on a banana boat, so Betty says."

"Well, that explains something," said Win. "I've been wondering why one or two of the big fellas have been throwing their weight about lately; they must have known he was safely out of the way, because they never knew when he was going to drop in and with Murphy himself, too."

The painter was muttering something now and Willie, taking it up, said, "Yes, talk about David and Goliath. Anyway, how long d'you think you're goin' to be here? Is it just for the night? Because if it is that can go by the board, but if it's for a week or more, then you must know the rules. Two and six a head for rent; bring your own bedding, buy your own food. Or, if you want to dish in with us, five shillings a week. Win there works it all out, and he'll feed you plain but well. There's only one rule, no overnight stays for lady friends. Of course"—he put on an air now—"you could have them up for afternoon tea, that's understandable; or they could look in to meet you and take you out for dinner, but don't bring them back." He was grinning widely now, then added flatly, "How long d'you intend to stay?"

"For a few days, perhaps a week, maybe longer. I don't know yet."

The question that was now thrown at him stumped him: it came from the painter, and aggressively, "Why don't you go back to your own people? They've certainly done you pretty well, I would say."

Andrew stared back at the man, and then quietly he said, "That's my business. I've got to work things out. The fact that I've found I have people . . . yet I must confess, with the exception of Betty, I don't like what I've found; but in some strange way I have a feeling of belonging, a feeling I've never experienced before. So I've got a lot to work out as to whether it's worth staying or going back."

No one spoke until Willie, drawing in a deep breath, said, "Well, that's settled. Now we know where we are. One more thing: we've got a good old woman who does our washing for a shilling a head, including pants, vests, two shirts, a towel and a few hankies. All right?"

Andrew didn't answer. The necessity for clean clothes had been taken care of by someone else; he had never even thought about it.

Dill Morgan now rose from the table and was about to move away when he half turned and looked at Andrew again, saying, "You said you paint. What did you mean?"

"Just that, I paint."

"Professionally?"

"I had two years in"—he almost said Edinburgh—"in an art school."

"Two years? Why didn't you carry on? Generally

takes a bit longer than that to turn out the . . . let's say, standard type."

"I didn't want to be a standard type. That's why I left. My taste in color didn't please the teachers there."

"Oh, I've heard that one before. Well, there's a room up above if you want to work." He raised his head toward the ceiling. "Can you lay your hands on your stuff?"

He thought a moment, then said, "Yes, some of it, in time."

Dill adopted Andrew's manner now, saying, "Well, in time you may like to come upstairs and see how a failed painter goes about his art."

"You're no failed painter," Willie put in. "All you need is somebody else to sell them, not that thieving bloke who gives you pin money, then sells them up town."

"Such is life, Willie. Such is life."

They were all moving from the table now when there came a knock on the door, and Win being nearest he opened it and exclaimed on a high note, "Oh, hello there, Delia. Come in. He's not ready; as usual, he talks too much."

"Hello, Win. Isn't it cold?"

"Well, I don't feel it, Delia. I prefer it to hot steaming dishwater. But there, that's life, as we all say."

She smiled at him, then looked across at Willie and said, "One of these days I'll drop down dead, for there you'll be at the bottom of the stairs waiting for me."

"Well, one thing I'll promise you, love, is I'll give you a nice funeral. And while I'm getting me coat on and making meself beautiful, say hello to our new lodger."

The girl turned and looked at Andrew, and when she said, "Hello, there," he inclined his head slightly toward her and said, "How d'you do?"

And at this the violinist laughed and repeated, "How d'you do?" only to be shouted down by Dill Morgan, crying at him, "One day your bloody ignorance will choke you. You know that?"

There was silence for a moment: then Mickey Fenwick quietly and apologetically said, "I meant no harm, and he understands." His head had jerked toward Andrew.

There was another silence, this time broken by Willie's voice, high now, crying as he came out of his cubicle, "Hello, How d'you do? Or Bob's your Uncle, take your choice; but how do I look?" He struck a pose, and it was the girl who answered on a laugh, "As you always look, like an apprentice bricklayer," which caused mixed laughter in the room until the girl, now looking fully at Andrew, said, "Betty won't be able to get round tonight; she's needed at home."

Again Willie's voice cut in: "Aye, I bet she is. How's the big fella?"

Delia now parted her red lips that showed scarlet against her olive skin, and said, "From what I saw of him, he's still in a bit of a maze. He can't get over someone hitting him and drawing blood. He's got a slit at the bottom of his skull. It isn't an inch long but it bled quite a bit, apparently. For once he didn't insult me or walk out of the room when I went in. He's in shock.''

''And one day he'll get another shock''—Willie's voice sounded angry now—''for I'll have a go at him meself.''

''I wouldn't do that,'' put in Win. ''Leave it to our new friend, Andrew here. He'll settle him.''

Again the room was full of laughter, but none was coming from Andrew; he was staring at the girl standing at arm's length from him: she was beautiful. He had never seen anything like her in his life before. Oh, he had seen half-castes, there were two in the academy. But this girl looked different. Her skin was what you would term a deep milk-chocolate color. Her nose was straight, her mouth beautifully shaped, and her eyes . . . well, her eyes had the slightest oriental look about them. Then there was that deep forehead and her black frizzy hair was in the same shape as Betty's blonde bouffant.

When she lifted a hand to her mouth as if to still her laughter, her palms, in comparison, were pale. But her fingers, indeed her hands entirely were beautiful: they were long and the nails were tapered. They were cared-for hands. And then there was her body under a coat that didn't seem to be touching her skin. She appeared wraith-like, at this moment not quite real to him as he stood in this very odd room among a very odd group of people.

He wasn't aware that Willie had moved to the

table until the hand came on his shoulder and his voice, with a playful note in it, but which still held a message, said, "Aye, she's beautiful. But she's not for sale, laddie. I'm her guardian, boyfriend, and as the old song says, I am her everything."

"And I am a painter." The words shot out. He hadn't meant to say that. He realized he should keep his mouth shut, at least for a time. He was new to this place; and they were being kind to him.

No one made a sound, until suddenly Willie tittered, then said, "Well, I'll be buggered!" and he looked at Dill Morgan, saying, "There's two of you now." Then, turning his head quickly toward Andrew again, he poked his head down to him as he said, "How old did you say you were?" And when the answer came, "Forty-two coming up forty-three, and can still do ten rounds," the room was once more filled with laughter, in which Dill Morgan's was the loudest now, leaving Willie to take hold of Delia's arm and to say quickly, "Let's get out of here; I'm losing." And they went out on the laughter. But no sooner had the door closed and Andrew had dropped into a chair than Win limped toward him and said, "You feeling bad again?"

"No, no!" he lied quickly; then added, "Head's still aching a bit."

"Then I'd get into your kip. You'll feel different in the mornin'. But by the way, in case you want to get up in the night and make a drink, I'll show you where the things are. Come on."

As Betty had taken him by the arm, so did Win

now, and the painter and the musician looked at each other, while Dill, in quite a conversational tone in which there was no aggressive note, said, "He thinks he's going to paint her."

Mickey Fenwick nodded as he said, "Yes, I guessed something like that . . . he was thunderstruck. But most people are when they first see her."

"Well, I hope he doesn't get on the wrong side of Willie, because he won't be as lucky as he was with the bruiser."

"I would say he's from some classy family, what d'you think?"

"Definitely some classy family. But if we sit back and wait, it'll all come out. It usually does."

"Yes, you're right, Dill," the violinist said, and as he rose from the chair he felt pleased, because it was a long time since the painter had given him a civil word. But there was one thing he had noticed: he had taken to the new addition; he wouldn't go for him and treat him as he did himself, and all because, in his own words, he prostituted his art by playing to the queues, instead of starving until he got into an orchestra.

4

After they had finished their tea in the restaurant, Jason lit a cigarette and looked across the table at Freddie and Gracie, and said, "I'm sorry; but then you knew it had to be done."

"When your separation is actually official, what will you do?"

Jason stubbed out his cigarette; then looking from one to the other, he said quietly, "Live with Maggie."

"Maggie?" They both spoke together. Then Gracie said, "You mean Marian's Maggie?"

"Which other Maggie is there?" Her father's voice was harsh now. "Of course Marian's Maggie."

"But she's . . . she's . . ."

He looked at his son, saying, "Yes. Yes, so much younger than me, twenty-five years to be exact, but we've been in love with each other for at least the last ten. However, unlike Janice and Robert we felt we shouldn't do anything about it, because it wouldn't be right. But during the last year I've said to myself, to hell with it! Life is quickly running out. I know I don't look my age but I *am* fifty-five; and she hasn't married, although she's had countless chances, simply because she's loved me."

Brother and sister looked down toward the table for a moment; and then it was Gracie who said, "Does . . . does Auntie Marian know?"

Jason smiled weakly now as he looked at her and said, "Oh yes, Auntie Marian knows. She's known from the beginning and has thought me a fool. And being my half-sister, she's had the privilege of telling me this a number of times."

"I . . . I suppose you'll live out there? It's a big house."

"Yes, Gracie, we'll live out there. In any case, we couldn't leave Marian alone, for she needs us both. And I love the place; it's been a haven of peace to me over the years. I don't think I could have stayed with your mother so long as I did if I hadn't had that respite."

Freddie now smiled at his father as he said, "I nearly got in before you."

"What!"

"I said, I nearly got in before you. I proposed to Maggie, you know."

"You did? You proposed to Maggie? When?" Jason's eyes were wide.

"Didn't she tell you? Oh, yes, I proposed to her." Freddie looked to the side now as if remembering, then went on, "I told her there was a slight difference in our ages, I knew that, but if she would wait until I was sixteen, then it would seem all right. It was only three years."

Freddie now watched his father's head droop as

he bit on his lip to prevent himself from laughing outright. But Freddie went on, "It didn't stop there, either."

"No?"

"No. When I was sixteen I reminded her, but not so enthusiastically as before. And I think I was relieved when she suggested we should wait a little while. And I agreed with her because then she seemed very old to me. What was she, nearly twenty-five?"

"Oh, Freddie; that is funny . . . but she's never told me of it: being who she is, she would consider it something very private and rather lovely."

Freddie colored slightly as he said, "Perhaps." Then he added, "She's rather attractive. I . . . . I think you're lucky, Dad. I only wish it wasn't making Mam so unhappy. It must have been yesterday morning she received the solicitor's letter, for she went berserk again. I don't know how Gracie here managed to hold her down until I got Grandfather from next door and he gave her a shot of something." He sighed now before adding, "I can't help but say I'm glad I've only got a few more days before term starts. But Gracie"—he jerked his head to the side—"she has to put up with it all the time. 'Tisn't fair, you know, Dad! And I'm going to say this: I . . . . I think you should have stuck it out, and stayed with her until you got her put into some place for her own good."

"Freddie!" Jason's voice held a bitter note. "I stayed there too long. That's been my trouble. I've been blackmailed for years with that bottle and

the threat of suicide, and God knows what else."
His voice had risen, and he glanced around the
restaurant before leaning across the table and
murmuring, "Would you rather have seen me up
for murder? Because that's what it would have
come to, and I'm not exaggerating. I stuck it year
after year until you were all settled in good positions, and even after that. But Christmas, and telling you all about the situation between Robert
and Janice, finished me, and I'm just waiting for
the moment when it is all exposed in the papers,
because there's an evil streak in her."

"Oh, Dad!"

He looked at Gracie's bowed head and said, "I
can't help it, Gracie, but that is the truth as I see it.
Anyway"—he suddenly straightened his back
and looked at his watch—"I must be going now;
my train leaves in half an hour."

Neither of them asked where he was going, for it
would be asking for the route they knew.

He had paid the bill and as they were all standing in the foyer of the restaurant he said quietly,
"You know you're more than welcome down there
at any time, for long or short stays. There's
enough room for a regiment."

Neither of them smiled or responded to the invitation. But when they were in the street Gracie
reached up and put her arms around his neck and
kissed him, and as she did so she whispered, "I
want you to be happy, Dad." And when he said,
"Thanks, my dear," there was a break in his
voice.

Next he was shaking his son's hand and as usual Freddie stated facts: "There's nobody very happy at the moment, is there?" he said. "Auntie Janice and Uncle Robert are in an awful state about Andrew."

"Yes. Yes, I know. Has nothing further been heard of him?"

"No; not since he went in a taxi one day, took most of his paints, brushes and easel, and packed a case with shirts and underwear and other necessaries, then told Patterson he was staying with his artist friend. Patterson, of course, got in touch with Uncle Robert, and he came straight down here; but he's seen neither hilt nor hair of him, and heard nothing until that strange phone call."

"Yes. Yes, that strange phone call." Jason was nodding now; then he added rather brightly, "But the main thing is, he's alive. And you know what I'd like to bet on: that he's been in search of his people and found them, and they're likely artists or something like that."

"But why couldn't he own up? Why couldn't he say?"

"Only he can answer that, Freddie. But look, I must hail this taxi."

He hailed the taxi; then before he closed the door, he said, "Think kindly of me, because I love you both very deeply."

As they walked away, neither of them made any comment: they were both dealing with their own thoughts. In Freddie's case it was of his father living with a girl not all that much older than Jessie. But Gracie's thoughts were running along a different channel: she was thinking of Andrew and his phone call to High Gully. Her Auntie Janice hadn't told her what Andrew had said, but her Uncle Robert had, for he had taken the call. Andrew had started the conversation by saying, "This is me, Father." And then there had followed the normal but worried inquiries from Robert: How was he? Was he all right? Was he coming home? Well, would he not give them his address? Any further questions Andrew checked by saying, "May I speak to Mother?"

To her he had said, "I shall always think of you as my mother; no one could ever replace you. To me you are beautiful, kind and good, and I love you and thank you for all you have done for me. Don't worry about me, I am all right. In fact, I am very well, and I may see you some day soon." And at that he had put down the receiver.

She missed Andrew. At times she ached to see him. The feeling for him had become intensified at Christmas. She had longed for him to be nineteen or twenty because then the two years between them wouldn't appear to be such a wide gap. Yet there was her father—a touch of bitterness entered into her thoughts now—going to live with a girl twenty-five years younger than himself. Why had she ever worried about being two years older than Andrew?

Sometimes she had the feeling that he was

quite near, in some house quite close by. One thing was sure; he was painting.

Freddie broke into her thoughts, saying, "We're all in a bit of a mess, aren't we; both houses? It's funny, but when I was little . . . well, not little, but younger, I used to think that High Gully and our house all belonged to one family . . . our family. But, strangely, I never fitted Grandma Montane into it. Isn't it amazing how she keeps herself secluded from all that's going on? Nothing seems to touch her: she acts like a dowager queen."

Further comment on their grandmother was immediately stifled, for Gracie had opened the front door and entered the hall, and there was the said grandmother, she who acted like a queen, shouting at them, "Where have you been? The doctor's upstairs."

"What's the matter? What's happened?"

It was Alice, holding onto her mistress's arm, who answered Freddie. "She's only tried to do herself in," she said, somewhat accusingly; "she shouldn't be left, somebody should be with her all the time."

The unfairness of this stirred Gracie to retort, "Then Alice, you should share your attention between the two houses. That might help."

"Oh, Miss Gracie, talking to me like that!"

"Oh, shut up!" Gracie tore off her hat and coat, threw them on a chair and ran upstairs, followed by Freddie. But as she ran across the landing toward her mother's room, the door opened and the doctor appeared and without any lead-up conversation, he said, "Get to the phone and call an ambulance."

At this, Freddie turned on his heels and ran back down the stairs, while Gracie followed the doctor into the bedroom immediately to gasp at the chaos that met her. Everything in the room that could have been moved and thrown about *had* been moved and thrown about. She had to step over a drawer out of which had spewed blouses and underwear; and glanced in amazement at the chest of drawers that had been pulled from the wall.

"Where's your father?"

She looked at the doctor's back as he bent over her mother and she said, "He's . . . he's gone to some friends in the country."

"I told him this would happen if he didn't do something. I'm only one voice. He should have insisted that she be put away, for her own good. Well, if the sherry hasn't killed her, that lot will have." He jerked his head toward the floor where four small bottles lay.

When Freddie entered the room and saw the chaos, he muttered, "Oh my God!" and the doctor replied, "Yes, but I don't think He is going to be much help in this case. Are they coming?"

"Yes; right away, they said."

"Well, they should be here in three minutes; they're quite near."

The doctor again took hold of Rose's hand and after a moment said on a lighter note, "Good; it's still there." Then, looking at Gracie, he asked, "Do you know what's brought this on? Anything more than usual?"

She couldn't say, "Yes, she would have had a letter from the solicitor, telling her that her husband was applying for a legal separation."

When she shook her head, he muttered, "Well, she was ready for it anyway. I'm not surprised; it's been going on too long. A stubborn woman, stubborn woman." Then, straightening up, he turned and addressed Freddie, saying, "Her father being just a stone's throw away, doesn't he look in?"

"She won't have anyone looking in, Doctor," and Freddie had to stop himself from adding, "You should know that by now."

When the sound of a commotion came to them from the landing, the doctor, taking command now, said, "Push that lot of debris out of the way," and he lifted his foot and pointed it to the drawers and bases and cosmetic bottles strewn on the floor, "and open the door, else they won't know where to come."

Gracie had never liked this doctor and at this moment she had the desire to yell at him, "You're as much to blame as anybody. You didn't exercise your authority, because you've got a weakness for the bottle yourself . . ."

Ten minutes later, after the stretcher had carried Rose from the house Emily, who was still in the hall, shouted at Freddie, "You get your father back here at once. Do you hear me? You know where he is, so phone him and tell him. Scandalous!''

Freddie answered not a word, but went out and banged the door behind him. And Alice, taking Emily's arm, said, ''Come along, dear. Come along.'' Yet that deep, ordinary commonsense voice that still remained Emily's foundation told her that Rose was just doing what she herself had done many years ago, and for the same reason: a protest against the outcome of love gone wrong.

Gracie walked slowly along the hospital corridor, feeling weighed down with guilt. Her mother hadn't died; and now she would live to carry on her feud. Oh, why hadn't she gone? She would have known nothing about it. She had lived in torment and misery for years and had become a source of torture to all those around her. She couldn't remember back to when there was an atmosphere of happiness in her home, but she could recall the sound that caused her thereafter always to sleep with her head half-buried under the pillow, with the noise of angry voices coming from a room along the landing.

The corridor led to a hall which she crossed to enter a waiting room. She felt she must sit down until Freddie came back; the nurse was taking details from him.

There were two people only in the room, and the sight of one of them brought her to a dead stop. Her voice came out on a high note as she cried, *''Andrew! Andrew!''*

His name brought him half up from the seat; then he dropped back again when Gracie stood in front of him, saying, "How wonderful to see you! You've had a bleeding? Oh, my dear!" She glanced at the girl sitting on the form to his side, then went on, "Oh, it *is* good to see you. We've been so worried. Wait till I tell Auntie Janice and Uncle Robert and . . ."

"Hold on a minute, Gracie!"

The terse words caused her to step back from him, saying, "Oh, I'm sorry. I do go on, don't I? Always did. And you never feel well after a bleeding." She again glanced at the girl sitting by his side, and wondered who on earth she was. Her mind was in a whirl. "Freddie's here," she said, more calmly now. "He's upstairs giving particulars."

"Particulars? Who's ill?"

"Oh." Now Gracie's body seemed to slump and her voice became dull-sounding, as she said, "Mother. She . . . she took an overdose."

"Oh, I'm sorry." Andrew had pulled himself to the edge of the form. "Oh, I am. When did it happen?"

"Just this evening."

"Sit down," he said, pointing to the seat. Then, before she had time to move, he apologized: "Oh; by the way, this is Betty," and saying this, he put his hand in the girl's, and the action was as if he had opened a door and her heart was dropping through into a depth filled with sadness. Then his voice came at her, saying, "I know you will be surprised, but she's my sister, my real sister."

Gracie's eyelids blinked and a smile spread over her face, even as she thought, Her! his sister? That girl! Yet she turned toward her and said politely, "How d'you do?"

"Quite well, if it stops rainin'."

Andrew shook the hand within his, saying, "Now, Betty, stop it! Don't be silly."

Gracie looked at the boy whom she loved, had always loved; except that now he seemed to be no longer a boy, but a young man, someone even older than Freddie.

He was smiling up at her and again he said, "Sit down. It's a long story."

After she had taken the seat he asked, "Is your father here?"

She shook her head as she answered, "No. He's down at Auntie Marian's. Well, he will be by now. We had had tea with him and when we got home we found the place all upset, and . . . and"—her head drooped—"she had taken some pills."

"I am sorry. Will she be all right?"

"Yes, they say she'll be all right," then quickly added, "You know, I always thought you were quite near, somewhere in London."

He turned and looked at her, and he found she had altered, too. She looked weary, but prettier than she used to be; and yet the word "pretty" didn't suit her: she had a lovely face and a lovely manner, so kind. Oh, dear, dear. Here he was again, his head was muzzy. He had lost a lot of blood this time, and of all the people to come across in the hospital she would have to be the one. Well, it would make no difference. Then there was Freddie; he'd have to talk to them both, and thinking thus, the muzziness seemed to be ripped away by a second cry of recognition, this time from Freddie: "Why, Andrew! Andrew! my dear fellow. Andrew."

He had taken both Andrew's hands in his and was immediately admonished by Gracie: "Stop shaking him; you'll start his bleeding again. You know how it is," she warned him.

"Where've you been all this time? Oh, 'tis good to see you. Oh, wait till I tell . . ."

"If I have my way, Freddie, and you, too, Gracie, you'll tell nobody. Look, can we go and get a coffee somewhere? I must talk to you."

Freddie and Gracie were both startled by the cheap-looking piece sitting next to Andrew saying, in no small voice, "You're not goin' in any place to have any coffee. You're comin' back and gettin' to bed. If they'd had their way in there you wouldn't have been let out tonight." She leaned across him now and thrust her face toward the brother and sister as she added, "You heard what I said, didn't you? He's not goin' anywhere; nor is he talkin' all that much. Get it!"

"Betty! be quiet. You know nothing about this."

"I know more than you think. I'm quick on the uptake, and I can tell you this for nothing: your two friends here are wonderin' why the hell you've taken up with me. I don't think she believes I'm your sister."

"Oh, dear, dear! be quiet." Andrew's voice was weary. Looking at the startled pair, he said, "You'll get used to her. She means well, but she's right: you don't really believe she's my sister. Oh, I didn't tell you, did I?" He was looking at Freddie, and he stressed: "She *is* my sister, my *real* sister. No adoption this time. And she's odd, as you can see, but she's wonderful, too." And he smiled as he pushed at Betty's shoulder.

They stared at him. This wasn't the Andrew they knew: he was speaking as they had never heard him speak before. His voice was the same, but his tone and the words and his manner belonged to someone they didn't know. When he had a bleeding at home their Aunt Janice put him to bed and cosseted him for at least two days. But here he was sitting in the dingy waiting room, his nostril packed to three times its normal size, his face as white as a sheet, and talking as they had never heard him talk before.

Another feature about him—a quickly formulated thought in each of their minds: he seemed at home, at ease, as if he had lived with people like this girl all his life. It was evident that if she *was* his sister, he had taken to her. Well, if there were a sister, thought Gracie, there would be a father and a mother, too. They must get to the bottom of this.

"Look," she said, "there's plenty of room at our house, why don't you . . . ?"

Andrew put out a hand and caught her wrist, saying, "I've got a home to go to, dear, and I'll be well looked after."

"We'll . . . we'll come with you, then."

"No, you'll not. Oh no!"

"Why not?" It was the girl speaking again. "Why not? In any case they'll ferret you out sooner or later. They'll only follow us tonight, won't you?" She looked straight at Freddie, and he, with a half smile on his face, admitted, "We just might; for one thing's sure, we're not going to lose sight of him now. His people have been most distressed, as we all have, wondering what he was doing, or what might have happened to him."

"They knew I was painting. I told them on the phone. Anyway, yes, you might as well come along. But one thing—" he now put his hands out to them both, saying, "please, do this for me: keep it to yourselves. Don't tell Mother and Father where I am or what I'm doing. Just don't mention me for a time."

They were both silent; then Gracie asked quietly, "Don't you intend ever going back home?"

He looked down for a moment before he answered her, "I don't know. Sometimes I long for the peace, other times I wonder how I've stood it all these years, pressing down the urge to fly those hills, those mountains, the barrenness of it and the beauty. The odd thing is the beauty never touched my feelings, never made me want to paint, never touched me in that way."

"Look . . . don't sit there yappin'; you should

be lyin' down. That nurse told you and that you should come back and have iron injections or something."

"Yes, or something." He went to pull himself up from the seat, and when Betty's arm was thrust under his oxter he didn't push her off. But as they all walked out of the room, he said to Gracie, "Don't you want to stay with your mother?"

"It wouldn't be any use: the doctor said she won't wake until tomorrow morning. We'll be here then, and Father, too . . . I hope." The last two words sank away.

After a ten-minute journey in a taxi they were mounting flight after dusty flight of stairs, causing Freddie's eyes to widen and Gracie's mouth to gape as their nostrils were assailed by the variety of smells, and even more so when they entered the big, odd-looking, musty-smelling room that seemed to be filled with men. Two were sitting at a table eating, one was standing at the end of the table cutting bread, and another, a big man and dust-covered, was about to go through a door at the far end of the room. But simultaneously they all stopped and stared at the group just entering the room, and their eyes held the same question, which Betty answered in her usual way: "Stop gapin', they don't eat raw meat," she snapped.

Then, as Andrew made for a chair to the side of the table, both the painter and the violinist rose to their feet. And it was Mickey who pushed his chair forward in Gracie's direction, and as she sat slowly down on it she muttered, "Thank you."

His elbow resting on the table, Andrew supported his head in the palm of his hand, and he muttered, "Well, Betty, get on with it. Make the introductions."

For answer, she came back quickly, "Well, what do I know about them?"

Andrew now looked up at Willie who had come to his end of the table and he asked him, "Did you ever know her, Willie, not to be able to make something up? They are my cousins, adoptive of course. Their father and my adoptive mother are half-brother and . . . half-sister."

"Well, how was I to know that?"

"Yes, you are right, Betty: how were you to know that?"

It was Willie who now took over, saying, "Well, any friend of Andrew's is welcome. My name is Willie Grabelly. This is my house, or flat or apartment, whatever you want to call it. I was born here." Then he tossed his head and said, " 'Tisn't mine. Like everybody else in the place, I rent it. But as I like company and—" he laughed now as he added, "bossing people about, 'cos that's me job you know, I'm on the buildin's, smashin' them up, not buildin' them, I let parts of this off to fellas. So"—he now nodded from Gracie to Freddie— "that's why it looks strange to you, I suppose, the cubicles an' things. But we're all good mates. This gentleman here"—he threw out his hand toward Dill—"is Mr. Morgan. He, like your cousin there, is a painter." Now he bent toward Dill and on a laugh he said, "But a different kind of painter, eh? Not so much splashing about as Andrew there." Then, turning to Mickey, he said, "Believe it or not, that one is a violinist, and a good 'un at that, if I say so. And if I had my way he'd be in Henry Hall's band."

As if greatly touched by this remark, Mickey hung his head.

When Willie, pointing now to the small man, said, "And here we have Mr. James Winterbottom"—he stressed the man's name—"who's cook, bottle-washer and Jack-of-all-trades, and he's just about to ask if you would like a cup of tea. Aren't you, Win?"

James Winterbottom smiled broadly; then, looking at Freddie, he said, "Yes, I can offer you a cup of tea, sir, real tea . . . but coffee . . . well, that will be of a sort."

"Thank you very much." Freddie paused, then looked down on Gracie, and she, making herself smile at the little man, said, "Yes, please. I would enjoy a cup of tea."

"Well now, that's all settled. So would somebody get our gentleman visitor a stool from the kitchen or offer him a bit of the form?"

"It's all right. It's all right." Freddie laughed. "I'm used to standing."

At this, Betty's voice broke in again: turning to Andrew, she said, "Now the introduction pantomime is over, you're gettin' yourself onto your bunk, aren't you?" and he, smiling at her, said, "Yes, nurse; I'll be very pleased to. Will you excuse me?"

He was looking toward the two people with whom he had practically grown up, and if they appeared like strangers to him at this moment, in their turn they were again trying to explain to themselves just how he appeared to them, for there was no vestige of the Andrew they once knew, except perhaps for the packed nostril. He could have been a much older relative of that boy whose eighteenth birthday they had celebrated last December.

When a backless chair was brought from the kitchen by Win, explaining as he placed it at Freddie's side, "The stool was too low," Freddie said, "Thank you, thank you. I'll be fine."

"Well, if I were you," Willie now put in, "I'd pull up to the table. You can talk better there. Those two are finished their meal; as for me, I'll go and get the dust off meself; and when I come back you won't recognize me." And he laughed as he added, "I've got a sister, you know, who won a beauty competition." And when Betty said, as one would in an aside, "And I've got an aunt who's a belly dancer," the room rang with laughter.

Andrew was leaning for support with two hands on the table while his body shook; then he slowly turned his head and looked at Freddie, and when he saw him covering his wide-open mouth he muttered, in fact almost spluttered, "You see what I mean. It's a new world." Then, as the laughter died down, he walked toward his cubicle unaided, having pushed Betty gently aside.

There followed a lull in the conversation until it became slightly embarrassing, and then Gracie, who had a natural gift for surmounting awkward moments, looked at Mickey and said, "Where do you play your violin, Mr. Fenwick?"

Mickey pursed his lips, glancing toward Dill, then at Gracie, and said, "Theatre queues, anywhere where there's anybody to listen, and be appreciative."

"Oh." There was a pause now before she spoke again: "I've heard some very good playing in the streets. There was Raymond Cranbury. I'm sure you've heard of him. That's where he used to play first, and . . . and the last thing I read about him, he was touring America."

"Yes. Yes, he was. But, you know, miss, nowadays there are not many old eccentric gentlemen picking up fiddlers and sending them to the academy. I've been waiting for one for a long time."

Dill Morgan now said, "You're young yet, there's plenty of time."

Mickey cast a grateful glance on the taciturn older man, but what he was going to say was checked by Freddie saying to Dill, "And you paint?"

"Yes," was the brusque reply; and after a short pause, he asked, "What do you do?"

With an almost deprecating shake of his head, Freddie replied, "Nothing really. Well, I'm up at Oxford. I . . . I go back next week for my last year."

There was another silence now before Dill asked, "What's your subject?"

"Mathematics."

"Mathematics?"

"Yes; very dry."

"You're going to teach?"

"Quite candidly, I don't know. I've reached that stage when I don't know what I'm going to do."

They all turned and looked at Betty now, who was sitting at the end of the table, for she was making a statement: "I'm good at figures, too. I can reckon up like nobody's business. I was goin' to go in an office at one time." When she paused and shrugged her shoulders Dill said, "You mean you were good at arithmetic; mathematics is not just counting up, Betty." And at this she came back at him, with, "Well, it's all figures, isn't it?"

"No." He shook his head.

"Well, you go on, clever clogs, and explain what it is."

Freddie wanted to say, "She's right in a way, for the theory of numbers is the basis of mathematics," but he was on delicate ground here so he turned to Betty now, saying, "I'm sorry, but I really can't explain it, not to make any sense. It's sort of analysing things, getting to the bottom of them, if you like, looking for patterns."

"Well," she came back sharply, "if you want to analyse things you've come to the right place. There's plenty to analyse in here. Just take that handsome film star—" and she nodded toward Willie, who was combing his wet hair as he entered the room, and he said, "What's she on about now?" which she brushed aside, saying, "You shouldn't be wearin' one of Andrew's shirts; you'll never get it buttoned."

"You mind your own damn business."

"It is mine. I look after his clothes."

As if Andrew had heard the altercation, he called from the cubicle, "Gracie! Freddie! Here a minute, please."

They rose hastily from the table, but when they reached the cubicle and found they had to edge their way in side by side along the low plank bed, they really could not believe what they were seeing: Andrew was propped up on a pillow and a cushion and he was covered by what looked like a red hospital blanket. He put his hands out to them and brought them bending down to him, then whispered, "Look, please don't worry about me. I'll tell you something"—his voice was very low—"I've never felt so free or happy in my life. I know it's an awful-looking place, but they're a very decent lot, couldn't be kinder, and all struggling to make a living. You two . . . and I, we know nothing about this kind of life; but at least, I'm learning. It's rough, it's primitive, it's disgusting at times, but there's an honesty and a kindness running through it that opens one's eyes. So please don't worry about me. And . . . do . . . do keep your promise and don't mention my whereabouts to the folks."

"Don't you ever mean to come back?" Gracie's voice was hardly audible, and Andrew's was much the same when he answered her. "Some day. Well, not go back to stay, but to visit them." Then he added, "Imagine Father's face if he came in that room. I can hear him immediately saying that not one of his workmen would deign to tolerate such quarters, and that his animals were better housed."

He was smiling at them, but it disappeared when Freddie said, "They are worried sick, Andrew. Just let us tell them we've seen you and that you're all right."

"No. No. They would get it out of you. Mother would. Oh yes, Mother would."

"Have you any money?" It was Gracie asking the question, and he nodded at her, saying, "Enough for the present. But I'm working hard and if things get desperate Dill will take me to his agent, who's a daylight robber, but who, nevertheless, keeps the wolf from his door.

"And, what's more, I've learned more about painting from him in the last months than I did in the two years in Edinburgh." He squeezed their hands now as he entreated, "So you won't, will you?"

They both shook their heads, but Freddie said, "No, we won't, but it's against the grain. Anyway, may we come here and see you now and again?"

"Oh, as often as you like. I never go out in the evenings and . . . and Dill, well, very rarely." His eyes seemed to rest a moment longer on Gracie as he said, "I'd be pleased to see you. Because there are times, I must confess, when I miss the old days, but just now and again when I'm like this." He was smiling now as he pointed to the padding sticking from his nostril. "And Mother used to make such a fuss. But she's got a good substitute—" he nodded toward the half-drawn curtain—"Betty; isn't she a star? A wonderful character." His lips spread into a broad smile now as he said, "She organizes my life."

"And everybody else's, I should imagine," whispered Freddie.

"Yes, just about." After a short silence he said, "She'll see you to a taxi."

"Oh, we won't trouble her."

Andrew nodded toward Gracie now, saying, "Well, it's either you don't trouble her, or somebody troubles you both before you get out of the district or even round the block. It's a tough area!"

Again they both shook their heads; then Gracie, bending further down, kissed him on the cheek, saying, "Good-night, dear. I'll keep popping in."

"Do that. Yes, do that."

It was as if those in the kitchen had been listening to every word, because there was Betty waiting for them with her coat on and a headscarf precariously covering her bouffant hair, and she greeted them abruptly, "You ready, then?"

"Yes. Yes."

After the round of good-nights and the final promise to call again, the three of them went out into the darkened street, and Betty muttered quietly, "If you see a group coming toward you, walk close together. And if they stop, leave the talkin' to me.''

It was on a laugh that Freddie said, ''Oh, definitely,'' but like a flash she came back with, ''Don't be so bloody sarky until you know what you're bein' sarky about!''

Following this the only thing to be heard was the sound of their own footsteps. No group appeared; nor did they meet anyone as they passed derelict buildings and negotiated an open, rubble-strewn piece of land. Then quite suddenly, they were in the main thoroughfare, and the relieved impressions of Freddie and Gracie were as if they were entering civilized society.

It was Betty who hailed a taxi, and when it drew to a stop she checked their goodbyes by saying, ''You'll not split on him, will you? because he's all right where he is. He's sortin' himself out from whatever life he had been leading; and he needed to. And what's more, he's me brother, me real brother, not by adoption.''

''You can trust us,'' said Freddie; ''and . . . and we do thank you for looking after him,'' and she answered flippantly, ''I should be working in the Battersea Dogs' Home.''

Betty watched the taxi drive away, then stood looking pensively into the throng of traffic.

She was considering her reactions to them both, and before she moved on she decided she liked him better than she did her. She was a bit snooty, and hadn't had much to say, except to

Andrew. And if she knew anything she had her eye on him all right: she recalled their meeting in the waiting room, all gooey she went, just like somebody at the pictures.

5

Freddie was on his way to lunch before meeting his father. He had crossed into Trafalgar Square, and was passing the National Gallery, when his head turned sharply as he saw the girl coming down the steps.

He was used to walking in London. He was used to brushing shoulders with all types of people. And her type was very common: the type that went overboard, lathered their faces with make-up, took fashion to stupid extremes, skirts worn very long or very short, and went in for outrageous colors; it was a commonness further emphasised by their voices; a type he had never really thought about, but had accepted was just part of London. Some accompanied the barrow boys. Most of them would work in shops. But none of them, he was sure, would ever go into ordinary service, as likely their mothers had. This was a different age into which had come the wireless and the talkies, and not only that, but color.

There she was tripping down the steps as if she was going into a dance. But what steps! those leading from the National Gallery. What on earth had she been doing there? she of all people!

She had reached the bottom but she hadn't noticed him, and he hurried forward, crying, "Hello! there."

She turned swiftly, blinked at him, then said, "Oh it's you."

"Yes, it's me." He looked up toward the steps. "Been to the National Gallery?"

She drew her chin into her neck, and in an assumed refined voice replied, "Yes, sir, I've been to the National Gallery. You now want to ask me, don't you, what I was doin' there? Me of all people! Don't you? That's what you want to ask?"

He laughed before he answered, "Yes; yes, I do."

"Well, I'll tell you. I wanted to look at the pictures, 'cos that is, you know, where they hang a lot of pictures, the National Gallery. Perhaps you didn't know that."

It was his turn now to draw his chin into his neck and to assume a manner: "Well, I'd 'eard of it, miss, I'd 'eard of it," he said.

Her attitude changed in a flash: "Don't mimic me!" she said. "I can mimic you, but please don't mimic me."

"Why not? Now, I ask you, why not? And anyway, why are we standing here talking like this? Tell me straight, why have you been in there?"

"Well, without any palaver, I can answer that question. Andrew and Dill are always talkin' about pictures, the merits of this an' the merits of that, an' this thing they call the Re'nais'sance. That's the right pronunciation, ain't it, Mr. Montane?"

"Yes, that is the right pronunciation, Miss Birchcomb."

"Well then, as I 'ad a bit of time to spare . . . it's one of me laryngitis days, you know."

His eyes widened and his head came forward as he repeated, "Laryngitis days?"

"It's a day off from work 'cos when me ma or me gran are not good, then I 'ave laryngitis. It is not like a disease, it doesn't last very long. I always go back within two days. I'm thinkin' I'd better cut it out, because Miss Whalebone Corset . . . I mean"—she shook her head—"that's a nickname we give to her who's over our department."

"Whalebone Corset?"

"Well, yes. You see her name's Concert an' she's as stiff as a ramrod and over forty, if she's a day, an' not married. Anyway, laryngitis is an excuse for gettin' orf. Most of 'em have bad backs." She grinned at him now. "I should 'ave picked on that, too, shouldn't I? because unless you 'ave an X-ray, they don't know if you're swingin' the lead or not."

Her language, her manner, the look of her, and that awful hair-do! She could be pretty, very pretty, but she had ruined it. The word that fitted her really was the one he had thought of earlier. Yes, she was common. He couldn't imagine meeting up with anyone who could represent the word more fully. But she had something else, a sort of attraction. He couldn't put a name to it.

And she had gone into the National Gallery to look at the pictures.

He said, "How did you enjoy your visit to the Gallery?"

There was a pause before she answered, "If you'd asked, did I enjoy my visit? I wouldn't've answered you, yes or no. But you said, 'How did I enjoy it?' Well, I've still got to sort that out in me mind. Some of the pictures I found very pleasing and I wanted to stand staring at 'em. But others were enough to make your knickers turn red, rapes an' things, an' two pictures with figures completely starkers. Oh, I suppose"—she glanced at him now—"you're used to all that. An' so, in a way, are we down our quarter, but it's more private like. I should imagine a lot of folks just go in there, not to learn about the art business, but to get goose-pimples, sort of."

He wanted to roar with laughter. Goose-pimples. What he said was, "You're right. I should imagine so, too."

"Anyroad, I just wanted to see what it was all about, 'cos I sit listenin' to them two at night and I can't butt in an' say anything, say me opinion like." Now she turned a grinning face toward him, as she said, "We 'aven't met but twice, 'ave we? But you'll 'ave recognized I like buttin' in."

"Yes. Yes, I sort of suspected you did."

He was taken by surprise when suddenly she said, "Well, 'ere we are. I've got to turn off 'ere."

"Wait! Are you . . . are you off all afternoon?"

"Yes; but I've got things to do at 'ome. Me ma's

not too good. It's funny, but when Andrew's bleedin' so is she."

"Does Andrew visit his mother?"

"No."

"No?"

"No; that's what I said, no. They didn't take to each other. And it's funny, I could understand him not likin' me dad, 'cos they 'ad the fight and 'e managed to knock him out; I mean, Andrew knocked me dad out. Oh, don't ask me how." She closed her eyes now. "You'll 'ear all about it if you go visitin' the flat. But let's face up to it, Andrew doesn't like me ma."

"But . . . but he's been looking for her for a long time, I think, wanting to . . ."

"Yes, wantin' to find out what she was like. Well, it didn't please 'im. His mother, or his adopted mother, must 'ave been . . . of course, not must 'ave, but is a different type altogether."

"But . . . but he likes you very, very much."

"Yes, I know he does." She nodded now, and there was a quiet smile on her face as she said, "I . . . I somehow seem more real to him, I think. I belong to him more—I'm the only one, you see— and . . . and I feel the same about him. I've now got a brother and he's got a sister."

He looked at his watch. It showed half-past twelve. Impulsively now he said, "I'm starving. There's no one at home to make meals now. I'm going to have something to eat. Will you join me?"

She stared at him hard before she said, "In a restaurant?"

"Yes. Yes, of course, in a restaurant."

And at this she shook her head, saying, "No. Ta. Thanks, but not like this. Me 'air's not done or anything. I'm goin' to 'ave it done this afternoon. Thanks all the same, but not like this."

"Well, we needn't go to a restaurant. Where do you usually eat?"

"Jonathan's pease an' pies, or bacon an' egg fry. They're good, an' plenty of it."

"All right, let's go to Jonathan's, wherever that is."

Again she stared at him and without moving, but she looked him up and down. He was tall, his clothes were well cut; he was wearing a trilby hat. Nobody need ask what class he came from. He left the same impression on her as Andrew had done when she first set eyes on him. He would stick out like a sore thumb in Jonathan's, just as she would in a restaurant, only more so in her case.

"All right, let's go. But mind, if there's any girls in there from my department, the one I'm in now, shovels and spades, you'll have to put up with them whistling."

"I think I would enjoy that. What do you mean by shovels and spades? Children's sea-side . . . ?"

"No, not children's seaside toys. Gardenin' stuff, down in the basement. If you open your mouth too much like I do, or you 'aven't got much up top, you're pushed off one of the counters on the first floor and into the basement . . . garden equipment. God! how I hate gardens."

His voice held surprise as he said, "You hate gardens?"

"That's what I said, I hate gardens. If a man comes down he asks for a shovel, but if a woman comes down it's usually . . . a spade . . . a lady's spade."

"Are there really ladies' spades?"

"Oh, aye, half the size of the men's. And it's usually the middle-class twits who play around with 'em. They'll sneak in, 'cos it's Woolworth's, you know. It's funny to hear them if they see somebody they know. And they're nearly all middle-aged, up from the country for a day, fat-arsed fannies the lot of 'em."

When her voice was cut off abruptly, he closed his eyes, stepped aside and almost overbalanced one of the ladies she had just represented, and profuse with his apologies he said, "Oh, I am sorry, madam. Are you all right?"

The lady smiled at him and walked on; whilst he had to take three or four hurried steps to catch up with Betty. Her head was lowered as she muttered, "I'm sorry."

He said nothing, for he couldn't speak: he was shaking inside with laughter, when suddenly his mind gave a jerk and told him that last night his mother had tried to commit suicide and that in a short while he would be seeing her. He swallowed deeply, and as she muttered, "You're so easy to

talk to, just like as if . . . well—'' her head came
up and her face looked angry and her voice
sounded the same as she said, ''I . . . I try to be
funny because it makes people laugh, for when
they laugh they forget themselves a bit. But that
wasn't funny, it was just coarse; and I know the
difference, an' that woman you nearly knocked
over might have heard and it would 'ave made her
feel awful, the same as I feel when people call me
common.'' She was looking ahead now and her
step was brisk. ''Oh, I know what they think of
me. Common an' funny, that's Betty. Well, if you
want to know somethin', I don't like it, either,
bein' thought common or bein' over-funny.''

They had come to a narrow street off the main
road, and he grabbed her arm and pulled her to
one side away from the passers by. And then,
taking her by the shoulders, he shook her, saying,
''Stop it! Stop dissecting yourself . . . pulling
yourself to bits.''

''That's what I mean.'' She was nodding at him.
''You thought I was ignorant an' all and that I
wouldn't know what 'dissecting' meant, so you
had to explain it by saying 'pulling yourself to
bits.' ''

''Nothing of the kind.'' His words were slow and
quiet now. ''And I don't think you're common.''
And now, in some strange way, he knew he
wasn't lying, or if he was it didn't matter. And now
there were words pouring out of him: ''As you
said, this is only the second time I've met you, but
it's as if I've known you for a long time. I like to

listen to you. I think that behind all the façade that you put on you're highly intelligent."

. . . Why should he suddenly think of Helen Clayton, who was in the same year at University, and to whom he could talk? Their minds were on the same level. He liked Helen. And only recently he had asked himself how much. Because he couldn't imagine himself spending his life with a woman who couldn't follow his thinking. And up till yesterday he had been looking forward to returning to college just for the thought of seeing her and enjoying one of their long exchanges again. But here he was going on rapidly, saying, "It's a pity I've got to go back next week . . . to Oxford. We could have got to know each other better. Still, there's five more days."

He took her hand now, saying, "Come on, pies and pease." Then he added, "The shovels and spades can wait."

She said nothing but walked by his side, her head down, her teeth rhythmically nipping at her bottom lip.

He had met his father at the station and had quickly endeavored to elaborate on what he had told him on the phone last night, and was somewhat surprised that Jason had made very little comment on it; in fact, that he had little to say about anything.

And now they were both standing near the hospital bed in a small side ward. The door was closed; but Rose's voice must have been audible in the corridor, for a nurse popped her head in and inquired, "All right?" Jason had nodded at her and answered, "Yes, nurse, quite all right." Then turning he looked down on Rose, adding, "But as usual."

"You won't get it. I've done nothing for which you can claim a separation."

"What about withholding conjugal rights, not only for the last six years but for some time before that. Also being a known alcoholic."

"I'm not an alcoholic."

Both Jason and Freddie turned and looked toward the door; then in a low but definite tone, Jason said, "Don't be silly, woman. What do you think has brought you here? I understand it wasn't so much the pills you took as all the drink you had taken beforehand. But then, you had measured both, hadn't you; just to frighten me, wasn't it? To start the blackmail again? Well, all I can say, Rose, is, the next time do it properly. The time is past for soft talk. It's your life. You can either take their advice, the advice that's been given you for years, and go for treatment, or you can continue to be the sherry sot which, in the end, will do the trick for you, because, from what I hear from the doctor, your liver is already damaged."

"I'll have you on your knees yet," she said, and then added, "You were born a bastard and you'll remain one," which made him turn quickly from the bed, and only Freddie's hand gripping his arm restrained his father from rushing from the room. But when his mother's voice went on, "What will you do if you get your separation, dear? Go and live with your half-sister? You've always hankered for that, haven't you? Your twin enjoys her filthy obscene life, but I'll spoil that if it's the last thing I do. I told you a few weeks ago that I would hold my hand about exposing them to the papers, that it was all up to you. Well, it's still up to you."

Freddie released his hold and Jason flung round and stared at his wife as he growled, "Well, Rose, I wouldn't hang on, because they are prepared for your onslaught. So, when you get up, do your worst. But I'd try to be sober before you allow yourself to be interviewed, because people might get the wrong ideas of why you are doing this."

Rose now pulled herself up from the pillows, yelling, "I'll spoil your little game, Jason Montane, some way or another. If I die, and I'll pick my own time for that, too, I'll haunt you."

"Do that, Rose. Do that. Whatever will make you happy, you do it," and Jason turned about, leaving Freddie standing with his head bowed, and feeling as if he were the rope in a tug of war, pulled first one way and then the other. His mother's deadly pale face, her clenched jaws, her clawing fingers on the bed cover, filled him with pity, yet at the same time he understood the strain his father had been under, coping with her for a long, long time.

He moved up the bed now and tried to take hold of his mother's jerking hand, but she pulled it away from him, saying, "You're all on his side, aren't you? Don't say you're not, because you would never have left me all on my own. The cruelty of it. You don't know him. You think he's nice and kind. He's not, he's cruel. Indifference can be the worst cruelty that one has to suffer. All he's ever thought about is his dear sister Marian, just to be near her. Oh, I know what's been going on."

"No, Mam; no, he never has. I know that. No, he hasn't."

Her body became still. "What do you mean, you know that?"

"Well, I know that he hasn't had those thoughts about Auntie Marian."

She narrowed her eyes at him. "Has he got them about anybody else?"

He shook his head. "I . . . I don't know."

"You do! You do!"

"No, Mam, no. I . . . I don't. Lie quiet now. Please, Mam." He bent toward her. "Do what they say. Do what they ask, it's for your own good. After the treatment you can be a new woman."

"Get out! Get out of my sight. You're another one who doesn't believe me. Why should I want to be a new woman? I don't drink. I take a glass of sherry now and again, but that's different; I don't drink."

A nurse appeared in the doorway and he turned quickly, saying, "All right, Mam, all right. Don't worry. Don't excite yourself. I'll . . . I'll come in tomorrow." And at that he hurried out.

Jason was waiting for him at the hospital door. They looked at each other but didn't speak until they were in the street, when Jason said, "Let's go somewhere and have a cup of tea."

They walked on in silence for some way until, hearing his father muttering, he turned to him.

"And to think that she once appeared so doll-like, so gentle, even pliable," Jason was saying; and he, too, turned to look at his son and to say, "You remember, Freddie: women have two sides. If they once suspect they don't own you completely they turn into devils. And another thing: never marry a woman until you ask yourself, if it came to the push, could you put up with her twenty-four hours a day, and I mean twenty-four hours; and if the answer is yes, then ask for how long." He sighed now; then after more muttering, added further, "Make sure you want her, you need her, and in every way . . . every way, mind, for a wife who can't be a friend will soon become a foe."

Doll-like, gentle, pliable: there was conjured up in Freddie's mind a picture of Betty. There was nothing doll-like about her. Oh no. Nor, as yet, had he detected any gentleness. As for being pliable, he couldn't imagine her ever being moulded by anyone from what she was into anything else. And yet she had something that was . . . Well, what?

He could put no name to the attraction she had for him; he only knew he wanted to be in her company again, to listen to her, to be enveloped in the atmosphere she created.

Yet, as she stood and must appear to others, it

was a pity that she would never change, for she did look a mess, he had to admit, and . . . and he had asked her to go to the pictures tomorrow night.

PART TWO
1937

1

It was June, 1937. He had come down from Oxford. The telegram, yesterday, sent on by the porter, had brought the news that he had been awarded a first. And now he was in his father's flat and being congratulated by the family: Steven, Jessie, and Gracie, and Steven was saying, "And you're off to a good start, with Uncle Robert getting you into Steerman's. That was part of his grandfather's old firm, I understand, and they've still got an interest in it. You're lucky, you know, boy, for jobs for graduates, no matter how brilliant, are few and far between."

"Chances are better than they were last year." His father was nodding at him now, and Steven said, "Yes, perhaps, but just for teaching. And then there are hundreds after the same jobs."

"It will all be different when the war starts," and Jessie's words immediately changed and held the subject of their attentions.

"What d'you mean, when the war starts?" said Freddie.

"According to the doctors"—she was smiling now—"four of them, they say that as sure as there'll be epidemics, there'll be a war. Doctor

Jones and Doctor Paisley were apparently walking the wards during the last war and they remember the atmosphere beforehand in the newspapers and such. They don't trust Germany; and who would with that Mr. Hitler shouting his mouth off. Anyway—'' she put out her hand across from her chair to the couch where Freddie was sitting and, patting his knee, she said, ''We're all very proud of you. Even old Steven here, who's as jealous as sin.''

''Don't be daft, Jessie! I'm not jealous. I'm only too pleased for him. I am.'' He thumped Freddie on the shoulder, saying, ''You know I am. That blooming nurse is a stirrer if ever there was one.''

''Well, you have always kept on saying you wished you had gone up.''

''Yes, but it was my own choice, and I chose right, didn't I, Dad?''

''You certainly did, where position and money are concerned. Where are they sending you next?''

''Italy, I think. There's a fellow wants a villa built exactly like the one he holidayed in. Some people have got more money than sense. I get a bit mad when I see the waste that money is put to. Then I have to tell myself it's giving me a job. But apart from all this,'' said Steven now, ''I would like to bring up this business about Andrew. I really think it's too bad to keep them in the dark up there. And Aunt Janice looked awful the last time I saw her. It must be almost three months since he phoned her and she can't understand why he won't show himself. And candidly, neither can I, when he agreed to see us—with the exception of you, Dad."

"Well, in that case," said Jessie, "you're a bit dull, for we've seen where he lives and whom he mixes with. And, more than that, you've met his mother and that frightful old hag of a grandmother. Then there's the vivacious Betty." She laughed now and looked toward Freddie before adding, "You still friendly with her?"

"Yes, Jessie, I'm still friendly with her, and determined to go on being friendly with her."

Surprisingly, the words brought no retort from the others, only silence, for there was something in Freddie's voice that expressed more than the words immediately implied, and now, quite quietly, he told them what it was.

"Now that I can see I've a good future ahead of me, I'm going to ask Betty to marry me."

Jason's mouth fell into a slight gape; Steven's eyes widened; Jessie laughed, a gentle laugh, but nevertheless with ridicule in it as she said, "Oh, Freddie; that's going a bit far, isn't it? All right, all right"—she held up a hand—"I've met her and she's jolly and full of personality, I admit. But she's an East Ender, the Cockney of Cockneys. They are what are called the salt of the earth, but that's among themselves . . . ."

She did not finish, because Freddie had risen sharply to his feet, saying, "Don't go on, Jessie. East Ender or Cockney or salt of the earth, or any other name you like to call her, let me tell you, she's worth all the people I've ever met, or am likely to."

"It's all right. It's all right, we understand," began Jason softly, but Freddie cut him off as he cried, "It isn't all right, Dad. And all I can say to you, Jessie, and to you, Gracie, too, you've been damned lucky you've never had to rough it. If you had you would have both gone under. You wouldn't have had the guts for it."

"Now! Now!" Jason came round the couch. "For goodness' sake, don't let us quarrel among ourselves. There's enough trouble outside. And I've got to say this to you, Freddie, when you're criticizing your sisters and making comparisons with regard to guts, which I'm translating into staying power, and patience, remember you've got to hand it to Gracie: it is she who goes home every night and has to put up with the racket there, because, we've got to face it, she's started again, the dry period didn't last . . . As for you, Steven, you won't go back, will you?"

"No, Dad. No. I couldn't stand it." Steven's head drooped and he turned away.

"Well, that leaves you, Jessie"—Jason's voice was curt now—"what about you? You could live out if you liked, now that you've passed your exams. So what about it, eh?"

Jessie turned her head away but made no reply.

And now Jason looked at Freddie, saying, "You've been down only five days and you've told me you're looking for rooms. So, I don't think you're the one to shout about guts."

Freddie hung his head for a moment and from that position he murmured, "Yes, you're right, Dad. But to get back to the point, whatever happens I mean to marry Betty . . . that is if she'll have me."

"You haven't asked her yet?"

He looked at Gracie now and shook his head as he said, "No, I haven't asked her yet. And when I put it to her, being who she is, she'll likely laugh in my face and say something similar to what you're all thinking, that such a match wouldn't work, that in fact it would be farcical. Unlike us here, she knows herself and faces up to herself. Anyway if you, Dad, can contemplate marrying a girl twenty-five years younger than yourself, I can't see from where the objection would come to my marrying a girl around about my own age but from a so-called lower class, because, chances being equal, they could both come off on the right side."

"Dear, dear. We are going into it," said Steven now. "It only needs me to drop a bombshell, and I might one of these days, because I've seen some beautiful dark-skinned ladies on my travels."

Freddie now smiled at his brother, saying, "Well, I'll bet you've never seen one like the big bricklayer has, she's a half-caste but weirdly beautiful, quite beyond description," and Gracie, breaking the tension still further, added, "Yes, you should come and have a look at her, but we'll engage an ambulance to carry you out once Willie sees you . . . Oh, I'll make a cup of tea," she said; "that's if you've got any in, Dad. Do you ever eat or drink here?''

"Sometimes.''

When Freddie followed Gracie to the kitchen, Jessie, rising from her seat, walked to the window and looked out for a moment before turning and facing her father and Steven. "He really means it about marrying that piece,'' she said. "She's as common as dirt. She knew I was onto her when I first saw her, and so she didn't take to me. She's of the same type as the woman scrubbing the hospital floors, a cheery cockney.''

"You'd be wise to keep your opinions to yourself, Jessie,'' Steven said; and Jason stared at his daughter and realized that he had never liked her; she was too much like her mother.

They were sitting in a quiet corner of the park. The sun was shining. In the far distance children were playing with a dog; they were going round and round in circles. Betty was looking toward them as she said, "You must feel wonderful knowin' that you've passed an' that there's a job lined up for you.''

"Stop evading the subject, Betty. I asked you a question, a serious question, and I'll repeat it, do you like me?''

Her body snapped round to him and she almost bawled at him, "Yes, I like you. I wouldn't be wastin' me bloody time walkin' out with you if I didn't like you.''

He smiled at her, saying, "Oh, we've been walk-

ing out, have we? That's another name for courting."

"It bloody well isn't."

"Stop swearing. I haven't heard you go at it for
some time."

"I 'aven't 'ad cause to go at it for some time.
But you get me goat, talkin' rubbish."

"Up till now I'm not aware that I've talked any
rubbish. All I've said is I want to ask you a question, and I asked you a question: Do you like
me?"

"Well, I've answered it. Satisfied?"

"No; far from satisfied, Betty. Now, look; come
off your high horse and lower your shield. All this
attitude of yours is just a cover-up, because you
know what's coming, don't you?"

"Well," she said, more quietly now, and she
poked her face toward him, "if you want us to go
on seein' each other, you won't go any further.
Understand? You're not daft or green. You know
what you're goin' to say can never get you anywhere, or me."

He gripped hold of her hands now and tugged
her toward him, and when their faces were almost
touching he looked into her eyes and said, "I love
you, Betty. I want you. I want you always near me.
I want to marry you. Oh—" As her body reared
from him he held her tighter and shook her arms
as he said, "Not straightaway, perhaps not for a
year or two, until I know where I am going in this
job and can set up a home. But I mean to . . .
set up a home, and with you. Because you do

care for me, don't you, more than just liking? Look at me."

At this, her head bowed and she wrenched her body from him, causing him to exclaim in surprise, "Oh! Betty, Betty. Don't! For the Lord's sake, don't cry. I couldn't imagine you . . ."

She was sniffling and groping for her handkerchief as she said, "No. No, you couldn't imagine me cryin', 'cos you know nothin' about me, not really, only this funny, brash, common piece that tickled your fancy."

"No! No!" He had his arm around her shoulders now. "You know that isn't true. Come on, dear, come on. Oh, anything, anything but make you cry. I never imagined."

She was facing him again. "No, that's what I said. You never imagined I could cry. Well, let me tell you somethin', Mr. Montane, I do a lot of cryin'. There's hardly a night goes by that I don't cry about one thing or . . . t'other."

"I'll never make you cry, Betty."

"Oh you"—her head wagged now—"you make me cry all the time, 'cos . . . 'cos all this business," and she now flung her hands wide, "can come to nothin'; an' you know it, you're playin' games."

"Oh, I don't know it." His voice was loud now. "And it's not coming to nothing. Here." He gripped her shoulders and pulled her round to him again. "As I see it at this minute, you wouldn't cry over me for nothing. Now, I've told you how I feel, but I haven't got words to express how deeply.

But I'm going to ask you, just simply, if you love me, or do you think you could love me?''

Her head drooped, her whole body slumped, and when she fell against his shoulder he held her tightly and stroked her silver-fair hair that was no longer sprayed and set into an unnatural stiffness. Then after a moment he lifted up her chin, and slowly he kissed her.

It was the first time they had kissed and it was of short duration. Then they were looking at each other and what she said now was, ''I'll never fit in, Freddie. An' your folks? Your father might accept me 'cos he's taken up with his own life, as you told me, but your nurse sister, never. We sparked off as soon as we met. She looked down 'er nose at me as if I smelt. I don't know about your older brother, what his reactions will be. But as for Gracie, oh well, Gracie likes me 'cos Andrew likes me. Whatever Andrew does it's all right with her 'cos she's so sotted with him.''

''Besotted.'' He was smiling now into her face.

''What?''

''It's besotted, not sotted. She is so besotted with him.''

''A . . . h''—it was a long drawn out sound—''that should prove somethin'. You see what I mean, yes . . . ?''

As she went to turn from him he pulled her to him again, kissed her once more on the lips, then said, ''That's only a beginning. You'll get used to it after a while.''

''You want me changed.'' Her voice was low

now and held a note of sadness. "Well, Freddie, I . . . I don't think I could ever change, not inside, not to keep it up. I can put on the manner, you know, I'm a good mimic, but just for a time. That isn't me."

"I know it isn't, dear, and I know it isn't the one that I want. I want the real you. But"—now he poked his face so close to hers that their noses touched and he moved his head backward and forward before saying softly, "but you're a smart little piece and you'll never say sotted again, will you?"

There was a slight grin on her face as she said, "You! still the clever bugger."

His head drooped now as he bit on his lip and muttered, "Oh, Betty; you are unique, you know."

She was laughing now as she said, "Well, don't try to explain that one, 'cos I know I am. There's only one of me an' I don't think they'll dig another up for a long time."

He was holding her tight now and they were rocking together. Then, pushing him from her, she said, "Let's talk serious, Freddie. Even lookin' at us we're like chalk an' cheese, that's without listenin' to us. Now, now." She wagged her finger in an admonishing movement at him as she went on, "Linkin' up with me could gradually cut you off from your folks. Oh yes, it could. An' be quiet, I must say this. But what's more important is my little lot. I could never leave me mother on 'er own. I'm fond of 'er, or perhaps a better way of puttin' it would be I'm sorry for 'er 'cos she's 'ad a rough time of it. So, I'd 'ave to see to 'er. Then there's me granny. But speakin' the truth now, I could put 'er into an old people's 'ome tomorrow without blinkin' an eyelid. She's never done or thought of anybody in 'er life but 'erself an' bein' respectable. Respectability. Oh, she's got a thing about bein' respectable, you wouldn't believe. That's why she pushed Mam into marryin' Dad. An' poor old Andrew was left on the doorstep, so to speak. That was a bloody awful thing to do."

He put in quickly, "But didn't you tell me some time ago that your father, in a letter, said this was his last trip on the banana boat?" He did not now laugh at the mention of the banana boat, but went on, "So I think your mother is his responsibility."

"Oh, yes, if he sticks to 'is word. But 'e's a flamin' liar half 'is time. It's odd"—she turned and looked at him—" 'e's a bruiser, a bully, 'e's everything I detest in a man, yet he cares for Mam. I think that's why he couldn't stand the thought of 'er 'aving a son. If it had been another daughter it mightn't 'ave been so bad, but the son was a male an' steppin' into 'is—" She paused then said in a more refined tone, "pre . . . serves."

This brought a sound of choking from him that ended on, "Oh, Betty!"

She said quietly, "I read a lot when I get the chance; but it's the pronouncin'. You see I don't hear people talkin' like what I read, very often."

She was again held tightly in his arms, and he muttered, "You are the most honest creature in the world," then added, "Don't worry about your mother. When the time comes we'll work out something . . . Oh, Betty, I do love you. I do, I do. It's a wonder I did as well as I did, that I even passed, because I couldn't get you out of my mind."

She was smiling into his face now as she said, "Did I interfere with your . . . 'nalysis?"

His laughter could have been heard at the far end of the park as he said, "Yes, Miss Birchcomb. You interfered with my analysis. But what's kept that in your mind, and to what does it refer?"

"Well, that night at the table when you said mathematics wasn't countin', I mean, wasn't just figures, an' you sort of 'ad to grope for things."

As if in wonder now, he held her at arm's length and as he looked at her face he saw it as beautiful and kindly, and loving and, what topped it all, intelligent.

Of a sudden he gripped her hand, pulled her to her feet, and cried, "Come on! Let's join the kids and the dog. Then we can grope our way through analysis as to why we did it."

She made no protest, just gave a hoot of a laugh, and then they were running hand in hand across the common, like two children who had just planned a life ahead and found it good.

Robert put down the phone and looked at Janice and, his voice as eager as his expression, he said, "That was Jason. He's found out where Andrew lives. At least, he's known for some time but promised not to tell. But now he thinks you should know. Andrew's been in hospital . . . he had a bleeding inside."

"Oh my goodness!" Janice closed her eyes and turned away, then said, "Is he still there?"

"As far as I can gather, no. He's living with a group of people and apparently has been very happy."

She looked at him and shook her head as she said, "We must go straightaway."

"No. No." He held up his hand. "I'm to go alone; Jason said the two of us would be too much. And . . . and the place where he's living . . . well, he seemed rather mysterious about it. Jason says he needs nursing, and as good as they are to him there, he's on his own quite a bit. So I'll get the late train, and I'd better start well before time, because there'll be drifts further along the road."

She came close to him now and took hold of the

lapels of his coat as if she were aiming to pull them together; but she kept her eyes cast down as she said, "It'll be lovely to have him back. I have missed him, and been so worried. He could have died and we would never have known."

"No; he wouldn't have died, dear"—he now stroked her cheek—"not in London where, apparently, he has been all the time, and surrounded by hospitals. Doctor Bracken has told you that you don't die of it unless you run out of blood. Once you can get that stopped, you're all right. But, of course, he wasn't thinking of bleeding inside."

"May I not go up with you?" Janice pleaded.

"No, no, my dear. You stay here. Jason was definite about it. Although he insists they've all been kind to him, he says we'll find the place rather a surprise. And he doesn't think you should go, not yet, anyway."

"Look, Robert, Jason forgets I was a nurse," Janice said a little tartly now; "and that I'm used to seeing all kinds of people in hospitals. Really!"

"Yes, my dear, I know; but not one that you've loved like you have Andrew. And he being our first child, he has become very special to you, and Jason knows this; and so, just let us thank God that we know where he is. Now, pack me a bag and I'll give Phil a shout to get me in."

"Oh, Johnny won't like that."

"No; well, Johnny will just have to put up with it, because if he doesn't stay indoors for another day or two he's going to be there for another few weeks with that chest of his."

"Will you be taking Patterson in with you?"

"No, of course not. What would I want Patterson for?"

"Only, my dear, that you said you would have to go in the day after tomorrow for a board meeting and the annual dinner."

"Oh, be quiet, woman, and go and tell Patterson to get my case packed."

She knew Jason was right, and so, softly now, she said, "Wouldn't it be wonderful to have him here for Christmas, with Alicia and John home from school?"

"Well, don't bank on it, dear. Just leave it for the time being. If he's happy where he is he might want to stay. You've got to face up to that."

It was eighteen hours later when the lights of the taxi showed up the grim exterior of the house, and that of its neighbors on either side.

The smell from the hall actually stung Robert's nostrils, and his own words came back to him as if he were denying them: "If he's happy where he is he might want to stay."

The very entrance to this place spelt poverty and dirt. He did not add the "degradation," because he had yet to meet the people with whom Andrew was living.

As they stood outside the door on the second floor they looked at each other through the dim light of the gas jet. And before Jason knocked, he whispered, "I warned you, Robert. But anyway, reserve judgement."

There was the sound of laughter and voices coming from the other side of the door, and Jason knocked twice before it was opened. Then James Winterbottom, looking up at the tall man, said, "Oh, good evening, sir." Then casting his glance to the other one, he paused before saying, "Come in. Come in."

The oddness of the room hit Robert as it did most people, but not so much as did the sight of the company sitting round the table, among whom was Andrew.

It was Andrew who rose to his feet first and, looking straight at Jason, was about to speak when Jason said, "I'm not going to make any excuses, Andrew; I thought it was time."

Robert moved two steps further into the room, and these brought him within a couple of yards of the table. And looking at the young man he thought of as his son, he said, "Hello, Andrew."

"He . . . hello, Father."

The name brought a startled movement from all those seated and a scraping back of chairs; but strangely, it wasn't Willie who took over and began to make the introductions, but Dill.

Looking at Robert, he said, "Will you take a chair, sir? And you, sir," and he glanced at Jason.

"Yes. Yes, thank you," said Robert when a chair was pushed toward him by a young man who smiled and said, "Somebody should do the introductions. I'm Mickey Fenwick, and that is Mr. Morgan." He put out a hand toward Dill. "And our friend here—" he now pointed to the other side of him, saying, "This is Mr. James Winterbottom." Then stretching out an arm toward Willie, he said, "But over all this is our boss and the owner of the flat. And as for the ladies," and he pointed to Betty, "Miss Betty Birchcomb and . . . and Miss Delia Moore."

Robert's eyes moved from the thin blonde girl to the equally thin, but startlingly beautiful colored girl, and he smiled at them. Then sitting down, he looked across at Andrew and said quietly, "It's nice seeing you, Andrew, and in such good company."

"It's nice seeing you, too, Father. It seems a long time. How's Mother?"

"Oh, excited; getting ready for Christmas again, and the others coming back from school. And—" he wetted his lips now before saying, "longing to see you." Then, looking around the group, he said, "Do please sit down else I'll feel that I'm intruding, which I suppose I am. But . . . but I'm grateful to Jason here." He looked up at his half-brother. "The best thing he's done for me for a long time was to break his promise to Freddie."

He now hitched the chair slightly forward toward the table as he said, "You were playing cards. I'm sorry I've interrupted." There was a pause before he added, "Do you all work in town?"

It was Willie now who came into his own, saying, "Yes, sir; but in our different ways. I'm a bricklayer by trade. I'm working with demolition gangs at the moment. And yes, as Dill said, this is my home and I've been pleased to share it with the fellas, an' definitely with Andrew, who," he laughed now, "thinks he's a painter. But as I've said to him, he's merely a splasher on of it," a statement which Dill could not let pass and so he dispersed any uncomfortable feeling the presence of the two visitors might have engendered by saying to Willie, "You wouldn't know a good picture if it was painted on your face." Then, turning his attention to Jason and Robert again, Dill said, "I'm a painter, but with ideas different from Andrew's. But he's light years ahead of me in some ways: he's of the avant-garde lot."

He now grinned at Andrew, who smiled back at him the while shaking his head. Then he said, "Mickey here introduced himself, he's a violinist," and he added on a cough, "without an orchestra, at present anyway. And Win, our Mr. James Winterbottom there, he's our sustainer with food and sees that we all wash behind our ears at least once a month," a statement which produced a slight titter, as he ended, "We five fellas live here and get on pretty well together, except when the girls interfere." He now indicated Betty, before adding quietly, "Betty, you will likely be surprised to know, is Andrew's sister."

When Robert turned his gaze quickly on the blonde girl, she looked back at him defiantly and spoke for the first time, saying, "Yes, that's right. It would surprise you; but I am Andrew's sister, his real sister," and again she firmly added the tag: "No adoption."

"Well . . . well, I'm very pleased to meet you."

Robert stood up and walked to her side and held out his hand; and after a moment's hesitation of surprise, she took it, and after shaking her hand Robert looked at Andrew, saying, "You found your people, then."

"Yes, Father."

"Are they a large family?"

"No. Betty is the only one besides me now."

Before Dill could finish the last of the introductions Willie put in, "And this is my girl." His hand was on Delia's shoulder.

Robert again put out his hand, and when it was taken he looked down into the deep, clear, brown gaze and his thoughts were summed up in two words, My God! For the unreal beauty of this slender piece of a girl, who seemingly belonged with that big rough hunk of a man, amazed him, and the possessiveness in Willie's voice, which always brought aggressiveness into his tone, was a warning, and it wasn't lost on him.

Tactfully, Mickey put in lightly, "They don't live here, sir. We've done our best to make them change their minds, but they both say they want drawing rooms," which caused Dill to prod Mickey hard into some awkward laughter. Then a silence settled on the room, to be broken by Robert rising again and looking across the table toward Andrew to say, "Would it be all right if I called in the morning . . . I mean, would you be in?"

"Yes. Yes, of course, Father." Andrew now walked round the table to stand by Robert, and as he looked up at him, he thought, Oh, if only you were my father and not that big lout; and with the thought came the realization that he loved this man, that he admired him and honored him; and this brought on a sudden desire, such as a child might have, of putting out his hand to him and saying, "Take me home. I want to see my mother."

Each week since he had come to live in this house he had paid a visit to his real mother, but the feeling he had first had for her remained: he was never at ease with her, nor she with him; and, moreover, he knew that she wished he had never put in an appearance. Also, recently, she had blamed him in an offhand way for the change that had apparently taken place in Betty. "She's not the same," she had said. "Gettin' too big for her boots," and she had used such phrases as "You should know your place, and if you should try to be what you aren't there'll be trouble for you, and you'll give yourself away in the end." No, he didn't care for his real mother. But the woman back there, that tall and comforting, beautiful woman, he loved her in much the same way as he loved Gracie; except that the love for Gracie was filled with desire, an eating-up desire.

"I'll see you in the morning, then, around ten?"

"Yes, Father, that'll be fine."

Jason, who had remained silent since his first few words, had also risen, and when he wished the company a general good-night, they nodded at him, but when Robert added, "I'll be pleased to meet you all again if I may," there was also silence for a moment, but then Dill answered, "We'd be happy to see you, too, sir, at any time."

On the landing and looking at his father, Andrew said, "I . . . I am pleased you came, Father."

"And I am, too, Andrew. Oh, yes, and I am, too."

"Father?"

"Yes?"

"Don't . . . don't bring Mother here."

"Oh, she'll want to come. She wouldn't mind."

Andrew lowered his head and said, "Well, I'll leave it to you."

Both men patted him on the shoulder now before turning and going down the stairs . . .

It was some minutes before Andrew re-entered the room, and Willie, addressing him straightaway, said, "Well, that's the second surprise today. It always goes in threes. But if you ask me, Andrew, you want your head looked into, 'cos if you've spent your life with blokes like them before coming here, well, it's beyond me. But anyway, stay or go, that's up to you. If I were you, though, I know what I'd do, and like a shot. In any case, you'll have to be looking for a place come January, we all will, because this is coming down, it's under orders. I heard that officially the other day. And I can't see old Lynch finding another house like this one: anyway, not one that we could adapt to our way of living and working."

They all remained silent; then Willie, putting his

hand on Delia's arm and almost lifting her from the chair, said, "Come on, love."

With their going, the others began to disperse, Dill up to the attic and Win into the kitchen, to where Mickey followed him, leaving Andrew and Betty at the table; and neither of them looked at the other as Andrew said, "It had to come sooner or later, Betty. That stay in hospital pointed the way. It was the first time it has happened in the stomach, and for a time . . . well, I didn't know where I was until they gave me the blood transfusion. And now they've told me it could happen again . . . well . . ."

"I know. I know." She was drumming her fingers on the table. "But . . . but I'm goin' to miss you. If only I didn't have to work, I could look after you."

He took a hold of her wrist as he said, "You heard the ultimatum from Willie. We'll all have to get out by January, and that's only five weeks away. It's going to be worse for the others than it is for us. You've got a home and I've got a home, and Delia's got a home. But the other four . . . well, they are going to find it difficult: there are times when Mickey can't pick up his rent, never mind his board; well, not in weather like this, anyway. Dill can manage because his pictures bring in enough for him to exist, only, of course, because it's cheap living here. At another house, the rent would be twice or three times as much. Win can earn enough. As for Willie . . . well, I don't see why he doesn't marry Delia and go and live with her people.''

''I've told you, the father won't have him. Of course, if the job was a steady one he'd manage all right. But there's not many more houses to knock down, around here, anyway. I expect they'll work things out for themselves,'' said Betty.

''But you'll be miles away in those hills an' it'll be ten to one I won't see you again.''

''Don't be ridiculous! Of course you'll see me again. You'll come up.''

''Huh! Don't be silly.''

''Freddie wouldn't come up without you. I know that.''

''That'll be another shock to them, won't it?''

''If I've told you once, I've told you a dozen times since we met, stop putting yourself down, because nobody else does.''

''Oh, you don't know what you're talkin' about. Just take Freddie's sister Jessie.''

''Oh, I know all about Jessie. Jessie is a born snob. She's like her mother and her grandmother. There's always one that picks up the family trait, and she certainly has taken after her mother. Right from the beginning I had little affection for Jessie.''

''But you love Gracie?''

They were looking at each other squarely in the face now, and he said, ''Yes. Yes, I love Gracie. But can you see me ever marrying her or anybody else and passing on this beastly business of mine? Your mother passed it onto me and . . .''

She stopped him here by saying sharply, "You never say 'our mother,' do you? It's always 'your mother;' and she's your mother, too, you know."

His head was bowed as he admitted, "Yes, I know, but we've never hit it off, have we? There's a wall between us."

"Of course there is. The way you were brought up built the wall, an' she knows she can never live up to you. I know how she feels. Anyway, regardin' marryin' Gracie; you'll have little say in it, for she'll marry you, 'cos she's a determined type. Bein' down in that dungeon for years, stickin' broken crockery together, has made her tenacious."

Betty put her hand out now and covered his where they were joined on the table, and softly she said, "You needn't necessarily pass on your blood problem; you can do what your mother an' father must have done when they found they couldn't have children. I don't know who was at fault, but I do think they were wise, when right from the beginning they decided to adopt. Well, you an' Gracie could do the same."

He looked at her hard now as he said, "Has Freddie not told you the reason they adopted?"

"No. Is there a reason?"

"Yes. Yes, and I'll tell you about it some day. Not now. You've had enough surprises for one night. Anyway, tell me, have you and Freddie fixed a date for your wedding?"

"Fixed a date? No. No, of course not. 'E's only been in that job a few months. 'E's not settled. Apparently they deal a lot with Germany and 'e seems to think that nothing is . . . well, stable. In any case, it'll be years before we get down to it, 'cos I've told him I must see to me mam; until me dad comes back, anyway."

"You're always having to think of somebody, aren't you?"

She made no comment on this, but what she said now was, "When d'you think you'll be leavin'?"

"Oh"—he shrugged his shoulders—"not straightaway. In a week or so. I'd like to be there for Christmas."

She nodded at him, saying, "I'll miss you."

"And I you, Betty. Oh yes, I you, because you've changed my life. You were the means of relieving me of a kind of burden I'd been carrying for years. The burden of not knowing who I really am. But now I know."

"And you're not ashamed?"

"Ashamed? No. No. The only thing is I'm grateful for the knowledge of myself that this year has brought about. Without it I would have had a brooding in me for the rest of my days. Now I feel free. And even . . . the bloody bleeding doesn't seem to matter very much." They now leaned their heads together and laughed. And when she said, "You even swear politely," the sound of their laughter filled the room and brought Mickey and Win from the kitchen, asking to be let into the joke.

3

As Dill came through the doorway, Win came out of his cubicle blinking the sleep from his eyes and Mickey stopped endeavoring to conquer a piece by Liszt on his violin. They both looked at him, asking eagerly, "How did it go?"

Dill, of different appearance today, was dressed in a navy-blue suit and highly polished black shoes. Only his hair seemed in disorder: the shortened front stood up over his brow like the peak of a cap; and before answering he repeated the question: "How did it go? As arranged, my dear fellows, as arranged." And when he flopped down into a seat Win said, "Would you like a cup of tea?"

"I would, but it can wait a minute. Sit yourself down."

Win duly sat down as he was bidden and he looked at Dill and, grinning, he said, "I've never seen you look so happy for years. In fact, I've never seen you look so happy ever before."

"Well, the reason I'm looking happy, lad, is because money talks. Money is power, and power commands, but it all stems from money."

"Well, you've got it?"

Dill looked at Mickey, then said, "Yes Mickey, I've got it, and how."

"Will it be a long job?"

"It could be a year, it could be two. As long as I've got a mind to spin it out, I think."

"Doing murals?"

He looked at Win and said, "Doing murals. There are twelve houses in the block. They have already gutted three of them, but they left the staircases, because they are beautifully wrought-iron spirals, you know." He demonstrated with his finger. "The walls have been stripped for damp and plastered and prepared, some of them, though, for paper.

"Before this I had been shown into an office. I don't think I was expected because the fella behind the desk reeked of toilet water and had a military air about him, and he looked at me as if I had come into the wrong place." He laughed now. "He seemed to take particular notice of my hair and I could hear him thinking, One of those! But you wouldn't believe the change in him when I said I was there to meet Mr. Anderson. He stressed, 'Mr. Anderson?' and I repeated and stressed, too, 'Yes, Mr. Anderson.' I may say he had risen to his feet by now and his voice had changed and he said, 'Will you please take a seat?' "

"I knew I was a bit early and while I waited we had nothing to say to each other, until suddenly there was a commotion outside the door. Then you should have seen the fella's face when Mr.

Anderson came breezing toward me, saying, 'Hello, Dill. You found your way through this maze, then?' Well, from then on things moved, and how. There were three departmental bosses that I could make out, then the clerks and oddments that seemed to tag onto the company.

"Anyway, Mr. Anderson took me next door and pointed to the walls. 'They are pretty high,' he said; 'you will need scaffolding. But I'll leave you to make your own arrangements. You'll know what to do. And over the holidays we'll go through some of your paintings to pick out those I would like you to transfer up there.'

"When I pointed out a dark corner on the stairway and suggested perhaps one or two of Andrew's efforts would light up that corner, he wasn't for it. No. He put it over that there had to be a similarity or uniformity in the work. On the second house, which is built almost the same as the first, he asked casually if I had yet found a flat. There had been no previous mention of flats," he seemed to insist, looking from Win to Mickey; "but I said just as casually, 'No, not yet; I hadn't had time to look around.' And then he turned to one of his men and said, 'I seem to remember a few years back, Henderson, there were quite decent quarters next door at number seven. It was after the war and I set my batman up as caretaker here. That, of course, was before your time. But they were quite nice rooms. They had been the housekeeper's apartments or some such.' " Dill had taken on Robert's manner of speaking, and laughed as he did. But now, his face straight, he said, "I can't help but say it. Although I like him— he's a nice man; he's a good man really; out to do kindness by stealth, one of those sort; but as I witnessed the fawning, yes sir, no sir, and the bowing and scraping, subservience at its worst, I realized that God or whatever people call God has no power. But money has, just money. If you've got money you can become a God, you can command. People will crawl to you. It's a bit sickening when I think that twenty years ago I would have got on my soap box about it, but not any more. Oh, no, I wouldn't look a gift horse in the mouth now, not me, for this particular gift horse has a wonderful set of teeth."

He laughed now, then went on. "Anyway, we went down into the basement of the house next door, and believe me, there was a suite of rooms. There was quite a bit of furniture in them, too. A bit damp, like the whole house, but who cares about damp when there's a big kitchen range in one of the rooms. It must have been the kitchen for the whole house. And electric plugs in the other rooms, three. They were likely the quarters of the hierarchy of below stairs. Anyway, our dear good friend said, 'Perhaps you could put these to use in the meantime until you have a look round.' To which I said, 'Yes. Yes, I'll do that.' Then he said to a fellow called Stevens, 'Perhaps you could get one of the boiler men to see if that flue's all right and a fire could be put onto help get the place warmed up.'

"Talk about from the sublime to the ridiculous. I was astonished now, because here was this man who must live in the lap of luxury—and just how much we're all going to find out soon—talking about having a flue cleared. Well, my conclusion of his character is that he is a very human human being. I understand he was an officer in the War and went through quite a bit, which probably accounts for the limp, and it likely knocked the sharp edges of wealth off him. Anyway, boys, I am to begin in the New Year, and I can't believe it. I can only say thank God for Betty and her discovering she had a brother. And oh, thank God for Andrew, too, for being the brother. Because the way things are he could have been a snipe and looked down his nose at the likes of us."

"Oh, I'm glad for you, Dill." Mickey's head was bobbing now. "That's one of us set up anyway."

"Well, there could be two or three set-up, because I've got to engage a helper, someone to carry my paints, et cetera. Because you know I'm not able to carry them myself." He laughed even gaily now before he went on. "So would you like the job?"

"Me?"

"Don't be so dim, you bloody fool. Who am I talking to? Not Win there, I'm talking to you."

Mickey bit on his lip, then said, "Thanks, Dill. Thanks a million. I don't mind admitting I was worried inside, because there's a lot like me, you know, under the arches."

"Good. Now, about this invitation, Win."

"Oh, I'll be all right, Dill."

"You won't be all right. And I can tell you, none of us will accept unless you come along. It's like the Three Musketeers: One for all and all for one."

"I can't, man. Thanks all the same, but I'll lose me job. He said I would, because it's their busiest time over Christmas. There's plenty'll be glad of it, he warned me."

"They're not lining up for a ten-to-six, standing over a sink, then cleaning up the bloody mess made by his revellers. Tell him, to hell with his job. He'll jump at you anyway when you come back, because he's never been able to keep anybody before he grabbed on you. So you tell him where to go. If not, we all stay here. Willie's of the same mind. Everybody's fixed, so don't spoil it. Betty says her mother's never had a bleeding for more than three months now and she's feeling better, and insists on her coming. I think our dear Mrs. Anderson, who had a talk with her, did something in that direction. And then there's Delia. My goodness! If her dear dark papa can allow her out of his sight, then any miracle could happen. Of course, he went to some trouble to find out where she was going and who these mad people were to invite that crazy lot from Lynch's lodging house. So, James Winterbottom, don't you spoil it for us. D'you hear? You tell him tonight, because the day after tomorrow we're off. Anyway, you know Andrew, they won't get him away from here unless you're with us. Your ticket's been bought and I'm not going to let that go to waste."

James Winterbottom got up from his seat and, his limp very much in evidence, made his way quietly to the kitchen.

"He would, you know, Mickey, he would have stayed on here by himself," Dill said quietly.

"He wouldn't have been by himself, Dill. I wouldn't have left him, either."

The two men looked at each other, one, who until now had been taciturn through failure, the other weak and timid through the same complaint; and they exchanged a look that embarrassed them both, understanding as it was.

As the occupants of Arthur Lynch's lodging-house, with Betty and Delia accompanying them, were driven along the snow-banked lanes, to see the fairy-like house that was High Gully standing on the rise, they gasped with amazement. And when they were ushered into the hall, where a roaring fire and the Christmas decorations greeted them, they were unable to find words to express their delight.

The welcome of Andrew by Janice, the house-keeper and the three maids was so effusive that Robert had to shout, "What about us? Don't we get a welcome, too?"

When the hubbub had died down a little, Robert said, "We're all frozen and we're thirsty and hungry. And you, Ginney, if you don't have a meal on that table within half an hour, you're for the road!"

"Yes, Mr. Robert. Yes, Mr. Robert. I'll pack me bags now," which caused further laughter. Then Janice called, "Bring in the hot drinks, Kathy," before turning to the guests now standing in a group as if for support, and saying, "Please make yourselves at home; and don't expect me to pamper you, or anybody else, either; you'll have to look after yourselves for half the time you are here!''

They all noticed that this tall, elegant lady had an arm around Andrew's shoulder, and that he had one arm around her waist; and he added, "Mother's right. In this barracks you've got to look after yourselves; and you'll find your legs worn out at the end of the day."

And now Janice was speaking again, addressing Freddie and Gracie, saying, "I'm not bothering with you two; you know where your rooms are. I'll tell you what you can do for me. I've put our friends"—she did not say "Andrew's friends" but "our friends"—"In the west wing. I can't say it's all that much warmer, only that it is not as cold as your end—there's two to a room—so you can take them up and let them choose . . . Ah, here come Kathy and Lynn with the life-savers."

When they had accepted the mugs of the hot toddy, it was Dill who appointed himself as spokesman for all the members of the group when he stood up from the plush-backed form that flanked one side of the great open hearth and said, "I . . . I would like to thank you, ma'am, for your invitation. We're all pleased . . . well, that isn't the right word, we're all delighted to be here, and most grateful."

"No more than we are to have you. You are . . . Dill, aren't you?"

"Yes, I am Dill, ma'am. And there's Mickey and Win and Willie, and, of course, Betty and Delia."

Smiling at the girls, Janice said, "By this time

tomorrow, I'll have you all sorted out." And now, addressing the young man she thought of as her son, she said, "And I'll run your bath, Andrew. Ten minutes, mind, that's all. Ten minutes. And you, Gracie! Come along with me."

Andrew looked from one to the other and sighed deeply, and Win asked quietly, "How on earth could you bear to leave all this, Andrew?"

"I don't know, Win. I don't know, but I'm only glad I did, because I would never have met you scurvy lot. You're the best thing that's happened to me in my life. I never knew there could be such comradeship or personal love." He reached over and took hold of Betty's free hand. Then he said, "I now know I'll be here for the rest of my life, and that I should be grateful. I *am* grateful, but I also know one other thing for sure: I'll miss you all. Yet I'll say, as will Mother and Father, that the house is yours whenever you want to visit, for I'll never be able to repay your kindness to me." And he added directly to Willie, "Like the Good Samaritan, Willie, you took me in."

"And he's taken you in ever since, overcharging you," Mickey put in on a laugh, in which they all joined.

It was Freddie who spoke now: "Well, if you're all warm inside, let's make for upstairs. It'll take a day or two for you to find your way around, I can tell you. But come on."

At the head of the broad, shallow staircase was a gallery overlooking the hall. "This is the main floor," he said. "My room's at that end and Gracie's is next to it. Andrew's is right opposite, next to Uncle Robert's and Aunt Janice's suite. That's all plain sailing. We now go this way." He led them to the end of the right-hand side gallery, and down a corridor, before saying, "Now watch out. There's three stone steps go up here." And when Willie stumbled on one and let out an exclamation, Freddie said, "Are you trying it out for demolition?"

They passed a number of doors before the corridor led into a smaller hall, where Win said, "How many rooms are there, Freddie?" and Freddie answered, "I couldn't say, Win, I really couldn't. The whole place goes back to God knows when and everybody's built a bit on. I suppose Uncle would be able to tell you."

Three bedrooms had been set apart for the visitors and each one caused "Ooh," and "Ah," and "Good gracious! Did you ever see anything like it?"

In each room a fire was blazing, and placed at the bottom of two single beds were velvet-covered easy chairs. There were matching curtains and bedspreads, and the mahogany wardrobes and dressing-tables were so large that, as Willie said, one lot would have taken up half the space in the flat.

It was as the door closed on the girls that Delia said, "It's a fairy tale, isn't it, Betty? I've never ever dreamt of anything like it. An' the kindness and the . . . the ordinariness of them, an' them being so wealthy. And all those servants who aren't really like servants. It's out of this world, don't you think?''

Betty was sitting in one of the chairs near the fire, and although she wasn't feeling the cold, she held her hands out to it as she thought, Yes, it is a fairy tale, an' yes, they're all so kind, but this has made the gulf even wider for me. They're so polite you don't really know what they're thinking. Still, we'll see. We'll see.

Six of the men were sitting in the smoke-room when Win remarked, ''Have we been here only twenty-four hours?'' He looked around. ''Did we only come last night? I . . . I feel I've been here weeks. I feel I've known them all my life.'' He laughed now, saying, ''The cook can't get over the speed at which I can wash dishes or even that I know how to cook. She asked me this evening if I'd like a job here and I said, 'Yes, thank you very much, ma'am.' And she said, 'Well, if I had my way it would be yours.' And I bet it would. Fancy working in that kitchen for the rest of one's life, being in this house for the rest of one's life! Andrew, I say again to you, how on earth could you leave this place?'' He did not wait for an answer, but went on, ''And the men outside, somehow they're not like ordinary workmen.''

''That's because you can't understand a word they say.''

He looked at Willie. ''Oh, yes I can,'' he said. ''You soon get used to it. Phil, the big one, Kilcullen, is his name, isn't it?'' He glanced at Andrew and Andrew said, "Yes, Phil Kilcullen. Now he takes a bit of understanding."

"Oh, it was he who said he didn't understand me. He said I talked like all the English foreigners."

Andrew glanced at the free-swinging pendulum of the clock on the mantelpiece and as it struck seven he said, "The train should just be in now. If this snow keeps on they're going to have a rough ride."

"Have you ever been snowed up for a time?" asked Dill now. And Andrew laughed and said, "Oh, yes, for weeks."

"Really?" It was Win speaking again. And now Freddie nodded toward him, saying, "Don't start hoping it's going to happen again now."

"Well, that's just what I was hoping," Win said, "I couldn't think of anything better happening to me." And quietly he said, "Miracles can happen. My grandfather said that to me. I remember him: he had a long white beard and I could bury my fist in it. And another thing he said was, 'Hope. Never let hope die in you. Whether in a pillory or a prison, hang onto hope.' " When he blinked as if coming out of a dream his head drooped and those who had lived with him for a number of years now realized that this was the first time he had mentioned having parents or from where he had sprung. All they had been told by him was, that through a purge he had landed in England and within a very short time both his parents had died, leaving his friends to surmise that it would

have been from starvation, and perhaps to pon-
der on his name, for it had become a bit of a joke
with them that on occasions he would still stress
his name Winterbottom.

To break the tension, Dill said, "Where are the
girls?"

"The last I saw of them, Delia and Gracie were
making for the nursery for a natter with Nanny, I
suppose," replied Andrew. "And I saw Betty with
my mother, and they were making for the rest-
room, Mother's rest-room. You have to be invited
there: it's no good knocking on the door, for you
won't be admitted. But as a privilege you are invited in, or ordered to appear for a telling-off." He
laughed now; then of a sudden, he said, "Oh,
damn and blast it!"

When Freddie quickly handed him a handkerchief Andrew said, "Now don't go and get
Mother, please. It's only a drip, nothing to make a
fuss about; but I'll go upstairs, in case Mother
does pop in."

"I'll come with you," Freddie said, and he left
the room with Andrew.

"I don't know how he puts up with it," Willie
said. "It would drive me mad. It must knock all the
stuffing out of him."

"Well, it does. We've seen that, haven't we?"
said Dill. "And no offense meant, Willie; but, looking back, I don't know how he stuck it in that
cubicle."

"Well, you're not the only one; I thought that
many a time." Willie was nodding at Dill now.

Win brought all their attention to him once again by saying, "Have any of you noticed that there's a difference in Betty? I don't know whether she's enjoying herself or not. She's very quiet, not Bettyish at all. And she's not like that with Freddie. Yet he's of the same stock as all them here."

"Betty's deeper than you think, than any of us think," Dill said quietly. "She knows it's chalk an' cheese, but she'll never stand being patronized, not Betty. . . ."

It was at about this time that Betty was being shown into Janice's private room, and Janice was saying, "It's nice to get away for a few minutes. This is my escape hole. I'm only allowed to be disturbed by a calamity." And now she smiled widely while looking at Betty, then added, "And they are not infrequent, I can tell you. Do sit down, dear."

Janice, too, sat down, in a high-backed, upholstered chair and, leaning back, she let out a long-drawn breath before she said, "It's odd about this room. No sounds penetrate it, and yet the walls are the same thickness as elsewhere. I understand that it was Robert's grandmother's domain and she used to spend a lot of time in here getting over the London season, in the days when they had seasons."

When Betty made no comment Janice said, "I've heard a lot about you, Betty. But I think it must have been exaggerated or that it wasn't true."

When she saw Betty's eyes narrow, she explained on a laugh, "Andrew emphasized that you were a most lively spark and very entertaining, and extremely kind and thoughtful. Regarding the last two," and Janice nodded now, "I am sure he was correct; but may I ask you why we haven't seen any of that liveliness since you came here?"

" 'Cos I feel out of place."

The straightforward answer nonplussed Janice for a time. Then she said, "But the others don't."

"I am not the others, ma'am, and I'm gettin' my eyes opened as to how things would be. You know that Freddie wants to marry me. Well, I was ready to go ahead, 'cos he talked me round; but bein' up here," she made a movement with her hand as if to encompass the whole house, then added, "and your way of life."

"But, my dear Betty, we're very ordinary, very homely."

"Oh, yes, yes, you make yourselves like that, and it's very kind of you. That's the word, *kind,* you're kind to everybody. But underneath you're bound to be askin' why on earth has 'e picked 'er?"

Janice brought herself forward to the edge of the chair and, leaning toward Betty, she said, "You know what I'd like to do now?" There was a slight pause before she added, "I'd like to shake you, shake some of the snobbishness out of you."

"Me? Snobby?"

"Yes, my dear, you, snobby. Now, let's come down to basics and let me tell you there's as much snobbishness in your class as in the one you think you're in now. You see, I haven't always lived up here. For years I worked in the East End of London in the hospital. For years I was bullied by sisters. And, let me tell you, there's no bully like an over-zealous ward sister. But, besides that, I had a good knowledge of the East End folk. You see, my father was a doctor and for years he had run a clinic down there; and I discovered that they tended to live in clans and they were more proud of their particular family or clan than any of the Scots up here are of theirs. The real meaning of a clan you'll find up here: you've only to read history to know there's been murder done by the clans. A clan is a form of snobbery. Yes. Yes, it is." She wagged her head at Betty, then said, "All right. All right. I admit I am not in your position and you feel you're on the other side of the tram-lines, but you've found someone who loves you dearly and is determined to marry you. Now it's up to you. If, through this false pride, because that's all it is, you're going to let him go . . ."

"No, it isn't false pride, ma'am. I've got none of that pride about me. Only I've always known I wasn't up to 'is standard, 'is way of livin'. An' coming up 'ere has emphasized that. And if I marry him I should 'ave to make meself change, and somehow I've always detested them that act as if they are somebody when they're not. I know I'll never be able to alter meself inside; all the time I would 'ave to be puttin' on a front."

Janice's face was straight as she said, "Well,

what do you think I've been doing for the last twenty years or more? Just that, putting on a front. My father being a doctor, I was brought up in what you call the middle class, but really the lower end of it. And, although I worked up to a position in the hospital where I could have been matron, like you, I was afraid of moving up into a different class." Now bending forward quickly, she caught hold of Betty's hand, saying, "Don't make the mistake that we did, my husband and I, and part. For seventeen long years we kept apart. We had a reason, a family reason: we were too closely related." She paused. "We were half-brother and half-sister. Yes, you can widen your eyes, dear. But how I regret those empty misera-ble years before we saw how ridiculous it all was. We only have one life. That's something to think about seriously, you know, just this one life. After all, we know nothing about another. But we do know we are here, and what I say to you now is, go on being yourself. But, like me, there are times when in company you'll have to act. My husband is a very important man, especially abroad, and I'm called upon from time to time to play the grand hostess, the lady of the manor, and I do it; but it isn't really me, because I'm still that proba-tioner who was scared out of her wits by the sis-ter."

They were gazing at each other now and smil-ing, and Janice said softly, "Make it all a play from now on, dear, and keep your real self for Freddie, because that's the part of you he fell in love with.

He has talked to me about you, and besides just loving you I know he admires you, and your honesty, and other good qualities. And for my part, I owe you a great debt, for as Andrew has told me, he would never have got by without you. Apparently he seems to know that if you hadn't got him out of your home, and your father had recovered from the surprise of being floored by a young whipper-snapper, he would have ended up in hospital himself and shipped ignominiously back here within a day or two. I was terribly upset when he left, but now I know it was the best thing that could have happened for him. You gave him the feeling of belonging, which unfortunately he had never *ever* experienced whilst in this house. But now he has adapted wonderfully. He has seen life from the bottom end and met some splendid people there. So, my dear, from now on, be yourself.'' She smiled and nodded, adding, ''I want to see the picture of you that Andrew has described. And my advice to you is, marry Freddie soon. But I had better warn you there are two people to be wary of. Freddie's mother who, as you know, is an alcoholic, and his sister Jessie. For there . . . talk about snobbery.'' Janice's head went back and she wrinkled her nose. ''She's a nurse, just like I was. But, my dear, I'm saying it and it's just between ourselves''—she was now whispering while there was a smile on her face—''she is what, in some societies, they call a crawler. And all I can say is, God help the staff if she ever works up to the position of sister and perhaps matron. Oh—'' her head jerked back again before she became still, and the thoughtful look appeared in her eyes as she said, ''It's odd, you know, how you like and dislike people right from the start. But she is my niece, yet the only one of Jason's family that I never could stand. Perhaps because''—her voice sank very low now to a confidential whisper—''she takes too much after her mother and grandmother and . . .''

She was about to add something further when the sound of a booming gong caused her to say, ''There it goes! That doesn't mean that dinner's in half an hour, only that cook's taken the joint out of the oven.'' She laughed as she stood up. ''And if it's all right and to her satisfaction, dinner will be in half an hour. If it isn't, then dinner is a little late. It could be an extra fifteen minutes or more. Come on, my dear.'' She put out her hand on Betty's shoulder, and Betty, looking up at this tall, gray-haired woman who had suddenly ceased to be the lady of the house dispensing salve to her guests, and was now a wise and motherly woman, said on a laugh, ''When you brought me into this room, I didn't know who I was or what I was gonna do. But as I go out I know I'm still me, come what may.'' Then after a short pause, she said, ''Thank you, ma'am.''

Janice made no reference to Betty's thanks, but said, ''Come along, my dear: I have to pay a visit to the nursery, and another to the kitchen; then I must get changed, by which time the half hour will be up and my husband and my brother and his friend will be on the doorstep."

"Could I do anything to help?"

"Yes, my dear." They were in the corridor now and Janice gave Betty a little push as she said, "Go and tell the fellows that you're back to normal," to which Betty answered, "Huh! if I do that they'll want to pack me off back 'ome for showing them up."

It was Christmas night, and the party was in full swing, although more than just a Christmas party it was a send-off do for Kathy Ferguson, the kitchen maid, who tomorrow, if they should be able to get down in the snow, would, with her future husband Billy McKenna, begin their journey to Glasgow to be married, and from there set out for America.

So the toasts had been running freely. The furniture in the hall and the drawing room had been cleared to one side to afford larger space for the dancers. The tin whistles and the fiddles had hardly stopped playing. Mickey hadn't intruded on them, except when asked to play solos for the company and on which Robert had commented so favorably to Jason, saying further that he must try and do something for the young fellow: there were avenues he was in a position to explore; and Jason had agreed.

Maggie had turned out to be a beautiful surprise. Although she had danced mostly with Jason, her contribution to the general entertainment was for her mimicry of well-known film actresses, and these were superb; but when she went adroitly into the Scottish idiom, the whole house resounded with laughter. And it was remarked upon, too, that Steven, as usual on his visits, was paying quite a lot of attention to the nanny, Miss Fanny Laidlaw.

And after Delia had sung in a sweet contralto voice, a surprise even to her tempestuous lover and guardian, there couldn't possibly have been a merrier and happier party in the whole of Scotland. And then the phone rang. It had rung a number of times before the passing maid picked it up and yelled into it, "Who is it? What d'you say? Doctor Nelson? Oh, Mr. Jason's father-in-law. Aye. Aye, I'll fetch him this minute. I'm sorry but I can hardly hear you for the carry-on."

She dropped the phone and ran into the drawing room, her head moving from side to side. But she soon picked out Mr. Jason at the far end—he was whirling the little fair-haired lassie off her feet—and she had to yell, "Mr. Jason. Mr. Jason. Ye're wanted on the phone. 'Tis your father-in-law."

"What is that, Lorna?" He was bending down to her.

"You are wanted on the phone, sir. 'Tis your father-in-law."

"Oh." He put his hand out and grabbed Betty's shoulder, saying, "Sit down before you fall; I'll be back to win my bet. Dance me off me feet, you said!"

He reached the hall with Lorna behind him, and she shouted at him again, "There's an extension in the master's study, sir. Ye'd be more able to hear better there."

"Yes. Yes, thanks, Lorna." He ran along the corridor to Robert's study. And once inside, with the door closed and the noise just a murmur in the distance, he leaned against it for a moment smiling to himself. The past few days had been the happiest he had known for many a long time. It had been a wonderful Christmas. He had pushed everything else to the background, determined to enjoy this short spell, if nothing else.

He sat down in the leather chair before the desk, then lifted up the phone and said, "Hello, there."

"Is that you, Jason?"

"Yes. Yes, it's me, Father-in-law. I couldn't get here any quicker. There's high jinks here tonight, such a party. What did you say?"

"I said, listen."

The smile went from Jason's face as he said, "I'm listening."

He heard a gulp, then John Nelson's voice saying, "She's dead!"

There was a long pause before Jason said, "What?"

"I said, Rose is dead."

He didn't say, "No! Oh no!" And his mind wouldn't admit to the callousness of his thinking, "Thank God!" he said simply. "How?"

"The usual way. She threatened it often enough, as you know."

"When did it happen?"

"I don't rightly know. She had been gone a number of hours before I found her, and then it was only because Mrs. Morton came and told me that she couldn't get in the back door. She had been off over the holidays, except that she popped in for an hour to tidy up. Rose usually opened the back door for her in the mornings any time after nine. Anyway, Rose had been here over the last two days and she had slept here. But last night she said she felt all right and thought she'd go home. The odd thing about it, Jason, is that she had been almost dry lately. Well, except for a couple of lapses and they weren't very bad. But there's something I must tell you and I don't know how far it's gone. I found three letters on the hall table. It's a good job I picked them up and that Mrs. Morton hadn't got in before me, because she would have likely put them in her pocket and then posted them later on. They were all to newspapers. And I don't know if there's any gone before."

"Oh, dear God!"

"Yes, that's what I said when I opened one. It was very long and very revealing. Anyway, don't hurry; there's nothing you can do. Her doctor came with another man, Fowler. He has a surgery in the square. And after that it was the usual procedure. She was taken to the mortuary."

"I am sorry. I really am."

"Oh, don't worry, Jason. I understand. You needn't be too sorry. I've had years of it, too, as you know. You haven't been blind. They were a pair, mother and daughter, possessive to the point of insanity. Drinking is a disease. But I think the desire to own someone else's body and soul is much worse, because it is this that sparks off the desire for an opiate. But as I've said, don't hurry. As long as you're here for the funeral. But about these letters, I'll hang onto them. I suppose the other two are similar to the one I read which was certainly an eye-opener with regard to Janice and Robert. Yet I've always had my doubts about many things. But we'll talk when you come."

"When will the funeral be?"

"Oh, I'll give it four days."

"I'll come back tomorrow, that's if we can get through. It's snowing heavily here."

"Don't worry. You'll have to tell the children and they'd better come with you."

"Of course. Of course."

The words now came slowly over the phone, "Such is life. But there's nothing so final as death, and it wipes out so many things."

When the line went dead Jason replaced the receiver, then held his head in his hands and the sound he made was like a groan. He felt guilty because he couldn't feel sorry. By the sound of it she went out aiming to leave disaster behind her. Robert's name was very much to the fore in international affairs now. It would just take something like that to blur it.

His father-in-law had been told that it had been Robert's grandfather who had objected to the original relationship between Robert and Janice; but that by the time they met again after all those years the grandfather had died, and so there was no obstacle to their marrying. Now he had read a different story. But he was a doctor and an understanding man.

But what about the newspapers?

He rose to his feet and walked to the door and when he opened it the sound of the merriment seemed even louder. And as he walked slowly down the corridor he thought, I must tell Robert and Janice, but the others I'll leave until tomorrow: they would never have enjoyed a night like this. There was Freddie glowing with love for his little cockney piece; there was Andrew and Gracie, each waiting for the other to speak; and there was Steven, his upright, matter-of-fact elder son, definitely paying court to Miss Fanny Laidlaw. And probably for the first time in their lives, and he wasn't going to spoil it. No; her going couldn't touch the lives of any of his children; nor his own.

He was free to marry Maggie, and he would do so at the earliest possible moment. Oh, yes, yes; he was no hypocrite. But there remained Robert and Janice, and their lives could be tainted through the viciousness of an unhappy woman. Rose had never been happy. Even during the first few months of their marriage she hadn't been happy. As she once said, she had been kept waiting too long, and there was a right time for everything.

5

Alice met him at the front door; the communicating door between the two houses had long been closed, upon Emily's command, following the departure of Steve.

"You've got it over, then?"

"Yes, Alice, I've got it over."

"Dreadful. Dreadful business. Somebody should have been with her all the time."

"Like a nurse or a guardian?"

"No, Master Jason." Her voice was a hiss now. "But I'll take the liberty to say, like a husband."

"Well, as usual, Alice, you've taken too many liberties in your time, and I'll thank you, from now on, to keep your liberties and thoughts to yourself."

Alice's head wagged from side to side and she said, "Well, I'll remember that, Master Jason; yes, I'll remember that . . . Your mother's waiting."

"Upstairs or down?" His tone was stiff.

"Downstairs."

"Thank you."

It was with a feeling of sadness that he entered the sitting room, for he had never before really crossed swords with Alice. She had been like one of the family. But that was the phrase: like one of the family; she had always been there as his mother's maid and companion, and so time and again had taken advantage of her position to speak her mind. But she had done so at the wrong time now.

His mother was sitting in her usual chair before a blazing fire, and she turned to him and in characteristic fashion dismissed the purpose of his visit by saying, "It must be still very cold outside. I always think sleet is colder than snow. Will you have a drink?"

"Yes, Mother, please, but not of tea or coffee."

"Oh. Oh, well, there's none in here." She turned her head from side to side as if to make certain of her words. "You'll have to get it from the dining room."

"It can wait."

He now pulled a chair up to the side of the fireplace and held his hands out to the blaze, and she watched him a moment before saying, "We're all very distressed."

"We are not all very distressed." He turned his head sharply toward her. "We are not all very distressed, Mother. You have known as well as I have that for years she had been drinking herself toward this end. And if she hadn't done it herself, her liver would have done it for her, so they tell me, in a very short space of time, too."

"You should have stayed with her."

"I stayed with her for years, Mother. I put up with her tantrums, her fighting, her filthy talk. Yes, she could use filthy language better than any street urchin.''

''I . . . I can't believe that.''

''Because you don't want to believe it.''

''No matter, she was your wife and you had a duty, and I think it was wrong of you . . .''

He was on his feet now, staring at her. ''Mother, I'm going to say this and I'll likely regret it, but I shall say it. You're the last person who should talk of anyone doing wrong, because everything that's happened has stemmed from your liaison that begot Janice and me; from pressing me into a marriage with Rose that you knew I had been trying to avoid for years. Then your supposed shock at Janice marrying Robert. It wasn't so much shock that wouldn't allow you to see her, but the fact that Father, or the man who acted as my father for years, loved Janice and, unknown to you, visited her whenever he could. But you ferreted that out, or dear Alice did for you. You couldn't bear the thought that anybody had stepped into your shoes where Steve was concerned. At bottom you are another Rose and her mother. You are all like cannibals. You're very sorry for Rose, aren't you? So you say. Well, I'm going to tell you something. But for the fact that her father opened one of the letters she had written to the papers, your name would now be splashed across the headlines: and the story would have detailed your affair as mistress of a well-known businessman, whose other mistress had beaten her up, and she had then been raped by the man, resulting in the birth of twins. Et cetera, et cetera; she didn't leave anything out. In a way, I think it's a pity that Father-in-law found the letters. They were going to three different papers. The only reason I'm glad he stopped them was that her main object was to expose Janice and Robert. So don't you dare talk to me about doing a bad thing. While you sit here in all your quiet magnificence, shutting out the world around you, living in the past that will never be yours again, just think of what I've said. You started all this. Janice said you used to put the blame on a hat, because it was a hat that attracted attention."

When she put her hand to her throat he turned quickly and, thrusting out an arm, supported himself against the mantelpiece. Oh, dear God! He hadn't meant to say any of those things.

Hearing the bell-rope being pulled he turned back quickly toward her, but saw that her face was quite impassive. And when Alice appeared in the doorway, she said, "Bring the decanter of whiskey, Alice, please, and two glasses."

Some minutes passed before either of them spoke. Then she said, "You've been wanting to say that for many a long day, haven't you, Jason? And you've said nothing that isn't with me every day. But I still maintain that you should have stayed with Rose, no matter what she was like, because she loved you."

"She didn't love me, Mother; she just wanted someone to possess, to be hers and to look after her and neither see nor speak to anyone else, especially a woman. Look at the maids she's dismissed in her time because she found us talking together. They were shown the door. The excuse was they had been insolent. It went on till I could stick it no longer.''

When her voice came back at him, saying, ''But your father would have stuck it,'' he almost yelled at her, ''He wasn't my father!''

''I'm well aware of that, Jason. Oh, well aware, because I can see traits of the other one in you.''

''Don't say that to me, Mother. He was a lazy, no-good, whoring sot—don't forget that I saw him—but as yet I recognize nothing of him in me, because I have neither charm of manner nor desire to rape. And now I'll give you something more, Mother, to get your teeth into. As soon as it is possible, I am marrying again, and this time to a woman twenty-five years younger than myself. Yes, that's opened your eyes. And I'll tell you something else. I stayed for years with Rose, aiming to keep her steady while all the time my feelings and heart were somewhere else. But there comes a time, there comes a limit to what one can stand.''

''Yes, Jason, you're right. There comes a time, a limit to what one can stand, and I think I've had enough for one day, don't you?''

He stared down at her but did not say, ''I'm sorry,'' because, as he saw her, she wasn't an old lady of eighty-four, but still the dominant, organizing mother he had always known. And on this he turned abruptly from her, and as he made to go out of the room he almost collided with Alice as she came in with a decanter and two glasses on a tray.

When the front door banged Emily said, "Pour out two glasses, Alice, and let us drink to the past, for that's all that's left to us now."

EPILOGUE

1941

She lay listening to the sound of the ack-ack guns and the distant *boom-boom* of the bombs. She wondered unemotionally when one would hit the house. She wished it would be soon, for she was very tired. She missed Alice. Oh, how she missed Alice. Was it only a week ago since she had died? And they intended to put her into a nursing home, that's what they said; to be looked after. She wanted Alice to look after her; nobody looked after her like Alice. Why had she to go so quickly? She shouldn't have left her. There was such a thing as willpower. She was using hers. She should have taught Alice about willpower. Oh, there was another *boom,* but it seemed further away.

She wished Steve would come. He had nearly come last night. She had seen him open the door. He hadn't come in. And the days were long and she heard no news now. Alice had always brought her the news, most of it gleaned from the maid next door. Oh, that next door. Why had she ever signed that house over to Jason as a deed of gift, all those years ago when he had married Rose?

Because now he didn't live in it, but lived with that young woman he had taken on, which was disgraceful. And they shared a home with his half-sister. They were all as thick as thieves. But that common piece next door and what she got up to! Alice had said she wouldn't believe it. Alice knew people, knew what class they belonged to, and she had said the blonde piece was as common as muck. And there she was married to Freddie, and it was he who owned that house now. In the War Office, Alice said he was. Doing special work. She called him a back-room boy, whatever that was. But there was his wife entertaining men all hours of the day, and the wireless and the gramophone blaring forth. It was supposed to be, Alice had said, because they were wounded. Some on crutches. Yet it didn't stop them dancing. The blonde piece wore a uniform, Alice had said. And she had colored friends. One big fellow had a colored wife. Did you ever! Then there was young Gracie up in that northern mansion or whatever, and now married to one of Janice's adopted children, and him with a disease. It shouldn't happen. It shouldn't be allowed to happen. And that wasn't all. No, that wasn't all. Only the day before she died, Alice had told her that she had watched a crowd going in there and that the high jinks went on until the bombs started to fall, when they all ran out. It was a party for a fiddler or some such, who was going to join some army entertainment. Some cripple fellow, too, who was a cook up at High Gully; they had brought him down to this party and he was taking a group of children back. Oh, of course, Janice would like to get her name in the papers again for taking in evacuees, just as she did some years ago when that man Hitler was turning the Jews out. Her house had been full of Jews then.

The only one who came to see her now was Jessie. She had never cared very much for Jessie. She always wanted what her eyes saw, did Jessie. And Alice had said she had her eye on one or two pieces of jewelry on the dressing-table. And it had been a very disturbing morning before Alice had had her attack in the afternoon, because they had found a number of pieces missing, and the only visitor who had been in the room had been Jessie.

Oh well, it didn't matter. Nothing mattered any more, only Steve. She wished Steve would come. John had been in to see her earlier. He was another one who had changed. Alice had said he seemed always to be gadding about, and him at his age.

That was another house she was sorry she had let go. When he died it would go to his son, who was somewhere in America. She had left this house to Alice, but Alice had gone on before her. And there was no other will, so it would go to Jason. Well, she didn't mind really, not now, for he came in pretty often. But it was he who was seeing about the nursing home.

The ack-ack guns had stopped. Why was it,

when we had won The Battle of Britain, or so they said, we hadn't stopped the Germans then? The raids had been worse since; they had come over night after night.

She had the sudden thought, hoping that they didn't bomb the house, because she would be all messed up with lime and that. And she was very particular about how she looked. Of course, it had been difficult this week without Alice. But what was she talking about? There was Alice standing by the bed. She said to her, "Where on earth have you been?" But Alice didn't answer; she just stood looking at her. She said, "I thought you had gone and left me. You know I can't do without you. We've been together for so long, haven't we? Right from the time I took you on as my lady's maid. You were so pleased, weren't you? And I recall you said that I had you for life. And you never broke your word, did you, Alice? Have you seen the master? He should be here now. I'll tell him that now you're back I needn't go into the nursing home." She sighed deeply now, and sank further into her pillows as she spoke aloud, saying, "It's been a long life, Alice. And I've been blamed for so much. But, you know, don't you? if I hadn't done what I did in the first place, nothing would have happened. Janice wouldn't be up in her magnificent highland house now. Jason wouldn't have his grand position in the Ministry and his children wouldn't all be going about their several lives. Lives start from an incident, don't they, Alice? Just an incident. The finding of a hat. Because that was the beginning of it, the finding of the hat up in the attic. Somebody had either been afraid of it or cherished it, because it had been carefully put away. It had a power, had the hat, and I burnt it. The day Janice left me for her half-brother, I burnt it. Yet, I've always been truthful with you, Alice, haven't I? And I must confess now that, although I did that, I was glad she had gone, because then I had Steve all to myself. He was mine once again. At least . . . at least, I thought he was . . .

"Oh, there you are, dear. I was just talking to Alice about you and about you being mine after Janice married Robert. But you still held Janice tightly in your heart, didn't you? And that hurt me. You thought I didn't know of your visits, didn't you, and your longing to see her? But I did. And I knew something else. She truly wasn't your daughter. She was no relation to you. And although you said you loved her as a daughter, I knew differently. And that's why I was jealous. They are going to put me into a nursing home, Steve. What are you smiling at? Yes, it's been a long time, but I knew you would come. I just said so to Alice. Did Alice tell you I was waiting? Alice knew me inside out, even more than you did.

"Oh dear, I'm so tired, so very, very tired. The bombs have stopped dropping and those pop-popping guns have stopped, too. Are you going to get into bed, Steve? Ah, yes that's nice. Just lie and hold my hand and Alice will put the light out.''

THE END